C000172207

'In Cook's hands, the crime novel moves firmly into literature'
*Peter Straub*

'Powerful and trenchant storytelling'
*Good Book Guide*

'Cook, writing in a wonderfully understated prose, calmly and
methodically builds everything up to a climax of multiple tragedies ...
bravura suspense writing'
*Crime Time*

'Terrific'
*Observer*

'Gripping, beautifully written, surprising and devastating. Thomas H.
Cook has long been one of my favourite writers'
*Harlan Coben*

## ALSO BY THOMAS H. COOK

### FICTION

*Blood Innocents*
*The Orchids*
*Tabernacle*
*Elena*
*Sacrificial Ground*
*Flesh and Blood*
*Streets of Fire*
*Night Secrets*
*The City When It Rains*
*Evidence of Blood*
*Breakheart Hill*
*Instruments of Night*
*Places in the Dark*
*The Interrogation*
*Taken* (based on the teleplay by Leslie Boehm)
*Moon over Manhattan* (with Larry King)
*Peril*
*Into the Web*
*The Murmur of Stones*

### NONFICTION

*Early Graves*
*Blood Echoes*
*Best American Crime Writing:* 2002 edition (ed. with Otto Penzler)
*Best American Crime Writing:* 2003 edition (ed. with Otto Penzler)
*Best American Crime Writing:* 2004 edition (ed. with Otto Penzler)

# THE THOMAS H. COOK OMNIBUS

## RED LEAVES
## MORTAL MEMORY
## THE CHATHAM SCHOOL AFFAIR

Quercus

First published in Great Britain in 2008 by
Quercus
21 Bloomsbury Square
London
WC1A 2NS

*Red Leaves* copyright © 2005 by Thomas H. Cook
*Mortal Memory* copyright © 1993 by Thomas H. Cook
*The Chatham School Affair* copyright © 1996 by Thomas H. Cook

The moral right of Thomas H. Cook to be
identified as the author of this work has been
asserted in accordance with the Copyright,
Designs and Patents Act, 1988.

All rights reserved. No part of this publication
may be reproduced or transmitted in any form
or by any means, electronic or mechanical,
including photocopy, recording, or any
information storage and retrieval system,
without permission in writing from the publisher.

A CIP catalogue reference for this book is available
from the British Library

ISBN 978 1 84724 120 7

This book is a work of fiction. Names, characters,
businesses, organizations, places and events are
either the product of the author's imagination
or are used fictitiously. Any resemblance to
actual persons, living or dead, events or
locales is entirely coincidental.

10 9 8 7 6 5 4 3 2 1

Typeset by Deltatype Ltd, Birkenhead, Merseyside
Printed and bound in Great Britain by Clays Ltd, St Ives plc.

# CONTENTS

# RED LEAVES

For Susan Terner,
courage under fire

Oh, return to zero, the master said.
Use whats's lying around the house.
Make it simple and sad.

Stephen Dunn, *Visiting the Master*

# PART I

When you remember those times, they return to you in a series of photographs. You see Meredith on the day you married her. You are standing outside the courthouse on a bright spring day. She is wearing a white dress and she stands beside you with her hand in your arm. A white corsage is pinned to her dress. You gaze at each other rather than the camera. Your eyes sparkle and the air around you is dancing.

Then there are the brief vacations before Keith was born. You are in a raft on the Colorado River, sprayed with white water. There you are, nearly blinded by the autumn foliage of New Hampshire. On the observation deck of the Empire State Building, you mug for the camera, feet spread, fists pressed to waists, like masters of the universe. You are twenty-four and she is twenty-one, and there is something gloriously confident in the way you stand together, sure and almost cocky. More than anything, without fear. Love, you have decided by then, is a form of armor.

Keith appears first in the crook of Meredith's right arm. She is lying in a hospital bed, her face bathed in sweat, her hair in disarray. Keith's small body floats in a swirl of bedding. His face is in profile, and a tiny pink hand instinctively reaches for something his closed eyes cannot see, his mother's loosely covered breast. Meredith is laughing at this gesture, but you recall that she was clearly struck by it, too, thought it a sign of high intelligence or early adventurousness, ambition, the drive to make a mark. You reminded her, joking, that her son was only a few minutes old. Yes, yes, of course, she said.

Here he is at two, unsteady on his feet, toddling toward the stuffed bear your brother, Warren, gave him that Christmas. Warren sits on the sofa, beside Meredith. He is leaning forward, his large pudgy hands blurred because he was clapping when you took the picture, clapping hard and fast, urging Keith forward like a good wind at his back. So lucky, Bro, he will say to you at the door before he leaves, so lucky to have all this.

7

You often pose before all you have. You stand with Meredith and Keith, who is six now and holds a plastic Wiffle ball bat. You are in front of the little house on Cranberry Way. You bought it on the slimmest of financial credentials, and Meredith predicted the loan would not be approved, and so, when it was, you uncorked a bottle of inexpensive champagne and toasted your new status as homeowners. There's the picture, you and Meredith with glasses raised, Keith standing between you, his six-year-old hand lifted in imitation, holding a glass of apple juice.

You build a business, buy a second, larger, house on a more secluded lot. In that larger house the holidays come and go. You carve turkey and hang ornaments on real trees, then later, fearing fire, on artificial ones. In photographs you wallow in holiday gift wrapping, and as the years pass, the pictures show your face aglow in the light of many birthday candles.

You buy Meredith a ring on your fifteenth anniversary and with Keith and Warren watching, you marry her again, this time writing your own vows. That night, in the bed's comforting darkness, she tells you that she has never stopped loving you, and it is all you can do not to weep.

You buy your son a simple, inexpensive bike for his tenth birthday, then an elaborate twelve-speed when he turns fourteen. He's not particularly mechanical, so you spend some time showing him the gears. After a while, you ask him if he'd prefer a less-complicated bike. He says he would, but that it has nothing to do with the gears. He prefers everything less complicated, he tells you, and the look in his eyes when he says this suggests that there may be hidden depths in him, unexpected complexities. You say nothing of this, however, but later you wonder if your son, the one who'd once rested so securely in the crook of Meredith's arm, has now begun to emerge from the comfortable cocoon you have so carefully woven around him. If so, you are pleased, and you are sure Meredith will be pleased.

Another year passes. Keith is almost as tall as you are, and Meredith has never looked more radiant. A warm satisfaction settles over you, and you realize that it isn't the house or the business that fills you with a sense of accomplishment. It is your family, the depth and balance it has given to your life, a quiet rootedness and sense of well-being your father never attained and which, for some reason at the end of that summer, you recognize as the crowning victory of your life.

And so you decide to take a photograph. You set up the tripod and call Keith and Meredith outside. You take your place between them, one arm over your son, the other over your wife. You have timed the camera. You see the warning light and draw them close in beside you. Ready now, you tell them – smile.

# ONE

*Family photos always lie.*

That's what occurred to me when I left my house that final afternoon, and so I took only two.

The first was of my earliest family, when I was a son, rather than a father. In the picture, I am standing with my mother and father, along with my older brother, Warren, and my younger sister, Jenny. I am smiling, happy because I've just been accepted to a prestigious private day school. But the other smiles now strike me as false, because even then there must have been fissures in the unruffled happiness they convey, beasts lurking just beyond the firelight.

By the end of that summer, for example, my father must have known that years of bad investments and extravagant spending had surely caught up with him, that bankruptcy and its accompanying humiliations were only a few short months away. I doubt, however, that he could have envisioned the full bleakness of his final years, the retirement home where he would sit hour upon hour, peering through the lace curtains, thinking of the grand house in which we'd all once lived, another asset lost.

Despite all this, or maybe because of it, my father meets the camera with a broad and oddly blustering grin, as if the old man felt his smile could protect him from the horde of angry creditors that was already gathering for a final assault. My mother's smile is more tentative – weak, hesitant, like a translucent mask beneath which her true face, though blurred, is yet still visible. It is an effortful smile, the corners of her mouth lifted like heavy weights, and had I been less self-absorbed, I might have noticed its tentativeness earlier, perhaps in time to have asked the question that later repeated so insistently in my mind, *What is going on in you?*

But I never asked, and so the day her car went flying off Van Cortland Bridge, it never occurred to me that anything might have been on her mind other than what she planned to cook for dinner or the laundry she'd left neatly folded on all our beds that afternoon.

My brother, Warren, stands sloppily to my left. He is only fifteen, but his hair is already thinning and his belly is wide and round and droops over his belt. Even at that age, he looks curiously past his prime. He is smiling, of course, and there is no hint of any reason why he shouldn't be, though I later had to wonder what fears might even then have begun to surface, the sense that certain already-planted seeds would bear grim fruit.

Finally, there is Jenny, so beautiful that even at seven she turned heads when she came into a room. Adorable, Warren always called her. He'd stroke her hair or sometimes simply look at her admiringly. Adorable, he'd say. And she was. But she was also quick and knowing, a little girl who came home from her first day at school and asked me why it was necessary for the teacher to repeat things. I told her it was because some people couldn't get it the first time. She took this in for a moment, thinking quietly, as if trying to incorporate nature's inequality within the scheme of things, calculate its human toll. 'How sad,' she said finally, lifting those sea blue eyes toward me, 'because it's not their fault.'

In this particular photograph Jenny's smile is wide and unencumbered, though in all the photographs after this one the cloud is clearly visible, the knowledge that it has already taken root in that fantastic brain of hers, microscopic at first, then no larger than a pinpoint, but growing steadily, taking things from her as it grew, her balance, her ringing speech, everything but her beauty, before it took her life.

She was the one I most often thought about after leaving my house that last afternoon. I don't know why, save that I suspected she might be able to understand things better than I could, and so I wanted to go over it all with her, trace the burning fuse, its series of explosions, seek her celestial wisdom, ask her, *Do you think it had to end this way, Jenny, or might the damage have been avoided, the dead ones saved?*

The evening of that final death, he said, 'I'll be back before the news.' Meaning, I suppose, the network news, which meant that he would be home before six-thirty. There was no hint of the ominous in what he said, or of anything sinister, no sense at all that the center had collapsed.

When I recall that day, I think of my second family, the one in which I am husband to Meredith and father to Keith, and I wonder what I might have said or done to stop the red tide that overwhelmed us. That's when I see another picture, this one of a little girl from another family, a school photograph used in a hastily distributed flyer, the little girl smiling happily below the cold black words: MISSING.

*Amy Giordano.*

She was the only daughter of Vince and Karen Giordano. Vince owned a modest produce market just outside the town limits. It was called

Vincent's Fresh Food, and Vince dressed himself as a walking advertisement for the place. He wore green flannel pants, a green vest, and a green cap, the latter two articles festooned with the name of the store. He was a short muscular man with the look of a high school wrestler who'd let himself go, and the last time I saw him – before the night Keith left for his house – he was carrying a brown paper bag with six rolls of film. 'My brother's family came for a week,' he explained as he handed me the bag, 'and his wife, she's a camera nut.'

I owned a small camera and photo shop in the town's only strip mall, and the pictures Vincent Giordano left that afternoon showed two families, one large, with at least four children ranging in age from approximately four to twelve, and which had to have belonged to the visiting brother and his 'camera nut' wife. The other family was small, a circle of three – Vince, his wife, Karen, and Amy, their only daughter.

In the pictures, the two families present themselves in poses that anyone who develops family photos taken at the end of summer in a small coastal town would expect. They are lounging in lawn chairs or huddled around outdoor tables, eating burgers and hotdogs. Sometimes they sprawl on brightly colored beach towels or stand on the gangway of chartered fishing boats. They smile and seem happy and give every indication that they have nothing to hide.

I have since calculated that Vincent dropped off his six rolls of film during the last week of August, less than a month before that fateful Friday evening when he and Karen went out to dinner. Just the two of them, as he later told police. Just the two of them ... without Amy.

Amy always reminded me of Jenny. And it was more than her looks, the long wavy hair I saw in her family photos, the deep-blue eyes and luminous white skin. Certainly Amy was beautiful, as Jenny had been beautiful. But in the photographs there is a similar sense of intuitiveness. You looked into Amy's eyes and you thought that she saw – as Jenny did – everything. To reporters, Detective Peak described her as 'very bright and lively', but she was more than that. She had Jenny's way of peering at things for a long time, as if studying their structures. She did this the last time I saw her. On that September afternoon, Karen had brought in yet another few rolls of film, and while I wrote up the order, Amy moved about the store, carefully examining what she found there, the small, mostly digital, cameras I stocked, along with various lenses, light meters, and carrying cases. At one point she picked up one of the cameras and turned it over in her small white hands. It was an arresting scene, this beautiful child lost in thoughtful examination, silent, curiously intense, probing. Watching her, I had a sense that she was studying the camera's various mechanisms, its buttons and switches and dials. Most

13

kids start by merely snapping pictures and grinning playfully, but the look on Amy's face was the look of a scientist or technician, an observer of materials and mechanical functions. She didn't want to take a picture; she wanted to discover how it was done.

'She was so special,' Karen Giordano told reporters, words often used by parents to describe their children. As a description it is usually exaggerated, since the vast majority of children are not special at all, save in the eyes of those who love them. But that doesn't matter. What matters is that she was Karen Giordano's daughter. And so on those days when I make my way down the village street, noting faces that from high above might appear indistinguishable as grains of sand, I accept the notion that to someone down here, someone close up, each face is unique. It is a mother's face or a father's; a sister's or a brother's; a daughter's or a son's. It is a face upon which a thousand memories have been etched and so it is differentiated from every other face. This is the core of all attachment, the quality that makes us human, and if we did not have it we would swim forever in an indifferent sea, glassy-eyed and unknowing, seeking only the most basic sustenance. We would know the pain of teeth in our flesh and the stinging scrape of rocks and coral. But we would know nothing of devotion and thus nothing of Karen Giordano's anguish, the full measure of feeling that was hers, the irreparable harm and irrevocable loss, the agony and violence that lay secreted, as we all would come to learn, within a simple promise to be home before the news.

# TWO

There was little rain that summer, and so when I heard the rumble of thunder, I looked up but saw nothing more threatening than a few high clouds, torn and ragged, pale brushstrokes across the blue.

'Heat lightning,' I said.

Meredith nodded from her place in the hammock, but kept her attention on the magazine she was reading. 'By the way,' she said, 'I have a departmental meeting tonight.'

'On a Friday?' I asked.

She shrugged. 'My thought, exactly, but Dr. Mays says we have to take a look at the year ahead. Make sure we understand our goals, that sort of thing.'

For the last eight years, Meredith had taught in the English department of the local junior college. For most of that time, she'd served as a lowly adjunct. Then suddenly, death had opened a full-time position, and since then, she'd assumed more and more administrative duties, gone off on professional days and attended seminars in Boston and New York. She had grown more confident and self-assured with each added responsibility, and when I think of her now, it seems to me that she had never appeared happier than she did that evening, relaxed and unburdened, a woman who'd found the balance of family and career that best suited her.

'I should be home by ten,' she said.

I was standing at the brick grill I'd built four summers before, an unnecessarily massive structure I enjoyed showing off for the loving craft I'd employed while building it. There were brick curves and brick steps and little brick shelves, and I loved the sheer solidity of it, the way it would hold up against even the strongest storm. I'd also loved every aspect of the work, the thick, wet feel of the mortar and the heaviness of the brick. There was nothing flimsy about it, nothing frail or tentative or collapsible. It was, Meredith later told me, a metaphor not for how things were, but for how I wanted them, everything lined up evenly, made of materials that were sturdy and unbending, built to last.

15

Our house, when I think of it now, had that same determined sturdiness. It was built of ancient wood, rough-hewn and very nearly petrified. The living-room ceiling rose at a forty-five-degree angle, supported by thick beams, and at the end of it there was a fireplace of gray stone. The grounds were also incontestably the product of a mind that sought security. The yard was thick with trees and wild brush that made it impossible to see the house from the road. An unpaved drive wound in a long lazy circle to the front of the house, then lifted up a short hill and circled back to the main road. It was possible to make the turn into the driveway and immediately disappear into densely covering forest. Save for that one break in the trees, no one would even have suspected that a family lived nearby. We lived on a desert island, as Meredith once said, in the middle of the woods.

I'd put on a couple of extra burgers because Warren had called earlier, sounding tired from his long day of house painting. I knew he hated spending Friday night alone, so I'd invited him over for a cookout. In recent weeks, he'd begun to drink more, and his fleeting efforts to 'find the right woman' had declined both in number and intensity. The year before he'd fallen off a ladder while repairing a patch of rotted shingles on the small two-story house he rented. The fall had broken his hip and he'd been laid up for nearly a month. There'd been no one to look after him, no wife or children, and so he'd moved into Keith's room for his convalescence, a period during which he'd played computer games and watched videos, usually adventure movies because, as he put it with a soft, self-mocking smile, 'I have a lot to keep my mind off of.'

He arrived at just before five, moving sluggishly up the winding walkway that led to the grill. Around him, in the lowering sun, the leaves were so brilliantly colored that he seemed to walk through a shimmering oil painting. The foliage had always been spectacular, but I most admired the Japanese maple I'd planted at the end of the walkway, its graceful branches, laden with red leaves, spread out like enveloping arms that seemed to draw you into its protective care.

'So, how's the chef?' Warren asked as he plopped down in a lawn chair a few feet from Meredith.

Meredith put down her magazine. 'He's only the summer chef,' she said lightly. 'He doesn't lift a finger when he's not at that grill.' She pulled herself out of the hammock. 'Got to get dressed,' she said, then bounded into the house.

'Dressed for what?' Warren asked.

'Department meeting,' I said.

The phone rang inside the house, and through the front window I saw Keith rush to pick it up, his movement considerably more sprightly than normal, so that I briefly sensed that the person at the other end might be the long-awaited girlfriend he'd no doubt been pining for. He talked briefly, then put the phone down and came to the door.

'Okay if I babysit tonight?' he asked. 'Mrs. Giordano can't get her usual one.'

I knew that Karen Giordano usually employed Beth Carpenter to babysit when she and Vince went out, but she sometimes called Keith when Beth wasn't available. He had filled in four or five times before that night, always home before eleven, usually with some story about Amy, how bright and well-behaved she was, deserving of the name he'd given her – Princess Perfect.

'You caught up with your homework?' I asked.

'Except algebra,' Keith said. 'Besides, it's Friday, Dad. I have the whole weekend.' He frowned as if I'd missed a cue. 'So, can I?'

I shrugged. 'Okay.'

Keith returned inside, where I glimpsed him through the window once again, speaking into the phone, a tall lanky boy of fifteen with a mop of curly black hair and skin so pale and soft to the touch it seemed very nearly feminine.

'You got a good kid there, Eric,' Warren said. He glanced over at the grill. 'Smells good.'

We gathered around the picnic table a few minutes later. Meredith was dressed in her professorial attire, complete with a silk scarf and black pumps with a modestly high heel. Keith wore his usual jeans and sweat-shirt along with the pair of worn tennis shoes he usually wore unlaced.

I remember that the conversation was rather limited that evening. I mentioned a roll of film I'd developed that morning, twenty-four pictures of the same goldfish. Meredith said that she'd come to like Dylan Thomas more than in the past, particularly his poem about a little girl who'd died by fire in London. 'He was asked to write a poem about this one little girl,' she said, 'but refused to do that and wrote something universal instead.'

Warren mostly complained that his hip still bothered him and that he might well require surgery in a year or two. He had always been one who needed sympathy, and sought it, the kind of man you'd think had been orphaned in his youth and thus was forever in search of a sweet maternal hand. My father had always found him soft and without ambition, called him 'day labor' behind his back, and warned my mother not to baby him, one of the few of his commands she had had the will to disobey.

As for Keith, he seemed even more quiet than usual, his head low over his plate, as if vaguely ashamed to look us in the eye. He had always been a shy boy, awkward and withdrawn, prone to injury, and with an early dislike of physical contact. He'd shunned sports, but not out of regard for some other activity, playing a musical instrument, for example, or because of some interest or hobby, but only because he seemed wary of being touched. But more than anything, he gave off a sense of something enclosed, drawn in upon itself, disinclined to reach out.

Meredith had more than once asked if I thought Keith should see someone. I was not averse to such a suggestion, but at the same time I had no idea whom Keith might see. And of course, the real question, it seemed to me, was not whether he was involved in sports or had friends, but whether he was or wasn't happy. But I had no way of knowing this, and so I let him drift, the first years of his adolescence passing quietly, almost silently, until they reached the end of that summer, and he sat, hunched over his plate, while Meredith raced to her meeting and Warren slumped in the hammock and I cleared the table and cleaned the grill.

'So, you gonna take me?' Keith asked as he came out of the house, now dressed for that cool autumn evening in khaki pants, wool shirt, and blue parka.

'You look very handsome,' I said.

He groaned, 'Yeah, right.'

'No, I mean it, you're growing into—'

He lifted his hand to stop me. 'So, you gonna take me?'

Before I could answer, Warren struggled out of the hammock. 'Let your father finish up, I'll take you.'

And so they left, my brother and my son, the two of them moving down the brick walkway through a dusky light, one wide and flabby, the other razor thin and erect, cutting through the air like a blade.

When they were gone I finished the cleaning, carefully scrubbed the grill's charred ironwork, then walked inside the house. Meredith had left a book on the table, *The Collected Poems of Dylan Thomas*. I picked it up, brought it over to my chair, and switched on the gooseneck lamp. Then I opened the book, looked up the poem she'd talked about at dinner, found it hard to follow, but interesting enough, especially the mournful sentiment at the end, that, according to the poet, 'After the first death, there is no other.'

I was snoozing in my chair when the phone rang a few hours later.

It was Keith. 'You don't have to pick me up,' he said. 'I'm gonna stay out for a while. Maybe hang out with some people.'

I'd never known Keith simply to seek out other people, but given his troubling solitariness, the news that he might have such an urge struck me as an encouraging sign of normality.

'So, when will you be in?' I asked.

'I don't know,' Keith answered. 'Before ... midnight, okay?'

'Okay,' I said. 'But no later. Your mother would be worried.'

'Okay, Dad,' Keith said.

He hung up and I went back to my chair, though not to *The Collected Poems of Dylan Thomas*. I had never had particularly refined taste in literature, although the occasional serious novel might gain a little ground among the nonfiction that was my usual fare. On this particular night, it was a book about an African tribe that had been displaced, moved from a region in which the tribesmen had been farmers to one in which they were reduced to gathering food among the sparse foliage that dotted otherwise rocky, inhospitable soil. As their condition had grown more desperate, their ancient religious and social institutions had collapsed. All that had once seemed so firm crumbled, all their habits and relations – everything. There was no solid human nature, the book said, there were only met and unmet needs, our deepest roots sunk in shifting sand.

I had just finished the book when Meredith returned home.

She seemed surprised that I hadn't gone to bed.

'Keith called,' I told her. 'He's going to be late.'

Meredith dropped her purse on the sofa and began pulling off her shoes. 'The Giordanos are making a late night of it, I guess.'

'No, he's already left there,' I told her. 'He said he might hang out with some people.'

She cocked her head quizzically. 'Well, that's an interesting development. Or it will be, if it's true.'

Her final words struck me as unexpectedly suspicious.

'True?' I asked. 'Why wouldn't it be true?'

She came over and touched my face, her gaze oddly indulgent, as if explaining life to a little boy. 'Because people lie, Eric.'

'But why else would he be out?' I asked.

She shrugged. 'Maybe he's buying drugs,' she said jokingly. 'Or maybe he's a Peeping Tom.'

I laughed, and so did she, since the image of our son lurking in the shadows, peering into windows, seemed comical, one of the many things we could not imagine him doing.

'I told him to be back home by midnight,' I said.

She reached for me. 'Let's go to bed,' she said.

Meredith often tossed restlessly for hours before finally dropping off, but that night was different. She fell asleep right away, like someone exhausted by a long day's labor. For a time, I watched her, pleased with how smart and lovely she was, how contented with the life we shared. By then, many of our friends had divorced, and those who hadn't seemed hardly better off, either snippy with one another or dismissive, the pleasure they'd once taken together now no more than a distant memory.

We'd met during her last year of college, dated for six months, then married. We'd lived in Boston for a time, where she'd taught at a local public school while I'd worked at a pharmaceutical company. We'd both hated our jobs, and so, a few months after Keith came along, we'd taken the plunge, moved to Wesley, managed to secure a loan, and bought the frame and photo shop. Meredith had stayed home with Keith for the first seven years, then taken a part-time teaching job at the junior college. As Keith grew older, she'd added to her teaching load, shedding her former household duties like a dry skin, becoming younger and more vibrant, it seemed to me, so that as she slept that night, it did not surprise me that her lips suddenly lifted in a quiet smile.

I was peering at that smile when I heard a car crunch to a halt at the far end of the drive. I sat up in bed, and glanced out the window. By then the car was backing onto the road, two beams of light sweeping across the undergrowth with a smooth, ghostly grace. Seconds later I saw Keith make his way down the unpaved drive that circled around to our front door, his pace slow and halting, head down as if against a hostile wind.

After a moment, he disappeared from view. Then I heard the metallic click of the front door, the sound of his feet as he made his way up the stairs, past our bedroom, and down the corridor to his own room.

He was just opening the door to that room when I stepped into the hallway.

'Hi,' I said.

He didn't turn toward me, but stood, facing the door, his body curiously stiff.

'Did you have a good time with your friends?' I asked lightly.

He nodded, the long strands of his hair shifting in a tangled curtain as he moved.

'Good,' I said.

As he eased around to face me, I saw that his shirttail was rumpled, as if it had been hurriedly tucked in. 'Okay if I go to bed now?' he asked a little curtly, but with no more than the usual teenage impatience.

'Yes,' I said. 'I just wanted to make sure you were okay.'

He quickly turned and disappeared into his room, leaving me alone in the dimly lit corridor.

I returned to my bed, now fully awake, feeling an inexplicable unease, a sense that something in the nature of things had quietly turned against me, undermining my long certitude, as if, beneath the house's firm foundation, I could feel a subtle trembling in the earth.

# THREE

The next morning Meredith was already up and making breakfast by the time I came into the kitchen.

'Well, hello, sleepyhead,' she said lightly.

The air was thick with the salty smell of bacon and brewing coffee, odors that mark a family man as surely as cheap perfume betrays a bounder.

'You're awfully energetic this morning,' I said.

Meredith forked a strip of bacon onto a paper towel to let it drain. 'I woke up starving. Don't you ever wake up starving?'

For some reason, I heard a faint sense of accusation in her question, the sense that my own early-morning lack of appetite was emblematic of deeper deficiencies. Did I lack ambition, too, she seemed to ask. And passion? Did I lack sufficient hungers?

She drew the bacon from the paper towel and took a quick bite. 'Yum.' She snapped at the dangling end of the bacon, tearing the meat away in small bites. Wolfishly. I half expected to hear her growl.

Or did she do any of this, I wonder now. Was it merely something I thought I saw? And even if it were really there, where does a man go with such odd presentiments, a sense, vague and ineffable, that you do not really know the one you know, that all your previous soundings have gone no deeper than the shallows.

I sat down at the table, picked up the paper, and glanced at the head-line, something about the proposed town budget. 'Keith got in late.' I idly turned the page, now looking for the ad I'd placed three days before. 'Around midnight, I guess.'

Meredith grabbed the pot from the coffeemaker and poured each of us a steaming cup.

'I heard him come in,' I added. 'But you were out like a light.'

She sat down, took a sip from her cup, then tossed her hair with an earthy flare, like a woman in a roadhouse. 'Beautiful morning,' she said. Then she laughed.

# THOMAS H. COOK

'What's so funny?'

'Oh, just some silly joke Dr. Mays told us at the meeting.'

'Which was?'

She waved her hand. 'You wouldn't think it was funny.'

'Why do you say that?'

'It's silly, Eric. You wouldn't like it.'

'Try me.'

She shrugged. 'Okay,' she said, 'it wasn't really a joke. It was a quotation. From Lenny Bruce.' She chuckled again. 'He said that the difference between a man and a woman is that when a woman is thrown through a plateglass window, she doesn't get up thinking about sex.'

'Dr. Mays said that?' I asked, surprised. 'Dr. Mays of the thick glasses and tweed jacket and white meerschaum pipe?'

Meredith took another sip of coffee. 'The very one.'

I folded the paper and laid it on the table. 'I'm surprised he's even heard of Lenny Bruce.'

Meredith snapped another strip of bacon from the plate and took a small bite. 'People aren't always what they seem,' she said.

'Not me.' I spread out my arms. 'I'm exactly what I seem.'

She started to respond, then caught herself and said, 'Yes, you are, Eric. You are exactly what you seem.'

Again, I felt the hint of an accusation of being flat, one-dimensional, by-the-book, dully transparent. I thought of my father, the mystery man, his unexplained absences from and abrupt returns to the family circle, his empty chair at the dining table, the vacant look in my mother's eyes when they inadvertently fell upon it. I drew my arms back in. 'And that's a good thing, right?' I asked.

'What's a good thing?' Meredith asked.

'Being what I seem,' I answered. 'Because otherwise you might be afraid of me.'

'Afraid?'

'That I might suddenly become someone else. A murderer or something. One of those guys who comes home from work one day and hacks his whole family to death.'

Meredith appeared faintly alarmed. 'Don't say things like that, Eric.' Her eyes darted away, then returned to me, sparkling darkly, as if the tables had been turned, and she had spotted the animal in me.

'I'm just making a point,' I told her. 'If people really weren't what they seemed, then we could never trust each other, and if that happened, the whole thing would fall apart, wouldn't it?'

She turned my question over in her mind and seemed to come to some conclusion about it, though she gave no hint of what the conclusion was.

22

Instead, she rose, walked to the sink, and looked out across the grounds, her eyes darting from the picnic table to the grill before settling on the wooden bird feeder, which hung from a nearby pine. 'Winter's coming,' she said. 'I hate winter.'

This was not a sentiment she'd ever expressed before. 'Hate winter? I thought you loved winter. The fire, the coziness.'

She looked at me. 'You're right. I guess it's autumn I don't like.'

'Why?'

She returned her gaze to the window. Her right hand lifted, as if on its own, a pale bird rising until it came to rest at her throat. 'I don't know,' she said. 'Maybe just all those falling leaves.'

A few of those leaves had already fallen, I noticed, as I headed down the walkway to my car. They were large and yellow, with small brown spots that looked vaguely disturbing, like tiny cancers in the flesh of the leaf.

Which is probably why I thought of Jenny as I continued down the walkway that morning. I couldn't imagine the icy tremor that had surely coursed through my mother and father when the doctor had first diagnosed the tumor. Or maybe it had felt like a blade, slicing them open, spilling any hope of future happiness onto the tiled floor. Jenny, the bright one, the one with the most promise, was going to die, and so there would be no family photographs of her growing up, acting in the school play, graduating, going to college, marrying, having children of her own. That was what must have struck them at that instant, I decided, that the life they'd expected, both Jenny's and their own, had just exploded, leaving nothing but acrid smoke behind.

I'd reached the car and was about to get in when I saw Meredith open the front door, her arm outstretched, waving me back toward the house.

'What is it?' I called.

She said nothing, but continued to wave, so I closed the door and returned to the house.

'It's Vince Giordano,' she said, nodding toward the kitchen phone.

I looked at her quizzically, then went to the phone. 'Hey, Vince,' I said.

'Eric,' Vince said starkly. 'Listen, I didn't want to upset Meredith, but I have to know if you ... if you've seen Keith this morning.'

'No, I haven't. He usually sleeps late on Saturday morning.'

'But he's home? He came home last night?'

'Yes, he did.'

'Do you know when that was?'

Suddenly, I felt my answer assume unexpected weight. 'Around midnight, I think.'

There was a brief silence, then Vince said, 'Amy's missing.'

I waited for Vince to finish the sentence, tell me what Amy was missing, a ring, a watch, something Keith could help her find.

'She wasn't in her room this morning,' Vince added. 'We waited for her to get up and come down, but she never did. So we went up to look ... and she was ... gone.'

I would later remember Vince's words not so much as words, but as a distant tolling, accompanied by a palpable change in the weight of the air around me.

'We've looked everywhere,' Vince added. 'All over the house. The neighborhood. We can't find her anywhere, and so I thought maybe ... Keith ...'

'I'll get him up,' I said quickly. 'I'll call you right back.'

'Thanks,' Vince said softly. 'Thank you.'

I hung up and glanced toward Meredith. She read the expression on my face and looked suddenly troubled.

'It's Amy,' I told her. 'They can't find her. She wasn't in her room this morning. They've looked everywhere, but so far, nothing.'

'Oh, no,' Meredith whispered.

'We have to talk to Keith.'

We walked upstairs together. I tapped at Keith's door. No answer. I tapped again. 'Keith?'

There was still no answer and so I tried the door. As always, it was locked. I tapped again, this time much more loudly. 'Keith, get up. This is important.'

I heard a low moan, then the pad of Keith's feet as he walked to the door. 'What is it?' he groaned without opening it.

'It's about Amy Giordano,' I said. 'Her father just called. They can't find her.'

The door opened slightly and a watery eye seemed to swim toward me like a small blue fish through the murky water of an aquarium.

'Can't find her?' Keith asked.

'That's what I said.'

Meredith pressed near the door. 'Get dressed and come downstairs, Keith,' she said. Her voice was quite stern, like a teacher's. 'Hurry up.'

We walked back downstairs and sat at the kitchen table and waited for Keith to come join us.

'Maybe she just went for a walk,' I said.

Meredith looked at me worriedly. 'If something happened to Amy, Keith would be the one they'd suspect.'

'Meredith, there's no point in—'

'Maybe we should call Leo.'

'Leo? No. Keith doesn't need a lawyer.'

'Yes, but—'

'Meredith, all we're going to do is ask Keith a few questions. When he last saw Amy. If she seemed okay. Then I'm going to call Vince and tell him what Keith said.' I looked at her pointedly. 'Okay?'

She nodded tensely. 'Yes, fine.'

Keith slouched down the stairs, still drowsy, scratching his head. 'Now ... what did you say about Amy?' he asked, as he slumped down in a chair at the kitchen table.

'She's missing,' I told him.

Keith rubbed his eyes with his fists. 'That's crazy,' he said, with a light, dismissive grunt.

Meredith leaned forward, her voice measured. 'This is serious, Keith. Where was Amy when you left the Giordanos' house last night?'

'In her bedroom,' Keith answered, still drowsy, but now coming a bit more to life. 'I read her a story. Then I went to the living room and watched TV.'

'When did you read her the story?'

'About eight-thirty, I guess.'

'Don't guess,' Meredith snapped. 'Don't guess about anything, Keith.'

For the first time the gravity of the situation registered on Keith's face. 'She's really missing?' he asked, as if everything up to now had been some kind of joke.

'What do you think we've been saying, Keith?' Meredith asked.

'Listen,' I said to him. 'I want you to think carefully, because I have to call Mr. Giordano and tell him exactly what you tell me. So, like your mother says, Keith, don't guess about anything.'

He nodded, and I could see that it had sunk in fully now. 'Okay, sure,' he said.

'All right,' I began. 'You didn't see Amy again, right? Not after you read her that story?'

'No.'

'Are you sure?'

'Yes,' Keith answered emphatically. His gaze darted over to Meredith. 'I didn't see her again.'

'Do you have any idea where she is?' I asked.

Keith looked suddenly offended. 'Of course not.' He glanced back and forth between Meredith and me. 'It's the truth,' he cried. 'I didn't see her again.'

'Did you see anything?' I asked.

'What do you mean?'

'Anything out of the ordinary.'

'You mean like … was she acting funny … or—'

'Funny. Strange. Unhappy. Maybe wanting to run away? Did she give you any hint of that?'

'No.'

'Okay, how about something else,' I said. 'Somebody around the house. Peeping Tom, that sort of thing.'

Keith shook his head. 'I didn't see anything, Dad.' His eyes swept over to Meredith, and I saw the first suggestion of worry in them. 'Am I in trouble?'

Meredith sat back slightly, the posture she always assumed when she had no immediate answer.

Keith held his gaze on Meredith. 'Are the police going to talk to me?'

Meredith shrugged. 'I guess it depends.'

'On what?'

Meredith remained silent.

Keith looked at me. 'On what, Dad?'

I gave him the only answer I had. 'On what happened to Amy, I suppose.'

# FOUR

Later I would try to define it, the uneasiness of those first few minutes. I would go over the phone call from Vince, the way Meredith and I had trudged up the stairs together then returned to the kitchen and waited for Keith. I would try to remember if I'd heard something during that otherwise silent interval, the sound of tiny insect teeth or a steady drip of water, small, insistent, relentlessly undermining. Now I know the chasm that yawned beneath the lives we had so carefully constructed. I hear a gunshot, a resigned murmur, and in those sounds all I didn't know flashes clear and bright.

But what *did* I know? The answer is clear. I knew nothing. And what do you do when you know nothing? You take the next step because you have to and because, in your ignorance, you can't possibly know how blind it is, the step you're taking, or how dire its unseen consequences.

And so after Keith returned to his room, I simply called Vince Giordano and told him exactly what my son had said, half believing that that might be the end of it for Keith, Meredith, and me, that whatever terrible thing might have happened to Amy Giordano, her spilled blood, if it had been spilled, would not wash over the rest of us.

'I'm sorry, Vince,' I said. 'I wish I could be more help, but Keith simply has no idea where Amy is.'

After a pause, Vince said, 'I have to ask you something.'

'Anything.'

'Did Keith leave the house while he was here with Amy?'

I had no way of knowing if Keith had left Vince's house at any point during the time he'd been there, but I suddenly felt the need to answer anyway, and so I gave an answer I deeply hoped was true.

'I'm sure he didn't,' I said.

'Would you mind asking him?' Vince's voice was almost pleading. 'We just can't figure out what happened.'

'Of course,' I told him.

'Just ask him if he left Amy ... even for a minute,' Vince repeated.

'I'll call you right back,' I said, then hung up and walked up the stairs, leaving Meredith alone and looking increasingly worried at the kitchen table.

Keith's door was closed but he opened it at my first tap, though slightly, so that only half his face was visible, a single eye peering at me through a narrow slit.

'Mr. Giordano wants to know if you left the house at any point last night,' I said.

The eye blinked languidly, like a curtain drawn down slowly then reluctantly raised.

'Well, did you?'

'No,' Keith answered.

It was a firm no, and yet his answer had come only after a moment of hesitation, or was it calculation?

'Are you sure about that, Keith?' I asked.

This time his answer came without hesitation. 'Yes.'

'Absolutely sure? Because I have to go back now and tell Mr. Giordano.'

'I didn't leave the house,' Keith assured me.

'It's not a big deal if you did, Keith. It's not the same as if you—'

'As if I what, Dad?' Keith asked, almost snappishly.

'You know what I mean,' I told him.

'As ... if I killed her?' Keith asked. 'Or whatever happened.'

'I don't believe you did anything to Amy Giordano, if that's what you're accusing me of,' I told him.

'Really?' Keith replied. His tone was petulant. 'It sounds like you do. Mom, too. Like both of you think I did something.'

'It only sounds that way to you, Keith,' I said, my tone now changing with his, becoming suddenly defensive. 'As a matter of fact, I told Mr. Giordano that you didn't leave the house before I came up here.'

Keith didn't look as if he believed me, but he kept his doubts to himself.

'Anyway, I have to call Mr. Giordano back now,' I said, then turned and quickly made my way down the stairs, Keith's door slamming sharply behind me, hard and unforgiving as a slap.

Karen Giordano answered the phone.

'Karen, it's Eric Moore.'

'Oh, hello, Eric,' Karen said with a slight sniffle that made me think she'd been crying.

'Has anything changed?' I asked.

'No,' she answered. Her voice was weak. 'We don't know where she is.' She was ordinarily a cheerful woman, but all her cheer had drained away. 'We've called everybody,' Karen continued. 'All the neighbors. Everybody.' Her voice softened still more and took on an oddly pleading quality, so that it struck me that dread was a kind of humility, an admission of one's helplessness, the fact that, in the end, we control nothing. 'No one's seen her.'

I wanted to assure her that everything would turn out fine, that Amy would suddenly appear out of a closet or from behind a curtain, shout 'April Fool' or something of the kind. But I had seen too many news stories to believe such a thing was likely. They really did vanish, these little girls, and if they were found at all, it was almost always too late. Still, there was one possibility. 'Do you think that she could have ... well ... could be maybe trying to ... make a point?'

'A point?' Karen asked.

'A statement,' I added, then realized that the word was ridiculously formal. 'Maybe, that she wants you to miss her so she—'

'Ran away?' Karen interrupted.

'Something like that,' I said. 'Kids can do crazy things.'

She started to speak, but suddenly Vince was on the line. 'What'd Keith say?' he asked urgently.

'He said he didn't leave the house.'

Vince released a sigh. 'Well, if that's what he says, then I have to call the police, Eric.'

'Okay,' I answered.

There was a pause, and I got the feeling that Vince was giving me, and perhaps my son, one last chance. So that's where we are now, I thought, he believes my son did something terrible to his daughter and there's nothing I can do to convince him otherwise, nothing I can say about Keith that he won't think tainted by my own protective fatherhood. Before I was a neighbor, a fellow tradesmen in a friendly town, someone he did business with and waved to and smiled at. But now I am an accessory to my son's imagined crime.

'I think you *should* tell the police, Vince.'

It surprised me that my response appeared to take him aback, as if he'd expected me to argue against it.

'They'll want to talk to Keith,' Vince warned.

'I'm sure he'll be happy to talk to them.'

'Okay,' Vince said, his tone strangely deflated, like a man forced to do something he'd hoped to avoid.

'Vince,' I began, 'if I can help in any—'

'Right,' Vince interrupted. 'I'll be in touch.'

And with that, he hung up.

\*

'That's all Vince said?' Meredith asked, as she walked me to the car a few minutes later. 'That he would be in touch?'

We brushed passed the Japanese maple, a gentle pink light filtering through its leaves.

'And that he's calling the police,' I said.

'He thinks Keith did something.'

'Probably,' I admitted.

Meredith remained silent until we reached the car. Then she said, 'I'm afraid, Eric.'

I touched her face. 'We can't get ahead of ourselves. I mean, there's no proof that anything has—'

'Are you sure you don't want to call Leo?'

I shook my head. 'Not yet.'

I opened the door of the car and pulled myself in behind the wheel, but made no effort to leave. Instead, I rolled down the window and looked at my wife in a way that later struck me as shockingly nostalgic, as if she were already drifting away or changing in some way, these the dwindling days of our previously unencumbered life together. For a moment everything that had gone before, the best years of our lives, seemed precariously balanced, happiness a kind of arrogance, a bounty we had taken for granted until then, death the only clear and present danger, and even that still very far away. And yet, despite such dark presentiments, I said, 'It's going to be okay, Meredith. It really is.'

I could see she didn't believe me, but that was not unusual for Meredith. She had always been a worrier, concerned about money before things got really tight, keeping a close eye on even Keith's most petty delinquencies, forever poised to nip something in the bud. I had countered with optimism, looking on the bright side, a pose I still thought it necessary to maintain.

'We can't go off the deep end,' I told her. 'Even if something happened to Amy, it has nothing to do with us.'

'That doesn't matter,' Meredith said.

'Of course it does.'

'No, it doesn't,' Meredith said, 'because once something like this happens, once they start asking questions ...'

'But Keith didn't leave the house until the Giordanos came home,' I said emphatically. 'So it doesn't matter about the questions. He'll have the answers.'

She drew in a long breath. 'Okay, Eric,' she said with a thin, frail smile. 'Whatever you say.'

She turned and headed back toward the house, a cool gust of wind sweeping the ground before her, fierce and devilish, kicking up those stricken yellow leaves I'd seen an hour earlier so that they spiraled up and up to where I saw Keith at his bedroom window, staring down at me, his gaze cold and resentful, as if I were no longer his father at all, no longer his protector or benefactor, but instead arrayed against him, part of the assembling mob that soon would be crying for his head.

'Morning,' Neil said, as I came into the store.

It was nearly nine, so I knew he'd already prepped the developers and dusted the stock. He was thorough and reliable in that way, the perfect employee. Best of all, he gave no indication of having any larger ambition than to work in my shop, collect his small salary, and indulge his few modest pleasures. Twice a year he went to New York to take in four or five Broadway shows, usually the big musicals whose glitzy numbers clearly thrilled him. While there, he stayed at a small inexpensive hotel in Chelsea, ate street food, save for his final night when he splurged on Italian, and usually came back with a new snow globe to add to his collection of travel mementos. Briefly he'd had a partner named Gordon, a round, bearded man who often appeared in community theater presentations, though only as a bit player, listed in the program as 'neighbor' or 'prison guard'. During the two years of their relationship, Neil's frame of mind had been closely tied to Gordon's severe mood swings, gloomy or cheerful depending, or so it often seemed, on the course of whatever show Gordon happened to be in at the time. Inevitably, they'd broken up, and since then Neil had lived with his ailing mother in a small house on one of the town's few remaining unpaved roads, an arrangement with which he seemed perfectly content, since, as he'd once told me, 'anything else would require too much effort.'

'Running late, boss,' Neil added.

I nodded silently.

Neil cocked his head to the right. 'Uh-oh, bad morning.'

'A little,' I admitted.

'Well, you'll perk up once the money starts rolling in. Speaking of which, I should probably go to the bank. We're low on change.'

He left a few minutes later, and while I went about the usual pre-opening routine, restocking shelves, a quick sweep of the sidewalk outside the shop, I thought about Amy Giordano and how Vince seemed determined to lay the blame for whatever had happened to her at Keith's door.

But there was nowhere to go with such thoughts. I had no idea what had befallen Amy, whether she'd run away or suffered some monstrous fate. And so I retreated to the refuge I usually sought when I was feeling uneasy about money or Keith's grades or any of a hundred other petty troubles.

It was at the rear of the store, my little refuge, no more than a large table, really, along with a square of particle board hung with a modest assortment of stained-wood frames. Little skill was needed to frame the family photos that came my way. Usually people chose colors they thought appropriate to the scene: blue for families on the beach; greens and reds for families in forest encampments; gold or silver for families posed beside the tall sea grass that adorns the nearby bay; white for photos taken while whale watching.

Framing these smiling, bucolic scenes never failed to relax and reassure me. But a frame is just a frame, and the life it holds is frozen, static, beyond the reach of future events. Real life is another matter.

The phone rang.

It was Meredith. 'Eric, come home,' she told me.

'Why?' I asked.

'Because,' she said, 'they're here.'

# FIVE

There were two of them, both dressed in dark suits, a tall, hawk-faced man named Kraus, and another, shorter and rounder, whose name was Peak. They were sitting in the living room when I arrived, and both smiled pleasantly as they introduced themselves.

'I understand,' Kraus began, 'that Mr. Giordano called you this morning?'

'Yes.'

We were all standing, Kraus's dark deep-set eyes leveled directly upon me; Peak a little to my left, seemed more interested, or so it seemed, in a family portrait I'd taken four years before, the three of us posed before Keith's sixth-grade science project, a plaster of paris sculpture of the body's internal organs, red heart, blue lungs, brown liver, and so on.

'Amy is still missing,' Kraus told me.

'I'm sorry to hear that,' I said.

Peak abruptly turned from the photograph. 'Interested in anatomy, is he?' he asked.

'Anatomy?'

'It looks like a science project,' Peak said. 'In the picture here. Organs?'

'Yes.'

'So, he's interested in that, your son?'

I shook my head. 'Not really, no.'

Kraus's smile was thin, anemic, forced rather than felt. 'So why did he do a project like that?' he asked

'Because it was easy for him,' I answered.

'Easy?'

'Other kids had much more elaborate projects,' I explained.

'He's not a great student then?'

'No.'

'How would you describe him?' Kraus asked.

'Keith? I don't know. He's a teenage boy. A little odd, maybe.'

33

'In what way is he odd?'

'Well, not odd exactly,' I added quickly. 'Quiet.'

Kraus looked at Peak and gave a faint nod, which brought the smaller man suddenly back into the game.

'No reason to be alarmed,' Peak said.

'I'm not alarmed,' I told him.

The two men exchanged glances.

'I suppose you'd like to talk to Keith,' I added, careful to keep my voice firm and confident, a father who has not the slightest doubt that he knows his son thoroughly. I wanted them to believe that nothing could have escaped my notice – that I had searched Keith's closets and the drawers of his bedroom bureau, smelled his breath when he came in at night, routinely dragged him to the family physician for drug tests; that I monitored the books he read, the music he listened to, the sites he visited on the Internet; that I had researched the family histories of the friends he hung around with; that only God could possibly know more than I did about my son.

'Yes, we would,' Kraus said.

'I'll get him.'

'He's not here,' Meredith said quickly.

I looked at her, puzzled. 'Where is he?'

'He went for a walk.'

Before I could say anything further, Kraus said, 'Where does he walk?'

For some reason, Meredith merely repeated the question. 'Where does he walk?'

Peak looked out the large window that fronted the thickly forested grounds behind the house. 'Back there, that's conservation land, right? No houses. No roads.'

'Yes, it's all conservation land,' I told him. 'No one can ever build back there or—'

'So it's very isolated,' Peak said. He turned back to Meredith. 'Is that where Keith takes these walks, in the woods back there?'

Suddenly the words 'these walks' took on an ominous quality and I imagined Keith as I knew Peak and Kraus imagined him, a figure crouching in the undergrowth, desperately digging in the moist ground, burying something that linked him to Amy Giordano, a bloodstained lock of hair.

'No, he doesn't walk back there,' I said quickly. 'You can't. The undergrowth is too thick and there are no trails.'

Kraus's eyes shifted to my wife, fixing on her an unsettling intensity. 'So where is he?'

'The baseball field,' Meredith answered. 'When he goes for a walk, he usually goes down to the baseball field.'

'There and back, you mean?' Peak asked.

Meredith nodded faintly, and I expected that to be the end of it, but Kraus said, 'When does he go for these walks? In the morning?'

'No,' Meredith answered. 'Usually in the afternoon. Or after dinner.'

'Not in the morning then,' Kraus said. 'Except this morning, right?'

Again, Meredith nodded delicately, like someone reluctant to give assent, but unable to withhold it.

'I noticed a bike at the end of the walkway,' Peak said. 'Is that Keith's?'

'Yes,' I said. 'He uses it to make deliveries for me after school.'

'Where does he make these deliveries?' Kraus asked.

'Anywhere in biking distance from my shop,' I said.

'And that would be where, Mr. Moore?' Peak asked.

'My shop is in Dalton Square,' I said.

'What does he deliver?' Kraus asked.

'Pictures,' I said. 'Of families, mostly.'

'Family photographs,' Peak said with a slight smile. 'Got a few of those myself.'

Kraus shifted his weight like a fighter preparing to deliver the next blow. 'How long has he been delivering these pictures?'

Again, there was a sinister, oddly accusatory, use of 'these', but I was no longer sure if the accusation was intended to incriminate Keith or if Kraus had now extended his accusatory tone to me.

'A couple of years,' I answered. 'There's no law against that, is there?'

'What?' Peak asked with a slight chuckle. 'Well, of course not, Mr. Moore.' He glanced toward Kraus then back to me. 'Why would you think that?'

Before I could answer, Meredith cut in. 'I'll go get him if you want me to.'

Peak looked at his watch. 'No, we'll do it. The ball field's on the way back to the station, we can—'

'No!' I blurted. 'Let me bring him here.'

Both of them looked at me, stonily silent, waiting.

'It would scare him,' I explained.

'What would scare him?' Kraus asked.

'You know, two men he's never seen.'

'He's a scared type of kid, your son?' Peak asked.

It had never occurred to me before, but now it struck me that in fact Keith was a 'scared type of kid'. He was scared he'd disappointed Meredith by doing poorly in school and scared he'd disappointed me by never having had a girlfriend. He was scared he wouldn't get into a good college, scared that he'd never find what he wanted to do in life or that he'd fail at the thing he did find. He had no friends, and I supposed that that scared him, too. Add them up, one by one, and it seemed that he was scared of almost everything, lived in a subtle crouch. And yet, I said, 'No, I don't think Keith's scared of anything in particular. But two men – police – that would scare anybody, wouldn't it?'

Again, Kraus and Peak glanced at each other, then Peak said. 'All right, Mr. Moore, you can go get him.' He regarded me distantly. 'No reason,' he repeated, 'to be alarmed.'

I expected to find Keith on Vernon Road, which fronts our house, then shoots directly to town, where it becomes Main Street, then winds another mile to the ball field, a distance of little more than three miles. But instead, I spotted him standing idly at the little playground near the town square, a place where people routinely bring small children to scrabble in the sandbox or race around the wooden castle. He was slumped against the playground's wrought iron fence, his shoulder pressed into it, rhythmically kicking at the ground with the toe of his shoe.

He didn't see me when I pulled up to the curb a few yards from the playground, so that by the time I'd gotten out of the car and walked across the lawn, it was too late for him to hide the cigarette.

'I didn't know you smoked,' I said, as I came up to him.

He whirled around, clearly startled, his gaze first on me, then darting nervously about the grounds, as if in fear of snipers.

I nodded toward the pack of Marlboros that winked from his shirt pocket. 'When did you start?'

He took a long, defiant draw on the cigarette, his body now assuming a sullen teenage swagger. 'I don't do it all the time.'

'So, in this case, what's the occasion?'

He shrugged. 'I guess I'm jumpy.' He let the cigarette drop from his fingers, lifted the collar of his parka, and in that instant he seemed to retreat to an earlier time, taking on the sullen hunch of a fifties teenager, a rebel without a cause.

'This thing with Amy,' I said. 'It makes everybody jumpy.'

'Yeah, sure.' He ground the cigarette into the dirt with the toe of his shoe, snatched the pack from his shirt pocket, thumped out another and lit it.

'It's okay to be a little nervous,' I told him.

He waved out the match and laughed. 'Oh yeah?'

'I would be,' I said.

'But there's a difference, Dad.' He took a long draw on the cigarette and released a column of smoke that narrowly missed my face. 'You weren't at her fucking house.'

He'd never used that kind of language in front of me before, but it didn't seem the right time to quibble about matters that now struck me as infinitely small. The last thing he needed, I decided, was a scolding.

'I have to take you back home,' I told him.

This appeared to disturb him more than my having caught him with a cigarette.

'I want to hang around here for a while,' he said.

'No, you have to come with me,' I insisted. 'There are a couple of policemen who want to talk to you.'

His face stiffened and an icy fear came into his eyes. 'They think I did it, right?'

'Did what?'

'You know, whatever happened to Amy.'

'There's no evidence that anything happened to Amy.'

'Yeah, but something did,' Keith said. 'Something did, or she wouldn't be missing.'

'Keith,' I said. 'I want you to be very careful when you talk to these cops. Think before you answer. And be sure you don't lie about anything.'

'Why would I lie about something?' Keith asked.

'Just don't, that's what I'm telling you. Because it's a red flag.'

He dropped the cigarette and crushed it with an odd brutality, as if he were angrily stomping the life out of a small defenseless creature. 'I didn't hurt Amy.'

'I know that.'

'I may be bad, but I didn't hurt Amy.'

'You're not bad, Keith. Smoking cigarettes doesn't make you bad.'

A dry scoffing laugh broke from him, one whose exact meaning I couldn't read. 'Yeah, right, Dad' was all he said.

Meredith had served Kraus and Peak coffee and cookies by the time I returned with Keith, but I couldn't imagine that she'd been able to do it in a way that actually made them feel welcome.

'This is Keith,' I told them as I ushered my son into the living room.

Both detectives rose and smiled and shook Keith's hand. Then they sat down on the green sofa, Keith opposite them in a wooden rocker.

'You don't have to stay,' Peak said to Meredith. He looked at me. 'You, either, Mr. Moore. This is just a friendly chat.' He smiled. 'If it were any more serious than that, we'd be reading Keith here his rights.' He glanced at Keith and the smile broadened. 'Just like they do on TV, right?'

Keith nodded slightly.

'I'd rather stay with my son,' I said.

Meredith opted to busy herself in her small office at the rear of the house, however, and so it was just three men and a teenage boy in the living room when the questioning began.

Then, almost immediately, it was over, with little more established than what I'd already told Vince Giordano, that Keith had not left Amy alone in her house, that he'd gotten home a little before midnight. The only new facts were that my son had walked from Amy's house into the village, then along its back streets, and finally over to the ball field where he'd sat alone on the bleachers for a time, then gotten up and walked home. At no time during this late-night sojourn had he talked to anyone. He'd called home at just before ten, he said. I'd answered the phone and he'd told me that he intended to stay out a little later than usual. I'd asked if he needed a ride, and he'd assured me that he didn't. At that point, he and I had agreed that he was to be home before midnight. Which, he told Kraus and Peak, he had been. The exact time, he said, was seven minutes before twelve. He knew this because he'd glanced at the large grandfather clock in the front foyer before going upstairs to his room.

As I listened to Keith's answers, I began to relax. Nothing Keith said surprised me and nothing contradicted my own understanding of his movements and activities that night.

'So,' Kraus said, 'after you hung around the ball field for a while, you went straight home?'

'Yes.'

'The ball field is only a few blocks from the Giordanos' house, isn't it?'

'Yes.'

'Did you pass their house again?'

'No.'

'You went straight home,' Peak said. 'Like do not pass go?'

Keith chuckled, but mirthlessly, a laugh I heard as a mocking response to Peak's reference.

And so it didn't surprise me that Peak's attitude immediately hardened. 'How'd you get home?'

'I walked.'

Peak's eyes were very still. 'You walked?'

'Yes,' Keith answered.

'You don't have a car?' Kraus asked.

'No,' Keith said. 'I couldn't drive anyway. I'm fifteen.'

'You have a learner's permit?' Peak asked.

'Yes.'

'How did you get to Amy's house?'

'My uncle drove me.'

Kraus took a notebook from his jacket pocket. 'What's your uncle's name?'

Keith looked at me as if asking if he should answer.

'His name is Warren,' I said. 'Warren Moore.'

'Where does he live?' Kraus asked.

'1473 Barrow Street.'

'Near the school,' Peak said. 'The elementary school.'

'Yes,' I said. 'Right next door, actually.'

'Where does he work?'

'He works on his own. He paints houses.'

Kraus jotted something in his notebook, then returned his attention to Keith. 'So your uncle drove you to Amy's house, and then, after Mr. and Mrs. Giordano came back home, you walked to town – have I got that right?'

'Yes.'

'And then you went to the ballfield, and after that you walked home?'

'Yes.'

'All the way from the center of town?'

Keith nodded.

'You didn't get a ride?' Kraus asked.

Keith shook his head. 'No.'

'But you could have called home, right, gotten a lift?'

'Sure.'

'Why didn't you?' Peak asked.

'I just didn't,' Keith answered. 'I don't mind walking.'

'Even that late?' Kraus asked.

'No,' Keith answered. He thrust his head backward and ran his fingers through the tangles of his hair. 'I like the night,' he said.

# SIX

*I* *like the night.*

Odd how sinister a simple remark can sound, the questions it can suddenly raise.

In what way, I wondered, did my son like the night? Did he like it because it brought him a certain peace? Or did he like it simply because it meant the end of another tedious day at school or at home? Or did he like it because it shielded him from view, because, clothed in its darkness, he could skulk about unnoticed, hidden beneath the hood of the blue parka? Did he like it like a saint in search of solitude or like a stalker in search of cover?

It didn't matter really. What mattered was that my son had gotten through it, so that it might end here, a hope I fully embraced as I walked the two detectives to their car.

Kraus got in behind the wheel, but Peak remained standing at the passenger door. He wore a dark green suit, and in the slant of bright sunlight that washed over him, he looked like a thick shrub.

'Mr. Moore,' he said, 'what is your experience with your son?'

'Experience?' I asked.

'In your exchanges, I mean. Day to day.'

'I still don't quite ...'

'Has he been truthful?' Peak asked.

Suddenly, I thought of the two beams of light sweeping across the ragged undergrowth and recalled that only moments before, Keith had said that he had not been driven home the night before. *Was that true?* I wondered now. But despite that jarring vision and its accompanying doubt, I said, 'As far as I know, he's always told me the truth.'

Peak watched me closely. 'About everything?'

'Well, I'm sure he's told a few little lies to me over the years,' I said. 'He's a kid, that's all. A little enclosed, but—' The look in Peak's eyes stopped me in my tracks. 'But normal,' I added quickly. 'A teenager, that's all.'

'Yes, of course,' Peak said.

He tried to appear perfectly satisfied by my answer, but I knew he wasn't. 'Well, thank you,' he said. 'We'll call if we need anything further.'

With that he settled into the passenger seat and the car pulled away.

Meredith was washing the detectives' coffee cups when I returned to the house, her movements strangely frantic, almost violent, like someone trying to erase an incriminating stain.

'Well, that was easier than I expected,' I told her.

'They'll be back,' Meredith said.

Her certainty surprised me. 'Why are you so sure of that?'

She had been facing the sink, her back to me, but now she whirled around. 'Because something always comes up, Eric.' There was a fire in her eyes, a sense that she was talking about more than Keith's connection, whatever it might be, to Amy Giordano's disappearance.

'What do you mean?'

'To spoil things' – her expression took on an indecipherable combination of anger and sadness, like someone mourning a death by freak accident – 'when things were so perfect.'

'Nothing is spoiled,' I said in a gentle, comforting tone, pleased that our life had seemed so perfect to her until now. 'Meredith, we don't even know what happened to Amy yet.'

She glanced away, settled her gaze briefly on the woods outside the window, two small birds in a hanging feeder. 'I just feel this terrible sinking,' she said softly.

I came over to her and drew her into my arms. Her body was stiff and brittle, a bundle of sticks. 'Nothing is sinking,' I assured her.

She shook her head. 'I'm just afraid, that's all. Afraid that it's all going to ... explode.'

With that, she stepped out of my embrace and made her way up the stairs. I made no effort to follow her. It wouldn't have done any good anyway. Under stress, Meredith preferred being alone, at least in brief intervals. There was something about solitude that calmed her, and so I left her to herself, walked out into the yard, sat beside the brick grill, and tried to reason through my impulsive decision to say nothing to the police or even to Keith about my oddly building suspicion that he'd lied to them. Even then, I wasn't sure why I'd done it, save that I'd found no way to address the matter without either drawing Keith deeper into suspicion or grilling him myself, an action I wanted to delay as long as possible in the hope that Amy would suddenly turn up safe and sound, and so there would be no need for me to confront Keith at all. It was an illusion that couldn't be justified, or even maintained for very long, and

I should have known that at the time. Since then I've learned that half of life is denial, that even in those we love, it's not what we see but what we choose to be blind to that sustains us.

I was still sitting in the same place when Warren's car made the lazy turn around the driveway and came to a halt in front of the house.

He got out and headed toward me, his gait far more determined than I'd ever seen it, an awkwardly charging bull.

'I just heard it on the radio,' he said breathlessly when he reached me. 'They're organizing a search. Volunteers. The whole town is gearing up for it.' His face was red and appeared a bit puffy, the way it looked after he'd been drinking.

'So,' he asked. 'Are you okay?'

'I just hope Amy turns up,' I said. 'Because if she doesn't—'

'Don't think about that,' Warren blurted.

This piece of advice did not surprise me. It was precisely the advice Warren had spent his life following. I recalled how he'd put my father's bankruptcy out of his mind, pretending that our precipitous fall into poverty had simply never happened. And so he'd obliviously urged me to hold to my plan to go to college, though there was no money for that. Years later, with my father now in a low-rent retirement home, he'd broached the subject of our starting a landscaping business. When I'd asked how he intended to come up with sufficient seed money, he'd replied, 'Well, you know, when Pop goes,' even though our father had long ago lost everything he had, everything he might have given us. Warren had reacted to Jenny's illness the same way, by simply refusing to face it. During the months of her dying, as she grew steadily weaker, losing one faculty after another to the growing tumor in her brain, Warren had talked on and on about a future she could not possibly have. 'When Jenny gets a boyfriend,' he'd say, or 'When Jenny gets to high school.' Only once, the afternoon of Jenny's death, when she lay mute and helpless, but none-theless frantically trying to communicate, had he actually looked stricken by her circumstances. In my mind I could still see the way he'd stood at the door as she squirmed and sputtered, unable to speak, but seized with a raw determination to make some final statement. I'd leaned down and put my ear to her lips, heard nothing but her feverish breathing until even that had ended and she sank into a coma from which she never awakened.

Now Warren was with me once again in a time of trial, and once again he was refusing to admit the nature of the problem or how grave it might be or yet become.

'So,' Warren said, 'I just wanted to tell you that it's going to be okay, Bro.'

There was no point in arguing with him, so I said simply, 'The police have already been here. Keith told them that he never left Amy's house and that he walked home alone.'

Warren plopped into a lawn chair opposite the grill and folded his hands over his belly. 'The police had to talk to him,' he said. 'But they wouldn't think he had anything to do with something bad.'

There it was again, mindless optimism, my brother's particular form of adaptation. He'd found a way to survive by taking in only the information that kept him afloat. In high school, he'd played the happy fat boy. In adulthood, the role of jovial alcoholic had fit like a glove. Now he was playing the steady family adviser, a role that clearly pleased him until I said, 'They'll probably talk to you, too.'

Warren smiled, but with a hint of nervousness. 'Me? Why would they talk to me? I'm not involved.'

'Of course you are, Warren.'

The faint smile now drooped. 'How?'

'You drove Keith to Amy's house,' I explained.

'So?'

'I'm just telling you that they know about it,' I said. 'They asked for your address. They have to talk to everybody, Warren. Anyone who had any contact with Amy in the hours before she disappeared.'

Warren said nothing, but his mind was clearly working hard.

'Did you have any contact with her?' I asked evenly.

'I wouldn't call it ... contact.'

'Did you see her?'

Warren didn't answer, but I knew from the look in his eyes that he had.

'Where was she?' I asked.

Warren's face grew very still. 'She was in the yard when I let Keith out in front of the house. Playing. She came up to the car.'

I leaned forward. 'Listen to me,' I said. 'This is serious business. So I'll tell you what I told Keith. When the cops come to you, when they ask you questions, think before you answer. And tell the truth.'

Warren nodded gently, obediently, like a child receiving grave instructions.

'Did you talk to Amy?' I asked.

Warren shook his head.

'Not even a quick hi?'

'I don't know,' Warren said.

'Think, Warren.'

He shrugged. 'Maybe something like that, like what you said. You know, a quick hi.'

'Nothing else?'

'No.'

'Are you sure?'

'Yes,' Warren answered.

I could see that he was worried now, but I also knew that this worry wouldn't last, his momentary fretfulness precisely that – momentary. Or so I thought. But to my surprise the veil of trouble didn't lift from my brother's face.

'Do you think they suspect me?' he asked.

'Why would they suspect you?'

Warren shrugged. 'I don't know,' he said weakly. 'Maybe they just do.'

I shook my head. 'They have no reason to suspect you, Warren,' I assured him.

But the pained expression remained on his face, an expression that reminded me of the look on Meredith's face, and on Keith's, so that it seemed to me that trouble had fallen upon my family like a net, leaving all our faces webbed in gray. 'Everybody's a little worried at the moment' – I placed my hand on his shoulder and gave it a brotherly squeeze – 'but it's nothing,' I said, 'compared to what Vince and Karen must be going through. A missing daughter, can you imagine?'

Warren nodded. 'Yeah,' he said quietly. 'Such an adorable little girl.'

# SEVEN

Here is the illusion – a normal day predicts a normal tomorrow and each day is not a brand-new spin of the wheel, our lives not lived at the whim of Lady Luck. And yet, now, when I recall the morning in question, a bright sunny morning, before that first ring of the phone, I see myself as living in a world that was almost entirely illusion. Then the phone rang and I heard Vince Giordano's voice, and suddenly the wheel stopped. Instead of falling on the number upon which I'd bet the full wealth and value of my life and which it had always landed on before, the red ball skirted past, made another circle around the wheel, and dropped into a very different slot. And like a gambler who'd won every spin before that moment, I stared, dazed, at the grim result of this latest turn of the wheel, and in my mind I set the wheel going backward, lifted the ball from the fateful slot, and sent it whirling back as if by sheer force of will it could be made to fall again where it had fallen so many times before. It was the afternoon of the day that Amy Giordano disappeared, but I refused to accept the fact that anything had changed.

And so, when I returned to the shop, I tried to appear normal, as if nothing were bothering me.

But Neil knew better. He attempted to hide it, but I often caught him glancing at me surreptitiously, as if I'd begun to manifest some curious symptom, a slight tremor in the hand, for example, or a peculiar tendency to stare into space.

'Something wrong, boss?' he asked finally.

By then the local radio stations had been reporting Amy's disappearance for several hours. People were searching her neighborhood, as well as more remote areas, particularly the woods that surrounded the subdivision where she lived. It was a big story, and so I knew that it was only a matter of time before the whole community would find out that Keith had been babysitting Amy the night of her disappearance.

'It's about Amy Giordano,' I said. 'Keith was at her house last night. Babysitting. The police spoke to him this morning.'

The layer of jovial self mockery with which Neil presented himself dropped away. 'I'm sure Keith didn't do anything wrong,' he said. 'Keith's very responsible.'

Keith was no such thing, and I knew it. Although he was supposed to come to the shop immediately after school each afternoon, he often showed up an hour late, usually with a grudging look on his face, wanting only to go directly home, then just as directly up the stairs to his room. If there were deliveries to be made, he would make them, but always sullenly. He was not responsible in his schoolwork or in his chores at home. When he raked leaves, he usually did little more than scatter them. When he took out the garbage, a few pieces always failed to make it into the can. There was something desultory in everything he did, and for the first time, this very desultoriness took on an oddly sinister character, an outward carelessness and indifference to order that struck me as perhaps emblematic of an inner, and far more serious, disarray.

Neil touched my arm. 'You don't have to worry about Keith,' he said. 'He's a good kid.'

It was typical of Neil to say whatever had to be said to ease my distress, and the only response I could think of was a quick, false 'Yes, he is.'

Neil smiled warmly, then returned to his work, though I noticed that each time the phone rang he tensed and glanced over at me worriedly.

Until just before two that afternoon, all the calls were routine, and during those few hours I felt the sweetness of the ordinary, of needs easily met, promises easily kept, a world of choices and decisions that demanded no great store of wisdom.

At 1:54 the phone rang.

It was Detective Peak. 'Mr. Moore, I wanted to let you know that—'

'You found her,' I blurted.

'What?' Peak asked.

'You found Amy,' I repeated.

'No,' he said. 'I wish we had. I'm just calling because I need your assurance that Keith will be around if we need to talk to him again.'

'Of course, he will.'

'This is an official request, Mr. Moore,' Peak said. 'Keith is now in your custody.'

*Custody.* The word was abruptly laden with grave responsibility.

'He won't go anywhere,' I told him.

'Good,' Peak said. 'Thank you for your cooperation.'

He hung up, but for a brief instant, I continued to press the receiver to my ear, hoping for another voice to come on the line, to tell me that Amy had been found, that she was alive and well, just a little girl who'd wandered out of her house, crawled into a storm drain, and gone to sleep.

'Boss?'

It was Neil. He was staring at me from behind a counter piled with small boxes of film.

'It was the police,' I told him. 'They want to make sure Keith doesn't go anywhere.'

Neil's lips parted, but he didn't speak.

I put down the phone. 'I think I should probably go home, Neil.'

'Sure,' Neil said. 'I'll lock up if you ...'

'Thanks.'

I walked to my car and got in, but didn't start the engine. Instead I sat, nearly motionless behind the wheel, watching people on the sidewalk, some alone, a few couples, a scattering of families with children. They strolled past the little shops with an air of complete casualness, like swimmers in the sea, untroubled, caught in that carefree instant before the dark fin breaks the surface and sends them thrashing toward shore.

Before I started home I snapped up my cell phone and called Meredith.

'Peak called me,' I told her. 'We have to keep an eye on Keith.'

She could tell by the tone of my voice that I was feeling shaky. 'That means they suspect him,' she said.

'I'm not sure you can draw that conclusion.'

'Oh please, Eric,' Meredith said, her tone faintly irritated. 'You can't live with your head in the sand forever. We have to face things.'

'I'm facing them, it's just that—'

'Where are you now?' she interrupted.

'I'm just leaving the shop.'

'Good. We need to talk.'

She was waiting in the living room when I arrived.

'It's all that's on the radio,' she said. 'A big story for this shitty little town.'

I had never heard her speak of Wesley in such a hateful way, as if she felt trapped by its smallness, ensnared and suffocating. Had she felt this way for a long time? I wondered. Had she sometimes awakened in the night and wanted to rush to the family car and drive away, out of Wesley, toward some bright horizon she'd never spoken of? In movies, people always had secret dreams, and I'd assumed that at least a few real people actually had them, but I'd never thought Meredith afflicted by such dreaminess. Now I wondered if she harbored some thwarted fantasy, dreamed of yellow-brick roads and princely palaces, of being king of some hill she'd never had a chance to climb.

She walked over to the sofa and sat down hard, as if she were trying to squash the world beneath her. 'They mentioned that Vince and Karen had gone out for the evening but not that there was a babysitter' – she shook her head – 'but that'll come,' she said crisply. 'There had to have been a babysitter. Amy was eight years old.'

'Was?' I asked darkly.

'You know what I mean.' She looked at me determinedly. 'I think we should call Leo.'

I don't know why I resisted, except that some part of me was determined to keep the gravest consequences at bay, a hope, foolishly held, that if I simply refused to take the next step then no one else would take it, either.

'Not yet,' I said.

'Why?' Meredith demanded.

'Because it'll make Keith look guilty,' I answered. 'You've seen how they do it on television. They say, "So-and-so has retained counsel." And people think, Okay the guy knows he did it and so now he's trying to protect himself.'

Meredith stood up, walked to the back window, and peered out into the woods. 'I hope you're right, Eric,' she said.

I let her cool a moment, then said, 'Do you think we should call the Giordanos?'

She shrugged.

'I think it would be a good idea,' I said. 'You know, to show our concern.'

I walked into the kitchen, took the phone, and dialed the number.

A strange voice answered, but one I recognized. It was Detective Kraus. I told him who I was and that I wanted to express my hope that Amy would be returned safely home and offer my help, my family's help, in finding her. I asked to speak to Vince. Kraus said he'd get him. I heard him put the phone down, then his footsteps as he walked across the room. I could hear voices, but they were low and distant. Then the footsteps returned.

'Mr. Giordano doesn't want to talk,' Kraus said. 'He's a little ... well ... upset.'

'Of course,' I said.

'Keith's around, right?' Kraus asked.

'Yes.'

'Because we have a few more questions for him.'

I told him that Keith would be more than willing to help in any way he could, then put down the phone. Meredith was watching me worriedly.

'Maybe you're right,' I told her. 'Maybe we should call Leo.'

*

Leo agreed to come over immediately, and so I went upstairs to talk to Keith.

The door to his room was closed and locked, as he'd insisted upon from the time he was thirteen. I'd never thought anything unusual about this. Teenagers were like that. They shut their parents out. It was a matter of asserting their independence, I supposed, part of the ritual of growing up and growing away. But now the fact that my son spent so much time in his room, at his computer, alone, behind a locked door, gave off an air of something hidden. What, I wondered, did he do in there? And in his solitude, what thoughts came to him?

I knocked at the door. 'Keith.'

I heard a strange scrambling, as if he were taken unawares and was now readying the room before opening the door, turning off the computer, closing drawers, perhaps quickly secreting things in his closet or beneath his bed.

I tapped again, this time more urgently. 'Keith?'

The bolt snapped back, then the door opened to its customary two inches, and the single blue eye appeared.

'We've called a lawyer,' I said.

The blue eye gave nothing away.

'Leo Brock,' I added. 'He's coming over in a few minutes.'

The blue eye stared at me without sparkle, a tiny pool of unmoving water.

'I need to talk to you before he gets here.'

Keith's voice was emotionless. 'What about?'

I looked at the slowly blinking eye and wondered if Keith had taken something, inhaled something, if this, too, was a part of him he had hidden from me.

'Open the door,' I said.

The door remained in place.

'What do we need to talk about?' Keith asked.

'Keith, open the door,' I insisted.

He hesitated briefly, then drew back the door, but instead of ushering me into his room, he came out into the corridor and quickly closed the door behind him.

'Okay,' he said. 'Talk.'

I looked at him closely. 'Are you okay?'

He laughed softly, almost mockingly. 'Yeah, great,' he said.

'I mean are you ... able to talk?'

He shrugged comically and grinned at me, but it was a cold grin, like a bitter clown. 'What do you want, Dad?'

'I want you to tell the truth, Keith,' I said. 'When Mr. Brock comes over here. Whatever he asks you, tell him the truth.'

'Like with the cops,' Keith said.

'Like I told you to do, yes.'

Again, he shrugged. 'Okay ... so?'

'The truth,' I repeated, this time sternly.

'The truth, right,' Keith said. His eyes narrowed slightly. 'Is there something else?'

'In every detail,' I said. 'What you did while you were at Amy's. Where you went after that. How you got home. The truth, Keith.'

'Yeah, okay.' He waved his hand, as if batting away a pesky insect. 'Can I go back now?'

I told him that he could, then watched as he slunk back behind the door and returned the bolt to its place, sealing himself off again.

Downstairs, Meredith was sitting at the kitchen table, drinking coffee, her long fingers fidgeting nervously with the top button of her blouse.

'What did he say?' she asked.

'Nothing.'

She took a sip from the cup. 'Typical.'

'What do you mean by that?'

'It's the same way he acted when we told him Amy was missing. No real reaction. A shrug. Like it was nothing.'

'He didn't know how to react,' I said.

Meredith didn't buy it. 'I don't know, Eric, there should have been some little expression of sympathy ... shock ... something.' She took another sip of coffee. 'He didn't ask a single question. Did you notice that?'

'He's afraid,' I told her.

She drew in a quick agitated breath. 'So am I,' she said.

I could see that clearly, her fear, and in that first visible dread, felt the touch of something yet more dreadful still.

'Are you all right?' I asked.

'How could I be all right, Eric?' Meredith asked. Her voice was edged in sarcasm. 'How can anything be all right?' She took an angry sip from the cup, grim, resigned, though I couldn't tell if this resignation had to do with Keith or me or herself, or just the life that was hers, the whole course by which she'd come to rest in a shitty little town.

I had no answer for her, and so I did what we often do when things seem beyond us, wrapped in total darkness, when we sense the approaching precipice.

I reached out blindly and took her hand.

# EIGHT

Leo preferred to meet Keith at our house rather than at his office because, as he told Meredith, 'Kids are less jumpy on their home turf.'

We'd known Leo for nearly fifteen years. When the time had come to buy the shop, I'd picked his name out of the local phone book, and he'd conducted the closing with such effortless competence that he'd handled all our personal and business affairs ever since. More recently, he'd also become something of a family friend. His wife, Peg, had died three years before, and since then Meredith had made a few attempts to match him up with various faculty members at the community college. Leo had never once called any of these women, however, and Meredith had finally gotten the message that he simply did not want to marry again. He was happy as a sixty-two-year-old widower, free to do as he pleased, take off on a whim.

He arrived at precisely 3:15, dressed in his customary jacket and tie, his shoes polished to a gleaming sheen.

'Hello, Eric,' he said when I opened the door.

I led him into the living room, where Meredith sat at the end of the sofa, her long legs primly crossed, hands in her lap, a rigid posture Leo noticed immediately.

'I know this is very disturbing,' he told her as he sat down on the sofa. 'But, believe me, it's much too early to suggest that Keith has anything at all to worry about.' He glanced around the room. 'Speaking of which, where is he?'

'In his room,' I said. 'I thought you might want to talk to us first.'

Leo shook his head. 'No, Keith is actually the person I need to talk with.'

It was a clear instruction to summon Keith downstairs.

'I'll get him,' Meredith said. She rose and headed up the stairs.

'This is all very strange,' I said after she'd left the room. 'Keith involved in something like this.'

'Naturally, it's worrisome,' Leo said. 'But nine times out of ten, everything can be cleared up very quickly.'

'You've handled this kind of thing before?' I asked.

Leo leaned back casually. 'What kind of thing is that?'

'A kid accused of something,' I answered.

'Has Keith been accused of anything?'

'Not exactly but ...'

'But what?'

'Well, he was the last person to see Amy.'

Leo shook his head. 'No, the last person to see Amy was the guy who took her.' He looked at me significantly. 'You need to keep that distinction firmly in mind, Eric.'

I nodded obediently.

Meredith returned, Keith dragging along behind her, looking tense, like someone already tried and found guilty who was now only awaiting the judge's sentence.

'Hi, Keith,' Leo said brightly. He rose and thrust out his hand with the exuberance of a patriot welcoming a soldier home. 'You look like you're holding up just fine.' He glanced at me, then offered Keith a wink. 'Not like your old man, huh?'

Keith smiled, but it was a smile I'd seen before, mirthless and rather resentful, as if the whole thing were a dreadful inconvenience, something he had to go through before he could get back to his computer game.

'Have a seat,' Leo said as he lowered himself back onto the sofa.

Keith sat down in the chair across the narrow coffee table. He looked at me, then back at Leo. In his eyes I saw nothing but a dull determination to endure the next few minutes, then slink back to the dark burrow of his room.

'So, I hear the cops came by,' Leo began. His tone was light, almost chatty. He might have been asking Keith about a favorite movie. 'They stay long?'

Keith shook his head.

'Good,' Leo said. 'They're not much fun to have around, are they?'

Again, Keith shook his head.

Leo flung one hand over the back of the sofa and with the other unbuttoned his jacket with a great show of casualness. 'What'd they want to know?'

'About Amy,' Keith said with a halfhearted shrug.

Leo's next question was carried on the back of a slight yawn. 'What'd you tell them?'

'That I put her to bed at around eight-thirty.'

'And that was the last time you saw her?'

'Yes.'

'When did you leave Amy's house?'

'When her parents came home.'

'And that would be?'

'Around ten.'

Leo leaned forward with a soft grunt and leisurely massaged his ankle. 'Then what?'

For the next few minutes, I listened as my son told Leo the same story he'd told the police – that he'd gone into the village, wandered the streets, lingered awhile at the ball field, then walked home. As he spoke, I let myself believe that he might actually be telling the truth, that perhaps I was wrong and hadn't really heard a car stop on the road that night, watched its lights sweep through the undergrowth, then draw away. I'd seen other parents find ways to deny the horrible possibility that their son or daughter might have done a terrible thing. In the past, the way they'd demonstrated such blind faith in their child's innocence had amazed me. But suddenly, when Leo turned to me and said, 'Were you awake when Keith came home?' I knew that I was now one of those parents, willing to do or say or believe anything that would hold back the grim tide of doubt.

'Yes, I was awake,' I answered.

'So you saw Keith when he came home?'

'Yes.'

'When did you see him?'

'I heard him come down the driveway,' I said.

Mercifully the next question – *Was he alone?* – never came, a blank I made no effort to fill in.

Leo smiled at me appreciatively. 'Good,' he said, as if I were a schoolboy who'd spelled the word correctly. He turned to Keith. 'I'll keep track of the investigation for you.' He leaned over and patted my son's knee. 'Don't worry about a thing.' He started to rise, then stopped and lowered himself back down on the sofa. 'One other thing,' he said, his eyes on Keith. 'Were you ever over around the water tower?'

I saw a dark sparkle in my son's eyes.

'Water tower?' Keith asked.

'The town water tower, you know where it is, don't you?' Leo said. 'About a mile outside town.'

'I know where it is,' Keith answered warily, as if it were a guilty knowledge.

'So, were you ever over that way?'

Keith shook his head. 'No,' he said.

With no further word, Leo got abruptly to his feet again. 'Well, I'll keep you all informed as this thing goes forward,' he said. He turned and walked to the door. 'Well, have a nice day.'

Meredith stepped forward quickly. 'I'll walk you to your car, Leo,' she said.

Seconds later I was alone in the living room, Keith upstairs, Meredith and Leo strolling down the walkway toward his impressive black Mercedes.

Briefly, I sat on the sofa, but anxiety soon overtook me, and I rose and walked to the front window. Meredith and Leo were standing beside his car, Leo nodding in that worldly way of his as he listened to Meredith. She seemed more animated than she'd been since Amy Giordano's disappearance, her hands fluttering about as if she were trying to catch an invisible butterfly. Then Leo said something, and her hands stopped their edgy flight, froze for a moment, and finally dropped to her sides like weights.

She listened as Leo spoke in what appeared to be slow, deliberate terms, her gaze fixed on him with great intensity until she abruptly glanced toward the house, the window where I stood, and in response to which, I stepped quickly out of view, like a peeper unexpectedly caught in the act.

I'd returned to the sofa by the time she came back into the house.

'Well, how do you think it went?' I asked.

She sat down beside me, calmer now, and less angry than before. 'We'll get through this, won't we, Eric?' she asked.

'What?'

'No matter what happens, we'll get through it.'

'Why wouldn't we?'

She appeared at a loss for an answer but said finally, 'Because of the strain, the pressure. Sometimes families break.'

'Or come together,' I said. 'Like those covered wagons when the Indians attack.'

Her smile was ghostly faint. 'Like covered wagons, yes,' was all she said.

I went back to the shop a few minutes later, hoping that Leo Brock was right, that there was nothing to worry about.

'Everything okay?' Neil asked.

'Well, we have a lawyer now,' I answered.

Neil received this in the way I'd offered it, as an indication that in some unknowable way things had grown more serious.

'If there's anything I can do,' he said.

I'd always thought Neil a somewhat inconsequential man, not because he was clownishly gay and effeminate, but because he was so excessively emotional, easily moved by tearjerker movies. But now that very excess struck me as sweet and genuine, an empathy that lay deep within him, like the marrow of his bones. And it struck me then that trouble was like a turn of a lens, a shift that brings everything into sharper focus. Suddenly, you see who cares and who doesn't, the genuinely kind and those who only fake their kindness.

'I just think that good people shouldn't, you know, have bad things happen to them,' Neil added. 'People like you and Meredith. Mr. and Mrs. Giordano. Innocent people. Like Amy.'

'Yes.'

'And Keith,' Neil added.

*Keith.*

I felt a catch, as if a stream deep inside me, one that had always been open and freely flowing toward my son, had abruptly narrowed.

'Yes, Keith,' I said.

Neil caught something in my eyes. 'I just hope Keith has someone to talk to,' he said, then edged away and pointedly busied himself with unpacking a box of camera cases.

I walked behind the framing counter and went to work. Several orders had come in during the previous afternoon. Neil had written them up on slips that gave the precise size and number of the frame required for each photograph. As usual, they were family pictures, save for one of a golden retriever as it loped along the shoreline. In one, a family was gathered on the steps of a small rented cottage, the father at the rear, tanned and shirtless, his arms draped over his wife's shoulders, two children seated on the wooden steps. In another, a much larger family was sprawled around a campsite, dappled sunlight falling through the overhanging limbs. Some were in bathing suits, and the teenage daughter's blond hair hung in wet curls as she dried it with a towel.

I read each slip, pulled the designated frame from stock, cut the glass, and leaned the completed work against the wall behind me. After that I wiped the counter and sat down on the short aluminum stool behind it.

I don't know how long I sat silently, waiting for the relief of an approaching customer, before I noticed the glossy edge of a photograph tucked just beneath the corner of the developing machine. It was crumpled badly, but when I placed it on the counter and smoothed it out, I saw that it was a picture of Amy Giordano. No doubt Neil had inadvertently dropped it on the floor some days before, one of the 'free doubles' we gave out with each order.

In the photograph, she was standing alone at the edge of a glittering blue pool, clothed in a one-piece red and white polka-dot bathing suit. An enormous beach ball rested beside her, beads of water clinging to its soft plastic sides. A crinkle in the photograph sliced Amy's body diagonally in a cruel, jagged line, so that her raised right arm appeared severed from her body, as did her left leg at midcalf. Other than this accidental bisection, there was no suggestion of Amy's fate, and yet I felt a sudden, terrible presentiment that she had been murdered, and in that instant, without in the least willing it, I saw Keith standing at the end of an imagined corridor that led to Amy's room, his hands closed in tight fists, fighting the impulse that raged within him, trying desperately to control himself, the urge so fierce that he felt it as a hand shoving him from behind, heard it as a voice shouting madly inside his head, the force growing ever more furious until he finally gave way before it, fixed his eyes upon the closed door at the far end of the shadowy hallway, drew in a long breath, and began to move toward it.

'Eric?'

I blinked quickly and glanced toward the voice, half expecting to find a demon standing there, horned and red-eyed, incarnate evil. But it was only Mrs. Phelps, holding two rolls of film in a slightly tremulous hand. 'I hope I can have this by Tuesday,' she said as she placed an eight-by-ten photo of her granddaughter on the counter before me. 'Isn't she lovely?' she asked.

I quickly pocketed the photograph of Amy and concentrated instead on the other little girl. 'Yes,' I said, 'she is.'

I closed the shop at the usual time, and headed back home. Meredith was just hanging up the phone when I came into the kitchen.

'I was talking to Dr. Mays,' she said. 'He's having a cocktail party next weekend. We're invited. Do you want to go? I think we should.'

'Why?'

'So we look ... normal,' Meredith said.

'We are normal, Meredith.'

'You know what I mean.'

'Yeah, okay,' I said. 'You're right. We can't let people think we have something to hide.'

She nodded. 'Especially now.'

'Now? What do you mean?'

'Now that we know why Leo asked Keith if he'd ever been to the water tower.'

'What are you talking about?'

'They found Amy's pajamas there,' Meredith said. She looked at me quizzically. 'Haven't you been listening to the radio?'

I shook my head. 'No, I guess I prefer to avoid things.'

To my surprise she said, 'Yes, you do. Keith's the same way.'

'What do you mean?'

'You're not confrontational, Eric. You're passive. So is he.'

'What does that mean, exactly?'

'It means what it says. That you don't confront things.'

'Like what?'

'Jesus, Eric, where should I begin? Like Keith's grades, for one thing. I'm the one who makes demands. And the way he just slouches around the house. I'm the one who gets on his back, makes him take out the garbage, rake the leaves.'

This was true. There was no denying it.

'And it's not that you don't think that he should do these things,' Meredith added. 'It's just that you don't want to confront him. That's the way you are, passive.'

I shrugged. 'Maybe so. I don't feel like arguing about it.'

'My point exactly,' Meredith said crisply.

Her tone struck me as unnecessarily harsh. 'Well, what had you rather me do, argue with him all the time? Argue with you? Make a big deal out of everything?'

'But some things are big deals,' Meredith shot back. 'Like whether your son is fucked-up or not. That's a big deal.'

'Fucked-up?'

'Yes.'

'How is Keith fucked-up?'

Meredith wagged her head in frustration. 'Jesus, Eric. Don't you see anything?'

'I see a teenage boy. What's so fucked-up about him?'

'He has no friends, for God's sake,' Meredith said emphatically. 'Lousy grades. No sense of direction. Have you ever seen a spark of interest in anything, the slightest sign of ambition?' She looked oddly defeated. 'When he graduates from high school, he'll work for you in the shop, that's what he'll do. He'll deliver pictures the way he does now, except that he'll use a car instead of a bicycle. Eventually, he'll take over Neil's job. And when you die, he'll take the shop over completely.' She made no effort to conceal her disappointment in such a course. 'That will be his life, Eric, a little frame and photo shop.'

'Like my life?' I asked. 'The poor, pathetic bastard.'

She saw that she had struck too deep. 'I didn't mean it like that. You had nothing. Your father went bankrupt. You had to fend for yourself. But Keith has all the advantages. He could go to any school, follow any star.'

I waved my hand and turned away. There was something in this I couldn't bear. 'I'm going for a walk,' I told her irritably.

'A walk?' Meredith asked. She looked at me quizzically. 'At this time of day? Where?'

I never went for walks, but I knew I had to get away. It didn't matter where I went, only that I got out of the house, away from Meredith and the sense of failure and disappointment that wafted from her like an odor.

I turned and headed for the door. 'The woods' was all I said.

In Frost's famous poem, they are lovely, dark, and deep, but the sun had not yet set on the woods that evening, and so every detail of the undergrowth was visible to me, save its function, which was to hide whatever lay beneath it.

There were no trails in the woods behind the house, no route through the bramble, so I made my way slowly, cautiously, pushing aside low-slung limbs and clinging vines.

I remember the things that came to mind as I walked: Amy's disappearance, Keith's interrogation, the trouble I feared might be ahead. But more than anything, when I think of that last lone walk, I consider not the bare facts I knew at the time, nor the problems I reasonably anticipated, but the darker currents I knew nothing of, nor could have imagined.

Now, so many years later, as I wait in the corner booth of a diner on a rainy autumn afternoon, I review the long course of my unknowing. Then the words return again, *I'll be back before the news,* and my body stiffens as if against a crushing blow, and I am once again in woods without a trail, and darkness is closing in, and there is no way to get back home.

# PART II

B eyond the diner window, the streets are crowded. Families mostly, cameras hanging from their arms. You have served them by the thousands. They ask only the simplest questions. They pull out their little canisters of film and ask how much it will cost to have their pictures developed. You quote them a price and if they're satisfied with it, they ask when the pictures will be ready. You answer that question, too, and in most cases the deal is done. You walk to the developing machine, open the canister, take out the film, feed it into the machine, and wait. The rollers inside the machine turn, the chemicals disperse. The motor hums. The minutes pass. Then the pictures emerge, shiny, new. They fall into the tray like brightly colored leaves.

The years go by, old customers drop away and new ones appear. You wonder if one of these new ones will recognize you, remember what happened, and ask a different question. Then one Sunday morning the phone rings, and you realize that a past without a future is a corpse, and that for a long time you have been dead. You want to rise from the grave, wrench something good from all that darkness, and so you say yes and make the arrangements.

But what will you say, you ask yourself, what will you say when you confront it all again? You want to end with wisdom, but you must begin without it because you had none when it began. You lived in a small town, lived a tidy little life. What you've learned since then, you've learned in increments, a treasure collected one coin at a time. And so you must chart the journey carefully, measure the pace, offer what you have gathered, and hope it will be accepted.

But first you must think it through again, return to that last moment, then double back to the days preceding it, how it happened that in a few short days everything fell apart. Yes, you decide, that's the way to tell it.

The waitress has no suspicion. She has seen other men like you, alone on a Sunday morning, sitting in the back booth, with nothing but a mug of coffee.

And so you feel safe here. And why not? You could not bring them back to life, could not repair the damage, and so you decided to make the best of it. You thought of leaving Wesley, but you didn't. You stayed because you believed there was a reason to stay, and that, in the end, you would find that reason. But the years passed, and you had begun to believe that you would never find it. Then the phone rang, and suddenly the reason was clear. You realized that, if nothing else, you could give a few things back, draw them like dried bones from your own buried past.

And so you have come here, to this diner, in hope of doing that, offering the paltry gift of the few dark things you know.

# NINE

*Suspicion is an acid,* that's one thing I know. Everything it touches it corrodes. It eats through the smooth, glistening surface of things and the mark it leaves is indelible. Late one night, I watched a rerun of one of the Alien movies. In one scene, the alien pukes up a liquid so corrosive it immediately eats through first one floor of the space station, then another and another. And I thought, it's like that, suspicion, it has nowhere to go but down through level after level of old trusts and long devotions. Its direction is always toward the bottom.

I knew that things had changed in my family, that Meredith had grown more volatile and Keith more defiant, but I wasn't aware of how much Amy Giordano's disappearance had affected other, seemingly neutral, people. She had been missing for three days by then, and there could be no doubt that everyone in Wesley now knew that Keith had been Amy's babysitter the night of her disappearance. Even so, I was totally unprepared for Mrs. Phelps's reaction.

She was in her early seventies and had been a regular customer since the shop opened. She had white or bluish hair, depending upon the competence of the beauty salon, and her teeth were false and thus unnaturally even and a bit too large for her mouth. She never came into the shop in anything but dressy clothes, usually with a silk scarf around her neck, her face fully made up down to the eye shadow.

She came into the store at just after ten. Neil was at the front counter, and she stopped to chat with him in that amiable way of hers. 'Neil's very nice,' she once said to me. But then, so was almost everyone, according to Mrs. Phelps. Her gardener was nice, for example, as was the Ecuadorian woman who cleaned her house. Summer was nice, but so were spring and fall. She'd never made particular mention of winter, but I had no doubt she could find some aspect of it that was nice, too.

She had come to pick up the large photograph of her granddaughter that she'd left for me to frame the preceding weekend, and the minute she came through the door I remembered that it wasn't ready. I'd begun framing it before closing on Saturday, and Neil had quite correctly taken the frame and photograph and placed them safely beneath the counter, where they'd remained, completely forgotten until now.

'I'm sorry, Mrs. Phelps,' I said when she walked up to the counter. 'I haven't finished the picture yet. I can have it for you later today.'

Mrs. Phelps smiled and waved her hand. 'Oh, don't worry, Eric,' she said. 'I'll come back for it later.'

'No, no,' I said. 'It's my fault for not having it ready. When Keith gets here, I'll have him deliver it to you.'

That's when I noticed an uneasy glimmer in Mrs. Phelps's eyes, a sudden, not very subtle wariness. I also knew the reason for it. Mrs. Phelps's granddaughter, the little girl in the photograph I had not yet framed, was staying with her. She was pretty, with long dark hair, and looked to be around eight years old, the same age and general appearance as Amy Giordano.

'Oh, you don't have to put Keith to that trouble,' Mrs. Phelps said. 'I'll drop by later this afternoon.' Her voice remained kindly and accommodating, a nice woman being nice, but there was a firmness in it, too, a clear refusal to allow my son ever to come near her granddaughter. I thought of the whales I'd read about, how the mother whale will place her vast bulk between the harpoon and her offspring. Mrs. Phelps was doing no more than that, protecting her granddaughter from the dark potential of my son.

'All right,' I said quietly. 'If that's what you'd prefer.'

'Yes, thank you,' Mrs. Phelps said politely. She took a step backward, her gaze now fleeing to any available object, the smile still on her face, but lifeless, frozen. She was embarrassed by what she'd just done but unwilling to take it back. After all, she must have thought, her granddaughter's safety was at stake.

'Around four then,' I said.

Mrs. Phelps nodded, turned, and walked rather hurriedly toward the door. She swept by Neil without nodding good-bye, and by the time she made it to the sidewalk I had the feeling that she was very nearly out of breath.

'Jesus,' Neil said to me. 'That was weird.'

I stared out the front window, watching as Mrs. Phelps walked to her car and got in. 'I don't think Keith should make deliveries anymore,' I said.

'It's just awful,' Neil said. 'Whatever happened to innocent until proven guilty? And Mrs. Phelps, of all people. So nice, and all that, but ...'

'It's fear,' I told him, though until that moment I hadn't realized to what degree suspicion was a form of fear. 'She's afraid of Keith. It's natural, I guess.'

'But there's no reason for her to be afraid of Keith,' Neil said.

I recalled the terrible vision I'd had a few days before, Keith moving down the shadowy corridor toward Amy's room. It was all I could do to keep from blurting the thought that came to me at that moment, *Dear God, I hope you're right.*

Neil seemed almost to have heard the grim prayer I'd managed not to utter.

'Keith couldn't have done anything to that little girl, Eric,' he said emphatically. 'He didn't have a car. Whoever took her, he had to have had a car. You don't just take a child from her house and walk away.'

I saw the twin beams of a car once again sweep across the undergrowth. 'I know.'

A stream of images sped through my mind, Keith slouching down the walkway, brushing past the low-slung limbs of the Japanese maple at its far end, moving stealthily up the stairs. I recalled the way he'd frozen at the sound of my voice, then stood facing the door, his rumpled shirttail hanging halfway outside his pants. For an instant, the thought of why his shirt had been pulled from his trousers was almost more than I could bear.

Neil touched my arm softly. 'Believe me, Eric, Keith's not a ...' He stopped, considered his words, then said, 'Keith wouldn't ... hurt a little girl.'

I nodded silently because there seemed nothing else to do, no words I could safely say. Then I went back to work. I framed Mrs. Phelps's photograph, then another and another as the hours passed and customers came and went, sometimes glancing in my direction, sometimes avoiding me altogether, both of which I found uncomfortable. It was a form of discomfort I didn't want Keith to experience, I decided, so at noon I called Meredith and told her that I thought it best that Keith go directly home after school until the matter of Amy Giordano was settled.

'I don't want him being looked at the way people are looking at me,' I said. 'Like an animal in the zoo.'

'Of course,' Meredith agreed. 'Besides, with him the look would be even worse.'

'What do you mean?'

Her answer chilled me with its unflinching starkness. 'Like the cage door is unlocked,' she said.

Warren arrived just as I was closing. He was dressed in coveralls, white cotton, dotted with paint. Bits of dried paint also clung to the wispy orange strands of his hair and dotted his hands and lower arms.

'Thought we might grab a beer, Bro,' he said.

I shook my head tiredly. 'It's been a long day, Warren. I think I'll just head home.'

Neil swept by, said hello to Warren, then made his way toward the old green Dodge he'd more or less inherited from his mother.

Warren laughed. 'Jesus, what a pansy,' he said. He looked at me, the smile now gone. 'I'd really like to have a beer, Eric.' He didn't wait for me to refuse a second time. 'The cops came by this house I was working on. Earl Bannister's place. They came right up to Earl and asked for me. Two cops. The ones that talked to you, I guess.'

'Peak and Kraus.'

'Sounds right,' Warren said. 'Anyway, that's not good, them coming up to Earl that way. I can't have cops coming around, asking for me while I'm on a job. Asking questions. Making it look like I'm ... involved in something.' His tone grew more tense and even a little resentful that he'd been drawn into circumstances he had not created but now knew no way to avoid. 'I'm a housepainter, for Christ's sake. In and out of people's houses. You got to be trusted in this business, not be on the job and a couple of cops show up.' His face reddened slightly. 'It's got to stop, Eric,' he said with sudden urgency. 'I mean, I can't let this go on. We have to talk about it, you know?'

He was working himself up, getting more and more agitated. It was one of Warren's traits, a continual escalation until his emotions peaked and he either started sobbing, as he did when he was drunk, or fell asleep, as he did when he was sober.

'All right,' I said. 'Let's go over to Teddy's.'

Teddy's was a small bar just a few doors down from my shop. Teddy Bethune, the owner, had died several years before, so that it was now run by his middle-aged daughter, a frowsy, irritable woman who had never made a secret of the fact that she actually preferred tourists to the boozy regulars who liked to sing old Irish songs, tell dirty jokes, and who continually regaled her with tales of how much more fun the bar had been before her father died.

'What'll you have?' Peg asked as she plopped two paper coasters before us.

We ordered two beers, grabbed the frosted bottles and headed for the booth at the back.

Warren took a long swig, then, before talking, decided on another. After that he put the bottle down on the table. 'Hits the spot,' he said.

'What did the cops want to know?' I asked.

'What I saw.'

'You mean, Amy?'

'Amy, yeah, and Keith.'

'Keith?'

'What he looked like.' Warren took another swig from the bottle. 'How he was acting. You know, like was he strange or anything that night. The short one was real interested in that.'

'Peak,' I said. 'What did you tell him?'

'Like you told me, Eric. The truth.'

'Which was?'

'That he was in a mood.'

I stared at my brother, appalled. 'Jesus, why did you say that?'

Warren looked at me, astonished. 'Say what?'

'That Keith was in a mood. What the hell does that mean, anyway, that he was in a mood?'

Warren looked the way he did when he was twelve, and I was eight, his younger brother berating him for some stupid blunder.

'I figured I needed to tell them something,' he said lamely. 'You know, give them something. You always got to give them something, right?'

'Why do you think that?'

Warren didn't answer, but I knew he'd gotten the idea from television or the movies.

I slumped forward and ran my fingers through my hair. 'All right, listen to me,' I said wearily. 'What exactly did you say?'

'Just what I told you,' Warren answered.

He looked vaguely frightened, like a little boy who'd screwed up his part in the class play, and I remembered how cruelly my father had dismissed him, and how, to please my father, and to feel in league with him, I'd often adopted the same attitude toward my brother, exaggerating his failures, mocking his small successes. I couldn't help but wonder if in some way I was still locked in that adolescent pattern.

'Listen, Warren,' I said, now trying for a less scolding tone. 'A little girl is missing. This town is small, and this thing is getting bigger and bigger. You've seen her picture all over. There's even one on the door of my shop. And ribbons now. Yellow ribbons all over town. That means the cops are under a lot of pressure. Their jobs are on the line. So they have to find Amy, dead or alive, and then they have to find whoever did this. See what I mean?'

Warren stared at me blankly.

'What I'm saying is that if they begin to think that Keith had something do with this, they'll hone in on him. They won't look anywhere else. They have to close the case.'

Warren nodded slowly, his big soft eyes blinking languidly.

'Which means that Keith being "in a mood" gives them something to think about, turn over in their minds, and so they start thinking, okay, we got this kid, a little weird, no friends . . . in a mood that night.'

'So things start to add up to the cops,' Warren said.

'Yes.'

He took another sip from the beer, then nodded toward my bottle. 'You not having any?' he asked, immediately shuffling off my warning, as well as any responsibility he might have for sinking my son deeper into police suspicion.

I pushed the bottle away. 'What else did you tell them?' I asked sternly.

Warren stiffened, like a lowly private at an officer's approach. 'Just that I drove Keith to the Giordanos' house,' he said. 'Amy was in the front yard. She came running up to the car. Then Keith got out and the two of them went inside.' He hesitantly took another sip of beer. 'Oh, and that I said hi to her.'

'Anything else?'

'They wanted to know how she looked with Keith.'

'Looked?'

'Like was she glad to see him, or did she act different when she saw him, like afraid, or backed away, stuff like that.'

'What did you say?'

'I told them I didn't notice how she looked. Then they asked me if he touched her, you know, in a funny way, like maybe he shouldn't have, that kind of touch.'

I dreaded the question but asked it anyway. 'Did he?'

'No.'

'Did he touch her at all?'

'He took her hand,' Warren said. 'He took her hand and led her inside.'

'And that's it?'

'Yeah.'

'Nothing else about Keith's mood?'

'No.'

'You're sure you didn't say anything else, Warren.'

'No, nothing,' Warren assured me. Another swig. 'What would I say?'

'I just need to know if there was anything else.'

Warren shook his head with childish exaggeration. 'Not a word, Eric.' He lifted his hand. 'I swear.'

'Okay,' I said. 'Okay, that's not too bad then, I guess.'

Warren took a swig and smiled like a little boy briefly in trouble but relieved now, all the burden lifted from him.

He chuckled. 'But I got to admit, they made me nervous, those cops.' He threw his head back, as if peering upward into the heart of some distant memory. 'People like that always make me nervous.'

I took a sip from my bottle, my own relief not all that different from Warren's, satisfied that he'd said nothing damaging about Keith.

'They all have the same look in their eyes, those guys,' Warren added. 'You know, suspicious.'

I glanced at my watch, anxious to get home.

'Like that guy who came by the house after Mom's accident,' Warren said. 'The one we had, you know, when we lived in the big house.'

He meant the house we'd lost, the one Dad had mortgaged to the hilt in his failed effort to regain financial ground, the one the bank had finally taken from us.

'I loved that house,' Warren added. 'Remember how we used to sail on the pond?'

'Yeah,' I said.

'We'd already lost it when this guy came,' Warren said. 'I was packing boxes and he ...'

'What guy are you talking about?'

'Some insurance guy.'

'I don't remember any insurance guy coming to the house,' I said.

'That's because you were with Aunt Emma.'

I had been twelve years old the summer of my mother's death, and I recalled how my father had driven me across town to stay with his sister until, as he put it, 'things calmed down.'

'I stayed with Dad, remember?' Warren said. 'Helping him pack.'

My father had often enlisted Warren to do such heavy work, so it didn't surprise me that he'd used him as a kind of packhorse when he'd had to clean the house out before its repossession.

'Where was Dad when this guy came to the house?'

Warren shrugged. 'You know Dad. He could have been anywhere.' He looked at the empty bottle, then raised his hand and ordered another. 'Anyway,' he said. 'With Dad not around, I didn't know what to do. But I figured, okay, this is just some guy from the insurance company, so, if he wants to talk to me, so what? I didn't see any harm in it.'

'So you talked to him.'

'Yeah. I was just a kid. He was a grown man. Big guy. You know, an adult. You don't say no, right?'

Peg arrived, plopped down Warren's beer then glared at me. 'You?'

'I'm fine,' I said.

She turned heavily and lumbered back up toward the front of the bar. 'Besides, he was just asking about general stuff,' Warren added. 'Like how things were.' He rolled the bottle between his hands, getting jumpy again, as if he suspected that I was laying some kind of trap for him. 'You know, was Mom okay. Stuff like that. Family stuff. I didn't think much about it then, but it sort of gives me the creeps now.'

'Why?'

'Because he seemed, you know, suspicious.'

'Suspicious of what?'

'Us. I guess. Things in the family. Between Mom and Dad. Like, were things okay between them.'

'He asked you that?'

'No, it was more a feeling I got, you know, like he was wondering if things were okay with them.'

'What did you tell him?'

'That everything was fine,' Warren said. 'Which is why I couldn't understand why Dad got so pissed when I told him about this guy. Told me to keep my mouth shut, not let this guy in if he showed up again.' He took a sip from the beer and wiped away a residue of white froth from his mouth with the back of his hand. 'I guess he told the guy the same thing, because he never came back after that one time.' He shrugged. 'So whatever it was, it got settled, right?'

'Sounds like it,' I answered. I glanced at my watch again. 'I have to get home, Warren.'

'Yeah, sure,' Warren said. 'I'll just hang around, finish my beer.'

I got to my feet. 'Just remember, if the cops talk to you again, be careful what you say.'

Warren smiled. 'You can count on me,' he said.

# TEN

Keith was in his room when I arrived at home.
'How'd he take it?' I asked Meredith. 'My not wanting him to make deliveries for a while.'

'I can't tell,' Meredith answered. She was in the kitchen, standing at the cutting board, running a knife across the fleshy surface of a late-summer tomato. Its juices ran out onto the board and added a tang to the air. 'He's just wears that same, flat face. No emotions. "Flat affect" – that's what they call it.'

'Who calls it that?'

'Psychologists.'

'He's a teenager,' I said. 'All teenagers have "flat affect".'

She stopped slicing. 'Did you?'

It was an unexpected question, but one I thought I could answer with a swift, decisive no. Then I recalled the moment when I'd been told of my mother's death, the way her car had plunged off a thirty-foot bridge. She'd been impaled on the steering wheel, a fact my father had not been reluctant to divulge, and yet, for all the gruesome nature of her death, I had simply nodded and walked upstairs to my room, turned on the phonograph, and listened to the album I'd just borrowed from a friend. Before now, I'd considered such behavior merely my way of choking off my grief, but now, thinking through it again, I couldn't be sure that I'd actually felt my mother's death as viscerally as I might have expected. At the funeral, for example, I'd sat silently beside my equally silent father, toying with my sleeve, while Warren sobbed uncontrollably, his fleshy shoulders shaking, huge tears running down his fat cheeks.

'Maybe I did,' I admitted. 'When my mother died, I didn't exactly fall apart.'

'But I thought you loved your mother,' Meredith said.

'I think I did,' I said. 'I mean, she was the one who wanted me to go to college, scrimped and saved.'

I remembered how, even in the midst of our worsening financial

71

situation, she'd hoarded a few pennies from each month's budget. She'd called it my college fund and had sworn me to secrecy, made me promise not to tell Warren and especially not to tell my father. It couldn't have been very much money, of course, and after her death I'd always assumed that my father had found it buried deep inside a closet or on the top shelf of the kitchen cabinet, then spent it in his usual way, probably on a final bottle of expensive brandy.

'I should have been really hurt by her death,' I said. 'But I don't remember being all that upset about it.' I recalled the slow, deliberate tone my father had taken when he broke the news, his voice even, emotionless. He might as easily have been informing me of a sudden change in the weather. 'My father didn't seem all that upset, either,' I added.

Meredith looked as if I'd just revealed a formerly hidden aspect of my character. 'Maybe that's where Keith gets it then.' She began slicing the tomato again. 'Anyway, it's not supposed to suggest anything, this flat affect behavior.'

'What would it suggest?'

'You know, that he's a monster.'

'Jesus, Meredith, Keith's not a monster.'

She continued to slice the tomato. 'That's what I just said.'

I sat down at the kitchen table. 'The cops talked to Warren. He told them Keith was in a mood that night.'

Meredith spun around, the knife frozen in her hand. 'What a fucking idiot,' she snapped.

'Yeah.'

'Goddamn it!'

'I know. I told him the next time to think before he spoke.'

'As if he could,' Meredith said hotly. 'In a mood, Jesus Christ!' She seemed to smolder as she stood, knife in hand, glaring at me. 'What's wrong with him, anyway? Is he just stupid, or is it something worse?'

'Something worse?'

'I mean, is he *trying* to get Keith in trouble?'

'Why would he do that?'

'Oh, come on, Eric.' She put down the knife. 'He's jealous of you. He always has been. You've always been the favorite. To your mother, but not just her. I mean, to this day, your father doesn't care if Warren comes by to see him. He never thinks about Warren. And then there's the fact that you have a wife, a son, a real family. What does Warren have? Absolutely nothing.'

All of this was true, but I had never considered its corrosive effects before, the terrible possibility that all the years of feeling small and unsuccessful, of living in a tiny rented house alone, might have corrupted some aspect of my brother's heart, poisoned him against me so that he secretly reveled in my current troubles, perhaps even sought to deepen them.

'Do you really think Warren would deliberately try to implicate Keith in this thing with Amy?'

'Yes,' Meredith answered bluntly.

The sheer force of her reply, the world of bitter envy it unearthed, was more than I could accept. 'I just can't believe he'd do something like that, Meredith,' I said.

Her gaze was withering, and beneath it I felt like a hopelessly clueless child. 'You don't have any idea how malicious people really are, Eric,' she said. 'And I don't think you ever will.'

There was no way to answer such a charge, and so I merely shook my head, walked into the living room, and turned on the television. The local news was just beginning. The lead story, once again, was about Amy's disappearance.

There'd been no developments in the case, the reporter said, but the police were busy following a few 'promising leads'.

*Promising leads.*

I glanced back to where Meredith stood at the entrance of the kitchen, her eyes fixed on the television screen.

'Promising leads,' she repeated sarcastically. 'I wonder how many of them came from dear old Warren.'

I turned back to the television. By then, the report had gone live, with Peak and Kraus before a bristling array of microphones, Peak out front, Kraus standing stiffly behind him. For the next few seconds, Peak brought reporters up to date. The police, he said, were following a number of leads. A hotline had been established, and some of the information gained from callers appeared 'credible'.

'Credible,' Meredith scoffed as she sat down on the sofa beside me. 'Not if it came from Warren.'

'Please, Meredith,' I said quietly.

Peak ended his update by saying that the Giordanos were being fully cooperative, that they absolutely were not suspects in Amy's disappearance, and that they'd recently turned over the family computer so police could see if Amy might have been contacted by 'suspicious individuals' on the Internet.

With that, Peak turned, and started to go back into police headquarters.

'Do you have a suspect?'

The question had come from the crowd of reporters gathered on the steps of the building, but when he turned, Peak appeared to recognize the reporter who'd asked it.

'We're looking at several people,' Peak said.

'But do you have one suspect in particular?' the reporter asked.

Peak glanced at Kraus, then faced the camera. 'We're building a case,' he said. 'That's all I can tell you.'

Then, almost like an apparition, he was gone.

'Building a case,' Meredith said. She looked at me worriedly. 'Against Keith.'

'We don't know that,' I told her.

She looked at me again in the way she'd looked at me when I'd denied my brother's ill intent. 'Yes, we do,' she said.

We had dinner an hour later, Keith slumped mutely in his chair, toying with his food, barely eating it. Watching him, I could not imagine Peak and Kraus building a case against him. In some sense, he appeared too pale and skinny to be considered a threat to anyone. But more than his physical weakness argued against his having done anything bad to Amy Giordano. Brooding silently at the table, aimlessly picking at his food, he gave off a sense of being innocuous, far too listless and desultory to have summoned the sheer malicious impetus required to harm a child. My son could not have hurt Amy Giordano, I decided, because he lacked the galvanizing energy necessary for such an act. He was too drab and ineffectual to be a child killer.

And so I forced myself to believe that the phantom suspect against whom the police were building their case had to be thick and burly, with a muscular body and short powerful legs. I wanted him to be a drifter or some visitor from another town. But barring that, I would have settled for anyone, as long as it wasn't Keith.

'How's school?' I asked, then regretted it since it was exactly the kind of inane parental question all teenagers dread.

'It's okay,' he answered dully.

'Just okay?'

He plucked a single green bean from the rest of them as if he were playing a solitary game of pick-up-sticks. 'It's okay,' he repeated, his tone now somewhat sharp, like a felon impatient with interrogation.

'Is there anything we need to know about?' Meredith asked in her usual no-nonsense tone.

'Like what?' Keith asked.

'Like about Amy,' Meredith answered. 'Are you having any trouble over Amy?'

He drew another green bean from the stack, peered at it as if he thought it might suddenly begin to squirm, then let it drop back onto his plate. 'Nobody says anything about it.'

'At some point they might,' Meredith said.

Keith picked lazily at a red pimple, but said nothing.

'Keith?' Meredith said insistently. 'Did you hear me?'

His hand dropped abruptly into his lap. 'Yeah, okay, Mom.'

He remained silent for the rest of the meal, then excused himself with an exaggerated show of formality and returned to his room.

Meredith and I cleared the table, put the dishes in the dishwasher, and finally returned to the living room where we watched television for a time. Neither of us had much to say, nor did either appear uncomfortable in the silence. There was, after all, nothing to talk about but Keith, and that was a subject that could not be raised without heightening the general level of anxiety, and so we simply avoided it.

A few hours later we went to bed. Meredith read for a while. I knew she was trying to lose herself in a book. That had always been one of her ways of coping. During her mother's illness, she'd read continually, but never more than at her mother's hospital bedside, where she'd devoured book after book in a frantic effort to keep her mother's approaching death at bay. Now she was using the same tactic to keep from dwelling on the grim possibility that our son might be in very deep trouble.

Before she finally turned out the light, it was clear that this time the tactic had failed.

'Do you think Keith should see a counselor?' she asked. She turned toward me and propped her head up in an open palm. 'There's one at the college. Stuart Rodenberry. Kids come to him with their troubles. People say he's very good.'

'Keith wouldn't talk to a counselor,' I said.

'How do you know?'

'He doesn't talk to anybody.'

'But everyone wants to reach out, don't you think, to someone?'

'You sound like a counselor, yourself.'

'I'm serious, Eric,' Meredith said. 'Maybe we should think about setting up something with Stuart.'

I didn't know what to say, whether counseling was a good or bad idea at this point, and so I simply said nothing.

'Look,' Meredith continued, 'Stuart's going to be at Dr. Mays's party on Friday. I'll introduce you. If you think Keith might respond to him, we can go from there.'

'Fair enough,' I said.

With that, Meredith turned out the light.

I lay in the darkness, laboring to fall asleep. But sleep eluded me, and as time crawled forward, my mind drifted back to my first family, which, for all its tragedies, seemed less besieged by trouble. A sister dead at seven, a mother impaled upon a steering wheel, a destitute father living out his days in a modest retirement home, an alcoholic brother – these were, for all their misfortune, not problems unknown to other families. Other families had yet different problems, but those, too, now struck me as common, ordinary. In comparison, Keith's situation was much darker and more sinister. I couldn't shake the image of him slouching out of the shadows and into the house that night, then stealthily trudging up the stairs to face the door when I spoke to him, as if he were afraid to look me in the eye. There was something familiar in the scene, a sense that I'd lived through it before. But try as I did, I couldn't bring the earlier moment back until I suddenly remembered how, on the morning before Jenny's death, Warren had returned from Jenny's room where he'd been more or less stationed by my father to see her through the night. It wasn't a job he'd wanted, and he'd tried to get out of it, but my father had in- sisted. 'You just have to sit by the goddamn bed, Warren,' he'd barked, a clear suggestion that any more complex task would have been beyond my brother's limited capacity. Warren had gone to Jenny's room at midnight, then returned to his own room when my mother relieved him at six in the morning. He'd looked lost and bedraggled as he trudged down the corridor in the dawning light, his heavy footsteps awakening me so that I'd walked out into the hallway, where I saw him standing, facing the door, just as Keith had, his eyes fixed and unmoving, unable to look at me when I'd asked about Jenny, muttering only, 'I'm going to bed,' before he opened the door to his room and disappeared inside.

It was the similarity in those two scenes that struck me now, one that went beyond the stark choreography of two teenage boys tired and bedraggled, walking down a hallway, standing rigidly before the closed doors of their rooms. There was a similarity of mood, tone, a sense that these two boys were laboring under similar pressures, both of which had to do, I realized suddenly, with the fate of a little girl.

My anxiety spiked abruptly. I drew myself from the bed, walked out into the corridor, then down the stairs to the unlit kitchen, where I sat in the darkness and thought each scene through again and again, trying to locate some reason beyond the obvious one as to why they so insistently bore down upon me.

It came to me slowly, like the building light of dawn, darkness giving way to gray, then to steadily brightening light. The real similarity was not between the two scenes, but between my brother and my son, the fact, hard though it was for me to admit, that in some sense I thought of both of them as losers in life's cruel lottery, locked in failure and disappointment, members of that despised legion of middle-aged drunks and teenage geeks whose one true power, I thought, must be their unheralded capacity to control their own consuming rage.

*He took her hand and led her inside.*

Warren's words suddenly called another scene into my mind, Keith summoned by the Giordanos to babysit this daughter they so completely loved. Amy Giordano. Raven-haired, with flawless skin, smart, inquisitive, her future impossibly bright and radiant, destined to be one of life's winners.

Keith's words tore through my brain in a sudden, chilling snarl – *Princess Perfect.*

In my mind I saw Keith take Amy's hand and lead her inside the house. Could it be, I wondered, that her beauty and giftedness worked on him like an incitement, everything about her an affront, her shining qualities always in his face, goading him from the general sluggishness that would have otherwise stayed his hand.

My own stark whisper broke the air. *'Could he have hated her?'*

I felt another anxious spike, walked out into the yard, and peered up into the nightbound sky where, in the past, I'd sometimes found comfort in the sheer beauty of the stars. But now each glint of light only reminded me of the mysterious headlights of the car I'd seen that night. Now I imagined a mysterious figure behind the wheel, Keith on the passenger side, then I added a frightful third image, a little girl crouched naked on the floorboard, tied and gagged, whimpering softly if still alive, and, if not, stiff and silent, my son's unlaced tennis shoes pressed against her pale, unmoving face.

# ELEVEN

It was a horrible vision, a fear for which I had no real evidence, and yet I couldn't rid myself of it. All through the night, I thought of nothing but that car, the ghostly driver, my son, all of it tied to the fact that Amy Giordano was incontestably missing and my growing suspicions that Keith had lied to me and to others for no reason I could figure out.

I alone knew about the car, of course, but by morning I also knew that it wasn't a knowledge I could keep to myself anymore. And so, just after Keith trooped down the stairs, mounted his bike, and headed off to school, I broke the news to Meredith.

'I think Keith may be hiding something,' I blurted.

Meredith had already put on her jacket and was headed for the door. She froze and immediately faced me.

'He said he walked home that night, but I'm not sure he did.'

'What makes you think he didn't?'

'I saw a car pull into the driveway up by the road,' I said. 'Then, just a few seconds later, Keith came walking down the drive.'

'So you think someone brought him home that night?'

'I don't know,' I answered. 'Maybe.'

'Did you see who the driver was?'

'No,' I answered. 'The car didn't pull all the way down the driveway.'

'So you couldn't tell if Keith got out of that car?'

'No.'

'Why didn't you tell me about this?'

'I don't know,' I admitted. 'Maybe I was afraid to—'

'Confront it?'

'Yes,' I admitted.

She thought for a moment, then said, 'We can't say anything about this, Eric. Not to the police or Leo. Not even to Keith.'

'But what if he lied, Meredith?' I asked. 'That's the worst thing he could have done. I told him that when I saw him in town the day the

78

police were here. Before I brought him back. I told him that he had to tell the truth. If he didn't, then he has to ...'

'No,' Meredith repeated sternly, like a captain taking charge of a dangerously floundering vessel. 'He can't take anything back. Or add anything. If he does, they'll keep at him. More and more questions. He'll have to lie again and again.'

I heard it like distant thunder, dark and threatening, inexorably closing in. 'Lie about what?'

She seemed to struggle for an appropriate answer, then gave up. 'About that night.'

'That night?' I asked. 'You think he knows something about – ?'

'Of course not, Eric,' Meredith snapped. Her voice was strained and unconvincing, so that I wondered if, like me, she'd begun to entertain the worst possible suspicion.

'The problem, Eric,' she added, 'is that if they find out he lied, there'll be more questions. About him. About us.'

'Us?'

'About why we covered it up.'

'We're not covering anything up,' I said.

'Yes, we are,' Meredith said. 'You've known about that car from the first night.'

'Yes,' I admitted, 'but it's not as if I was trying to cover up something Keith did. Like hiding a bloody hammer, something like that. It was just a car. Keith might not even have been in it.'

Meredith glared at me, exasperated. 'Eric, you sat in our living room and listened to two cops question our son. You heard his answers, and you knew that one of them might have been a lie, but you didn't say anything.' Her eyes flamed. 'It's too late to take any of this back, Eric.' She shook her head. 'It's too late to take anything back.'

For a moment I couldn't tell exactly what she was talking about, what, among perhaps scores of things, could not be taken back.

'All right,' I said. 'I won't say anything.'

'Good,' Meredith said. Then, with no further word, she whirled around, opened the door, and fled toward the car, the heels of her shoes popping like pistol shots on the hard brick walk.

Despite Meredith's conclusion that we couldn't say anything about the car I'd seen pull into our driveway that night, I thought of calling Leo Brock and telling him about it. But I never did. Meredith would no doubt argue that it was because I knew Leo would be irritated that I'd withheld something from him and I didn't want to confront that irritation.

But the reason is simpler even than that. The fact is, by midmorning

I'd entered an irrational state of hope that it might all simply go away. This hope was based on nothing, and because of that I've come to believe that we are little more than machines designed to create hope in the face of doom. We hope for peace as the bombs explode around us. We hope the tumor will not grow and that our prayers will not dissolve into the empty space into which we lift them. We hope that love will not fade and that our children will turn out all right. As our car skids over the granite cliff, we hope, as we fall, that a cushion will receive us. And at the end, the last fibers of our hope throb for painless death and glorious resurrection.

But on that particular morning, my hope was more specific, and I have no doubt that it sprang from a groundless feeling that things were getting back to normal. Customers came and went, but none of them looked at me in precisely the same way as Mrs. Phelps had the day before. Instead, they nodded polite greetings, smiled, looked me dead in the eye. Perhaps the case was growing cold in their minds, the events distant, their former urgency dissipating. Perhaps my customers had come to accept the fact that Amy was missing and we might never know what had become of her. If this were so, then soon the flyers with Amy's picture would peel from the town's shop windows. The yellow ribbons would unravel and fall to the ground, to be picked up and tossed into the garbage. For a time, the people of Wesley would vaguely consider that my son might have had something to do with Amy's disappearance, but day by day, the stain of their suspicion would fade, and eventually his association with whatever had happened to Amy Giordano would fade as well, and we would all be back to where we were before that night. That was the illusion I allowed myself all that morning, so that by the time I came back from lunch, got out of my car, and headed toward the shop, I half believed that the worst was over.

Then suddenly, like a creature rising from dark, brackish water, he was there.

I saw him get out of the delivery van he used to haul his fruits and vegetables, the bright green cap and vest, his lumbering, muscular figure oddly hunched, like a man carrying a huge invisible stone.

'Hello, Vince,' I said.

I could see what the last few days had done to him, the toll they'd taken. His eyes were red with lack of sleep, and large brown crescents hung beneath them. His face looked as if it were hung with weights, everything pulled down slightly.

'Karen didn't want me to talk to you,' he said. 'Cops probably wouldn't like it, either.'

'Then maybe it's not a good idea,' I said.

He steadied himself with a shifting motion, and had it been Warren, I would have suspected he'd been drinking. But as far as I knew, Vince Giordano was not a drinking man, especially one who'd have a bag on at one-thirty in the afternoon.

'Maybe it's not,' he said. 'I don't know, maybe it's not.' He glanced toward my shop, then back at me. 'But I got to.'

He'd always had a ruddy complexion, but now I noticed that the side of his face looked as if it had been roughly scraped. I pictured him clawing at himself with an agonizing desperation, like an animal gnawing at its paw, frantic to escape the metal trap.

'Karen can't have more kids,' he said. 'Amy was hard. And after her, Karen can't have another one.'

I nodded softly, but I could feel my skin tightening, becoming armor. 'I'm sorry, Vince.'

His eyes glistened. 'I got to have Amy back,' he said. 'She was all we had, Eric. All we'll ever have. And we got to have her back ... one way or the other.' Again his eyes fled from me. He sucked in a long trembling breath, but continued to stare out across the parking lot. 'If she's in some' – his voice broke – 'some ditch or something, you know?' He looked at me pleadingly. 'You know?'

'Yes,' I said quietly.

'Some ditch where ... animals can ... where—' He suddenly staggered forward, leaned into me, buried his face in my shoulder, and began to sob. 'Oh, Jesus,' he cried. 'I got to have her back.'

I draped a single arm over his shoulder, and he drew away quickly, as if stung by an electric charge. 'You tell him that, okay?' he said. 'Keith.' His eyes were dry now, a desert waste. 'You tell him that I got to have her back.'

'Keith doesn't know where Amy is, Vince,' I said.

His gaze fixed on me like two hot beams. 'Just tell him,' he said.

I started to speak, but he spun around and made his way to his truck, his short powerful arms sawing the wind mechanically, like a furious wind-up doll.

'Keith doesn't know anything,' I called after him.

Vince didn't turn, and when he reached his van, he yanked open the door and pulled himself in behind the wheel. For a moment, he sat, head dropped forward, eyes downcast. Then he turned toward me, and I saw the depth of his pain and knew beyond doubt that his world had shrunk to the dark, pulsing nucleus of Amy's loss. All that had mattered to him before no longer mattered. Nor did all that still mattered to others touch him now. I heard his words again, fraught with desperate warning, *I got to have her back*. Beneath the anguish, there was a festering rage. Vince would level cities, vaporize oceans, burn all the fields of earth to hold Amy in his arms again, hold her dead or alive. For him, all existence weighed no more than sixty pounds, stood no higher than four feet. Everything else was dust.

I didn't want to go into the shop after that, didn't want Neil to see how shaken I was. He'd ask questions I didn't want to answer. And so I walked to the other end of the mall and dialed Leo Brock.

'I had a little ... confrontation with Vince Giordano,' I told him.

'When?'

'Just now.'

'Where?'

'In the parking lot outside my shop.'

'What did he say?'

'That he wants Amy back,' I answered. 'He told me to tell that to Keith.'

'I see.'

'He thinks Keith did something, Leo,' I added. 'He's convinced himself of that.'

There was a pause, and I could almost hear the tumblers of Leo's brain.

'Listen, Eric,' he said at last. 'The police seem to think that there's something wrong. Something somebody isn't telling.'

'What do you mean?'

'That's the most I could get out of my source,' Brock said. 'Nothing concrete. Just a feeling that something's wrong.'

'With Keith?'

'With something,' Leo said. 'The guy who tells me these things, he just gives hints.'

'Something wrong,' I repeated. 'Where would they come up with an idea like that?'

'I don't know. Maybe they got a tip.'

'A tip? From whom?'

'It could be anybody,' Leo answered. 'It could have come from that hotline they've set up. You know how that works. Anonymous. Anybody can call in, say anything.'

'But the cops don't have to believe it, do they?'

'No, they don't,' Leo said. 'But if it has any credibility, then they're apt to look into it. Especially in a case like this. Missing girl. They're under a lot of pressure, Eric, as I'm sure you know.' He paused, like a priest in the confessional, using silence as a spade, digging at me. 'So, if you know of something ... wrong.'

I choked back the reflex to tell him about the car. 'This isn't enough,' I said. 'This isn't enough for me to go on, this business of something being wrong. Jesus Christ. It could be anything. Something "wrong". Jesus, could they get more vague?'

'Which is why I'm asking,' Leo said.

'What exactly are you asking, Leo?'

'Eric, listen,' Leo said evenly. 'This business of Vince Giordano, don't worry about that. I can get a restraining order in two seconds. But understand, on this other matter, the police are going to be looking into things.'

'What things?'

'Whatever looks promising from their point of view,' Leo said. 'They don't have to go in only one direction. If something comes in, like on that hotline, they can run with it. It could be anything. Some rumor. This is a police investigation, Eric, not a trial. The rules aren't the same.'

I shook my head. 'Hotline. Jesus Christ. Just something somebody says over the phone, and—'

'That's right,' Leo interrupted. 'So let me ask you this, is there any reason why someone out there might want to hurt you or Meredith?'

'By doing what? Blaming this whole thing on Keith?'

'Perhaps that. Or maybe just by planting stories.'

'What kind of stories?'

'Any story that might get the attention of the police.'

I laughed coldly. 'Like we're drug dealers ... or Satanists?'

Leo's tone was grave. 'Anything, Eric.'

Suddenly I felt drained, all my energy dissipated, my earlier optimism flattened like an animal on the road. 'God,' I breathed. 'My God.'

'I don't know what this "something wrong" is,' Leo said. 'My guess, it's probably nothing. But they don't need much, the cops. Not in a case like this.'

I lifted my head slightly, like a battered fighter rallying before the next bell. 'Well, the answer is no,' I said. 'There is nothing wrong.'

After a pause, Leo said, 'All right.' He cleared his throat roughly. 'Do you want me to take action regarding Mr. Giordano?'

I saw Vince's stricken face bury itself in my shoulder, felt the tremble of his sobs. 'No,' I said. 'Not yet.'

'All right,' Leo said again, his tone the same as seconds before, carrying a hint of disappointment. 'But let me know if he approaches you again.'

'I will,' I assured him.

He hung up with no further word, but a mood continued to reverberate around me, weird suggestions about 'someone out there' who might want to hurt me or Meredith or Keith, strike at our little family circle, rip it apart. I heard a whispered voice, anonymous and malicious, recorded on the police hotline, mouthing accusations of incest, abuse, all manner of deviance, but the longer the list became, the more I dismissed the dark accusing voice. Charges had to be proved, after all. Suspicion alone could not destroy anything.

Or could it?

Suddenly another question sliced through my brain, one directed not toward Keith or Meredith, as should have been expected, but to the mysterious man who'd shown up at the house, asked Warren questions, come on an insurance matter only a week or so after my mother's car had shattered the guardrail of the Van Cortland Bridge and plunged into the icy stream below.

What, I wondered with an inexplicable sense of dread, had he been looking for?

# TWELVE

For the first time in years, I didn't want to go home that night, though even then, despite my anxiety, I had no idea that before long I would be leaving my home for good.

I saw it for the last time on a chill October day. The closing was set for that afternoon, and the new owner, an attorney with a young wife and two small children, was anxious to move in. I walked through the swept and empty rooms one by one, first the kitchen and living room, then upstairs to the bedroom Meredith and I had shared for so long. I looked out its frosted window to a carpet of fallen leaves. Then I walked out into the corridor where I'd faced Keith that night, passed through the door he'd slunk behind, and stared out the window over which he'd once hung a thick impenetrable shade, the one I'd finally ripped down in a fit of rage, my words at that moment once again echoing in my mind, *No more fucking lies!*

Perhaps I'd actually begun to sense that steadily approaching violence the evening I decided not to go home directly after work, but called Meredith instead, told her I was going to be late and tried to lose myself in the repetitive labor of safely enclosing idyllic family photographs within neat square walls of perfectly stained wood and painted metal. Or perhaps I'd begun to feel that the protective walls that had once surrounded my own family, both the first and the second, were beginning to crumble, and that if I could simply ignore the leaks and fissures, then it would all go away and Amy would be returned to Vince and Karen and I could return to Meredith and Keith and by that means escape the ghosts of that other family, Dad and my mother, Jenny and Warren, who'd already begun to speak to me in the same suspicious whisper I imagined as the voice on the police hotline, sinister, malicious, ceaselessly insisting that something at the heart of things was wrong.

I don't remember how long I remained in the shop after closing, only that night had fallen by the time I locked up and walked to my car. Neil had lingered briefly, needlessly shelving stock, so that I knew he was keeping an eye on me, ever ready to provide what he called a friendly shoulder. He left just after seven. I worked another hour, perhaps two, time somehow flowing past me without weight or importance, so that I felt as if I were adrift on its invisible current, a frail rudderless craft moving toward the distant haze behind which waits the furiously cascading falls.

I sat down behind the wheel, but didn't start the engine. All the stores in the mall were closed, and briefly I peered from one unlit shop window to the next. What was I looking for? Direction, I suppose. I knew that strange suspicions were now rising like a noxious mist around my first family, but I also knew that I had to let them go, concentrate on the far more serious matter that now confronted my second family. So, what was I looking for? Probably a way of thinking through the current crisis, putting it in perspective, running the various scenarios, everything from Amy found to Amy murdered, from Keith exonerated to the look on his face as they led him into the death chamber. No thought was too optimistic nor too grim for me that night as I careened from hope to gloom. The fact is, I knew nothing concrete, save that I'd seen a car at the end of the driveway then Keith moving through the darkness toward home.

Suddenly, Leo Brock's voice sounded in my mind: *Were you ever over around the water tower?*

Keith's answer had been typically short – *no*.

And yet, between the question and the answer, something had glimmered in my son's eyes, the same dark flaring I'd seen when he'd said that he'd walked home alone the night of Amy's disappearance.

I'd let all of this go for days, despite the fact that Amy's pajamas had been discovered in the general area of the tower, a fact I'd hardly thought about until that evening, when I suddenly felt the urge to go there, see the place for myself, perhaps even find some small thing, a lock of hair, a scrap of paper, that would lead me to her. It was an absurd hope, as I knew even then, but I'd reached the point where absurdity joined with reality, my son accused, however vaguely, of a terrible crime, and I unable to feel certain that he was not also guilty of it. That was the pressure that drove me forward, made me start the engine, drive out of the parking lot in front of my shop, turn right, and head toward the northern edge of town where, within minutes, I could see the top of the water tower glowing softly in the distance, motionless, cylindrical, like a hovering spacecraft.

The unpaved road that led to the tower was a bumpy winding one that grew ever more narrow as I drove down it. Two walls of green vines crept in from both sides of the road, sometimes clawing at my window like skeletal fingers.

The road curled to the left, then made a long circle around the looming tower and the high metal legs that supported its enormous weight. There were no formal parking spaces, but I could see indentations in the surrounding vegetation, places where cars had pulled in and parked with sufficient regularity to leave their ghostly images in the undergrowth.

I followed the road on around, then stopped, backed into a phantom space, and cut my lights. Now there was nothing to illuminate the darkness but the beams that swept down from the outer rim of the tower.

For a time I sat in that covering darkness, my gaze moving about the softly illuminated area beneath the tower. It was weedy and overgrown, and the wind rippled softly through the grasses. Here and there bits of litter tumbled briefly in these same breezes, then gently came to rest.

I saw nothing that I might not have expected of such a place. It was lonely and deserted and far off the beaten track, but beyond these common characteristics, it might have been reproduced in a dozen other towns throughout the region. They all had their own water towers, and nothing distinguished this one from those others except my gathering sense that it was used in some way, a designated meeting place, the sacred territory of a secret society. I half expected to see animal bones scattered about the grounds, the remains of some occult group's bizarre religious sacrifices.

That thought gave me an eerie chill, the feeling that I'd stumbled into someone else's territory, the way casual hikers are said to stumble onto marijuana patches in the middle of otherwise perfectly innocuous fields and meadows. Could it be, I wondered, that Amy Giordano had been brought here not merely because it was secluded, but for some specific purpose? My imagination fired luridly, and I saw her standing, stripped and bound, surrounded by a circle of robed figures, all of them mumbling satanic incantations as they slowly circled her. Then, in my mind's bizarre scenario, she was laid upon a makeshift altar, silver blades raised high above her as the incantation reached a fever pitch. Then the knives came down one at a time, each figure taking his appointed turn until –

That was when I saw the light.

It came down the same unpaved road I'd taken only minutes before, headlights bouncing jerkily as the car bumped toward the tower. At the tower, it circled slowly, the shadowy driver staring straight ahead as the car drifted past mine, so that I caught the face only in brief black silhouette.

Clearly, he was familiar with the place, because he drove directly to what seemed a preordained spot, then stopped, backed up, and turned off his lights.

I had backed deeply into the undergrowth, and so I doubt that he saw me as he passed, though surely he must have glimpsed the front of my car when he backed into his own place. If so, my presence did not in the least alarm him. Through the eerie haze cast beneath the tower, I saw him as he sat in the shadowy interior of his car. He did not get out, and for a time he remained almost completely still. Then I saw a slight movement and after that, the fire of a match and the glowing tip of a cigarette, rhythmically brightening and dimming with each inhalation.

The minutes passed, and as they did, the man became less sinister. I imagined him a harmless night owl, maybe plagued by an unhappy home, and so he'd found a place where he could sit alone, undisturbed, and either think things through or let his troubles briefly slip his mind altogether.

Then, out of the darkness, a second car made its approach, moving slowly, its headlights joggling through the undergrowth until it made the same slow turn, found its place, and backed in.

A woman got out, short and somewhat overweight, her blond hair hanging stiffly, like a wig. She walked to the second car and pulled herself in on the passenger side. Despite the darkness, I could see her talking with the man. Then she leaned forward, curling downward, and disappeared from view. The man took a final draw on his cigarette and tossed it out the window. The woman surfaced briefly, and I think they both laughed. Then she curled forward and disappeared again, this time without resurfacing until the man suddenly thrust his head backward and released what even from a distance I recognized as a shuddering sigh.

I wanted to leave, of course, to skulk away unseen, because there is a kind of intrusion that comes very close to crime. I felt like a thief, someone who'd broken into a secret chamber, and for that reason I remained in place, my head down, my eyes roaming here and there, avoiding the two cars that rested in the darkness several yards away. The sound of a car door returned me to them. The woman had gotten out of the man's car and was heading back toward her own. On the way, she grabbed the purse that dangled from her shoulder, opened it, and put something inside. Seconds later, she pulled away, the other car falling in behind her, both cars making their way around the circle, through the grasping vines, and back out onto the main road.

Even then, I stayed in place for fear that if I left too soon I might come upon one or the other of them and reveal what I'd seen at the tower.

Five minutes went by, then ten, and at last it seemed safe to leave. I drove back to the main road and headed home to where I knew I would find Meredith reading in bed and Keith secreted in his room, listening to music or playing his computer games. I thought I knew the things that were on Meredith's mind, either Keith or some problem at the college. But Keith was much more of an enigma now, a boy who smoked, cursed, perhaps even lied to the police and me about – I couldn't even say how many things he might have lied about. I only knew that I couldn't stop my own growing suspicion that the anonymous caller on the police hotline had been right, that there was something wrong.

# THIRTEEN

The next morning Keith left for school at his usual time. From the front window I watched as he mounted his bicycle and pedaled up the short incline to the main road. Physically, he was burdened by nothing more than the book bag that hung at his back, but I couldn't help but consider the other weights he bore – confusion, isolation, loneliness. Still, these were no more than the usual burdens of a teenage boy, and I worked to dismiss any doubts that they might not be the only ones he carried.

'Well, I guess no news is good news.'

I turned to see Meredith standing a few feet behind me, her gaze following Keith as he made his way up the incline and disappeared behind a wall of forest undergrowth.

'Nothing new from the cops,' she added. 'I guess that's a good thing.'

I continued to peer out into the woods. 'I suppose,' I said dryly.

She cocked her head to the right. 'You sound pessimistic, Eric. That's not like you.' She came over and drew me around to face her. 'You okay?'

I smiled weakly. 'I'm just tired, that's all. Thinking about everything.'

'Sure,' Meredith said. 'And it couldn't have been a very good experience, Vince Giordano coming up to you like that.' She placed her hands on either side of my face. 'Listen, we'll go to Dr. Mays's party tomorrow night, get out of this gloom, have a good time. We both need it, right, a chance to relax?'

'Yes.'

With that she kissed me, though dartingly, spun around, and headed up to our bedroom to finish dressing.

I remained at the window, watching the morning light slant through the overhanging trees. I had never actually noticed how beautiful it was, the small piece of woodland that surrounded our house. For a moment I recalled the day we'd moved in, how before unloading the truck we'd taken a moment to stand and look around, Meredith with Keith beside her, how bright the day had been. How on that day, as we'd huddled together in this perfect wood, we had all been smiling.

It was a Thursday morning, and so, rather than drive directly to the shop, I headed for the retirement home where my father had lived for the past four years. I'd dropped in on him at exactly the same day and time since he'd first taken up residence there. Even in old age, he'd maintained his aversion to what he called 'untimely surprises', by which he meant everything from a gift offered on any but appropriate occasions to unscheduled visits by either of his two sons.

That morning he received me as he always did, in a wheelchair parked on the home's broad front porch. Even in winter, he preferred that we sit outside, though in recent years, he'd given in a little on that one, and so from time to time I'd found him in the front room, his chair placed a few feet from the fireplace.

'Hello, Dad,' I said as I came up the stairs.

'Eric,' he said with a crisp nod.

I sat down in the wicker rocker beside his chair and glanced out over the grounds. They were roughly tended, dotted with crabgrass and dandelions, and I could see how much they offended him.

'They'll wait for frost to kill the weeds,' he grumbled.

He'd always been a stickler that the spacious grounds surrounding the grand house on Elm Street were always perfectly manicured. He'd hired and fired at least ten groundskeepers during as many years. They were lazy or inept, according to him, though he'd never permitted my mother to so much as pick up a spade to correct their deficiencies. Her job had been to maintain my father, see to it that his suits were pressed, his desk cleared, his dinner on the table when he triumphantly returned home each evening. A woman's work, he'd pointedly declared, is always to be done on the inside.

'I guess you heard about Amy Giordano,' I said.

He continued to stare out across the unkempt grounds.

'The little girl who disappeared,' I added.

He nodded, but with little interest

'I guess you've also heard that Keith was babysitting her that night,' I said.

My father's lips jerked downward, 'He was bound to get in trouble,' he said sourly. 'This or something else.'

I'd never guessed that my father had any such opinion of my son.

'Why do you think that?' I asked.

My father's eyes drifted over to me. 'You never stood up to him, Eric,' he said. 'You never made him mind you. Same with Meredith. Hippies.'

91

'Hippies?' I laughed. 'Are you kidding me? I was never a hippie. I went to work when I was sixteen, remember? I didn't have time to be a hippie.'

He turned back toward the yard, his eyes now strangely hard. 'From the first time I saw him, I knew he'd be trouble.'

In all the fifteen years of my son's life, my father had never expressed such a grim notion. 'What are you talking about?' I demanded. 'Keith has always been a good kid. Not the best grades, but a good kid.'

'Looks like a bum,' my father growled. 'Like he lives on the street. Lazy. Like Warren.'

'Warren's been good to you, Dad.'

'Warren is a bum,' my father sneered.

'When he was a kid, he worked his ass off for you.'

'A bum,' my father repeated.

'He did all the heavy lifting around the house,' I insisted. 'Every time you fired yet another landscaper, he took up the slack – mowed, cut the hedge. You even had him paint the house one summer.'

'Looked like a melted cake when he finished,' my father snarled. 'Dripping all over. Splotches. Couldn't do corners. Messed up the lattice-work. Everything sloppy.'

'Okay, so he didn't do a professional job,' I said. 'But he was just a kid, Dad. Sixteen years old that last summer.'

That last summer. I remembered it with almost disturbing clarity. My father had been gone for days at a time, off to New York or Boston in search of cash. My mother had kept the house running by sheer will, secretly borrowing money from Aunt Emma, according to Warren, cutting corners at the grocery store, driving thirty miles to buy clothes at the Catholic thrift shop in a neighboring town.

'You refused to admit how bad things were,' I reminded him. 'You came back from New York with two new suits from Brooks Brothers.'

My father waved his hand dismissively. 'Nobody went hungry.'

'We might have,' I said. 'If it hadn't been for Mom handling the household budget.'

My father laughed coldly. 'Your mother couldn't handle anything' – he waved his hand – 'worthless.'

'Worthless?' I asked, angry that he would say such a thing about a woman who'd spent her life taking care of him. 'If she was so worthless, why did you have her insured?'

My father's head jerked to attention. 'Insured?'

'Warren said there was insurance. When Mom got killed.'

'What would Warren know about that?'

'The insurance man came to the house,' I said.

92

I saw my father's face tighten slightly.

'He came one day when Warren was packing everything after the bank took the house.'

My father laughed dryly. 'Warren's nuts. There was no insurance man.'

'According to Warren he was asking about our family, how things were between you and Mom.'

'Bullshit!' my father grumbled, his voice now a low growl, like a dog driven into a corner.

I started to speak, but his hand shot up, stopping me. 'What does a drunk like Warren know? His brain is soaked in alcohol.' He lowered his hand, leaned back in his chair, and glared out over the weedy yard. 'Nothing,' he said bitterly. 'When that old woman died, I got nothing.'

'That old woman?' I repeated. 'Jesus, Dad, she was devoted to—'

'Devoted to me?' my father bawled. His head rotated toward me with an eerie smoothness, and a caustic laugh burst from him. 'You have no idea,' he said.

'About what?'

My father chuckled to himself. 'You don't know a thing about her. Devoted, my ass.'

'What are you getting at?'

His laughter took a still more brutal turn, becoming a hard, hellish cackle. 'Christ, Eric.' He shook his head. 'You always put her on a pedestal, but, believe me, she was no fucking saint.'

'A saint is exactly what she was,' I insisted.

His eyes twinkled with some demonic inner light. 'Eric, trust me,' he said. 'You have no idea.'

I was numb when I left him a few minutes later, numb and floating like a feather in the air. After his outburst, my father had refused to say anything more about my mother. It was as if their married life was a brief, unpleasant episode for him, a game of poker he'd lost or a horse he'd bet on that came in last. I remembered the effusive show of love and devotion he'd always put on for the well-heeled business associates who occasionally dropped by for a game of billiards or to sip his expensive scotch while they talked and smoked cigars in the grand house's well-appointed parlor. 'And this is my beautiful bride,' he'd say of my mother by way of introduction. Then, in an exaggerated gesture of adoration, he'd draw her to his side, cup her narrow waist in his hand ... and smile.

It was just after ten when I arrived at the shop. Neil was already at work, as usual. A less-observant man might not have noticed any change in my demeanor, but Neil had always been quick to gauge even the subtlest alteration of mood. He saw the distress I was laboring to hide, but when he finally addressed the matter, he was miles off the mark.

'Business will pick up,' he said. 'People are just ... I don't know ... they're strange.'

*Strange.*

The word abruptly swept away all my defenses, all my efforts to keep my fears in check. The dam broke, and I felt myself hurling forward on a rush of boiling dread, every dark aspect of the last few days now rising before me, demanding to be heard.

'Something wrong, boss?' Neil asked.

I looked into his hugely caring eyes and felt that I had no one else to go to. But even then, I had no idea where to begin. There was too much boiling within me now, too much hissing steam. I could barely sort one troubling doubt from another. And so I drew in a quick breath, trying to center myself and concentrate on the most immediate matter before me. Which surely, I decided, was Keith.

'I'd like to ask you something, Neil,' I began tentatively.

'Anything,' Neil said softly.

I walked to the front of the shop, turned out the CLOSED sign and locked the door.

Neil suddenly looked frightened. 'You're going to fire me.' His voice edged into panic. 'Please don't, Eric. I'll correct whatever it is. I need this job. My mother, you know. Medicine. I—'

'It's not about the job,' I assured him. 'You do a great job.'

He looked as if he were about to faint. 'I know it wasn't a great summer, businesswise, but ...'

'It has nothing to do with the shop,' I said. I stopped and drew in a fortifying breath. 'It's about Keith.'

Neil's face grew very still.

I could find no alternative to simply leaping in. 'What do you know about him?'

'Know about him?' Neil asked, clearly a little baffled by the curious urgency he heard in my voice.

'About his life.'

'Not very much, I guess,' Neil answered. 'He talks about music, sometimes. What bands he likes, that sort of thing.'

'Has he ever talked about girls?' I asked.

'No.'

'How about friends? He doesn't seem to have any friends.'

Neil shrugged. 'He's never mentioned anyone.'

'Okay,' I said. 'How about the people he delivers to. Have you ever heard any complaints?'

'What kind of complaints?'

'Anything about him, anything he did that seemed ... strange.'

Neil shook his head violently. 'Absolutely not, Eric. Never!'

I looked at him pointedly. 'You're sure?'

'Yes, I'm sure.'

I nodded. 'Okay,' I said. 'I just thought he might have come to you. I mean if—'

'If what?'

'If he had any ... problems he wouldn't know how to deal with.'

'What kind of problems?' Neil asked. He looked genuinely baffled. 'I mean, he wouldn't talk to me about girls, right?'

'I guess not.'

He looked at me curiously. 'It bothers you, doesn't it? That Keith doesn't have a girlfriend?'

I nodded. 'Maybe a little. Meredith says it does, but I'm not so sure. I mean, what if he doesn't have a girlfriend. He's just a kid. That doesn't mean he's—'

'Gay?'

'No,' I said. 'Not just that.'

Neil heard the awkwardness in my voice, the sense of trying to weasel out of the truth. 'Do you think Keith's gay?'

'I've thought about it,' I admitted.

'Why? Has he said anything?'

'No,' I answered. 'But he seems angry all the time.'

'What does that have to do with being gay?' Neil asked.

'Nothing.'

No one had ever looked at me the way Neil did now, with a mixture of pain and disappointment. 'Yeah, okay,' he said softly.

'What?'

He didn't answer.

'What, Neil?'

Neil laughed dryly. 'It just seems like you thought maybe if Keith was gay, he'd have to be angry. Hate himself, you know, that sort of thing. A lot of people have that idea. That a gay guy would have to hate himself.'

I started to speak, but Neil lifted his hand and silenced me.

'It's okay,' he said. 'I know you don't believe that.'

'No, I don't,' I told him. 'Really, Neil, I don't.'

'It's okay, Eric,' Neil repeated. 'Really. It is.' He smiled gently. 'Anyway, I hope everything works out all right for everyone,' he said quietly. 'Especially for Keith.'

He turned back toward the front of the shop.

'Neil,' I said. 'I didn't mean to . . .'

He didn't bother to look back. 'I'm fine' was all he said.

For the rest of the day, customers came and went. Neil kept himself busy and seemed determined to keep his distance from me.

At five the color of the air began to change, and by six, when I prepared to lock up, it had taken on a golden glow.

The phone rang.

'Eric's Frame and Photo.'

'Eric, they're coming here again,' Meredith told me.

'Who?'

'The police. They're coming to the house again.'

'Don't panic,' I said. 'They were there before, remember?'

I heard the fearful catch in her breath. 'This time they have a search warrant,' she said. 'Come home.'

# PART III

You stop now. You take a sip of coffee. You are halfway through the story you intend to tell. You realize that you have reached the moment when the lines you thought ran parallel begin to intersect. You know that from here on the telling will become more difficult. You will need to speak in measured tones, make the right connections. Nothing should blur, and nothing should be avoided. Particularly the responsibilities, the consequences.

You want to describe how the history of one family stained another, as if the colors from one photograph bled onto another in an accidental double exposure. You want to expose this process, but instead you stare out at the rain, watching people as they stand beneath their soaked umbrellas, and consider not what happened, but how it might have been avoided, what you could have done to stop it, or at least to change it in a way that would have allowed lives to go on, find balance, reach the high wisdom that only the fallen know.

But the wheels of your mind begin to spin. You can feel them spinning, but there is nothing to do but wait until they find traction. Then, without warning, they do, and you understand that all you can do is go on, start at exactly where you left off.

# FOURTEEN

*C*ome home.

    I often repeat the words in my mind. I recall Meredith's caught breath each time I repeat them, hear the icy dread in her voice.

I hear other things, too – a whispery voice, a gunshot – and with those sounds I recognize that I've gone through all of it again, reliving every detail from that first night when Keith and Warren strolled down the walkway and disappeared behind the Japanese maple to the moment when I passed under that same tree for the last time. In retrospect, I suppose, everything seems inevitable, the whole course of events summed up in the grim irony of that line of poetry I read while I waited for Keith to come home from Amy Giordano's house that night – *'After the first death, there is no other.'*

But there was.

I drove home quickly after Meredith's call. The sun was just setting when I pulled into the driveway, the air beneath the spreading limbs of the Japanese maple already a delicate pink. Meredith met me halfway up the walkway.

'I sent Keith into town. Because I needed to concentrate on writing a lecture. That's what I told him. He knows not to come back for a few hours.' There were tiny creases at the sides of her eyes, as if she'd aged several years during the brief time between her phone call and my arrival. 'I didn't tell him the police were coming over. I was afraid he might do something. Hide something.'

I looked at her quizzically.

'It could be anything,' she added. 'Some dirty magazine, pot, anything he wouldn't want them to see. And if he did that, you know, not even thinking about it, it would still be obstruction of justice.'

'I see you've talked to Leo.'

'Yes,' Meredith said. 'I told him I was going to send Keith to the store, keep him out of his room. He thought it was a good idea.'

'Because he doesn't trust Keith,' I said. 'That's why he thought it was a good idea.'

Meredith nodded. 'Probably.'

'Is he coming over?'

'Only if the cops want to question Keith.' She looked at me worriedly. 'I don't want to talk to them, either. Especially Kraus. On the phone, he sounded hard – like we're the enemy?' She looked at me pleadingly. 'Why would he act like that, Eric?'

'Maybe he doesn't think we're exactly ordinary,' I said cautiously. 'Did Leo mention the hotline? Things people might have said?'

'Said about what?'

'About us,' I told her. 'He has a source somewhere. With the police, I guess. And this source, whoever it is, told him that the police had gotten the idea that there was something wrong. Those were his words – *something wrong*. He thought somebody might have called on the hotline, told the cops something about us.'

Meredith looked stricken, helpless, a small creature caught in a vast web.

'Leo has no idea what might have been said,' I added. 'But with the police under all this pressure, he's worried they'll believe just about anything they hear about us.'

Meredith remained locked in grim silence, but I could see her mind working.

'Maybe someone saw that car pull into our driveway.'

'Maybe,' Meredith muttered.

'And there's something else they might have seen,' I told her. 'Remember when Leo asked Keith if he'd ever been around the water tower? I'm not sure Keith told the truth when he said no.'

'What makes you think he didn't tell the truth?'

'Just the look in his eyes,' I said. 'It was the same one he had when he told the cops he came home alone.' I shrugged. 'Anyway, the water tower, it's sort of a meeting place … for men and … prostitutes – or at least I think they're prostitutes. She was putting something in her bag. My guess is it was money.'

Meredith looked dazed.

'I went there,' I said. 'To the water tower. Leo brought it up, and then the way Keith looked when he said he'd never been there, I just got curious.'

'And you saw all this?' Meredith asked. 'These men and—'

'Yes,' I answered. 'I don't know why Keith goes there. I mean, if he does. Maybe he just watches. Maybe that's his … outlet.'

For a moment. Meredith seemed unable to deal with the tawdriness of what I'd just told her. 'Okay, so there's this place and people go there. But why are you so quick to believe that Keith goes there ... to watch ... or for any other reason?'

I had no answer, and she saw that I had no answer. 'Oh, Eric,' she said exhaustedly. 'What's happening to us?'

Meredith had put on her tightly controlled, professorial face by the time Peak and Kraus arrived. They brushed past the limbs of the maple and strode down the walkway at a leisurely pace, chatting to each other like two men on their way to the local tavern.

I met them at the door, and the instant I opened it, I noticed that their easy manner changed to one of cool professionalism. Now they stood erect, with somber faces, hands folded in front of them.

'Sorry to trouble you again, Mr. Moore,' Peak said.

Kraus nodded to me, but said nothing.

'How do we do this?' I asked. 'I've never had my house searched.'

'We have a warrant for the house and grounds,' Peak explained. 'We'll try not to disturb anything unnecessarily.'

'So I just let you in, is that it?'

'Yes.'

I stepped back, swung the door open, and let them pass into the living room where Meredith stood, her body completely rigid, eyes not so much hostile as wary.

'Keith isn't home,' she said. 'We haven't told him about this.'

'We won't be long,' Peak said with a weak smile.

'Where do you want to start?' I asked.

'Keith's room,' Peak said.

I nodded toward the stairs. 'Second door on your left.'

Meredith and I walked into the kitchen while Peak and Kraus searched Keith's room. Meredith made a pot of coffee, and we sat at the table and drank it silently. For that brief interval, we merely waited, held in suspension, staring at each other briefly, then drawing our gazes away. We might have been figures in a pantomime of a couple who'd been together too long, knew each other too well, and so had fallen into a final muteness.

Over the next few minutes, other officers arrived, all of them in uniform.

From our place in the kitchen, we watched as they poked about the yard, as well as the conservation forest that stretched for several acres behind our house. Two hours passed before Peak and Kraus came back down the stairs. Two young uniformed officers trailed behind them, carrying sealed bags stenciled in black letters: EVIDENCE.

I had no idea what the bags contained until Peak handed me a slip of paper on the way out. 'That's the inventory of what we took from Keith's room,' he said. 'And of course we'll bring back anything that has no evidentiary value.'

Evidentiary value, I thought. Evidence against Keith.

I glanced up the stairs and saw a uniformed officer coming down, carrying my son's computer.

'The computer in Keith's room,' Peak said. 'Is that the only one in the house?'

'No,' I said.

'I'm afraid we'll have to look at them all,' Peak said.

'There's one down the hall, in my office,' Meredith said. 'And I have a computer at college. Do you want to seize that, too?'

'Nothing is being seized, Mrs. Moore,' Peak answered mildly. 'But to answer your question, no, we have no need to take your computer.' He paused, then added significantly, 'At least, for now.'

The police left a few minutes later, just as Keith was coming down the drive on his bike. He pulled over to the side, got off the bike, and watched the cars go by.

'What did the cops want this time?' he asked as he came into the house.

'They searched your room,' I told him. 'They took a few things.' I handed him the inventory.

He scanned the list with surprising lack of interest until suddenly his eyes widened. 'My computer?' he cried. 'They have no right—'

'Yes, they do,' I interrupted. 'They can take anything they want.'

He looked at the inventory again, but now with a sense of helplessness. 'My computer,' he muttered. He slapped the paper against the side of his leg. 'Shit.'

Meredith had been standing silently a few feet away, observing Keith no less intently than I was. Now, she stepped forward. 'Keith, it's going to be okay.' Her tone of sympathy surprised me, as if she somehow understood his fear, knew what it was like to be threatened with exposure. 'It really is.'

Now it seemed up to me to state the hard facts of the case. 'Keith?' I asked, 'is there anything on that computer? Anything ... bad?'

He looked at me sourly. 'No.'

'Have you been in touch with Amy?'

'In touch?'

'E-mail.'

'No,' Keith said.

'Because if you have, they'll find that out,' I warned.

He laughed almost derisively. 'They would already know that, Dad,' he scoffed. 'They took the computer from Mr. Giordano's house, remember?'

I realized that Keith could only have known that the police had taken a computer from Amy's house if he'd actually been following news reports of the investigation. That the police had taken the Giordanos' computer had been mentioned on the evening news the night of her disappearance, and appeared only once in print, a brief notation in the local paper. From the beginning, he'd feigned indifference, even boredom, with the police. But clearly he had been keeping an eye on what they were doing.

'I asked you a question,' I said sharply.

'That's all you ever do,' Keith shot back. 'Ask me questions.' His eyes glittered angrily. 'Why don't you just get to the one question you really want to ask. Go ahead, Dad. Ask me.'

My lips jerked into an angry frown. 'Don't start that, Keith.'

'Ask the question,' Keith repeated insistently, offering it as a challenge. 'We all know what it is.' He laughed bitterly. 'All right, I'll ask it.' He cocked his head to the right, and switched to a low, exaggeratedly masculine, voice. 'So, Keith, did you kidnap Amy Giordano?'

'Stop it,' I said.

He continued in the same mock fatherly tone. 'Did you take her someplace and fuck her?'

'That's enough,' I said. 'Go to your room.'

He didn't move, save for his fingers, which instantly crushed the inventory. 'No, Dad, not until I ask the last question.'

'Keith . . .'

He cocked his head back and pretended to suck on an imaginary pipe. 'So, my boy, did you kill Amy Giordano?'

'Shut up!' I shouted.

He stared at me brokenly, his tone now soft, almost mournful. 'You believed it from the very first, Dad.' With that, he turned away and walked slowly up the stairs.

I looked at Meredith, noticed that her eyes were glistening. 'Is he right, Eric?' she asked. 'Did you believe it from the beginning?'

'No, I didn't,' I told her. 'Why would I?'

She turned my question over in her mind, working it silently until she found the answer. 'Maybe because you don't like him,' she whispered. 'Oh, I know you love him. But maybe you don't like him. It's what people do in families, isn't it? They love people they don't like.'

I heard footsteps on the stairs, then the front door closed loudly.

'He's going for one of those walks, I guess,' I said.

*Those walks* – Peak's words soured in my mouth, sounding suspicious, vaguely ominous, as they had when I first heard them.

'He's just trying to deal with it the only way he can,' Meredith told me. 'Which is alone, I guess.'

Keith was already at the end of the walkway, moving swiftly, shoulders hunched head down, as if against a heavy wind.

'We'll never be normal again,' Meredith said quietly.

It was a dark pronouncement, and I refused to accept it.

'Of course, we will,' I said. 'All of this will go away once Amy Giordano is found.'

She kept her eyes on Keith, watching intently as he mounted the small hill and moved on up toward the main road. 'We have to help him, Eric.'

'How?'

'Get someone for him to talk to.'

I thought of all my first family must have held secret, of its legacy of drink, unhappiness, and an old man's bitter cackle. Anything seemed better than that. 'What was the counselor's name?' I asked. 'The one at the college?'

Meredith smiled softly. 'Rodenberry,' she said. 'He'll be at the party tomorrow.'

# FIFTEEN

Dr. Mays lived in an old sea-captain's house only a few blocks from the home in which I'd grown up and which had seemed happy to me, at least until Jenny's death. After that my mother had sunk into a deep gloom, while my father's financial losses grew more and more severe, so that within the year the house itself had gone on the block. But none of that dreary history returned to me as we swept past the old house that evening. Instead, it was my father's dismissive outburst that played upon my mind – *You have no idea.*

He'd said it as an accusation but adamantly refused to clarify what he meant. Perhaps, I thought, my father was merely grasping for attention, his undefined charge against my mother was only his way of asserting himself when faced by her hallowed memory. If this were true, he'd chosen a crude method of gaining ground. But he'd always been reckless with his words, prone to vicious insult, and so it was perfectly in character for him to lift himself by bringing my mother down. And yet, for all that, I couldn't help wondering what he'd meant in saying that my mother hadn't been devoted to him. I'd seen nothing but devotion – patient and abiding. She had overlooked all his faults, stood by his side as his little empire shrank and finally disappeared. She had defended him no matter how outrageous his actions or negligent his fatherhood. How could it be that through all those years I'd had no idea of her?

'We'll just act normal,' Meredith said as I pulled the car up in front of Dr. Mays's house.

I offered a quick smile. 'We are normal,' I reminded her. 'We don't have to act.'

She seemed hardly to hear me. Her gaze was fixed on the house, the guests she could see milling about inside, her expression intense and oddly searching, like a woman on a widow's walk, peering out into the empty sea, hoping for the first fluttering glimpse of her husband's returning ship.

'What is it, Meredith?' I asked.

She turned toward me abruptly, as if I'd caught her unawares. 'I just hope he's here,' she said. 'Stuart.' She seemed to catch something odd in my expression. 'So we can talk to him about Keith,' she explained. 'We *are* going to do that, aren't we? That's what we decided.'

'Yes.'

Dr. Mays greeted us at the door. He was a short bald man, with wire spectacles.

'Ah, Meredith,' he said as he pumped her hand, then looked at me. 'Hello, Eric.'

We shook hands, and he ushered us into a spacious living room where several professors stood with their wives and husbands, sipping wine and munching little squares of cheese. We all stood by the fireplace for a time, exchanging the usual pleasantries. Then Meredith excused herself and drifted away, leaving me alone with Dr. Mays.

'You have a terrific wife, Eric,' he said, his eyes on Meredith as she approached a tall man in a tweed jacket who stood beside a thin woman with straight black hair.

'We feel very fortunate to have her with us,' Dr. Mays added.

I nodded. 'She loves teaching.'

'That's good to hear,' Dr. Mays said. He plucked a celery stalk from a plate of assorted cut vegetables and dipped it in the small bowl of onion dip that rested on the table beside him. 'I hope she doesn't find me stodgy.'

Across the room, Meredith laughed lightly and touched the man's arm.

'Not at all,' I said. 'She's always telling me some joke or story you've told.'

Dr. Mays appeared surprised. 'Really?'

I laughed. 'She loved the one about Lenny Bruce.'

He looked at me quizzically. 'Lenny Bruce?'

'The one about the difference between men and women,' I said.

Dr. Mays shrugged. 'I'm afraid I don't know that one.'

'You know, the plateglass window.'

Dr. Mays stared at me blankly. 'She must have heard that from someone else,' he said.

There was another burst of laughter from across the room. I looked over to see Meredith with her hand at her mouth, the way she always held it when she laughed, her eyes bright and strangely joyful, so different from the way she'd been only a few minutes before. The man in the tweed jacket laughed with her, but the woman beside him only smiled quietly, then took a quick sip from her glass.

'Who are they?' I asked. 'The people with Meredith.'

Dr. Mays looked over at them. 'Oh, that's Dr. Rodenberry and his wife, Judith,' he said. 'He's our college counselor.'

'Oh, yes,' I said. 'Meredith has mentioned him.'

'Brilliant man,' Dr. Mays said. 'And very funny.'

He gave me a few more details about Rodenberry, that he'd been at the college for five years, turned a moribund counseling service into a vibrant school function. After that, Dr. Mays said he had to mingle and stepped over to another group of teachers.

I took the opportunity to make my way across the room, where Meredith still stood, talking to the Rodenberrys.

She glanced over as I approached her.

'Hi,' I said softly.

'Hi,' Meredith said. She turned to Rodenberry and his wife. 'Stuart, Judith, this is my husband, Eric.'

I shook hands with the two of them, smiling as warmly as I knew how. Then there was a moment of awkward silence, eyes shifting about, Rodenberry's back and forth between me and Meredith, his wife's eyes darting toward me, then quickly away.

'I've mentioned this situation with Keith to Stuart,' she said.

I looked at Rodenberry. 'What do you think?' I asked.

He considered the question briefly. 'Well, Keith's certainly under a lot of pressure.'

That seemed hardly an answer, so I dug deeper.

'But do you think he needs professional help?' I asked.

Again Rodenberry appeared reluctant to answer directly. 'Perhaps, but only if he's willing to accept it. Otherwise, counseling would just add to the pressure he's already under.'

'So how can we tell?' I asked. 'If he needs help, I mean.'

Rodenberry glanced at Meredith in what appeared a signal for her to jump in.

'Stuart feels that we should raise the subject with Keith,' she said. 'Not present it to him as something we think he should do, but only raise it as a possibility.'

'And see how he reacts,' Rodenberry added quickly. 'Whether he's immediately hostile, or if he seems amenable to the idea.'

'And if he seems amenable?' I asked.

Again, Rodenberry's gaze slid over to Meredith. 'Well, as I told Meredith,' he said, now returning his attention to me, 'I'd be more than happy to provide whatever help I can.'

I started to add some final remark on the subject, but Rodenberry's wife suddenly withdrew from our circle, her head turned decidedly away, as if shielding her face from view.

'Judith has been ill,' Rodenberry said quietly once his wife was out of earshot. Again he looked at Meredith, and in response she offered a smile that struck me as unexpectedly intimate, which Rodenberry immediately returned.

'Anyway,' he said, now returning his gaze to me. 'Let me know what you decide about Keith.' He drew a card from his jacket pocket. 'Meredith has my number at school,' he said as he handed me the card, 'but this is my private number. Call it anytime.'

I thanked him, and after that Rodenberry walked across the room to join his wife beside a buffet table. Once there, he placed his arm on his wife's shoulder. She quickly stepped away, as if repulsed by his touch, so that Rodenberry's arm immediately fell free and dangled limply at his side.

'I think the Rodenberrys have problems,' I said to Meredith.

She watched as Rodenberry poured himself a drink and stood alone beside the window, where Dr. Mays joined him a few minutes later.

'Dr. Mays didn't remember that Lenny Bruce remark,' I said.

Meredith continued to stare straight ahead, which was odd for her, I realized, since her tendency was always to glance toward me when I spoke.

'The one about the plateglass window,' I added.

Her eyes shot over to me. 'What?'

'You didn't hear it from Dr. Mays,' I repeated.

Meredith glanced back into the adjoining room. 'Well, I heard it from somebody,' she said absently.

'Maybe from Rodenberry,' I suggested. 'Dr. Mays says he's very funny.'

'Yes, he is,' Meredith said. Her eyes glittered briefly, then dimmed, as if a shadowy thought had skirted through her mind. 'He'll be good with Keith' was all she said.

We left the party a couple of hours later, driving more or less silently back to our house. The light was on in Keith's room, but we didn't go up or call him or make any effort to find out if he was really there. Such surveillance would only have struck him as yet more proof that I thought him a criminal, and his mood had become far too volatile to incite any such added resentment.

And so we simply watched television for an hour, then went to bed. Meredith tried to read for a while, but before too long she slipped the book onto the floor beside the bed, then twisted away from me and promptly fell asleep.

But I couldn't sleep. I thought about Keith and Meredith, of course, but increasingly my thoughts returned me to my first family – Warren's story of the insurance man with the odd questions, the strange remark my father had made, his bitter assertion that I had no idea about my mother.

Could that be true? I wondered. Could it be true that I had never known my mother? Or my father? That Warren, for all our growing up together, remained essentially an enigma?

I got up, walked to the window, and peered out into the tangled, night-bound woods. In my mind, I saw the car that had brought Keith home that night, its phantom driver behind the wheel, a figure who suddenly seemed to me no less mysterious than my son, my wife, my father and mother and brother, mere shadows, dark and indefinable.

'Eric?'

It was Meredith's voice.

I turned toward the bed but couldn't see her there.

'Something wrong?'

'No, nothing,' I told her, grateful that I hadn't turned on the light, since, had she seen me, she would have known it was a lie.

# SIXTEEN

Leo Brock called me at the shop at eleven the next morning.
'Quick question,' he said. 'Does Keith smoke?'

He heard my answer in the strain of a pause.

'Okay,' he said, 'what brand does he smoke?'

I saw the face of the pack as Keith snatched it from his shirt pocket.
'Marlboro,' I said.

Leo drew in a long breath. 'And he told police that he never left the
house, isn't that right?'

'Yes.'

'For any reason.'

'He said he never left the house,' I told him. 'What's happening, Leo?'

'My source tells me that the cops found four cigarette butts outside the
Giordanos' house,' Leo said. 'Marlboro.'

'Is that so bad?' I asked. 'I mean, so what if Keith went out for a
smoke?'

'They were at the side of the house,' Leo added. 'Just beneath Amy's
bedroom window.'

'Jesus,' I breathed.

In my mind I saw Keith at the window, peering through the curtains
of Amy's window, watching as she slept, her long dark hair splayed
out across her pillow. Had he watched her undress, too? I wondered.
And while doing that ... done what? Had he gone to the water tower in
search of similar stimulation? Before that moment, I would probably have
avoided such questions, but something in my mind had hardened, taken
on the shape of a pick or a spade, prepared to dig.

'So they think he was watching her,' I said.

'We can't be sure what they're thinking.'

'Oh come on, Leo, why would his cigarettes be there, at her window?'

'Not his,' Leo cautioned. 'Just the brand he smokes.'

'Don't talk to me like a lawyer, Leo,' I said. 'This is bad and you know it.'

'It doesn't help things,' Leo admitted.

'They're going to arrest him, aren't they?'

'Not yet,' Leo said.

'Why not?' I asked. 'We both know they think he did it.'

'First of all, no one knows what was done,' Leo reminded me. 'Remember that, Eric. Whatever the police may be thinking, they don't know anything. And there's something else to keep in mind. Keith didn't have a car. So how could he have taken Amy from her house?'

I made no argument to this, but I felt the water around me rise slightly.

'Eric?'

'Yes.'

'You have to have faith.'

I said nothing.

'And I don't mean that in a religious way,' Leo added. 'You have to have faith in Keith.'

'Of course,' I said quietly.

There was a pause, then Leo said, 'One final ... difficulty.'

I didn't bother to ask what it was, but only because I knew Leo was about to tell me.

'Keith ordered a pizza for dinner that night,' Leo said. 'The pizza guy delivered it at just after eight. He said that when he arrived, he didn't see Amy, but Keith was there, and he was on the phone.'

'The phone?'

'Did he call you that night?'

'Yes.'

'When did he call?'

'Just before ten.'

'Not before?'

'No.'

'You're sure about that,' Leo said. 'You're sure that Keith only called you once that night.'

'Only once,' I said. 'At around ten.'

'And that's when he told you he'd be late and that he wouldn't need a ride, correct?'

'Yes.'

'Because he had a ride?'

'No,' I said. 'He said that he could get a ride.'

'But not that he had one?'

'No, not that he had one.'

'Okay,' Leo said.

'So who was he on the phone with?' I asked. 'When the pizza guy was there.'

'I'm sure the police have the number,' Leo said. 'So it won't be long before they tell us.'

We talked a few minutes longer, Leo doing what he could to put the best light on things. Still, for all his effort, I could sense nothing but a spiraling down, a room closing in, slowly dwindling routes of escape.

'What happens,' I asked finally, 'if they never find Amy?'

'Well, it's awfully hard to convict when there's no body,' Leo answered.

'I wasn't thinking of that,' I told him. 'I mean, Keith would have to live with it, wouldn't he? The suspicion that he killed her.'

'Yes, he would,' Leo answered. 'And I admit, cases like that, without any definite resolution, they can be painful to all concerned.'

'Corrosive,' I said softly, almost to myself.

'Corrosive, yes,' Leo said. 'It's hard, when you can't get to the bottom of something.'

I had never known how true that was before that moment, how little whiffs of doubt could darken and grow menacing, urge you forward relentlessly, fix you in a need to find out what really happened. 'Otherwise your whole life is an unsolved mystery,' I said.

'Yeah, it's just that bad,' Leo said. 'You become a cold-case file.'

*A cold-case file.*

I remember thinking that that was precisely what I was becoming, and that for the rest of that day, as I dealt with customers, framed a few pictures, I felt a fierce urgency building in me, a need to know about Keith, the life he might have hidden from me, the terrible thing I could not keep myself from thinking that he might, indeed, have done.

Just before I closed, I called Meredith and told her what Leo Brock had earlier told me. I expected her to be irritated that I hadn't called before, accuse me once again of refusing to confront things, but instead she took the latest development without surprise, as if she'd been expecting it all along.

'I have to work late tonight,' she said. Her voice struck me as oddly wistful, like a woman who'd once lived in a perfect world, known its beauty and contentment, a world that was no more and would never be again. 'I should be home by eleven.'

I was on my way to my car a few minutes later when I noticed Warren's truck parked outside Teddy's bar. I guessed that he was probably drinking earlier and earlier, his usual pattern before plunging into a full-blown binge. In the past, I'd never been able to prevent his periodic dives, and because of that I had more or less stopped trying. But suddenly, faced with my own family problems, I found that I could see his more clearly.

The contempt my father had so relentlessly heaped upon him had stolen away any shred of self-confidence he might otherwise have grasped, then the tragedy of Jenny's death, and after that, my mother's fatal accident. Perhaps, I told myself, he was not so much one of life's pathetic losers, as simply a man who had lost a lot.

He was sitting in the back booth, his paint-spattered hands wrapped around a mug of beer.

'Hey, Bro,' he said as I slid into the seat opposite him. He lifted the beer. 'Want a frosty?'

I shook my head. 'No, I don't have much time. Meredith's working late, so I have to get home, make dinner for Keith.'

He took a sip of the beer. 'So,' he said. 'How's tricks?'

I shrugged. 'The same.'

'And this thing with Keith?'

'I have the feeling the cops are focusing on him.' I added no further details, and typically, Warren didn't ask.

Instead he said, 'They jump to conclusions, the cops. It only takes some little thing.' He laughed. 'But, that's the way we all are, right? Obsessed.'

'Why do you say that?'

'You know, the way some crazy idea won't stop nagging at a guy.'

Warren often spoke of himself in the third person, as 'a guy'.

'What crazy idea is nagging at you, Warren?' I asked.

I thought it was probably something about Keith, but I was wrong.

'For some reason I keep thinking about Mom,' Warren said. 'You know, how upset she was toward the end.'

'Well, why wouldn't she be?' I said. 'She was losing her house.'

'That wasn't it,' Warren said. 'She never liked that house.'

'She never liked the house?'

'No, she hated it,' Warren said. He took a sip of beer. 'It was too big, she said, too much to take care of.'

'I didn't know she felt that way,' I said.

'The house was for Dad,' Warren said. 'Part of the show. He wanted it because it made people think he was a big important guy.' He glanced away, then back to me. 'You seen him lately?'

'I see him every Thursday.'

Warren smiled. 'Dutiful,' he said. 'You've always been dutiful with Dad.'

He made duty sound oddly disreputable. 'I don't want him to feel abandoned, if that's what you mean.'

Warren took a hard pull on the beer. 'I dropped in on him this morning,' he said. He looked at me with a bitter grin. 'He said he never wanted to see me again.'

'What? Why?'

'Because of what I told you, that insurance guy.'

'Dad doesn't want to see you again because of that?' I asked unbelievingly.

'Yup,' Warren said, now trying to make light of it. 'Funny world, huh, Eric?'

I waved my hand. 'He'll get over it.'

Warren shook his head adamantly. 'No, he won't. Not this time. I really pissed him off.'

'But it was nothing,' I argued.

'Not to Dad,' Warren said. 'He got in a real lather about it.'

I recalled the look on my father's face when I'd broached the same subject with him, and suddenly I realized that the part of me that wished to avoid things, the part Meredith had long recognized, was dead. My suspicion had begun with a subtle itch, but now it was a raging affliction, a thousand bleeding sores I couldn't stop digging at.

'What's he hiding, Warren?' I asked bluntly.

Warren's eyes fell toward his hands.

'Warren?'

He shrugged.

I leaned toward him. 'You were there that summer,' I said. 'What happened?'

Warren looked up shyly. 'Dad thought she did something,' he said. 'Mom.' He glanced about as if to make sure no one else was listening. 'Something with this other guy. You know what I mean.'

'Mom?' I was astonished. 'What other guy?'

Warren took a sip. 'Jason Benefield. The family lawyer, remember? Used to come over with papers for this or that.'

I recalled him as a tall, well-dressed, and very courtly man with a great shock of gray hair, handsome in the way of old boats, rugged, worn, but graceful.

'Do you think it was true, what Dad thought?' I asked.

'Maybe,' Warren said. He saw the surprise in my face, how little I'd believed it possible that he noticed anything. 'I'm not stupid, Eric,' he said. 'I can see things.'

'What did you see exactly?'

'That Mom was ... that she liked this guy,' Warren answered. 'And that he felt the same way about her.' He finished the drink and waved for another. 'At first I didn't know what to think about it, you know? Mom and this guy. But then I knew how Dad treated her, like she was nothing except when his cronies came over. And so I just thought, Well, okay, good for Mom, you know?'

Peg arrived with Warren's beer. He smiled at her, but she didn't smile back.

'Bitch, huh?' Warren muttered after she'd stepped away. 'But then, they all are, right?' He gave a quick self-mocking laugh. 'At least to me.'

'What made Dad suspect her?'

Warren ran his fingers through what was left of his hair. 'Somebody tipped him off.'

'Who?'

He hesitated, and so I knew I wouldn't like the answer, but comfort no longer mattered to me. 'Who?' I repeated sternly.

'Aunt Emma,' Warren answered. He took a long drink, glanced into the dying foam, then looked at me. 'She saw Mom and Jason together. I mean, not in a bad way. Like in bed, or something like that. Mom would never have done anything, you know, at home. But one day Aunt Emma came over to bring some tomatoes from her garden. She heard Mom and this guy talking.' He shrugged. 'You know, the way people talk when there's something between them. You don't have to hear the words.'

'And Aunt Emma told Dad?'

Warren nodded, returned his gaze to the glass, remained silent for a moment, then looked up. 'He beat the hell out of her, Eric. I knew it was coming, so I took off. When I got back, Dad was sitting in the living room, drinking. Mom was upstairs. She didn't come down until the next morning. That's when I saw what he'd done to her.' He seemed to return to that grim day. 'I got real upset. I wanted to hit him. Like he hit her. I wanted to beat the shit out of him.' He shook his head. 'But I didn't do anything. I didn't even mention it.' His eyes glistened slightly. 'I never had any nerve, Eric. All Dad had to do was look at me, and I crumbled.'

I shook my head. 'I had no idea about any of this.'

Warren nodded. 'You couldn't have done anything, anyway. Nobody could do anything with Dad. Besides, he was good to you.'

'Yes, to me,' I admitted. 'But you had to—'

Warren waved his hand to silence me. 'Oh, don't worry about me and Dad. Then or now. Hell, I don't care if I never see him again.' He took a long pull on the beer, one that left no doubt that it was my father's anger that had hurled him off the wagon. 'Water under the bridge.'

Except that it wasn't. At least not for me.

'I keep thinking about things, Warren,' I told him. 'I know it's because of this thing with Keith. But I keep going back to our family, too.'

Warren laughed. 'Why bother? They were gone before you grew up. Mom. Jenny. You were still a kid when they died.'

'But I don't want to be a kid anymore,' I told him. 'I want to know what you know. About everything.'

'I told you what I know.'

'Maybe there was more,' I said.

'Like what?'

'Like that insurance man you told me about. Why would he have come around the house, asking questions about Mom and Dad?'

Warren shrugged. 'Who knows?'

'Dad told me there was no insurance on Mom,' I said.

'Then I guess there wasn't any insurance.' He took a sip of beer. 'Jesus, what difference does it make, anyway?'

'It makes a difference because I want to know.'

'Know what?'

The words fell like stones from my mouth. 'If he killed her.'

Warren's eyes grew very still. 'Jesus, Eric.'

'Fucked with the car some way. The brakes.'

'Dad didn't know anything about cars, Eric.'

'So, you don't think—'

Warren laughed. 'Of course not.' He peered at me as if I were very small, a creature he couldn't quite bring into focus. 'What's the matter with you? Dad kill Mom? Come on, Eric.'

'How can you be so sure?'

Warren laughed again, but this time, mirthlessly. 'Eric, this is nuts.'

'How do you know?' I repeated.

'Jesus, Eric,' Warren said. 'This is weird.'

'What if he killed her?' I asked.

Warren remained silent for a moment, his gaze downcast, as if studying the last small portion of beer that remained. Then he said, 'What good would it do, even if you found out he did?'

'I don't know,' I said. 'But as it stands, everything seems like a lie.'

'So?'

'I don't want to live like that.'

He drained the last of the beer. 'Eric, everybody lives like that.' He grinned and the grim seriousness of our former discussion simply fell away from him. 'Lighten up, Bro – everybody's fake.'

I leaned forward and planted my elbows on the table. 'I want to know the truth.'

Warren shrugged lightly. 'Okay, fine,' he said wearily. 'Knock yourself out. Hell, Dad's a pack rat. Kept everything in that old metal filing cabinet, remember? Wouldn't throw it away, or anything in it. Heavy fucking thing. Remember the trouble we had moving it into your basement?' He drained the last of the beer and looked at me drowsily. 'If he had a policy on Mom,' he said, 'that's where it would be.'

# SEVENTEEN

T he next night, after Meredith and Keith had already gone to bed, I quietly made my way to the basement. It was a gray metal filing cabinet, the one in which my father had kept his records and which Warren and I had removed from the little house my father had lived in before I'd finally convinced him to take up residence at the retirement home.

I'd taken him to Shelton Arms on a snowy January day, then returned to the house and helped Warren pack up Dad's belongings and transport them to the basement where they'd rested undisturbed until now.

My father's old rolltop desk stood beside the cabinet. I opened it, pulled over a plain metal chair, took out a stack of files from the top drawer of the cabinet, and began to go through the yellow crumbling papers I found inside, the records of my father's many failed enterprises along with his increasingly desperate attempts to salvage them.

But that was not the history I was looking for. I didn't care that my father had failed, that his business dealings were shadowy, that he'd squandered thousands of dollars to keep up appearances, joined expensive clubs at the very time my mother was scouring local thrift shops in order to keep her children clothed.

None of that mattered because I wasn't looking for evidence of bad business decisions or foolish investments. I was Peak and Kraus, my gaze, like theirs, focused by suspicion, looking for evidence of a crime.

It emerged slowly, like a body rising through layers of accumulated silt, the excruciating details of my father's ruin. The decline began in the late sixties as his real estate holdings were decimated by soaring interest rates. Steadily, for five years, he defaulted on one mortgage after another, his banker friends no longer willing to extend further credit, so that he lost both residential lots and commercial properties, his wealth dropping from him like petals from a wilting rose.

By the fall of 1974, he had nothing left but the family house, itself mortgaged to the gills, literally sinking in a slough of debt. I was twelve

119

years old that autumn, now attending the expensive private school my father had denied Warren, a little boy dressed in his school uniform, complete with navy blue blazer with brass buttons, the crest of Saint Regis embroidered on the breast pocket.

Each night, I returned to a house that was disappearing, though I didn't know that at the time. Warren stayed in his room most of the time, and Jenny had begun complaining of terrible headaches. My mother made increasingly modest meals, which she served at a table my father hardly frequented anymore. 'He's in New York,' my mother would explain, 'on business.'

The disastrous nature of that business was apparent in the papers I rifled through that night, applications for loans and their subsequent denials, threatening letters from lawyers and creditors and even local tradesmen, all of them demanding payment ... or else.

Under such a barrage, men have been driven to suicide or simply run away, in either case leaving their families to fend for themselves. But on rare occasions some men take a third, far more drastic, option. They kill their families.

Until that night, it had never occurred to me that at some desperate moment, with the fifth scotch of the evening trembling in his hand, my father might actually have considered this final course.

Then, suddenly, it was there, the terrifying suggestion that he had.

A suggestion, not evidence, and yet it stopped me cold, so that for a long time, I simply stared at what I'd stumbled upon, the real estate section of the *Los Angeles Times*, dated April 27, 1975, and wondered how this particular section of a paper from a city several thousand miles away had come into my father's hands, and why, halfway down column three, he had drawn a red circle around a particular advertisement, one offering a 'neat, clean, studio ... suitable for bachelor.'

*Suitable for bachelor.*

In what way, I wondered, had my father planned to be a bachelor again?

Was it only that he'd considered option one, abandonment?

Or had he considered option three as well, a final, irrevocable break that would truly leave him free?

I didn't know, couldn't know, and yet, in my current state of mind, one the shadowy basement perfectly mirrored, I found that I could neither dismiss the possibility that my father had truly contemplated our murders nor suppress my need to discover if he actually had.

And so I continued through his papers, watching with an ever-deepening sense of desperation as his circumstances grew more dire. As the weeks of that last disastrous year passed, the dunning letters became more threatening and my father's responses increasingly laced with fabrications. He began to invent correspondence with 'anonymous backers', to claim sources of revenue he did not have, and to pepper his letters with the names of important people – mostly politicians – who were, he said, 'getting in on the ground floor' of whatever wholly fanciful enterprise he was at that moment proposing. The line between delusion and reality appeared to fade, and because of that, I could no longer tell if he was outright lying or if he had begun to believe his own fantasies.

Then, in yet another stack of business correspondence, this one interspersed with yellowing family photographs, I found a letter from my father's sister, Emma. It was dated February 3, 1975, a short two and a half months before my mother's death. One line in particular caught my attention: *'As you say, Edward, these current straits are due entirely to Margaret's outrageous spending.'*

My mother's outrageous spending? On what had my mother spent outrageously? I knew the answer all too well. She had spent 'outrageously' on used clothes at the Catholic thrift shop, on bruised vegetables at the market. She'd spent on bent cans and day-old bread. Despite our dwindling resources, she had tried with all her might to keep her children decently clothed and fed. During the year of Jenny's death, she had bought absolutely nothing for herself. Not so much as a hat or an earring.

That my father could blame my mother for his own financial mismanagement was deplorable enough. But the line he'd scrawled in the margin beside my aunt's comment was worse: *'Now let her get me out of it.'*

Me.

Not us.

So what exactly were we – his wife and three children – to my father, I wondered. The answer was implicit in his use of 'me'. We were nothing.

We were nothing, and so he could go to New York, pick up a copy of the *Los Angeles Times,* pull out the real estate section, peruse it casually on the train back to Wesley, circle an ad for a neat clean studio, 'suitable for bachelor'.

And how might he regain his bachelorhood?

The darkest possible scenario immediately unspooled in my mind: my father waiting until deep in the night, then moving silently downstairs to his office, opening the rolltop desk, unlocking a small wooden cubicle, and drawing out the pistol he had always kept there. The very pistol which, as if in some miraculous vision, glimmered darkly before me, still in the cubicle where he'd left it. Had he reached for it, as I now did, then taken it up the stairs to where his family slept, as my family also did, he would have been but three quick shots from freedom.

But if that had ever been his plan, why had he not done it? Others had.

Men like my father, ruined in business, in dread of humiliation, men who'd lost everything, and so, on a cool evening had decided to start over in the most profound and devastating way a man can seek deliverance. They had methodically murdered their families. Why had my father refused to take that road? Why had he not even decided on the less awesome route of simply climbing on a plane or train or bus and vanishing into the night?

I knew that his remaining with us had nothing to do with love. My mother's power over him had faded with her beauty. He felt nothing but contempt for Warren. And Jenny, for whom he'd seemed to have a true affection, had only just died. That left me, and so, briefly, I entertained the notion that his hopes for me had provided the one force that held us together. He had, after all, sent me to the best school, and when he talked about my future, it was always in the brightest terms. I would go to an Ivy League college, become a powerhouse in some business or law firm. I would be the son he'd dreamed of, proof of his worth, as much an ornament as my mother's beauty had once been.

But by April 1975, even that dream was surely dying. There would be no money for an Ivy League education, as my father must have known, and without it how could I fulfill his vision of a rich, successful son?

For a moment, I considered my father's predicament. He was bankrupt, saddled with a family he cared little for, his daughter already dead.

Why then had he stayed with us?

The answer occurred to me instantly. He'd stayed because somewhere in the dark tangle of his business and family relations, he had found a way out.

The single line he'd written in the margin of his sister's letter now returned to me in a sinister whisper. *Now let her get me out of it.*

In a vision, I put myself in my brother Warren's place on that long ago summer afternoon. I am sitting on the grand staircase, reading a book. The doorbell rings. I answer it. A tall lean man in a dark suit draws a gray hat from his head and stares at me with small, quiet, sparklingly inquisitive eyes. His voice is calm, soothing, like Peak's: *No reason to be alarmed.* He is from the insurance company, he says, investigating something, that much is clear, though he doesn't tell me what he's looking into. And so I let him in, as Warren did, then go back to the stairs, my book. He leaves after a few minutes. He does not tell me what he was looking for, and the years go by and I marry and have a son and never ask him what he sought that day.

But now I know, and within only a few minutes it is in my hands, buried among other papers, but not deeply. Like a body hurriedly covered with leaves and fallen branches, the lightest digging brings it up, not a policy exactly, but a letter to my father, informing him that the life insurance policy on his wife has been approved in the amount of two hundred thousand dollars.

'Eric?'

I looked up and saw Meredith standing at the bottom of the stairs. I hadn't heard her come down them, the soft tread of her feet muffled by the stormy currents in my own mind.

'What are you doing down here?' she asked in a voice that seemed faintly alarmed, like she'd stumbled upon some oddity in me that called other, once-stable, characteristics into question.

'Just going through some old stuff,' I answered.

She peered at the pile of papers that lay strewn across the desk. 'What are you looking for?'

I quickly glanced down and noticed a photograph. 'This,' I said, lifting it from the pile for her to see.

It was a family photograph, the last one taken of all of us together. My father and mother on the front steps of the big house, their three children lined up in front of them, Warren on the left, Jenny on the right, me in the middle.

Who had I been then? I wondered as I glanced at the picture. How much had I known that year? How much had I refused to know? And not just about hidden things, the insurance policy, my mother's grief, but about the most obvious aspects of life in the big house. Had I once considered how cruelly Warren was treated or that Jenny sometimes had headaches and fell for no reason at all, or that my mother often sat silently at the kitchen table, toying distractedly with a crushed napkin? Had I once glanced out the window of the fancy bus that whisked me to Saint Regis each morning, looked out as the big house grew small in the distance, and allowed myself to confront the possibility that something might be wrong?

I looked at my wife, noted the wariness in her gaze, and Leo Brock's words sounded in my mind, the disturbing intimation that all was not well in my own house, either, and that someone out there knew it.

*Something wrong.*

For a moment, I imagined the source of that discomforting remark, saw a phantom person pawing through my papers as I'd just pawed through my father's, full of suspicion but with no real evidence. I suddenly felt an annihilating fury at whomever it was who'd phoned the police hotline, a rage that was not in the least calmed by the fact that I could not even be sure that there was such a person. And yet I believed that there was, believed it so powerfully that I instantly imagined the caller's voice as something between a lascivious whisper and the hissing of a snake. The caller's profile emerged no less fully formed – a fat puffy face, with thick moist lips and a day's growth of facial hair. I could even see the outline of his room, dirty and disheveled, littered with grease-stained paper napkins and empty pizza boxes. He was a bachelor, this man, lonely and hateful, someone who'd seen either me or Meredith or Keith and fixed some sullen and resentful part of himself upon us. He had created histories for us, I decided, and ran those histories through his mind, sneering at a family whose imagined perfection he despised.

'You don't want me to see it?'

I came out of my reverie to find Meredith now at the desk, tugging at a picture I had reflexively resisted letting go.

'Of course, you can see it,' I said. I released the photograph and watched as Meredith gazed at it expressionlessly.

'Why were you looking for this particular picture?' Meredith asked.

I shrugged. 'I don't know,' I said. 'Maybe because it was the last time everything seemed' – the final word cracked something deep within me – 'right.'

She handed the picture back to me. 'Are you going to stay down here all night?'

I shook my head. 'No,' I told her. 'Just a little longer.'

She turned and headed back up the stairs, head bent forward slightly, her hair dangling in dark waves on the side of her face. At the top of the stairs, she stopped and stood on the landing. For a moment, I thought she might come back down to me, take a deep breath and—

*Confess?*

I stared at her, stunned by the word that had suddenly popped into my mind. What had Meredith done that required confession? And yet, there it was, the idea thrown up from some murky depth inside me, suspicion now flowing into empty space, filling it with a sharp, acrid smoke, so that I felt trapped in a furiously overheated room, flames licking at me from all directions, with no way to douse the ever-rising fire.

# EIGHTEEN

Monday morning I got up early, walked to the kitchen and made coffee. For a long time I sat alone at the small oval table that overlooked the front yard. I recalled the previous night's search through my father's papers, the incriminating documents I'd found among them, and felt again a searing need to get to the bottom of what, if anything, had actually happened to my mother. At the same time I knew nowhere to go with what I'd found. I recalled how Meredith had come down to the basement, the strange accusation my mind had seized upon, the licking flames that had suddenly sprung up all around me, which I now laid at the feet of the undeniable strain I'd been under since Amy Giordano's disappearance. It was this tension that had created the false fires I felt still burning in me, I decided, fires which, when the mystery of her circumstances was finally resolved, would surely weaken and gutter out.

Keith came down the stairs at just past seven. He didn't bother to come into the kitchen. He'd never been hungry in the morning, and neither Meredith nor I any longer insisted that he eat something before going to school. And so on this particular morning, like most others, he simply swept down the stairs and out the door to where his bike lay on its side in the dewy grass, mounted it, and pedaled away.

He'd already disappeared up the hill when Meredith came into the kitchen. Normally by this time she would be fully dressed for work, so it surprised me that she was still in her housecoat, the belt drawn tight, her feet bare, hair in disarray. She hadn't put on the usual light coat of makeup either, and I noticed dark circles under her eyes. She looked tense and unrested, worn down by what we'd been going through.

'I'm not going in to work today,' she said. She poured a cup of coffee, but instead of joining me at the table, walked to the window and stared out into the yard.

Her back was to me, and I admired her shape, the way she'd so carefully maintained it. She had broad shoulders, and long sleek legs, and despite her drawn appearance, I knew why men still turned when she came into the room.

'Keith's already gone,' I told her.

'Yeah, I saw him out the window.' She took a sip of coffee and kept her eyes fixed on the front yard. 'I'll just call it a personal day,' she said. 'They don't ask questions when you take a personal day.'

I walked over to her, wrapped my arms loosely around her shoulders. 'Maybe I'll take off, too. Go to a movie or something. Spend the whole day. Just the two of us.'

She shook her head and pulled out of my arms. 'No, I have to work. It's not that kind of personal day.'

'What work?' I asked.

'I need to write a lecture. On Browning.'

'I thought you'd written all your lectures. Wasn't that what all those late nights at the library were about?'

She returned to the coffee machine. 'All but Browning,' she said. 'I have the notes here.'

'Any chance of finishing it by afternoon? We could go for a long walk together.'

'No, I won't be finished by then,' she answered. She came over to me and pressed an open palm against the side of my face. 'But I'll cook a nice dinner. French. With candles. Wine.' She smiled thinly. 'We might even persuade Keith to join us.'

I drew her hand away and held it lightly. 'What about Rodenberry?'

Her eyes tensed.

'Are we going to talk to Keith about him?'

My question seemed to put her at ease. 'I think we should,' she said.

'All right.'

I left her, walked upstairs, and finished dressing. She was sitting at the kitchen table, sipping from her cup, when I came back down.

She smiled when she saw me. 'Have a nice day,' she said.

Detective Peak was waiting for me when I arrived at the shop. This time he was dressed casually, in a light flannel jacket and open-collar shirt. As I came toward him, he edged away from the side of the building and nodded.

'I wonder if we could have a cup of coffee,' he asked.

'I've already had my morning coffee,' I answered coolly.

'Just one cup,' Peak said, but not in the distant professional tone he'd used with Meredith. Instead, there was now something unexpectedly fraternal in his manner, as if we were old war buddies and so could talk to each other in full trust and confidence.

'You'll be able to open on time,' he added.

'All right,' I said with a shrug.

We walked to the diner at the end of the block. It was owned by the Richardsons, a couple who'd moved to Wesley from New York only a few years before. They'd shunned the sleek art deco look of city diners and tried for a homey design instead, wooden tables, lace curtains, porcelain salt and pepper shakers in the form of a nineteenth-century sea captain and his wife. Before that morning, I'd hardly noticed the décor, but now it struck me as false and unnatural, like a bad face-lift.

'Two coffees,' Peak said to Matt Richardson as we took a table near the front window.

Peak smiled. 'May I call you Eric?'

'No.'

The smiled vanished. 'I have a family, too,' he said. He waited for me to respond. When I didn't, he folded his arms on the table and leaned into them. 'It's my day off,' he added.

I immediately suspected that this was Peak's new approach and that it was meant to soften me up, a way of telling me that he'd taken a special interest in the case, was trying to be of help. A week before, I might have believed him, but now I thought it just an act, something he'd learned at police interrogation school.

The coffees came. I took a quick sip, but Peak left his untouched.

'This doesn't have to go any further,' he said. His voice was low, measured. It conveyed a sense of guarded discretion. 'Absolutely no further.'

He drew in a deep preparatory breath, like a man about to take a long dive into uncertain waters. 'We found things on Keith's computer.'

My hands trembled very slightly, like shaking leaves. I quickly dropped them into my lap and put on a stiff unflappable face.

'What did you find?' I asked.

Peak's face was a melancholy mask. 'Pictures.'

'Pictures of what?' I asked stonily.

'Children.'

The earth stopped turning.

'They aren't illegal, these pictures,' Peak added quickly. 'They're not exactly child pornography.'

'What are they?'

He looked at me pointedly. 'You're sure you don't know anything about these pictures?'

'No, nothing.'

'You never use Keith's computer?'

I shook my head.

'Then the pictures have to be Keith's,' Peak said. He made a show of

127

being genuinely sorry that the pictures had turned up. Part of his new act, I decided, his effort to suggest that he'd come to me in search of an explanation, one that would get Keith off the hook. I had a photo shop, after all. Maybe I was interested in 'art pictures'. If so, as he'd already assured me, nothing would go further.

'The children are all girls,' Peak continued. 'They look to be around eight years old.' He bit his lower lip, then said, 'Nude.'

I felt the only safety lay in silence, so I said nothing.

'We've talked to Keith's teachers,' Peak said. 'He seems to have self-esteem problems.'

I saw Keith in my mind, the limp drag of his hair, how unkempt he was, the slouch of his shoulders, the drowsy, listless eyes. Was that the posture of his inner view of himself, hunched, sloppy, worthless?

'Low self-esteem is part of the profile,' Peak said.

I remained silent, afraid the slightest word might be used against my son, quoted by the prosecution, used to buttress the case, contribute to conviction.

'Of men who like children,' Peak added.

I clung to silence like the shattered bow of a sinking boat, the only thing that could keep me afloat in the rising water.

'Do you want to see the pictures?' Peak asked.

I didn't know what to do, couldn't figure out Peak's scheme. If I said no, what would that mean? And if I said yes, what would he gather from that?

'Mr. Moore?'

I raced to figure out the right answer, then simply tossed a mental coin.

'I guess I should,' I said.

He had them in his car, and as I made my way across the parking lot, I felt like a man following the hangman to the waiting gallows.

Peak got in behind the wheel. I took my place on the passenger side. He picked up the plain manila folder that rested on the seat between us. 'We printed these off Keith's computer. As I said, they're not illegal. But I'm sure you can understand that they're a problem for us, something we can't ignore.'

I took the envelope and drew out the pictures. The stack was about half an inch thick, twenty, maybe thirty photographs. One by one, I went through them, and just as Peak said, they weren't exactly pornographic. All of the girls were posed alone in natural settings, never indoors, little girls in bright sunlight, their tiny budding breasts barely detectible on their gleaming white chests. Naked, they sat on fallen trees or beside glittering streams. They were sometimes shot from the front, sometimes from the rear, sometimes their whole bodies in profile, standing erect, or sitting, knees to their chins, their arms enfolding their legs. They had long hair and perfectly proportioned bodies. They were beautiful in the flawless, innocent way of childhood beauty. None, I guessed, was more than four feet tall. None had pubic hair. All of them were smiling.

So what do you do at such a moment? As a father. What do you do after you've looked at such pictures, then returned them to the manila envelope, and lowered the envelope back down upon the car seat?

You do this. You look into the closely regarding eyes of another man, one who clearly thinks your son is, at best, a pervert, and at worse, a kidnapper, perhaps a rapist, a murderer. You look into those eyes and because you have no answer to the terrible accusation you see in them, you say simply, 'What about his room? Did you find anything?'

'You mean, magazines ... things like that?' Peak asked. 'No, we didn't.'

I hazarded another question. 'Anything connected to Amy?'

Peak shook his head.

'So where are we?'

'We're still investigating,' Peak said.

I looked at him evenly. 'What did you hope to get by showing me those pictures?'

'Mr. Moore,' Peak said evenly, 'in a case like this, it always goes better if we can stop the investigation.'

'Stop it with a confession, you mean,' I said.

'If Keith voluntarily gives us a statement, we can help him,' Peak said. He studied my face for a moment. 'The Giordanos want their daughter back. They want to know where she is, and they want to bring her home.' He drew the envelope up against the side of his leg. 'And, of course, they want to know what happened to her,' he added. 'If it were your child, you'd want that, too, I'm sure.'

He was into the depths of his kinder, gentler ruse, but I'd had enough. 'I assume we're done,' I said sharply, then reached for the handle of the door. Peak's voice stopped me dead.

'Has Keith ever mentioned a man named Delmot Price?' Peak asked.

I recognized the name. 'He owns the Village Florist Shop. Keith delivers there sometimes.'

'And that's all you know about them?'

'Them?' I asked.

'We traced the call,' Peak said. 'I'm sure your lawyer has told you about it. The one the pizza deliveryman saw Keith making at the Giordanos'. It was placed to Delmot Price.'

I started to speak, then stopped and waited.

'He knows Keith quite well,' Peak added significantly.

I saw the car draw into the driveway as it had that night, its twin beams sweeping through the undergrowth, then Keith as he made his way down the unpaved road, brushed past the Japanese maple, and came into the house.

'Were they together that night?' I asked.

'Together?'

'Keith and Delmot Price.'

'What makes you think they were together?' Peak asked.

I couldn't answer.

'Mr. Moore?'

I shook my head. 'Nothing,' I said. 'Nothing makes me think they were together.'

Peak saw the wound open up in me. I was a deer and he was an archer who knew he'd aimed well. I could almost feel the arrow dangling from my side.

'Did you know Keith had a relationship with this man?' Peak asked.

'Is that what he has?'

'According to Price, it's sort of a father–son thing.'

'Keith has a father,' I said sharply.

'Of course,' Peak said softly, 'but he talks to Price, you know, about himself, his problems. That he's not happy. Feels isolated.'

'You think I don't know that about him?'

Peak seemed to be peering into my brain, looking through its many chambers, searching for the clue to me.

'I'm sure of one thing,' he said. 'You want to help Keith. We all want to help Keith.'

It was all I could do to keep from laughing in Peak's face because I knew it was an act, scripted, a carefully laid trap to get me to incriminate my son; Peak had been moving at just the right pace, dropping little bits of information, then holding back, waiting. Which he was doing now, his eyes very still until he blinked slowly, released a small sigh, then said, 'Did you know that Keith steals?'

I drew in a quick breath but did not reply.

'Price caught him stealing money from the cash register in his shop,' Peak said. 'Keith begged him not to say anything, and that's how they started talking.'

I pretended to scoff at the outrageous nature of this latest charge. 'That's ridiculous,' I said. 'Keith has everything he needs. And in addition, I pay him for the work he does at the shop.'

'Not enough evidently.'

'He has everything he needs,' I insisted. 'Why would he steal?'

Again, Peak waited for just the right amount of time before releasing his next arrow. 'According to Price, he's trying to get enough money to run away.'

'Run away? To where?'

'Anywhere, I guess.'

Meaning, anywhere as long as it was away from me, from Meredith, from the burden of our family life.

'When was he going to do it?' I asked icily.

'As soon as he got enough money, I suppose.' Peak leaned back and raked the side of his face.

'Unless this whole thing about Keith stealing isn't true,' I said quickly. 'Have you thought of that? Maybe Price is lying. Maybe Keith never took anything.'

'Maybe,' Peak said. 'Why don't you ask him?'

He was setting me up, and I knew it. He was setting me up to do his work for him, interrogate my son.

'What have you asked him, Mr. Moore?' Peak said. 'Have you asked him directly if he hurt Amy Giordano?'

He saw the answer in my eyes.

'Have you asked him anything about that night?'

'Of course, I have.'

'What?'

'Well, for one thing, I asked him if he had any reason to think that Amy might have run away,' I said. 'Or if he'd seen anything suspicious around her house. A prowler, something like that.'

'And he said no, right?'

I nodded.

'And you believed him, of course,' Peak said. 'Any father would.' He leaned toward me slightly. 'But Keith's not exactly who you think he is,' he said gravely.

It was all I could do not to sneer. 'Yeah, well,' I said, 'who is?'

# NINETEEN

*Yeah, well, who is?*

I had never said anything so disturbing, and for the rest of the morning, as it echoed in my mind, I recalled similar sentiments I'd heard of late: Meredith's *Because people lie, Eric;* Warren's *Everybody's fake.* That I would remember such painful statements didn't strike me as particularly unusual. What was incontestably alarming was that this time I'd made such a statement myself. Why? I couldn't find an answer. All I knew was that each time I tried to think it through, examine the tortuous changes I could feel in myself, I returned to a single gnawing memory. Again and again, like a loop of film continually unfolding the same image, I saw Jenny that last time, mute, dying, her eyes full of a terrible urgency as she pressed her lips to my ear. Clearly she had been struggling against all odds to tell me something. In the years since her death I'd imagined it as some great truth she'd glimpsed on the precipice of death. But now, I wondered if that urgent communication might have been no more than some similarly dreary truth: *Don't trust anyone or anything – ever.*

I thought of Keith, the way I'd found him smoking sullenly near the playground, then of the things Peak had told me, that he had 'a father–son thing' with Delmot Price and that he was a thief and planned to run away. All of this had come as a complete surprise, facts, if they were facts, which I couldn't have guessed, and which, if true, pointed to the single unavoidable truth that I did not know my son.

Suddenly, out of nowhere, a boiling wave of anger washed over me, anger at myself. What kind of father was I, really, if Keith had found it necessary to find another man, confide in him, reveal his most secret plans?

I had always felt terribly superior to my own father, far more involved with my son than he had ever been with any of his children. Even during Jenny's last days he'd made overnight business trips to Boston and New York, assigning Warren to stay at her bedside, see her through the night, a job my brother had made no effort to avoid, save on that last night, as

I recalled now, when he'd emerged from Jenny's room looking old and haggard, a boy who, from his pale, stricken appearance on that gloomy morning, looked as if he'd seen the worst of things.

But now I wondered if, in fact, I was any better at fatherhood than my own father had been. When was the last time I'd actually talked with my son? Sure, we chatted over dinner, exchanged hasty asides as we passed each other in the hallway. But that was not real talk. Real talk bore the weight of hopes and dreams, tore away facades, and let each face shine in revealing light. Real talk was about life, the way we try to get through it, make the best of it, what we learn along the way. This kind of talk Keith had saved for Delmot Price, the man he'd gone to because he could not come to me, and who, if I were to begin to get a handle on my son before it was too late, I knew I would have to seek out, too.

Delmot Price wasn't hard to find, and the moment he saw me come through the door of his flower shop, he looked like a man who'd suddenly found himself in the crosshairs of a rifle scope.

He'd been wrapping a dozen long-stem red roses as I came into the shop. I stood off to the side and waited while he completed the task, took payment, and with a quick smile, thanked the woman whose roses they were.

During that time, I noted how gracefully he moved, his white hair gleaming in the overhead light, his long fingers folding the silver foil just so, tying the gold ribbon with a perfect knot. His fingers moved like dancers in a flowing and oddly beautiful choreography. There was no room for the slightest misstep, they had that kind of precision. And so it was obvious that in Keith, Price had not found a boy who was like himself, the way an English teacher might find a student with the same literary aspirations the teacher had once known as a youth. But instead, Delmot Price had found his opposite in Keith, a graceless, slovenly boy with tangled hair and a sullen smirk, a boy he'd befriended not out of admiration but because he pitied my son, felt sorry for how awkward and isolated and utterly directionless he was, how in need, as Price must have supposed, of a father.

He came toward me like a man wending his way out of a perfumed garden, weaving through swollen buds and broad-petaled flowers.

'Mr. Moore,' he said. He started to offer his hand, then stopped, unsure if I'd take it.

And so I offered mine.

'I don't mean to intrude,' I said.

He nodded, stepped to the door, turned the OPEN sign to CLOSED, and ushered me to the rear of the shop where we stood discreetly hidden behind a wall of ferns.

'The police talked to me,' he said. 'I suppose you know that.'

'Yes.'

'Just so you know, I don't believe Keith had anything to do with the disappearance of that little girl.'

'I don't, either,' I said, then realized that in part this was a lie, and so, I added, 'but he's done troubling things. He stole from you.'

Price nodded softly.

'Why does he want to run away?' I asked.

Price hesitated, like a doctor just asked how long a precious relative actually has to live. 'He's not happy, Mr. Moore.'

'Can you be more specific?'

I could see him working toward an answer, searching through a lifetime of words, images, experiences, looking for just the right one.

'Let me put it this way,' Price said at last. 'I have a greenhouse at my home, and most of the time, when I order a particular seed, it comes just the way it's supposed to. If I order a rose, I get a rose. But once in a while, I get something I didn't order, maybe don't even like. Geranium, something like that. I plant the seed, hoping for a rose, and up comes a geranium. At that point, I have to change the plan. I can't feed it and water it like I would if it were the rose I'd hoped for. I have to say, Okay, it's a geranium. It'll never be a rose. But at least I can raise it to be a healthy geranium. See what I mean? I have to adjust, because I didn't get what I ordered.'

'Keith thinks I want a different son?' I asked.

'No,' Price said. 'He knows you do.'

'Okay, but what good would running away do?' I asked.

'None, probably,' Price said. 'Which is what I told him. "No matter where you go," I said, "it goes with you."'

'What goes with him?'

'Your low opinion of him.'

He saw that he'd delivered a stomach-emptying blow.

'I had the same problem with my son,' he said quickly.

'Did he run away?' I asked.

Price's eyes glistened suddenly. 'No,' he said. 'He killed himself.'

A vision of Keith doing the same shot through my mind. I saw him in his room, opening the Swiss Army knife I'd given him for his thirteenth birthday, sliding its now-rusty blade across his pale wrists, watching as the crimson stream flowed down his arms and puddled between his bare feet, watching it dully, merely waiting for the final sleep to come upon him, his face expressionless, indifferent to the worthless life he was ending, doing all of this with an utterly flat affect.

'I'm sorry,' I whispered.

'I was like a lot of fathers, I had great plans for my son,' Price told me. 'The trouble is, they weren't *his* plans.'

'What are Keith's plans, did he tell you?'

Price shrugged. 'I'm not sure he has any. Except this idea of getting away.'

'He can't do that now,' I said. 'Not after Amy. He has to know that.'

'I'm sure you've made it clear.'

I realized that I'd done no such thing, and that the reason I'd not done it was no more complicated than the fact that I simply didn't like talking to Keith, seeing his dead, dull eye peering at me through the slit of his open door. The weight of the truth hit me like a hammer – the fact was, my son simply and undeniably repulsed me. I hated the way he slumped around, the tangle of his hair, the listlessness that overwhelmed him, the sheer dull thud of him. I hated all that, but had tirelessly labored to give no sign of it. Instead I had cheered his every modest achievement, praised and photographed his ridiculously infantile science project, patted him on the back so often and with such false force that my hand had grown numb with the practice. I had worked hard to conceal what I really thought, and I had failed utterly. For all his seeming obliviousness, Keith had seen through me, divined and suffered silently the full depth of my contempt.

Price touched my arm. 'It's not your fault, the way Keith feels,' he assured me. 'I can see how much you love him.'

'Yes, of course,' I said, then shook hands, said good-bye, turned, and walked through the scented air with my wife's words echoing in my head – *Everybody lies.*

Meredith was on the phone when I arrived at the house a few minutes later. I heard her voice as I opened the door, no doubt surprising her, since it was still early in the day and I wasn't expected back until the end of it.

'Gotta go' I heard her say, then the snap of her cell phone closing shut. She'd sunk it into the pocket of her housecoat by the time she greeted me.

'Oh, hi,' she said as she walked out of the kitchen. She smiled. 'I was just making another pot of coffee.'

On the counter behind her, I noted the coffee machine sitting idly, the first morning pot still half full.

'You're getting to be a purist, I guess,' I told her.

She looked at me quizzically.

'A coffee purist,' I explained. 'Never drink coffee that was brewed more than two hours before.'

She laughed, but tensely. 'Oh,' she said, 'is that the rule for coffee snobs?' She tossed her hair. 'Where do you hear things like that, Eric?'

'Television, I guess.'

For a moment, we faced each other silently. Then Meredith said, 'So, what are you doing home so early?'

'Peak was waiting for me when I got to work,' I told her.

Suddenly she paled. 'The hotline,' she blurted. 'Someone's spreading—'

I shook my head. 'No. This is not about the hotline. They found out a few things about Keith. Things we have to talk about.'

I turned, walked into the living room, and sat down on the sofa.

Meredith trailed behind and took the chair opposite me.

'Peak told me two things,' I began. 'That Keith has been talking to someone. Delmot Price. He owns the Village Flower Shop. Anyway, Price caught Keith stealing from him. They started talking about it. Keith told him that he was stealing because he needed money.'

'Needed money?' Meredith asked.

'To run away,' I added grimly. 'That's why he was stealing.'

She was silent for a long time, like someone hit between the eyes, dazed, groping to regain her balance.

'Peak talked to his teachers, too,' I added. 'They say he has a problem with low self-esteem.' The last piece of information was the hardest, but I had no choice but to deliver it. 'That's part of the profile, he says ... of a child molester.'

Her eyes began to dart around, as if the air was filled with tiny explosions. 'The car,' she said tensely. 'Do you think it was Price?'

'No,' I said. 'I talked to him right after Peak left. He's a good man, Meredith. He had a son like Keith.'

'What do you mean, like Keith?'

'A kid with this problem, you know, esteem,' I said. 'Only worse. He killed himself.'

Meredith's lips parted wordlessly.

'Price was just trying to help Keith,' I said. 'A shoulder to cry on, that's all.'

Meredith shook her head slowly.

'It gets worse, Meredith. They found some pictures on Keith's computer. Little girls. Naked.'

Meredith's right hand lifted to her closed lips.

'Not pornography exactly,' I added. 'But bad enough.'

She stood up. 'This is terrible,' she whispered.

'Keith can't run away,' I told her. 'We have to make sure of that. No matter what he was planning before, he can't do it now. The police would think he was running away from this thing with Amy. They would never believe that—' I stopped because for a moment the words were too painful to bear. Then, because there was no choice, I said them. 'That he was running away from us.'

She nodded heavily. 'So you have to talk to him, Eric.'

'We both do.'

'No,' Meredith said firmly. 'It would look like we were ganging up on him.'

'All right,' I said. 'But I'm going to tell him everything Peak told me. Everything Price told me. And I'm going to ask him who brought him home that night. I want an answer to that.'

Meredith released a weary breath.

'I won't take some bullshit story, either,' I said. 'This is getting worse and worse, and he has to know that.'

'Yes,' Meredith said. She seemed far away, and getting farther, like a boat unmoored and drifting out into the open sea. 'All right,' she said. Then she turned and made her way down the corridor to her small office, where I imagined she remained, waiting anxiously for her son to come home.

# TWENTY

It was nearly four in the afternoon when Keith appeared.

During the hours before I finally saw Keith pedal down the unpaved driveway, I tried to find the best way to approach him. I remember how clumsy my mother had always been at such interrogations. She would ask Warren about some misdeed. He would deny it. She would accept his denial, and that would be the end of it. My father, on the other hand, had relentlessly pursued him, puncturing each alibi, watching sternly, his eyes gleaming with superiority as my brother steadily sank deeper into the mire of his own inept little falsehoods. If Warren claimed to have been watching television when some small misdeed had been committed, my father would whip out the *TV Guide* and demand to know exactly what Warren had been watching. If Warren were clever enough actually to have named a program, my father would rifle through the pages until he found the show and then demand that Warren tell him precisely what, exactly, the show had been about. He'd always managed to be two or three steps ahead of Warren, waiting for him like a mugger in a dark alleyway, poised to strike.

But Warren had been easy to frighten and confuse. After only a few minutes under my father's inquisition he would invariably surrender, confess what slight crime he'd committed, then accept whatever punishment my father decreed. Warren had always been pliant, straining to please, contrite, eager to say or do whatever my father commanded.

I knew I could not expect the same of Keith. His mood was volatile, resentful, sullen. At the slightest provocation, he might bolt out of the room, storm into the night, make his run for it. More than anything, what I feared as I watched him slip off the seat of his bike and trudge up the walkway toward the house was that in the end it would turn physical, that in order to prevent him from running away, I would have to use force.

He didn't see me when he came through the door. He tossed his book bag on the stairs, whirled to the right, and strode into the kitchen. I heard him open the refrigerator. There was a clink of bottles, the sound of one being opened. I assumed he'd taken a bottled water or a soda, but when he slouched back into the foyer, I saw that he held a beer.

When he saw me sitting in the living room, he stared at me evenly, waiting for a challenge, then tilted back his head, took a long swig, and wiped his mouth with his sleeve.

'You're not of drinking age, Keith,' I reminded him.

'That right?' he asked with a smirk. 'Well, by the time I'm old enough to drink, I'll be in jail, so, like they say, what the fuck.' He grinned at me defiantly, took another swig, then pressed the bottle toward me. 'Care for a drink, Dad?'

I stood up, walked over to him, and yanked the bottle from his hand. 'We need to talk,' I said. 'In your room.'

'My room?' He laughed dismissively. 'No way, Dad.'

I placed the bottle on the table beside the door. 'Your room,' I said evenly. 'Now.'

He shook his head with exaggerated weariness, turned, and made his way up the stairs with a slow exhausted gait, like a boy who'd worked in the fields all day, rather than one who'd spent the last seven hours sitting in a classroom.

At the door of his room, he turned to me. 'You're not going to like it,' he said. 'It's not like all neat and orderly.'

'I don't care what it looks like,' I told him.

With that, Keith opened the door to his room and stepped inside.

I followed behind, stepping into a level of clutter and disarray that I'd fully expected. The only surprise was that between the window and the small desk that had once held his computer, he'd hung a thick black cloth, which was clearly meant to block the monitor from view. The walls of the room were covered with torn-out magazine pictures of people dressed in Goth attire, black jeans and black T-shirts, stringy hair dyed black, blackened eyes and lips and fingernails.

'Like the décor, Dad?' Keith asked with a brutal laugh. 'Glad you came to visit?'

I whirled around to face him. 'Delmot Price and I had a little talk this morning,' I said.

Keith slumped down on the unmade bed and idly picked up a magazine. 'So?'

'The police have talked to him, too,' I added. 'They know you called him the night Amy disappeared.'

Keith flipped a page of the magazine, licked his finger, and flipped another. 'I just wanted to talk,' he said.

'About your plan to run away?'

Keith gave no sign that the fact that I knew about his plan in the least bothered him. He continued to stare at the magazine.

'Look at me, Keith,' I said sharply.

He lifted his eyes languidly.

'Put the magazine away.'

He flipped the cover, tossed it across the room, and made a great show of staring me directly in the eye.

'First off, don't even think about leaving town,' I said. 'That's all the cops would need right now.'

Keith kicked off his shoes, pressed his back against the wall, and folded his arms over his chest.

I pulled the chair away from his desk, planted it in the center of the room, and sat down so that we were now eye to eye.

'I need some answers, Keith,' I said.

Keith said nothing but continued to stare at me sullenly.

'They found pictures on your computer,' I said.

I looked for some sign that the shock of having the pictures discovered had shaken him but saw nothing but his cold metallic stare.

'Why did you have those pictures, Keith?'

His silence was like a cocked gun.

'Little girls,' I said. 'Naked.'

He closed his eyes.

'Why did you have pictures of little girls on your computer?'

He shook his head.

'They found them, Keith,' I said firmly. 'They found them on your computer.'

He continued to shake his head, eyes still closed.

'You know what that looks like, don't you? How bad it looks. With Amy missing.'

He began to breathe with exaggerated force, rhythmically, like a pant.

'Keith, are you listening to me? They *found pictures*!'

He was breathing in short gasps, loud and furiously, like a diver gearing up for a frightening plunge.

'They showed them to me, Keith,' I said. 'Little girls. Seven, eight years old.'

Suddenly the gasping breaths ceased, and his eyes shot open. 'What else?' he hissed. 'What else, Dad? I know there's more.'

'Yes, there is,' I said hotly, as if he'd challenged me to make a stronger case against him. 'I want to know who brought you home the night Amy disappeared.'

He stared at me silently for a moment, and I expected him to yell back some ridiculous reply, but instead something appeared to unravel deep within him, as if he were suddenly in the motions of a final letting go. 'Nobody brought me home.'

I leaned forward threateningly. 'I saw a car pull into the driveway, Keith. Up on the road. It pulled in. I saw the lights. Then it backed up and drove away. That's when I saw you coming down the drive.' I lifted my head and looked him dead in the eye. 'Who brought you home in that car, Keith?'

'Nobody,' Keith answered softly.

'Keith, I have to know the truth,' I said. 'I have to know about those pictures. And I have to know about that car.'

'I didn't have any pictures,' he said with surprising firmness. 'And nobody brought me home that night.'

I felt nearly drunk with exasperation, dazed and staggering. 'Keith, you have to tell me the truth.'

Without the slightest warning, a wrenching sob broke from him. It seemed to come from an unexpected depth, a sob that all but gutted him. 'Fuck me,' he cried. He dropped his head forward then brought it back against the wall so hard that the force rattled the shelf that hung above him. 'Fuck me!'

'Jesus, Keith, can't you see I'm trying to help you?'

'Fuck me,' Keith cried. He jerked forward, then, like a body caught in a seizure, he slammed his head back against the wall.

I shot out of my chair and jerked the black cloth from the wire. *'No more fucking lies!'* I screamed.

Keith thrust forward, then slammed back again, his head pounding violently against the wall. He seemed caught in an uncontrollable spasm, his body moving like a puppet in the hands of a murderous puppeteer.

I grabbed his shoulders and drew him tightly into my arms. 'Stop it, Keith,' I pleaded. 'Stop it!'

He began to cry again, and I held him while he cried, held him until he finally stopped crying and slumped down on the bed, where he wiped his eyes with the palms of his hands, then looked up and started to speak. That for a moment I thought he'd decided to come clean, admit what there was to admit about the pictures, the car that had brought him home that night. Even at its worst, I thought, it would be a relief to have it out, done with, known. It was the suspense that was killing us, slowly, hour by hour, like a long drawn-out strangulation.

'Keith, please tell me,' I said softly.

His lips sealed immediately, and his eyes were dry now. 'I didn't do anything,' he said softly. He closed his eyes slowly, then opened them again. 'I didn't do anything,' he repeated. He slithered out of my arms and sat bolt upright on the bed, no longer broken. I felt him harden before my eyes. 'May I please be alone now?' he asked stiffly. 'I'd really like to be alone.'

I knew there was no point in challenging him further. The moment had come and gone. This had been my chance, and his, but nothing had come of it, and it was over.

I walked out of the room and down the stairs to where Meredith now sat in the living room.

'Nothing,' I said. 'He denied everything.'

Her eyes took on a kind of animal panic. 'He has to tell you the truth, Eric.'

'The truth, yes,' I said.

I glanced at the outline of her cell phone in the shallow pocket of her robe and considered all that now demanded to be truly known, things my father had told me, things Warren had told me, things Keith had told me, all of them now in doubt. In my mind I saw them posed together, Meredith and Keith, along with my other family, the living and the dead, Warren and my father, my mother, Jenny. They stood on the steps of the lost house, shoulder to shoulder, as in a family photograph.

None of them was smiling.

# PART IV

A figure appears beyond the diner's rain-streaked window, and for a moment you think it is the one you're waiting for. You recall it in photographs, but so much time has passed that you can no longer be sure that you would recognize the eyes, the mouth, the hair. Features sharpen then blur as they mature, and time has a downward pull, creating folds where none existed when the photographs were taken. And so you scan the onrushing faces, preparing your own, hoping that time has not ravaged your features so mercilessly that you will go unrecognized as well.

You notice a little girl, her hand tucked inside her mother's, and it strikes you that everyone was young back then. You were young. So were Meredith and Warren. Keith was young and Amy was young. Vincent and Karen Giordano were young. Peak was no more than fifty; Kraus no more than forty-five. Even Leo Brock seems young to you now, or at least not as old as he seemed then.

The figure who first called your attention vanishes, but you continue to stare out the window. An autumn wind is lashing the trees across the way, showering the wet ground with falling leaves. You think of the Japanese maple at the end of the walkway and recall the last time you saw it. It was fall then, too. You remember your last glance at the house, how your gaze settled on the grill. How desolate it looked beside the empty house, its elaborate and sturdy brickwork awash in sodden leaves. You wonder if you should have taken a picture of the cold grill, the unlit house, something to replace the stacks of family photographs you burned in the fireplace on your last day there. In a movie, a character like you would have fed them one by one into the flames, but you tossed whole stacks of them in at once. You even tried not to look at the faces in the photographs as the fire engulfed them, turning every life to ash.

# TWENTY-ONE

Over a week passed after my confrontation with Keith. Day after day, as I worked at the shop, I waited for the call from Leo, the one that would tell me that Keith was going to be arrested, that I should go home, wait for Peak and Kraus to arrive, warrants in hand, and read my son his rights, then, one man at each arm, lead him away.

But when it came, the phone call from Leo brought just the opposite news.

'It's looking good, Eric,' he said happily. 'They're running tests on those cigarettes they found outside Amy's window, but even if it turns out they can prove Keith smoked them, so what? There's no law against a kid going out for a smoke.'

'But he lied, Leo,' I said. 'He said he didn't leave the house.'

'Well, contrary to popular belief,' Leo said, 'lying to the police is not technically a crime. And as for those pictures on his computer? Same answer. They were completely harmless.'

Pictures of nude little girls didn't strike me as harmless, but I let it go.

'So, what happens then, if they can't arrest him?' I asked.

'Nothing happens,' Leo answered lightly.

'It can't just go away, Leo,' I said. 'A little girl is missing and—'

'And Keith had nothing to do with it,' Leo interrupted. He spoke his next words at a measured pace. 'Nothing to do with it, right?'

I didn't answer fast enough, so Leo said, 'Right, Eric?'

'Right,' I muttered.

'So like I said, it's good news all around,' Leo repeated cautiously. 'You should take it as good news.'

'I know.'

'So, is there a reason you're not?'

'It's just that this whole experience, it's dredged up a lot of things,' I told him. 'Not just about Keith. Other things.'

'Things between you and Meredith?'

It seemed an odd question. I'd never discussed the state of my marriage with Leo, yet something 'between you and Meredith' was the first thing that had entered his mind. 'Why would you think it's something between me and Meredith?' I asked.

'No reason,' Leo said. 'Except that a case like this, it can create a certain strain.' He quickly moved on to another subject. 'Everything else okay?'

'Sure.'

'No harm to your business, right?'

'Just the usual off-season lull.'

There was a pause and I sensed that something bad was coming.

'One thing, Eric,' Leo said. 'Evidently Vince Giordano's pretty upset.'

'Of course, he is,' I said. 'His daughter is missing.'

'Not just that,' Leo said. 'Upset with the way the case is going.'

'You mean, about Keith?'

'That's right,' Leo said. 'My people tell me he went ballistic at headquarters yesterday. Demanded that Keith be arrested, that sort of thing.'

'He thinks Keith did it,' I said. 'There's nothing I can do about that.'

'You can stay clear of him,' Leo said in that paternal way of his. 'And make sure Keith does, too.'

'All right,' I said.

'Warren, too.'

'Warren?' I asked, surprised. 'Why would he have anything against Warren?'

'Because Keith doesn't have a car,' Leo told me. 'So Vince figures it had to be the two of them.'

'Why would he think that?'

'We're not dealing with reason here, Eric,' Leo reminded me. 'We're talking about a distraught father. So just tell everyone in your family to stay clear of Vince. And if any of you happen to run into him, like at the post office, something like that, just keep to yourself, and get out of sight as soon as possible.'

There was a brief pause, then Leo spoke again, his voice now unexpectedly gentle. 'Are you all right, Eric?'

A wave of deep melancholy washed over me; my life, my once-comfortable life, was fraught with danger and confusion, along with a terrible mixture of anger and pain. 'How could I be all right, Leo?' I asked. 'Everyone in town thinks Keith killed Amy Giordano. Some anonymous caller tells the cops that there's "something wrong" with me or Meredith or Keith. And now I hear Vince has gone nuts and that none of us can go anywhere without fear of running into him. It's a prison, Leo. That's where we all are right now. We're in prison.'

Again there was a pause, after which, Leo said, 'Eric, I want you to listen very carefully to me. In all likelihood, Keith is not going to be arrested. That's good news, and you should be happy about it. And if some nut calls the hotline? Big deal. And as far as Vince Giordano is concerned, all you have to do is stay away from him.'

'Okay,' I muttered. What was the point of saying more?

'Do you understand what I'm telling you?'

'Yeah,' I said. 'Thanks for calling Leo.'

Leo was clearly reluctant to hang up. 'Good news, remember?' he said, addressing a schoolboy in need of a change of attitude.

'Good news, yes,' I said, though only because I knew it was what he wanted to hear. 'Good news,' I repeated, then smiled as if for a hidden camera in my shop, planted by Leo, so that even at that moment he could see my face, appreciate the smile.

My working day came to an end a few hours later, but I didn't want to go home. Meredith had told me that she'd be working late at the college, and I knew that Keith would be secreted in his room. And so I called Warren, hoping he could join me for a beer, but there was no answer.

That left only my father, and so I went to him.

He was sitting inside, by the fire, curled in a wheelchair, his emaciated frame wrapped in a dark red blanket. In his youth, he'd gone all winter without once putting on an overcoat, but now even a slight late-September touch of fall chilled him.

'It's not Thursday,' he said as I came up the stairs.

I sat down in the wicker chair beside him. 'I just felt like dropping in,' I told him.

He stared into the flames. 'Warren talk to you?'

'Yeah.'

'That why you're here?'

I shook my head.

'I figured he'd go whining to you, try to get me to change my mind, let him come over again.'

'No, he didn't do that,' I said. 'He told me you had an argument, that you said you didn't want to see him again, but he wasn't whining about it.'

My father's eyes narrowed hatefully. 'Should have done it long ago,' he said coldly. 'Worthless.'

'Worthless,' I repeated. 'That's what you said about Mom.'

He peered about absently, like a man in a museum full of artifacts he had no interest in.

'Speaking of which,' I said. 'You lied to me, Dad.'

149

He closed his eyes wearily, clearly preparing himself for yet another series of false accusations.

'You said you didn't take out an insurance policy on Mom,' I continued. 'I found it in your papers. It was for two hundred thousand dollars.' When this had no visible effect on my father, I added, 'Why did you lie to me about this, Dad?'

His gaze slid over to me. 'I didn't.'

A wave of anger swept over me, fueled by exasperation. My father was doing the same thing Keith had done a week before.

'Dad, I found an application for a life insurance policy,' I snapped.

'An application is not a policy, Eric,' my father scoffed. 'You should know that.'

'Are you denying there was ever such a policy?' I demanded. 'Is that what you're doing?'

A dry laugh broke from him. 'Eric, you asked me if I took out a policy on your mother. I said I didn't. Which is the truth.'

'Once again, Dad, are you saying there was no life insurance policy on Mom's life?'

'As a matter of fact, Eric, I'm not saying that at all.'

'So there was one?'

'Yes.'

'For two hundred thousand dollars?'

'That was the amount,' my father said. 'But does that mean I took the policy out?'

'Who else would?'

'Your mother, Eric,' my father said flatly. 'Your mother took it out.'

'On herself?'

'Yes.' His eyes glistened slightly, though I couldn't be sure if the glistening came from some well of lost emotion, or if it were only an illusion, merely a play of light. 'She took it out without telling me,' he added. 'She had a ... friend. He helped her do it.'

'A friend?'

'Yes,' my father answered. 'You met him. A family friend.' His smile was more a sneer. 'Good friend of your mother. Always coming around the house. Glad to be of help, that was Jason.'

'Jason,' I said. 'Benefield?'

'So, you've heard about him?'

'Warren mentioned him,' I explained.

'Of course,' my father said with an odd, downward jerk at the corners of his mouth. 'Anyway, he's still alive. You can ask him. He'll tell you I had nothing to do with that policy. And for your added information, I wasn't the beneficiary of it, either.'

I couldn't tell if this was a bluff, but I suspected that it was, and moved to expose it. 'Where did the money go?' I asked.

'What money?'

'The money that was due after Mom died.'

'There was never any money, Eric,' my father said. 'Not a penny.'

'Why not?'

He hesitated, and in that interval, I imagined all the worthless get-rich-quick schemes into which he had probably poured the money, a bottomless pit of failed businesses and bad investments.

'The company denied the claim,' he said finally.

He squirmed uncomfortably, and I knew he was trying to get off the hook. So I bore in.

'Why did the company deny the claim?' I asked.

'Ask them yourself,' my father shot back.

'I'm asking you,' I said hotly.

My father turned away from me.

'Tell me, goddamn it!'

His eyes shot over to me. 'Insurance companies don't pay,' he said, 'when it's a suicide.'

'Suicide?' I whispered unbelievingly. 'You're telling me that Mom intended to run off that bridge? That's ridiculous.'

My father's glare was pure challenge. 'Then why wasn't she wearing a seat belt, Eric? She always insisted on wearing one, remember? She made all of you wear them. So why, on that particular day, when she went off that bridge, did she not have hers on?'

He read the look in my eyes.

'You don't believe me, do you?' he asked.

'No, I don't.'

'Then look at the police report. It was all right there – the whole story: how fast she was going. The way the car went straight into the guardrail – everything. Including the fact that she wasn't wearing a seat belt.' He shook his head. 'There were witnesses, too. People who saw what she did.' A contemptuous laugh broke from him. 'Couldn't even pull off a simple suicide scheme without fucking it up.'

'Don't lie to me, Dad,' I warned. 'Not about this.'

'Go look at the fucking report, if you don't believe me,' my father snarled. 'There's a copy in my files. You've been digging around in them anyway, right? Dig some more.'

I couldn't let him go unchallenged. 'Speaking of your files,' I said. 'I found a letter from Aunt Emma. She blames Mom for spending you into bankruptcy.'

My father waved his hand. 'Who cares what my nutty sister writes?'

'It's what you wrote that bothered me.'

'Which was?'

'A line you scrawled in the margin of Aunt Emma's letter.'

'I repeat, "Which was?"'

'"Now let her get me out of it."'

My father laughed. 'Jesus, Eric.'

'What did you mean by that?'

'That Emma should get me out of it,' my father said. 'She's the "her" in that note.'

'How could Aunt Emma get you out of it?'

'Because her goddamn husband left her a fortune,' my father said. 'But true to form, she never spent a dime of it. And she wouldn't have given me a penny, either. When she died, she still had every dollar that old bastard left her. Close to a million dollars. You know where it went? To a fucking animal shelter!'

He laughed again, but bitterly, as if all he had ever known of life amounted to little more than a cruel joke.

I waited until his laughter faded, then, because I couldn't stop myself, I asked the final question. 'Did Mom have an affair? Warren said she did. With that man you mentioned, Benefield. He said Aunt Emma told you about it.'

For a moment, my father seemed unable to deal with this latest assault. 'What is this all about, Eric? All this business about insurance policies, affairs. What have you been thinking?' He saw the answer in my eyes. 'You thought I killed her, didn't you? Either for money or because I thought she was fucking around. One or the other, right?' He released a scoffing chuckle. 'Does it matter which one it is, Eric?' He didn't wait for me to answer. 'This is all about Keith, isn't it?' he asked. 'You can't bear to think that he may be a liar and a murderer, so you've decided to think it about me.' He remained silent for a few seconds. I could see his mind working behind his darting eyes, reasoning something through, coming to a grave conclusion. Then he looked at me. 'Well, if you're so fucking eager to find the truth about this, Eric, here's a truth you might wish you hadn't heard.' His grin was pure triumph. 'I wasn't the beneficiary of your mother's insurance policy. You were.'

I stared at him, thunderstruck. 'Me? Why would she ... ?'

'She knew how much you wanted to go to college,' my father interrupted. He shrugged with a curious sense of acceptance. 'It was the only way she could make sure you had the money you needed.'

I didn't believe him, and yet at the same time what he said made sense. In the grips of that dire uncertainty, I realized that there was absolutely nothing I could be sure of. I saw the car's yellow beams sweep through the undergrowth and thought of Keith's lie. And here was my father telling me that my mother had driven the family station wagon off a thirty-foot bridge, a story that could just as easily be used to shift my own suspicions concerning my mother's death safely away from him.

I got to my feet. 'I'm leaving,' I told him.

This time, my father made no effort to stop me. 'Suit yourself,' he said.

'I'm not sure I'll be coming back, Dad,' I added sourly.

He stared at the fire. 'Have I ever asked you to come here?' His eyes slithered over to me. 'Have I ever asked you for one fucking thing, Eric?' Before I could answer he whipped his eyes away and settled them angrily on the lashing flames. 'Just go.'

I hesitated a moment longer, let my gaze take him in, the bony shoulders beneath the robe, the shrunken eyes, how at this moment he had absolutely nothing, a penury deeper than I'd have imagined possible only a few days before. But I could not approach him now, felt not the slightest inclination to regain any footing for us. And with that recognition, I knew that this was the last time I would see my father alive.

I took in the scene with a quick blink of the eye, then wheeled around and returned to my car. Slumped behind the wheel, I hesitated, glancing back toward the bleak little residence where I knew my father was doomed to slog through what remained of his days. He would grow brittle and still more bitter, I supposed, speaking sharply to anyone who approached him. In time, both staff and fellow residents would learn to keep their distance, so that in the final hour, when they came and found him slumped in his chair or faceup in bed, a little wave of secret pleasure would sweep through the halls and common rooms at the news of his death. Such would be his parting gift to his fellow man – the brief relief of knowing that he was gone.

# TWENTY-TWO

As I drove toward home, mother's long ordeal returned to me in a series of small grainy photographs that seemed to rise from some previously forgotten album in my mind. I saw her standing beneath the large oak that graced our neatly manicured front lawn. I saw her walking in the rain. I saw her lying awake in a dark bedroom, her face illuminated by a single white candle. I saw her in the dimly lit garage, sitting alone behind the wheel of the dark blue Chrysler, her hands in her lap, head slightly bowed.

In fact, I had only glimpsed these images of my mother's final weeks, glimpsed them as I'd hurried past her on my way to school or returned from it, far more interested in the day's boyish transactions than in the adult world that was eating her alive.

But now, as evening fell, I tried to measure the weight that lay upon her: an unloving and unsuccessful husband, a beloved daughter dead, a son – Warren – saddled with his father's contempt, and me, the other son, who barely saw her when he passed. So little to leave behind, she must have thought, as she sat behind the wheel in the shadowy garage, so little she would miss.

For the first time in years, I felt burdened beyond my strength, desperate to share the load with another human being. It was at that moment, I suppose, that the full value of marriage proclaimed itself. I had laughed at a thousand jokes about married life. And what a huge target it was, after all. The idea that you would share your entire life with one person, expect that man or woman to satisfy a vast array of needs, from the most passionate to the most mundane – on its face, it was absurd. How could it ever work?

Suddenly, I knew. It worked because in a shifting world you wanted one person you could trust to be there when you needed her.

It was a short ride down Route 6, no more than twenty minutes. The college sat on a rise, all brick and glass, one of those purely functional structures architects despise, but whose charmlessness is hardly noticed by the legions of students who obliviously come and go. It was a junior college, after all, a holding cell between high school and university, unremarkable and doomed to be unremembered, save as a launching pad toward some less-humble institution.

I pulled into the lot designated VISITORS, and made my way up the cement walkway toward Meredith's office. In the distance, I could see her car parked in the lot reserved for faculty, and something in its sturdy familiarity was oddly comforting.

Meredith's office was on the second floor. I knocked, but there was no answer. I glanced at the office hours she'd posted on the door, 4:30 to 6:30. I glanced at my watch. It was 5:45, so I assumed Meredith would be back soon, that she'd gone to the bathroom or was lingering in the faculty lounge.

A few folding metal chairs dotted the corridor, places where students could seat themselves while waiting for their scheduled appointments. I sat down, plucked a newspaper from the chair next to me, and idly went through it. There was little about Amy's disappearance, save that the police were still 'following various leads'.

I perused the paper a few more minutes, then glanced at my watch. It was 6:05. I looked down the empty corridor, hoping to see Meredith at the end of it. I even imagined her coming through the double doors, munching an apple, the early-evening snack she often took in order to quell her appetite before coming home.

But the corridor remained empty, and so I went through the paper again, this time reading articles that didn't interest me very much, the sports and financial pages, something about a new treatment for baldness.

When I'd read the last of them, I put down the paper and again looked at my watch. 6:15.

I stood up, walked to her office, and knocked again on the unlikely chance that she hadn't heard me the first time. There was no answer, but I could see a sliver of light coming from inside. She'd left the lights on, something she wouldn't have done if she hadn't been planning to come back.

On that evidence, I returned to my chair and waited. As the minutes passed, I thought again of my father, the terrible things he'd told me, which I suddenly believed were true. I don't know why I came to that conclusion as I sat waiting for Meredith that evening, only that with each passing second, the certainty built, and one by one, every dark suspicion took on a fatal substance. I believed that my mother had had an affair. I believed that she'd taken out an insurance policy on herself. I believed that she'd committed suicide. But at the same time, I also believed that my father had wanted her dead, might even have toyed with the idea of killing her, perhaps even killing us all.

I felt the air darken around me, thicken like smoke, felt my breathing take on a strange, frantic pace, as if I were being forced to run faster and faster along an unlit path, to leap obstacles I could barely see and twist around gaping pits and snares. A kind of rumbling shook me from within, distant as a building storm, and I found myself staring at the sliver of light beneath Meredith's door wondering if perhaps she were actually inside, knew I was in the corridor, but remained behind the locked door ... hiding.

But from what?

I stood suddenly, jerked up by my own volcanic anxiety, marched to the door, and knocked again, this time harder, more insistently. Then, out of nowhere, her name broke from my lips in a strange, animal cry – 'Meredith!'

I realized that I'd called her name much more loudly than I'd intended. I could hear it echoing down the hall. It sounded desperate, even theatrical, like Stanley Kowalski screaming for Stella.

I took a deep breath and tried to calm myself, but my skin felt hot, and beneath it, hotter still, as if deep inside, a furnace was being madly stoked.

It was past 6:30 now, and as I looked at the otherwise inconsequential time of day, it took on a fatal quality, like the hour of execution, the prisoner now being led out. It was as if I had given my wife until that moment to explain herself, which she had failed to do, and so was now condemned.

I strode down the corridor, taking the stairs two at a time, and plunged through the doors out into the crisp, cold air. For a moment, the chill cooled my burning skin, but only briefly, because in the distance, at the end of the lot, in the space between her car and a sleek BMW, I saw Meredith standing with a tall slender man.

Rodenberry.

I darted behind a nearby tree and watched them with the skulking silence of a Peeping Tom. They stood very close to each other, talking intimately. From time to time Rodenberry nodded, and from time to time, Meredith reached out and touched his arm.

I waited for them to draw together into each other's arms, waited like a man in a darkened theater, waited for the kiss that would seal both their fates.

It didn't matter that it never came. It didn't matter that after a final word, Meredith simply turned and walked to her car, and that Rodenberry, with the same casualness, got into the gleaming BMW. It only mattered that as each of them drove away, I heard the click of the police hotline, then the whisper that came through the line, and knew absolutely who had spoken and what had been said.

When, in the throes of crisis, you have nowhere to go but to a lawyer, you should realize just how depleted you have become. But I was far from realizing anything that night, and so I went to Leo Brock.

His office was modest, simply a small brick building tucked between a gourmet deli and a hardware store. His far more impressive Mercedes was parked in a space reserved for it behind the office.

His secretary had already gone home for the evening, but the door to his office was open, and I found Leo in the leather chair behind his desk, feet up, idly thumbing a magazine.

'Eric,' he said with a big smile. 'How's it going?'

He must have known that it could not have been going very well if I were here, standing before his desk, looking shaken, like a man who'd stared into the pit and seen the dreadful face of things.

'You had another run in with Vincent?' he asked immediately.

'No.'

He drew his feet from the top of the desk, and in that gesture I read just how dire I appeared to him. 'What is it, Eric?' he asked.

'That thing on the hotline,' I said. 'What was it?'

He unnecessarily slid the magazine to the corner of his desk. 'It was nothing,' he said.

'What do you mean nothing?'

'Eric, why don't you sit down.'

'What do you mean, nothing, Leo?'

'I mean it had nothing to do with the case.'

'Keith's case.'

'The Amy Giordano case,' Leo corrected.

'But you know what it was?'

'I have an idea.'

'What was it?'

'As I said, Eric, it had nothing to do with the case.'

'And as I said, Leo, what the fuck was it?'

He looked at me as if sparks were flying off my body, gathering in glowing clusters on his oriental carpet.

'Eric, please, have a seat.'

I recalled how he and Meredith had stood together in the driveway of the house, speaking in what now seemed secretive tones, how Leo had nodded to her reassuringly, how my wife's hands had then dropped limply to her sides as if she'd just shuffled off a heavy weight.

'I knew from the beginning,' I said.

'Knew what?'

'Knew that Meredith told you.'

Leo looked at me with what was clearly a fake expression of bafflement.

'That first day,' I said, 'when you came over to talk with Keith. Meredith walked you to your car. That's when she told you.'

'Told me what?'

'Told you that there were things in the family,' I said. 'Things that were ... wrong. I even know why she did it. She was afraid that in the end it would come out anyway. What she didn't know is that other people knew. At least one person.'

Leo leaned back in his chair and opened his arms. 'Eric, I don't have a clue what you're talking about.'

'At the car, the two of you,' I explained.

'Yes, she walked me out to my car, so what?'

'That's when she told you.'

Leo looked both worried and exasperated, like a man before a cobra, wary, but also growing tired of its dance. 'You're going to have to be a tad more specific as to exactly what it is you think she said to me on that occasion.'

I recalled Meredith's voice as I'd come home that afternoon, taking her by surprise, the quick way she'd blurted, 'Gotta go,' then sunk the phone into her pocket. A series of memories followed that initial recollection: Meredith working late at the college; the wistful tone in which she'd said, 'It will be the last time'; how it hadn't been Dr. Mays who'd told her the Lenny Bruce story; the fact that Mays had described Stuart Rodenberry as 'very funny'. Last, I saw Meredith once again in the parking lot with Rodenberry, pressed closely together, as I saw it, but duly cautious not to touch.

'That she was having an affair,' I said quietly, like a man finally accepting a terrible, terrible truth. 'That's what the police heard on the hotline. That Meredith is having an affair.'

Leo stared at me mutely, a pose I had no doubt was part of a deception. He was almost as much in league with Meredith as Rodenberry, all three of them arrayed against me, determined to keep me in the dark,

'Here's another guess,' I said sharply. 'The person who called the hotline was a woman, wasn't it?'

Leo leaned forward and peered at me closely. 'Eric, you need to calm down.'

I rebuked him with a harsh cackle. 'The wife of the man Meredith is supposed to be having an affair with, that's who called.'

Leo now looked as if deep in thought, unable to decide between two equally difficult choices.

'A pale little wisp of a thing named Judith Rodenberry,' I added.

Leo shook his head. 'I don't know what you're talking about, Eric,' he said.

He was lying, and I knew it. Again, I recalled that first day, when Meredith had walked him to his black Mercedes, the two of them standing there in the driveway, half concealed by the spreading limbs of the Japanese maple, but not concealed so much that I hadn't seen the way Meredith's hands fluttered about like panicked birds until a few no-doubt well-chosen words from Leo stopped them in their frenzied flight. What had he said?, I wondered now, then instantly put the words into his mouth: *Don't worry, Meredith, no one will find out.*

'Did you hear me, Eric?' Leo said firmly. 'I have no idea what you're talking about. The hotline matter, it had nothing to do with Meredith.'

'What then?' I challenged. 'What did this person say? What was this "something wrong"?' I felt like a vial filled to the brim with combustible materials, everything poised at the volcanic edge. *'Tell me the fucking truth!'*

Leo slumped back in his chair and seemed almost to grow older before my eyes, more grave in his demeanor than I had ever seen him. 'Warren,' he said. The "something wrong" is Warren.'

# TWENTY-THREE

In all the years I'd gone there, the scores and scores of times, I'd never noticed anything. But now as I turned onto Warren's street, I noticed everything. I noticed how close his house was to the elementary school, how his upstairs window looked out over the school's playground, how, from that small, square window, he could easily watch the girls on the swings, see their skirts lift and fold back as they glided forward. He could stand behind the translucent white curtains and observe them clamoring over the monkey bars and riding up and down on the seesaw. Or, if he wished, he could stare down at the entire playground, take in small gatherings of little girls at a single glimpse, keep track of them as they played, pick and choose among them, find the one that most interested him and follow her like a hunter tracking a deer caught in the crosshairs of his scope.

As I closed in upon his house, I thought of other things, too. I recalled that Warren preferred to work on weekends and take Wednesdays and Thursdays off, both school days, days when the little girls of the elementary school would be frolicking on the playground. I remembered how he never minded working holidays, when school was out, and how each year, he seemed to dread the approach of summer, when school would no longer be in session. He had reasons for all these preferences, of course. He didn't mind working weekends, he said, because he didn't have anything to do anyway. He didn't mind working holidays because holidays depressed him, which, in turn made it harder for him to resist the bottle. He dreaded summer because it was hot and muggy, and he didn't like to work in heat and humidity.

In the past, his reasons had always made perfect sense to me. Now they seemed fabrications, ways of concealing the fact that what my brother wanted to do more than anything was to stand at his window and peer down at the elementary school playground and watch little girls at play.

These thoughts led me to a yet darker one, hurling my mind back to the month when Warren had been holed up at my house with a broken hip. Holed up in Keith's room. With Keith's computer. I could almost hear the tap of his fingers on the keys as I had so many times when I'd walked by the closed door of Keith's room when Warren was staying there. At the time, I'd assumed that Warren was playing some mindless computer game.

Then I thought of the pictures Detective Peak had shown me, pictures taken from Keith's computer, and remembered the anguish of Keith's denial, the way he'd banged his head against the wall, how fiercely he had fought off the horror of my accusations. Now I knew that it had been Warren all along, Warren who'd sat hour after hour cruising the Internet for pictures of little girls. The only question now was what he saw in them. What in the twisted circuitry of my brother's mind allowed him to drag these little girls from the safety of their childhoods and harness their small undeveloped bodies to his adult desire?

I tried to recall if I'd ever seen the slightest sign of such a dark perversity. I went back through the days and years of our youth, the times we'd been together in the presence of small children, and searched for some glimmer in Warren's eye, a look I might not have understood at that earlier time, but which I would easily recognize now. Had his gaze ever followed a child across a yard or down a street? Had he ever stopped in midsentence at a little girl's approach? Had he ever so much as mentioned a neighborhood kid, someone's little sister, perhaps, or a visiting cousin?

I could find no instance of any such early indication, not one occasion when Warren had seemed anything but an awkward boy, lacking in self-confidence, slow in his studies, incompetent on the playing field, the butt of countless school-yard jokes. He'd been all these things, and in one way or another I'd always felt sorry for him. But now I felt nothing but revulsion, a creepy sense that this boy had grown into an utterly repulsive man.

I pulled into Warren's driveway behind the battered truck he used in his work. Its open bed was scattered with paint cans and spattered drop cloths, and two equally spattered wooden ladders were strapped to its sideboards, loosely tied and drooping, as I would have expected from Warren. All his life he'd done things haphazardly, with little attention to detail, following a course as wobbly as his footsteps when he'd had too much to drink. Even so, I'd always had a brother's affection for him, overlooked his lassitude, his drinking, those parts of his life that were basically pathetic. But now a vile shadow covered him, my suspicions so intense, and in their intensity, so brutal, that I couldn't ignore them.

And yet, for all that, I sat behind the wheel for a long time, sat in Warren's weedy driveway, unable to move, staring at the small bleak house he'd lived in for fifteen years. His door was closed, of course, but a sickly yellow light shone from the upstairs room he called his bachelor lair. He'd furnished the room with a motley assortment of furniture, along with a television, a computer, and a refrigerator just large enough to hold a few six packs of beer. He'd lit the place with lava lamps at one point, then a series of garish paper lanterns, but these had ultimately given way to the single uncovered ceiling light and the flickering of his computer screen.

The image of Warren's dissolute body slumped in an overstuffed chair, his doughy face eerily lit by the computer screen sent a piercing melancholy through me. I saw the weary run of my brother's life, the corrosive nature of his most guarded secret, the unspeakable cravings that ceaselessly gnawed at him. One by one the photographs Detective Peak had found on Keith's computer surfaced in my mind, little girls in nature, naked, innocent, incapable of arousing anything but a child-man. But that was what Warren was, wasn't he? Stunted in every way a man can be stunted, dismal in his own sickly underdevelopment, a wretched, pitiable creature, hardly a man at all.

But none of that, I decided, changed what he had done. He had come into my house, lived in my son's room, and while living there, had poisoned Keith's computer with pictures of naked little girls. And when Keith's computer was seized by the police, he'd kept the fact secret that such incriminating material might still be floating about in its unknowable circuitry. He had sat back silently, knowing full well that the pictures the police found would be laid at Keith's door.

Suddenly, whatever pity I'd felt for Warren vanished, replaced by a stinging anger that he had been perfectly willing to feed my son, his own nephew, to the dogs.

When he answered the door, he was clearly surprised to see me. His eyes were watery and red-rimmed, his cheeks flushed. There was an odd grogginess and imbalance in his posture, so that he seemed almost to teeter as he stood before me in the doorway.

'Hey, Bro,' he said softly. He lifted his hand, his finger tightening around a can of beer. 'Want a drink?'

'No, thanks.'

'What's up?'

'I need to talk to you, Warren.'

A gray veil fell over his eyes. 'The last time you had to talk to me, I didn't like it very much.'

'It's more serious this time,' I said grimly. 'Something the police found out. Something about you.'

I wanted the look in his eyes to be genuine surprise, because if I saw surprise, then I knew I would force myself to entertain the hope that it

162

could all be explained, every detail of what Leo had told me as I stood, dumbstruck in his office. I wanted Warren to explain away the fact that school officials had reported him for staring out his window at the playground, to explain the pictures on Keith's computer, all of it miraculously a mistake. But I didn't see surprise. I saw resignation, a little boy who'd been caught at something disreputable. There was a hint of embarrassment, too, so that I thought he might actually come out with it without my asking, simply tell me to my face that he knew what I was talking about, and that, yes, it was true.

But instead of an admission, he simply shrugged, stepped back into the foyer of his house and said, 'Okay, come in.'

I followed him into the living room, where he switched on a standing lamp, plopped down on a cracked Naugahyde sofa, and took a quick sip of beer. 'Sure you don't want one?' he asked.

'I'm sure.'

He sucked in a long breath. 'Okay, shoot,' he said. 'What's on your mind, Bro?'

I sat down in the wooden rocker a few feet away, a relic from the grand house, probably an antique, but worthless now because Warren had taken no care to protect it from scrapes and cuts. 'They found pictures on Keith's computer,' I began.

Warren lowered his gaze, all the proof I needed that he'd done exactly what I suspected.

'They were of little girls,' I added. 'Naked little girls.'

Warren took a long pull on the beer, but held his gaze on the floor.

'Keith says he never downloaded any pictures like that,' I added. 'He absolutely denies that they're his.'

Warren nodded heavily. 'Okay.'

'The police checked on when the pictures were downloaded,' I said though I had no real proof of this. To this bluff, I added another. 'You can do that, you know. You can find out.' I watched Warren for any sign that he might come clean. 'The exact dates. Literally, to the minute.'

Warren shifted uneasily in his chair, but otherwise gave no hint that he could see where I was going with all this, how relentlessly I was closing in.

'They were all downloaded a year ago, Warren,' I said. I could not be sure of this, but in my dark world, a lie designed to expose other, darker lies seemed like a ray of light. 'Last September.' I looked at him pointedly. 'You remember where you were last September?'

Warren nodded.

'You were staying in Keith's room,' I told him. 'You were using Keith's computer. No one else was using it.'

Warren lowered the beer to his lap, cradling it between his large flabby thighs. 'Yeah,' he said softly.

I leaned back in the chair and waited.

'Yeah, okay,' Warren said.

Again, I waited, but Warren simply took another sip of beer, then glanced over at me silently.

'Warren,' I said pointedly. 'Those pictures are yours.'

One fat leg began to rock tensely.

'Little girls,' I said. 'Naked little girls.'

The steady rock grew more intense and agitated.

'And then I learned that some people at the school have complained about you,' I said. 'In the past, I mean. Complained about you watching the kids. Somebody reported that on the police hotline.'

'I just look out my window, that's all,' he said. The leg rocked violently for a few more seconds then stopped abruptly. 'I wouldn't hurt a little girl.' He looked lost, but more than that, inwardly disheveled, a crumpled soul, but for all I knew this was no more than a ruse.

'Then why do you watch them, Warren?' I demanded. 'And why did you download those pictures?'

Warren shrugged. 'They were pretty, the pictures.'

A wave of exasperation swept over me. 'They were little girls, for Christ's sake!' I cried. 'Eight years old. And they were naked!'

'They didn't have to be naked,' Warren said weakly, his voice little more than a whine.

'What are you talking about?' I barked. 'They were naked, Warren.'

'But they didn't have to be, that's what I'm saying.' He looked at me like a small child desperately trying to explain himself. 'I mean, I don't ... need them to be naked.'

'Need?' I glared at him. 'What exactly do you need, Warren?'

'I just like to ... look at them,' he whimpered.

'Little girls?' I fired at him. 'You need to look at little girls?' I bolted forward, my eyes like lasers. 'Warren, did you know those pictures were on Keith's computer?'

He shook his head violently. 'I didn't. I swear I didn't. I tried to—'

'Erase them, yes, I know.' I interrupted. 'The cops know it, too.'

'I can't help it, Eric.'

'Can't help what?'

'You know, looking ... at ...' He shook his head. 'It's sick. I know it's sick, but I can't help it.' He began to cry. 'They're just so ... adorable.'

*Adorable.*

The word leaped in me like a flame. 'Adorable,' I repeated, all but shaking with the vision my mind instantly created, Warren coming out of Jenny's room that final morning, his face wreathed in what I had taken for exhaustion, but now saw as a scalding shame. 'You always said that about' – I saw my sister as she lay in her bed later that same afternoon, her eyes darting about frantically. She'd seemed desperate to tell me something, her lips fluttering in my ear, until suddenly they'd stopped and I'd glanced back toward the door and seen Warren standing there, head bowed, his hands deep in his pockets – 'about Jenny.'

He saw it in my eyes, the searing accusation that had suddenly seized me.

'Eric,' he whispered. He seemed to come out of his stupor, all the day's accumulated drink abruptly draining from him. It was as if he'd been dipped in icy water, then jerked out of it to face a reality colder still. 'You think ... ?'

I wanted to howl *no! no!*, deny in the most passionate and conclusive terms that I had the slightest suspicion that he had ever harmed Jenny, that even his most desperate urge would have stopped at her bed, her helplessness, that as she lay dying, pale and wracked with suffering, he could not possibly have found her ... adorable.

But the words wouldn't come, and so I only faced him silently.

He stared at me a moment in frozen disbelief. Then he shook his head wearily and pointed to the door. 'I'm done with you, Eric,' he said. His wet eyes went dry as a desert waste. 'I'm done with everything.' He pointed to the door. 'Go,' he said, 'just go.'

I knew nothing else to do. And so I rose, walked silently out of the room and back to my car. As I pulled out, I saw the light flash upstairs in Warren's bachelor lair and imagined him there alone, sunk in this new despair, wifeless, childless, motherless, fatherless, and now without a brother, too.

I drove back home in a kind of daze, Meredith, Warren, Keith – all of them swirling around in my head like bits of paper in foaming water. I tried to position myself somehow, get a grip on what I knew and didn't know, the dreadful suspicions I could neither avoid nor address, since they were made of smoke and fog.

I pulled in the driveway a few minutes later, got out of the car, swept pass the branches of the Japanese maple and headed on down the walkway to the front door.

Through the window, I saw Meredith clutching the phone. She seemed very nearly frantic, her eyes wide in an unmistakable look of alarm. I thought of the other time I'd come upon her abruptly, the way she'd blurted, 'Talk to you later,' and quickly snapped her cell phone shut and sunk it deep into the pocket of her robe. I had caught her again,

I supposed, and, with that thought, fully expected her to hang up immediately when she heard me open the door.

But when I opened the door, she rushed over to me, the phone trembling in her hand. 'It's – Warren,' she said. 'He's drunk and' – she thrust the phone toward me almost violently – 'Here,' she blurted. 'He's yours.'

I took the phone. 'Warren?'

There was no answer, but I could hear him breathing rapidly, like someone who'd just completed a long exhausting run.

'Warren?' I said again.

Silence.

'Warren,' I snapped. 'Either talk to me or get the fuck off the phone.'

The silence continued briefly, then I heard him draw in a long slow breath.

'Bro,' he said softly, 'your troubles are over.'

Then I heard the blast.

# TWENTY-FOUR

The ambulance and police had already arrived by the time I got to Warren's house. The whole neighborhood strobed with flashing lights, and a yellow tape had been stretched across the driveway and along the borders of the yard.

I had called 911 immediately, though even at that moment, I wasn't sure exactly what Warren had done. He'd been drunk, after all, and on such occasions in the past, he'd not been above making some melodramatic gesture in order to win me back. Once, as a boy, he'd taken a plunge off a high embankment after I'd yelled at him. He'd pulled similar stunts after my father had laced into him for one reason or another. It was a pitiful attempt to regain whatever he thought he'd lost in our affection, and it had never worked. Warren had never been one to learn from experience, however, and even as I watched the flashing lights that surrounded his house, I half expected to see him stagger out into the yard, arms spread in greeting, all bleary good cheer. *Hey, Bro.*

But as I closed in on the house, I knew that this time, it was different. The front door was wide open, and Peak stood, backlit by the light of the foyer, scribbling in a small notebook.

'Is he okay?' I asked as I came up to him.

Peak sank the notebook into his jacket pocket. 'He's dead,' he told me. 'I'm sorry.'

I didn't shudder at the news, and even now I can hardly recall exactly what I felt, save the curious realization that I would never see my brother alive again. A moment ago, he'd spoken to me. Now he was utterly and forever silent. If I thought or felt more than this at that moment, then those feelings were too vague and insubstantial to make a sustained impression.

'Do you want to identify him?' Peak asked.

'Yes.'

'Mind if I ask you a few questions first?'

I shook my head. 'I've gotten used to questions.'

He drew the notebook out of his pocket and flipped it open. 'You spoke to him just before he did it, right?'

'I heard the shot.'

This did not faze Peak, and for a moment it struck me that he probably thought it a way of gaining the sympathy he was not inclined to offer.

'What did he say?'

'That my troubles were over,' I answered.

'What did he mean by that?'

'That he wouldn't be a bother to me anymore, I guess.'

Peak looked at me doubtfully. 'You don't think this had anything to do with Amy Giordano?'

'Just the pictures you found on Keith's computer,' I said. 'They were his.'

'How do you know?'

'Warren stayed at our house while he was recovering from a broken hip,' I said. 'He stayed in Keith's room.'

'That doesn't mean the pictures were his,' Peak said.

'I know they weren't Keith's.'

'How do you know?'

I shrugged. 'Why would Warren have done this if the pictures weren't his?'

'Well, he might have thought we'd shift away from Keith,' Peak said. 'I mean, he all but confessed, didn't he?'

'No, he didn't,' I said. 'Except that the pictures were his. But he said they weren't ... sexual. That he didn't use them that way.'

'Then why did he have them?'

'He said he just thought the kids were ... adorable.'

Peak looked at me squarely. 'Do you think he had anything to do with Amy Giordano being missing?'

I gave the only answer I could be certain of. 'I don't know.'

Peak looked surprised by my answer. 'He was your brother. If he were capable of something like that, kidnapping a little girl, you'd know it, wouldn't you?'

I thought of all the years I'd spent with Warren and realized that for all we'd shared, parents, the big house we'd lost together, the joint trajectories of our lives, for all that, I simply couldn't answer Peak's question, couldn't in the least be sure that I knew Warren at all, or knew any more than his glossy surfaces. 'Can you ever know anyone?' I asked.

Peak released a long frustrated breath and closed the notebook. 'All right.' He glanced inside the house, then back at me. 'You ready to make the identification?'

'Yes.'

Peak turned and led me up the stairs, then down the short corridor to Warren's room. At the door, he stepped aside. 'Sorry,' he murmured. 'This is never easy.'

Warren had pulled a chair up to the window, facing out toward the elementary school's dimly lit playground. His head was slumped to the right, so that he looked as if he'd simply gone to sleep while staring out the window. It was only when I stepped around to face the chair that I saw the shattered mouth, the dead eyes.

I don't know what I felt as I stared down at him during the next few seconds. Perhaps I was simply numb, my tumorous suspicion now grown so large that it was pressing against other vital channels, blocking light and air.

'Was that all he said?' Peak asked. 'Just that your troubles were over?'

I nodded.

'How about before he spoke to you? Did he talk to anyone else in your family?'

'You mean Keith, right?' I asked.

'I mean anybody.'

'Well, he didn't talk to Keith. He talked to my wife briefly, but not to Keith.'

'What did he say to your wife?'

'I don't know,' I told him. 'When I got home, she handed me the phone. Then Warren said that my troubles were over – nothing else. When I heard the shot, I called 911, then came directly here.'

'You came alone, I noticed.'

'Yes.'

Peak looked as if he felt sorry for me because I'd had to come to the scene of my brother's suicide alone, without the comfort of my wife and son.

'Do you want to stay a little longer?' he asked finally.

'No,' I told him.

I gave Warren a final glance, then followed Peak back down the stairs and out into the yard where we stood together in the misty light that swept out from the school playground. The air was completely still, the scattered leaves lying flat, like dead birds, in the unkempt yard.

Peak looked over toward the playground, and I could see how troubled the sight of it made him, the fear he had that some other little girl was still in peril because whoever had taken Amy Giordano was still out there.

'I read that leads get cold after a couple of weeks,' I said.

'Sometimes.'

'It's been two weeks.'

He nodded. 'That's what Vince Giordano keeps telling me.'

'He wants his daughter back,' I said. 'I can understand that.'

Peak drew his gaze over to me. 'We're testing the cigarettes. It takes a while to get the results.'

'And what if they were Keith's?'

'It means he lied,' Peak said. 'He told Vince Giordano that he never left the house. He said he was inside the whole time.'

'And he was,' I said, a response that struck me as wholly reflexive.

Peak returned his attention to the deserted playground, held his gaze on the ghostly swings and monkey bars and seesaws. He seemed to see dead children playing there.

'What if your son hurt Amy Giordano?' He looked at me very intently, and I saw that he was asking the deepest imaginable question. 'I mean, if you knew he did it, but also knew that he was going to get away with it, and that after that, he was going to do it again, which most of them do, men who kill children. If you knew all that I've just said, Mr. Moore, what would you do then?'

*I would kill him.* The answer flashed through my mind so suddenly and irrefutably that I recoiled from this raw truth before replying to Peak. 'I wouldn't let him get away with it.'

Peak seemed to see the stark line that led me to this place, how much had been lost on the way, the shaved-down nature of my circumstances, how little I had left to lose. 'I believe you,' he said.

Meredith was waiting for me when I got home, and the minute I saw her, I recalled the way she'd stood with Rodenberry, and all my earlier feelings rose up, hot and cold, a searing blade of ice.

'He's dead,' I told her flatly.

Her hand lifted mutely to her mouth.

'He shot himself in the head.'

She stared at me from behind her hand, still silent, although I couldn't tell if it were shock or simply her own dead center that kept her silent.

I sat down in the chair across from her. 'What did he say to you?'

She looked at me strangely. 'Why are you so angry, Eric?'

I had no way to answer her without revealing the murky water in which my own emotions now washed about. 'The cops will want to know.'

She bowed her head slightly. 'I'm so sorry, Eric,' she said quietly. 'Warren was so—'

Her feelings for Warren sounded like metal banging steel. 'Oh please,' I blurted. 'You couldn't stand him.'

She looked stunned. 'Don't say that.'

'Why not? It's the truth.'

She looked at me as if I were a stranger who'd somehow managed to crawl into the body of her husband. 'What's the matter with you?'

'Maybe I'm tired of lies.'

'What lies?'

I wanted to confront her, tell her that I'd seen her and Rodenberry in the college parking lot, but some final cowardice, or perhaps it was only fear that if I broached that subject, I would surely lose her, warned me away. 'Warren's lies, for one thing. Those pictures the cops found on Keith's computer. They were Warren's.'

Her eyes glistened slightly, and I saw how wracked she was, how reduced by our long ordeal, her emotions tingling at the surface.

'Leo told me about it,' I went on. 'He said Warren had been caught watching kids play at the elementary school. He'd stand at the window of his little "bachelor lair" and watch them. With binoculars. It was so fucking obvious the school complained about it. The principal went over and told Warren to stop it. So when this thing with Amy Giordano happened, somebody called the police hotline and told them about Warren.'

'So that's what it was,' Meredith said. She seemed relieved, as if a small dread had been taken from her. She remained silent a moment, gazing at her hands. Then she said, 'Warren couldn't have done something like that, Eric. He couldn't have hurt a little girl.'

Her certainty surprised me. She had never cared for my brother, never had the slightest respect for him. He was one of life's losers, and Meredith had never had any patience for such people. Warren's drinking and self-pity had only made it worse. But now, out of nowhere, she seemed completely confident that Warren had had nothing to do with Amy Giordano's disappearance.

'How do you know?' I asked.

'I know Warren,' she answered.

'Really? How can you be so sure you know him?'

'Aren't you?'

'No.'

'He was your brother, Eric. You've known him all your life.'

Peak had said the same thing, and now I gave the same reply. 'I'm not sure you ever know anyone.'

She looked at me, puzzled and alarmed, but also alerted to something hidden. 'Warren said you came over to his house. He said you had a quarrel.'

'It wasn't exactly a quarrel,' I told her.

'That's what he called it,' Meredith said. 'What was it then?'

'I talked to him about the pictures.'

'What did he say?'

'That they weren't really sexual.' I shook my head. 'He said he just liked looking at the pictures. That the kids were ... adorable.'

'And you didn't believe him?'

'No.'

'Why not?'

'Oh come on, Meredith, he fits the profile in every aspect. Especially the low self-esteem part.'

'If low self-esteem is a big deal, then you'd better mark Keith for a pedophile, too.'

'Don't think that hasn't crossed my mind.'

Now amazement gave way to shock. 'You think that?'

'Don't you?'

'No, I don't.'

'Wait a minute,' I yelped. 'You're the one who first had doubts about Keith.'

'But I never thought it was a sexual thing. That even if he hurt Amy, it wasn't because of sex.'

'What then?'

'Anger,' Meredith answered. 'Or maybe a cry for attention.'

*A cry for attention.*

This sounded like the sort of psychobabble that would come from Stuart Rodenberry, and I bristled at the thought that Meredith was arguing with me through him, using his professional expertise and experience against me.

'Oh, bullshit,' I said sharply. 'You don't believe a word of that.'

'What are you saying, Eric?'

'I'm saying that from the minute Amy disappeared you thought Keith was involved. And I don't for a fucking second believe you thought a "cry for attention" had anything to do with it.' I looked at her hotly. 'You thought it was in the family. Something he inherited. Connected to me. To Warren.' I laughed brutally. 'And you were probably right.'

'Right? You mean because you've decided that Warren was a pedophile?' Her gaze was pure challenge. 'And what, Eric, makes you so sure of that? A few pictures on his computer? The fact that he liked to watch kids play? Jesus Christ, anybody could—'

'More than that,' I interrupted.

'What then?'

I shook my head. 'I don't want to go into this anymore, Meredith.'

I started to turn away, but she grabbed my arm and jerked me around to face her. 'Oh no, you don't. You're not walking away from this. You accuse Keith of being a pedophile, a kidnapper, and God knows what else. You accuse me of suggesting that something awful is in your family.

You do all that, and then you think you can just say you're tired and walk away? Oh no, Eric, not this time. You don't walk away from an accusation like that. No, no. You stand right here and you tell me why you're so fucking sure of all this bullshit.'

I pulled away, unable to confront what I'd seen in Jenny's room that morning, then conveyed to Warren in a single glance, how, upon that accusation, he must have finally decided that the world was no longer a fit place for him.

But again Meredith grabbed my arm. 'Tell me,' she demanded. 'What did Warren or Keith ever do to—'

'It has nothing to do with Keith.'

'So, it's Warren then?'

I gazed at her desolately. 'Yes.'

She saw the anguish flare in my eyes. 'What happened, Eric?'

'I thought I saw something.'

'Something . . . in Warren?'

'No. In Jenny.'

Meredith peered at me unbelievingly. 'Jenny?'

'The day she died I went into her room. She was trying desperately to tell me something. Moving all around. Lips. Legs. Desperate. I bent down to try to hear what she was saying, but then she stopped dead and pulled away from me and just lay there, looking toward the door.' I drew in a troubled breath. 'Warren was standing at the door. He'd been with Jenny that night and . . .' I stopped. 'And I thought maybe he—'

'Jesus, Eric,' Meredith gasped. 'You said that to him?'

'No,' I answered. 'But he saw it.'

She stared at me as if I were a strange creature who'd just washed up on the beach beside her, a crawler of black depths. 'You had no evidence of that at all, Eric,' she said. 'No evidence at all that Warren did anything to your sister' – there was a lacerating disappointment in her gaze – 'How could you have done that? Said something like that without . . . knowing anything?'

I thought of the way she and Rodenberry had stood together in the parking lot, their bodies so close, the cool air, the night, the rustle of fallen leaves when the wind touched them. 'You don't always need evidence,' I said coldly. 'Sometimes you just know.'

She said nothing more, but I felt utterly berated, like a small boy whipped into a corner. To get out of it, I struck back in the only way that seemed open to me.

'I saw you tonight,' I told her.

'Saw me?'

'You and Rodenberry.'

She seemed hardly able to comprehend what I was saying.

'In the parking lot at the college.'

Her lips sealed tightly.

'Talking.'

Her eyes became small, reptilian slits. 'And?' she snapped. 'What are you getting at, Eric?'

'I want to know what's going on,' I said haughtily, a man who knew his rights and intended to exercise them.

Fire leaped in her eyes. 'Wasn't Warren enough for you, Eric?' she asked. 'Isn't one life enough?'

She could not have more deeply wounded me if she'd fired a bullet into my head, but what she said next was said with such utter finality that I knew nothing could return me to the world that had existed before she said it.

'I don't know you anymore,' she added. Then she turned and walked up the stairs.

I knew that she meant it, and that she meant it absolutely. Meredith was not a woman to make false gestures, bluff, halt at the precipice, or seek to regain it once she'd gone over. Something had broken, the bridge that connected us, and even at that early moment, when I was still feeling the heat of her eyes like the sting of a slap, I knew that the process of repair would be long, if it could be done at all.

# TWENTY-FIVE

Warren was buried on a bright, crisp afternoon. My father had told me flatly that he had no intention of going to the funeral, so it was only the strained and separating members of my second family, along with a few people Warren had gotten to know over the years, regulars at the bars he frequented, who came to say good-bye to him.

Meredith watched stiffly as the coffin was lowered into the ground, Keith at her side, looking even more pale and emaciated than usual. He'd reacted to Warren's death by not reacting to it at all, which was typical of Keith. Standing at the grave, so small a force beside the tidal wave of his mother, he looked incapable of weathering any of life's coming storms. I could not imagine him ever marrying or having children or adequately managing even the least complicated and demanding aspects of life.

When the funeral was over, we walked out of the cemetery together, Meredith's body so rigid, her face so stonily composed, holding down such sulfuric rage, that I thought she might suddenly wheel around and slap me.

But she didn't, and so, as we all passed through the gate of the cemetery, I suppose we looked like a normal family, one whose members shared grief and joy, made the best of whatever life sent our way.

At least that is certainly how we appeared to Vincent Giordano.

He was standing outside his delivery van, its door oddly open, as if in preparation for a quick getaway. His eyes were no longer moist and bloodshot, not at all like the day he'd approached me outside the photo shop. He stood erect, rather than stooped, and there was nothing broken or beggarly in his posture. He pulled away from the van as we approached our car, his body rolling like a great stone toward us.

I looked at Meredith. 'Get in the car,' I told her, then turned to Keith. 'You, too.'

By then Vince was closing in.

'Hello, Vince,' I said coolly.

Vince stopped and folded his large beefy arms over his chest. 'I just came to tell you it won't work.'

'I don't know what you mean.'

'That brother of yours shooting himself,' Vince said. 'It's not going to get that son of yours off the hook.'

'Vince, we shouldn't be having this conversation.'

'You heard what I said.'

'It's in the hands of the police, Vince. And that's where it should be.'

'You heard what I said,' Vince repeated. 'That kid of yours is not going to get away with it. You can hire a fancy lawyer, do whatever else you want to, but that kid is not going to get away with it.' His eyes flared. 'My little girl is dead.'

'We don't know that.'

'Yes, we do,' Vince said. 'Two weeks. What else could it be?'

'I don't know,' I said.

He looked over my shoulder and I knew he was glaring at Keith.

'They found his cigarettes at Amy's window,' Vince said. 'Outside her window. He said he didn't leave the house. So, whose cigarettes are they, huh? Tell me that. Why did he lie, tell me that!' His voice rang high and desperate, reaching for heaven. 'Tell me that. You or that fancy lawyer you hired to protect his fucking ass!'

'That's enough,' I said.

'It's your whole goddamn family that's screwed up,' Vince screamed. 'A brother watches kids in the playground, looks at dirty pictures of little kids. That's where that son of yours got it from. The family. In their blood.' He was seething now. 'You should all be wiped out!' he cried. 'Every goddamn one of you!'

I felt his hot breath on my face, turned quickly, strode to my car, and got in. For a moment we locked eyes, and I saw how deeply Vince Giordano hated me, hated Keith, hated the neat little family he'd watched come through the cemetery gate, the kind of family he'd once had and which had been taken from him, he felt certain, by my son.

We drove directly home, Meredith trembling all the way, terrified that Vince would follow us there. From time to time, she glanced at the rear-view mirror, searching for his green van behind us. I had never seen her so frightened, and I knew that part of her fear was that the husband she'd once trusted had changed irrevocably.

At home, she wanted me to call the police, but I had leaped to so many conclusions of late, that I refused to leap to another one.

'He's just upset,' I told her. 'He has a right to be.'

'But he doesn't have a right to threaten us,' Meredith cried.

176

'He didn't threaten us,' I reminded her. 'Besides, the police won't do anything. They can't unless he does something first.'

She shook her head in exasperation, no doubt convinced that here again I was simply refusing to confront the obvious truth that Vince Giordano was a dangerous man. 'All right, fine,' she snapped, 'but if anything happens, Eric, it's on your head.'

With that, she stormed down the corridor to her office and slammed the door.

I built a fire and for a long time sat, staring at the flames. Outside, autumn leaves gathered and blew apart at the will of the wind. The gray air darkened steadily, and night finally fell. Yet Meredith remained in her room, and Keith in his.

It wasn't until early evening that one of them, Keith, finally joined me in the living room.

'So, are we not going to have dinner?' he asked.

I drew my eyes from the fire and faced him. 'Nobody feels like cooking, I guess.'

'So, what does that mean ... like ... we don't eat?'

'No, we'll eat.'

'Okay.'

'All right,' I said. I got to my feet. 'Come on, let's go get a pizza.'

We walked out of the house and down the brick walkway, past the shadowy limbs of the Japanese maple.

The drive to Nico's took only a few minutes, and on the way, Keith sat on the passenger side, looking less sullen than before, as if he were beginning to emerge from the tiresome irritation of his teenage years. A light played in his eyes, a hint of energy, or perhaps some spark of hope that his life might one day be less plagued with trouble. I recalled a line I'd read somewhere, that we must be able to imagine redemption before we can achieve it.

'I'd ask you how things are,' I said. 'But you hate that question.'

He looked over at me and a faint smile fluttered on his lips. 'I was going to ask you that. I mean, Mom's really mad at you, right?'

'Yes, she is.'

'What about?'

'She blames me for being too suspicious.'

'Of her?'

'Of everything, I guess,' I answered. 'I have to try harder, Keith. I have to get more evidence before I jump to conclusions.'

'What were you suspicious about?'

'Just things.'

'So, you won't tell me?'

'It's between your mother and me,' I said.

'What if I told you something. A secret.'

I felt a chill pass over me.

'Would you tell me then?' Keith asked. 'Like, an exchange? You know, father and son?'

I watched him closely for a moment, then decided that where I'd gone wrong with Keith was in failing to recognize that despite his teenage aloofness, the sullen behavior that fixed him in an angry smirk, there was an adult growing inside him, forming within the brittle chrysalis of adolescence, and that this adult had to be recognized and carefully coaxed out, that it was time to confront not Keith's immaturity, but the fact that he was soon to be a man.

'Okay,' I told him. 'An exchange.'

He drew in a long breath, then said, 'The money. It wasn't for me. And what I told Mr. Price – about running away – that wasn't true.'

'What was the money for?'

'This girl,' Keith said. 'We're sort of ... you know. And she has it really bad at home, and I thought, okay, maybe I could get her out of it. Get her away from it.'

'Am I allowed to know who this girl is?' I asked.

'Her name is Polly,' Keith said shyly. 'She lives on the other side of town. Those walks I go on. At night. That's where we meet.'

'The other side of town,' I repeated. 'Near the water tower.'

He looked surprised. 'Yes.'

I smiled. 'Okay, I guess it's my turn. This thing with your mother. The things she's so mad about. It's that I accused her of having a lover.' I felt a tight ball of pain release its grip on me. 'I didn't have any evidence, but I accused her anyway.'

He looked at me softly. 'You believed I hurt Amy Giordano, too.'

I nodded. 'Yes, Keith, I did.'

'Do you still think that?'

I looked at him again and saw nothing but a shy, tender boy, reserved and oddly solitary, fighting his own inner battles as we all must, coming to terms with his limits, which we all must do, struggling to free himself from the bonds that seem unnatural, find himself within the incomprehensible tangle of hopes and fears that is the roiling substance of every human being. I saw all of that, and in seeing that, saw that my son was not the killer of a child.

'No, I don't, Keith,' I said. Then I pulled the car over and drew him into my arms and felt his body grow soft and pliant in my embrace and my body do the same in his, and in that surrender, we both suddenly released the sweetest imaginable tears.

Then we released each other and wiped those same tears away and laughed at the sheer strangeness of the moment.

'Okay, pizza,' I said as I started the car again.

Keith smiled. 'Pepperoni and onion,' he said.

Nico's wasn't crowded that night, and so Keith and I sat alone on a small bench and waited for our order. He took out a handheld video game and played silently, while I perused the local paper. There was a story about Amy Giordano, but it was short and on page four, relating only that police were still in the process of 'eliminating suspects'.

I showed the last two words to Keith. 'That means you,' I said. 'You're being eliminated as a suspect.'

He smiled and nodded, then went back to his game.

I glanced outside, toward the pizza delivery van that rested beside the curb. A deliveryman waited beside the truck. He was tall and very thin, with dark hair and small slightly bulging eyes. He leaned languidly against the front of the truck, smoking casually, and watching cars pull in and out of the parking lot. Then suddenly he straightened, tossed the cigarette on the ground, hustled into his van, and drove away.

'Pepperoni and onion,' someone called from behind the counter.

Keith and I stepped up to get it. I paid for the pizza, handed it to Keith, and the two of us headed for the car. On the way, I glanced down to where the deliveryman had tossed his cigarette. There were several butts floating in a pool of oily water. All of them were Marlboros.

I kept that fact to myself until we reached the exit of the parking lot. Then I stopped the car and looked at Keith. 'The night you ordered pizza for you and Amy, did you order it from Nico's?'

Keith nodded. 'Where else?'

'What did the guy who delivered it look like?'

'Tall,' Keith said. 'Skinny.'

'Did you happen to see the guy who was standing outside the delivery van a few minutes ago?'

'No.'

'He was tall and skinny,' I said. 'Smoked one cigarette after another.'

'So?'

'He smokes Marlboros.'

Keith's face seemed to age before my eyes, grow dark and knowing, as if the full weight of life, the web of accident and circumstance in which we all are ensnared, had suddenly appeared to him.

'We should call the cops,' he said.

I shook my head. 'They've probably already checked him out. Besides, we don't even know if it's the same guy who came to Amy's house that night.'

'But if it is,' Keith said. 'He might still have her.'

'No,' I said. 'If he took her, she's long dead by now.'

Keith was not convinced. 'But what if she's not. Shouldn't we at least try?'

'We have nothing to go on,' I told him. 'Just that a guy who delivers pizzas from Nico's also happens to smoke the kind of cigarette you smoke, along with millions of other people. Besides, like I said before, the police have already questioned him, I'm sure.'

I couldn't be certain that Keith accepted my argument, but he said nothing more, and we went the rest of the way home in silence.

Meredith was in the kitchen when we arrived. We set the table together, then sat talking quietly, and during those few minutes I came to believe that for all the terrible disruptions our family had suffered during the past two weeks, we might yet reclaim the normal balance we had once possessed. I wanted to believe that Meredith's anger toward me might dissipate as Keith's resentment had seemed to dissipate, that we might regain our common footing as a family, if for no other reason than that we were all simply too exhausted by events to hold each other at knifepoint any longer. Anger takes energy, I told myself, and unless its devouring fire is steadily and continually stoked, it will cool to embers soon enough. It was for that reason perhaps more than any other that I decided simply to let things go, to say nothing more about Amy Giordano or Warren or Rodenberry, to hold back and wait and hope that after Amy Giordano had finally been found and the shock of Warren's death and the accusing finger I'd so recklessly pointed at Meredith had grown less painful, we might come together again as a family.

After dinner, Keith went to his room. From below, I could hear him pacing about, as if worrying a point, trying to come to a conclusion. Meredith heard him, too, but said nothing about it, and so the source of Keith's anxiety never came up that evening.

We went to bed at just before ten, Meredith's back to me like a fortress.

'I love you, Meredith,' I told her.

She didn't answer or turn toward me, but I hoped that in the end she would – that in the end we would survive.

She went to sleep a few minutes later, but I remained awake for a long time before finally drifting off.

By morning, Meredith seemed slightly less brittle, which gave me yet more hope. Still, I didn't press the issue, but instead remained quiet and kept my distance.

Keith left for school at his usual time, and a few minutes later I went to work. The day passed like most days, and I reveled in the simple uneventfulness of it. Keith got home at just after four and found a message on the phone, telling him that I'd decided it was time for him to start making deliveries again. He got on his bike, pedaled to the shop, and gathered up the deliveries for that afternoon. There were a lot of them, but I had no doubt that he'd still be able to get them done and get back to the shop before I closed for the day.

It was nearly six when I finally closed the shop and headed for my car; at almost that very same moment, Vincent Giordano had locked the front door of his produce market, then picked up his cell phone and called his wife, telling her not to worry – he'd be home before the news.

You see it suddenly, the face. It swims toward you out of the crowd, so utterly clear and distinct and achingly recognizable that it blurs all other faces. It drifts toward you with wide, searching eyes and streaming hair, like a head carried in a crystal stream. She lifts her hand in greeting when she sees you seated in your booth beside the window. Then she moves down the aisle toward you, a face you have not seen in years and remember most from the flyer you taped on the window of your shop, a face that seemed to hang from a jagged fence of big black letters – MISSING.

'Thank you for doing this, Mr. Moore,' she says.

'I would do anything for you, Amy.'

She is twenty-three, her face a little fuller than before, but with the same flawless skin. You see that she is adorable, your mind returning, after so many years, to the word Warren used, and from which you judged him suspect in crimes both near and distant.

'I'm not sure what I'm looking for,' she says.

She draws a dark blue scarf from her head and lets her hair fall free. It is shorter than it was then, with no hint of wave, and you recall how it fell well below her shoulders the last time she was in your shop. You remember the penetration with which she peered at the cameras on display, as if touching the knobs and dials with her inquiring mind.

'I'm getting married, I suppose that's part of it,' she says. 'I just want to ... settle everything before I start a family of my own.'

She waits for a response, but you only watch her silently.

'Does that sound crazy?' she asks. 'My wanting to talk to you?'

'No.'

She peels off her raincoat, folds it neatly, and places it on the seat beside her. You wonder if she's going to pull out a notebook, begin to take notes. You're relieved when she doesn't.

'I've told Stephen everything,' she says. 'Stephen's my fiancé. Anyway, I told him everything about what happened. At least, everything I remember.' She sits back slightly, as if you are giving off waves of heat. 'Maybe I just wanted to say thank you.'

'For what?'

'For noticing things,' she says. 'And for doing something about it.'

I recall the sound of Keith's footsteps in his upstairs room, his soft tread across the carpet, back and forth, back and forth, how, during those lonely minutes, he must have been trying to decide what he should do, weighing what I'd earlier told him, weighing it all the next day before finally dismissing it, and in that fateful dismissal, becoming for all time a man.

'I didn't do anything about it,' I tell her.

'Yes,' she says. 'That was Keith.'

'Only Keith.'

I see what I could not have seen at the time. I see my son at school, see him glance at the pay phone in the lunchroom, stop, think it through again, then dial the number he'd seen posted on flyers in the school lobby and on shop windows throughout the town, a number used for rumors, wild notions, false sightings, vicious gossip, unfounded suspicions, and occasionally, very occasionally, the shattering possibility of salvation. I hear the voice, which I had always judged weak and irresolute, but which now sounds powerful in my mind, forceful, confident, determined.

'I just wish it had all happened before' – her eyes hold the immemorial regret of our kind, the iron door that closes with each movement of the second hand – 'I want to tell you how sorry I am.'

Her father's words echo in my mind – *I'll be home before the news.*

What had he meant by home? I wonder suddenly. Had he meant the house he'd shared with his wife and daughter? Or had it been some other home he expected to reach, the place where he hoped to find peace, or at least forgetfulness?

'It was all so terrible,' she says. 'So unfair. Especially since Keith had already called the police.'

You hear your son's voice, hear it as clearly as when Peak played it for you three days later.

*'This is Keith. Keith Moore, and last night my dad and I went for pizza at Nico's and we saw a man who might have delivered pizza to Amy Giordano's house that night, and he smokes Marlboro cigarettes, and I just think you should at least go talk to him because, you know, well, maybe it's not too late ... for Amy.'*

Now images rise from the gray depths. You see the man taken into custody, a little girl carried up basement stairs and out to a waiting ambulance, her long dark hair tangled and matted with filth, one eye swollen shut, her lips parched and cracked. You hold this image in your mind as you stare at the face that faces yours, healed by time, the lips moist, hair immaculately clean and neatly combed.

'He would have killed me really soon,' she tells you. 'He'd already dug the grave.'

You have no doubt that this is true, that had your brave and noble son not made his lonely, lonely choice, Amy Giordano would be dead.

'I only wish I could have thanked Keith.'

Now the final hours of your family life pass before you in a series of photographs that were never taken, but which you have carried all these years in the grim portfolio of your mind. You see Keith on his bicycle, pedaling back from his deliveries. You see him turn into the parking lot, holding one leg out as he always did, the photo shop in the background. You see him coast down the hill toward the shop, a green van now entering the frame. You see the slender barrel inch from the van's open window, a hunting rifle, complete with scope. You see your son in the crosshairs, his arm lifted, waving to you as he hurtles toward the shop, where you stand, staring helplessly, until the awful sound reverberates, and your son rises from the seat of his bike, rises as if rudely jerked from it by an invisible hand and hurled backward onto the dark pavement where he lies writhing as you run toward him.

'I don't know why he did it,' she says. 'My dad.'

You see yourself in pictures now. You see yourself collapse beside your strangely still son, gather his lifeless body into your arms, then shudder as another shot rips the otherwise ghostly silent air, and your eyes dart toward the sound, and you see a second body, slumped over the wheel of Vincent Giordano's green van.

'He did it,' you say, 'because he loved you.'

Her eyes glisten, and for a moment the two of you flow one into the other and become a single, irremediable ache.

'I'm sorry, too,' you tell her.

And it's true, you are sorry for Amy, and for Karen who never married again, and for Meredith who could not hold on to anything after Keith's death, could not live with you or even in the town where you'd made a family and briefly a good life, and so she had drifted first to Boston and then to California and then to some third place from which she has sent no word.

'Well,' Amy says, 'I just felt that I wanted to see you and tell you how sorry I am for everything that happened.' She shakes her head. 'There was just so much ... misunderstanding.' She starts to get up.

'No, wait,' you tell her.

She eases back into the seat and peers at you quizzically.

'I want to talk to you,' you tell her. 'You're getting married, about to have a family of your own. There are things, Amy, you need to know.'

She nods. 'I know there are,' she says.

'I'd like to help,' you tell her. 'Give you the benefit of what I've learned.'

'Okay,' she says, then waits, ready to receive whatever gifts you have.

You think of Warren, Meredith, Keith, the family you briefly held, then doubted, and finally lost. You recall your final glimpse of your house, the winding walkway that led from the driveway to the front door, the sturdy grill, the Japanese maple you'd lovingly planted so many years before, how on that final day you'd glanced at the ground beneath it, so baffled now, so tormented by doubts and suspicions that you could no longer tell whether you saw a pool of blood beneath its naked limbs or just a scattering of red leaves.

You close your eyes, then open them, and all of that is gone, and you see only Amy.

'I'll start at the end,' you tell her. 'The day I left my house.'

And then, as in a family photograph, you smile.

# MORTAL MEMORY

FOR
Maria Eugeina Caballero, David Delgado,
Carlo and Rachel Malka and
Pablo Martinez-Calleja in Madrid
AND FOR
Charles Radanovich and
Antonio Perez-Melero in New York

# ONE

This much I remembered from the beginning: the floral curtains in their second-floor bedroom pulled tightly together; Jamie's new basketball at the edge of the yard, glistening in the rain; Laura's plain white bra lying haphazardly in the grass behind the house, the rest of our clothes, drenched and motionless as they hung from the line above it.

And I remembered this: two men in a car, both in the front seat; the one behind the wheel younger, smaller, bareheaded; the other wearing a gray hat, breathing hard, smoking. It was the older one who first spoke, drawing his wire-rimmed glasses from his eyes, then wiping them with a white handkerchief as he shifted around to face me. Before Rebecca, I'd never been able to remember what he'd said to me, although, over the years, I'd imagined many different things, lines no doubt picked up from television or movies, but which had never struck me as exactly right.

Before Rebecca, I hadn't even been able to recall how long I'd actually stayed in the back seat of the car, although I'd always sensed that the light had altered during the time I'd remained there, a change which could have only come about slowly, as evening fell. I remembered a thickening gray as it gathered around the bare, autumnal trees. I even remembered shadows lengthening and growing darker as the hours passed, but given the thick cloud cover of that late afternoon, it couldn't have been real. Still, this false impression of shadows lengthening and growing dark lingered through the years, stubbornly remaining while other, vastly more important things, began to blur and fade.

More than anything, I remembered the rain. It had fallen steadily all that day, puddles growing larger and larger, streams tumbling like tiny mountain rapids along the slanting gutters of the suburban streets. It was a fall rain, cold and heavy, the sort that sinks into the bones, making them feel thick and soggy. All day, while I'd sat at my desk in school, I'd listened as it spattered against my classroom windows. Outside, it fell in great gray veils across the playground and the schoolyard, finally gathering in dark pools beneath the swings, the seesaws, the dripping monkey bars. It kept me in when I wanted to be let out, and I remember glancing longingly at the sodden softball field, the thick clouds that hung above it, the slender, wiry rain. Now, when I think of it, it strikes me that almost every impression I retained of that day had something to do with confinement.

That day: November 19, 1959.

The car I sat in as evening fell was dark blue and had a faintly sweet, yet dusty smell, probably caused by the cigarette and cigar smoke the upholstery had collected over the years. There was a chrome ornament on the hood, a bird with its wings spread, a common design in those days. I remember the bird because I focused on it from time to time, watching it rather than the men who sat silently in the front seat. It was very beautiful, or at least it seemed so at the time, a point of gleaming silver in the gloomy air, a vision of release, a creature taking flight. It seemed odd that it should be attached to anything, least of all to the flat metal hood of the car in which I sat while the rain thudded down upon it, throwing large drops of water onto the bird's uplifted, but unmoving wings.

The car itself rested in the driveway of my house. I don't know what kind of car it was, but I've always imagined it as a Ford or a Chevy. It had blackwall tires, and its interior was dark blue. Instead of the usual radio with small chrome dials, it had a strange metal box with a black microphone that dangled above the floorboard. I could sometimes hear static coming from the box, but I don't remember hearing a voice. As far as I recall, neither of the men in the front seat ever picked up the microphone. Instead, they seemed to sit rigidly in place, silent, heavy, like carved figures.

I sat mutely behind them, my short legs drawn up beneath me in the back seat of the car. Through the space between the garage and the eastern corner of the house, I could glimpse a small patch of the backyard. I could see the wooden fence my father had erected before I was born, and a portion of the metal swing set, which my brother and sister had outgrown, but which I still used at certain idle moments to entertain myself. Beyond it was the clothesline, sagging heavily with its burden of soggy clothes, and beneath them the white tangle of my sister's bra.

The house was made of plain red brick. It had a faintly Tudor design, two-storied, with a gabled roof and dark green exterior shutters that were purely ornamental. A straight cement walkway led to the front door. Two front doors, actually. One of glass with an aluminum frame, the other of wood, painted white with a brass knocker shaped in the figure of a hand holding a small metal sphere. I remember how gently the long fingers appeared to hold on to the ball, as if about to release it.

There were other ornate touches. Flowers, for example, which my mother had planted not only all around the house, but in two circular gardens on either side of the cement walkway. She grew roses, tulips, and azaleas of various colors, and I remember her stooped over them awkwardly, almost in a squat, dressed in a loose-fitting red housedress, poking at the ground with a small spade. She was thirty-seven, but in pictures she appeared considerably older. She was thin and blonde, and her face had many sharp angles. I remember her as being tall, but she was actually five foot four. Before Rebecca, I didn't remember the sound of her voice, except that it was rather high, or the touch of her hand, except that it seemed vague and hesitant, or anything at all of the heart that had beaten beneath the red housedress, not even the fact that, according to the coroner's report, it had weighed nearly fifteen hundred grams.

And so, through all the years that followed her death, my mother remained an insubstantial presence, a figure carved from beach sand, tentative and impermanent.

Her sister Edna was another story, and it was she who finally came to retrieve me from the car, the two men handing me over to her casually, without ever asking her to produce a single article of identification.

She would have had the proper identification, of course. She was a cautious, correct woman, and knowing what would be expected of her that day, she would have brought a driver's license or a library card along with her. But neither of the two men who sat in the front seat of the car bothered to ask her who she was. The young one simply said, 'You must be the sister,' then nodded toward me and added, 'Okay, you can take him then.'

And so it was my aunt who came to me that day. My father had always called her 'the maiden aunt' or 'the spinster', though I doubt that he meant anything cruel in using such phrases. She was forty-two years old and unmarried. It was as simple as that. Others might have felt differently, using the same words to point out that my aunt had failed in her central mission to attract and keep a man. But my father admired her solitude, I think, along with her capacity to endure a certain subtle scorn.

She was dressed in a thick cloth coat that day, her dark hair pulled back in a bun which seemed to hang like a swollen berry from beneath the curve of her broad-brimmed black rain hat.

The back door of the car swung open and I slid out of the seat and into her care. She didn't pull me into her arms, but took my hand instead, and then strode swiftly across the rain-soaked yard to her waiting car, jerking me along hastily, so that I nearly stumbled as I trotted along beside her.

Her car was an old green Packard, and as she hustled me into its front seat, I glanced toward my house, Jamie's basketball suddenly floating into my view like a tiny orange planet. As the car pulled away, I got up on my knees in the seat and turned to look out the rain-streaked window toward the house in which I'd lived all my life. There it stood, in all its forlorn and broken gloom. I suppose by then I knew more or less everything that had happened within its various rooms during the last few hours. But all that had gone before it, the long march we had all made to that day in November, remained beyond my scope.

'Face forward, Stevie,' Aunt Edna commanded sternly. 'Don't look back.'

Before Rebecca, I never had.

But now, I think that memory is the consolation prize we get for each day's death, the place we go to edit and rewrite our lives, to give ourselves another chance. Perhaps, in the end, that was all any of us ever wanted, just another chance. My father, my mother, Laura, Jamie, all of us locked up together in that house on McDonald Drive. From the street, it didn't look like a prison, but I know now that it was one, and that although I didn't hear them at the time, the sounds of my childhood were sliding bars and clanging doors.

Perhaps Aunt Edna had already sensed all that, and fearing the worst, warned me never to look back.

She was a middle-aged woman the day she rushed me across the yard to her waiting car, but she seemed ancient to me. Once at her house, she fed me a light dinner of chicken and white rice. I sat at the table, nibbling at the food, stunned into silence by what I already knew. I remember that she looked at me for a long time, as if trying to find the right words. Then she gave up, and simply muttered, 'I'll figure something out.'

But she never did, and I think part of the reason for her failure ever to 'figure something out' with regard to me was that in some way I scared her. Without doubt, there were occasions during the short two months that I lived with her when she would gaze at me distantly, with an unmistakable apprehension, and I think that at those moments she was searching for the dark seed she thought must one day bloom in me, the ember that hadn't been entirely consumed in the burning ruin of my family, but which still floated in the smoky atmosphere, dense, acrid, waiting to ignite.

Once, late at night, I wandered downstairs and into the kitchen, took the long carving knife from its drawer and headed across the room to the bowl of apples that sat beside the old tin sink. I had only moved a few steps when I saw Aunt Edna step out of the darkness of the adjoining room. Her eyes were on the knife, rather than my face, and I could tell she was fighting a terrible impulse to snatch it from my hand.

'Put that back,' she commanded.

'I was going to have an apple,' I told her.

'It's too late to eat something,' she said evenly. 'It's bad for your stomach.'

For a tense, trembling instant, we stared at each other, the long knife still held tightly in my fist, her eyes now shifting from its blade to my face.

'Put it back, Stevie,' she repeated.

I obeyed immediately, of course, but I never forgot the look in Aunt Edna's eyes, the way she seemed to sniff some poisonous vapor in the air around me.

Years later, when I told my wife the story, she said only, 'How macabre,' and went back to her work. I know now that instead of such a light dismissal, she should have stopped me dead, stared at me and asked, 'Was she right, Steven? Is it in you, too? What can we do to root it out?'

For years I believed that my mother should have demanded the same answers from my father, as if that one frank exchange might have saved us all.

My mother, Dorothy Coleman Farris, age thirty-seven.

During the brief time that I lived with Aunt Edna, she rarely mentioned my mother. When she did, she always referred to her as 'poor Dottie', as if 'poor' and 'Dottie' were melded together in her mind, impossible to separate. There were even times when I suspected that Aunt Edna finally blamed my mother for everything that happened that day in 1959.

That was something my Uncle Quentin, the tall man in work clothes who picked me up at Aunt Edna's only two months after I arrived there, never did. Instead, he spoke fondly, and even a little comically, of my mother. And so, over the years, as his memories of her surfaced in one story or another, my mother began to emerge as a gentle and somewhat gullible person who, as a child, had always fallen for Quentin's tricks, believed his outrageous lies, and generally served as the butt of his harmless jokes. 'Dottie always looked on the bright side,' he told me once. Then added with a helpless shrug: 'That was her downfall, you might say.'

What did he mean by that?

He never said, and so I was left with only the vision of my mother as a person so ordinary she seemed featureless, bland, a bubble in a sea of bubbles.

Her school reports, which Aunt Edna had, and which were passed on to me when she died, revealed a similar figure to the one Quentin painted. There was a pattern of C's dotted from time to time with a B or a B–, but nothing higher. Her fifth-grade teacher summed her up: 'Dorothy is a very nice child, always kind and friendly. Her work is adequate, and she is always punctual. It is pleasant to teach her.'

Nice. Pleasant. Punctual. Even at their best, these are not the towering virtues. They leave out courage and adventurousness. But more than anything, they leave out passion. There is nothing to suggest that anything ever moved my mother with great force. Perhaps, in the end, that's what Aunt Edna always meant by calling her 'poor Dottie', that she was poor in spirit, that she had no inner will, that perhaps even on that November day, she'd gone to her death like a slave to her quarters, head bowed, arms hung, eyes scarcely noting the black tail of the lash.

But could any life have really been so spiritless and void? After all, at one point, this same 'poor Dottie' met a boy named Billy Farris, tall with jet-black hair, and when he asked her on a date, she accepted. Perhaps, on those evenings during the bright Indian summer of 1940, when they'd walked down to the old movie house on Timmons Street, or along the edges of the little stream that ran through the town's carefully tended park, perhaps on those quiet, humid nights, she'd found herself momentarily aglow with something strong, new, irresistible. Isn't it possible that there were moments early on, in the first blush of infatuation, when she had loved my father with the kind of love depicted in those little books they found beside her bed, tales of high romance in exotic places, Fiji, Paris, Istanbul? When his hand first brushed her breast, or drew slowly up her thigh, isn't it possible that even 'poor Dottie' lost her breath?

Without Rebecca, I never would have known.

Even so, however, I would have known a little. I would have known that she married Billy Farris and later bore three children. And yet, despite such knowledge, I find that I still can't imagine her on those nights of conception, when Jamie and Laura and I were, in effect, born. I can't imagine her naked beneath a man, or over him, or beside him, as they move together on the bed.

She was on a bed that day, too, lying where he put her, her arms folded neatly over her chest, eyes closed, feet side by side, her stack of romance novels arranged neatly beside the bed, as if at any moment, she might roll over, pluck one from the floor, and immediately lose herself in the soap opera glamour of a beach romance.

It was Aunt Edna who identified her. From the back seat of the detective's plain, unmarked car, I saw two men in black rain slicks lead her down the walkway and into the house. A few minutes later I heard a hollow, wrenching sound come from inside the house. It wasn't so much a scream as a low, painful wail. It was then that the older detective turned and spoke to me, although, until recently, I could not remember what he said.

Aunt Edna was at the blue car a few minutes later, her jaw set, her lips so tightly closed that when the young detective asked if she was 'the sister', she could only nod silently in response.

It would be many years before I saw what Aunt Edna saw that afternoon, my eyes lingering hypnotically on the body of my mother, how it was so carefully and respectfully laid out with perfect formality.

Other pictures showed that the same care had not been taken with my brother.

Jamie Edward Farris, age seventeen.

He was tall and lanky, with glistening black hair. In pictures, he appears rather thin, with a pale face and large, dark, nearly clownish lips. His eyes were a milky brown, like his mother's, with thin eyebrows, and short dark lashes. Like hers, Jamie's face gave the sense of having been composed of various parts selected from other faces, the eyes too dull and faded to go with the glossy black hair, the nose too flat to fit in with the high cheekbones and narrow forehead.

Jamie and I were typical 'older' and 'kid' brothers. We shared the same room, the same bunk beds. We often annoyed and frustrated each other. In the evening, we listened to music together, always records selected by Jamie, and sometimes played Chinese checkers on a bright tin board. From time to time, he would try to teach me things, the guitar on one occasion, and how to use a cue stick on another.

But despite all that, we were never really close. There was a sullenness in him, a sense of subdued explosion which kept me at arm's length. Wanting a room of his own, resentful that Laura had always had one, Jamie often made me feel unwelcome in his presence, as if I were an unwanted intrusion.

But even more than he resented me, Jamie resented my sister. 'Laura gets her own room because she's a girl,' he often sneered at those times when she would return home with some small school triumph. It was a maliciousness and envy of my sister which I didn't share and probably despised. In any event, I don't recall missing him a great deal after his death, certainly not in the way I missed Laura, longed for her and called her name at night.

Still, I do remember Jamie quite well. I remember that he often seemed listless, drowsy, the heavy lids drooping slowly as he sat at his desk, the head following not long after that, nodding almost all the way down to the open textbook before it bobbed up suddenly, and he began to study once again. More than anything, he seems to have been one of those people who feel estranged from their own existence. There were even times when he appeared to dangle above his own life, unable to touch ground, find direction, move in a way that he'd willed himself. Had he lived, I doubt that much would have come of him, for even as a boy, he seemed to have inherited that lethargy and lack of spirit that was so visible in the woman in the red housedress.

Even so, as I must add in a final qualification, he was not entirely in-animate. There were things that truly interested Jamie. He could spend long hours practicing his guitar, despite the fact that there was never any noticeable improvement in his ability to play it. He liked to fish, and he, Laura, and I would sometimes walk to the pond a half-mile or so from our house, cast our bait into the water and wait – usually for hours – before finally returning home with nothing. Even before Rebecca urged me back, I remembered those little fishing trips surprisingly well, the shade of the trees, the small boats that skirted across the nearly motion-less water, the bell on the ice cream truck that made three rounds per afternoon, even when the driver knew that on this particular stop, there'd be no customers but the Farris kids.

What else of Jamie?

Only a few scattered items. I remember him rushing to hide something in his desk as I came unexpectedly into the room we shared. I remember him breaking a guitar string and cursing, then, his anger quickly spent, meticulously stringing another.

And finally, there is this, which I remember more vividly than anything else, perhaps because it occurred only two days before he died. I was riding my bike down the block toward home when I saw him standing by the mailbox at the edge of our yard. I waved as I sped by, but he did not wave back. Instead, he continued staring, a little anxiously, up the street. He was clearly waiting for the postman to arrive, but I never learned what he was expecting in the mail. Perhaps it was a letter from a sweetheart we never knew about, or some item from a mail-order house that came three days later. Perhaps it was no more than a signed photograph from a movie star.

Whatever it was, Jamie was waiting for it nervously, and it was there that my mind had chosen to leave him, a figure waiting, tall and gangly, his black hair tangled and unwashed, his languid, nearly lightless eyes fixed expectantly on the road ahead. Better there, than sprawled across the floor of our little room, his face a bubbly mass of shattered flesh, the side of his head blown away, and hanging in a red, glistening flap over his hunched shoulder.

And finally, there was Laura.

As the years passed, I continued to remember her best of all. I remem-bered her with every sense impression. I remembered the sweet smell of her hair, how soft her hands were when they touched my face, the taste of her skin when I kissed her. I remembered the edginess and restless-ness that sometimes came into her voice, rebellion building in her like a wave.

Laura was sixteen. She had my father's black hair, as I do, but with features that were absolutely her own. Her eyes were dark brown, almost black when she walked beneath the shade, and her skin was a glowing white. Her lips were full and when she was cold, or when she cried, as she often did suddenly and explosively, for reasons I could not have fathomed, they turned a soft violet.

Even as a child, I recognized that there were powerful emotions in Laura. Something in her soul was always trembling. She seemed to stand on a ledge, looking down, at times with fear, at times with longing. Had she lived, I have sometimes thought, she might have ended up a teenage suicide. A great-aunt on her mother's side, Quentin later told me, had shot herself in a small cottage in Maine, and when he pulled a dusty family album from its ancestral shelf and pointed the woman out, the resemblance between the lost aunt and my sister was astonishingly deep. There was the same nervous tension in her eyes, the corners of the mouth drawn down along the same narrow lines, a certain stiffness and rigidity in the stance, as if rigor mortis were already setting in.

Remembering Laura now, the melancholy that at times consumed her, it's easy to see the ebb and flow of chemistry, to blame everything on the time of life she shared with my brother, he nearing the end of adolescence, she at its scorching core. But I believe that Laura suffered from more than a stage of development. There was something deeply wrong, askew, unbalanced. At night, she would often walk about the house, ghostly and forlorn, like some distraught maiden out of one of my mother's romance novels. To Jamie, it was an annoyance, and often, when he heard her footsteps in the hallway, he would yell at her harshly, demanding that she return to her room, then lean over the edge of his upper bunk, glance down at me, and rotate his index finger at the side of his head, whispering vehemently: 'She's nuts.'

Nuts, perhaps, to Jamie, but to me she was the most mysterious person in the world. The nightly rambling that irritated him, enchanted me. I sensed that there were secret regions in her, lost rooms, labyrinthine caverns. I know now that I was in love with my sister, and that the feelings I had for her, and even the way her memory still from time to time overwhelms me, that all of this was part of an early romantic attachment, a longing that I experienced as a natural adoration, something that all boys felt for their older sisters. I have since learned that it was no such thing, that the excitement which I felt in her presence, the way my breath stopped when I heard her pass my closed door, the way I stole glances even at her shadow on the wall, that all of this had its roots in the first inchoate gropings of desire.

I once said as much to Quentin. 'I loved my sister,' I told him. 'Yes, of course you did,' he said. 'No, Uncle Quentin,' I added pointedly, 'I *loved* my sister.' He waved his hand and laughed. 'You were only nine years old, Steve,' he said, then stood up and headed for the bathroom, something he always did when the conversation suddenly took a turn he didn't like.

But he knew.

I think he always knew that our house, the one with the dark green shutters and neat Tudor roof, held within its prim walls the most primitive and violent hopes, needs, and fears. And so he pulled me away from it, as if it were a whirling saw or an exposed electrical wire, snatched me away, and brought me north to the idyllic sterility of coastal Maine, to a landscape that seemed frozen in a rigid self-control. 'You have to keep a tight grip on everything,' he once told me. 'Remember what happens when you don't.'

Remember, in other words, my father.

William Patrick Farris, age forty-four.

What I could never fathom was how much Laura loved him, how powerfully she was drawn to him, how much she craved his admiration. Often, in her nightly wanderings, she would move down the stairs to the small solarium which led off from the living room. My mother had placed a few plants there, mostly indistinguishable green vines, along with two white wicker chairs and a glass-topped table. I remember seeing the two of them together in that room, sitting silently opposite each other in the early hours, light gathering outside, while their eyes remained steady, their faces nearly motionless, as if after hours of struggle, they'd finally come to a grave understanding. At those moments, they seemed to share a peculiar exhaustion, their eyes glassy from lost sleep, their skin pale, muscles limp from too much strain.

Even as a young boy, watching them secretively from my place at the top of the stairs, I had felt a mysterious connection between them. Their voices at such moments were always soft, and when they touched each other, it was with an eerie grace.

Later, I imagined that it was at these dawn meetings that she must have revealed herself to him, told him all those secrets she would never have told me.

And so, even before I came to hate my father for what he did to my family, I had envied his relationship with Laura, the whispery conclave the two of them shared, a society that excluded and infuriated me. I wanted to know exactly what kind of power he had over her, break the code by which they spoke to each other, usurp his place in her esteem.

A few weeks before she died, I saw them together in the solarium for the last time. Laura was sitting on the floor, her back pressed against my father's long, thin legs, her hands resting loosely in her lap while he sat above her in the white wicker chair, gazing out into the early morning light. For once, she looked rested, almost serene, her eyes opening and closing slowly as if she were about to fall asleep.

As for the way my father looked at that moment, I can only say that I'd never seen a man who looked more troubled. It was as if the very thing that had brought Laura such peace that morning had filled my father with an all but unbearable anguish.

Perhaps, even then, he had sensed how she would end.

This way: lying on her back, faceup, her white arms stretched over her head, splattered with blood, two fingers and half the palm of the right hand blown away, as if she'd thrust it toward him at the moment he had fired.

Her legs spread wide apart as if in a vulgar pose, her white bathrobe pulled upward from her soiled bare feet, revealing her thighs and a thin line of white cotton panties.

Her chest blown open, ribs shattered like bits of porcelain, her flesh torn and mangled as if a bomb had gone off behind her heart.

Her mouth flung open, red and gaping, giving her face an attitude of grave surprise, one corner of the white towel she'd wrapped around her wet hair hanging limply, almost clownishly, over a single, blue, wide-open eye.

Along with Jamie and my mother, Laura died at approximately four in the afternoon. It was almost two hours later that Mrs. Hamilton, a neighbor from across the street, saw my father walk out of the house, climb into the Ford station wagon, and drive away. He was wearing a black raincoat and an old floppy hat. He was not carrying anything, not so much as a small overnight bag.

During those long two hours in which he remained in the house, my father washed my mother's body, changed her into a pair of blue pajamas, and arranged her neatly on the bed. After that, he made a ham sandwich and ate it at the small table in the kitchen. I know it was his sandwich, because in the police photographs, there was a ring of raw onion on the side of the plate. No one but my father ate raw onion. He drank a cup of coffee, leaving both the plate and the cup in the sink as he always did, as if expecting them to be washed later, as normally they would have been.

He didn't pack anything, because he left with nothing; not so much as a pair of socks was missing from his closet.

He didn't reenter either Laura or Jamie's rooms. He made no attempt to clean up the frightful mess that had been made of them.

And yet, for no apparent reason, he remained in the house for a full two hours, alone, silent, surrounded by nothing but the bodies of his murdered wife and children.

What had he been waiting for?

When I became old enough to ponder that question seriously – I was probably around Laura's age, sixteen – I came up with a great many possibilities. He was waiting for some mysterious phone call. Or he was waiting to go to the airport at just the right time to catch some flight he'd booked weeks in advance. He was waiting to be picked up by gangsters, foreign agents, Communists. My own theory changed each time I considered the question.

Then, rather suddenly, on a spring day as I sat on a rock watching the waves, I arrived at the answer that had no doubt come to the police and Aunt Edna and Uncle Quentin long before, but which they'd kept to themselves, perhaps hoping that the question would never actually occur to me, that I would never seek its answer. But I did seek it, and it did come: he was waiting for me.

Once it had occurred to me, the answer was entirely obvious. Under ordinary circumstances, I would have been home from school by three-fifteen in the afternoon, just as Jamie and Laura would. But I'd gone to Bobby Fields's house instead, a play date my mother had known about all week, but of which my father knew nothing.

And so for nearly two hours my father had waited for me.

It's possible that he might have waited as long as necessary had not Mrs. Fields made two phone calls to the house on McDonald Drive. According to the statement she later gave police, she made the first call at around 5:30 P.M. When no one answered, she called again twenty minutes later. There was still no answer.

Five minutes or so after that last call, Mrs. Hamilton from across the street saw my father walk through the rain to the Ford station wagon, get in, and drive away.

A half hour later, Mrs. Fields decided, after a good deal of protest from Bobby and me, that she couldn't take me to the movies without getting parental permission first. She then drove directly to my house, and while Bobby and I remained in the back seat, she got out of the car and walked to the side entrance, which was nearest to the driveway, the one that led directly into the kitchen. She knocked at the door, glancing in as she did so, and saw a plate with a curl of raw onion and a coffee cup in the kitchen sink. Glancing idly to the left, she also saw a shotgun laid lengthwise across the small cutting board my mother kept in the corner beside the basement door.

I remember seeing her raise her hand to knock a second time, then stop, the hand motionless in the air, and turn back toward the car.

Before Rebecca, I remembered nothing else about that day except for the other car, the one with the two policemen in it, the older one turning toward me, drawing his glasses from his face, wiping the rain from the lenses with a white handkerchief, his lips parting to make a statement which, before Rebecca, time or shock had swept away.

# TWO

Even now, when I return to my dead family, it's always by way of my father. It's as if he stands at the gate of my memory, the border guard of a dark frontier.

It was a border I rarely approached during the years that followed the murders, a frontier I almost never entered. It was the 'terra incognito' of the medieval maps, the place where 'there be dragons', as the ancient cartographers declared.

And so, over the years, I had not looked back. Because of that, everything had faded – Jamie, my mother, even Laura to some degree. Only my father had remained in stark relief, grim and unfathomable, the ultimate enigma.

Of all the questions Rebecca later asked about him, she never asked the easiest one, the one for which my life had provided two different answers: *What did your father do?*

Until I was nine, the answer came quickly, without that momentary twinge of dread or embarrassment that later accompanied it. I simply replied that my father owned a hardware store.

I could remember the store very well. It was on Sycamore Street, and it had two large windows, which my father stuffed with anything that came to hand: hammers, saws, lengths of rope. In general, he stacked smaller items in the window to the right of the door, and larger ones, like enormous red tool-boxes or shiny aluminum ladders, in the one to the left. He took no pains to make the windows attractive, or to display the goods in any particular way. He simply lumbered absently from the back of the store, his arms filled with anything he'd found in reach, and deposited it all neatly, but randomly, in the front windows. As far as I recall, the only regard he ever paid was to the seasons. From time to time he would shove a wheelbarrow into the fall window, the perfect tool for gathering leaves. In winter he would replace it with the snow blower that would remain in the window for the next four months. Beyond that, he seems to have had no theme in mind, no organizing principle.

Inside the store, the usual implements and materials hung from the walls, such things as rakes, shovels, and axes. Smaller items were gathered in wooden bins, nails, bolts, lengths of coiled wire and the like. The only thing I ever noticed in the store that seemed out of place was the single Rodger and Windsor racing bicycle which my father kept in the left rear corner of the shop, cordoned off from everything else, as if it were only for display. It was a fancy touring bicycle, imported from England, and each time the latest model was sold, my father would replace it, tediously assembling it himself in the basement of our house, then transporting it to the store in the back of his small brown delivery van.

The Rodger and Windsor was the only kind of bike my father ever stocked. It was always red, and it never appeared to matter that he sold no more than three or four of them during the entire year. The fact is, he seemed to love it, or at least to feel for it some kind of strange devotion.

More than anything, I think now, he loved the process of putting it together. It was a difficult and painstaking labor, and he worked at it for many hours without stopping. It was strange to see him alone in the basement, stooped over a disconnected wheel, meticulously tightening each spoke, then turning the wheel, and methodically tightening each of them again. As a working style, it was completely different from his usual habit, which was hasty and sloppy and impulsive, the way he arranged the windows of the store or tossed different-sized nails into a common bin, everything done offhandedly, without a thought.

The look on his face was different, too. Normally, it was rather ex-pressionless, but when he worked on the Rodger and Windsor, it took on a wonderful intensity and concentration, as if he found something rapturous in the process of assembly. Perhaps in this, as in everything else, it was the building rather than the completion which attracted and sustained him.

In any event, I remember seeing him at work toward the end of October. The latest bike had arrived a week before, but he'd been occupied in trying to straighten out some entanglement with the Internal Revenue Service. The woman who'd done the store's books for several years had left a few weeks earlier, and without her, he'd been entirely at sea as he'd labored to give the IRS the information it had suddenly demanded. Normally, he would have set to work on the new Rodger and Windsor immediately, but because of the government paperwork, he'd been prevented from unpacking the bike for almost two weeks.

When he finally got to it, however, he went at it with the same persist-ence that he always applied to this task, working many hours at a time, always at night, with nothing but the single, naked bulb which hung above to help him make his hundreds of minute adjustments. I remember seeing him hunched over a length of bicycle chain, tapping at it with a small hammer, while his other hand caressed it with an eerie gentleness and affection. He was wearing his customary gray flannel shirt and trousers, and he had thrown the black sweater he often wore over the bike's chrome handlebars. It hung there like a dried animal skin while my father continued at his tapping, unaware that I stood not far away, poised, as he would be three weeks later, on the third step from the bottom.

For a long time, he didn't see me. Then, suddenly, he lifted his head and turned his eyes toward me, his gaze lingering on my face, but very dully, the way Jamie sometimes stared at his open textbook. For a time, his expression remained blank, the face of a mannequin in a shop window, colorless, with dim, unlighted eyes.

'Hi, Dad,' I said.

He didn't answer at first, but after a moment, he smiled very softly, then said in a low, broken voice, 'This is *all I want.*'

This is all I want.

Neither that evening, as I went back upstairs, nor in the years to come, did I ever give the slightest thought to what he might have meant by that. And yet, almost without my realizing it, it had always suggested to me that on that particular October night, a full three weeks before the murders, my father had already determined that we were going to die, that he was going to remove everything that stood between him and whatever it was he wanted out of life.

*What did your father do?*

After that day in November, the question took on a completely different significance. After that day, he could no longer be defined by what he 'did' for a living. He could no longer be reduced to the man in the hardware store on Sycamore Street. What he 'did' was kill his family.

But as I'd watched Mrs. Fields walk to the kitchen door, knock, start to knock again, but grow rigid instead, then return to the car, I hadn't realized that the strained, tortured look on her face was the same one I would see from now on when I answered the question truthfully. What did your father do? He killed my mother, my sister, and my brother, then waited in the kitchen to kill me.

It was all in Mrs. Fields's face that afternoon, the world's response to my father, the dread and horror his image would conjure up forever.

I could see her eyes in the rearview mirror as she wheeled the car into her own driveway, tense, darting, as if desperately trying to avoid her own terrible conjectures. Bobby was bouncing playfully on the seat beside me, the rain blowing against the car window, pounding at it with huge gray drops. Mrs. Fields opened the back door and pulled him out, almost violently, so that he squealed 'Mom,' then ran into the house. I looked at her curiously, trying to determine if I'd done anything to cause the strain and alarm I could see in her face. She lifted her hand toward me, the painted red fingernails like little arrows of light in the shadowy interior of the car.

'Come out, Stevie,' she said, still offering her hand.

I took it reluctantly, let it tug me out into the rain, then bolted for the front door of the house. Bobby was waiting for me down the hall. He motioned me into his room. He didn't bother to close the door, and so I could hear Mrs. Fields on the phone a few feet away. She was clearly distressed. She was calling for help.

For help, but not for the police. She called Mrs. Hamilton instead. I could hear her voice, hesitant, restrained, and although I can't be sure that I gathered the words in exactly, I know the kind of call it was:

'Hello, Jane? This is Mary Fields.'

'Oh, hi, Mary.'

'Jane, I was just over at Dottie Farris's house. Stevie is with me, and I was bringing him home. And well ... I went to the door, the one at the kitchen, and I saw ...'

It was only at that moment, Mrs. Hamilton would say later, that she remembered the three muffled booms that had swept through the sheeting rain that afternoon, the second rapidly following the first, the third coming several minutes later.

Several minutes.

What, during those several minutes, did Mrs. Hamilton, the gray, overweight wife of the town's only Presbyterian minister, think was going on across the street at 417 McDonald Drive?

Several minutes.

Later, when I began my search, I read those two words in the thick file which the Somerset, New Jersey, Police Department finally allowed me to see: 'Witness stated that although the second shot followed closely after the first, there was a duration of several minutes between the second and final shots.'

And then this: 'Witness stated that the television program *Queen for a Day* had just ended, and therefore estimates the time of the last shot at between 3:55 and 4:00 P.M. EST.'

And so, all across the Eastern Seaboard, *Queen for a Day*, with its bilious host and tacky audience applause meter, had just ended when the last member of my family died.

*What did your father do?*

Years later, looking at a series of police photographs while two uniformed officers watched me warily from the other side of the room, I tried to reconstruct the grim choreography of my family's murder:

From them it seemed clear that Jamie had been the first to die. In the pictures, a set of bloody tracks lead from Jamie's room down the upstairs corridor to Laura's. She'd probably been near the window when she heard first the deafening roar which came from Jamie's room, then footsteps moving down the corridor, and last the sound of her own door as it opened toward her. Reflexively she turned toward it, and saw my father standing there, the barrel of his shotgun lowering toward her. Against its blast, she raised her hand, perhaps to shield her face, or perhaps in a pleading motion which he immediately refused.

From Laura's room, the tracks, still thick with blood, lead directly to the room opposite Laura's, the master bedroom, the one with the floral curtains. He must have found it empty, because my mother was not killed in that room. There were no spattered walls, no blood-soaked carpet for the police to photograph in that dimly lighted bedroom.

The tracks head back down the corridor, down the stairs, into the living room, and through it to the small solarium, where they move into it a little way, then turn and head out again. It is a line of trajectory which could only mean one thing. That my mother was trying to escape, but witlessly, never thinking of leaving the house, too passive even to make that final domestic break.

The tracks then move back through the living room, a little wider now, for he is searching for her desperately, taking longer steps, perhaps in fear, or rage. Certainly, he is moving faster.

The tracks are seen in the dining room next, then in the kitchen. Still, she eludes him. He wheels around, leaving a slender mark on the tile floor to indicate the fierceness of his turn, how for just an instant, he lifted almost entirely from the ground, whirling on the backs of his heels.

The tracks move again, toward the door that leads to the basement, then down the wooden stairs toward its flat cement floor. At the third step from the bottom, they stop.

Because of the hard rain which had been falling for hours by late that afternoon, water had seeped into the basement, a small lake gathering near the middle of the room. My mother passed through that puddle several times, her watery trail making a bizarre and illogical pattern on the cement floor. Perhaps she ran about, zigzagging in her terror, while he stood on the third step, laboring to bring her into his sights.

At last, she came to rest in a back corner, behind the huge cardboard box in which she'd once stored our Christmas decorations. It was there that he raked her with a third and final blast.

All of this, then, was what my father did.

And in the years that followed, it was to this single horrendous act

I had reduced him. All his life had collapsed into a single savage and explosive instant. I couldn't imagine his life before or after it. My father was frozen forever as he had stood upon that third step, his shoes still glistening brightly with my brother's and my sister's blood.

But there had been a life before that one murderous instant. Not a great life. Not a life of high achievement, or even noble failure. But a life nonetheless, the kind that most of us live, plain but sturdy, building day by day a structure that holds up.

My father, as I came to discover, was a country boy. Throughout all his early years, he lived on a small farm in rural New York. Each day, he did the chores common to children on a farm. He gathered eggs, milked cows, cleared the weeds that sprouted intransigently among the neatly proportioned rows of the family garden. In the summer he swam in the great blue lake several miles away. In the fall he went to a country school named for Daniel Webster where he learned to read and write sufficiently to carry out the basic tasks of life. Later, when he was fourteen, he transferred to the high school in the nearby town of Highfield. It was named for a local boy who'd died in the Spanish-American War, and my father graduated from it at somewhere near the middle of his class in June of 1931. In the class photograph, taken at the town ball field on graduation day, he is positioned on the back row, the fifth boy from the left, his black hair greased back, staring at the camera with an ordinary smile. Inside the high school yearbook for that same year, a slender volume made of cheap paper and bound in leatherette, and which I found in one of the boxes I inherited from Aunt Edna, he is said to have been a member of the baseball team. A picture shows him individually, dressed in a flat black suit and bow tie, his nickname printed underneath: *Town Crier.*

Town Crier. What had his classmates meant by that? Was there something in him that suggested warning and alarm, a sense of being startled from one's sleep? Had the faces of his classmates ever grown taut as they stared into my father's youthful eyes? When some of them later read of what he did, were there a few among them who had not been surprised?

I wondered about his parents, too. In photographs they are a sturdy, farming couple, plain in that way that makes plainness seem beautiful, noble, and even a little superior to more sophisticated and elaborate things. At night, when the lights were out, and they lay together in the darkness, had they ever voiced the slightest concern for some odd look or disturbing word they'd noticed in their only son?

During all his early years, my father lived with his parents on the same small farm. It was nestled in a grove of trees, with a broad expanse of field on either side. The house still stands, and only a few weeks before Rebecca, I visited it for the first time. Peter, my nine-year-old son, had spent the summer at a camp in upstate New York, and around the middle of August, Marie and I drove up to the camp to pick him up and bring him back home. I had a Volvo station wagon then, and we piled all his belongings into it and headed back toward Connecticut.

I hadn't intended to visit the little house where my father grew up, but on the way to the expressway I saw a small sign for Highfield. I recognized the name, although I'd never been there. My father's parents had died within a year of each other when he was only twenty-five, and evidently he'd never felt the need to visit the farm after that. I don't think he ever took my mother there, or Jamie or Laura. At his parents' death, it appeared to have dissolved from his mind.

But it hadn't dissolved from mine, and according to the sign, it was only twelve miles away. Even so, I continued straight ahead, expecting to turn onto the expressway well before I reached the town. It was Marie who stopped me, looking quizzically in my direction only a few seconds after we passed the sign.

'Highfield,' she said finally, her eyes drifting over to me. 'Isn't that the town your father came from?'

I nodded silently and kept driving.

'He was born there, right?'

'On a little farm right outside it.'

'When did he leave?'

'When he graduated from high school, I think.'

Marie turned back toward the road. She knew about my father, of course, and I think that something in him, his sudden, inexplicable murderousness, had always interested her. Early on, she'd asked a great many questions about what he was like, probing like an amateur, somewhat Freudian detective, looking for *the reason*, as if there were some twisted secret in his past, which, if unearthed, would bring everything to light.

'Wouldn't you like to see the house?' she asked after a moment.

'Why would I want to do that?'

'Because he was your father,' she answered.

I glanced in her direction. 'I think you're the one who wants to see it.'

She shook her head. 'No. You do.' She smiled. 'It's only natural. Why don't we drop by?'

I shrugged. 'Okay,' I said.

And so I didn't get on the expressway that afternoon, but headed toward Highfield, then drove through it, searching for the small road that Quentin had long ago described, a road that wound off to the right at the end of a stone wall.

The road came up shortly, looking like little more than a cattle trail through a green field. A narrow sign marked it with the words I'd seen on the letters my father had written to his parents during the brief time he'd lived in New York City: Lake Road.

I slowed as I neared the sign, stopped just before I got to it and looked at Marie. I remember very well the clipped, undramatic exchange that followed:

'Should I?'

'Why not? ... It's just a house.'

And so it was. Just a house, run-down a bit, but otherwise as I might have expected. The yard was neatly mowed, and a line of flowers had been planted along the small walkway which led to the front door. Two large trees kept the grounds heavily shaded. It had a gravel driveway, but no garage, and as I got out of the car, I could see an old wooden fence, weathered and dilapidated, which, I suppose, my father had helped build.

I left Marie and Peter in the car, walked up the small walkway to the house and knocked at the door. The woman who answered it was middle-aged, plump, her hair pinned up behind her head. She was wiping her hands with a dishcloth bordered with small red flowers.

'Hello,' I said.

She nodded, neither friendly nor unfriendly, simply curious to know who I was.

'My name is Steven Farris,' I told her.

'Uh-huh,' she said.

'This is a little strange,' I added, 'but years ago my ...' I choked briefly on the word, but nonetheless got it out. '... father lived here, in this house.'

The woman smiled. 'Oh,' she said and, without another word, swung open the door. 'I guess you'd like to see it then.'

'Well, I don't want to disturb you.'

'No, not at all,' the woman said. She leaned out the door slightly. 'That your family?' she asked, eyeing the people in the Volvo.

'Yes.'

'They want to come in?'

'I guess so,' I told her, then turned and waved Marie and Peter toward the house.

We were only there for a short time. Marie engaged the woman in conversation, the two of them finally heading up to the second floor, while Peter sat indifferently in the foyer, lost in one of his electronic games.

And so, for a moment, I was alone in my father's house. Not alone physically, of course, but alone in the way that I could look at it without distraction.

At first, I wandered into the living room, glancing at the old fireplace, the neatly arranged furniture, the varnished wooden floor. A great number of family photos hung from the walls, sons in uniform, daughters in communion dresses, and later, grown older now, these same boys and girls with strangers at their sides, children on their knees, the boys with moustaches or thinning hair, the girls with wrinkled eyes. Time went forward on the wall, and hair retreated even more, faces grew more slack. The children left their parents' knees to dress in uniforms and bridal gowns, choose strangers from a world of strangers, have children of their own.

'Steve, you want to look upstairs?'

It was Marie's voice. She was standing on the staircase, leaning over the rail. 'His room must have been up here,' she said.

I headed toward her, walking up the stairs, touring the house now as if it were a black museum, my father's room cordoned off as Washington's or Lincoln's might have been, all the furniture in place, but with an atmosphere altogether different, sinister and grave.

Marie was standing at the end of the short corridor, poised beside an open door, the woman standing beside her, smiling sweetly.

'This must have been it,' Marie said. 'There are only two bedrooms up here, and the other one's big, so it must have been for his parents.'

It was the amateur detective at work again, and as I walked to where Marie stood like a guide waiting for a straggling tourist, I remember resenting how flippantly she had come to regard the story of my father, treating it more as a childhood tale, an imagined horror. Of course, I'd been partly to blame for that, answering her questions matter-of-factly, without emotion, like a reporter who'd covered the story, rather than a child who'd lived it. Perhaps, because of that, she'd come to think that the whole dark history meant little to me, that I no longer felt its grisly power.

And yet, for all that, Marie didn't go in my father's room, but remained outside, waiting in the corridor.

I have often wondered why. Was there something in that tiny room that warned her away, the ghost of the black-haired boy his friends called *Town Crier*?

In any event, I went in alone, stood on the circular hooked carpet at the center of the room, and turned slowly to take it in. I felt nothing. Everything that might have given me some sense of my father had long ago been removed. His bed was gone, along with whatever he might have tacked to the walls, maps or photographs or pennants. If he'd ever had a desk or chair, they were gone as well. In their place, the new owner had put a small worktable and wooden stool. The table was covered with spools of different-colored yarn, along with an assortment of needles and brass clips. 'I make things for the crafts fairs we have up here,' the woman said as she stepped up beside me. Then, glancing about the room, she added, 'It makes a nice little work space, don't you think?' She smiled. 'Very cozy.'

She offered coffee and cake after we'd all gone back downstairs, but neither Marie nor I felt inclined to take her up on it. Instead, we thanked her for her generosity, returned to the car, and headed home, the old house growing small in my rearview mirror before it finally vanished behind a sudden curve.

It was dark by the time we reached Old Salsbury. Peter was asleep in the back seat. I took him up the stairs and laid him on his bed, then sat down beside him and ran my fingers through his hair. I had seen my father do the same to me, and certainly he'd done it to Laura and Jamie as well. There had been a gentleness in him, a guardianship and care. That murder might finally flow from such a source seemed inconceivable to me.

I left Peter to his sleep, and walked across the hallway to where Marie sat at her dressing table, applying her nightly oils and creams. I took off my clothes, placing everything neatly on the little wooden valet which stood on my side of the bed, and crawled beneath the covers. The sheets were very cool, as I prefer them, but later Marie drew in beside me, her body heating them, so that I pulled away from her, finally edging myself precariously toward the far side of the bed.

I rarely dream, or if I do, I rarely remember my dreams. But that night I had not so much a dream as what I would call a visitation. It was not a visit from my father. There was no shotgun-toting figure moving toward me from the depths of a smoky corridor, the subject of my childhood nightmares. In fact, there was no one in my dream at all. At least, no one but myself. And yet, it was so powerfully rendered, so elaborately detailed, that I could easily recall it the following morning.

In the dream, I awakened slowly, rather than the way I usually do, with a sudden start. It was a luxurious restfulness from what appeared to have been a state of great exhaustion. The dream gave no hint as to what had tired me so, but only that I had slept a long time, and was now rising with a natural and unhurried rhythm.

The room was very bright, but it was not my room, nor any room in which I'd ever been. It seemed a bit drab, but also strangely atmospheric, so that I felt completely at home in it, as if living there were my natural state. There was a large wooden bureau, the plain metal bed on which I had slept, and a sink. A pair of wrinkled towels hung over each side of the sink, and a slender full-length mirror hung from the wall beside it.

In my dream, I got to my feet languidly and walked toward the window. On the way, I glanced at the mirror. What I saw did not alarm me. I had about a three-day growth of beard, and I was wearing a white, sleeveless T-shirt and baggy brown trousers. I was barefoot, but I could see a pair of old shoes beneath the bed, one set of laces a little frayed, but otherwise in good repair.

At the window, I parted a pair of ragged white curtains and looked out. The sun was very bright, and I remember sensing that it was midday. Beyond the window, there was a large, dusty city, a conglomeration of rust-colored shingled roofs and distant church towers. In the streets below, I could see signs written in a foreign language, and hear men laughing in an outdoor tavern. Over their laughter, I could make out the sound of guitars, strummed softly by men I could not see, and the lilting cry of what I took for a wooden flute.

I awoke while still standing at the window. Nothing at all happened in the dream. And yet, it awakened me, not languidly, but with the usual sense of being startled. Dawn had not broken, and so I felt my way through the continuing darkness until I made it into the hallway. I switched on the light, walked past Peter's room, then down the stairs to the kitchen. There was a can of soda in the refrigerator, which I opened and poured into the huge mug Peter had given me the previous Christmas, porcelain with German figures on it, smiling milkmaids and old men in lederhosen.

I drank silently, the dream still lingering in my mind, as if it were an afterimage which needed only a bit more time to fade. But as the minutes passed, and I followed the first soda with a second, it still held its place in my mind, all its details fully intact, everything from the tiniest scratches I had seen on the old bureau to the notes I'd heard played on the flute I'd never seen.

I couldn't finish the second soda, and after a while, I walked back upstairs, crawled into bed again, twisted about uncomfortably for a few minutes, then returned to the kitchen. I switched on the light, and as I did so, my eyes caught on the half-filled mug I'd put in the sink. It sat near the drain, upright, but out of place, just as my father's unfinished cup of coffee had rested in nearly the same position on that November day, as if waiting still for Mrs. Fields to see it. It was then that it struck me that the dream had come from him, that it was a message – although still cryptic and unreadable – from my father.

*What did your father do?*

Even that night, after the visit to my father's house and the dream that followed it, even then, it was still someone else's question.

It was Bobby Fields's question when we met the first day of first grade, and to which I'd been able to give the simple reply that I would lose forever in only a few years: 'He owns a hardware store.'

It was Jerry Flynn's question when I was ten, and living in Maine, and when he asked it, he meant Uncle Quentin, whom he assumed to be my father.

It was Sally Peacock's question when I went out on my first date and had to explain, because there seemed no way to avoid it, that my father had left me years before and so, at the moment, I had no idea what he 'did'.

It was Marie's question that long night we first made love, and I told her in full and ghastly detail exactly what my father had done on that November day.

And at last, as it must always be with sons, it was my question, too.

# THREE

The usual breakfast atrocities occurred the Monday morning after we brought Peter back from camp. Peter dropped or spilled nearly everything he touched, and Marie became increasingly exasperated with him, finally screaming at his back as he trudged, hunched and angry, out into the backyard.

Once he'd left, she turned her wrath on me, her eyes narrowing lethally, as if taking aim.

'Why don't you ever say anything to him?' she demanded harshly. 'Why do I have to do all the yelling?'

'I don't care what he spills,' I told her with a shrug. 'It doesn't matter to me.'

It was a reply which only concentrated her anger by focusing it on me.

'It's because you don't have to clean it up,' she shot back. 'If you had to clean it up, then you'd care.'

I started to offer something in return, but she whirled around and strode out of the kitchen, tossing a wadded paper towel into the plastic garbage can beside the door.

It was typical of Marie to storm out of a room rather than engage in a longer confrontation. Even our first real argument had been a clipped and stifled affair, again with Marie leaving rapidly, this time from a car, but with the same air of unavoidable flight. Over the years I'd come to think of it as a way of avoiding some invisible line she feared to cross, a form of self-control.

I left around fifteen minutes later, waving to Peter as I headed for the car. He sat, slumped in a chair beside the pool, and as I went by, he waved back halfheartedly, then offered a knowing smile, as if we were allies in some war we waged against the central woman in our lives.

I backed slowly out of the driveway, glancing only briefly toward the house. I could see Marie at the window of our bedroom on the second floor. She'd thrown open the curtains and was standing in the full morning light, her arms folded tightly below her breasts, so that their round upper quarters were lifted and exposed beneath the partly open gown. It was a stance my mother would never have assumed, and I remember thinking, as I pulled out of the driveway, that for 'poor Dottie' bedroom curtains were meant to be tightly closed. As for the woman poised behind them, a plain red housedress would do just fine.

There were other differences between Marie and my mother, as well, and on the way to my office that morning, I silently, and almost unconsciously, catalogued them.

Marie was stern and demanding, while my mother had suffered from a general lack of will, one so severe, I think, that it had even prevented her from disciplining her children. Thus, instead of ordering us to do things, help around the house, choose the proper clothes, keep our mouths shut when others were talking, she'd simply allowed us to find our own way through the maze, directionless and uninstructed.

Unlike Marie, who was self-assured and confident in her abilities and opinions, my mother had seemed to doubt her own adulthood, doubt even those of its prerogatives which my father had taken for granted and exercised with full authority.

My father.

The memory that suddenly returned him to me that morning, as I drove to work, appeared ordinary enough at first. It was clear and vivid, the setting laid out perfectly in my mind:

We had all been in the backyard, Laura and I tossing a ball back and forth while Jamie lounged in a small yard chair, leafing through some sort of sports magazine. As the minutes passed, the pitches became wilder and faster, with Laura lobbing the ball toward me at weird angles, or heaving it in a high and uncontrolled arc over all our heads.

Inevitably, one of her throws went way off, the ball crashing down onto Jamie's magazine, knocking it first into his lap, then onto the ground.

The ball startled and frightened him, and his sudden panic had no doubt embarrassed him as well, and so he leaped to his feet, angrily strode across the yard, grabbed Laura by the shoulders, and started screaming at her. She fought back, pushing him away violently and yelling into his face. I ran over to her, trying to get between the two, and started screaming just as loudly.

We were still going at it when we heard the door open at the back of the house and saw our father step out onto the small veranda which overlooked the backyard. He didn't say a word, but only stood, his hands holding firmly to the railing of the veranda, as he peered down at us.

All our attention was trained upon him, all our eyes lifted up, as if he were descending from the clouds. A complete silence fell over the backyard as the three of us stood in place, saying nothing, only watching him as he watched us during that brief, oddly delicious instant before he turned and walked away.

What had we felt at that moment?

As a child, it would have been impossible for me to say. But that morning, as I unexpectedly recalled this single incident with all the detail of something that had happened only minutes before, it seemed to me that I had felt the sweet and awesome luxury of a hand that stayed my hand. I had sensed my father's restraining firmness, and because of it, perhaps because of nothing more than his exercise of it, I had loved him deeply and inexpressibly. The solitary killer who'd crouched beneath that mask of paternal care and responsibility had never appeared to me. Instead, I'd glimpsed only that part of him that was beautiful and grave and unreachable, that figure of a father, steadfast and enduring, that all men wish to have and wish to be.

And so, it struck me that morning that my father's life had to have been a vast deception, a lie he'd lived in while he'd lived with us, harboring whatever resentment and bitterness it was that had finally boiled over on that day in November.

I was still thinking about him when I got to the office a few minutes later.

The architectural offices of Simpson and Lowe were on the top floor of a five-story cubicle structure made of steel and tinted glass. It was a purely functional design, and no one but Mr. Lowe, the firm's sole surviving founder, ever liked it. Over the years the rest of us had either resented it or been embarrassed by it, thinking it a rather unimaginative structure, unlikely to impress prospective clients, especially those who might be interested in more innovative designs for their own projects.

But despite all our criticism, Mr. Lowe had remained firm in his commitment to it, stubbornly holding on out of loyalty to its aging pipes and circuits, its squeaky hinges and buckling tile. Wally had been arguing for years that we should move the whole operation to the new business center north of the city, but Mr. Lowe had always refused, shaking his head with that enormous dignity he still maintained despite the palsy that rocked his hands. 'Don't abandon things,' he once told Wally scoldingly at the end of one of these discussions. Then he rose and left the room, knowing that Wally remained behind to mutter against him resentfully, but wholly indifferent to anything he might say, as if all his malicious whisperings were nothing more than a light desert breeze.

Wally was already at his desk, meticulously going over the details for a new office building, when I arrived that morning.

'Another day at the venerable old firm,' he said with a wink as I passed his desk.

I'd worked as an architect for Simpson and Lowe for almost fifteen years by then, and I realize now that it was no accident that I chose architecture as my profession, even though I had no great ability at geometry or drawing or any of the other skills the work requires. Rather, I chose it because it fulfilled an abiding need, appealed to one of the deeper strains of my character, my desperate need for order. For all its creativity, architecture is finally about predictability. It runs on what is known, rather than what is not. In a fully executed building, one knows with a comforting certainty exactly what the materials will do, their durabilities, the precise level of strain which each can bear and still hold on to its essential shape and function. It is a world which has no room for chance, which has doggedly eliminated the speculative and hypothetical from its principal calculations. Reality is its basis. It makes room for nothing else.

Before Rebecca, it was home.

I was working at my desk, when Wally appeared before me, a peculiar expression on his face.

'There's someone here to see you, Steve,' he said. 'Rebecca something. I lost the last name. I think I was in a daze.'

'What are you talking about?'

'Go see for yourself.'

She was in the small waiting room, seated on a dark red sofa, her face very serious as she rose. She put out her hand and I shook it as she introduced herself, her voice deep but not masculine, a fine, somber voice, though somewhat edgy, distant, intensely formal.

'My name is Rebecca Soltero,' she said.

'Steve Farris. Did we have an appointment?'

'No, we didn't,' Rebecca answered. 'I believe in doing things face-to-face. That's why I didn't call or write you first.'

She was very direct, a woman with a mission, though I had no idea what it was.

'What can I do for you?' I asked.

'I've come about your father.'

She could not have said a stranger thing, nor one more utterly unexpected. It was as if he had suddenly materialized again, magically, in the form of a beautiful woman.

'My father?'

For an instant, I thought perhaps the police or the FBI, or some other agency, had actually begun to look for him again, had, in a moment of unconscious whimsy, assigned an alluring woman to track him down, bring him back, and make him pay, at last, for what he'd done to his family.

219

'But you must know that my father ...'

'Yes. That's why I want to talk to you,' Rebecca said. 'I'd like to hear what you remember about him.'

'Why?'

'I'm writing a book about men who've killed their families,' she said.

It was strange, but until that moment, I'd never thought of my father as one of a type, a member of some definable human subcategory. Instead, he'd always come to me as a lone wolf, cut from the pack and set adrift by the awesome nature of his crime. I'd never seen anything in him that suggested a common thread, a link with the rest of us.

'I've already done a lot of work,' Rebecca added, 'particularly with one of the men who investigated the case.' She stepped back slightly, as if to get a better view of me, or the room, or something else she might later want to describe. 'You probably remember him,' she said. 'He remembers that you sat in the back seat of the car and that it was raining.'

I could see the silver bird as the rain crashed down upon its outstretched wings.

'His name is Swenson,' Rebecca went on, 'and he remembers turning around and saying something to you.'

At that instant, I remembered everything exactly as it had happened that day. I saw the black arms of the windshield wipers as they floated rhythmically over the rain-swept glass, the curling smoke that came from the other one's cigar, the big, white face as it turned toward me, Swenson's pudgy pink thumb gently rubbing the lenses beneath a slightly soiled white handkerchief, his voice low, wheezy: *One day you'll be all right again.*

'He had red hair,' I blurted suddenly.

'It's more of an orange-white now,' Rebecca said. 'His health is not very good.'

She described him briefly. Despite his illness, he was still large, she said, with very intense green eyes. He had a gentle manner, but she had sensed great reserves of fortitude and courage. She said that he'd looked long and hard for my father, had followed scores of leads, but that finally, after several years, he'd been told to let it drop, that there was no more money to pursue an unsolvable case. He'd retired not long after that, his health failing steadily, so that during her interview with him, he'd sat near an oxygen tank, taking quick breaths through a plastic mask. It was a condition that reminded me of Quentin's final days.

'My uncle died like that,' I told her. 'Some sort of respiratory thing.'

'That would be Quentin Coleman, the man you lived with in Maine?'

'That's right.'

Rebecca said, 'I know it's sudden, the way I've just shown up here at your office, but I hope you don't mind.' She paused, then added, 'I'd like to talk to you for a longer time. It's up to you, of course.'

'To tell you the truth, Miss Soltero,' I said, 'I don't know if I could be of much help to you. I was only nine years old when it happened.'

'But you remember your father, don't you?'

'No, not much.'

She looked at me very intently. 'Are you sure?' she asked.

It was more than a question, and even at that moment I recognized that part of it was a challenge, and part an accusation, the notion that if I didn't help her unearth my father's crime, then I was, to some degree, a partner in it, his cowardly accomplice.

'Would you be willing to meet me again, Mr. Farris?' Rebecca asked directly.

She had drawn the line in the dust. Now it was up to me either to cross it or drift back, draw away from her, but even more critically, to draw away from my father, to close the door forever in his ghostly face. There was something in such a grave finality that I couldn't do.

'Well, I guess we could talk,' I replied, 'but I still don't think I'll be able to remember much.'

Rebecca smiled quietly and put out her hand. 'Thank you,' she said. 'I'll call you.'

She left directly after that, and I went back to my desk and began working up a preliminary design for a small library in neighboring Massachusetts.

Within an hour the clouds had broken. From my desk I watched the morning air steadily brighten until it reached a kind of sparkling purity at midday.

I ate my lunch in the park, watching the swans drift along the edges of the pond, until Wally suddenly plopped down beside me, stretched out his thick, stubby legs, and released a soft belch.

'Oops. Sorry, Stevie,' he said. 'It's the spaghetti. It always repeats on me.' He patted his stomach and went on about other foods that had the same effect upon him – popcorn, melon, a vast assortment – until, near the end of a long list, he stopped, his eyes fixed on a figure he saw moving along the far edges of the pond. 'Well, I'll be damned,' he said wonderingly. 'Christ, that's her, Steve.'

'Who?'

'Hell, it's been ten years. I don't know her name right off.'

'Who are you talking about?'

'That woman, there.'

He nodded, and I glanced over in the direction he indicated. I could see a tall, thin woman as she strolled beside the water. She was wearing a plain, dark blue dress. Her hair had once been very dark, but was now streaked with gray. Her skin looked very pale, almost powdery, as if she were slowly disintegrating.

'Yolanda, that's it,' Wally blurted. 'Yolanda Dawes.'

'Who is she?'

'You kidding me, Steve?' Wally asked unbelievingly. 'Hell, man, she's the evil home-wrecker, the menace on the road.'

'What are you talking about?'

'She's the broad that killed Marty Harmon.'

I turned toward her as if she were a creature out of myth, the scarlet woman of immemorial renown. She'd reached the far end of the pond by then, the bright midday light throwing a dazzling haze around her as she strolled along its smooth, rounded edge.

Wally had returned to deeper interests, plucking at his nails with a tiny clipper. 'Even way back then, she never struck me as something to get all that worked up about,' he said absently. 'But she sure killed old Marty Harmon, just as sure as if she'd put a bullet in his head.'

I hadn't thought of Marty in years, but it was not hard to conjure him up again. We'd come to work for Simpson and Lowe at nearly the same time, and although he was older than I, we'd both been novices at the firm. Because of that we'd socialized together, usually going out for an hour or so after work on Fridays, a custom that neither Marie nor Marty's wife had ever seemed to mind.

Marty's wife was named LeAnn. Before marrying Marty, she'd spent most of her life in Richmond, Virginia. They'd met while Marty was in the navy, married, then moved north, where Marty felt more comfortable. By the time he joined Simpson and Lowe, they'd had two children, a boy of eleven and a girl of nine. I don't recall their names, but only that they were both strikingly blond. By now their hair has darkened. In all likelihood, they have married, and have children of their own. Perhaps, had I kept in touch, I might have been of some assistance to them, since, like me, they were destined to grow up without a father.

As a fellow-worker and, to some extent, a friend, Marty was self-effacing, witty, and very kind. He was not a terribly ambitious man, and he might never have become a partner. But he was highly competent, great with detail, organizational and otherwise, and socially adept enough never to embarrass himself or anyone else by his behavior at office parties or other business functions.

Our favorite place was Harbor Lights, a little bar-restaurant on the outskirts of town. The interior was decked out like the inside of an old whaling boat, complete with oars, coils of thick gray rope, and a few rusty harpoons. For almost two years, we went there at least two Friday evenings out of each month. We talked business and office gossip, the usual end-of-the-week banality. Marty seemed to enjoy the time we spent together, loosening his tie, and sometimes even kicking off his black, perfectly polished shoes. We talked about sports a great deal, and sometimes about our families. Marie was pregnant by then, a child we later lost to miscarriage in its second month, and Marty sometimes fell into the role of the older, more experienced man, warning me of the changes that would inevitably come with fatherhood.

'But all the changes are worth it,' he told me cheerfully, 'because being a father, it's a different kind of love.'

He was always reassuring, and even after the miscarriage he continued to talk about parenthood, clearly encouraging me to try again.

Then, without a word, our Friday meetings came to an end. At first I thought that, after two years, Marty and I had simply come to that point when there was nothing more to discuss and so had drifted in other directions.

I might have felt that way forever if LeAnn hadn't called me three months later. It was just past midnight on a Friday, and her voice was strained.

'Steve, have you seen Marty tonight?'

'No.'

'You didn't meet him at that restaurant you go to?'

'No, LeAnn. Why?'

She didn't say. She never said. But something in the tone of her voice that night suggested to me that the snake which seems to lie coiled at the center of so many lives had suddenly struck out at her.

'LeAnn, has something happened?'

She didn't answer.

'LeAnn? Are you all right?'

'Yes,' she said, then immediately hung up.

She'd lied, of course. She wasn't all right. She'd dropped from girlhood into womanhood as if through a scaffold floor. 'Boys come to manhood through mastery,' Rebecca would write years later, 'girls come to womanhood through betrayal.' So it was with LeAnn Harmon.

The following Monday, I found Marty already at the office when I arrived. He looked haggard, his shoulders slumped, as if under heavy weights, as he shambled toward me.

'LeAnn said she called you,' he said. 'What did you tell her?'

'What could I tell her, Marty?'

He nodded helplessly. 'I should have mentioned something to you, Steve. I'm sorry you got pulled into it.'

'I didn't know what to do.'

'No, of course not,' Marty said. 'There's nothing you could have done.'

He walked wearily to his desk, then pulled himself in behind it. He didn't speak to me again that day, and only rarely after that, as if I'd become a source of embarrassment to him, something he'd rather have been rid of.

For the next month, Marty worked steadily and well, but during those intervals when he wasn't completely engaged, he looked lost and distracted. At noon, he would wander into the small park across from the office and take his lunch alone. From the window beside my desk, I could see him on the little wooden bench beside the pond, dressed in dark pants and a white shirt, the sleeves rolled up to the elbow, the black-rimmed glasses like a mask over his eyes.

I talked to Marty for the last time about three weeks later. It was at our old haunt, Harbor Lights. I found him sitting alone at a booth near the back. He was smoking a cigarette, his other hand wrapped around a glass of scotch. The jacket of his suit lay in a disordered lump beside him, and he'd yanked his tie down and unbuttoned the top two buttons of his shirt.

'You know what the trouble with men like us is, Steve?' he asked. 'We think we can handle anything.' He leaned forward, squinting in my direction. 'But there is a force, my friend,' he said with a sudden vehemence. 'There is a force that none of us can handle.'

I never asked him what that force was, and after a while, he finished his drink, took a long draw on his last cigarette, then got to his feet and walked away, giving my arm a quick, comradely squeeze as he headed for the door.

There was a small hotel a few blocks from Harbor Lights. It had a neat mid-Atlantic design, all wood and white paint, with bright red shutters. The door had panes of inlaid glass and the sign which hung beside it showed a teenage boy in Colonial dress, red vest and tri-corner hat, a snare drum hanging at his side.

At 11:15 A.M. the following day, Marty checked into room 304 of that hotel. Twenty minutes later, he shot himself.

Marty was buried a few days later, and only a month after that, LeAnn returned to Richmond with her two blond children. I never saw any of them again.

'Yolanda Dawes,' Wally said again, shaking his head, as he sat on the bench beside me. 'Doesn't look like the black widow, does she?'

I glanced toward her again, my eyes lingering on the wistful, beguiling grace her body had assumed as she made her way along the water's edge.

Wally smiled. 'That's the trouble with black widows, buddy,' he said, 'they never do.' He grunted as he stood up, adding nothing else as the two of us walked back to work.

For the rest of the afternoon, I concentrated on the little library in Massachusetts, then left for home at around five-thirty.

When I arrived, Peter was shooting hoops into the basket I'd nailed to the garage door years before. He hardly noticed as I walked by, merely nodded briefly, fired a quick 'Hi, Dad,' and continued with the game. I could hear the ball thudding like an irregular pulse as I went on past the garage and up the stairway that led to the side entrance of the house, the one that opened onto the kitchen.

Marie was in her office down the hall, working at her computer and listening to Brahms's violin concerto, the only one he ever wrote, a work that Marie liked more than any other, obsessively buying each new rendition as soon as it was released.

'How'd it go today?' I asked.

She barely looked up from her keyboard. 'Okay,' she said idly. 'You?'

'Fine,' I told her, paused a moment, then added, 'Nothing new.'

In that brief pause, I'd thought of Rebecca, considered mentioning her visit to Marie, then decided not to. It had all been done in an instant, a choice made in favor of concealment, even though there'd been nothing to conceal. I realize now that it was a choice made out of a subtle yearning to have a secret in my life, something hidden, tucked away, a compartment where I could keep one treasure for myself alone. The fact that this 'treasure' was a woman meant less to me at the time than that it was clandestine and mysterious, a secluded back street I wanted to walk down.

'Go change, then,' Marie said, her eyes still fixed on the monitor. 'We need to start dinner.'

I headed upstairs to the bedroom, pulled off my suit and tie, and returned downstairs. Marie and Peter were already in the kitchen.

'Okay, let's get started,' she said, handing me a wooden salad bowl.

Making dinner together was a ritual Marie had long ago established, a 'family time' that was busy and productive, a moment when we had to 'face' each other, as she said, without the distraction of a game or television. Over the years it had become routine, something I neither looked forward to nor dreaded, a fact of life like any other, open, above-board, beyond the allure of the unrevealed.

# FOUR

The light in the bedroom was dark gray when I woke up the next morning. Marie had already gotten out of bed. I could see a little sliver of light under the door of the adjoining bathroom. I closed my eyes, heard the toilet flush, then, a few seconds later, the soft scrape of the bathroom door as she opened it.

'It's time, Steve,' she said firmly.

I didn't open my eyes. I didn't want to open them. I wanted to sink back into my sleep, but a heaviness in my chest nudged me awake. It was as if someone were sitting on me, looking down.

'Steve, it's time.'

Her voice was more insistent, and I knew that she'd keep at it until she saw me climb out of bed. I opened my eyes and glanced toward her. She stood at the bedroom window, a figure in silhouette, the curtains flung open behind her.

'Get up, Steve.'

I pushed the covers aside and got to my feet.

Marie looked satisfied and headed for the door. On the way she said, 'It's raining. Can you drive Peter to school this morning? I have to see a client in Bridgeport.'

I waved my hand. 'Yeah, okay, I'll drop him off on my way to work.'

Marie turned and left the room as I staggered toward the bathroom, then disappeared inside. I could hear her as she moved spiritedly along the corridor, then trotted down the short flight of stairs that led to the first floor.

My own pace was slower. The heaviness I'd felt in my chest had managed to creep into my arms and legs, drawing me downward like metal weights.

Peter was already at the table when I finally came downstairs a few minutes later. He'd poured himself a bowl of cereal and was staring at it without interest.

'Mom's already gone,' he told me.

'She had to go to Bridgeport.'

'So you're taking me?'

'Yeah.'

Peter ate the rest of his cereal while I drank a quick cup of coffee, then went back upstairs. I finished dressing, carefully knotted my tie, gathered up the office materials I'd brought home the night before, and returned to the kitchen.

Peter was standing at the door that led from the kitchen to the driveway, tall for his age, and slender, as I had been, but with his mother's straight, determinedly erect posture. Behind him, I could see the rain as it drove down through the trees that bordered the driveway, and against its gray veil he appeared almost ghostly, his large round eyes blinking slowly, like an owl's.

It was a floating, disembodied look that reminded me suddenly of Jamie, of the strange vacancy that had sometimes come into his face, lingered a moment, then dissolved into the pinched and irritated expression that was more usual with him. I remembered that during the last months of his life, those oddly resentful features had hardened into a mask of teenage hostility and sullenness, a face my father had finally aimed at directly, then reduced to a pulpy, glistening mass.

I glanced away from Peter, as if expecting to see his face explode as Jamie's had, then motioned him out the door, following along behind at a cautious distance, my shoulders hunched against the rain.

In the car, Peter sat silently, staring straight ahead, his face no longer locked in that strange innocence and helpless doom I had suddenly associated with my murdered brother. I looked at him and smiled.

'Everything going okay at school?' I asked.

He nodded.

'Good,' I told him.

Glancing toward him from time to time as I drove toward his school, I could easily remember him as a little boy, warm and glowing, his hair even lighter, a silver sheen. In the mornings he'd had the habit of crawling into bed with Marie and me, inching his head under my arm, then glancing up with a bright, sometimes toothless, smile.

Strangely, that remembered smile brought Jamie back again, and I recalled the only bit of conversation I'd ever been able to recall between him and my father. We'd all been heading through an indistinct countryside, toward somewhere I don't remember. My father was at the wheel, I in the middle, and Jamie pressed up against the passenger door. We'd been riding together silently, as we usually did, when suddenly my father had turned to Jamie. 'You don't smile much,' he said.

Jamie's eyes shot over to him resentfully. 'What did you say?'

My father appeared to regret having brought the subject up. 'Nothing,' he muttered, returning his eyes to the road.

But Jamie wouldn't let it go. 'What did you say?' he repeated.

'Just that you don't smile much,' my father answered.

Jamie gave him that familiar pinched, irritated look. 'I smile,' he said curtly, as if my father had accused him of something he felt obliged to deny.

'Good,' my father answered quickly, then let the subject drop.

But not before he'd briefly leveled his two light blue eyes on my brother, aiming them steadily at his face.

I shuddered, and my hands curled tightly around the steering wheel, as if to bring my body back to the present. It was a tactic that worked so well, I sensed that I'd used it before, but unconsciously, to prevent the emergence of such brief memories, rather than to return from them.

Once at the school, Peter got out quickly, with a child's enthusiasm, opening the door before I'd come to a full stop, then dashing through the rain to where a group of other boys huddled together beneath an aluminum awning. The bell was ringing as I pulled away.

I drove slowly toward my office. The rain grew somewhat lighter, but to the south I could see a line of clouds, low and heavy with rain. It struck me that the clouds lay between Old Salsbury and Bridgeport, and that Marie was probably driving under their low canopy at that very moment. It was then that I remembered that we'd not really said good-bye that morning. I'd heard the scrape of the bathroom door as it opened, then her voice telling me to get up, repeating it when I didn't. After that, nothing.

Marie Olivia Farris. Age, thirty-nine.

I'd met her during my last year in college. I was living in New York then, a small flat in the East Village. At night I worked as a waiter in a restaurant in Little Italy. It was frequented by a well-heeled assortment of mobsters and mid-level show people, whom the owner, Mr. Pinaldi, liked to identify. 'You know who you're serving, don't you?' he'd sometimes ask fiercely as I passed with a full tray.

Often I did know, but that particular night I didn't have the slightest idea and told him so.

Mr. Pinaldi looked at me as if I'd just walked out of the Amazon, knew nothing of the civilized world. 'The one with the bright red tie, that's Joey Santucci,' he said in a vehement whisper. 'He's a button man for the Brendizzi gang. He whacks people, kid. He blows them away.'

My eyes had reflexively shot toward the customer.

Joey Santucci was sitting at a round table, with two women on either side, one middle-aged, like Joey, the other much younger, and a large man who was dressed in a dark suit. The older woman was overweight, with flabby arms, and had an enormous white flower in her hair. She had a smoker's voice, hard and gravelly, and I took her for some old whorehouse madam Santucci had met years before. The second woman sat directly across from Santucci. She was no more than a girl, really, with dark brown hair and an olive complexion. She did not laugh when the others did, and at times, she cast disdainful glances toward the older woman, though always reserving the fiercer and more contemptuous ones for the man with the bright red tie. She was already halfway through her shrimp cocktail when I heard her call him 'Dad'.

There was nothing to distinguish any of them, and I probably would have forgotten them immediately if it hadn't happened.

It was very late, and the restaurant was nearly empty. I had just stepped up to take their dessert orders when he came through the door, a short, small-boned, wiry little man with a thin moustache. He had dark, gleaming eyes, quick and feral beneath the slouchy gray hat. He opened the door very wide as he came in, and a whirl of snow swept in behind him, then lay melting on the checkered tile floor as he moved smoothly to the bar.

I watched him as he propped his elbow up on the bar, then glanced back toward me.

'I'll just have a dish of chocolate ice cream,' the young one said.

I wrote the order on my pad, a quick squiggle of lines, then glanced back toward the bar.

The little man slid off the stool and now stood beside it, brushing snow from the shoulders of his overcoat as Sandy, the bartender that night, leaned toward him. I saw the little man's mouth twitch, then Sandy nod, turn around, and pull a bottle of scotch from the shelf.

A voice drew my attention from him.

'Just an espresso,' the older woman said.

The man pulled himself up on one of the barstools, but did not actually appear to be sitting on it. Rather, he seemed to be floating on a cushion of air, his body tilting right and left, while he drew his eyes over to the mirror behind the bar, then focused them with a dire intensity on the reflection of the man in the red tie.

'Bring me a brandy,' Joey Santucci said.

I glanced down at the pad, scribbled the order quickly, then looked back toward the bar. The little man had wheeled around on the stool, facing me silently, his hands deep in the pockets of the snow-flecked overcoat. His eyes moved from Santucci to the man in the dark suit, the one who had ordered nothing after dinner, and whom I took for Santucci's bodyguard.

I turned, walked around the table, and headed back toward the kitchen.

I could see the man at the bar spin slowly around as I passed him, his eyes trained on the mirror again, the four seated figures he could see very clearly in the glass.

Louie snapped the dessert order from my hand as I came through the double doors. He was grumbling angrily.

'That bunch at table six ever going to leave?'

'I don't know.'

'Chocolate ice cream. That fat cow ordered dessert?'

'The espresso is for her.'

Normally I would have dropped the liquor order on my way to the kitchen, but I had not done that, I realized suddenly, because something had warned me away, had unnerved me.

'Well, go get the drink, Steve,' Louie said sharply. 'I'll have the dessert ready by the time you get back.'

I stepped toward the door, following Louie's instructions. I walked slowly, haltingly, the air growing thick around me. I made it all the way to the door, then pressed my face up against the little square of glass that looked out onto the dining room. I could not move any farther.

'What's the matter, Steve?' Louie asked after a moment.

I didn't answer. Through the small square window, I could see the man at the bar, his hands still deep in his overcoat pockets, the untouched drink resting before him, its amber reflection winking in the mirror, the now motionless eyes trained determinedly on the oblivious, unthinking family.

'Steve?'

I didn't look back at Louie. I felt the words form in my mouth, but I'm not sure I ever actually said them: 'He's going to kill them.'

I began to tremble. I could feel myself trembling. It was a sensation of helplessness, of being something small and delicate before a line of black, rumbling clouds. To the left, I could see the little man as he brought one hand from his coat, stretched his fingers slowly, then returned it to the pocket. A few feet away, the young girl fiddled with her napkin, looking out of sorts, while her mother toyed coquettishly with her husband's bright red tie.

'Steve, what's the matter?'

It wasn't Louie's voice this time, but a young woman named Marie who'd only come to work a few days before. She had reddish-brown hair, very straight, and her eyes were deep-set and dreamy, exactly the kind that in movies the leading man always yearns to kiss.

'What's the matter?' she asked.

I didn't look at her. I kept my eyes trained on the little man at the bar. 'He's going to ...'

'Who?'

She saw the order slip quivering in my hand, snatched it from me, then burst through the door and out into the dining room, striding boldly up to the bar, where Sandy took it from her, reaching thoughtlessly over the little man's untouched glass.

I was still standing rigidly by the door when she came back into the kitchen. The little man had drunk the scotch in one quick gulp and was heading for the door. A few feet away, Joey Santucci gave his wife a kiss while his teenage daughter looked on sourly.

I felt myself collapse, as if every muscle had suddenly been ripped from its mooring. I was actually sliding helplessly toward the floor when Marie grabbed me by the arm, drew me over to the small bench beside the cutting table, and lowered me into it.

'You want me to call a doctor, Steve?' she asked urgently.

'No.'

'Are you sure?'

I nodded. 'I'm sorry. It was just something that reminded me of ...' I couldn't keep back the words. '... of my father.'

It was hours later, nearing dawn, and we were in bed in her apartment on MacDougal Street before I finally got the whole story out. I cried and cried, and so she held me through all that sleepless, gorgeous night.

And twenty years later, she'd walked out of our bedroom and down the stairs, and neither of us had thought to say good-bye.

I'd been at my desk for no more than an hour when the phone rang.

'Mr. Farris?'

'Yes.'

'Rebecca Soltero. I was wondering if you might be able to meet me for lunch today.'

'Well, it would have to be a short lunch,' I said. 'And near the office.'

'That would be fine,' Rebecca said. 'I'd just like to get a few biographical details before we do the other type of interview.'

She meant the kind, of course, that would return me to my father.

'All right,' I said. 'There's a small café on Linden, just down the block from my office. It's called Plimpton's.'

'Yes, I saw it yesterday,' Rebecca said. 'What time?'

'I can meet you at twelve-thirty,' I told her.

She was already waiting for me when I arrived an hour or so later. She was wearing a long dark skirt with matching jacket and a white blouse. Her earrings were plain gold hoops. She wore no other jewelry.

I nodded crisply as I sat down. 'I wasn't expecting to hear from you quite so soon,' I said cautiously.

She nodded. 'I know,' she said, 'but I'm at that point where I need a little background information.' She took a small notebook from her jacket pocket. 'Information about you, I mean,' she added. 'Biographical details, that sort of thing.'

'And the other interviews,' I said, 'they'll be focused on my father?'

'Along with your family,' Rebecca said. 'I'd like to have portraits of each of them.'

'How many interviews do you expect to need?'

'It depends on how much you remember,' Rebecca answered.

'Well, how long are you planning to stay in Old Salsbury?'

She looked at me very determinedly. 'I live in Boston,' she said, 'but I'll stay here as long as I need to.' Her eyes returned to the notebook. 'I know that you lived with your aunt in Somerset for a while after the murders,' she began. 'How long?'

'Two months.'

'And that's when your uncle came to get you?'

'Yes.'

As I spoke, I remembered the morning Quentin arrived at Aunt Edna's house, the old truck shuddering to a stop in her gravel driveway. I'd been stacking dominoes on the carpet in the living room, and when I looked up I saw Aunt Edna part the translucent blue curtains which hung over her large picture window, release a weary sigh, and shake her head, as if the sight of him alone was enough to exasperate her.

He entered the house seconds later, a large man with a round belly and thick legs. He was wearing rubber boots which rose almost to his thighs, and a gray, broad-billed cap that looked like the type worn by locomotive engineers.

He hardly noticed Aunt Edna, but strode powerfully over to me, jerked me into his arms, and said, 'Well, Stevie, ready to live a man's life now, are you?'

From the corner of my eye, I could see Aunt Edna looking at both of us crossly, her arms folded over her chest. 'Put him down, Quentin,' she said sternly, 'and come on into the kitchen. We have things to talk about.'

They'd talked about me, as I told Rebecca over lunch that day, a conversation I'd heard from just behind the closed door:

'As I said on the phone, it's not working out here, Quentin,' Aunt Edna said. 'That's the long and the short of it.'

'I told you I'd take him, Edna,' Quentin told her. 'I know you don't want him.'

'Well, it's not exactly that I don't ...'

'Besides,' Uncle Quentin interrupted, 'he's better off with a man.'

There was a brief silence after that, but finally I heard my aunt say, 'All right, take him.'

And he had, the two of us rattling for hours along well-traveled roads before turning onto the more deserted one that led out to Quentin's house by the sea.

'He was an older man, wasn't he?' Rebecca asked.

'Late fifties.'

But he'd seemed much older to me, his hair entirely gray, his face heavily furrowed with deep wrinkles about his eyes and the corners of his mouth.

'Did you get along well, the two of you?' Rebecca asked.

We had, but he had brooked no whining, no grieving, no self-pity. The past was past in his book, and only a fool or a coward dwelled upon its scattered ruins.

'He tried his best to do things with me,' I told Rebecca, 'things a father would have done.'

And so we had camped out from time to time, and fished in the local ponds. In the summer, he took me swimming, snoozing on the shore while I bounced about in the water.

The problem was his health. My first impression of him had been that he was vigorous and robust. But actually, he was rather frail. In the winter, he suffered from long, dreadful colds, and seemed particularly susceptible to digestive problems. He called whiskey his 'medicine' and drank as much as he liked as often as he liked, though in all the years we lived together, I never saw him drunk.

I don't think I ever really knew him, as I admitted to Rebecca, but I did remember one incident when I was twelve, something which made me think that there was something deeply wrong with Quentin, something which seethed just below the surface.

It happened on a fall day, with the sky very low, hanging like a flat gray ceiling above my head. I'd been working on the front porch, mending some of the lobster cages which Quentin had hauled in the day before. It was tedious, uncomplicated work, no more than a matter of hammering in a few loose nails. I'd finished up within an hour or so, and after that I wandered around the house to the backyard. Years before, Quentin had built a small wooden shed there, a ramshackle structure which he used partly as a work space, partly as a storehouse for his fishing supplies. In the fall, he went there to mend his nets, and he'd gathered a huge pile of them together in the corner.

The shed had a few small windows, and that afternoon I absently walked over to one of them and glanced in. Quentin was sitting on a stubby wooden bench, working to separate two tangled nets. His face seemed very taut and impatient, and I noticed that his fingers were trembling. His face had taken on a reddish tint around the cheeks and his eyes appeared to glisten slightly, as if he were about to cry. Suddenly he threw the nets down, then picked them up again and began to sling them about, whipping them violently at the shed's skeletal supporting beams. I could see small puffs of dust come from the posts as the nets bit into them and hear the hard slap of the cord as it whipped about furiously.

In a moment, he stopped, then collapsed, exhausted, onto the spindly wooden stool he'd been sitting on before it all began. His head dropped slightly, and he wiped his mouth with his hand. His shoulders were lifting high and rhythmically, so I knew it had taken almost all his breath to groan the single word he said into the dusty interior of the shed.

'It was a woman's name,' I told Rebecca.

She glanced up from her notebook, her face very still, intense, searching. 'A woman's name?'

'Yes,' I said. 'But I have no idea who she was.'

She seemed to consider the story a moment, turning it over in her mind. Then she sat back slightly, as if to regain her focus.

'When did you leave Maine?' she asked.

'Not until I went to college. Aunt Edna had sold the house on McDonald Drive and put the money in an account for me. That's what I used to pay for college.'

'And after college, you never lived in Maine again?'

'Only for a little while. I went back to take care of Quentin. He was dying by then.'

Old and frail and drinking far too much, he'd needed me to stay with him during the last weeks of his life, and so, directly after leaving college, I'd returned to the little house by the sea.

Quentin hadn't died quickly. It had taken a long time. Nor had he approached death gracefully. Instead, a bitterness and rancor had slowly overwhelmed him, filling his days with mean-spirited discourses on the inadequacies of life.

For nearly three months, I listened as he lay out on the back porch, staring fiercely at the sea, while fuming against and damning to hell almost everyone he'd ever known. He railed against his own parents, against Edna, against a host of double-dealing business partners. One by one the names passed his lips carried on a curse. Except one.

'He never said anything bad about my father,' I said to Rebecca. 'Not a single word.'

Rebecca looked surprised.

'As a matter of fact,' I added, 'the only thing he ever said about my father was sort of complimentary.'

'Complimentary?'

'One night, he was really having a bad time,' I went on. 'He was railing about things, as usual. But all of a sudden he stopped. Then he looked at me, and he whispered, "Ah, your father, Stevie, he really took it by the balls."'

Rebecca said nothing, but I could see something moving behind her eyes.

I shrugged. 'He died ten days later,' I added. 'I never knew exactly what he meant.'

Rebecca lowered her eyes toward her notebook, wrote something there, and then looked up at me. 'Did he ever mention the woman again?' she asked. 'The name he said in the shed that afternoon?'

I shook my head. 'No,' I answered, then smiled lightly. 'I guess she'll always be a mystery.'

Rebecca did not return my smile. 'Like a lot of things,' she said, but with a curious unease and sense of strain, as if it were a fate she was still unwilling to accept.

# FIVE

It was nearly a week before I heard from Rebecca again, and I remember that the days passed slowly, like soldiers in a gray line. During that interval, I often thought about the life my family had lived on McDonald Drive. I recalled how, when I was very small, Laura had taken me out to the swings and played with me for hours. My father had often sat in a small wrought-iron chair and watched us. 'Don't swing him too high,' he would caution at those times when Laura's natural energy would get the better of her and she'd send me hurtling skyward, my feet soaring into the summer air.

There were other memories, too. I could recall my mother piddling about in the garage, moving small boxes from one place to another. She seemed always to be hunting for something small and inconsequential that eluded her again and again, a pruning fork or a spool of thread. Jamie would joke about it from time to time. 'Everything she touches disappears,' he once said with a mocking grin.

There'd been a fireplace in the living room, and I remembered the sounds the fire made in the winter, along with the rhythmic thump of the axe when my father chopped wood beneath the large maple tree in the backyard.

Smells returned. Laura's nail polish, the raincoat that Jamie often hung wet in the closet we were forced to share, my mother's cooking, always bland and unaccented, the smell, I often thought, of little more than boiling water. And last, my father's hands, the strange odor that always came from them, and which, one night during that week before Rebecca called again, I actually mentioned to Marie.

'Like soil,' I said suddenly, as we sat at the dinner table one evening. The words had come from nowhere but my own mind. We'd not been talking about my father, or anything even remotely connected to him.

'What are you talking about, Steve?' Marie asked.

I felt embarrassed, surprised by the level of my own distraction.

'I was thinking about my father,' I explained quickly. 'The odor of his hands.'

'Why were you thinking about that?'

It was the perfect chance to tell her about Rebecca, her book, the meetings I'd had, the ones I expected to have in the future. And yet, I found that I couldn't do it.

'I don't know,' I told her. 'Sometimes, things just pop into my head. This time, it was my father.' I shrugged. 'No reason.'

And so, it had begun.

It was a Thursday afternoon, and I was at the drafting table in my office at Simpson and Lowe when Rebecca called to arrange another meeting.

'It's Rebecca Soltero,' she said.

'Yes, I know.'

'I was wondering if you might have an evening free this week?'

'Most of my evenings are free,' I told her.

She didn't seem surprised to hear it. 'Well, we could meet tonight, if you want.'

'All right.'

'Where?'

I suggested a small restaurant north of town. In the past I'd gone there alone in the late afternoon, simply to sit in the generally quiet atmosphere and have a drink before going home. At times I would do a little work, perhaps add a line or two to the drawing of the 'dream house' I had been elaborating and modifying for years, and vaguely hoped to build one day. It was a house of floating levels and dreamy, translucent walls, of rooms that melted into other rooms. It was impractical and unrealizable, a structure bereft of all those mundane pillars and supporting beams without which it could not hope to stand.

She arrived promptly, carrying a black briefcase, and wearing a dark red silk blouse and a long black skirt. She'd added a bolero jacket, also black, unnecessary in the unusual warmth of that long Indian summer, but worn, I think, in order to conceal or diminish the more obvious contours of her body.

'Thanks for meeting me again, Mr. Farris,' she said as she sat down.

'Steve,' I said. 'It's no trouble.' I glanced about the room. 'It's a nice place, don't you think?'

It was a garden restaurant, made of glass and hung with vines. Small fountains sprouted here and there among the foliage.

'A sort of Garden of Eden effect,' I added.

'Yes, it's fine,' Rebecca answered briskly.

The waitress stepped over, a young woman named Gail, with whom Wally claimed to have had a brief affair, though he probably hadn't. I ordered a beer on tap, Rebecca a glass of red wine. Gail glanced at Rebecca, then at me. She grinned knowingly, as if privy to a secret.

'When do you have to be home?' Rebecca asked after Gail stepped away.

'Home?'

'You're married, aren't you? With a son?'

I nodded. 'A family man,' I said, then added, 'My son is nine years old. His name is Peter.'

'And your wife's name?'

'Marie.'

Rebecca smiled quietly, but with a certain quickness that made it clear that she had only a passing, casual interest in my present family, that her entire focus was on the other one that had been destroyed.

The drinks came promptly, and I lifted my glass casually for the customary toast. She raised hers as well, but when I moved to touch my glass to hers, she drew it away quickly, almost in an act of self-defense, and took a quick sip.

'I've been working on the book for three years,' she said, after returning the glass to the table.

I nodded silently, watching the steady gaze of her eyes. They were dark eyes, sensual, but not dreamy, and there was nothing in the least sultry about them. They were the eyes of an explorer, searching, determined, curiously ruthless. I imagined them in the face of Pizarro or Cortés.

'I finally settled on five cases,' she went on. 'At this point I've finished four of them.' She opened the black briefcase she'd placed on the table between us and drew out a large manila envelope. 'I thought you might like to see the ones I've already studied.'

'See them?'

'Well, I brought photographs of the men, and the victims,' Rebecca explained. 'I've also written short summaries of each crime. You can read them if you like.'

She hesitated, her hand poised to open the envelope, her eyes leveled upon me, sensing the chilly dread that had suddenly gripped me as my eyes fell upon the yellow envelope.

'Of course, if you'd rather not do any of this ...'

I rushed to assure her that she didn't need to be delicate with me. 'No, no, I think I should know about the others,' I told her.

She took a smaller envelope from the larger one, opened it, and pulled out a short stack of photographs. The one on top was in black and white, and it showed a tall, slender man as he leaned idly against the fender of a dusty pickup truck.

'This is the first man I studied,' Rebecca said. 'Harold Wayne Fuller. Age, thirty-seven.'

That was all she said as she turned the photograph toward me.

In the picture, Fuller was dressed in loose-fitting trousers and a plain white shirt, its sleeves rolled up beyond the elbows. He wore a dark-colored baseball cap with the initials 'AB' on the front, and a slender baseball bat dangled from his right hand.

'He was a steelworker in Birmingham, Alabama,' Rebecca said, 'a union leader, very respected by the men he worked with. As a young man, he played professional baseball for a few years, but a knee injury finally made him quit.'

Her tone was very matter-of-fact, even a little rushed, as if this were a task she was anxious to get through.

'He had been married to his wife, Elizabeth, for fourteen years,' she continued. 'They had two daughters, ages twelve and thirteen. Both girls attended the local school, and both were good students. No one at the school had noticed any signs of emotional disturbance in either one.'

She stopped, watching me as I continued to stare at the picture.

The face of Harold Wayne Fuller was the face of Everyman. It was plain and flat and impossible to read. There was no sign of dementia or murderous intent, of anything lurking beneath the surface, tightening the fingers around the baseball bat.

Rebecca let my eyes linger on the photo a while longer, then drew it away to expose the one that lay beneath it.

'This is the couple together,' she said.

The second photograph showed Fuller and his wife on their wedding day, a picture taken outside a large gray public building, probably by a stranger, and which showed them smiling brightly, Fuller in a baggy double-breasted suit, his arm draped over his wife's nearly bare shoulders.

'Fuller married Elizabeth in the summer of 1952,' Rebecca added. 'She had their first daughter, Emily Jane, the following year.'

Once again Rebecca drew the photograph away to reveal the one beneath it.

'This is Emily Jane,' she said. 'Age, nine.'

In the small, black-and-white picture, Emily Jane Fuller was standing beside the same dusty pickup truck which had been captured in the first picture, the baseball bat her father had been holding now leaning against the truck's closed door, her father no doubt behind the camera now, aiming it steadily at his daughter.

After a few seconds, Rebecca slid the picture away, bringing a fourth photograph into view.

'A second daughter, Phyllis Beatrice, called 'Bootsie', was born a year later,' she said.

In the fourth photograph, 'Bootsie' stood in a nondescript living room, dressed in a cowboy skirt and blouse, her long hair partly concealed by a large, western hat.

'Bootsie belonged to the same square-dancing club her mother attended,' Rebecca said. 'They seem to have been very close.'

I let my eyes rest on the picture for a time, then glanced up toward Rebecca.

'Did he kill them all?' I asked.

Rebecca nodded. 'With the baseball bat,' she said. 'The police still have it stored in their evidence locker.'

'They kept everything they took from my house, too,' I said. 'I don't even know exactly what they took. I just know that they never gave anything back.'

'No, of course not,' Rebecca said. 'The case is still open.'

I dismissed the thought of it. 'Open? That's just a formality. They can't ever officially close an unsolved murder case. There's no statute of limitations on murder. But they're never going to find my father. It's been thirty-five years since he did it.'

Rebecca said nothing. She took a second, small envelope from the larger one and handed it to me. It was identical to the first, and as I drew it from her hand, I heard her call the man's name and age, though without expression, as if doing an inventory.

'Gerald Ward Stringer. Age, forty-one.'

The second set of pictures was arranged in exactly the same order as the first, more or less chronologically.

'The summation of the case is under the photographs,' Rebecca said.

I nodded, my eyes already settling on the first picture.

Gerald Ward Stringer sat in a recliner, shirtless, legs stretched out, his bare feet aimed at the camera, his belly pouring over his beltless trousers. He was nearly bald, a shiny star of light gleaming on his forehead, the result no doubt of the reflected flash that had been used to take the picture. He was smiling, very broadly, the happy fat man in his cluttered lair. The room in which he sat was paneled in pinewood. A few mounted animal heads hung from the walls that surrounded him, and I could see a rack of hunting rifles hung between a deer and a fox. A safari hat, one side of its bill turned up raffishly, dangled from one of the deer's upturned antlers.

Rebecca gave her narration as I leafed through the photos.

'The murders occurred six months after this picture was taken,' she said. 'Stringer killed Mary Faye, his wife of nine years, and his three sons: Eddie, four. Tyrone, six. And Jimmy Dale, seven.'

She waited a moment, then added softly, 'With a rifle, as you've probably already figured out.'

As if realizing that I didn't want to read the summations she'd written, she continued on, relating the details of the case, describing what had actually happened on February 11, 1967. As she did so, I found that I could see it all quite graphically in my mind.

Gerald Ward Stringer had come home from one of a string of small, very successful bakeries that he owned in Des Moines, Iowa, at the usual time of seven-thirty. He'd gone to work at five o'clock that morning, and he was, as he later told police in a description of himself that was eloquently simple, 'a very tired man.'

Mary Faye worked as an office clerk at a local brewery, and she had been at work all day, too. When Stringer arrived home, he found her sleeping on the sofa in the den, one leg hanging over the side, her right foot almost touching the floor, her body in the exact position in which the police would find her several hours later, and which Stringer described as looking 'sort of like a big towel that somebody had just thrown onto the couch.'

The children, all three of them, were in the basement. Tyrone and Jimmy Dale were playing at the miniature pool table they'd gotten for Christmas two months before, while Eddie played with a set of Tinker Toys on the large square of outdoor carpet which covered the basement's otherwise cold, cement floor.

For nearly an hour, Stringer sat in the den only a few feet from his sleeping wife. From time to time during that fateful hour, Miss Zena Crawford, the woman who rented the small apartment over the Stringers' two-car garage, looked down from her window and glanced into the Stringer family house. From her position over the garage, she had a commanding view of the den and kitchen. In the den, she saw Gerald Ward Stringer as he sat silently in the big recliner. He sat upright, his hands in his lap, rather than the usual reclining position in which she'd glimpsed him at other times.

At 8:20 P.M., Miss Crawford heard Tyrone calling to his mother, asking her to unlock the door that separated the basement from the upper floor of the house. She looked out the window and saw both Tyrone and Jimmy Dale at the basement window, the one which looked out at just above ground level, and which was situated almost directly below the window in the den. She glanced up and saw Mrs. Stringer rustle slightly on the sofa, as if the voices of her children were awakening her.

Having seen nothing that alarmed her, Miss Crawford turned from the window, took a couple of steps toward her small kitchen, then heard a shot. She returned to her window, glanced down, and noticed that the blinds in the Stringers' den had been lowered. She looked down at the small basement window just in time to see Tyrone and Jimmy Dale as they turned away from her, back toward the basement's interior darkness, as if in answer to someone's call. They lingered at the window for an instant, then shrank away from it. Seconds after the two boys had left the window, Miss Crawford heard three shots.

Rebecca paused a moment after she'd finished her narrative. She was watching me closely, no doubt because this particular crime resembled my father's a bit more closely than the first. It had been committed with a firearm, and three of the murders had taken place in a basement, which, on the surface, appeared to resemble the sort of place in which my mother, too, had died.

'Do you have any questions?' she asked tentatively as she returned the pictures to their envelope.

'No.'

Rebecca pulled out a third envelope.

'Herbert Malcolm Parks,' she said. 'Age, forty-three.'

She said nothing else, now clearly preferring that I read the summaries she'd attached to the photos rather than listen to her own narration of the events.

The summary was neatly typed on plain white paper, and it was very succinct, giving the details briefly and without the slightest literary adornment.

Herbert Parks was a real estate agent in San Francisco. On June 12, 1964, he'd suddenly been stricken by an upset stomach while sitting at his downtown office. After complaining of the pain to several fellow agents, he'd driven to his home in Mill Valley, and there murdered his wife, Wenonah, age thirty-eight, and his two daughters, Frederica, twelve, and Constance, seven. Mrs. Parks had been shot once in the back of the head. The two girls had been forced to drink orange soda in which their father had dissolved several rat control pellets which contained cyanide. All three bodies had been stacked one on top of the other in the walk-in closet off the master bedroom.

The murders had occurred at approximately two-thirty in the afternoon, and as a result, there was no Miss Crawford to glance out her window and see something strange going on at the house next door.

Nonetheless, there were witnesses of a type. George McFadden, an electrical lineman perched high above the street only a few yards from the house, saw Parks's dark gray Mercedes pull into the driveway at approximately two that afternoon. According to McFadden, Parks had not gotten out of the car right away, but had remained behind the wheel, 'as if waiting for some kind of signal' before entering the house.

A few minutes later, two young girls had come from the house, both of them moving toward the car. The smaller one, who must have been Constance, darted enthusiastically toward her father, while the larger one, Frederica, held back. Parks had already gotten out by the time they reached him, and, once again according to McFadden, he took each of them into his arms, hugged them for a long time, then, hand in hand, his shoulders slightly hunched, led them back into the house.

No one else saw or heard anything after that.

After reading the summation, I turned to the photographs. Arranged once again in the established order, the first picture showed Herbert Parks in a dark double-breasted suit. It was a professional photograph, done at a studio, and the smaller marks and blotches which must have been on his face had been air-brushed into oblivion. He had gray hair at the temples, but otherwise jet black, and for the purposes of the photo he appeared to have pulled a single curl down so that it dangled, slightly greased in fifties matinee-idol style, near the center of his forehead.

There were only two other photographs. The first, just under the studio picture of Herbert Parks, showed his wife posed beside the same dark Mercedes which George McFadden saw pull into the driveway on the afternoon of June 12, 1964. She was wearing a light blue blouse, its ends tied in a knot across her waist, a pair of jeans, rolled up to mid-calf, and white tennis shoes. She was holding a water hose and a red plastic pail, and seemed to be pretending to wash the car.

The last picture was from the family's personal Christmas card of the year before. Both Herbert and Wenonah Parks were in the photograph, but the focus of the picture, its heart and soul, was the two little girls they held in their arms. Constance was clearly laughing, but Frederica seemed to stare pensively toward the lens, her tiny mouth firmly set in place, not so much frowning, as refusing to smile, her eyes oddly vacant, her arms wrapped tightly around Wenonah's slender neck.

Rebecca noticed how my eyes lingered upon her, then spoke:

'He put her on top.'

'You mean, in the closet?'

'Yes. She was larger than Constance, but he stacked her on top, and folded her hands over her chest. The others were just sprawled across the closet floor.'

I remembered how my father had done something odd as well, how he'd washed my mother's body and arranged it carefully on the bed while leaving Laura and Jamie to lie in their ugly, smelly pools of coagulating blood. And as I remembered it, my eyes drifted back to Frederica, and suddenly I thought I knew why she had clung so desperately to her mother in the Christmas card photo, why she had, as George McFadden had mentioned, 'held back' from running heedlessly to her father on the day he had assigned to kill her.

'It was because she knew,' I said, almost to myself, but loud enough for Rebecca to hear me.

She looked at me curiously. 'Knew what?'

'That it was coming,' I told her, 'that her father was going to kill them.' I looked at her pointedly. 'There must always be someone who knows what's about to happen, don't you think? Not everyone can be entirely in the dark.'

'Why not?' Rebecca asked.

'Because so much is going on,' I said. 'In the family, I mean. Surely someone has to sense it.'

Rebecca looked at me squarely. 'Did you?'

'No.'

'Did Laura or Jamie?'

It was odd to hear their names again, to hear them spoken of as if they once had actually existed, had lived and observed the life around them, rather than simply as the faceless victims of my father's crime.

I shook my head slowly. 'I don't think so.'

'And your mother?'

It was strange, but at that moment, I suddenly suspected that somehow, through all the mists that must have clouded and thwarted and befuddled her, 'poor Dottie' must have known that my father was approaching some dreadful line, and that if he crossed it, he might kill us all.

'She might have known,' I said quietly.

'What makes you think so?'

A memory invaded me, and I recalled how often she'd gone off to her bedroom, closed the door and remained there for hours, as if locking herself away from him, from us, from whatever it was she could feel heating the air inside the little mock Tudor house on McDonald Drive.

'She spent a lot of time in the bedroom,' I told Rebecca.

Even as I said it, I wondered what dreadful possibilities my mother might have envisioned while she lay alone on her bed. In her mind, had she ever seen him coming up the stairs, the shotgun in his hand? And if she had glimpsed such a thing, had she ever considered packing us into the car and taking us away before it was too late?

'But if she did suspect something,' I said, 'she didn't do anything about it.'

Except to let us drift, I thought with a sudden bitterness, let us slide into destruction because she was unable to summon up even enough will to throw off her red housedress, gather us into the station wagon, and take us away from him.

As all of this swept over me, I found that I suddenly blamed my mother as much as, maybe even more than, I blamed my father. The cool rancor and cruelty of my next remark amazed me.

'My mother was very weak,' I said. 'She was a nothing. She could have left him, but she didn't.'

'Had he ever been violent with her?' Rebecca asked.

'No.'

'With any of you?'

'No, never,' I said. 'He would sometimes get irritated. Especially with Jamie. But he never raised his hand against any of us.'

To my surprise, Rebecca didn't ask any more questions. Instead, she simply handed me another envelope.

'This is the last one,' she said.

I took the envelope from her and read it quietly.

Hollis Donald Townsend. Age, forty-four.

On July 12, 1961, Hollis Townsend, a certified public accountant and avid foreign-stamp collector who lived and worked in Phoenix, Arizona, returned with his family from a two-week vacation at Yellowstone National Park. A neighbor, Sally Miller, who came out to welcome them back, placed the time at 3:35 P.M. For the next few minutes, while Hollis Townsend unpacked the car, she spoke to his wife, Mary Townsend, thirty-seven. During this brief time, as she later told police, the Townsend children, Karen, five, and Sheila, eight, had played with the family dog, a large collie named Samson.

Nearly nine hours later, at around midnight, Mrs. Miller was awakened by a single shot, followed rapidly by two others. She rose, walked to her window, glanced out, and saw Hollis Townsend as he stepped out of the house, turned left, and headed for the garage. He had a large suitcase, one which appeared to be very heavy, since Townsend needed both hands to drag, rather than carry, it across the lawn. He was dressed in the same beige trousers and short-sleeved knit shirt he'd been wearing earlier in the day, an indication that he had not gone to bed, although, as Mrs. Miller told police, all the lights in the house had been off for more than two hours.

What had he done in that darkness?

Rebecca's summation gave a short but graphic answer. For one thing, he'd written several letters, all of which he'd eventually thrown into the kitchen wastebasket. The letters, written in Townsend's pinched script, alluded to an 'inadequacy' which he had to face, the inadequacy, as he put it, 'of life, of what I can't find in it somehow.'

At some other point during the night, Townsend had poured gasoline in every room in the house, drenching carpets and furniture, and leaving a trail which began in the kitchen, then led through the rooms on the ground floor before heading up the stairs to where his family lay sleeping obliviously. At the last moment, however, he had not lit a match, but had simply dragged his enormous suitcase out across the lawn, leaving the house intact behind him, the bodies of his wife and two children still lying in their own beds.

Each had been shot one time. Karen and Sheila had been shot in the back of the head, Mary through the forehead, presumably because, unlike her daughters, she slept on her back rather than her stomach.

Only two photographs were attached. The first showed Hollis Townsend beside the family swimming pool. He was wearing only a bathing suit, and he appeared to be beating his breasts comically, in a mocking imitation of Tarzan.

The second photograph was of Mary Townsend. She was kneeling down, her arms around her small daughters. It was a picture that had undoubtedly been taken during the family vacation at Yellowstone. Old Faithful, the park's most famous geyser, could be seen exploding from a cloud of steam behind them.

Without comment, I returned the summation and photographs to their envelope and handed it to Rebecca. She took them from my hand, placed them in her briefcase.

'I think that's enough for tonight,' she said abruptly.

I was surprised. 'I have more time,' I told her.

She began to gather her things together. 'I'd rather start fresh next time,' she said. 'The questions I want to ask you would take a long time to answer, and I'd rather not go into them now.' She closed the briefcase and started to rise.

I touched her hand. 'Why my father?' I asked. 'Why did you pick him?'

She drew her hand away from mine, leaned back slightly, and gave me her reasons so smoothly and matter-of-factly that she seemed to be quoting a long passage she'd written beforehand.

'Well, all the cases you've read about have a few things in common,' she said. 'None of them had serious money problems. None of them had medical problems. None of them had lovers. There were no "other women" in their lives. All of them committed their murders in their family homes. All of them had planned the murders beforehand. Nothing about them was sudden or impulsive. These were not acts of rage. The killings were quick and clean.'

She paused, as if waiting for a question, then went on when I simply watched her silently.

'And last, these men all tried to escape,' she said. 'They didn't kill themselves, as some family murderers do. They tried to get away instead, to escape. None of them succeeded, except, of course, your father.'

As if in a sudden vision, I saw him. Through the rain, his hat pulled down, water dripping from its sagging brim, I saw my father move toward the family car, saw him as Mrs. Hamilton must have seen him, her eyes peering toward the street from behind the blue curtains that hung from her living room window.

'Yes, he did succeed in that,' I said. I smiled ironically. 'He would be an old man now.'

Rebecca nodded, a small green leaf brushing against the side of her face.

'An old man,' I repeated, though without emphasis, a simple mathematical determination. The others swam into my mind, Fuller, Stringer, and the rest.

'What are you looking for in these men?' I asked.

The question appeared to sink into her face like a dye.

'I want to find out what it was in life that they couldn't bear,' she said.

'And because of that, killed their families?'

'Yes.'

I looked at her, puzzled. 'And you think that in each of them it was the same thing?'

She peered closely into my eyes, as if trying to gauge what my response might be to her next remark. 'The same thing,' she said finally, 'in almost every man.'

I was still going over that peculiar remark when I got home a few minutes later. It was still early, and Peter was in the small family room watching some sort of situation comedy on television.

'Where's your mother?' I asked him as I strolled into the room.

'In her office.'

'Did you have dinner?'

'She fixed one of those cheese things.'

I walked out of the room, down a short corridor, and opened the door to Marie's office. She looked up, startled.

'Please don't do that, Steve,' she said.

'Do what?'

'Come in like that. Through the door all of a sudden.'

I laughed mockingly. 'What do you think I am, Marie, some crazed axe murderer?'

She did not seem amused. She went back to her work without saying anything else.

I remained at the door, looking at her. She was typing something at her computer, something that was probably businesslike, but uninspired, a bid for the job in Bridgeport, I supposed, a banal proposal for interior design. I compared it to the project upon which Rebecca had embarked, a far more profound investigation of a far deeper interior. Marie's work seemed small and inconsequential compared to that, scarcely more than the busywork of a life that had settled for too little, a life that had been lived ... like mine.

Without warning, an odd sense of desolation suddenly overwhelmed me, and I left Marie to her work, walked to the kitchen, snatched the cheese thing from the refrigerator, and ate it pleasurelessly at the dining room table.

When I'd finished, I returned to the family room. Peter was still watching television, and for a few minutes I watched along with him, an action picture of some sort, all car chases and shattering glass.

He went to bed at ten, without speaking, a slender figure in red pajamas padding up the carpeted stairs to a room he had come to consider as his private domain, and which his mother and I had been forbidden to enter without permission.

I remained in the family room, my mind in a kind of featureless limbo until Rebecca's final remark came back into my mind, and I began to think over the cases she'd written about. I saw Harold Fuller leaning on his baseball bat, Gerald Stringer sitting rigidly upright in his big recliner, Herbert Parks slowly walking his two daughters hand-in-hand back into the house, Hollis Townsend beating his breasts beside the bright blue pool. What was it in any of these men that so fascinated her?

Finally, inevitably, I thought about my father, too, asking the same questions I thought Rebecca must be asking: Who was he? Why did he do it? From what dark, volcanic core had so much murder come?

At that early stage, I couldn't have answered any of these questions. Still, I felt the urge to pursue them, to press on toward finding some kind of solution to the mystery of my father's crime. Certainly, part of that urge came from Rebecca, but part of it also came from me, the need to touch the center of something, to reach the final depth ... no matter where it lay.

# SIX

'Steve, it's seven-thirty.'

It was Marie calling from downstairs.

I got up slowly, showered, and dressed.

Marie and Peter were seated at the breakfast table. Peter was chattering on about some atrocity his teacher had committed against another student. As he talked, Marie watched him quietly, nodding from time to time as she chewed a final bit of toast.

When Peter had finished, we all fell silent, and after a moment, I found myself remembering those other family breakfasts I'd had so long ago at the little oval-shaped Formica table on McDonald Drive. Often, we'd all fallen silent, too, sitting for long stretches in a gloomy quiet. But it was not a moment like that which came back to me. Instead it was one of those rare occasions when my father and Laura, normally so withdrawn from the rest of us, had talked quite openly at the breakfast table, chatting with a rare spiritedness and candor, as if they were alone.

Laura had begun it, talking about some report she'd been working on in her geography class. It had had to do with an Oriental country. I don't remember the particular place, but only that my sister had spoken almost mystically about the beauty of the land, the strangeness of the people, all those bizarre landscapes and customs which would have fascinated any sixteen-year-old girl as high-strung and curious as Laura.

In any event, she'd finished by saying that she intended to go there at some point in her life, an ambition, as I noticed, which had spontaneously and very powerfully appealed to my father. As much as I ever saw his love pour out to her, I saw it at that moment in the little kitchen. It was a look of unqualified admiration, but a look that also seemed a kind of plea that she hold forever to this longing for distant things and lost, mysterious places.

Jamie saw it, too, however, and something in it infuriated him.

'You're never going anywhere,' he sneered at Laura. 'Who do you think you are, some kind of princess?'

Laura glared at him angrily. 'Oh, shut up, Jamie,' she snapped.

'Just big ideas, that's all,' Jamie fired back. 'You're not going any-where.'

'I said, shut up, Jamie,' Laura screamed, 'just shut up.'

It continued in this way for some time, both Jamie and Laura growing hotter by the minute, my mother lamely attempting to quell the riot, but with her usual lack of force.

I don't know exactly at what point I became aware that my father had left the room. I hadn't seen him rise, walk around the table, and disappear into some other part of the house. It was as if he'd simply vanished.

The battle continued in his absence, growing more furious and abusive by the moment. My mother left after a time, coughing slightly, as if escaping from a smoke-filled room. I remained in my seat, of course, watching the battle like a child, fascinated by the flames. I was still there when it died away suddenly, and both Laura and Jamie moved out into the open air, Jamie to the basketball hoop, Laura to a chair in the backyard.

Later, coming from the upstairs bathroom, I glimpsed my mother as she lay on her back in the bed, one hand at her side, the other balanced palm up on her forehead, as if she were wiping a line of sweat from her brow.

A terrible silence had descended upon the house by then, one which no one seemed willing to break, as if this sullen, unhappy peace was the only kind of quiet we could know. I remember that in order not to break it, I had actually tiptoed down the stairs.

I was near the bottom of them when I saw my father sitting alone in the solarium. His legs stretched out before him, his arms hanging limply at his sides, he no longer looked like that commanding figure who'd once stepped out onto the balcony and brought all of us to attention.

At that point I might have thought him broken, I suppose, a pitiful shell in gray work clothes, but suddenly he looked over at me, and the man I saw was not weak, nor timid, nor lacking in resolve. Rather, he seemed to smolder with a strangely building purpose, the eyes small, intense, deeply engaged, the jaw firmly set. It was a face I'd seen in old cowboy movies, a man about to draw.

Now, as I sat in the silence of my own kitchen, my eyes moving slowly from Peter to Marie, I wondered if it was at that precise moment that my father had decided that he would bear no more, that he would kill us all.

'These men,' Rebecca would later write, 'shouldered all they had been taught to shoulder, until their shoulders broke.'

Until their shoulders broke, and they reached for the pistol, the base-ball bat, the pellets encrusted with cyanide. Until their shoulders broke, and they stood on the third step and followed the little watery footprints as they led toward the empty cardboard box ... and fired.

Or was it only the slow wearing away she wanted to explore, the long descent toward that explosive second when the shoulders cracked and the savagery began?

'What are you thinking about, Steve?'

I glanced toward Marie. 'What?'

'You looked like you were thinking about something.'

'Just something at work,' I said.

Marie took me at my word and didn't press the matter. She went back to her breakfast, and after finishing it, walked upstairs to finish dressing.

I walked to my car and drove to work. Wally was leaning against my desk when I arrived. He handed me a note.

'Phone message,' he said with a leering grin.

I glanced at the message: 'Call Rebecca,' and then a number.

'Thanks,' I said to Wally, as I pocketed the note and slid in behind my desk.

Wally continued to stare at me knowingly. 'So, is she a nice woman, Steve?' he asked with a quick wink.

'Very,' I told him, but without emphasis, in the same way I might have said it of a business acquaintance.

Wally grinned. 'Glad to hear it,' he said, then walked away.

I dialed the number, and Rebecca answered the phone right away. 'Hello.'

'It's me.'

'Who?'

'Steve Farris.'

'Oh, Steve, thanks for calling,' she said. 'Listen, I was wondering if we might meet again this Friday.'

For the first time, I felt the pull of her voice as something alluring.

'I suppose so.'

'The same place? Around five?'

'Okay.'

Rebecca thanked me, then hung up. I went back to my work, but even as I continued sketching the design for the Massachusetts library, I felt both Rebecca and the task she had set herself lingering in the air around me. It gave a peculiar energy to my thoughts, a direction that hadn't been there before. It was as if, before Rebecca, a space had existed in my mind, empty and featureless, but which I had always felt as an odd, persistent ache. And so, as the days passed, and I went through the routine of work and home, I looked forward to my meeting with Rebecca as a wounded man might have looked forward to the first soothing touch of a doctor or a nurse.

I was relieved to see her when she arrived that Friday afternoon.

She was wearing a white blouse and dark green skirt that fell nearly to the floor. I noticed the skirt most: 'It's very beautiful.'

'Thank you,' Rebecca said. She was just that crisp and dismissive, a mode of behavior that her beauty had no doubt taught her, to be distant, restrained, to slap the hand long before it made its first uncertain movement toward her. She opened her briefcase and reached for something inside it, speaking at the same time, though with her eyes averted, focused on the papers her long brown fingers were riffling through.

'I brought a few pictures,' she said.

'Pictures of the murders?' I asked.

A certain wariness came into her face, as if she didn't want to rush me into a terrain that she knew I would find horrible.

'I have those pictures, too,' she said, 'but they're not for today.'

I watched her as she placed the pictures in a small stack at her right hand. It was obvious that she'd already arranged them in the order she thought appropriate. She shifted slightly in her seat, and I could hear the sound of her body as it rustled against her dark green skirt. It was a soft but highly detailed sound, crisp and distinct, like the crunch of bare feet moving softly over leaves.

She plucked the first picture from the stack and moved it slowly toward me. It was of my father when he was in his late teens. He was standing at the bus station in Highfield, dressed in blue jeans and a plaid shirt, his traveling case dangling from his hand.

'That must have been taken the day he left home,' I said.

'He went to New York, didn't he?' Rebecca asked.

'Yes.'

'Do you know anything about how he came to make that decision?'

At the time, I didn't. But I've learned a great deal since then. There was a box of letters and other papers which he left behind. Aunt Edna had stored them in her attic, and when she died, they came to me. For years they moldered in our basement, but when I finally began to look through them, I discovered, among other things, the world my father had confronted in his youth.

The Depression had been in full swing, of course, so that by the time he'd graduated from high school, he'd had few prospects in a town like Highfield. Because of that he'd gone to New York City, looking for work along with thousands of others, and had ended up in a dingy rooming house on Great Jones Street.

After Rebecca, when I finally visited that place, I found a plain, six-story brick building that had long ago been converted into a drafty, dilapidated warehouse. My father's room had been on the top floor, little more than a converted attic which he'd shared with several other men, a grim hall without a stove or a refrigerator, where the beds were hardly more than bunks, thin mattresses on wire springs.

From the room's dusty window, I could see the same brick street my father must have seen. The man who let me do it, standing in the doorway, watching me suspiciously as he puffed at a stubby black cigar, must have thought it odd that a son would wish to do such a thing, retrace, at such distance, the journey of his father. But he was willing to let me in anyway, escorting me up the stairs, and opening the long-closed door to a musty, unlighted room.

I didn't know exactly what part of the room my father had used as his small space. The beds had been removed years before, leaving only a bare floor and a scattering of loose boards. A great many names had been carved on the wooden walls and supporting beams, and for a while I looked for my father's name among them. I found J. C. Paxton and Monty Cochran and Leo Krantz and a host of other solitary males, but there was no sign of William P. Farris, or Bill Farris, or even W.P.F.

He'd lived there for nearly a year. Each night, from his small window, he'd seen the men in the street below, brooding by their open fires, tossing wooden slats into the flames while they grumbled about the state of things.

Dutifully he'd written home once a week, the letters preserved by his parents, then passed down to him, and finally, because of Mrs. Fields's second phone call, the one that made him quickly pull on his coat and hat and head for the waiting station wagon, also passed on to me.

They weren't chatty letters, and they suggested that my father hadn't felt much excitement about being in New York. They were informative, but little else. In them he mentioned the attic on Great Jones Street, but not that he shared it with a crowd of other itinerants. He talked about the weather, but only in the most general terms, days described as cold or hot, rainy or clear. The word 'pleasant' recurred, as did the word 'nasty', but all the more detailed descriptions were left out.

Left out too was the sense of limited horizons that must surely have overwhelmed him from time to time. He'd been a boy of only nineteen, alone in an enormous city, living in a dreary attic with nearly a dozen other people, men probably older than he, broken and displaced men, fleeing shattered homes. At night, he must have listened to their tales of bad luck and betrayal, perhaps from his own dark bunk, too young and inexperienced to join in the talk or to be treated as an equal.

Since Rebecca, I've often imagined him in such a posture, lying faceup on his grimy mattress, his pale blue eyes fixed on the ceiling, the murmur of voices curling around him while he tried to calculate his next move, a man locked in a grim and airless solitude.

But that day months before, as I stared quietly at the photograph Rebecca had placed before me, I saw only an empty-faced young man, a face without a past, almost a fictional character, one whom murder had created.

'I never heard my father talk about New York,' I said. 'I never heard him talk very much about Highfield, either.'

Rebecca didn't press me for more. Instead, she drew the photograph away and revealed the one beneath it, a picture of my mother as she stood beside a low stone wall. She was dressed in a light-colored skirt and blouse, her hair shining in a bright summer light.

'She looks about eighteen,' I said.

'Do you know anything about her youth?' Rebecca asked.

'I can't even imagine her as young,' I said. 'She always seemed so old to me.' I thought a moment, then added, 'I think she was probably a very depressed person. Clinically depressed.'

'Why do you think that?'

'She never seemed to have any energy. There was something faded in her, like she needed someone to brush the dust off her shoulders.'

Rebecca nodded toward the photograph. 'She seems to have a lot of energy in this picture,' she said. 'She looks quite vivid.'

I looked at the photograph again. My mother was smiling very cheerfully at the camera. She seemed not only young, but free, lighthearted, happy. There was a flirtatiousness in the way she leaned back against the stone wall, in the girlish tilt of her head, in the 'come hither' look she offered to the camera.

'Who took this picture?' I asked.

'I don't know,' Rebecca answered. 'They were among the pictures the police took from your house on McDonald Drive. No one ever claimed them, and so Swenson let me go through them. Most of them had dates and locations written on the back, but this one didn't.' She shrugged. 'I don't know why.'

My mother's face appeared to beam toward me, her joy sweeping out like a wave. 'I think I know why,' I said quietly. 'It was because she knew exactly where and when it had been taken, and knew that she'd never forget that particular moment.'

Rebecca said nothing. Instead she waited for me to continue, to call up some other memory of my mother.

'I don't have anything else to say about her,' I said after a while. 'She never talked about her youth. She never seemed to want to talk about it.'

'Why not?'

'Well, maybe she didn't want to be reminded of it,' I said, though without much certainty, mere conjecture. 'Maybe she didn't like to compare it to what her life became.'

'Which was?'

'Drudgery,' I said without hesitation, returning now to the woman of my most recent memories, the one in the red housedress, who piddled in the flower garden and lost herself in romance novels.

Rebecca nodded quickly, then slid the photograph to the side, revealing the one just under it.

It had been taken the day my father married my mother and it showed the two of them outside a small church. My mother stood beneath his arm, smiling brightly. My father seemed to be drawing her closely to his side, smiling, too.

Rebecca tapped my mother's face gently. 'Did he talk about her?' she asked.

I shrugged. 'Not to me.'

I was still looking vacantly at the same picture when Rebecca slid another one up beside it, the one taken years later, which showed my mother on the bed, her face and body neatly scrubbed, hands folded, dead.

I realized, of course, that it was the contrast Rebecca wanted, perhaps for the initial shock of it, or perhaps for something deeper, the sense that for 'these men' and their murdered families, life had been a long descent from some initial happiness to a murderous despair.

I looked at both pictures for a long time, shifting my concentration from one to the other before finally glancing up at Rebecca.

'What do you expect me to say?' I asked.

She didn't answer.

I tapped the picture of my father and mother on their wedding day. 'They seem happy together, don't they?'

Rebecca nodded, then looked at me significantly. 'Did you know that your mother was pregnant the day she got married?'

My eyes shot over to Rebecca. I was astonished. 'She was?' I asked, unbelievingly.

'According to the records, Jamie was born on October 7, 1942, only seven months after your parents were married,' Rebecca told me. 'He weighed nearly nine pounds, so he couldn't have been premature.'

I looked at the wedding photograph again, my eyes concentrating on my mother, the 'poor Dottie' of Aunt Edna's vision, and yet a woman who, in her youth, had done at least this one daring thing. She had slept with a man who was not yet her husband, an act that had seemed beyond the reach of the woman I remembered.

'We never know them, do we?' I said. 'Our parents.'

'It depends on what they're willing to reveal,' Rebecca answered.

I glanced at the photograph, this time settling on the tall, commanding figure of my father. He was dressed in his army uniform, the green garrison cap cocked raffishly to the right. 'He must have been on leave,' I said, unable to think of any other comment.

'Do you have his army records?'

'I don't know,' I answered. 'Are they important?'

'Well, I like to have a basic chronology of each man's life,' Rebecca answered.

'I'll look for it,' I told her, though unemphatically, my eyes still set firmly on my father's beaming face, on how happy he seemed. 'He doesn't seem to mind the idea that he's about to be a father,' I said.

'No, he probably didn't mind that at all,' Rebecca said. 'These men rarely do.'

I could see 'these men' more fully now. I could see them in their game rooms and their basements, in their trucks and station wagons, standing in their driveways and out beside their glittering blue swimming pools, men with baseball bats and rifles, who later killed their families in inconceivable acts of annihilating violence. Step by step, they were becoming less abstract to me, less headlines glimpsed in newspapers than faces emerging slowly from a pale white cloud.

I shook my head as I studied my father's smiling face on his wedding day. 'I would never have guessed that my father would have ended up as one of "these men", as you always call them,' I said.

For a moment I stared at the two pictures together, the wedding photo, and next to it my mother's motionless body, imagining the slow crawl of time that divided them, the invisible span of days and months and years that stretched from the smiling bride to the immobile corpse so neatly laid out behind the closed bedroom curtains. Suddenly, I saw my mother alive again, squatting by the little flower garden in the early evening, digging at the ground with her rusty spade as my father's brown van pulled into the driveway.

Often during those last weeks, he had not gotten out of the van immediately, but had remained inside, sitting behind the wheel, watching my mother silently while he smoked a cigarette, his light blue eyes piercing through the curling fog as they settled frozenly on my mother like the cross hairs of a telescopic sight.

'I can't imagine why he did it, Rebecca,' I said.

She looked at me pointedly, but said nothing.

'But I think he knew why,' I added.

I told about the time I'd gone down into the basement not long before the murders and found my father at work on the bicycle. I described his body clothed in gray flannel, his hands working steadily at the bicycle until they'd stopped abruptly, and he'd looked up at me, his eyes eerily motionless and sad, but utterly clear at the same time. I told her about standing on the third step, watching my father silently until he'd finally noticed me, lifted his eyes and held me in his gaze for a long moment before telling me cryptically that 'this' was all he wanted.

Rebecca did not write any of it down in the little pad she'd placed at her right hand. She merely listened attentively until I repeated my inevitable conclusion.

'I think my father was very conscious that there was something missing in his life,' I told her. I recalled his face again, the way he'd looked that night, the unreadable sadness I'd glimpsed in his eyes.

Once again my eyes swept down to the photograph, my father's face shining toward me from the picture taken on his wedding day. There was no doubt of his happiness on that day, of the delight he'd felt. He had the look of a man who believed that he'd accomplished something.

'Something missing,' I repeated as I glanced back up at her again. 'Which made him want to kill us all.'

Rebecca's next question surprised me. 'Why do you think he didn't kill you, Steve?'

'I think he intended to,' I told her, 'but that he got scared off by the phone calls.'

'The ones Mrs. Fields made,' Rebecca said. She took a pen out of her briefcase and held it over the blank page of her notebook. 'So you don't think he spared you because he had some special feeling for you?' she asked. 'Or maybe even because you were his youngest son.'

'Well, he killed his oldest son,' I said, 'so why wouldn't he have killed me?' I shook my head. 'No, I don't think he intentionally spared me. I think that if I'd come home on time that afternoon, he'd have killed me just like he killed the others.'

She paused a moment before asking her next question. 'What's your most vivid memory of your father?'

I hesitated before answering, though not in an attempt to keep her in suspense, but only because, at first, I wasn't sure. Finally, I said, 'I remember how much my sister loved him.'

Rebecca's eyes softened, as if this gentle answer had reached her unexpectedly.

'I don't know what she saw in my father,' I added. 'He always seemed so ordinary to me.'

The word 'ordinary' appeared to surprise her.

'I mean, he didn't have any special skills,' I explained. 'He wasn't a great talker, or anything like that. The only thing that ever really interested him was those bicycles of his.'

Rebecca looked at me curiously. 'Bicycles?'

I nodded. 'He imported very expensive racing bikes from England. Special ones. Rodger and Windsor. They were always red, he sold them in that little hardware store he owned. It was like some kind of obsession. He would assemble them himself, and he was always down in the basement doing that.'

'Down in the basement? Would your sister sometimes go down there?'

I'd never thought of it before, but Rebecca's question brought it all back.

'Yes, she would,' I said. 'I'd sometimes hear them talking together.'

Even at that moment, with Rebecca sitting across from me as evening fell outside the glass windows, I could hear those voices as if they were still lifting toward me, rising like smoke through the floor. They were soft voices, almost in whispers, secretive, intimate.

'Do you have any idea what they talked about?' Rebecca asked.

'I don't think Laura ever told me.'

I let my mind drift back. I could see Laura moving across the living room, her bare feet padding across the beige carpet, her long dark hair flowing down her back as she headed for the door that led down the stairs to the basement. I could hear my father's hammer tapping just below me, then the sound of Laura's feet as she walked down the stairs. It was at that point, as I remembered, that the tapping had always stopped. Stopped entirely, and never started again until Laura had come back up the stairs. The memory produced a faintly alarming realization.

'She was the only one in the family who could draw him away from that obsession he had with bicycles,' I said. 'I guess you could say she was the only person who had any real power over him.'

'What kind of power?'

'I don't know.'

'Well, there are only a few kinds,' Rebecca said, ticking them off one by one. 'There's money, of course, and love. Kinship. Desire.' Rebecca stared at me intently. 'And duty. These men are always dutiful.'

I nodded. 'Yes,' I said. 'My father was dutiful.'

As I spoke, I saw him join the ranks of these other men. Like them, he'd been dutiful down to the last second. For a moment, I envisioned him as a ghostly, scooped-out man in gray flannels, trudging wearily up the aisle of the hardware store, his arms laden with tools or boxes of nails. I wondered how often during that long walk up the same dusty aisle he'd searched for some way out of his vast responsibilities, a pathway through the bramble, before he'd settled upon murder. I imagined him making another choice, to live and let us live, going on, year after year, growing old and gray and bent as he sat behind the wheel of the brown van. I imagined my mother aging into a crippled husk, unable to bend any longer over her desolate little flower garden. I saw Jamie fattening into middle age, Laura drying into a parched doll. Had my father seen all that, too? Had he glimpsed the whole dark game, seen it play out move by move in a process so unbearable that he'd finally settled on murder as a way to break the rules?

'Very dutiful,' I repeated. 'Despite the way life is.'

'The way life is?' Rebecca repeated, as if puzzled by the phrase.

'You know, the way people live,' I said. 'Going to work every day. Sticking to the same job. Coming home at the same time. Day after day, the same rooms, the same faces.'

Rebecca began to write in her notebook. I watched her hand, the slender fingers wrapped delicately around the dark shaft of the pen. I'd heard the strange contempt which had risen into my voice as I'd described the mundane nature of everyday life, and as I watched Rebecca's pen skirt across the open page of her notebook, I felt that somehow I had exposed myself. It was an uneasy and unsettling feeling, and for an instant I regretted that I'd ever agreed to talk to her.

'You know, sometimes I'm not really sure I can go on with this,' I said.

She looked at me squarely. 'You can stop whenever you want.'

But I knew that I couldn't in the least do that. I knew that I'd become enamored of a mystery, that I wanted to feel the edgy tension and exhilaration of closing in upon a dangerous and undiscovered thing.

For a moment, I let my eyes linger on her as she wrote, her head bent forward slightly, the long dark hair falling nearly to her pen. When she looked up again, I thought I saw a subtle recognition in her face, an uneasiness that made me glance away, my eyes fleeing toward the large glass window to my left and the darkening landscape beyond it. Far away, I could see night descending over the distant hills. It seemed to fall helplessly, out of control, to spin and tumble as it fell.

# SEVEN

Night had fully fallen by the time I got home. Marie and Peter were in the kitchen, both of them working at the evening's dinner, Marie chopping onions, Peter shaping hamburger patties.

She stopped as I came through the door and looked at me closely. 'You look tired,' she said.

'There's a lot of work at the office,' I told her.

'Are you going to be staying late often?'

'Maybe.'

She nodded, then returned to the cutting board. 'I finished the bid this afternoon.'

'Bid?'

She glanced at me, puzzled. 'The Bridgeport bid,' she said, 'the one I've been working on so long.'

'Oh, right,' I said. 'You think you'll get the contract?'

She shrugged. 'Maybe. You never know.'

I began to set the table, one of the 'family time' jobs that had fallen to me. Peter continued slapping at the raw meat, making a game of it.

'Do it right,' I told him, a little sharply.

Marie looked at me, surprised by the edginess in my voice. 'Are you okay, Steve?'

I nodded. 'Yeah, why?'

She didn't answer. Instead, she returned to her work. 'I thought it might be nice to visit my parents tomorrow,' she said after a moment. 'We haven't seen them in several weeks.'

I nodded. 'It's fine with me.'

'So you don't have to go in to work tomorrow?'

'No.'

Marie smiled. 'Good,' she said, 'we'll have a nice day in the country, then.'

Peter finished making the hamburger patties and handed them to Marie.

'Good job, Peter,' she said lightly, as she took them from him.

We ate dinner shortly after that, then Peter went to the den to watch television while Marie and I cleaned up the kitchen.

'What exactly are you working on now?' she asked.

'A library for a little town in Massachusetts,' I answered.

She looked surprised. 'And that's what kept you at the office tonight?'

'Yeah,' I said. 'Mr. Lowe has a personal interest in the project. It's for his hometown, and so I want it to be right before he sees it.'

The real reason for my being late in coming home swam into my mind, and I saw Rebecca's face staring at me questioningly. I remembered the request she'd made for more information about my father's life, the chronology she was trying to construct, her interest in his army records.

'Do you remember when Aunt Edna died, and we went to her house, and found that box of papers that had belonged to my father?'

Marie nodded.

'You took it out of the car when we got back,' I reminded her. 'Do you remember what you did with it?'

'It's in the basement,' Marie answered. 'I wrote "Somerset" on the side of it. I think it's on the top shelf.' She looked at me curiously. 'Why?'

'I thought I might look through it,' I answered. 'I never have.'

Marie smiled half-mockingly. 'You're not gearing up for a midlife crisis, are you, Steve?' she asked. 'You know, trying to get in touch with yourself, going back over things?' The smile broadened. 'Reliving your "significant life experiences", that sort of thing?'

I shook my head. 'No, I don't think so. I'm just curious about what's in the box.'

My answer appeared to satisfy her. She turned to another subject, something about Peter wanting to try out for the school basketball team, and not long after that she joined him in the den. I could hear them laughing together at whatever it was they were watching.

I walked down the corridor to the stairs that led to the basement. The box was exactly where Marie had said it would be, on the top shelf, the word SOMERSET marked in large, block letters. I dragged it down and carried it back upstairs to my own small office.

I put the box on my desk and opened it. Inside, I could see a disordered mound of papers. They were all that remained of my father, a scattering of letters, documents, a few photographs. I doubted that there could be anything among them that Rebecca would find useful.

I started to reach for the first of the papers when I glanced up and saw Marie at my office door.

She was looking at the box. 'Well, you sure didn't waste any time finding it,' she said.

261

'It was where you said it would be.'

She smiled. 'Peter wants you to come into the den.'

'Why?'

'So we can all watch his favorite show together.'

I didn't move.

'You got home very late tonight,' Marie added. 'I think he sort of missed you.' She stretched her hand toward me. 'Come on,' she said softly.

I rose slowly, reluctantly, and went with her. We walked down the corridor together. In the family room, I watched television with my wife and son, talking occasionally, laughing when they laughed, but only out of duty. The force that had once compelled me to such small acts of devotion was already losing speed.

We left the house at around ten the next morning. The drive north toward the Massachusetts border was along winding, country roads. Peter sat in the back, working with a portable video game, while Marie leaned against the door on the passenger side, the window open, the rush of air continually blowing through the red highlights in her hair.

Was she beautiful?

Marie would insist that I say no. She would insist that I admit that it was beauty which formed the grim core of what happened in the end, her own beauty either faded or familiar, Rebecca's either new or in full bloom. She would insist that it was desire which drove me forward, desire alone, since, as she would say to me that final night, 'It was never love ...'

We arrived at her parents' small country house only an hour or so after leaving Old Salsbury. It was a medium-sized, wooden house, painted white, with a large, wraparound porch. In his retirement, Carl had taken up furniture making, and in typical style, had overdone the labor, making far more plain wooden rocking chairs than were strictly needed. As I pulled into the unpaved driveway, I could see several of them on the front porch or scattered randomly about the lawn, rocking eerily when a strong burst of wind swept down from the mountains.

For all the abundance of empty chairs, Carl was sitting on the front steps of the house when we pulled up. Marie had called her mother earlier that morning and let Amelia know that we were coming, but from the pleasantly surprised look on Carl's face, I realized that she'd never gotten around to telling him to expect us.

He rose slowly, pulling himself up by one of the wooden banisters which bordered the stairs, then waved broadly as we all got out of the car. He was a tall man, with narrow shoulders and long, thin legs. He wore a pair of light brown flannel work pants and a short-sleeved checkered shirt. From a distance he appeared to have a thick head of snowy white hair, but up close, his pink scalp easily showed through it. I'd first met him only a month or so after meeting Marie, the two of us driving up from New York City. He'd tried his best to be lighthearted that evening, but even then, he'd had the aging factory worker's sense of the bulkiness of things, their ironclad inflexibility.

Marie made it to him first, pressing herself into his arms, then kissing him lightly on the cheek.

'Hi, Dad,' she said.

He held her tightly for a moment, as old people sometimes do, never knowing which embrace will be the last. Then he turned to me and shook my hand with his firm, industrial grip.

'How you doing, Steve?' he asked.

'Fine.'

It was Peter's turn then, and Carl all but yanked him from the ground.

'You got a girlfriend yet?' he demanded.

Peter had not had time to answer before Amelia's voice came booming toward us from above.

'Don't ask personal questions, Carl,' she snapped, but in a friendly, joking tone. She shook her head with comic exasperation. 'What am I going to do with him?'

She was a tall, slender woman, with thin arms and a somewhat hawkish face. She seemed to hop down the stairs toward us, nervous and bird-like. Once at the bottom of them, she swept Peter into her arms, then Marie. Finally she turned to me, gave me a quick, no-nonsense hug, then firmly pushed me away.

In her youth, Amelia had been a great beauty, locally renowned, and I assumed that the glancing, cautious way she had always embraced and separated from me was a holdover from those bygone days when her slightest touch had given too strong a signal to the breathless men who'd flocked around her. According to Carl, these same men, old now, with shaking heads, still spoke of her in the social club downtown. 'They still can't get over that I had her every night,' he'd once told me with a wry, self-satisfied grin, then added significantly, 'And she was just eighteen years old, Steve. Can you imagine that?'

Now she was seventy-one, still tall and dignified, like her daughter, but with withered skin, iron-gray hair, and hasty, nervous eyes that glanced about restlessly, as if trying to get a glimpse of where it had all gone.

We followed her into the house, all of us climbing up the stairs toward the open front door. Carl brought up the rear, pulling himself up by means of the old wooden rail.

Marie and her mother disappeared into the back of the house while Carl and I sat down in the front room. I looked at him silently, smiling amiably, as I watched him ease himself down into the overstuffed chair by the piano. A mild heart attack had shaken him three years before, and only last summer he'd fallen in the garden behind the house, and, unable to get up, had wallowed in the tomato plants for nearly ten minutes before Amelia had finally spotted him and come running to his side.

Now, as I watched him, he seemed to age almost by the minute, his hair whitening, his skin wrinkling, his long legs drawing up under the cuffs of his trousers.

For a moment he remained silent, then he nodded idly toward the piano.

'You don't play, do you, Steve?' he asked, a question he had asked me several times before, always forgetting my answer.

'No,' I said.

'Amy used to play,' Carl said. He drew in a deep breath and let it out in a quick, exhausted rush, as if the burden of holding in his breath were becoming too much for him. 'She played for the Knights of Columbus,' he went on. 'At a dance one night when Jimmy Doyle didn't show up.' He winked boyishly. 'She wasn't that good, but she gave it a good try.'

I smiled.

'All you can ask, right?' Carl added. 'To give it a good try.'

'I suppose so.'

'It's the same for life,' Carl said. 'You can't do more than give it a good try.'

I nodded softly, letting my eyes drift away, hoping that with that gesture I could avoid giving Carl any further encouragement toward sharing his philosophy. In the past few years, as old age had overtaken him, he'd become increasingly homespun and folksy, dotting his conversation with empty truisms that annoyed Marie, but which Amelia seemed hardly to notice.

'I wouldn't say Amy was at a professional level,' Carl went on. 'But she was pretty good.' He pulled a red handkerchief from the back pocket of his trousers and began to wipe his face, his eyes drifting over the room.

It was a room that Amelia dominated entirely, pictures of her lined up on top of the piano or hanging from the walls, all of them taken much earlier, in the days of her youthful glory. She'd been her father's favorite, and probably her mother's, too, and she'd grown up beneath the gaze of a thousand desperately admiring eyes. From that spawning pool of frantically beseeching men, she'd selected a factory worker named Carl. It had been a choice which had baffled, disturbed, and finally embittered her parents. In the end, they'd entirely rejected Carl, an experience he'd never forgotten. 'My wife's parents froze me out,' he told me that first weekend when Marie brought me to his home. 'My wife was so pretty, you see. They thought that was her ticket to a brighter future, you know? Then, poor thing, she got tied up with me.'

It was precisely that brighter future that seemed to shine from the photographs which cluttered and overwhelmed the room, all of them taken during Amelia's glory days, first as a little girl in her father's arms, later as an adolescent growing toward a stunning womanhood, and finally as a young woman posing by the lake on that single, breathless day her beauty reached its frail, already fading peak.

I drew my eyes away from that last picture and toward the woman herself as Amelia suddenly came back into the room. She was carrying a large picnic basket, and Marie and Peter were standing just behind her, both of them holding a few lightweight folding chairs.

'We thought we'd go on a picnic,' Amelia said. Her eyes swept over to Carl. 'What do you think, hon? Just a short walk over to the spring?'

Carl nodded. 'Yeah. I'm up for that,' he said, already pulling himself to his feet.

I looked at Marie. She was smiling at Carl with great cheerfulness and affection, which were still on her face when she turned to me.

'Okay with you, Steve?' she asked.

'Sure.'

The spring was small, and it flowed in gentle curves through a glade of trees. It was no more than a short walk from the house, but Carl's pace was slow and halting, so it was almost twenty minutes later when we reached the shady embankment Amelia had already designated for the picnic.

By that time it was early afternoon, the sun still high and very bright in a cloudless blue. Amelia and Marie spread a large checkered cloth over the grass and began to take the various sandwich meats and breads out of the basket. Peter opened the folding chairs and after a while we were all seated comfortably by the water.

'It's pretty here, don't you think?' Amelia asked, though to no one in particular.

Marie nodded, her eyes on me. 'Dad and I used to fish in this little stream.'

Carl chuckled. 'You never caught anything though, did you, Marie?'

Marie shook her head. 'How could I? All I had was that little plastic pole, remember? The one you bought at the dime store downtown?'

'He bought you that for Christmas one year,' Amelia added, 'and you had to wait several months for the ice to break before you could use it.' She glanced at Carl. 'I told you it would drive her crazy giving her a thing like that in the winter, a thing she couldn't play with right away.'

Carl laughed again as he glanced toward Marie. 'It did just about drive you crazy, too,' he said. 'We went fishing the first day the ice broke up.' He shivered. 'It was cold as hell.'

In my mind, I could see them by the little spring, the winter thaw barely a few days old, a snowy border on both sides of the stream, the trees bare and creaking in the frozen breeze as they dipped their hooks into the icy, fishless water.

'You really kept at it, though,' Carl said to Marie admiringly. 'We must have stayed out here a couple hours. You just wouldn't go back in.' He looked at Amelia. 'How old was she that year, Amy?'

'Six,' Amelia answered, almost wistfully. 'She was six years old.'

I looked over at Peter, remembered him at six years old, a little boy with reddish cheeks and gleaming eyes. It was the year I'd taken him to the state fair in Danbury, taken pictures of him as he was led about on a small, spotted pony, fed him hot dogs and cotton candy until he'd finally puked behind a huge green circus tent.

I laughed suddenly at the thought of it.

Marie looked at me, a smile playing on her lips. 'What are you laughing about, Steve?'

'I was just remembering the first time we took Peter to the Danbury Fair.'

I could see the whole day playing through Marie's memory, sweet, almost delectable, even down to the last unsavory moment. 'He threw up,' she said, 'behind this big tent.'

Peter grimaced. 'I did?'

Carl waved his hand. 'Everybody throws up,' he said. He leaned back in his chair and lifted his face upward slightly, as if trying to get some sun.

'Careful there, hon,' Amelia warned. 'Don't tip back too far.'

Carl waved his hand as he leaned back a bit farther. 'A man's got to take a risk, right, Steve?' he said as he pressed himself back farther, Amelia watching him steadily, growing tense until he bolted forward suddenly and caught her eyes in his.

'Scared you, didn't I?' he joked.

Amelia's face relaxed. 'He's always trying to get at me,' she said, her eyes now on me. She began a story about some other occasion when Carl had 'gotten her', as she put it, then followed with another.

While she spoke, I felt my mind drift away, drift along the shaded stream, as if skating lightly across the glassy surface of the water. I could hear Amelia's voice, as well as the laughter of the others as she continued with her tale. I heard names and places, dates, weather reports, ages. I could even feel the overall warmth of the moment we were all sharing, its calmness, pleasure, and serenity.

And yet, I could also feel myself moving away from it, down the softly winding stream, its twin banks gliding smoothly along either side, as if I were being carried on a small canoe. Overhead, I could see the flow of the trees as they passed above me, flowing like another stream, this one suspended surreally above my head. Slowly, almost without my realizing it, the stream became a sleek blue road, winding through a maze of suburban streets, neat lines of houses flowing past on both sides, until, in the distance, I could see the mock Tudor house at 417 McDonald Drive. It was silent, and not at all threatening, and as I continued to drift toward it in my mind, I could feel a grave attraction for it, an excitement at drawing near it, as if it were a place of assignation.

A burst of laughter brought me back, loud and wrenching as a sudden gunshot. I blinked quickly and stared around me. Everyone was laughing – Marie, Peter, Carl. Everyone but Amelia, who, as I noticed, was staring directly toward me with steady, evaluating eyes.

'Where were you, Steve?' she asked.

I shrugged. 'I don't know.'

She didn't seem to believe me. Her eyes remained very still, her face framed by the swirling circular maelstrom of her old straw hat. 'Just in some other world, I guess,' she said, in a strangely cool and brooding voice.

I nodded, but added nothing else.

Amelia returned her attention to the others. Carl was telling some story about Marie as a little girl, and a few feet away Peter was listening very attentively, as if surprised by the fact that his mother had ever been a child.

I listened attentively too, though from time to time my eye would return to the spring, follow a leaf as it flowed through the dappled shade until it disappeared around the nearest bend.

Toward the end of the afternoon, we repacked the picnic basket, gathered up the folding chairs, and returned to the house. Carl and Amelia walked in the lead, arm in arm, chatting quietly on the way. I could not make out any of what they were saying to each other, but from the quiet glances they exchanged it seemed one of those intimate, deeply familiar conversations one sometimes sees in older people, the sense of completedness, of everything having passed the trial stage.

Marie walked along beside me, her arm in mine, her head pressed lightly against my shoulder. She seemed contented, happy with how the day had gone, with the choices she'd made in her life so far, with me as her husband, with Peter as her son. It was the kind of satisfaction that seemed complete in itself, rather than the product of a thinly disguised resignation.

As we neared the house, Peter shot ahead, running through the tall grass, his blond hair glistening in the sunlight. I felt Marie press her head more firmly against my shoulder.

I glanced down at her.

She was staring up at me affectionately, as if marveling at her own contentment. Then she lifted her face toward me and kissed me on the mouth. Bathed in such sweetness and familiarity, the product of such a long and enduring love, it should have been the single most thrilling kiss I had ever known.

Toward evening, Carl made a fire in the old hearth, and we all sat around it, talking quietly. Marie sat beside me on the sofa, her feet balled up beneath her, her shoulder pressed up snugly against mine. Peter slept next to her, his head resting delicately in her lap.

'Everything going okay at work, Steve?' Carl asked idly, by then puffing on the white meerschaum pipe Marie had given him the preceding Christmas.

'Yeah,' I said.

'He'll probably be made a partner soon,' Marie said.

Carl looked at her. 'How about your business?'

'It's fine,' Marie told him. 'I put in a bid for a job in Bridgeport last week.'

I glanced over toward Amelia. She was rocking softly in one of the chairs Carl had made, but her eyes seemed not to move at all as she stared at me.

'So I guess everything's okay, then?' she asked.

I nodded. 'Yes, it is.'

I expected her to smile, or give some sign of satisfaction, but she didn't. She turned toward the fire instead, and held her eyes there, the light playing on her face in the way of old romantic movies.

We left an hour later, Peter piling groggily into the back seat while Marie and I said good-bye. Carl hugged each of us in turn, then stepped back to allow Amelia to do the same.

'Nice seeing you again,' she said easily, then glanced over at me. 'Be good, Steve,' she told me in a voice that seemed stern and full of warning.

Marie sat close to me on the drive home, breathing softly as we drove through the dark countryside. Once back in Old Salsbury, we led Peter to his room, and watched, amused and smiling, as he collapsed onto his bed.

Later, in bed ourselves, Marie inched toward me, stroking me slowly. We made love sweetly and well, with that correctness of pace and expertise that only custom can attain. After that, Marie moved quietly into a restful sleep.

Toward dawn I felt her awaken slightly. She lifted her head in the early light, smiled, kissed my chest, then lowered her head down on it again and closed her eyes. While I waited for the morning, I stroked her hair.

So it was never love, as she would say to me that last night, it was never love ... that was missing.

Marie was still sleeping in the morning when I got up and headed downstairs to my office. It was smaller than Marie's, since I'd always done most of my work at Simpson and Lowe, while Marie did most of hers at home. It contained little more than a drafting table, a large light, and a few metal filing cabinets.

I sat down at the table, pulled out the latest plans for my dream house, and began to go over the details again, searching for places where I could remove yet another enclosed area from what was already an impossibly airy and unreal space. But as I worked, I found myself increasingly unable to concentrate on the plans before me. It was as if the dream house had become, at last, pure dream, nothing more than idle whimsy, an idea for which I no longer felt any genuine conviction. It was Rebecca and her search that seemed real to me now, and I even allowed myself to hope that from time to time Rebecca might sense my presence beside her, silent, determined, armed as she was armed, with the same grisly instruments of night, the two of us equally committed to tracking down 'these men', poking at the ashes they had left behind, closing in on their distant hiding places.

I remembered the photograph she'd shown me on Friday afternoon. I saw my father standing in the open, his army cap cocked to the side. The smile on his face had seemed absolutely genuine. It had given his face an immense happiness, a joy and sense of triumph that I'd never seen before. Not in life. Not in any other photograph. That day, April 1, 1942, I realized with complete certainty, had been his finest moment.

Rebecca had already noted that my mother had to have been pregnant with Jamie by then, but it wasn't the fact of my brother's technical illegitimacy which struck me suddenly. It was something else, a curious memory of something that had happened when I was eight years old, a year or more before the murders, but which I could now recall very clearly.

It was a spring day, and my father had been doing some kind of repair work in the basement. He'd asked Laura to bring him something from the garage. Laura had gone to find it, but after several minutes, she still hadn't come back into the house, and so my father had turned to me.

'Go get Laura,' he told me.

I went up the stairs, out the kitchen door, and into the garage, expecting to find Laura still searching through the usual disarray to find whatever it was my father wanted. But she was sitting in a far corner instead, her body in a dusky, yellow light. A pile of blue papers was scattered at her feet, all of them spilling out of a small shoe box that had obviously fallen from the shelf overhead. She had one of the light blue pieces of paper in her hand, but she was no longer reading it. She was simply sitting motionlessly, deep in thought, her eyes lifted toward the dark, wooden ceiling.

I called to her, but very softly. 'Laura?'

She looked at me directly, her body still motionless, except for the way her fingers slowly curled around the blue paper, as if to conceal it.

'What do you want, Stevie?' she asked stiffly.

'Dad wants you,' I told her.

She drew her hands behind her, the blue note disappearing behind her back. 'Tell him I'll be there in a minute,' she said. 'I have to clean up this mess.'

I did as she told me, and for a while my father seemed satisfied that Laura was on her way. But later, with his typical impatience, he finally headed up the stairs and out to the garage. I followed behind him, a dog at his heels.

Laura was still in the same corner as we entered the garage, the same blue paper in her hand. She tried to hide it again, which surprised me, since I'd never before seen her try to conceal anything from my father.

His eyes fixed on the paper. 'What is that?' he asked.

Laura didn't answer.

My father walked through the dusky light and drew the paper from Laura's fingers.

From my place at the front of the garage, I watched as he read it. When he'd finished, he turned to me.

'Go play, Stevie,' he said.

I was in the backyard a few minutes later when the two of them came out of the garage. Laura was nestled beneath my father's arm, and they were walking slowly toward the house.

My mother came home a short time later. She'd been grocery shopping, I remember, and as she headed up the stairs, her arms around an enormous brown bag, my father stepped out of the house, took the bag from her, and returned it to the car. Then he motioned for her to follow him and the two of them walked past me and over to the very edge of the yard. I was too far away from them to make out any of what they said, but I remember having the distinct feeling that they were talking about the blue papers Laura had found in the garage.

After a while they walked back toward the house. They were still talking, and as they passed, I heard my mother say, 'You told her not to ...' She didn't finish, because Jamie suddenly came rushing around the corner of the house. At the sight of him, both my father and my mother froze, each of them staring at him with such frightened, startled looks that I had sensed even then that the blue papers, and everything that had happened since I'd seen Laura reading them, had had something to do with Jamie.

During the next few days, however, the entire incident slipped from my mind. Everything returned to its normal pattern, except that my mother seemed even more subdued. There were times, forever after that, when she seemed to flee from any notion of command. Steadily over the next few years, she became more vaporous, slowly giving up the prerogatives of wife and mother so that in the end she seemed more like some distant relative we'd saved from poverty or shame, one who lived with us but had no standing among us, no office or authority, incontestably by then the 'poor Dottie' of my aunt's unforgiving judgment.

But for the rest of us, nothing seemed to change, and as I sat at my desk that morning, remembering the blue papers, it struck me that I wouldn't have remembered it at all if something else hadn't happened, something which I always believed was connected in some way to what had been written in them.

It was about three months later. My father had recently put a redwood picnic table under the large maple tree that stood beside the rear fence, and Laura and I had begun meeting there to play Monopoly or checkers or some other game. That particular day, Laura had begun to teach me chess. Slowly, with infinite patience, she introduced me to each piece. I had only played checkers before, and it was not easy for me to get a grip on this much more complicated game.

We'd been at it for nearly an hour before Jamie strode across the backyard and sat himself down on the bench beside me.

Laura hardly registered his presence. Instead, she continued to concentrate on teaching me the game. Jamie watched sullenly while she did it, as if evaluating each word my sister spoke, each gesture she made, second-guessing and inwardly ridiculing her, at times even smiling snidely when she got something slightly wrong or out of order and had to correct herself.

As the minutes passed, I could feel the air heating up and turning sour around us. It was as if the peaceful little island that Laura and I created when we were together had been invaded by a poisonous wind.

Finally, the storm broke.

'You're doing it all wrong, Laura,' Jamie snapped. 'It's stupid the way you're teaching him.'

Laura didn't so much as look at him. She picked up the knight, and began to explain its move.

'You're going to screw it up, as usual,' Jamie barked.

Laura's eyes shot over to him. 'You're not supposed to talk like that in front of Stevie.'

'I'm trying to keep him from being a loser, Laura,' Jamie fired back. 'The way you're teaching him this game, he'll play it like a sissy.'

Laura's eyes narrowed lethally. 'Nobody asked you, anyway, Jamie,' she hissed angrily. 'Nobody asked you to come over here and bother us.'

Jamie leaned toward her threateningly. 'I don't have to be asked,' he said. 'It's my yard, too, you know.'

For a flaming instant, Laura glared at him with a terrible ferocity. Then she turned her attention back to the game, but not before muttering a single, indecipherable phrase. 'Sort of,' she said.

It had been said under her breath, but loud enough for us to hear it.

'What did you say?' Jamie demanded.

Laura didn't answer. She picked up one of the knights and pressed it toward me. I could see that it was trembling in her hand.

'What did you say, Laura?' Jamie repeated, only this time in a tone that was more than teenage anger. Cold. Severe. A prelude to explosive rage.

Laura locked her eyes on mine. 'This is the knight,' she said evenly, 'it moves like this.' She lowered the knight to the board and demonstrated the move.

Jamie continued to stare at her with a terrible, quivering hatred. I remember bracing myself, my own mind racing to decide what I would do if he lunged forward and hit her.

But he did no such thing. After a few more impossibly tense seconds, he simply rose silently and left us, a lean, disjointed figure striding awkwardly across the green summer lawn.

Laura had resumed teaching me about the knight by the time Jamie had finally disappeared into the house. She went directly to its moves, to various ways of using it. She didn't try to explain what she'd meant with that angry, nearly whispered 'Sort of', and I never heard her say anything so cryptic to Jamie after that.

So what had my sister meant that day beneath the maple tree?

For well over thirty years, it was a question I'd never asked. Then, that Sunday morning, as Peter and Marie slept upstairs and I sat at my desk, with both Rebecca and her mission steadily gaining force in my own mind, I tried to find out. I went to the box I'd brought up from the basement the day before, hoping that the answer might be there.

Within a matter of only a few minutes, I discovered that it was.

# EIGHT

Three days later, Rebecca had hardly taken her seat across from me at the restaurant before I handed her the document I'd found in the box. She took it from my hand and began to read it. What I gave her that evening was something she'd already asked for, my father's army records. After the war, he'd taken a few college classes under the GI Bill of Rights. A short application process had been required, and he'd submitted several forms to prove that he'd been in the army. One of them was a listing of his whereabouts during all that time. It began with Newark, New Jersey, where he'd been inducted in June of 1940, and ended with New York City, where he'd been mustered out on a medical discharge, an injured knee, in May of 1942. All the places my father had lived during those two years of military service were listed in the document, along with all of his official leaves. What it showed unmistakably was that he had lived at Fort Bragg, North Carolina, from July of 1941 until April of 1942, when he'd been given leave to return to New Jersey, and where, on April 1, he'd married my mother in a civil ceremony in Somerset.

When Rebecca finished reading, she looked up, her face very still. She had instantly put it together.

'Jamie was not your father's son,' she said.

'No, he couldn't have been. My father was in North Carolina when my brother was conceived.'

'And so he must have known that he wasn't the father of the child your mother was carrying. Even on the day he married her,' Rebecca added wonderingly.

'Yes, he had to have known that.'

She thought a moment, then asked, 'So who was Jamie's father?'

'I don't know,' I answered. 'How could I know? It all happened a long time before I was born.' Then something occurred to me. 'Do you have the pictures you showed me last time?'

'Yes.' Rebecca took them out and spread them across the table.

I lifted the one that showed my mother posed alluringly against the stone wall and handed it to Rebecca. 'I think maybe the man who took this was Jamie's father,' I said. 'I mean, look at my mother, at the way her face is shining.'

Rebecca let her eyes dwell on the picture as I continued.

'I think my mother was in love that day,' I said. 'She was satisfied in every way. I don't think my father ever made her feel like that.'

Rebecca returned the photograph to the table. She remained silent.

'Reading all those romance novels, that was the way my mother went back to that time in her life,' I told her. 'She never forgot him. She never forgot the way he made her feel.' I glanced over at the picture of my father. 'Maybe that's what my father couldn't bear, that he was going to live the rest of his life in the shadow of my mother's first love.'

'Which might explain your mother's murder, and perhaps even Jamie's,' Rebecca said. 'But what about Laura?'

I had no answer, and after a moment, Rebecca's eyes returned to the picture of my father on his wedding day. 'Even though he must have known about the child, he looks very happy in this picture,' she said.

'He was happy, I think,' I admitted. 'It's the only picture he ever looked that happy in.'

She thought a while longer, then returned her attention to the military document that had revealed everything. 'Where did you find this?'

'In some papers my aunt left me,' I said, 'but there was something else I couldn't find.'

I told her about the blue papers, the ones Laura had found in the garage that day, the ones, I felt sure now, that had told her everything about Jamie, that he was only 'sort of' a member of our family.

'So Laura knew,' I said when I'd finished, 'and she used that knowledge against Jamie at least once.'

I went through the story of the argument beneath the maple tree.

'Do you think Jamie knew what Laura meant?' Rebecca asked.

'I don't know.'

Rebecca considered everything I'd told her for a few seconds. 'What were the blue papers?' she asked finally. 'They weren't documents, were they?'

'No ... I think they could have been love letters,' I answered slowly, 'from Jamie's real father. Letters she couldn't part with.'

'Even at the risk of their being found.'

'Yes.'

And so all my old surmises about my mother had been wrong. 'Poor Dottie' had swooned to someone's touch, had caught her breath, taken a stunning risk, and in doing that had lived for just a moment the life she only read about from then on, in novels piled beside her bed.

Rebecca leaned back in her seat and remained very quiet for a long time. She was still thinking about my mother, I believe, but my mind had shifted over to my father, to the smiling figure in the photograph, triumphant on his wedding day.

'He must have loved my mother a great deal to marry her knowing that she was already carrying another man's child,' I said.

Rebecca didn't look so sure.

I remembered the look on my father's face the night I'd gone down into the basement, stopped on the third step, and watched him work silently on his latest Rodger and Windsor until his eyes had finally lifted toward me. I heard his words again: *This is all I want.*

'Or maybe all he ever wanted was just a wife and kids,' I said.

Rebecca looked at me. 'Except that he killed his wife, and two of his children,' she said sharply, 'slaughtered them one by one, in cold blood.'

It was at that moment that the full ruin of my family struck me in all its horror. In a weird, nightmarish vision, I felt myself pass effortlessly through the walls of 417 McDonald Drive as if they were nothing more than stage scrims, solid at one moment, dreamily transparent at the next, so that I could see through the whole house at a single glance, see one day's death unroll before me in far more grisly and exact detail than I had ever been able to imagine it before.

My father's old brown van glides into the rainswept driveway, its slick black tires throwing arcs of water into the air behind them. From its gloomy interior, my father's face stares at me from behind the van's black, serrated wheel, his eyes glowing from its gray interior like unblinking small blue lights. He does not linger inside the van, but emerges quickly and determinedly, then walks at a measured, unhurried pace toward the side door of the house. Once inside, he slaps his old gray hat softly against the side of his leg, sending a shower of shimmering droplets across the gleaming, checked tile of the kitchen floor. For a single, suspended moment, he stares about the room, taking in its empty, lifeless space, his face a rigid, wooden mask, with nothing moving in it but his eyes. They settle finally on the basement door.

He walks down the stairs to the tall metal cabinet he has always used to store his tools. He opens it in a single smooth, untroubled movement, all indecision long behind him, and withdraws a long object which years ago he had stored away, wrapping it in brown paper and binding it hap-hazardly with a length of frazzled twine. At the small workbench he had once used to assemble his Rodger and Windsor bicycles, he unwraps the shotgun and lays it out across the wooden worktable. For a few seconds he strokes its wooden stock deliciously, as if it were a woman's smooth, brown thigh.

Upstairs, each in their separate rooms, those who are about to die continue through the iron motions of their quickly dwindling lives.

Alone in his room, Jamie hunches over his desk, working mightily to keep his attention on the biology textbook the police photographs would later show still open on his desk.

A few feet down the corridor, Laura emerges from the bathroom, her body wrapped up in her long white robe. She enters her own room, walks to the small dressing table by the window, and begins to run a brush through her long dark hair.

Across the hallway, my mother rises from her bed. She stares about wearily, still in the fog of her late afternoon nap. She plucks one of her romance novels from the table by the bed and heads softly down the corridor to the stairs, moving down them slowly just as my father, still in the basement several feet below, presses two red, cylindrical 12-gauge shells into the twin chambers of the shotgun.

Upstairs, Jamie grimaces, shakes his head, closes the text, thinks better of it, and wearily opens it again.

Laura makes a final sweep through her hair, then opens the center drawer of her dressing table. She withdraws a tube of lipstick, pulls off its shiny cap, and leans in closer to the mirror as she brings its dark red tip to her mouth.

Below them, in the basement's faded light, my father turns and begins his ascent up the plain wooden stairs that lead to the kitchen.

Now on the first floor, clutching at the collar of her red housedress, my mother turns to the right and advances into the living room just as my father reaches the top of the basement stairs. She is in the solarium, easing herself down into one of its white wicker chairs by the time he steps out into the kitchen, the long black barrel of the shotgun weaving as he glances, very briefly, out the window toward the rain.

For a single, breathless instant, I see all motion stop, as if at that final, precipitous moment, my family had been given one more chance. I feel like screaming at them from my great distance: 'Stop, please stop! We can find some other way!'

They do not hear me.

They begin to move again.

My father mounts the stairs toward the second floor, his eyes staring toward the upper reaches of the house until he passes the threshold and confronts a dimly lighted hallway and three closed doors.

Behind the first door to the right, Jamie fidgets at his desk. He leans back, peers out the window, finds no relief, and slowly returns to the open book.

Behind the second, Laura remains at her dressing table. She reaches into the dresser again and takes out a light green plastic compact. She looks at it, clearly displeased by its babyish appearance. She opens it anyway, takes the small beige pad from inside, and begins to rub it softly across her cheek.

Downstairs, my mother remains slumped in one of the little solarium's white wicker chairs. She lets her eyes drift up from the book for a moment, then stares out at the rain as she absently fingers a small green leaf on a hanging fern.

I see my father as he begins to move down the upstairs hallway, his eyes on the first door to his right. He shifts the shotgun into position as he nears Jamie's door.

Inside the room, Jamie turns as that same door opens seconds later. He stands up as my father enters, moving his desk chair against the back wall as he steps away.

Below, in the solarium, my mother's body bolts forward with the roar of the first blast. Her lips part as she draws in a startled, unbelieving breath. The book slips from her lap and flutters to the floor.

Above her, Jamie's body wheels to the left. His face disintegrates as his body lifts from the floor with such force that one of his tennis shoes flies off and slams against the side of my lower bunk, leaving a small, rubbery mark against its light, pine finish.

In the adjoining room, Laura freezes for an instant, as if locked in place by the horrific tumult she can hear next door. She stands up, stares about wonderingly, and lets the light green plastic compact drop from her fingers, its small round mirror cracking softly as it hits the floor.

Below her, my mother rises, stricken, from her chair. Her shoulder brushes against the curtain of long green vines. Her right hand rises, trembling, to her throat.

Upstairs, my father is on the move again. He strides toward the second door, a cloud of smoke trailing behind him as he closes in upon it.

Another blast shakes the house, and my sister's body plummets backward, the palm and two fingers of her right hand flying away as her chest explodes in a fine pink spray.

Through the translucent walls of the house on McDonald Drive, I see all that had been denied, diminished, or somehow brushed aside accumulate in the grim mortification of my mother's face.

Above her, my father breaks open the breech of the shotgun and draws out its two spent shells. In slow motion, I see their slender red cylinders slip from his long fingers and tumble through the thick, powdery air.

The reins which had held my mother in place for so long snap as if cut away by a flying dagger, and she bolts from the solarium and rushes toward the kitchen. Once there, she spins around wildly, unable to focus, too driven by terror to initiate a logical scheme to save her life.

Above her, my father moves from room to room, looking for her in their bedroom, their bathroom, everywhere. Time is passing while he hunts for her, the several minutes that Mrs. Hamilton noticed between the second shot and the last.

Time is passing, while my mother spins like a human top in the kitchen, spins and spins, until her eyes catch on the basement door. She darts toward it frantically, instinctively, an animal's flight to the underground safety of its earthen burrow.

My father is already coming down the stairs before she opens it. He is already in the solarium by the time she reaches the basement's cement floor. She is spinning again by the time he closes in upon the kitchen. She has already padded through the basement's puddled water and taken her place behind the cardboard box by the time he descends toward her from the dark at the top of the stairs. He stops on the third step from the bottom.

There is a third horrendous blast.

*Queen for a Day* comes to an end.

The vision ended abruptly, and I felt as if I'd been hurled against a bare wall. Reflexively, I jerked backward, my breath coming in quick, wrenching gasps. I could feel long lines of sweat move down my chest and back. A wave of tingling sharpness swept across my body.

In a kind of blur, I saw Rebecca lean toward me, her hand reaching across the table.

'Steve? Is something wrong?'

I shook my head, but fiercely, in a kind of manic up-and-down motion.

Rebecca stood up immediately. 'Let's go outside,' she said, then tugged me to my feet and led me out into the night.

For a moment, I leaned against a wall, still breathing heavily, unable to talk.

'Do you want to stop?' Rebecca asked. 'You don't have to go on with this.'

I shook my head.

'Are you sure?'

I nodded.

'Then let's go to my place,' Rebecca said. 'It's more private. We can just talk, if you want. About something else.'

She walked me to my car, then pointed to hers. 'Just follow me,' she said.

I fell behind her, keeping a close distance, first through the town, then out toward the lake, the yellow beams of my headlights rising and falling as we moved along the wavy, unpaved road. I felt self-conscious and embarrassed, as if I'd cracked under too little pressure. There were moments when I wanted to turn around, to disappear into the darkness. But at the same time I was driven to continue, to follow Rebecca all the way, as if my father were in the car beside her, riding along, his blue eyes staring out into the nightbound trees.

I'd calmed myself down considerably by the time I reached Rebecca's cottage. It rested deep in a grove of trees, the lake only a matter of yards away, so that as I got out of my car, I could hear its waves lapping softly against the shore, which calmed me even more.

Rebecca didn't wait for me to join her, but walked quickly to her door. As I approached, moving across the moist grass, I could hear the keys tinkling softly as she drew them from the pocket of her skirt. She faced the door, her back to me, the long dark hair falling to her shoulders as she searched for the right key.

She found it quickly, opened the door, and turned on the small lamp that rested on a table beside it. I followed her inside, then stood silently, watching her as she moved about the room, depositing her things in various places, the briefcase on the table by the window, her small black handbag in a chair by the door. A few feet away, I could see her bed, cluttered and disheveled, through a partially open door.

'Would you like something to drink?' Rebecca asked.

'No, thanks.'

She nodded toward a chair to my right. 'Sit down.'

I did, then watched as she took a seat opposite me, drawing her legs up under her in a gesture that seemed casual and unstudied, as if she'd become somewhat more at ease in my presence.

'I'm sorry about what happened in the restaurant,' I told her.

'What did happen, exactly?'

'I saw it all. The murders, I mean. The way he killed them one by one.'

'How much do you actually know about the murders?' Rebecca asked. 'How they were done, that sort of thing.'

'Not much, really,' I admitted. 'I know he used a shotgun.'

'So what you "saw" – I mean at the restaurant a few minutes ago – that wasn't based on anything you knew?'

'No.'

'You never actually saw any of the bodies, right?'

'No,' I answered. 'I never went inside that house again.' I shrugged. 'I used to say that I never saw any of my family alive again, but actually, I never saw any of them at all.'

I could remember a few things about that morning, however, and I told Rebecca what they were. I remembered my mother standing at the kitchen counter as I raced by her on my way to school. And Jamie walking far ahead of me, his cap pulled down against the morning rain. And I remembered Laura, the feel of her fingers wrapped around mine as we walked toward school together. 'Bye, Stevie,' she'd said, as she'd dropped me off at my school, then moved down the sidewalk, a slender girl with long dark hair, a body disappearing into a net of rain.

'Laura was the last one I saw,' I told Rebecca.

'And she was walking alone? Not with Jamie?'

'They never walked together.'

'But they went to the same school, didn't they, the one a few blocks from the grammar school where you went?'

'Yes, but they never walked together,' I said. 'I always walked with Laura.'

'Who did Jamie walk with?'

'Nobody,' I said. 'He didn't have any ...' I stopped, remembering something. I waited until it was clear in my head, then I told Rebecca.

'Someone put flowers on his grave,' I said. 'Not my mother's or Laura's. Just Jamie's.'

'When?'

'Just before I left for Maine with Uncle Quentin,' I answered. 'Aunt Edna took me over to the cemetery so that I could say good-bye. They'd all been buried side by side, with Laura on one side of my mother and Jamie on the other.'

It had been a cold, snowy day, the wind snarling around us as we'd climbed the low hill that led up to the graves. It had played havoc with Aunt Edna's long black coat, whipping at it madly while she struggled forward, tugging me along with her, sometimes harshly, so that I'd tripped occasionally and gone facedown into the snow. 'Get up, Stevie,' my aunt had kept saying. 'Get up! Get up!'

It had taken us almost five minutes to reach the graves, and by that time Aunt Edna was exhausted. She clutched irritably at her coat and glared down at the three snow-covered mounds, each with its own gray stone. My eyes were drawn to the one on the right, to Laura's grave. A layer of snow nearly covered her name. I could make out only the large, ornate 'L' and the faint outline of the final two letters. The date of her birth was completely covered, but I could see the word 'November' carved below it, though the date and year were covered with snow.

Aunt Edna jerked my hands. 'Say good-bye, Stevie,' she snapped.

Obediently, I whispered, 'Good-bye, Laura,' then repeated the process with my mother and, at last, with Jamie.

'That's when I noticed the flowers,' I told Rebecca. 'They were small, blue flowers, and the wind had nearly stripped them, but I could see a few buds, nonetheless. There were no flowers on the other graves, just on Jamie's.'

'Where did you think they'd come from?' Rebecca asked.

To my surprise, I recalled exactly where I thought they'd come from. 'Well, I remember looking at them and thinking to myself, "He's still here."' I stopped and looked at her somberly. Even to me, it seemed too bizarre to be true. 'I was only nine,' I admitted, 'so who else could I have possibly thought might put them there? Who else would have cared enough to do it – and who was still alive – except my father?'

'Did your father care for Jamie?' Rebecca asked directly.

'I think he tried to, yes,' I said.

'You never noticed him showing any particular resentment toward him?'

'No,' I said. 'Even now, knowing what we've learned, I still don't re-member seeing any great resentment toward Jamie on my father's part.'

'But they didn't get along, did they?'

'No, they didn't.' I thought a moment, then added, 'But Jamie was not a lovable person, and he was always after Laura, always belittling her. And since my father loved Laura so much, I'm sure that Jamie's behavior made it hard for my father to reach out to him.' I glanced toward the window, fixed my eyes on the dark lake beyond it, the wild currents I imagined to be swirling just beneath its black, unmoving surface. 'It was getting all tangled up,' I said quietly.

'What was?'

'Us. All of us. We were getting all tangled up in things.'

For a moment, I saw my father as I'd often seen him, standing alone by the fence, smoking. There were times when I'd awakened near dawn, gone to the bathroom down the hall, then returned to bed. As I'd crawled back beneath the covers, I'd sometimes glimpsed him there, a solitary figure, standing in the smoky gray of early morning light, very still and deep in thought, as if he were trying to find a way out.

'Maybe that's what he couldn't bear,' I said.

'What were you getting tangled up in?' Rebecca asked.

The answer came to me without hesitation. 'In each other,' I said. 'All knotted up in each other.' I considered my answer longer, then added, 'And in love, or faking it, anyway.'

'Faking love?'

'Yes. Pretending to love, when we really didn't. That's the hardest thing in life. Imagine doing it for years.' I saw my father by the fence again, caught in his arctic solitude. 'The way my father did.'

Rebecca said nothing, but I could see a growing intensity in her eyes, as if I had alerted her to something.

'The men you're studying, they were all doing that, weren't they?' I asked. 'They were all faking love.'

Rebecca responded with a question of her own. 'If that was true, that your father was faking love, when did that begin?'

'I don't know for sure,' I admitted. 'But I knew who he loved the least.'

So did Rebecca, and to demonstrate it, she drew another picture from her stack. It showed Jamie's body sprawled across the floor, his head like an exploded melon, scattered in bits and pieces across the floor and wall.

'Poor Jamie,' I said softly. 'He had no idea what was coming toward him.'

I remembered all the times my father had gone out and shot baskets with my brother, how often even that had ended in some kind of brawl, ended with Jamie stomping up to his room, slamming the door behind him. At those times, my father had often lingered beneath the net, the ball bouncing up and down on the cement drive, rhythmic as a heartbeat, while he stared vacantly toward the backyard. I could see the look on his face, an expression of helplessness and bafflement, as if he were lost in a terrible bramble, pricked and bleeding, with no way out.

'My father was confused,' I told Rebecca. 'Maybe, in the end, he just wanted to get out of that confusion.' I looked up at her emphatically. 'Things were heating up in our house,' I told her. 'Tension. Hatred. Maybe he couldn't find any other way to clear the air.' I considered it a moment. 'So he just blasted his way out.'

'A sudden explosion, is that what you're saying?' Rebecca asked. 'That your father just blew up one afternoon?'

I nodded.

Rebecca said nothing.

'Maybe Jamie was the focal point of that confusion,' I added after a time, 'the center of the storm, you might say, but not the whole thing.'

'Did you ever see them talking?' Rebecca asked. 'Jamie and your father?'

I shook my head. 'No.'

'So they weren't faking love anymore?'

'No, they'd gone beyond that point, I think,' I said.

It struck me that perhaps this was the line that my father, and all these men, had finally crossed, the one that divided genuine from counterfeit devotion. Somewhere, they had decided that they would no longer live behind their own paternal mask, that the long masquerade was over.

My eyes drew over to the picture of my father on his wedding day, the luminous smile that adorned his face. 'Maybe that's where the fakery began,' I said as I tapped the photograph softly, 'from right here, from the very first day.'

Rebecca watched me silently.

'So that his whole family life was a lie,' I added quietly, in a voice that was even, controlled.

In a rush of images, I saw all the postcard moments of our family life, the holidays spent together, the bloated turkey on Thanksgiving, the lighted tree at Christmastime. I saw all our little celebrations, saw my father as he'd stood beside the blazing candles of countless birthday cakes. Each in turn, I watched him lift us into the uncluttered air, Jamie when he turned five, Laura the day she won the fourth-grade spelling bee, me on the day I first rode my bike without training wheels.

'All a lie,' I repeated softly, my lips hardly parting with the words. 'Can that be possible?'

Rebecca's eyes fell toward the picture of my brother in his ruin, a gesture that gave me the only answer I required at the time.

# NINE

A week passed before we met again. As always, it began with a phone
call to my office, and it ended with the two of us seated in the front
room of her cottage by the lake.

From the beginning, it was clear that during the intervening days,
Rebecca had thought a great deal about our last conversation. She began
with a reference to it.

'We were talking about faking love,' she said, as she took a seat opposite me. 'You were saying that your father might have faked it from the
beginning.'

I nodded.

'What about his love for Laura?' Rebecca asked. 'Was he faking that,
too?'

I shook my head determinedly. 'No. Absolutely not.'

Rebecca took a picture from her briefcase and handed it to me. It
showed Laura as she lay on her back, her chest blown open, her soiled
feet pressed toward the camera. I gave the picture back to her.

'I don't care what that shows,' I told her. 'I saw his face when he was
with her. She relieved him. She gave him the only happiness he may have
had in our family.'

I could tell Rebecca remained doubtful.

'I know that my father loved Laura,' I repeated, almost wistfully.
'Because I loved her too. Especially toward the end. Especially that last
year when it became ...' I hesitated to say it, but found that I couldn't
keep it back. '... romantic.' I shrugged. 'Or at least that's the way it
felt.'

Laura was sixteen that year, and so beautiful that there were times
when I'd catch her in my eye, and simply stop, dead still, and watch
until she passed from view. So beautiful that I'd begun to dream about
her. They weren't the sweaty, lustful fantasies of teenage boys, but the
atmosphere was always luscious nonetheless, a sensual world of glades
and humid leaves, warm mists and jungle fragrances.

In dreams, Laura came to me in such places. Of course, it was never really Laura, but only a presence I recognized as her, a smell, a taste, but never the person that she really was, the teenage girl who ate dinner across the table from me, and slept in the room next door. Still, it was a powerful presence, and after each dream, I was left with the odd sensation of her actually having passed through me, like a wind through a cloud, leaving me in a strangely suspended state of excitement and delight. The following morning, while she ate her eggs obliviously across the table, I would smile inwardly, remembering my dream, and with the strange sense that I'd cunningly stolen something from her during the night, then triumphantly slinked away.

'I was in love with my sister,' I said. 'If we'd been allowed to grow up together, I'm sure I would have found another romantic object.' I shook my head. 'But she died at the height of her power over me, and so, I had all this love left over, like money I couldn't spend.'

'You couldn't spend it with your wife?'

'It's not the same.'

I half expected Rebecca to lean toward me and begin a wholly different inquiry, but she didn't. Instead, she looked at me very shrewdly, as if taking some part of me in for the first time. Then she said, 'I know.'

For a moment, we stared at each other softly. During that brief time, I felt an undeniable connection to her, a sense of having shared the same dark space. But it lasted only an instant, for almost immediately, Rebecca shifted in her seat, as if to break free of some invisible net.

'How about Laura?' she said. 'Did she have a "romantic object" in her life?'

I suppose it was not until that moment that I fully realized just how much I'd buried since the murders, how much I'd repressed.

'Yes, she did,' I said. 'A boy named Teddy Lawford.'

Rebecca drew a small pad from the table beside her chair. 'Was he from Somerset?'

'No. They met on Cape Cod. My father had rented a cottage there for the last week in August 1959.' The nearness of that day in November struck me. 'It was just three months before the murders.'

Rebecca's eyes tensed slightly, but she said nothing. Instead, she merely allowed me to continue, her pen still poised above the white paper which bore nothing but Teddy Lawford's name.

'Teddy was seventeen,' I began.

As I spoke, I could see him quite clearly in my mind, tall and lanky, with light brown hair. He had grayish eyes that seemed to change depending on the light, something Laura had later commented on. His amiable, divorced father was a large, beer-barrel of a man who'd spent his life selling auto parts in Boston. He'd rented the cottage next to ours for the summer, and Teddy had watched a series of families move in and out of it over the preceding weeks, some staying no longer than a few days before they were replaced by another. But we had been the first, I later heard Mr. Lawford say, who'd shown up with a lovely girl nearly his son's age.

'I think Teddy's father was anxious for him to meet someone,' I said.

Rebecca looked at me. 'You mean a girl his son could have a sexual experience with?'

'Yes, probably,' I answered. 'He must have seen Laura at some point, although I don't know exactly when that might have been.'

Perhaps from behind the tattered paper shades of his own cottage, perhaps from the screened porch that looked out over the sea. In any event, Mr. Lawford had no doubt glimpsed her, had let his eyes settle upon her body as she moved along the side of the house, or strolled through the tall green sea grass to the beach below, all the time brokenly aware, as he must have been, that she was well beyond him, that he was too old and bald and fat to inspire anything but repulsion in such a beautiful young girl, but that she might make a suitable offering for his son.

'Mr. Lawford invited us over to his cottage the second night we were on the Cape,' I said. 'My mother hadn't really wanted to go. Jamie, either. But both of them had finally come along with the rest of us.'

It was early evening, and a gorgeous red sun was lowering on the horizon. I'd never seen a sunset on the sea, or even the kind of deep blue light that descended upon us that evening. It was warm, and Laura was dressed in a pair of white shorts and a dark green blouse, its ends knotted at the front. I remember that Teddy came to attention as she walked into the backyard, his dark eyes clinging to her like talons.

'Teddy fell for my sister at first sight,' I told Rebecca. 'They hadn't even spoken, but he was crazy about her.'

'So it wasn't exactly love,' Rebecca said.

I shook my head. 'Love? No, it didn't have time to be love.'

But it was very powerful nonetheless, and it grew unabatedly during the entire evening, as Laura and Teddy inched their way into a different universe. The contrast between them and the rest of us must have been amazing. Jamie sat morosely by himself, dully watching the sea. My father and Mr. Lawford talked idly and passionlessly of business matters, my mother listening to them silently, her hands folded in her lap. As for me, I scuffled with Mr. Lawford's cocker spaniel, both of us rolling mindlessly across the sandy lawn.

And yet, even as I rolled around that evening, I could sense the emergence of a new state of being, a world that had suddenly sprung into

existence, and which floated in the air between Teddy Lawford and my
sister. I didn't know what it was, but only that it was something that had
been mysteriously created, and that its movements were infinitely fast.

'It wasn't love,' I told Rebecca once again. 'But once you'd felt it, you
wouldn't want to live without it.'

Rebecca lifted her face slightly. 'It was romance,' she said firmly.

'Well, whatever it was, Teddy was in the full grip of it. He came over
to our house the very next morning.'

He was dressed in a pair of cutoff blue jeans and a white T-shirt, the
sleeves rolled up above his shoulders. I saw him lope across the yard,
pause a moment at the little stone walkway that led to our house, then
bolt forward, as if, in those few hesitant moments, he'd thought it all over
and decided the issue once and for all.

Though it was still early, Laura had been awake for a long time. I'd
glimpsed her sitting alone on the screen porch, then later strolling absently
in the backyard, making odd, aimless turns, her long hair blowing in the
early morning breeze. Despite the chill, she'd gone into the yard wearing
nothing but the bottom of her bathing suit beneath a loose-fitting blouse,
purposely leaving behind her thin blue wind-breaker, the one she'd
tightly wrapped around herself while she'd remained on the porch.

'Laura had gone out to attract Teddy,' I told Rebecca. 'You might
say, to display herself. She was very beautiful that summer, and I'm sure
Teddy was completely overwhelmed by that.'

And so, that morning I watched as Teddy bounded down the walkway
toward our cottage, not even able to control his stride. I was at the window,
and it was only a few feet from there to the door, but Laura was at the
door even before I could get to it, answering his knock instantly. A wave
of white light swept over her when she opened it, and for a moment, as I
watched, she seemed encased in its radiance. She stood quite still, talking
to him, her hands toying nervously with the loose ends of her blouse. I
can still remember the words that passed between them, so ordinary they
seemed to burst in the heated air:

'Oh, hi, Teddy.'

'Hi, Laura. Have you already eaten?'

'No, not yet.'

'There's a little diner down the road. It's not so great, but I go there for
breakfast. You want to come with me?'

'Well, my father's still asleep, you know?'

I had come up quite close to them by then, walking very slowly from
the window to the door, listening intently as I moved toward them.

Laura looked at me, and I noticed that, despite the chill, small beads of
sweat had formed a moist line across her upper lip.

In an instant, she was gone, the two of them disappearing behind a curve in the road. She hadn't asked my father's permission. She hadn't said so much as a 'see you later, Stevie' to me. It was as if a mighty wind had picked her up and blown her out the door.

'She was completely swept away,' I told Rebecca. 'I couldn't imagine what was going on in her. I couldn't believe that she'd just left without saying anything to my father.'

He woke up an hour later, fully alert, the way he always did, as if, each morning, he returned to himself in a sudden, startling realization. He was dressed in a pair of blue trousers and a checked shirt, and he barely offered a passing wave as he headed for the kitchen. I heard him making a pot of coffee, then, after it was made, I saw him walk out onto the back porch and stare out across the field of high, green sea grass that stretched almost to the beach. The morning light was even brighter by then, and it framed him eerily as he stood, his back to me, peering out toward the bay, the black mug of coffee rising and falling rhythmically before he finally spun around, as if alerted by some sound, and looked at me:

'Where's Laura?' he asked.

'Laura?' I repeated hesitantly, stalling for time, but remembering the look she'd given to me as she'd left with Teddy, a look that had unmistakably commanded me to lie. 'I don't know, Dad,' I answered. 'I haven't seen her.'

He nodded slowly and lowered himself into one of the rusty metal chairs on the back porch. It was only then that the oddity of his initial question struck me. How had he known that Laura was not in the house, not sleeping in her bed like his wife was? I know that the question rose in my mind that morning, but only in a child's mind, quick, glancing, devoid of further investigation. It was not until I'd related the whole story of that morning to Rebecca that the answer actually occurred to me.

'He had expected to find her waiting for him on the porch,' I told her. 'And when he walked out onto the back porch and saw she wasn't there, he knew something was wrong.'

'What did he do?'

'He had another cup of coffee.'

And another and another, while the sun rose steadily and my mother slept mindlessly, and I wandered in the backyard, glancing apprehensively toward him from time to time. Something had gone wrong, and I knew it; some mysterious and confusing element had entered into our lives. I could see it in my father's face. For even though his features remained very still, I could sense that wheels were spinning wildly behind them.

My mother got up at around ten that morning, but she didn't join my father on the back porch. Instead, she mechanically made breakfast for

289

herself, the usual boiled egg and toast, then walked out into the living room and ate it absently, as if it were merely tasteless fodder, fit for nothing but the maintenance of life.

I went out to play in the backyard. Mr. Lawford's spaniel spotted me and ran over for another round of tussling in the grass, and this occupied me fully for quite some time. The strange dread I'd felt vanished in the frolic, and so it was not until I saw my father come to his feet that I even noticed that he still remained on the back porch.

He stood very tall, a lean man with wavy black hair, the checked shirt billowing slightly as he came out into the yard. He didn't notice me at all, but walked directly to the edge of the yard, the place where it began its sharp decline toward the beach.

I walked over to him and stood at his side, looking down, as he did, toward Laura.

'Laura came back about an hour later,' I told Rebecca, 'but not by way of the road. She came up the beach instead, and she was alone.'

Alone, because she must have known that whatever lie I'd come up with to tell my father, it surely hadn't included Teddy.

Standing beside my father, I could see her moving slowly, her head bowed slightly, as if she were looking for shells. She was barefoot, her brown leather sandals dangling from one hand, as she waded through the weaving lines of white lacy foam.

'There she is.'

That was all my father said, and it was no more than a whisper, three words carried on a single, expelled breath. Then he returned to the house, without waiting, as I did, for Laura to make the hard climb up the stairs along the sandy hill to our cottage.

She was out of breath by the time she reached me, her long hair slightly moist with sea spray. She wasted no time in getting to the subject:

'I saw Dad up here.'

'He went back into the house.'

'What did you tell him?'

'That I didn't know where you were.'

'Good. Thanks, Stevie.'

'Where were you, Laura?'

She didn't answer me, but only walked directly back to the house and joined my father on the small back porch. While I played in the backyard, I could see them sitting together, their faces gray behind the screen, smoke from my father's cigarette drifting out into the summer air.

A few hours later we all went down to the beach, trudging cautiously through the deep sea grass, my father lugging a huge picnic basket, Jamie dragging along behind, looking as morose as he had the preceding day.

Teddy came bounding down a few minutes later. My mother invited him to have one of the ham sandwiches she'd made, and he accepted without hesitation. For a time, he chatted amiably with us all, although his eyes often fell upon Laura with a deadly earnest. Neither of them gave the slightest impression of having met earlier that morning, but I remember having the distinct impression that my father knew that they had. Perhaps Laura had told him while the two of them sat behind the gray screen. Or perhaps he'd sensed it in the looks that sometimes passed between Teddy and Laura while we all sat together on the blanket my mother had spread over the sand.

It was very hot that day, and not long after lunch, Laura, Teddy, and I all went into the water for relief. My mother, who never swam, gathered everything up and wandered back to the house, leaving my father alone on the beach. He sat there for several hours, his long legs sticking out of a dark blue bathing suit, watching us distantly, with that strange attitude of concentration which I'd only seen in the basement before, and which I associated only with the assembling of fancy European bicycles. And yet it was there on his face, that look of intense study and attention.

It was not directed at me, of course, but at Laura and Teddy as they moved farther and farther out into the sea. Glancing toward them from time to time, I would see hardly more than two heads bobbing happily in the blue water, although I am sure now that my father saw a good deal more.

Rebecca looked at me quizzically. 'What more did your father see?' she asked. 'I mean besides what was obvious, two teenagers attracted to each other.'

'I'm not sure, but I think it was something about life.' I remembered Rebecca's earlier remark about what she was looking for in these men. 'Maybe something unbearable,' I added.

I could see my father's face as it had appeared that day. Although in his youth he'd been a pale, skinny boy, middle age had filled him out a bit. He was still slender, of course, but his face had aged into an unmistakable handsomeness, his sharper features less bird-like, the eyes more deeply set and piercing. His curly black hair framed his face well, and when the wind tossed it, as it did that afternoon, it gave him a wild, curiously appealing look. Because of that, I realized that I'd been completely mistaken in what I'd just told Rebecca. 'No, he didn't look like a man about to break,' I said. 'He didn't look like that at all.'

I watched her quietly for a moment, certain now that I was following behind her in some strange way, covering ground she'd already covered.

'My father wasn't some little gray man who crumbled under pressure,' I said finally. 'Why have I always wanted to think of him that way?'

I instantly thought of the other men Rebecca had chosen for her study. None of them had been inept or inconsequential; none had seemed to lack a certain undeniable dignity.

I saw my father again as he'd appeared that day on the beach, his legs stretched out before him, leaning back slightly, propped up on his elbows, his eyes focused on Laura and Teddy as they bounced up and down in the heaving waves.

In my imagination, his features took on a classical solidity and force, almost the military bearing of one who had chosen to defend the city, no matter what the cost.

I looked at Rebecca, amazed by my own reassessment. 'My father had a certain courage, I think.'

It was then that the utter loneliness of my father hit me with its full force, the darkness within him, his long silence, the terrible hunger he carried with him into the basement night after night, and which, I realized now, Laura had sensed as well, and perhaps even tried to relieve from time to time, like someone visiting a prisoner in his cell.

Rebecca looked at me questioningly. 'Did something happen on the Cape, Steve?' she asked.

I nodded. 'Yes.'

Rebecca seemed almost reluctant to continue, as if she felt herself being drawn down in a world even she was not quite prepared to enter. 'Do you want to stop now,' she asked, 'or do you want to go on?'

'I want to go on, Rebecca.'

And so I did.

I told her how Teddy and Laura had spent almost all their time together after that first morning, how my mother had remained almost like an invalid, reading her romance novels, how, at last, my father had seized the gray back porch like a conquered province, sitting hour after hour in the little metal chair, his eyes trained on the sea.

Finally, I arrived at the place where I'd been heading all along, that last night on Cape Cod.

'Nothing really strange happened until the end of that week,' I began, 'the night before we headed back to Somerset.'

Early that afternoon, it had begun to rain. By evening, it had developed into a full summer storm, with sheets of wind-blown rain slapping against the cottage's rattling windowpanes. While the rest of us retreated into the house, my father remained on the back porch, still in that same chair, his eyes fixed on the violently churning sea.

'Lost in thought, that's how I'd describe him,' I told Rebecca. 'Lost in thought.'

'But you don't know what he was thinking about?'

A possibility occurred to me: 'Killing us, perhaps.'

'Why would you think that?'

'Because, over dinner that night, he did something cruel to my mother.'

She'd called him in to a hastily prepared dinner of hot dogs and baked beans, and he'd taken his usual seat. He looked preoccupied, intensely engaged in something within him. He remained silent while the rest of us chatted, mostly about the things that still had to be done before we could leave the next morning. A couple of times during the meal, Laura had tried to engage him, but he'd only answered her in quick, terse phrases, little more than a yes or no, sometimes not even that, but only a brisk nod of the head.

My mother had watched all of this for some time, yet had said nothing. Finally, she got up and headed back to her chair in the living room, inadvertently leaving one of her novels on the table near my father. She was almost all the way out of the room when he called to her suddenly:

'Dottie.'

She turned quickly, as if surprised by the sound of her name in his mouth, unsure of the context in which he'd used it, already gathering her red house-dress around herself more tightly:

'Dottie.'

My mother had already turned all the way around to face him before he spoke to her again. She didn't answer him, but only stood, very still, as if waiting for his next word.

My father added nothing else for a moment, and I remember he looked regretful that he'd called her name at all. Still, he had started something which he could not help but finish:

'You forgot to take your book, Dottie.'

And with that, he picked it up and hurtled it toward her violently, its pages flapping hysterically in the air until it struck my mother in the chest and fluttered to the floor.

My mother stared at him, stricken, and my father seemed to collapse beneath her broken, helpless gaze. His face was ashen, as if mortified by what he'd done. He stood up, walked over to where the book lay lifelessly on the floor, retrieved it, and handed it to my mother:

'I'm sorry, Dottie.'

She took it from him, retreated into the living room, and slumped down in her accustomed position. The book lay in her lap. She made no effort to read it that night. Instead, she remained in her chair, the yellow lamplight flooding over her, her eyes fixed on the small painting that hung on the opposite wall.

I gave Rebecca a penetrating look as the thought struck me.

293

'She knew it was coming,' I said. 'From that moment, I think, she knew he was going to kill us.'

Rebecca didn't question this. She jotted a note in her black book and looked back up.

'What was Laura's reaction to what your father did?' she asked.

I remembered the look on her face in great detail. She had been sitting across from me, so that the book had flown between us as it hurtled toward my mother. Laura's eyes had followed it briefly, then shot over to my father. What I saw in them astonished me.

'It was admiration,' I told Rebecca. 'Laura looked at my father as if he'd done something gallant, like he was some kind of knight in shining armor.' I released a sharp, ironic chuckle. 'All he'd done was throw a book at a helpless woman,' I said. 'That's not exactly Sir Lancelot, is it?'

'Then why did Laura look at him that way?'

'I don't know.'

She didn't seem to believe me. 'Are you sure you don't know?'

'What are you getting at, Rebecca?'

Before she could answer, I already knew. It had undoubtedly been admiration that I'd seen in my sister's eyes, but I hadn't guessed the nature of what it was she admired until that moment.

'Action,' I said. 'She admired him for actually doing something. It was hostile, and it was cruel, but at least it was *something*.'

It was perhaps the same thing Quentin had admired not long before he died, muttering about how my father had 'taken it by the balls'. I thought about it a little while longer, remembering the softness in my sister's eyes, the love she had for my father, the small, almost undetectable smile that had quivered on her lips as she'd glanced over at him that night. It led me to the final moment of my narrative.

'That wasn't all my father did that night,' I said.

Rebecca looked at me thoughtfully. I knew that she could hear the slight strain that had suddenly entered my voice as I began:

'It was much later that night, and ...'

I'd already been in bed for several hours when I heard someone moving softly in the adjoining room. I crawled out of bed, walked to the door, and opened it. In the darkness, I could see Laura as she headed stealthily toward the back porch, through its creaking screen door and out into the yard. Her posture was different than I'd ever seen it, slightly crouched, as if she were trying to make herself smaller, less easily seen.

I followed her as far as the back porch, then stood, staring through the gray metal web of the screen. I could see my sister as she made her way across the wet grass, the white folds of her nightgown rippling softly in the wind that came toward her from the sea. In that same wind, her long

294

hair lifted like a black wave, falling softly to her shoulders and down her back.

I remember that I pressed my face into the screen, as if trying to pass through it bodilessly, like a ghost, and float out toward the tall green reeds into which she had wholly disappeared.

I stood for a long time by the screen, half expecting Laura to reemerge from the sea grass, perhaps with a shell in her hand, or some article she'd forgotten to retrieve from the beach earlier in the day.

But she didn't come back, and so, after a moment, I drew away from the screen and turned back toward the house.

That was when I saw my father.

He was sitting motionlessly in the far corner of the porch, his long legs folded under the metal chair, his light blue eyes oddly luminous in the darkness. In the eerie stillness, he looked like a serpent sunning itself on a stone, but entirely inverted, drawing warmth and comfort from the darkness.

He didn't speak to me at first, but merely let his eyes drift over to me, hold for a moment, then leap back to their original position, peering out at the wall of gently waving reeds. Then he spoke:

'Go back to bed, Stevie.'

'Where's Laura going?'

'Go back to bed.'

His eyes returned to me, and I felt myself shrink back, moving away from him cautiously and fearfully, as if he were coming toward me with a knife.

Within seconds I was back in my room, but I couldn't sleep. My mind latched on to Laura, to her white gown billowing in the breeze, and I remember feeling frightened for her somehow. Normally, the fear would have come from the simple knowledge that she was out in the darkness alone. But that wasn't the origin of my dread. It was him. It was the feeling that he was going to go after her, stalk her in the reeds, do something unimaginable.

I looked at Rebecca, shaken suddenly by my own unexpected insight. 'So I was really the one who knew all along that he was going to kill us,' I told her. 'I was the one who sensed it. Not my mother or Jamie or Laura.'

Rebecca's face was very still. 'Go on,' she said.

And so I did, relating the story in as much detail as I could recall, reliving it.

After a time I walked back to the porch, although very stealthily, intending only to peer surreptitiously around the corner of the door to assure myself that my father was still there, that he hadn't followed my sister into the reeds.

But he was gone, the chair empty, a cigarette butt still smoldering in the little ashtray he kept beside it. I knew that he hadn't returned to the bedroom he shared with my mother. I don't know how I knew this, but it was as clear to me as if I'd seen him disappear into the tall grass or heard the creak of the screen door as it closed behind him. I knew, absolutely, that he'd decided to go after my sister.

I stood, frozen on the porch, poised between the warmth of my childhood bed and the darkness beyond the house. I don't know what I thought, if I thought anything at all. Perhaps I was already beyond thought, already operating at a more primitive level, sensing the storm that was building within my father the way an animal lifts its face to the air and senses danger in the bush.

'What did you do?' Rebecca asked.

'I went after my father.'

A curious expression rose in Rebecca's face. 'You weren't thinking of it as going after Laura?'

'No.'

And it was true. Even as I opened the screen door and stepped out onto the wet lawn, I knew absolutely that I was pursuing my father rather than moving to protect my sister, that my intent, shadowy and vaguely understood, was to join him in the tall grass, commit myself to whatever it was he had committed to the moment he'd crushed the cigarette butt into the ashtray beside his chair and headed out into the night.

The grass was tall and still wet with rain, and the blades, as they pressed my arms and legs, felt very cool and damp. The ground was soft, and I could feel my feet sink into it slightly with each step. The reeds had parted as my father had moved through them, leaving a wide trail for me to follow, already crouching as I went forward, moving slowly and secretly, as if I already had much to hide.

The trail led down the hill toward the sea. I could hear the waves tumbling not far away, but I couldn't see them until the clouds parted suddenly and a broad expanse of light fell over the beach. It was then that I glimpsed my father's head, saw his tangled black hair and sharp, angular face just for an instant before he sank down, squatting over the wet earth. I could tell by the motionlessness of the grass that he'd stopped, and for a moment, I stopped as well and stood, sinking imperceptibly into the rain-soaked ground.

For a little while I listened intently, my head cocked like some primordial creature. I could hear only the waves as they tumbled toward shore a few yards away and the wind as it swept through the reeds that surrounded me.

I don't know exactly when I began to move forward again, or why, or what I was thinking as I did so. I remember only the sudden desire to penetrate more deeply into the green wall and the inability to draw back once I'd begun to move again.

I walked slowly, very silently, as if stalking a prey almost as cunning as myself. I remember shifting to the right somewhat, because I didn't want to come upon my father. I'd glimpsed his position in a wedge of light, and I carefully edged myself away from him as I continued to slink forward through the reeds.

I didn't stop until I heard a shifting in the grass, the slow, rhythmic friction of blades rubbing softly against other blades. As I continued forward, I could hear someone breathing, then two people breathing in short, quick spasms.

I stopped and peered out, gently drawing away the curtain of reeds that blocked my vision. That was when I saw her.

'Laura,' Rebecca whispered.

'Yes.'

At first my sister's body appeared to me in a blur of white and black, her long hair shifting back and forth over her naked shoulders. She seemed to be rising and falling on a completely separate cushion of pale flesh. I could only partially see the body beneath her, the one which shuddered violently each time my sister rose and fell above it. It came to me only as a headless ghost, white against the dark ground, moaning softly each time my sister lifted the lower part of her body then eased herself down upon him again.

I could see his slightly hairy thighs, the nest of dark hair into which they disappeared, and finally the long pale shaft that seemed to pierce and then withdraw itself from the body of my sister.

It was 1959, I was nine years old, and so I'm sure I didn't know what was happening there in front of me. Still, I knew that it was something powerful, occult, primitive, and at last profoundly private. I felt the need to withdraw, to sink back into the reeds and return to my bed, but something held me there, and for a moment, I continued to watch, shamed perhaps, but also mesmerized by the spectacle before me.

I don't know how long I watched, but I do remember that during that time the idea that my father could be anywhere near such a scene completely left me. I remained fixed on the two bodies, as if dazzled by the continually building intensity of their motions, the rising force and deep needfulness I could hear in their breathing.

Suddenly, my sister arched her back and released a long, luxurious sigh. She shook her head, and her dark hair brushed back and forth along the lower quarters of her naked back. Then she fell forward in a spent, exhausted motion, the wall of her flesh suddenly collapsing so that I could see the green reeds beyond her, and deep within those reeds, my father's pale blue eyes, motionless and vaguely hooded, with nothing at all in them of the voyeur's seamy lust, but only staring toward mine in an instant of unspeakable collusion.

For a few seconds, we continued to stare frozenly at each other while Laura and Teddy hurriedly dressed themselves, took a final, strangely passionless kiss, then rushed away, Laura moving up toward our cottage, Teddy toward his.

Once both of them were out of sight my father stood up and started walking back to the cottage. I trailed after him, just a few feet behind. He didn't look back at me. Perhaps he was too ashamed. I will never know.

Rebecca peered at me unbelievingly. 'You mean that he never said anything to you about that night?' she asked.

'No.'

'Did he seem different after that?'

'Yes, but not toward me,' I answered. 'Only toward Laura.'

Rebecca's pen remained motionless above the still nearly blank pad. She'd taken very few notes, but I knew she'd absorbed every bit of my story, every nuance and detail.

'How did he change toward Laura?' she asked.

'He got even closer to her,' I answered. I considered it a moment, trying to find precisely the right word. 'He became ... more tender.'

For the first time Rebecca looked vaguely alarmed, as if the word had caught her by surprise.

Still, it was undoubtedly the right word to describe the change that came over the relationship between Laura and my father during the few weeks before he killed her.

'They were very tender with each other after that night on the beach,' I said. 'They'd always been very close, but they got even closer for a while.' I did a quick calculation in my head. 'My sister had seventy-nine days to live.'

The starkness of the number, the brevity of my sister's life, shook me slightly, but only slightly, not with the disoriented unease I'd experienced in the restaurant days before.

Still, Rebecca noticed the reaction. 'This is hard, I know,' she said.

Her eyes were very soft when she said it, and I knew that I wanted to touch her, and that everything about such a grave desire seemed right to me at that moment, while everything that stood in the way of its completion, the whole vast structure of fidelity and restraint, seemed profoundly wrong.

'Rebecca, I ...'

I stopped, quickly glanced away from her, and let my eyes settle once again on the lake beyond her window. The clouds had parted by then, and the moon was bright against its ebony surface. It gave the sense of a world turned upside down, of the past devouring the future, of all life's elements twisted and inverted, so that I seemed to be staring down into the waters of the sky.

# TEN

It was nearly midnight by the time I got back home that evening. I'd expected to find Marie either working in her office or asleep. But she was waiting in the den instead, sitting beneath the reading lamp, her face very stern when she spoke to me.

'Where have you been, Steve?' she asked.

I looked at her innocently. 'What do you mean? I've been at work.'

'You mean at the office?'

'That's right.'

'I called the office,' Marie said. 'I spoke to Wally. He said that ...'

'I was doing a site inspection,' I interrupted quickly. 'At that office complex on the north side of town.'

She looked at me a long moment, and I could see the wheels turning, the whole machinery of her suspicion fully exposed in her eyes.

'A site inspection at night?' she said doubtfully.

'We began it in the afternoon,' I told her. 'Then we had a long meeting in the general contractor's trailer.'

For a moment she seemed vaguely embarrassed, as if by her own dark thoughts. 'Oh,' she said, her voice less accusatory, though a strained quality lingered in it. Then she smiled faintly. 'Well, anyway, I'm glad you're home,' she said.

'Me, too,' I told her, though I knew it was a lie, that I wanted to be with Rebecca instead.

'Any more questions?' I asked half jokingly.

'I guess not.'

I offered a quick smile, then headed upstairs. It was a gesture of flight, I recognized, a darting-away from the seaminess of the lie I'd just told Marie, perhaps even a flight from the uneasiness and foreboding I'd felt at the moment of telling it.

Once alone in the bedroom, I thought of my father, of the way he'd hurled the book at my mother's chest that night on Cape Cod. I wondered if he'd felt the same restriction I felt now. Had there been some place outside his home that had called to him with an irresistible urgency? Later on that balmy summer night on Cape Cod, as I remembered now, I'd glimpsed him in the yard, standing beside my mother in the moonlight, his arm draped loosely around her shoulder. They'd returned from a long walk, and for a moment, as they'd stood together in the darkness, they'd actually looked like a couple in love. For a moment, he'd drawn her in more closely and kissed her hair. I wondered now if that gesture had been nothing more than part of a vast deception. Had my father really wanted to be with her that night? Had he wanted to be with any of us? Or had he secretly yearned for another life, one in which every moment was filled with challenge and surprise, a life from which we blocked him simply by being alive?

I thought of each of us in turn. I saw Jamie in his sullen anger and isolation; Laura in her reeling moods, walking the house in the blue twilight; my mother forever locked within the folds of her red housedress; myself, a small, ordinary boy, indistinguishable from any other. Last I saw my father, still distant and mysterious, a figure walking behind us, the grip of the shotgun nestled, almost gently, in his hands.

I remembered Rebecca's purpose again, her search for whatever it was in life that these men had been unable to bear, and in my father's case it occurred to me that the unbearable thing for which Rebecca was still searching might have been nothing more mysterious than ourselves, that we were, each of us, in our own individual lives, unbearable to him, the living proof that his life had come to nothing.

I walked to the bedroom window, parted the curtains, and looked out. The lights from the suburban street seemed dull and lifeless. For years I'd been able to look out that same window without the slightest sense of disturbance. Now the very look of it made me cringe, for it seemed to me that my life, like all the other lives around me, possessed only the manageable level of risk, and no real jeopardy at all. Lived within its confines, we hunted the appropriate game, settled for the reachable star. We made the roads straight and flat. We turned on the light before we headed down the corridor, and grabbed the railing as we inched cautiously down the padded stairs. We grew old in a world of shallow breaths, feared both gasps and sighs.

And yet, for all that, the very next morning I went on with my routine as if nothing were changing in my life. I sat at the breakfast table and made small talk with Marie and Peter. Dutifully, I asked about Marie's latest bid, about Peter's work in school. But even as I listened to them, their voices sometimes faded, their faces drifted off into a blur, as if they were becoming mere white noise.

'Finish up, Peter,' I heard Marie say as she got to her feet, 'you're going to be late for school.'

I remained at the table while Marie went upstairs to finish dressing and Peter darted to his room to get his jacket. Seconds later, I heard him dash by me. He gave me a quick 'Bye, Dad,' then bolted out the door.

'Are you still here?' Marie said later when she came into the kitchen.

I looked at her. 'What time is it?'

I could see that the question struck her as odd. 'You're wearing a watch, Steve,' she said.

'Oh,' I said, then glanced down at it, but didn't move.

'Shouldn't you be leaving?' Marie asked.

'Yeah, I guess.'

I got up and went to my car. As I began to guide it out of the driveway, Marie came out of the kitchen and walked toward me. I stopped the car as she came near.

'You don't look well, Steve,' she said worriedly. 'Do you want to stay home today?'

I shook my head. 'No, I'm fine,' I said with a small, dismissive smile.

Marie didn't smile back. 'You need to take care of yourself, Steve,' she said in a voice as full of real concern as I'd ever heard, a voice that should have comforted and relieved me, but didn't.

I shrugged. 'I'm fine,' I repeated, then let the car begin to drift away again.

She said nothing more, but simply stepped away from the car and watched, without waving good-bye, as I glided down the driveway. Now, when I think of her, I often see her in that pose, standing in the grass, her arms folded over her chest, watching silently as I drifted from her sight.

Once at my office, I went directly to my desk and began working on the library I'd been designing. But even as I worked, adding lines and filling in details, I felt that I was continually returning to the house on McDonald Drive. Curiously, I no longer dreaded these returns. Instead, I seemed to move back toward that lost place with an increasing sense of rendezvous and complicity. My companion was always Rebecca, and I sometimes felt that I was walking hand in hand with her through the separate murder rooms. I could hear her voice, as if in whispers, pointing out details, the open textbook on Jamie's desk, my sister's bare feet. The bodies of my dead family seemed to lie sensually before us, as if we were joined in the rapture of my father's crime.

It was over a week before I saw her again, and it seemed an infinitely long time. Each time the phone rang on my desk, I hoped that it would be she, whispering to me with a grave intimacy, as if we were lovers, bursting with breathless communications.

She called on a Wednesday afternoon, and we met at her cottage the following evening. I expected to exchange a few pleasantries, but Rebecca got right down to business instead.

She'd gotten some additional information from Swenson, she told me, and even as we began where we'd left off the week before, I sensed that she was holding something back. Even so, I didn't press the point. By then I'd become quite willing to go at whatever pace Rebecca set. Perhaps I'd even sensed that to know everything Rebecca knew would dull the intensity of the journey we were making together – something I didn't want to happen. What I wanted was to feel that intensity and peril all the time, to tremble forever at the edge of some sudden, apocalyptic discovery.

And so I followed Rebecca's lead, anticipating nothing, merely letting her questions guide me back.

'You said that things became more tender between your father and Laura after that night on the beach,' she said.

'Yes.'

'But they'd always had a close relationship, hadn't they?'

'Yes,' I said. 'But he seemed to pay even more attention to her after that. It was almost as if he were studying her, trying to get an idea of what was going on inside.'

'And you only noticed this change after you'd returned from the Cape?'

'Yes.'

We'd gotten back on a Monday night, Labor Day 1959, all of us crammed into the dark brown station wagon. My father drove, of course, while my mother sat in the front seat, her right shoulder pressed tightly up against the door, her face pale and bloodless as she stared straight ahead. Her eyes seemed lifeless, drained of light, and the sallow skin of the face that surrounded them made her look like a department store mannequin.

Laura and I sat together in the back seat while Jamie lay crouched up and constantly complaining in the small square of trunk space that lay just behind us. He had absented himself as much as possible from the rest of us during the preceding week, but this last effort at self-imposed exile was certainly his most extreme, a punishing act of ostracism which Laura found ridiculous and contemptible, but which my father, lost in his own thoughts, seemed hardly to notice.

We'd planned to leave early that Monday morning, but things had gotten scattered and confused during the day, and we'd finally pulled away from the little cottage at nearly four in the afternoon. By that time, the off-Cape traffic had reached its dreadful end-of-season peak, and we'd staggered along toward the Sagamore Bridge at a snail's pace, inching down the highway one jerk at a time, Jamie groaning uncomfortably with each movement of the car.

It was nearly midnight by the time we got back to the house on McDonald Drive, but my father didn't seem particularly tired. He pulled himself briskly out of the old station wagon and immediately began to unload the week's supplies while my mother staggered wearily into the house, then up the stairs to the bedroom.

Laura regarded my mother's bedraggled retreat into the house as nothing more than a way of avoiding the work involved in unpacking the car, and she clearly resented it.

'Why doesn't Mom help unpack?' she demanded sharply as my father handed her a large cardboard box. 'The rest of us have to work at it.'

My father did not reply. He simply drew another box from the back of the car while he listened as Laura railed on about my mother.

'Why is she so special?' she asked hotly. 'Why does she get to go up to bed?'

Once again, my father refused to answer her. Instead, he yelled for Jamie, tossed him a heavy box, and commanded him to take it into the basement. Then, when Jamie was safely out of sight, he turned toward Laura, his eyes staring pointedly into hers. There was a kind of fierceness in his gaze, and I remember being quite drawn by the strangeness of it, as if he were about to pronounce some vital truth that he'd kept to himself all these years, waiting for the right moment to reveal it. But when he spoke, no such great truth emerged. Instead, after he'd settled his eyes on Laura for a moment, he said to her, almost in a whisper, but very distinctly nonetheless, and with that air of unchallengeable authority he often had, 'You should know.'

Rebecca wrote the words in her notebook, then looked at me. 'Where were you when your father said that?'

'I was standing next to Laura.'

'What did Laura say?'

'She didn't say anything.'

'What do you think your father meant by, "You should know"?'

'I have no idea,' I told her. 'But Laura knew what he meant. I know she did, because of the way she reacted.'

I was standing only a few inches from her. I saw her fire her final question, then heard my father's reply, his voice neither sharp, nor angry, nor resigned. Instead, it seemed to carry a sense of severe scolding which struck Laura like a slap in the face, so that she shrank back from him immediately and lowered her eyes. Then, almost in the same motion, she stepped toward my father again, placed her hand very briefly on his shoulder, then turned and made her way into the house. She did not come back out to help us unload the car, but remained inside with my mother.

'Actually *with* my mother,' I told Rebecca emphatically. 'In the same room with her, not just the same house.'

It wasn't until we'd finished unloading the car that I finally returned to the house. My father and Jamie continued putting various things away in the garage outside, but that was heavy labor, unsuited for a nine-year-old boy, and so I'd left them and gone back inside. It was nearly one in the morning by then, and I was very tired and wanted to get in bed as soon as possible.

I'd passed the threshold of the stairs and was headed down the corridor toward the room I shared with Jamie when I saw Laura and my mother. It was enough to make me stop.

'They were together in my mother's room,' I told Rebecca. 'Sitting side by side on the bed. I'd never seen my sister sit that close to my mother. It seemed very strange.'

They were facing away from me. My mother had changed into her red housedress, and she was bent forward slightly, as if she were about to pick something up from the floor. I could see that Laura had draped her arm over my mother's shoulder comfortingly, and though I didn't know it then, the soft shaking motion I noticed in my mother's body undoubtedly was caused by the fact that she was crying.

Rebecca looked up sharply from her notebook. 'Crying?' she asked.

'It must have been that,' I said. 'I don't know what else it could have been.'

'But what was she crying about?'

'I don't know. Maybe it was some sort of delayed reaction,' I said. 'You know, delayed from earlier, when my father had thrown that romance novel at her.'

'And Laura was comforting her, you said?'

'Well, not exactly,' I answered, remembering it with a fierce clarity.

Rebecca looked at me, puzzled.

'It wasn't real,' I said, 'the sympathy. None of what Laura was doing was real. Not the way she'd slung her arm over my mother's shoulder. Probably not even the words she must have said to her while they sat on the bed together.'

Rebecca looked at me doubtfully. 'How do you know that?' she asked.

'By the way my sister looked at me,' I answered, glimpsing that look again, a chill moving over me, as if a ghost had suddenly drifted past, brushing my shoulder with its pale robe.

'It was a strange look,' I added.

In all the years I'd known her, Laura had never glared at me in such a forbidding way as she did that night. I'd climbed the stairs wearily, innocently seeking only the shortest route to my bed. I hadn't meant to eavesdrop. And yet, as Laura's head swiveled slowly in my direction, I saw her face stiffen hideously, her eyes take on a dreadful anger.

'She looked like an animal,' I told Rebecca, 'trapped, like a creature driven into a corner.'

Rebecca jotted a note into her notebook, but didn't speak.

Even then, as I told Rebecca about that one brief incident, the look in my sister's face chilled me, and I remembered that during the few seconds she'd stared at me, I'd felt as if I were under fire, bullets slamming toward me, chewing up the floor beneath my feet, riddling the plaster wall behind me, spewing dust into the air.

'I all but dove into my room,' I said, 'just to get out of her sight.'

But I'd done more than that. Once in my room, I'd locked the door behind me, then pressed my back against it like some terrorized child in a grade-B horror movie.

I'd still been standing in the same position a few minutes later when I felt the doorknob turn.

'Stevie? You in there?'

It was Jamie.

'Stevie?' he called again. 'Stevie, you in there?'

I opened the door, glancing around his lean body toward the empty corridor. The door to my mother's room was closed. To my right, only a few feet down the dark corridor, the door to Laura's room was closed too, though I could see a line of bright light just beneath it.

'What's the matter with you?' Jamie demanded irritably. 'You hiding something? Why was the door locked?'

I shrugged, unable to come up with an explanation that would have made any sense to him. 'I didn't know it was locked,' I said finally.

To my surprise, Jamie didn't challenge the completely illogical nature of my answer, perhaps because the childhood sense of the magical and miraculous which lingers on in adolescence was still so much a part of the way he saw the world that he could casually accept the otherwise impossible notion that doors could sometimes lock themselves.

In any event, he merely walked to the bed, pulled himself up to his upper bunk, and lost himself in one of the sports magazines that were always piled in a jagged stack at the foot of his bed.

For a long time, I remained in the room, sitting in the lower bunk. The weariness I'd felt before as I'd trudged up the stairs had disappeared, and in its place I could feel nothing but a disquieting tension. After a time, it drove me from my bed to the window. By that time, Jamie had fallen asleep, the sports magazine still open on his chest.

It was a clear summer night, and I could see the whole shadowy stretch of the backyard as if it were illuminated by a pale blue light. It was very warm, as well, and the window was fully open, a light breeze rustling the curtains quietly.

I don't know how long I stood by the window, but after a time, I heard the door at the side of the house – the kitchen door, the one that Mrs. Fields would approach only a few weeks later, then shrink back from in sudden dread – I heard it open, then close, and after that, the muffled sound of footsteps as they moved down the short flight of stairs to the walkway which divided the house from the garage and which led in a gentle curve to the backyard.

My father appeared seconds later, walking alone over the dark green lawn. He was taking long, slow strides, as he moved from the western to the eastern corner of the yard, then back again, a cloud of white smoke trailing behind him like the pale exhaust of an old steam engine.

I don't know exactly how long he paced the yard alone that night, but only that after a few minutes, I heard the kitchen door open again.

This time it was Laura.

She came around the corner of the house, dressed in her white sleeping gown, her long dark hair hanging in a black wave down her back. She was barefoot, and I could see her white feet as they padded across the dark green grass toward where my father stood, now leaning slightly against the solid wooden fence he'd built along the rear edge of the yard.

He didn't turn toward her, although he must have heard the door open, just as I had heard it. He didn't turn because, unlike me, he already knew who'd opened the kitchen door.

'It was obviously a prearranged meeting,' I told Rebecca, 'something the two of them had already planned.'

Rebecca didn't look surprised, and I could tell from her face that she'd fully accepted the conspiratorial nature of my father and my sister's relationship, its eerie sense of secret conclave.

'Laura walked over to him,' I went on, 'and the two of them stood by the fence and talked for a long time.'

From just behind the plain white curtains, while my brother lay snoozing a few feet away, the sports magazine rising and falling to the rhythm of his breath, I watched as my father and sister talked quietly, but very intently, their eyes resting steadily upon each other.

It was probably exactly that feeling of intensity that kept me posted by the window during the next few minutes. It was in every element of their posture, in every glance that passed between them, even in the sharp whispers I could hear but not make out, as if their voices were distant instruments scraping at the air.

They were in plain sight, of course, both of them posed starkly against the moonlight, and yet I felt the inexplicable need to hide behind the white shroud of the bedroom curtains. I didn't know why, but only that despite their outward show of openness, the fully illuminated yard, even the nearly ostentatious brightness of my sister's gown, the predominant mood of their meeting was surreptitious and collusive. Perhaps even a little arrogant, as if they both presumed with perfect certainty that the rest of us were sleeping in the dark house, that no matter what they said or how loudly they said it, neither Jamie nor my mother nor I would hear or see anything.

'If was as if, as far as they were concerned, we were already dead,' I said.

Rebecca glanced down at her notebook, as if trying to avoid my eyes. 'Did you ever get any idea of what they talked about that night?' she asked, but in a voice that was deliberately flat.

'No.'

But I suspected even then that it was something of the deepest significance to them both. My father had remained rigidly in place throughout the conversation, his eyes focused intently on my sister. For her part, Laura had remained almost as motionless as my father. From a distance, she appeared locked in a stony, reptilian stillness which went against the often frantic quality of her movements, the fidgety fingers and continually bouncing feet. It was as if this stillness had been imposed upon her by the gravity of what was transpiring between them, the sheer awesomeness of its content.

'So you never heard any part of what they said?' Rebecca asked, as if she were still in doubt about the truth of my first answer.

'Well, only a few words at the very end,' I admitted, 'but that was after they'd come back into the house.'

I'm not sure how long they'd talked together before my father suddenly nodded sharply, as if in conclusion, then began walking back toward the house. Laura walked beside him, her hand holding to his arm. When they had made it almost halfway across the yard, my father stopped, looked down at my sister for a moment, then lifted his right hand and very gently stroked her hair. It was a gesture that seemed to melt her, so that she leaned toward him and buried her face in his shoulder. My father looked away from her, as if unable to bear what he'd seen in her eyes. Then, in a slow, surprisingly dramatic movement, he lifted his face toward the bright, overhanging moon. They stood in just this position for a long time, she in her pale gown, he in his stone-gray work clothes, the light washing over them, so that they looked vaguely like marble figures, motionless and cold.

308

Then they separated and walked, without touching, back toward the kitchen door. Seconds later, I heard them pad up the short flight of stairs toward their separate rooms.

I ran to the door of my room and opened it slightly. Through the small slit, I could see my father and Laura as they mounted the stairs, moving slowly, until they came to a stop at the top of the landing. For a brief, suspended instant, they stood, facing each other silently.

Then my father said, 'Are you all right?'

And my sister said, 'Yes, I'm fine.'

With that, they headed up the corridor, moving directly toward my room. I shrank away from them, not wanting to be seen, and eased my door back so that it was almost closed when they passed. Because of that, I could see only the broad outlines of their two bodies as they swept by my door, featureless and without detail, little more than gliding shapes.

I heard my father say, 'Tomorrow.'

And my sister said, 'So soon?'

My father did not answer her. Or, if he did, it was later, in some place beyond my hearing. For after that, I heard nothing but the sound of his feet as they moved on down the carpeted hallway, then the sound of his bedroom door as it opened and closed.

Minutes later, I heard Laura open the door to her own room, so I know that for a short time she stood alone in the unlighted corridor. I don't know why she waited for those few extra minutes, or what thoughts played through her mind as she stood in the darkness outside her room, as if afraid to go in alone.

'And that's all you heard them say?' Rebecca asked.

'Yes.'

She glanced down at her notes, quietly, thoughtfully, as if she were processing and rearranging information that she alone possessed. Watching her, I felt as if she'd rowed out onto a dark lake, leaving me on shore.

'The "tomorrow" your father talked about,' she said finally, 'that would have been the first Tuesday in September?'

'I suppose.'

'The first day of school,' she added, almost to herself. Then she came back to me suddenly, her dark eyes darting over to mine. 'Did anything unusual happen that next day?' she asked. 'Did you notice any change in anything?'

'No,' I said.

Again, Rebecca appeared to draw into herself, her mind deep in thought, as if she were unable to accept what appeared to be the routine notion that 'tomorrow' had been nothing more than my father's idle reference to the beginning of school, and Laura's whispered reply just a schoolchild's regret.

I leaned forward slightly. 'Should I have seen something different that day?' I asked. 'Was something going on?'

She didn't answer, but only flipped back a few pages in her notebook, scanning the lines she'd written until she found the right one.

'You said before that when Laura and your father were down by the fence, that they hadn't been concerned that anyone in the house might be watching them,' she said.

'That's right.'

'You said that it was as if they thought the people in the house were already dead.'

I knew then what she was getting at. 'How long had he been planning it, Rebecca?'

'Maybe longer than you think, Steve.' She waited, trying to gauge how the latest information might affect me. 'At least three or four months,' she said finally.

'How do you know that?'

'Because of something Swenson found,' she told me. 'Travel brochures. A lot of them.'

Occasionally, I'd seen my father reading an adventure novel, always slowly, taking weeks to slog through each one. I'd also seen him idly turning the pages of the local newspaper. But I'd never seen him browsing through anything that resembled a travel brochure.

'He found quite a few of them in that little office your father had at the rear of the store,' Rebecca added, without emphasis.

It was little more than a stockroom, as I recalled then, small and cramped, but more secure, with many locks. It was the place he'd kept the unassembled Rodger and Windsor bicycles before bringing them home. Once or twice I'd seen him there with Nellie Grimes, the book-keeper he'd hired some years before, but on all other occasions, he'd been in the room alone. Because of that, it was easy for me to think of it as the place of his solitude, the cluttered little room which he'd set aside for his plotting, the careful working out both of his crime and his escape.

'These brochures,' I said. 'Where did they come from?'

'He got them through the mail,' Rebecca answered. 'There was no indication that he ever went to a travel agency.'

I shrugged. 'I don't ever remember seeing any travel brochures around the house.'

'That's because they weren't mailed to McDonald Drive,' Rebecca said. 'They were all mailed to the hardware store downtown.' She paused

310

a moment, then added, 'Some had been mailed as long as three months before the murders.'

I leaned back, as if unable to absorb this latest bit of information, the full-blown proof, as if any had still been necessary, of my father's plot.

'The brochures were from all over,' Rebecca said. 'Mexico, Europe, Asia, South America. That's why they weren't much help to the police.'

'So they never had any idea where he went?'

'Not until they found the car,' Rebecca said.

'That was in Texas, wasn't it?' I said tentatively, only vaguely recalling something Quentin had told me. 'Near the Mexican border?'

'Right on the border, actually,' Rebecca said. 'In Laredo.'

I nodded. 'That's right,' I said. 'I remember that Quentin told me about them finding the car.'

'Swenson brought it back,' Rebecca said, 'but no one ever claimed it.'

So that it still sat in the shadowy corner of the police garage in Somerset, as Rebecca went on to inform me, a dark, eerie symbol of my father's flight. I could see it there, rusting, abandoned, the odor of my father's cigarettes still lingering in the ragged brown upholstery, dust gathering on the black, serrated wheel where he had laid his hands.

'You could claim it if you wanted,' Rebecca added softly.

I shook my head wearily. 'No, I don't want it,' I whispered.

But I remembered it, nonetheless, as I told her.

Then I related a time when my father had driven all of us far out into the woods, to where an old cabin, not much more than a log shack, sat in a primeval forest.

It was probably four years or so before the murders, and we'd all gone out in that same old car in which he'd later made his escape – Laura and Jamie and I scrunched up together in the back seat; my mother, looking vaguely content on the passenger side; my father, his big hands on the wheel, smiling with a kind of gleeful adventurousness as we bumped along the barely passable road.

He'd stumbled upon the cabin while hunting as a boy, and I suppose there was something about it which had suddenly called him back. 'I want to show you all something,' he'd said at the breakfast table that morning.

We hit the road about an hour later, drove for a long time, paved roads eventually giving way to unpaved ones, then at last on to what were little more than ancient logging trails. It was already early in the afternoon by the time we finally reached the cabin.

It was set in a deep wood, near a winding brook, and I could tell by the way my father looked at it that it represented something to him, perhaps his ideal of a forest paradise, remote, primitive, and uncomplicated. When he looked at it, his face took on the kind of expression I would later see in paintings of the saints when they saw God, that here before them was the true, abiding majesty. That day, he even seemed like them, saintly, a father out of the great book of fatherhood, a man of mythic kindness and commitment, capable of making an epic sacrifice.

He played with us in the forest, a long game of hide-and-seek, in which we skirted behind bushes and fallen trees, while my mother watched us from her place on the cabin's small, dilapidated porch. We played tag, and he ran after us, lifting Laura into the air each time he caught up with her, their faces nearly touching as he lowered her to the ground again.

Toward evening, it began to snow, and while the rest of us gathered up our things and prepared to leave, my father walked out into the woods again and stood alone among the trees, his arms lifted slightly, hands open, catching snowflakes in his palms.

As I finished relating this episode, I realized that my eyes had grown moist.

'I'm all right,' I assured Rebecca quickly, gathering myself in again. 'I just got a little nostalgic, I guess.'

It was more than that, though. I'd entered a new realm of feeling in regard to my family's slaughter. I realized that it was no longer the explosive instant which horrified me, as it had in the restaurant days before, but the long decay of love, the slow stages of its dissolution.

I could see that Rebecca understood that, but what she could not have known was that only part of my anguish was connected to the dark reliving of my family's death. The rest had to do with me, the volcanic discontent I had come to feel in the presence of everything that had grounded and sustained me in the past. It was as if that airy, unreal dream house I'd been working on for so long was now the only one in which I wanted to live. It was without walls. It had no foundation. It was pure fantasy. And yet it seemed right in a way that made everything else seem wrong.

After a moment, my eyes settled upon Rebecca. 'They actually saw the monster, didn't they?' I asked. 'My father and the rest of them? Whatever it was that was eating them alive, they actually looked it in the eye.'

Rebecca didn't answer me directly, but grew distant, perhaps even apprehensive. 'Maybe we should end the interview for tonight, Steve.'

'Why?'

'I just think it would be best,' Rebecca said firmly, leaving no doubt that the interview was over.

She walked to the door, opened it, then followed me out into the darkness, slowly walking me to my car as a swirl of leaves played at our feet.

'I'm sorry this is so hard for you,' she said.

'It's a lot of things, Rebecca,' I admitted. 'It's not just my past.'

At the car, I stopped and stood very near to her. I could almost feel her breath.

'When do you want to meet again?' I asked.

She watched me hesitantly, but said nothing.

I smiled. 'Don't worry, Rebecca. I'll go all the way through it with you.'

She nodded. 'In all the other cases, there were no survivors,' she said. 'I guess I should have known how hard it would be for you, but I just hadn't had the experience before.'

'It's okay,' I assured her.

I opened the door and started to get in, but she touched my arm and drew me back around to face her.

'You should only go as far as you want to, Steve,' she said. 'No farther.'

'I know,' I told her.

I could feel her hand at my arm, and I wanted to reach up and hold it tightly for a long time. But I knew that close as it seemed to me, her hand might as well have been in another universe.

'Well, good night, then,' she said as she let it drop from my shoulder.

'Good night,' I said, then got into my car.

It was still early, so I stopped off at a small restaurant and had a sandwich and a cup of coffee before going home.

Marie was at the sink when I walked into the kitchen. Peter was at the table, chopping celery.

'You're home early,' Marie said. 'We're making a tuna dish.'

'I've already eaten,' I said idly.

Marie's eyes shot over to me. 'You've already eaten?'

I nodded obliviously.

'You got off early and didn't come home to have dinner with Peter and me?' she asked, in a voice that struck me even then as deeply troubled, as if in this small twist of behavior she'd already begun to detect the approach of her destruction.

'I guess I did,' I said, then added defensively, 'Sorry. I just wasn't thinking.'

Marie looked at me brokenly, but I did nothing to ease her distress.

'I'm going to lie down for a while,' I said, then headed up the stairs.

Once upstairs, I lay down on the bed, my eyes staring at the blank ceiling. Below me, I could hear Peter and Marie as they continued to make their dinner together. Below me, as I realize now, they were shrinking. I should have seen it, like a murderous vision, as I lay alone on my bed that evening. I should have seen Peter fleeing down a dark corridor, Marie cringing behind a cardboard box. I should have seen the circle tightening, felt the first bite of the noose.

But that evening I felt nothing but my own distress. I remembered Rebecca as she'd stood beside me only a short time before, and I knew that I'd wanted to draw her into my arms. Perhaps, at the time, I'd even imagined that she was all I really needed to solve the riddle of my life. But I realize now that Rebecca was only the symbol of those other things I had wanted even more.

'In the deepest and most inchoate longings of these men,' Rebecca would later write, 'there was a central yearning to be embattled, a fierce need for a fierce engagement, so that they saw themselves in that single, searing instant not as killers slaughtering women and children, but as soldiers in the midst of battle, men heroically and perilously engaged in the act of returning fire.'

It was months later, and I was alone, when I read that passage. By then, I was wifeless, childless, homeless. Everything was gone, except my one need to 'return fire' as my father had, in an act of sudden and avenging violence.

# ELEVEN

During the last days of October, as fall retreated and the first wintry rains began, I felt as if some sort of countdown had begun. It wasn't a radical change, only a shift in direction, a sense of moving into the final phase of something. There was a helplessness about it, a feeling that I no longer controlled my life, that perhaps, a creature of disastrous circumstances, I had never actually controlled it. It seemed my father had destroyed that web of connections which might have given me context, a place to stand in the world. After that, I'd drifted here and there, but always in reaction to something outside myself. I was an accidental architect, an accidental husband, an accidental father – an accidental man.

'They felt their lives were dissolving, didn't they?' I said to Rebecca at one of our meetings toward the end of October.

Her reply went to the center of how I'd come to feel. 'No,' she said. 'They felt that in some way they had never lived.'

But rather than thinking of myself at that moment, my mind focused once again on my father, and I remembered how, in the days preceding the murders, he'd seemed to sink into a profound nothingness. For many hours he would sit alone in the solarium, silent, nebulous, hardly there at all. At other times, he would stand by the old wooden fence, his hands deep in his pockets, staring emptily across the lawn. At the very end, he had even stopped answering the phone when it rang at the house on McDonald Drive. It was as if he could no longer imagine that the call might be for him.

'He'd become a worthless shell,' I told Rebecca at one point. 'He'd been stripped of everything by then.'

It was the word 'stripped' that seemed to catch in Rebecca's mind. She repeated it slowly, as if it had conjured up something even darker than my father's crime.

'Stripped to the bone,' I said assuredly. 'There was nothing left of him.'

I recalled the dreadful baiting which Jamie had continued to inflict on

Laura, and how, in the last weeks, my father had sat by and let it go on day after day. The force that had once moved him to defend my sister had dissipated.

Rebecca didn't challenge my description of my father's disintegration, but I could see that it disturbed her. For a time, she even seemed curiously disoriented, as if she'd lost her way somehow. At the next meeting, her questions skirted away from the final days of my family's life. Instead, she concentrated on other issues, our routines and schedules, the division of chores, all the minutiae of my family's existence.

Then suddenly, during the second week of November, she regained her direction. It was as if after standing poised at the edge of something for a long time, she'd now decided to plunge over the side.

I arrived at her cottage late on a Thursday afternoon. She'd already started a small fire in the hearth, and it was blazing warmly when I arrived.

'It's cold out,' she said as I came through the door.

I nodded and began to take off my coat.

'I like November,' she added. 'I think it's my favorite month.'

It struck me as an odd choice. 'Why?'

She thought a moment. 'I guess because it's cold enough to make it clear that winter really is coming,' she said, 'and that we need shelter.'

I shook my head. 'Too rainy,' I said. 'Too confining.' I shook my shoulders uncomfortably. 'It gets into your bones.'

I sat down in my usual seat, then waited for Rebecca to ease herself into the chair across from me.

But she didn't do that. She took a seat at the table by the window instead, her briefcase already open before her. For a few seconds, she hesitated, her eyes glancing first out the window, then back to her briefcase, then at last to me.

'Do you remember saying that these men had actually seen the monster?' she asked. 'That they'd looked it in the eye?'

'Yes.'

'We have to do that, too,' she said. She picked up a single photograph and handed it to me. 'We have to look it in the eye.'

It was a picture of my father standing in front of the hardware store on Sycamore Street. It had been taken the day he'd opened the store, and all of us were with him. I, an infant, slept obliviously in my mother's arms, while Jamie and Laura seemed to hang like small sacks from my father's hands.

It was the first photograph she'd shown me in which we were all together, and something in it frightened me so much that I actually drew back from it unconsciously, as if it might strike out at me.

I handed the picture back to her. 'Okay,' I said. 'Now what?'

She looked at me evenly. 'As a picture, a family tableau, it's practically idyllic,' she said.

'Yes, it is. So what?'

'We've been through each of the relationships in your family,' Rebecca said. 'Now we have to look at the possibility of something outside the family that might have had some bearing on the murders.'

It was then I knew that we were racing toward the end of it. She'd gotten as much information about my family as she expected to get from me. Her final task was simply to assure herself that in getting the story of my family as it related to its destruction, she'd gotten the only story there was, that there were no loose ends, that my father fully and completely conformed to her archetype of 'these men'.

'You mean another person?' I asked. 'Someone connected to my father? A lover, something like that?'

'Yes,' Rebecca said.

The very idea seemed preposterous to me. It was as if I could accept the fact that my father had slaughtered his family more easily than the notion that he might have loved someone outside the circle of that destruction.

'I don't think he was the type to have another woman,' I said offhandedly. 'Of course, a love affair is not something he would have talked about with a nine-year-old boy.'

Rebecca looked at me. 'Would he have talked about it with Laura?'

The question brought back a quick play of memory.

'Maybe,' I said. I remembered how, during the weeks before her death, my sister had appeared to stiffen and grow cold toward my father, to give him unmistakably hostile glances. I'd noticed the change at the time, but been unable to understand it.

'I can say that things did change between Laura and my father,' I added. 'At first, after we came back from Cape Cod, they seemed closer than ever. But not long after that Laura withdrew from him.'

Suddenly I saw this change as the key to everything. The last link my father had had with us, his love for my sister, had abruptly broken. His one and only tie to us had snapped, setting him free to kill us all.

I remembered the look on my sister's face when she'd glanced at my father from time to time during the last month of her life. The sense of admiration that I'd always seen in her eyes was entirely gone. It had been replaced by something deeper and far grimmer.

'She seemed very disappointed in him,' I said. 'It was as if she'd come to despise him.'

Rebecca said nothing.

'Maybe that was what my father couldn't bear,' I added after a time, 'the fact that he'd lost Laura.'

'Or that she'd simply come to love someone else,' Rebecca added cautiously, 'the way teenage girls inevitably do.'

I saw my sister again in the long green reeds, the arch of her white back in the moonlight.

'You mean Teddy Lawford?'

'He wrote quite a few letters to Laura,' Rebecca told me. 'Swenson found them in one of the drawers of her dressing table.' She reached into the briefcase and withdrew a single sheet of paper. 'Laura wrote him back, too,' she said, as she handed me the paper. 'This is a copy of the last letter she wrote to him.'

'Where did you get it?' I asked as I took it from her hand.

'Swenson got it from Teddy when he went up to Boston to interview him about the murders.'

'Swenson interviewed Teddy? Why?'

'He considered him a suspect for a while,' Rebecca said. 'But Teddy had been at the University of Michigan on the day of the murders.' She nodded toward the letter. 'It's dated November 15.'

While Rebecca looked on, I read what was probably the last letter my sister ever wrote:

Dear Teddy:

Hi, I hope you are okay, and that everything is still going well at college. I wish I could say things are better here, but they're not. They're worse than ever. Jamie's a bastard, like always, and Stevie's just a kid. My father stays in the basement, but I don't go down there anymore. If I ever see you, I'll tell you what he did. I don't want to say it in a letter. Someone might see it, and I don't know what he would do if that happened. He's such a fake, Teddy, such a cheat.

Teddy, sometimes I get really scared. I feel like something's going to happen, but I don't know what.

Damn, this is a depressing letter. I'm sorry, but it's just the way I feel. Maybe something will brighten me up in the next few days. If it does, I promise to write and let you know.

Love,
Laura

Once I'd finished reading, I handed the letter back to Rebecca. She kept it in her hand, waiting for me to speak. When I didn't, she repeated the line that had struck her as the most important: '"If I ever see you, I'll tell you what he did."' Her eyes bore down upon me. 'What do you think Laura meant by that?'

'I have no idea.'

'"Fake." "Cheat." Why would she use those words?'

I realized that Rebecca had gone full circle, returning to her original point. 'Another woman, you mean,' I said. 'You think it's possible that he was cheating on my mother, and that Laura found out, and somewhere in all that, he decided to kill us?'

Rebecca didn't answer, but I could tell that her earlier questions had been generated by more than speculation.

'If your father had a lover,' she said, 'then he can't be included in my study.'

'Yes, I know, Rebecca,' I said. 'But is there some reason why you think he might have had another woman other than Laura's letter?'

She hesitated a moment, looking at me with an expression which always signaled the fact that she was about to reveal something she had previously kept hidden. 'Well, there's a detail that always bothered Swenson,' she said. 'He was never able to track it down exactly, and I think you're the only person who might know what it means.'

'What detail?'

'The fact that almost five months before the murders your father bought two tickets on a flight to Mexico City,' Rebecca answered, the revelation completed. She glanced down at her notebook. 'He made the reservation on June 15, 1959. The flight was scheduled to leave from Idlewild Airport in New York City.'

'On what day?'

She looked up at me. 'November 19.'

I felt a sharp pang. 'The day of the murders,' I said.

'But he canceled those same tickets over a month before the murders,' Rebecca added. 'On October 10. So, on November 19, as far as we know, he had no travel plans.'

I repeated the most relevant aspect of what she'd told me. 'But the main thing is that before that, he'd reserved two tickets, not just one.'

'He made the reservation in his own name,' Rebecca said pointedly, 'one for him and one ...' She stopped for a beat, '... for someone else.'

'And this "someone else",' I said, 'there was no name?'

Rebecca shook her head. 'He made the reservation by phone, and he never gave a name for the second person.'

'For his lover, you mean.'

'If he had one,' Rebecca said doubtfully.

'You don't think he did?'

'If I'd thought that, I wouldn't have gotten this far in studying him,' Rebecca said. 'Even Swenson was never able to trace him to any other person.' She shrugged. 'Everything about your father points to a family man.'

'Everything except that ticket.'

'Yes.'

I let it all pass through my mind slowly, trying to think if I'd ever seen the slightest sign that my father had had his own version of Yolanda Dawes, some pale, slender female with thin, spidery arms, the mythical destroyer of homes. I thought of various possibilities. There was Mrs. Hamilton, the minister's wife who lived across the street, but she was far older than my father, matronly and overweight, hardly a candidate for romance. Next door, Mrs. Bishop, even older, lay bedridden with rheumatoid arthritis. There were other women in the neighborhood, younger, sleeker, their legs tightly bound in the pedalpusher pants so common at the time, but it didn't seem possible that they would have cast a longing glance at the middle-aged man in gray work clothes who sometimes cruised by in his old brown van.

Then, quite suddenly, I thought of someone.

'Well,' I said hesitantly, not wanting to emphasize the point, 'there was this one woman who worked for my father.'

Rebecca's eyes bored into me. 'Who?'

'Her name was Nellie Grimes,' I said. 'I didn't know her very well.'

'Was she a neighbor?'

'No. She just worked for my father.'

A divorcée, with a three-year-old daughter, Nellie had begun to work in the hardware store in the fall of 1956. My father had needed someone to straighten out the store's tangled bookkeeping system, but after doing that, Nellie had stayed on to handle the part of the business my father despised, the dismal mountain of paperwork involved in keeping the store stocked, billing credit customers, even paying the store's own bills. He'd never liked any of the minutiae of running his own small business, and after Nellie came on, he'd turned all of it over to her. Thorough and highly organized, Nellie had quickly become indispensable to my father, a woman, as I'd once heard him describe her, 'of many talents'.

'"Of many talents",' Rebecca repeated as she wrote the phrase in her book. 'Who did he say that to?'

My own answer surprised me. 'My mother.'

'So your mother knew about Nellie Grimes?'

I labored to dismiss the disquieting notion that there might have been an edge of cruelty in my father's description of Nellie, as if he were bent upon making the contrast between 'poor Dottie' and a woman of 'many talents' as painful as he could.

'Well, she knew who Nellie was,' I answered casually. 'All of us knew who she was, that she was this woman who worked for my father.' I shrugged. 'But I don't think it occurred to any of us that there might have been something going on between them.'

I thought of all the times I'd seen my father and Nellie together, simply standing in one of the store's cluttered aisles, or hunched over Nellie's desk in the back, the two of them trying to straighten out some incongruity in the books. Everything had always looked perfectly normal between them. Neither had ever exhibited the slightest sense of a clandestine relationship, of secret hideaways or kisses stolen behind a potted palm.

'It always seemed like an ordinary, professional relationship,' I said.

Rebecca gave me a penetrating look. 'Then why did you bring her up?'

'Just as a possibility,' I answered, dismissing it at the same time. 'Nothing more than that.'

But it was more than that.

I knew that it was more because of the force with which Nellie had suddenly returned to me. I hadn't thought of her in years, and yet I saw her exactly as she'd appeared during the time she'd worked for my father.

She was a short, compact woman with curly light brown hair, always neatly dressed, her lips painted a bright, glossy red. She had called me Skipper for some reason, and at the little birthday party my mother threw for me three months before her murder, Nellie gave me a blue captain's cap with a large golden anchor stitched across the front. Her daughter was named May, and at the party she'd stood, looking a bit confused, in a lacy white dress, a small, willowy child with long, blond hair and a vacant look in her light green eyes.

'Why did this woman in particular come to mind, Steve?'

'Opportunity, I suppose,' I said. 'I mean, they were alone in the store a good deal. It would have been easy for him.'

'Would that have been enough for your father to have an affair?' Rebecca asked. 'Just that it would have been convenient?'

The word 'affair' struck me as an inappropriate one to use in terms of any relationship my father might have had with Nellie. It seemed too worldly and sophisticated a word for either one of them. Had the 'affair' existed at all, it would have been carried out in cheap motel rooms off noisy, commercial roads. Or, perhaps, even worse, just a quick, sweaty tumble in the back of the hardware store. As such, it didn't strike me as the sort of thing my father would have done.

'No, I don't think so,' I told Rebecca. 'Besides, he never struck me as being driven in that way. Toward sex, I mean, just for itself.' I thought a moment longer, my father's face returning to me, clothed in the curling smoke that had always seemed to surround him. 'Love might have attracted him, though.'

'Could your father have gotten that from Nellie Grimes?' Rebecca asked.

I considered Nellie carefully once again, recalling the round face and hazel eyes, the somewhat large and rolling hips, but more important, the buoyancy of her manner, the uncomplicated happiness and jollity that seemed to pour from her, and which was so different from the general gloominess and withdrawal which characterized my mother.

I nodded. 'Maybe,' I admitted.

My father kept a small army-surplus cot in the back of the store, and for an instant I saw him lying upon it, wrapped in Nellie's somewhat flabby arms, his old gray work clothes stripped away and bundled sloppily in a pile beneath the creaking springs of the old metal cot. It was not a vision I could sustain, however.

I shook my head. 'I can't give you any particular reason, Rebecca, but I just don't think my father would have been attracted to Nellie Grimes.'

'Do you know what happened to her?' Rebecca asked. 'There's no indication in the investigation that she was thought of in connection with the murders.'

'Well, she wasn't working at the store when it all happened,' I explained. 'She'd stopped working for my father by then.'

'When did she stop?'

I tried to recall the time exactly, but found that I could come up with only a general approximation. 'Toward the end of the summer,' I said. 'Sometime in the middle of August, I think.'

'Do you know why she left?'

'No.'

'Do you know where she went?'

'I don't know that either,' I said. 'But I do remember the last time I saw her.'

It had been in the railway station downtown. My father had driven her and May, who was six years old by then, to the train late one summer afternoon, and I had come along with them, May and I bouncing about in the back of the van, along with a varied array of battered old suitcases, while my father and Nellie sat up front, talking quietly.

My father had been dressed in his usual work clothes that day, but Nellie had dolled herself a bit in a black polka-dot dress to which she'd added a round, pillbox hat with a short black net that hung from her forehead to just beneath her upper lip, and which, though long out of style, had given her an unmistakable air of mystery.

Once at the station, my father had lugged the suitcases to the appropriate ramp, then we had all waited for Nellie's train. It had not been long in coming, and during that short interval, my father and Nellie had smoked cigarettes and talked quietly while May and I darted here and there among the other passengers. I caught none of the conversation that passed between them except, at the very end, as the train was already pulling into the station, its cloud of billowing steam pouring over them, I saw my father take a plain white envelope and press it into Nellie's hand. He said nothing at all, but the look which passed between them at that instant was very beautiful and grave, deeper than a casual farewell.

For a moment, I labored to bring back those two lost faces. I saw my father peering down at Nellie, his large, sad eyes settling delicately upon her as he placed the envelope in her hand, then gently folded her fingers around it. She was staring up at him, pressing her face closer to him as if reaching for his lips. She seemed to strain toward him unconsciously for a moment, then to pull back, instantly aware that he would not bend toward her, not so much as a single, tender inch.

Then she stepped away, bent down to me, lifted the black net from her face, and kissed me softly on the cheek. 'Bye, Skipper,' she said. She looked at me a moment, then smiled brokenly, and added, 'Maybe someday.' After that, she quickly grabbed May's hand, and the two of them disappeared into the train. My father and I hoisted the bags on after her, but she was not there to take them from us, and I had the strangest sense that she was just inside the first car, standing with her back pressed against its cold metal wall, crying.

'There might have been something between them,' I told Rebecca, 'but only on her side, not his.'

'So you don't think that second ticket to Mexico could have been for Nellie?'

Because there seemed no other, more likely, candidate, I let myself consider the thought once again, probing at it almost academically, using little bits of logic and deduction to piece together my father's phantom love affair.

Then a chilling thought occurred to me.

If it was true that the two tickets to Mexico had been for my father and Nellie, then what had they planned to do with May?

For an instant, I saw her exactly as I'd seen her that day in the train station, a little girl in a burgundy dress, disappearing into the gloomy, rattling depths of the railway car. A few months later had she died as my mother, Laura, and Jamie had died? In some distant city, perhaps even at the same time, had Nellie Grimes done to her daughter what my father had done to Laura?

From the grim notion of such a murder, it was easy for me to imagine it in all its awesome detail.

I could see May in her room, playing with her doll, a record on the little dark red plastic music box she had carried with her onto the train that day. She was humming along with its scratchy tune while she dressed a pink, rubbery doll whose heavy lids closed each time the head was tilted back. Alone, sitting Indian-style on the checkered quilt that covered her bed, humming to herself while her fingers tugged softly at the doll's little wool dress, she barely looked up as the door to her room crept open and Nellie Grimes stepped into it as if from a cloud of thick gray smoke.

I sat back in my seat, startled by the vividness of my own imagination, by the way it had driven me toward a firm and uncompromising denial.

'No, that second ticket couldn't have been for Nellie,' I said with absolute certainty, 'because two tickets would mean that they'd have had to kill May, and I don't believe my father would have had anything to do with such a murder.'

Rebecca looked at me cautiously. 'You don't think he would have had anything to do with the murder of May Grimes even though he had been willing to kill ...'

'The rest of us, yes,' I said. I shook my head at the absurdity of my own reasoning, but I couldn't rid myself of the notion that, for all he'd done to my mother, Laura, and Jamie, my father would not have brought May Grimes within that murderous circle.

'He wouldn't have killed May,' I said again. 'He killed us because we'd done something to him. We weren't like May. We weren't ... innocent.'

I stopped, stunned by the hard and unforgiving judgment I had just rendered upon my murdered family. I tried to draw my scattered thoughts into a coherent whole. 'It's just that we were unhappy,' I said finally, giving up. 'Desperately unhappy.'

I stopped again, waiting for the next question, but Rebecca knew I'd supply the story anyway.

'I think my mother tried to kill herself once,' I said softly, 'but I can't be sure.' I drew in a long, weary breath, then continued. 'It was toward the end of October,' I said. 'I know because it was the night of the fireworks. It was sort of a village Indian summer celebration. The town had this big festival in October, and we always went together, the whole family.'

It had been a clear, unseasonably warm night, and I was dressed in just a pair of jeans and a T-shirt. The town fireworks display went off at nine, and for a few blazing minutes we'd all watched as the dark sky exploded with brilliant shards of multicolored light. It had lasted for only a short time, certainly no more than ten minutes, and yet, during that interval we'd actually seemed like a family that might endure, taking the days in ordinary stride, weathering the usual storms.

After the fireworks, we went to a local diner, and my father ate quite heartily, which was unusual for him. So unusual, in fact, that it seemed curiously faked, as if he were acting a part, forcing himself to appear less troubled than he was. My mother sat beside him, and from time to time, while Laura and Jamie and I dined on our usual hamburgers and french fries, my mother and father talked quietly to each other.

'We got home around eleven that night, I suppose,' I went on. 'My mother looked very tired. We all noticed it. Jamie actually took my mother's arm as she got out of the car. Laura saw it, too. After my mother had sat down in the living room, she went into the kitchen and made her a glass of warm milk.'

'And your father?'

'He didn't do anything,' I said. 'He just sat across from my mother until we all went upstairs to bed.'

As always, Jamie fell asleep almost instantly. I could hear him snoozing contentedly in the upper bunk. Laura was more high-strung, and that night, like many other nights, I heard her walking about in the room next door long after everyone else had fallen asleep.

But that night, I heard something more than the familiar sounds of Jamie's breathing and Laura's rustling about in her own room. I heard the door of my mother's bedroom open softly, a tiny squeak I had long ago recognized, but had rarely heard at such a late hour. I got up at once, walked to the door of my room, and opened it. In the corridor, I could see my mother as she came out of her bedroom, then, without turning on the light in the hallway, made her way slowly down the stairs. She was all the way down the stairs before I ventured out of my room. I walked down the same corridor, but stopped at the top of the stairs. From there I could see the light in the downstairs bathroom go on, and hear my mother as she opened the white wooden medicine cabinet that hung above the sink.

'What did you do?' Rebecca asked.

'I waited until she started back up the stairs,' I told her. 'Then I just went back to my room.'

But I didn't fall asleep, and about two hours later, I heard the same squeaking hinge that told me my parents' bedroom door had opened once again. Just like before, I walked to the door of my room, opened it slightly, and looked out. From that position, I could see my mother as she staggered toward the staircase once again. But this time she was weaving unsteadily and moaning softly, her arms wrapped around her stomach.

I started to move toward her, perhaps to help her down the stairs or to wherever it was she was trying to get to that night, but then I saw my father come out of the bedroom. For a moment, he stood very still in the doorway, watching her silently, his light blue eyes glowing, cat-like, in the moonlit hallway. Then, as if in response to a sudden signal, he rushed toward her, gathered her into his arms, and walked her back into their bedroom.

I remained at my door for a long time, but I didn't see either my mother or my father again that night. I could hear my mother coughing and gagging, and I knew that she was in the bathroom that adjoined her room, probably bent over the sink or the toilet. After a while, I returned to my own room and lay down on the lower bunk.

'At the time,' I said, 'I thought it was just a bad stomach.'

Rebecca looked up from her notes. 'Why did you ever come to think it might be something else?' she asked.

'Because of what happened the next morning.'

I had gotten up early, just at dawn, a little boy needing to go to the bathroom. The light was pouring through the high window to the right of Jamie's desk, and some of it spread out into the hallway when I opened the door and headed for the downstairs bathroom.

It was located to the left of the stairs, just off the kitchen, and when I reached the bottom of the stairs I saw my father working furiously inside its cramped space. He was going through all the drawers of the small cabinet that we used to store such things as toothpaste and extra rolls of toilet paper. The door of the mirrored medicine chest that hung above the small white porcelain sink, and which my mother used to store the family's various medicines, was open. My father had assembled a large number of bottles and plastic pill containers along the rim of the sink, and he was intently reading the labels of each of them in turn, his eyes squinting fiercely as he read. After reading a label, he would either return the container to the medicine chest or drop it into the plain gray shoe box he'd placed on top of the toilet.

'So from all this, you've come to believe that your mother had tried to kill herself that night?' Rebecca asked.

'Yes.'

'And that the next morning your father had tried to find out what she'd used so that he could get rid of it?'

I nodded. 'Because later that morning, I saw him put the shoe box in his van.'

Rebecca scribbled a few notes into her notebook, then glanced up at me. 'When did you see your mother again?'

'Later that day,' I answered. 'She looked very weak. Like an old woman, frail.'

But she looked more than weak, more than frail. She looked devastated.

I had arrived home from school just a few minutes earlier and was busily making myself a peanut butter sandwich when I saw her make her way shakily down the stairs. The house was empty save for the two of us. Neither Laura nor Jamie had gotten back home yet, and my father was still at work in the hardware store downtown.

'She must have heard me fiddling around in the kitchen,' I told Rebecca. 'That's probably why she came down.' In my mind, I saw her drag herself down that long flight of stairs, still exhausted and probably in some kind of pain, so that she could say the three barely audible words as she drew herself into the kitchen.

'"Welcome home, Stevie", that's what she said to me. That's all she said. Just "Welcome home, Stevie".' I shook my head. 'Poor Dottie,' I said. 'She died in that same old red housedress she wore when she came down to the kitchen that afternoon.'

Rebecca's pen stopped dead. 'No, she didn't,' she said. 'She was killed in a regular skirt and blouse.'

'She was?'

'Yes,' Rebecca said. 'Why did you think she'd been wearing the red housedress?'

I shook my head, astonished and a little unnerved by my own weird conjectures. 'I don't know why I thought that,' I said.

Rebecca watched me with a kind of eerie wariness, as if, perhaps, she already did.

# TWELVE

Peter was at the small desk in the den, intently tracing a map, when I got home from my evening with Rebecca. It was part of that night's schoolwork, and he was working at it diligently, as he always did. He barely looked up as I passed, and when he did, a fringe of blond hair fell over his right eye.

'Hi, Dad,' he said, then returned to the map.

I nodded toward him as I headed on down the corridor. I could see the light shining in Marie's office, and some part of me wanted to avoid it, to slink up the stairs, away from her increasingly uneasy gaze. But the stairs themselves rested at the end of the corridor. Only a ghost could have made it past her door unseen.

She was behind her desk, as usual, a classical piece playing softly in the background, something I didn't recognize.

'How's it going?' I asked casually as I stopped at her door.

She glanced up and smiled somewhat tiredly. 'Fine,' she said. She was wearing her reading glasses, but she took them off to look at me thoughtfully for a moment, her face very quiet, one part of it in shadow, the other brightly illuminated by the lamp at her right.

'Everything okay?' I asked.

'I suppose so,' Marie answered in a strange, uncertain reply.

'All your projects moving along?'

It clearly struck her as a spiritless question, with an answer neither wanted nor expected, but she did not make an issue of it. Instead, her mind appeared to shift to a more casual concern. 'I thought we might call out for a pizza for dinner,' she said.

I nodded. 'Fine with me.'

The thoughtful look returned, studious, concentrated, as if she were trying to read something written on my forehead. 'You've been getting home at such odd hours for the past few weeks, it's hard to know exactly when to cook,' she said.

I nodded. 'We're finishing up a few big drafting jobs at the office,'

I told her, though she had not asked for any further explanation of my unusual absences.

'Finishing up?' she asked. 'So things should be back to normal soon?'

'Yeah, pretty soon.'

She smiled, though a little stiffly. 'That's good,' she said.

'Anything else?' I asked.

The question seemed to strike her as more serious than I had meant it. She looked at me solemnly. 'Should there be?'

I shook my head. 'Not that I know of.'

'Okay,' Marie said, but with an unmistakable tone of resignation, as if a chance had been offered, but not taken. Then she reached for the phone, though her eyes never left me. 'With anchovies?' she asked, in a voice that sounded unexpectedly sad.

'Yeah, that's fine,' I told her, drawing away from the door. 'I just need to go wash up.'

I walked up the stairs to our bathroom and washed my hands. As I did so, the phrase Marie had used, 'back to normal', lingered uncomfortably in my mind. For Marie, it meant the return to a precious predictability and routine. To me, however, it meant the end of something exciting and full of unexpected discovery. As I dried my hands that evening, I felt like a man who'd lived for many years on a deserted island, only to spot, for a single, shining hour, the approach of a long white ship, the dream of rescue growing wildly with each passing moment, until, after an excruciating interval of anticipation, the great ship had drifted once again toward the far horizon, and, at last, disappeared beneath the flat gray of the sea.

'Steve?'

It was Marie calling from downstairs, but I couldn't answer. I stood, as if transfixed by the misty glass of the bathroom mirror.

'Steve, the pizza's here.'

The pizza had arrived, and moving as if on automatic pilot, I went downstairs, paid the delivery boy, and brought the large square box into the kitchen.

Peter and Marie gathered around, and I methodically gave each of them a slice, then got one of my own, eating it silently with them at the kitchen table.

Across from me, I could see Peter's blond head lowered over his plate, but I didn't think of him, or of Marie. Instead, I returned to my father.

I saw him in his long silences, in the lair he'd made for himself in the gray basement. I saw him as he watched each of us go through our daily, unexalted lives, and I wondered at the process by which we had been reduced to nothing in his eyes. Nothing, at least, beyond profound intrusions. Had he spent night after night in the house on McDonald

Drive, listening mutely to our squabbling, and thought only of how he might be released from us, set free, at last, to go to ... what?

Was it to his own, still undiscovered version of Rebecca?

Was it the pain of not being with her that he had, at last, found impossible to bear?

It was hard to imagine, and yet I had no choice. I wondered if during the long, drab dinners at our kitchen table, my father had dreamed of a 'someone else' while he'd listened absently to our quarreling or our dull school day gossip. Had he dreamed of spiriting her away to his own dream house, a cottage in the hills, perhaps? And each time, had that rapturous vision foundered on the banks of our daily bickering and mundane pettiness?

I remembered that as a child, I'd noticed moments when my father had stared vacantly out the window or sat in isolation in the little, vine-draped solarium. Perhaps, on those occasions, he'd let himself be carried away by the intensity of his need.

I also saw him in his van, staring at my mother as she crouched over her flower bed, and I marveled at how easily I could put Marie in the place of 'poor Dottie', how easily I could shrink her down to a small, dry pebble.

Later that same night, as I walked out into the backyard, my feet trudging through the dry, steadily accumulating leaves, I thought again of how lost my father had looked as he'd sat alone in the brown van. I saw his face, deep-lined and webbed in misery, but with a terrible edge of purpose within it, his eyes shining through the smoke, cold and without pupils, mere round, ice-blue orbs.

After a time, I returned to the house. I watched television with Peter, then chatted with Marie for a few minutes after he had gone to bed, a dull conversation which appeared to annoy her after a while, so that she finally marched up the stairs and went to bed.

I went to my office, sat down at my desk, and began to add a few passionate but unreal lines to my 'dream house'. The house had become even more vague and insubstantial during the last few weeks, with turrets and towers and unsupported balconies, a house that could exist only in a world that had forsaken gravity, along with all the other laws that govern earthbound things.

It was the phone that finally interrupted me. I picked it up, and to my immense surprise, it was Rebecca.

There was something urgent in her voice, and for a moment I allowed myself the fantasy that she had been seized by the same deep yearning for me that I had so long felt for her.

'It's me,' she said.

'Yes, I know.'

'I won't be able to meet with you on Wednesday afternoon. I have to check on a few things.'

I could clearly hear her reluctance to say more. I could also hear the sound of engines in the background, the rustle of passing voices.

'You're at the railway station,' I said.

'No, the bus station,' she said. 'I'm going to Somerset. To see Swenson.'

'When will you be back?'

'By Saturday.'

'So we can meet at the usual time that day?'

'Maybe a little later, if that's all right,' she said. 'I'll let you know.' I heard a pneumatic door as it opened. The strain returned to Rebecca's voice. 'I've got to go,' she said. 'My bus is leaving.'

Then she hung up.

The phone was still in my hand when Marie came to the door. She was dressed in a sleek, white sleeping gown, her hair in disarray.

'Who was that?' she asked drowsily.

I said the first name that occurred to me. 'Wally,' I told her.

She seemed to awaken suddenly, the veil of sleep dissolved. She looked at me, puzzled. 'So late?' She glanced at the clock which hung on the wall to her left. 'It's past midnight.'

I shrugged. 'He just wanted to talk about a problem we'd run into earlier today.'

She smiled, but distantly. 'I didn't think Wally ever cared that much about anything at work.'

She knew him well, and she was right. Wally had never been the type to give his work a second thought once he'd left the office. He'd been a bad choice, but I was stuck with him.

'He's been a little more concerned with things lately,' I said. 'Maybe he's a little worried, too.'

'About what?'

'I don't know,' I said with a shrug. 'Mr. Lowe's opinion of him, I guess.'

Marie smiled at the mention of Mr. Lowe's name, a quiet, respectful smile.

'Anyway, we straightened it all out,' I added quickly.

'Good,' Marie said. She looked at me softly. 'So, are you coming to bed soon?'

'It won't be long,' I assured her.

She nodded and drew herself back out into the corridor. 'Good night, then,' she said as she disappeared into its darkness.

I sat back in my chair and let my eyes settle on the telephone. Marie had already vanished from my mind, but merely by staring at the phone I could all but feel Rebecca's breath still surging toward me through its stiff black lines.

I got up early the next morning. While still in bed, I reached up and touched my face. I could feel the scratchy texture of my morning beard, and it reminded me of the dream I'd had a few weeks before, a dream of waking up in a place I didn't recognize, a small room with an old sink and a battered armoire. I remembered the short white curtains and the warm, tropical breeze that had lifted them languidly, revealing a rust-colored landscape of tiled roofs and dark spires.

A few minutes later, I walked downstairs. Everything in my house, I realized, looked old and encrusted, and had lost its power of attraction. It was a feeling which Rebecca had already begun to explore. 'For these men, perhaps, for all men,' as she finally wrote, 'the sense of permanence in human relations rarely issues a truly romantic call, rarely speaks in thrilling whispers or attains the electrifying jolt of a lover's voice.' The capacity to imbue long and enduring relations with just that kind of highly charged romanticism, she added, 'was the single greatest achievement of the female imagination.'

Whether true or not of all men, Rebecca's insight was true enough of me. For it was undoubtedly the 'thrilling whisper' rather than the 'sense of permanence' that I wanted as I stood among all the things and people who'd gathered around my life.

'You tossed a lot in bed last night,' Marie said as she came down the stairs.

I gave her a weak smile. 'I've got a lot on my mind,' I told her. I didn't add anything else, but merely allowed her to assume that my recent agitation was related only to my work, that there was nothing growing in me that she should fear.

Peter came bounding down the stairs a few minutes later. He wolfed down the cereal Marie had poured into the bowl, then headed out to the driveway for a couple of hoop shots before he left for school. I could see him playing happily in the sun as he leaped about the cement driveway, ducking and swooping, pretending that the opposite team was closing in upon him.

'You know, he's a pretty good basketball player,' I said as Marie rose and headed for the stairs.

She turned toward me and smiled weakly. 'Like his dad was,' she said, almost wistfully, as if remembering the former life of a loved one who had already died.

She was still upstairs when I left the house a few minutes later. I passed

Peter on the way to my car, stopped to make a couple of shots, then drove away. In the rearview mirror I could see his hair shining in the early morning sun.

I arrived at my office a few minutes later. I had barely gotten to my desk when Wally stepped up to it.

He smiled brightly and slapped me on the shoulders. 'You got lucky, old chap,' he said.

'What do you mean?'

'I have to go into New York today, and Mr. Lowe told me to take you along.'

'To do what?'

'I'm delivering the latest drawings on the Global Apartments project,' Wally told me. 'Old Man Lowe thinks you should be there in case there are any questions.'

Normally I would have dreaded such a trip. My love was drawing in my private cubicle, the seclusion of creating isolated forms. I hated meetings of all kinds, especially client meetings. But that day such a ride into the city struck me as a respite, a way of regaining the strength which had been drained from me during the night.

We took the old U.S. 1 rather than the highway, moving through shady Connecticut villages until we reached the crowded suburbs of New York. Wally drove in his usual style, casually, with his arm slung out the open window. He was about twenty pounds overweight, and his reddish hair had thinned considerably since the days he and Marty Harmon and I had first worked together at Simpson and Lowe, but there was still a raw and vulgar boyishness about him, a quality that appeared to attract some people as much as it repelled others. The young secretaries often flirted with him openly, while the older ones, married or looking toward marriage, thought him a pathetic clown.

That day, as we drove through the bright, still summery, air, Wally lit one cigarette after another, often bobbing the lighted tips wildly as he spoke. He related tales of his various jobs, his youth, finally his travels, either alone on business trips, or with his wife and family.

'You don't get out much, do you, Steve?' he asked at one point. 'Out of Old Salsbury, I mean.'

'Not much.'

'When was the last time you were in New York?'

'Years ago. I can hardly remember.'

Wally shrugged, letting the subject drop.

I thought of the night before, the excuse I'd made to Marie about Rebecca's call.

'Listen, Wally,' I said as we headed through the last stretch of road that led into the city, 'if Marie ever mentions anything about my getting a call from you late last night, I ...'

Wally's eyes shot over to me. 'You need an alibi, Steve? Someone to cover for you?'

'Well, it's just that last night ...'

'She called, right?' Wally said with a slow smile. 'She always does, in the end.'

'Who does?'

'The other woman,' Wally said flatly. 'She always says she'll never call you at home, but she always does.'

'This was a little different,' I said quickly.

Wally looked at me pointedly. 'It couldn't have been too different,' he said, 'or you wouldn't have had to lie about it, would you, old buddy?'

He was right, of course. But only partly right. For though Rebecca was not my lover in any technical sense, she had come to represent one: the flight from life's heaviness, the possibility of escape.

'So is it love?' Wally asked lightly.

I didn't answer.

Wally's smile broadened. He didn't press the question, but settled instead for a different one. 'It's the woman who came to see you in the office that day, am I right?'

I nodded faintly, reluctantly.

'Whew!' Wally said, pretending to wipe a line of sweat from his forehead. 'Hot, hot, hot.'

I watched the road, adding nothing, feeling neither shame nor the absence of shame, but only the disquieting sense that I had cheapened the nature of my own feeling for Rebecca by being unable to explain it.

'Does she live in Old Salsbury?' Wally asked.

'A little ways outside it.'

'Do you see her a lot?'

'Not too often.'

Wally shrugged. 'Well, just tell her to ease up on the old home phone, you know?' he said. Then he grinned impishly, one worldly man to another. 'Either that, or keep me well-informed in case ...' He stopped. 'What's your wife's name?'

'Marie,' I said.

Wally nodded briskly, then finished his sentence. 'In case Marie calls me up sometime to find out where the hell you are.'

'She'd never do that,' I assured him. 'She'd never try to track me down.'

'Don't kid yourself, buddy,' Wally said. 'If she starts really chewing at it, she'll track you down all right.'

I shook my head. 'No, she wouldn't,' I told him. 'She'd rather die first.'

Suddenly I felt my eyes grow cool and vacant, and there must have been something in my voice, because I felt the car veer to the right, then come to a noisy halt along the bank of the road. I turned toward Wally. He was staring at me worriedly.

'Whoa, now, buddy,' he said.

I glanced at him quickly, defensively, as if some part of a secret plot had been uncovered.

'You look a little weird, Steve,' Wally added. He reached over and squeezed my shoulder. 'You don't want to let things get out of hand, you know?'

'What do you mean?'

'With this woman,' Wally said, 'the one who's fucking your mind.' He looked at me pointedly, giving me his best advice. 'You don't want to burn the house down, you know?'

'Burn the house down?'

He smiled indulgently. 'The first time a woman comes flying into things, it really jerks your tail into a knot, I know,' he said. 'But then, when that one's gone, another one comes along, and after two or three times like that, you realize that it's all just fun and games, that there's no need to get all knotted up about it.'

I shook my head. 'It's not like that with me,' I told him. 'It's not just fun and games.'

He laughed at my boyish innocence. 'So, I guess you're one of these men that has to take it seriously, right?' he asked.

I didn't answer. I had no answer.

Wally watched me soberly. 'Listen, Steve, you can play around with this woman, have your fun and all that, but when it's all over, you need to go home and warm your feet at the same old fire.' He waited for me to answer. 'I'm talking about your wife, Steve.'

'Marie,' I said, but my voice was little above a whisper.

Wally gave me a penetrating look. 'You have to be careful and not get things mixed up, that's what I'm saying.' He paused a moment, his eyes watching me closely. 'When they get mixed up, bad things can happen,' he added darkly. 'Remember Marty Harmon?'

I nodded silently.

'He was one of these men that couldn't keep things straight,' Wally told me firmly, 'and look what happened to him.'

Suicide, of course, had 'happened' to Marty, but it had never occurred to me that I was in the least like him, or that I might ever reach such a state of physical and spiritual exhaustion. It wasn't death I wanted, it was a different life.

The realization that swept over me at that instant was as close as I had ever come to a full understanding of how far I had been swept out to sea, of how deep my discontent actually was.

'I can't go back,' I muttered weakly.

'To wherever you were before this woman, you mean?' Wally asked. 'Of course you can.'

I shook my head slowly.

Wally leaned toward me, his eyes intent, troubled. 'Listen, I'm trying to give you some advice, Steve,' he said sharply. 'I gave Marty the same advice, and he didn't take it either.' He stopped, looked at me very severely for a moment, then added, 'I mean, you don't want to end up like ...' He stopped again. 'I mean, when your father ...'

I stared at Wally, stunned not so much that he would make a connection between me and my father, as that he would actually say it to my face.

'I don't even remember who told me about it,' Wally said, his voice softer now, conciliatory, 'and, believe me, I don't mean ...'

'That I could murder my family?' I asked harshly.

'No, no, no, no. I would never have said that, Steve,' Wally answered. 'It's just that when you see a man hurting, well, you see a man who might lose control.' He shrugged. 'I just keep remembering Marty, you know? He wasn't a bad guy. He was just a guy that got it all screwed up.'

'I'm not Marty Harmon,' I said firmly. 'And I'm not my father either.'

Wally looked at me quietly, resigned that there would be no point in continuing the conversation. 'Okay, Steve,' he said at last, 'we'll just drop it, okay?'

'Yeah, let's do.'

With that, Wally edged the car back onto the road and drove on silently. We never spoke seriously again, nor did he ever mention my father, my family, or even the unknown woman he has no doubt come to blame for their destruction.

Now, when I remember that afternoon, I think of it as the last chance I had to save us all. I knew that Rebecca was leaving, that her study was very nearly done, that very, very soon my life would go 'back to normal', with nights at home with Peter and Marie, days at work, summer visits to that very lake along whose bank Rebecca's cottage still rested in a grove of trees.

So what would have been missing in a life lived like that? Certainly not love, as Marie was soon to tell me. Certainly not comfort. There would have been no ignominy in my return to normal.

What would have been missing? The mythical dream house without walls or firm foundation. The thrill of awakening in an unknown country, the exhilaration of an endless setting forth. Surprise. The allure of the unexplored. And finally, love, at its sharpest instant, the moment when it fuses with desire.

Much would have been missing.

But not everything.

# THIRTEEN

Rebecca returned to Old Salsbury the following day just as she'd said she would. It was a Saturday, but I wasn't at home when she called. Neither was Marie. It was Peter who answered, then later gave me the message.

'A woman called,' he said. 'She asked for you. She left her name and number.'

He'd written it down on a small square of white paper, which he handed to me dutifully.

I glanced at the paper, pretending that I didn't recognize the name he'd written in large block letters beside the number: REBECCA.

'Did she say what she wanted?' I asked casually.

Peter shook his head. 'She just wanted you to call her back, I guess.' He shrugged and darted away.

A few seconds later, as I sat at my desk, dialing Rebecca's number, I saw his lean body as it darted across the backyard and disappeared around a tall, nearly leafless tree.

She answered immediately.

'It's me,' I said.

'Yes, hi,' Rebecca said. 'I just wanted to let you know that I'd gotten back to town.'

'Was it a worthwhile trip?'

'Yes.' Her voice seemed to tighten somewhat. 'There were some new developments.'

'I'm surprised to hear that. I thought you already knew everything.'

'Sometimes it's just a question of one thing leading to another.'

'Well, what did you ...'

'Not now,' Rebecca interrupted quickly. 'We'd planned to meet today. Can you make it in the evening? Say, around seven?'

'All right.'

'Okay, see you then,' Rebecca said as she hung up.

I held the receiver for a moment, almost as if it were her hand. I felt it cool, then let it go, and walked out into the backyard and stood beside the covered pool.

Peter was poised on the other side. He smiled a moment, then lifted his arms until his fingers touched. He held himself suspended in that position for a moment, pretending he was about to dive onto the broad black tarpaulin that stretched across the now empty pool.

'Good form,' I said. 'You look like a real pro.'

He seemed pleased by my attention. 'They're teaching us at school,' he said. Then he ran over to me, his blond head bobbing left and right.

'What if there were water in the pool,' he said, 'and one time I started to drown?'

'I'd come in after you.'

'What if there were sharks in the water?'

'I'd come in after you,' I repeated.

He smiled broadly, then dashed away again, this time around the far corner of the house.

Marie returned an hour later. She looked tired as she got out of the car and headed toward the house. From my place in the den, I could see her move wearily up the stairs that led to the kitchen and disappear inside the house. I expected her to join me, but she never did, and so, after a time, I went to look for her. She was not in her office, so I went upstairs.

I found her in our bedroom, lying faceup on her side of the bed, her arms folded neatly over her chest. She'd kicked off her shoes, but otherwise she remained in the same formal business clothes she'd worn to New Haven earlier in the day. A bright shaft of light fell over her from the parted curtains, and I could see small bits of dust floating weightlessly in the flooding light.

'How'd it go?' I asked.

She did not open her eyes. 'Not great. They didn't like some of the designs.'

'They never like them in the beginning,' I told her. 'They have to be critical at the first presentation; otherwise they feel like they're being led by the nose.'

Marie took a deep breath, then let it out slowly. 'I'm tired,' she said.

'It was a long day,' I said, 'the drive alone, you know?'

She opened her eyes and gazed at me softly. 'Let's go out to dinner tonight, Steve,' she said, almost plaintively, as if asking a favor, 'just you and me.' She smiled. 'We could use a night out, don't you think?'

It was a simple request, not much asked nor expected, and yet I couldn't grant it. Rebecca would be waiting for me at her cottage. It was to her that I had to go.

I shook my head. 'I can't, Marie,' I said. 'I have to go into the office.'

Her eyes narrowed. 'On a Saturday night?'

'It's the final meeting on that library,' I said. 'I have to finish the designs.'

She looked at me doubtfully. 'On a Saturday night?' she said again.

'I'm supposed to be at the office by seven,' I told her. 'Wally's coming in, along with a few guys from the drafting department. We're going to work through the night if we have to.'

Her eyes lingered on me a moment, then she turned away and closed them again. 'You'd better start getting ready then,' she said. 'It's almost six.'

I walked over to the bed and sat down beside her. 'I have a little time,' I said.

She didn't answer, but only continued to lie stiffly beside me.

I touched her cheek with the side of my hand.

She drew her face away instantly. 'No, no,' she said, a little brusquely, 'I want to rest.'

I stood up and walked into the adjoining bathroom. Once there, I showered and dressed myself. Marie was still lying on the bed when I came back into the bedroom. She didn't stir as I left her, didn't so much as open her eyes.

Peter was in the family room when I got downstairs.

'Why are you all dressed up?' he asked, as I stepped in to say good-bye.

'I have to go into the office,' I said.

'When will you be back?'

'Not until late. There's a lot to do.'

He smiled jokingly. 'So I guess I shouldn't wait up for you, huh?'

I shook my head. 'No, I don't think so.' I waved good-bye, then headed outside.

I'd already backed the car nearly halfway toward the street when I glanced back toward the house. I could see the gray eye of the television as it glowed dimly toward me from the shaded window of the family room. It gave me the eerie sense of being watched, and so I let my eyes retreat from it, drifting upward, along a wall of brick and mortar, until our bedroom came into view and I saw Marie standing at the window, watching me from afar. For a single, delicate moment, we stared mutely at each other, two faces peering outward, it seemed to me, from two different worlds. Then, her eyes still gazing at me with the same penetrating force, she lifted her arms very gracefully, like the wingspread of a great bird, grasped the separate edges of the bedroom curtains, and slowly drew them together. They were still weaving slightly as I let the car drift on down the driveway and out into the street.

*

'Hi, Steve,' Rebecca said as she opened the door. She stepped aside to let me pass.

I took a chair not far from the window. Outside, I could see the still gray surface of the lake. It looked like a sheet of slate.

Rebecca took the chair opposite me, so that we faced each other directly, as if we were about to begin some kind of intensely demanding game.

'We're close to the end, I think.'

Something in my face must have puzzled her, because for a moment she stopped and regarded me closely. 'We've gone through each member of your family,' she explained, 'and their relationships.'

I nodded but said nothing.

'There are things I'll never know, of course,' she added. 'Your father still seems very mysterious to me.'

'My father,' I repeated softly. Curiously, I suddenly thought of him almost as a rival for her attention, a dark, majestic figure whose profound experience of life and death utterly dwarfed the humdrum banality of my own.

I felt the need to bring him down. 'Are you sure he's worth knowing any more than you already do?'

'Yes, I am.'

'But you're sure he fits your criteria, aren't you?' I asked. 'You're sure that Nellie Grimes, for example, had nothing to do with the murders.'

She nodded. 'Yes, I'm sure of that,' she answered.

'You found her, didn't you?' I said. 'You found Nellie.'

She shook her head. 'Not exactly. Nellie Grimes died eight years ago. But I found her daughter, May. She lives not far from Somerset.'

'How did you find her?'

'Through Swenson.'

'I thought he hadn't known anything about Nellie.'

'He's never mentioned her to me, that's true,' Rebecca told me, 'but only because he'd never thought of her as actually connected to the case.' She paused a moment, then went on. 'After the murders, Swenson talked to a lot of people who'd known your father. He was trying to get some idea of where he might have gone after the murders. One of the people he talked to was Grimes.' She reached into her briefcase and handed me a picture of a woman standing on a small wooden porch. 'She was living in Hoboken,' she went on. 'Swenson remembered seeing May playing in the backyard despite the drizzle. He said her dress was muddy, and that her hair was wet and stringy, but that Nellie didn't seem to care.'

It was hard to imagine May in such a state, or her mother's indifference to it. In all my other memories of them, they'd been dressed as well as they could afford to be, always neat and clean, as if waiting to be put upon display.

'Nellie Grimes was not doing very well at that point,' Rebecca added.

'What did she say about my father?'

'She said that he'd always been very kind to her,' Rebecca answered, 'and that he'd given her some money when she'd left Somerset.'

In my mind I saw the envelope pass from my father's hand to Nellie's.

'She also told Swenson that she didn't believe your father had killed his family,' Rebecca added.

'Then who did?'

Rebecca shrugged. 'She only said that she was sure it was someone else,' she said. 'Then Swenson asked her directly if your father might have been involved with another woman, and she said absolutely not. She told him that she knew for a fact that your father was not that kind of man.'

I remembered the way Nellie's face had lifted toward my father that day in the train station, and I suspected that it had lifted toward him in just that same tempting way many times before. In isolated places, no doubt, where no one could have seen him answer to the intensity of such a call, but he'd drawn back on those occasions, too, resolutely, with his own unfathomable pride.

Rebecca looked at me as if she expected me to contradict her, then added, 'May also had a very high opinion of your father.'

'But she was just a child,' I said. 'What could she have known about him?'

'Actually, she remembered him quite well,' Rebecca said. 'Very clearly, even down to the gray work clothes he always wore.'

For a moment it struck me as intimate knowledge, and I felt a strange resentment toward May Grimes, as if she'd usurped my place as the sole surviving witness.

'How would she have known anything about my father?' I asked.

'May evidently spent a lot of time in the hardware store,' Rebecca continued. 'There was no place for her to go after school, so she played in the back room. Sometimes your father would come back there and try to entertain her a little.' She smiled. 'May remembered that he bought her a Chinese checkers set and that they used to sit on the floor and play together.'

I could not bring the image to mind very easily, my father sitting on the bare cement floor with a little girl, playing Chinese checkers, trying to help her pass the long boring hours of a winter afternoon.

'She remembered something else,' Rebecca said, the tone of her voice changing. 'They were playing together one afternoon. May thinks it was just a few weeks before the day your father took her and her mother to the train station.' She paused a moment, as if hesitant to go on. 'They were alone in the back room,' she continued finally. 'May had been staring at the board, making her next move. When she finished it, she looked up and noticed your father staring at her. She said he looked different, very sad. She asked him if there was anything wrong. He didn't answer exactly. He only said, 'This is all I want.''

I felt my skin tighten, but said nothing.

Rebecca watched me cautiously, gauging my mood. 'I remembered you telling me that he'd said the same thing to you.'

'In exactly the same words.' I shook my head helplessly, my father's mystery still as dense as it had ever been. 'What was going on in him?' I asked, though very softly, a question directed toward myself as much as toward Rebecca.

Rebecca, however, actually offered an answer. 'At that point, when he said that to you in the basement,' she said, 'he was probably very depressed.'

I could see that she was leading into something.

'Depressed about what?'

'Well, he'd finalized his plan by then, of course,' she said. 'He'd canceled the two plane tickets, for example.' She looked at me significantly. 'He did that on October 10.'

I knew then that the 'new developments' she'd mentioned on the phone earlier had to do with those two mysterious plane tickets. She'd tracked down their enigmatic meaning and was about to lay her findings before me like a parting gift.

'Why did he cancel those tickets?' I asked. 'You know, don't you?'

Rebecca leaned forward, settling her eyes on me with a deep, probing gaze. 'You remember the night before you came home from the Cape? You saw your father and mother talking together, and he had his arm around her.'

'That's right.'

'And the next night, the night the family got back to Somerset, you saw your father and Laura beside the fence in the backyard.'

I nodded.

'You said that they looked as if they were engaged in a very serious conversation,' Rebecca went on. 'Then later, you saw them come up the stairs, and it was at that point that you heard a few words pass between them.'

'That's right.'

Rebecca drew her black notebook from the briefcase. 'I want to be sure

I have this exactly right.' She flipped through the notebook until she found the page she wanted. 'This is what you heard,' she said. Then she quoted it: 'Your father: "Tomorrow." Laura: "So soon?" Your father: "Yes."' She looked up. 'The "tomorrow" that your father mentioned would have been September 3.'

'Yes.'

'Let me ask you again: do you remember anything about that morning?' Rebecca asked.

I tried to recall it, but it remained a blur of activity. My mother had prepared the usual breakfast of cereal and toast, and after eating, Laura, Jamie, and I had all gone back upstairs to finish getting ready for school. The only thing that seemed different was the fact that my father had still been at home when we'd all left the house about a half hour later.

'My father stayed home that morning,' I said to Rebecca. 'He usually left before we did, but that morning, he didn't.' I drifted back to that day again, but only far enough to regain one last, minuscule detail. 'He was sitting at the kitchen table as I passed,' I added. 'I was racing for the door, you know, excited to be going back to school, but he shot his hand out, grabbed my arm, and stopped me. "Kiss your mother good-bye, Stevie," he said. And so I did.'

Rebecca looked as if I'd just confirmed something that had only been a conjecture before.

'He'd never asked me to do that before.'

'And then you went to school just like always?' Rebecca asked.

I nodded. 'Yes, we all went together. Well, at least Laura and I did. Jamie always went ahead of us.'

'Did you and Laura talk about anything in particular that morning?'

'No,' I said. 'We just walked to school like always. She left me at my school, then walked on to hers, about three blocks down the road.'

'When did you see Laura again?'

'She was waiting at the corner for me right after school,' I said. 'She always did that.'

For a moment, as I remembered her standing on the corner waiting for me that afternoon, her books in her arms, her long dark hair falling over her shoulders, I felt her loss again, but this time with a piercing depth, as if all the conversations I might have had with her in life, all the good and comforting times we might have had together, had suddenly swept over me in a great wave of imagined days. I saw us share all that we had not been allowed to share, the keenest experiences of adulthood, marriage, parenthood, the approach of middle age, all that my father had abruptly and mysteriously canceled as surely as he'd canceled those two plane tickets to Mexico.

'I loved my sister,' I said, though barely above a whisper. 'And I think she loved me.'

Rebecca's next question came at me like a slap in the face. 'And Jamie,' she asked, 'did you love him?'

I answered without hesitation. 'No.'

'Did anyone in the family love him?'

'I don't think so,' I answered. 'He always seemed alone.'

Alone in his bunk, alone at his desk, alone beneath the tree in the backyard, always alone.

'So Jamie never waited for you after school?' Rebecca asked.

'No, only Laura did that,' I answered. 'She was always there, waiting on the corner, just like she was that first day of school.'

Despite the warmth of the weather, as I recalled then, the first leaves of autumn had already begun to drift down upon us. I saw them fall slowly, but thickly, as Laura and I made our way down Ontario Street, and I felt a great sadness settle upon me, like the leaves.

'The leaves were falling,' I said to Rebecca. 'They were very red.'

But they could not have been red, I realized. I was not thinking of leaves. I was thinking of my sister's death, and Jamie's and my mother's. I was thinking of their thickly falling blood.

'Did you and your sister talk much on the way home that afternoon?' Rebecca asked.

'Not that I recall.'

'You walked silently, all the way home?'

Something came back vaguely, a tiny detail. 'No, I don't think we walked all the way home together that day,' I said slowly, unsure. 'I think she went into Oscar's, that little convenience store on the corner.'

Rebecca looked at me doubtfully. 'Why would you remember that?' she asked.

'Because it was so unusual,' I answered. 'But I do remember it now.'

I saw Laura turn to me, felt her hand release mine. 'Go on home, Stevie,' she said. 'I'll be there in a minute.' Then she walked away, moving slowly toward the convenience store, and finally disappearing inside of it. As I headed home, I saw her standing by the window, her eyes fixed on me, as if she were waiting for me to leave.

'So you walked the rest of the way home by yourself?' Rebecca asked.

I nodded. 'Laura told me to go on home without her, and so I did.'

'Was Jamie home when you got there?' Rebecca asked.

'No,' I said. I could feel it returning to me slowly, a picture of that afternoon. 'No one was home,' I added, 'not even my mother.'

It had never occurred to me before, but for the first and only time I could remember, my mother had not been at home when I arrived from school. I had returned to an empty house.

'I was alone in the house for a while,' I said, 'then Laura arrived, and Jamie a few minutes after that.'

Jamie had gone directly to our room, but Laura had walked into the solarium instead. Later, when I'd approached her, skipping jauntily across the living room carpet, she'd looked up at me fiercely, and snapped, 'Stop it, Stevie.' Then she'd turned away, letting her eyes drift out toward the empty street.

'Laura was not in a very good mood that afternoon,' I told Rebecca. 'I could tell that something was bothering her.'

Rebecca glanced down at her notebook. 'When did your mother get home?'

'Soon after the rest of us, I guess,' I told her. Then I remembered something else. 'My father brought her. They came home in his van.'

Once again an odd certainty swept into Rebecca's face. She leaned forward and began to dig through the briefcase, finally withdrawing several sheets of paper. It looked like a report of some kind, very official, with all the pages stapled together in the left-hand corner.

'This is the autopsy report on your mother,' she said. 'I had never read it because the cause of her death was so obvious.' She flipped back the first two pages. 'But while I was with Swenson yesterday, he made an aside about your mother being "doomed anyway".' She lifted the report toward me. 'When I asked him what he meant, he gave me this.'

She'd already turned to the page that mattered. She'd even underlined the relevant passage. I read it, then handed the report back to her, dazed.

'She had a brain tumor,' I said, astonished. 'Is that why she tried to kill herself?'

Rebecca nodded. 'Probably.'

I saw my mother as I'd seen her that night, trudging wearily down the stairs, shoulders bowed, head down, a single shaky hand gripping the wooden banister. How alone she must have felt at that moment, how sealed within a black solitude.

'Your mother's doctor told Swenson that your mother had come in for an X-ray examination on September 3, and that your father had come with her,' Rebecca said.

'September 3,' I said, laboring to make those connections I was certain Rebecca had already made. 'So when my father and Laura had that conversation by the fence the night we got back from the Cape, he was telling her that my mother was sick, and that she was going for an examination the next day?'

'Probably,' Rebecca said. She looked back down at her notebook, read a few pages to herself, then glanced back up at me. 'The doctor said that your mother arrived on schedule for her appointment. He remembered that your father brought her in, and that later, when the examination was over, he came to pick her up.'

'Yes, he brought her home that afternoon,' I told her.

Rebecca seemed hardly to hear me. 'Over the next few weeks the doctor had several conversations with your father,' she went on. 'The kind of conversations male doctors had with men in those days.'

'What do you mean?'

Rebecca seemed surprised by the question, as if any further explanation should have been unnecessary. 'Well, in certain cases a doctor and the husband of a female patient would get together to decide just how much a wife should know.'

'And so this doctor, he talked to my father about my mother's illness, but not to her?'

'Yes,' Rebecca said. 'According to Swenson's case notes, the doctor told your father that your mother's tumor was inoperable, and after that, they discussed quite a few alternatives. The doctor called several specialists in the field. He got back answers that weren't very encouraging.'

'I see.'

'And finally, on October 10, the doctor told your father that there was nothing that could be done,' Rebecca said, 'that your mother was going to die.' Her eyes drifted down to her notebook, then back up to me. 'The two tickets to Mexico City were canceled that same afternoon.'

The realization swept over me like a lifting breeze. 'So the second ticket was for my mother,' I said. 'He'd planned to take her away at some point, a surprise vacation, something like that.'

Rebecca nodded. 'There was no other woman, Steve.'

For a brief interval, I thought it all over again, everything Rebecca had just revealed. There was still something that didn't fit, and after a moment, I realized what it was.

'But when we were unloading the car the night we got back from Cape Cod, and Laura started complaining about my mother, my father snapped at her, remember? He said, "You should know."'

Rebecca looked at me without expression.

'And Laura went up to my mother's room and sat down on the bed beside her and put her arm around her.'

Rebecca nodded.

'Well, my father couldn't have meant that Laura should know about my mother's illness,' I said, 'because Laura couldn't have known about it that night. She hadn't been told yet.'

'Probably not,' Rebecca admitted.

'But she went up to my mother's room anyway,' I added. 'So she must have known something.'

Rebecca glanced down at her notes, as if expecting to find an answer there.

'And if my mother was already dying, why did my father bother to kill her?' I asked.

Rebecca sighed. 'There's still something missing, isn't there? Swenson thought so, too. He never thought it all added up. He never found a motive.'

'A reason for my father to have done it, you mean?'

'Yes.'

'Well, that's what you're still looking for, isn't it?'

Rebecca stared at me in earnest. 'I know what it was in all these other men,' she said, 'but I'm still not sure about your father.'

I said nothing, but only looked past her, out toward the lake. Night had nearly fallen by then, but beyond the water, I could still make out a dark line of thunderclouds as they rumbled in from the west.

'Motive is everything,' Rebecca said, though only to herself. 'There's no question that your father did it. His fingerprints were all over the shotgun. There were no other fingerprints.' She thought a moment longer, then glanced toward me. 'The only question is why?'

I continued to watch the wall of dark gray clouds as it closed in upon us. My father's face swam into my mind, then dissolved almost instantly, a figment, an enigma.

'It may rain tonight,' I said softly, as if to avoid any further inquiry into the foggy labyrinth of his mind.

Rebecca nodded. 'It was raining that day in November,' she said thoughtfully. Her mind seemed to latch on to an unexpected possibility. 'Maybe something happened that day in particular. Maybe something happened that brought it all together.'

'And sent my father over the edge, you mean?'

'Yes.'

I remembered the changing faces of my father, those features that slowly descended from the joy of his wedding day to the bleakness with which he'd stared toward my mother from the smoke-filled cab of the old brown van.

'I don't think so,' I told Rebecca. 'I don't think something just happened that day, something out of the blue, that caused my father to pick up that shotgun.'

Rebecca nodded. 'No, probably not,' she said. Then she pulled a single sheet of yellow paper from her briefcase. 'All right,' she said, 'let's start

348

again. Let's start from October 10, the day your father learned that your mother was dying. We'll go from there to the end.'

I said nothing, but merely waited for her to guide me back toward that day, as I knew she'd always planned to do.

'Your mother was dying,' Rebecca began. 'How did things change in the family because of that?'

'I never knew she was dying,' I told her. 'No one ever told me. And I don't think Jamie knew, either.'

'Why do you think that?'

'Because he was the same old Jamie up until the moment my father murdered him,' I said. 'He was always up in his room, always alone. Nothing changed with Jamie.'

'So you don't think he ever found out about your mother?'

'I don't think so,' I said. 'He certainly never changed in his attitude toward her.'

'What was his attitude?'

'That she was a maid,' I said, 'someone who washed clothes, cooked meals, vacuumed up that gray grime that my father was always tracking up from the basement.'

'That's the only way Jamie saw your mother?'

'More or less. I don't think he gave her much thought.'

Rebecca wrote my observations down in her notebook, then glanced up again. 'Do you think Laura ever knew just how serious your mother's illness was?'

'Oh, yes, of course she did,' I said.

I saw my sister in the solarium once again, sitting sullenly in the wicker chair as she had that September afternoon, snapping at me to 'stop it', without adding what must have been the final, unsaid portion of that sentence: 'Don't you know your mother's sick, don't you know she may be dying!'

'Laura looked quite upset the afternoon before my mother came home,' I told Rebecca. 'And after that, for the next few days, she looked very strange.' I shrugged. 'At the time, I couldn't have known what was bothering her, but I did notice that she seemed ...' I stopped, searching for the right word. 'She seemed dazed,' I said finally, 'like she couldn't quite figure out what to do, how to handle it.'

'Did she treat your mother differently after that?'

'Yes,' I said. 'For a time, she treated her much more gently.'

Rebecca's eyes narrowed questioningly. 'What do you mean, "for a time"?'

Even though it had been my own phrase, it struck me as being almost purposely vague, just as it had clearly struck Rebecca as being so.

'Well, for the first few weeks, Laura was very gentle and helpful,' I explained.

It was easy for me to recall all the little gestures of kindness my sister had made toward my mother during that brief time. She'd helped her in the kitchen, gone shopping with her on Saturday afternoons, and had been generally more tender toward her than she'd ever been.

'But that kindness didn't continue?' Rebecca asked.

'No, it didn't,' I said. 'It lasted for a few weeks, more or less until my mother tried to kill herself.'

'How did it change after that?'

'Laura seemed to withdraw from her,' I said. 'From my father, too. At about the same time.'

'That would have been around the middle of October, then?'

I nodded.

'Jamie was the only one who stayed the same during all those weeks,' I added, then thought a bit more of it, remembering how often he'd begun to bait my mother, too, as if one target were no longer enough for his steadily building spitefulness and anger. 'Actually, I think he got a little worse,' I said. 'He was sharp with my mother during those last weeks, but he also began to pull away entirely. From all of us, I mean. It was as if he couldn't stand being in the same house with us anymore.'

Growing more sullen with each day, bitter in what must have been a terrible, homebound loneliness, I remembered that Jamie had begun to absent himself almost entirely from the family during the last weeks of our time on McDonald Drive. He'd never joined us in the little den anymore, or even gone on those rare family outings to the drive-in movies. Instead, he'd sealed himself in his room, remaining there for hours at a time, coming down only to eat quickly, and after that, trudging up the stairs again.

'Toward the end,' I told Rebecca, 'Jamie was just a face in the hallway or on the other side of the dinner table. My mother didn't like to be around him. Neither did I. And, of course, Laura hated him.'

'You left out your father,' Rebecca reminded me. 'What did he think of Jamie during this time?'

Once again I recalled the moment years before when all three of us, Laura and Jamie and myself, had erupted into noisy battle in the backyard. My father had stepped out onto the second-floor patio and stared down silently, bringing the conflict to an immediate end. Even from that distance, I could tell that his eyes had swept smoothly from my upturned face to Laura's, then back to mine, leaving out the third point in what should have been the triangle of his assembled children. Even in that moment of disciplinary concern, his eyes had not once moved toward

Jamie. The following years, it struck me now, had only widened the abyss which separated them.

'I think that toward the end, my father just gave up on Jamie.'

'In what way?'

'Gave up trying to love him, to be a father to him.'

'Do you think Jamie felt that "giving up"?' Rebecca asked.

'Yes,' I said.

And for the first time, I saw Jamie captured in the deep well of his isolation. Not really his father's son, yet unaware of that dreadful fact, he had been kept outside the circle of our kinship, a prodigal and an outcast. To have killed him in so lonely and bereft a state, the only one among us who had never loved nor been loved by another, struck me as the single, saddest aspect of my father's crime.

A wave of empty, helpless grief must have passed over me at that moment, because when I looked back toward Rebecca, she appeared almost frightened by what she saw in my face.

'We don't have to finish everything tonight,' she said.

Finish everything. Those were the words she used. And so I knew that within hours, perhaps minutes, I would be returned to that dreadful state of 'back to normal' to which Marie had seemed to look forward with such anxious anticipation. I felt a pall descend, the atmosphere thickening and congealing around me. My destiny was being sealed. I was being buried alive. It was almost more than I could bear.

'Do you want to stop for the night, Steve?' Rebecca asked.

I lifted my head. 'No, let's finish it tonight,' I told her, now anxious to finish everything, to leave Rebecca behind, to go on to whatever it was that awaited me, and to do it quickly, cleanly, without ever looking back.

She nodded, glanced down at her notes, let Jamie slip back into his long oblivion, and renewed her focus upon Laura.

'You said that Laura treated your mother very gently for a time,' she began.

'It was just a brief change,' I said quickly, already pushing toward the next question, driving forward relentlessly, almost a man in flight.

'And after that how did Laura treat her?'

'She went back to the same attitude she'd always had toward her,' I answered. 'She seemed resentful of her. She avoided her most of the time, but once in a while, she would say something rather harsh.'

'Harsh? Like what?'

'I can't remember any specific word,' I told her crisply, almost curtly, urging her on at a steadily accelerating pace.

'You don't remember any particular episode of harsh treatment?' Rebecca asked.

'No.'

'Did Laura act this way in your father's presence?'

'No. Never.'

'And you said that this change occurred about a month or so after you got back from Cape Cod?'

'Yes.'

'In early October then?'

I nodded.

Rebecca wrote the date down in her notebook. 'But your father didn't change, is that right?'

'No, he didn't.'

'Do you recall any particular incident between them? Some special act of kindness?'

'No.'

Rebecca continued to pursue the point. 'Did anything at all strike you as different in your family during this time?'

'No.'

'So as far as you know, nothing at all changed in the family during the month before the murders?'

I shook my head. 'Nothing.'

And yet, as I sat there, responding to Rebecca's questions with clipped, one-word answers, I could nonetheless feel the slowly building sense of doom that had begun to invade those final days. A heaviness had descended upon us, as if the house at 417 McDonald Drive had been filled with a thick, transparent gelatin through which Laura, Jamie, my mother, and even my father moved slowly and trudgingly, like weary, exhausted creatures, struggling to draw what were their final breaths. One by one, each of them isolated from the other, I saw them all a final time: Jamie, embittered by successive waves of rejection, entombed behind the closed door of his room; Laura slouched sullenly in the wicker chair of the solarium; my mother in her bed behind the tightly drawn floral curtains, a bomb already lit inside her brain; and finally my father, alone now in the basement, bereft, solitary and morose, slowly turning forward the thin black wheel. They had all been dying during those last weeks, I realized, like flowers past their season.

It began to rain, and Rebecca rose and closed the window. 'And so everything remained the same up until the last day?' she asked as she returned to her seat.

'The last day,' I repeated, remembering it now as fully as I thought I ever would.

'It was raining,' I said.

It was raining, and had been raining for days. The lawns along

McDonald Drive were brown and soggy. Rain battered against the windowpanes of our rooms and thumped down loudly against the mock Tudor gables. The white cords of the basketball net hung limply in a gray, sodden web. The day before, my mother had hung our laundry beneath a bright mid-morning sun, but now, drenched and rain-beaten, it drooped heavily toward the saturated ground. Alone among all our clothes, only my sister's bra had been set free by a sudden burst of wind. It lay in a mangled, mud-spattered pile beneath a line of bathroom towels.

'Did everything seem normal that morning?' Rebecca asked.

'Yes, everything seemed "normal",' I said evenly, almost choking on the word. 'We were all back to *normal* on that last day,' I said bitterly, my voice coming through nearly clenched teeth. 'Maybe that's what my father couldn't bear.'

I saw Rebecca's face stiffen. 'What do you mean?'

'Maybe that's why he killed them,' I said coldly. 'Because the kind of life they represented made him sick.'

Rebecca's eyes narrowed. 'What kind of life are you talking about, Steve?' she asked, but warily, as if she were closing in on a dangerous animal she'd studied and knew well.

'A pinched, little life,' I said, brutally, the raw edge of my own vast discontent piercing through the mask behind which I'd hidden so long. 'A dull, stupid life, with nothing in it that lifted him, that gave him hope, that had some possibility of escape.'

Rebecca's face filled with recognition. 'Escape from what?' she asked.

'From *them*,' I blurted. 'From the way they were killing him before he decided to take it by the *balls* ... and kill *them* instead.'

The words seemed to hit her like bullets. She drew away from me, her eyes glaring fiercely. Her lips parted, but she didn't speak. Instead, she closed her notebook with an abrupt finality.

'I think we can end it here,' she said, in a steely voice, her tone beyond any feeble gesture I might make at either apology or explanation.

I started to speak, but she rose instantly, walked to the door, and jerked it open. 'I'll send you all the materials I've collected on the case,' she said tensely.

I remained in my chair, my own last words washing over me like a hot wave.

'Rebecca, I ...'

She remained at the door, her body rigid. 'I'll also send you a copy of the book,' she added.

I knew that all she might have felt for me before that moment – respect, esteem, perhaps even some affection – had been reduced to this single, brutal and explosive kernel. She'd seen the face of 'these men' in my face, and there was no way for me to creep back into my former self.

And so I nodded to her as I passed, saw her eyes dart away, then stepped out into the rain.

# FOURTEEN

I walked out into the rain, moving resolutely toward my waiting car. I didn't glance back toward Rebecca's cottage to see if she lingered by the door or watched me leave from behind the short white curtains of her tiny living room.

I could feel an immense emptiness within me, a sense of having been filled for a time, then gutted absolutely. As I drove down the curving road which led from Rebecca's cottage, I felt that some part of me had been blasted away by the same fire that had taken my mother, my brother, and my sister to their isolated graves.

It was still raining heavily when I pulled onto the main road, the leaden drops coming toward me like a hail of silver bullets, splattering onto the hood and windshield of the car, sending small bursts of water back into the dense, nocturnal air.

For a while, I drove on determinedly, biting down on my aching emptiness, trying to remove all the preceding days from my mind. I wanted to forget that I'd ever met Rebecca Soltero, heard her voice, or entertained a single one of her darkly probing questions. I wanted to forget all that she'd unearthed in me, the hunger and dissatisfaction along with the gnawing, nearly frenzied, urge to burst out of the life my own choices had created, as if in one, explosive act I could erase and then reconstitute an existence which, without explosion, offered no way out.

The lights of Old Salsbury glimmered hazily through the weaving veils of rain. I swept through its slick, deserted streets, past shop windows crowded with blank-faced mannequins and on toward its prim outer wall of white Colonial houses. I felt my head drift backward almost groggily, my mind reeling drunkenly in a fog of pain. I had never known so deep an anguish, or experienced so complete a sense of irredeemable collapse.

The house was dark when I pulled into the driveway. For a time I didn't go in, but remained in the car, instead, poised motionlessly behind the wheel, staring hollow-eyed at the black, unblinking windows. For a moment I closed my eyes, as if in an effort to make it all disappear, the whole intransigent structure of my life. When I opened them again, I realized that they were moist, glistening, that I had, against the force of my will, begun to cry.

I waited for a long time after that, waited to regain a stony composure. Then I got out of the car and walked toward the short flight of cement steps that led to the side entrance of the house. I could feel the rain slapping ruthlessly against me, but I walked slowly anyway, so that by the time I entered the house, my hair hung in a wet tangle over my forehead.

Down the corridor I could see a light burning softly, and for an instant, I thought that Marie must still be working in her office. Then I realized that the light was coming from farther down the hallway, from my office, rather than Marie's.

She was sitting very erectly in the black leather chair behind my desk, the surreal outlines of my mythical dream house spread out before her. When she spoke to me, only her mouth seemed to move; the rest of her body, her arms, her hair, the clean, classically drawn lines of her face, everything else appeared to hold itself firmly within a marble stillness.

'Where have you been, Steve?' she asked.

'At the office, you know that.'

She shook her head firmly. 'You weren't at the office.'

'What are you talking about, Marie?'

She looked at me as if this last, despicable lie was hardly worthy of attention. 'I went to the office,' she said.

I started to speak, but found that I had no words. I felt my lips part, but no sound came. I knew that I was helpless, literally naked, before her. She was armored in the truth, and I was a worm wriggling beneath its dark, approaching shadow.

'Peter fell out by the pool,' she said. 'He hit his head.'

'Is he all right?' I asked quickly.

'He's fine,' Marie answered stiffly. 'That's not the point now.'

I knew what the point was. I could sense it hurling toward me like the head of a spear.

'I had to take him to the hospital,' Marie went on. 'The doctor wanted him to stay there a little while, and I thought you'd want to come and be with him.'

'Well, of course I'd want to ...'

She lifted her hand to stop me. 'I drove to the office to get you, Steve, but you weren't there. No one was there except the night watchman. He told me that no one had been in the office all night.' Her eyes narrowed slightly. 'Not Wally or any of those other men you said were going to meet you there.'

I struggled to save what I could see sinking in the murky gray water, my wife, my son, sinking away from me forever.

'Marie, I was ...'

'I know where you were,' Marie said coolly, though without rancor, and entirely without fear, calm and self-possessed, ready to amputate the diseased and frightful limb.

'You were with her,' she said, lifting a small square of white paper toward me.

From my place in the doorway, I could see the large block letters Peter had printed so neatly across the page: REBECCA.

I shook my head. 'Marie, it's different, it's ...'

She rose gracefully, like an ancient woman warrior, beleaguered, betrayed, her forces wounded all around, but still in full command. 'I guess I always expected that you'd have some little fling somewhere along the way,' she said, then added, 'most men do.'

'Marie, I ...'

Again her hand rose, palm out, silencing me.

'But I never expected you to forget us, Steve,' she said, 'I never expected you to forget Peter and me.'

I said nothing.

'And you did that,' Marie said. 'You forgot us. Maybe only for a little while, but an hour would have been enough.'

She stepped out from behind the desk and headed for the door. The force of her character pressed me out into the corridor as she swept by me, marched down the hallway, then ascended the stairs. As she disappeared up them, I would have died to hold her, died to kiss her, died to have been the man she had always expected me to be.

I was still standing, stunned and speechless, when she came down the stairs again, this time with Peter sleeping in her arms. I could see the white bandage with its single spot of blood wrapped around his delicate blond head. I knew that she was going to her parents' home in the mountains. She would stay with them awhile, but only long enough to get her bearings. Then she would make her life over again, in some other place, perhaps even with some other man. Certainly, she would never come back to Old Salsbury or to me.

'Marie,' I said softly, calling to her.

She turned as she reached the door, glancing back toward me, her face framed by the dark window, the space between us completely silent except for the hollow patter of the rain.

'Marie,' I said again.

She looked at me almost mercifully, no longer as a husband, but only as another man who had lost his way. 'Things weren't perfect,' she said.

'They never are.' She watched me for a moment longer, as if in grave regret that what had been so obvious to her could have been so lost to me. 'Things were missing, I know that,' she added. 'Things always are.' She paused, her two dark eyes upon me like the twin barrels of a shotgun. 'But it was never love, Steve,' she said in her final words to me, 'it was never love that was missing.'

She turned then, and headed out into the rain. I walked down the corridor, parted the curtains, and watched as she laid Peter down in the back seat, then drew herself in behind the wheel. As she let the car drift down the driveway, I saw her eyes lift toward our bedroom window, close slowly as the car continued backward, then open again as it swung to the left and out into the slick, rainswept street.

Within an instant, she was gone.

For the next few hours, I wandered the house like a man who had awakened in a foreign city. Nothing looked familiar anymore. I heard ghostly, floating voices that seemed to speak to me in a language I had once understood, but which my long neglect had made incomprehensible, a language of connection, of duty, of belonging, a language which spoke of things present, rather than things missing, and as I listened to that language, I yearned for the oldest and most familiar objects in a house that was suddenly brand-new.

I don't remember into exactly what part of that house I had wandered when, hours later, I heard the knock at the door.

Two men were standing on the small porch when I opened it, one younger, bareheaded, one older, with glasses and a large gray hat.

'Steven Farris?' the older one said.

I nodded.

He reached into the pocket of his rain-soaked jacket and brought out a small, yellow badge. 'Could you come with us, please?'

I rode in the back of a dark, unmarked car. I don't remember anything being said between the time I got in and the moment when the car finally pulled in behind a large brick building that I didn't recognize. I'm sure they spoke to me, but I can't remember what they said.

It was still raining when the car stopped and the older one turned to me.

'Are you ready, Mr. Farris?' he asked.

I must have nodded, because he got out immediately and opened the rear door of the car.

I followed him up a cement ramp, through a pair of double doors, then down a long corridor which ended at a flight of stairs.

'Just down here,' the older one said.

We went down the stairs together, then into a small, green room where two metal stretchers rested side by side against the far wall.

By the time we reached them, the younger one had joined us. Still, it was the older one who drew back the white sheet that covered what was left of Peter's face.

I nodded. 'My son,' I said.

He covered him again, then stepped over to the other stretcher and repeated the same slow movement, drawing back the stiff white cloth.

She lay on her back, stiffly, her arms pressed neatly against her sides. 'My wife.'

The sheet drifted back over her unmoving face.

The older one turned, and I followed him out of the room and back to the car. I took my place in the back seat and rode silently through the darkness, past the winding, unexpected curve that had brought my family to its death.

It was nearly dawn by the time the car pulled into the driveway again, returning me to my empty house. For a moment I continued to sit in the back seat, motionless, unable to move, as if paralyzed. During that interval, I don't remember seeing or hearing anything. Then, as if in response to a signal I couldn't see, the older one turned toward me, his eyes gazing at me softly. 'It's terrible right now, I know,' he said, 'but in the end, you will find your way.'

*You will find your way.*

In my mind, I heard those words many times in the days that followed. I heard them as I paced the empty, voiceless rooms of my house or sat beside the covered pool, watching the late fall leaves gather on the dull black tarp. I heard them as Mr. Lowe, by then aware of exactly why my wife and son had been on the road that rainswept night, watched me disappointedly from the small square window of his office.

*You will find your way.*

I heard the words again and again, but still I couldn't find my way.

Things began to fall apart. I couldn't sleep, and barely ate at all. I burned my 'dream house' plans, and sat for long, dull hours in the family room, the dim green eye of the television watching me from its place across the room. All my former occupations fell away. I couldn't read, couldn't draw, couldn't engage in conversation. At work, I sat at my desk, a silent, eerie specter, warily watched by the others as if at any moment I might pull a pistol from beneath my jacket and do to them what they all knew my father had done to my mother, brother, sister. At times, I would see the same, distant apprehension in their eyes that I'd sometimes glimpsed in the eyes of Aunt Edna so many years before, a suspicion that my father's poisoned blood had been passed on to me.

But although my fellow workers at Simpson and Lowe couldn't have known it, they had nothing at all to fear from me. The revenge that was steadily building in my mind was not in the least directed toward them. I'd found another figure upon whom I'd begun to concentrate all my grief and rage.

William Patrick Farris.

During the weeks immediately following what everyone continually referred to as 'the tragedy', I came to hate my father more than I'd ever hated him. I hated him for more than the ancient crime of my family's murder, hated him for more than what he'd done to my mother, Laura, and Jamie. I hated him for what he'd done to me.

Done to me, yes.

For it seemed to me at that time that my father had brought everything to pass, that almost everything could be laid ultimately at his door. Had he not killed my family, Rebecca would never have come to me, and Peter and Marie would still be alive. Even more, however, I blamed him for the poison in my own blood, for what I'd inherited from him, the dark impulsiveness and cataclysmic discontent that had led him to kill my mother, Laura, and Jamie, and which he had bequeathed to me. I thought of Peter and Marie, and went through the steps by which I'd murdered them as surely as my father had killed his own wife and children. It was a legacy of blood, passed down from father to son, and because of it, as I reasoned at last, it was necessary for both of us to die.

Night after night, I went through the packet of papers and photographs Rebecca had sent me by then. I no longer felt them as a link to her, but only as a way to keep alive my hatred, both of my father and myself. One by one, I stared at the photographs or read over the police reports. I savored each blood-soaked image, drank in every word, my eyes heavy in the early morning light, but glaring still at each macabre reminder of the hideously destructive nature I had inherited from him.

I grew bloated on our evil. I could think of nothing else. I lost my job, sold my house, and moved into a cheap hotel, but I didn't drink or sink into madness. That would have dulled the fierce edge I wanted more than anything to retain in what was left of my life. I didn't want to forget what the two of us had done. I wanted to remember every harrowing detail until the time of our executions.

Slowly, the plan emerged. I would track him down by moving through the places he'd moved, looking steadily for some clue both as to how he had been formed and where he might have gone.

As the weeks passed, I journeyed back to the little house in which he'd lived out his solitary youth, then to the hard-scrabble warehouse on Great Jones Street, and finally along the dreary line of small New Jersey towns through which he'd wandered, looking for work, finding none, moving on, in a trail that struck me, even then, as terribly forlorn.

I went through all the papers my Aunt Edna had left me, searching for addresses where he'd lived, references to places he'd been. I went to rooming houses that were now libraries, cafés that were now clothing stores, rural meadows that were now bald, grassless tracks of suburban housing. I traced names: cousins, co-workers, people he'd lent money. I found them living in back rooms, asylums, basements, old hotels. I found them dead, as well, wild boys and dancing girls reduced to names carved in gray stone.

I lost track of time. Hours glided into days, weeks into months. My father's trail, never warm, and mostly fanciful, grew cold, and in the end I was left with a list of names and dates and places that were no more able to guide me to him than the random scribbling I might read from a bathroom wall.

In the end, you will find your way.

It was the older detective who'd said that to me as I'd sat, dazed and unmoving, in the rainy driveway that night. But now, when the words returned to me, I realized that they were carried on a different voice, the one which had guided Rebecca before me, and which, after so many years, so much brutal evidence, still dared to suggest that something didn't fit.

It was easy to find him. Swenson, after all, was not hiding from anyone.

A woman met me at the door. She wore a green dress dotted with small white flowers, and her hair was pulled back into a frazzled reddish bun.

'My name is Steve Farris,' I told her.

It was a name she clearly recognized. She stepped back and eyed me with a keen vigilance from behind a pair of large, tortoiseshell glasses.

'I guess you want to see Dave,' she said.

I nodded. 'Is he here?'

'Sure he is,' the woman said. 'He can't get out anymore.' She stepped away from the door. 'Come on in,' she said. 'He's in the back.'

I followed her down a short corridor, then into the shadowy bedroom where he lay. His condition seemed worse than Rebecca had described. Propped up by three large white pillows, he sat in a small metal bed, his lower body covered by a worn, patchwork quilt, the air around him little more than a cloud of medicinal fumes. There was a cylindrical orange oxygen tank at his right, and as I entered, he drew its yellow plastic mask from his mouth and watched me curiously.

'This is Steve Farris,' the woman said.

Swenson nodded to me, then swung his head to the right, as if trying to get a somewhat better look at me.

361

'You need anything, Dave?' the woman asked.

Swenson shook his head slowly, his eyes still leveled upon me.

The woman walked over to his bed, drew the blanket a little more snugly over his stomach, and disappeared out the door.

During all that time, Swenson's eyes never left me.

'The son,' he said finally in a breathless, ragged voice.

'Yes.'

He motioned for me to take a seat near the bed, then returned the mask to his mouth and took in a quick, anxious breath. The face behind the mask was pale and ravaged, though his green eyes still shone brightly from their deep sockets.

'Rebecca thought you might come by here,' he said, after he'd withdrawn the mask again.

'She did?'

He inhaled a long, rattling breath, lifted the mask again, then let it drop. 'She said there were things you might want to know.' His pale skin seemed strangely luminous in the gray light, as if a small candle still burned behind his eyes. But it was the eyes themselves that I could still recognize from that moment he'd turned to face me so many years before, those same eyes settling quietly upon me as I'd sat stunned and silent in the back seat of his unmarked car.

'Smart woman, Rebecca,' Swenson said shakily, his head drifting slightly to the left. 'Very smart.'

'Yes, she is.'

The green eyes bored into me, a young detective's eyes, swift and penetrating, but now embedded in a slack, doughy face. 'What do you want to know about your father?' he asked.

It was a question which, as I realized at that moment, had never actually been asked of me, and which I'd never actually asked myself. What *did* I want to know? Why *had* I come so far in order to know it?

'I want to know what really happened,' I told him. 'I want to know exactly what my father did.'

'That day, you mean?' Swenson asked. The mask rose again, the great chest expanded beneath the patchwork quilt, then collapsed. 'November 19, 1959,' he added, as the mask drifted down and finally came to rest in his lap.

He'd said the date not to impress me with his memory, but to suggest how it had remained with him through all the passing years, how he'd never been able to rid himself of his own, gnawing doubt, the persistent and irreducible presence of something in that house that didn't fit. And yet, at the same time, he seemed reluctant to begin, as if still unsure of where it might finally lead.

'My father had planned it for a long time, hadn't he?' I said.

Even as I said it, I saw our lives dangling helplessly over the fiery pit of my father's dreadful calculations. One by one, it seemed, he'd weighed the separate elements of our lives and deaths. Like a Grand Inquisitor, he'd heard the evidence while staring at my red-robed mother from the smoky fortress of his old brown van, or tinkering with his latest bicycle in the chill dungeon of the cement basement. One by one, we'd come before him like prisoners naked in a dock. Day by day the long trials had stretched on through the months, until, in a red wave of judgment, he'd finally condemned us all.

After that final condemnation, as I supposed at that moment, it had been only a matter of working out the technical details. Perhaps he'd considered various weapons for a time, carefully weighing the advantages of knives, guns, poisons, before finally deciding on the shotgun for no better reason than that he'd bought it years before, that it rested quietly in the green metal cabinet in the basement, that it was ready-to-hand.

'How long had he been planning it, do you think?' I asked Swenson, coaxing him forward, as one might nudge a man, ever so subtly, toward the edge of a cliff.

Swenson shrugged. He started to speak, but stopped abruptly, and returned the mask to his mouth. He took in a long breath, then let it out in a sudden, hollow gush. 'If he planned it early, then he must have changed his plans,' he said.

I said nothing, but only waited, as it seemed to me I had in one way or another been waiting all my life.

'Did Rebecca think he had a plan?' Swenson asked.

It was odd how far she seemed from me now. I saw her poised over her black briefcase, withdrawing papers in her usual methodical manner, showing me only what was relevant at that particular moment, conceal-ing all the rest. I could recall the tension of my lost desire, but only as something remembered by another man, a story told by someone else, so that now when she came forward in my mind, it was as little more than a messenger sent to me by my father.

'I think so,' I told him.

He looked vaguely surprised to hear it. He stared at me quietly, his breath coming in long hard pulls and quick exhalations. 'Well, maybe he did,' he said. The mask lifted, lingered for a moment at his mouth, then fell again. 'But maybe he didn't.' He tried to go on, but his breath could not carry the weight of another sentence. He took a quick inhalation, then added, 'He got away, that's for sure.'

'All the way to Mexico,' I said.

Swenson nodded. 'Using nothing but back roads,' he said, 'or we'd have picked him up for sure.' He coughed suddenly, a hard, brutal cough, his face reddening with the strain. 'Sorry,' he said quickly, then returned to his story. 'He left all his money in the bank.' He looked at me pointedly as he drew in another aching breath. 'Does that sound like a well-thought-out plan?'

I looked at him, puzzled, my eyes urging him to go on.

Swenson shifted uncomfortably, the large head sinking and rising heavily, its little wisps of reddish hair floating eerily in the veiled light. 'He left the house at around six o'clock.'

In my mind I could see him go almost as clearly as Mrs. Hamilton had seen him, a figure in a gray hat, carrying nothing with him, not so much as the smallest bag.

'He went downtown to the hardware store after that,' Swenson said. A short cough broke from him, but he suppressed the larger one behind it. 'Several people saw him go in, but since he owned the place, nobody made anything of it.'

'What did he do in there?' I asked.

'He cleaned out the cash register,' Swenson answered. 'Took every dime.' The mask rose again, then fell. 'Then he went to that little store near your house.'

'Oscar's?'

Swenson nodded. 'He bought a lot of food and stuff for the trip.' He stopped. The mask climbed up to his mouth, settled over it for a long, raspy breath, then crawled back down into Swenson's lap. 'And he made a phone call.'

'A phone call?'

'From that little phone they had out front,' Swenson said, without emphasis. 'We don't know who he called,' he added, 'but the kid that was standing behind him, waiting to use the same phone, was sure that he never got an answer.'

'Someone else,' I said in a cold whisper, 'he was calling someone else.' The face of Nellie Grimes came toward me, lifting slowly, gently, as if offering a kiss.

Swenson's great head drifted to the left. 'Someone else, that's right.'

'Rebecca told me that you spoke to Nellie Grimes,' I said.

Swenson returned the mask to his lips, sucked in a long breath, then let it drop unceremoniously from his mouth. 'It wasn't her.'

'Then who was it?'

Swenson wagged his head wearily. 'I don't know.' He brought the oxygen mask to his mouth again, took in a long, noisy breath, and let it fall back into his lap.

I could feel a tidal fury sweep over me as I imagined him at that phone, still working feverishly to carry out his escape. It was a rage which Swenson could see in its full, thrusting hatred, and it seemed to press me back roughly, like a violent burst of wind.

'You're looking for him, aren't you?' he asked.

I stared at him icily, but did not speak.

'You want to kill him for what he did that day,' Swenson said. He seemed neither shocked nor outraged by the truth he'd come upon. By then, no doubt, he'd slogged through a world of death. His only word was one of caution.

'There'll be more to do after that,' he said.

'What do you mean?'

He lifted the mask to his face, leaned into it, and took in a long, rattling breath. 'Someone else,' he said when the mask lowered again, 'like you've already said.'

'Someone else, yes,' I asked. 'Someone waiting for him at an airport or a bus station, or just on a corner, waiting for him to pull up in the car.'

Swenson shook his head slowly, ponderously, as if there were heavy weights inside his head. 'No,' he said. 'Someone who was already with him. Someone in the house.' He looked at me intently. 'Someone helping him.'

I stared at him, astonished. 'Helping him?' I whispered. 'Helping him kill us?'

Swenson nodded. 'We followed your father's tracks down into the basement,' he said. 'They were very bloody, and they went all the way down to the third step.'

'Yes, I know.'

'But that was as far as they ever went,' Swenson added laboriously, wheezing loudly now. 'The only tracks on the basement floor were the little ones your mother made through those pools of water that had seeped in from the rain.'

I nodded, waiting, as I knew I must, for the thing that didn't fit.

'But if your father had fired at your mother from the third step,' Swenson added, 'then he would have riddled the box she'd hid behind.' His head shifted back and forth, as if with the weight of what he knew. 'But that box wasn't hit at all,' he added. He brought the mask to his face and sucked in a long, mighty breath. 'It hadn't been moved, either,' he added as he lowered it slightly, 'because if someone had moved it, it would have left a smear of blood.' He looked at me pointedly as he returned the mask to his mouth, took a long, heavy breath, then lowered it again. 'Someone walked around that box and shot your mother,' he began again, his voice high and tremulous now, breaking with the effort these last words had cost him. 'Maybe brought her back up the stairs, too,' he added, 'because there were no tracks from your father's shoes that went below that third step.'

'Did you tell Rebecca this?'

He nodded.

'What did she say?'

'She said he must have changed before he went downstairs,' Swenson answered.

'Is that possible?'

'Well, we found his bloody shoes and clothes in the bathroom upstairs,' Swenson said. 'And there was that small amount of time between the second shot and the last one.'

'Was that long enough for him to have changed his clothes, then walked down to the basement and killed my mother?' I asked.

Swenson looked at me solemnly. 'Rebecca thought so.'

'Do you?'

For a moment, he seemed to review the whole terrible choreography of my family's murder, his head lifting slightly, as the mask dropped into his lap.

'No,' he said finally, 'I think there was some . . .'

A quick breath left him, and he leaned back into the pillows, brought the plastic mask to his mouth, and drew in a tortured, wracking breath. 'Someone else,' he said, on what seemed like his final breath, the mask returning quickly to his mouth, his eyes peering motionlessly over its rounded, plastic rim, watching me, animal-like, as if his green, amphibian eyes were poised just above the surface of a murky pool.

Someone else.

As I drove back toward my hotel room that afternoon, I thought of nothing but those words. I remembered that Nellie Grimes had used the same words in her interview with Swenson. She had insisted on my father's innocence, then ascribed the blame simply and mysteriously to 'someone else'.

My lips parted in the only answer I could offer at the time. 'The other woman,' I whispered.

But who?

It was nearly night when I arrived back at the hotel. As I headed across its dank, cluttered lobby, the little bald desk clerk who'd regarded me so suspiciously over my long stay unexpectedly motioned me toward the reception desk.

'There's a package for you,' he said, then reached beneath the desk and handed me a small, rectangular box.

It had been sent first to my house in Old Salsbury, then to the offices of Simpson and Lowe, and finally forwarded to me here. For a single, surreal instant, I sensed that it had come from my father, some macabre remembrance he'd sent to mock and torment me, a blood-encrusted strand, perhaps, of my mother's hair. I tucked the package quickly under my arm, took the stairs up to my third-floor room, and tossed it, unopened, on the bed.

It lay there for a long time while I sat beside the window, staring out at the deserted street, still trying to reason out the identity of the unknown woman who, in the end, had helped my father destroy not only one, but both my families. Step by step, I once again walked the paces of my father's crime, following the bloody tracks Swenson had followed, a trail that led from Jamie's room to Laura's, and finally down the basement stairs to where two women had waited for him, one crouched behind a cardboard box, the other standing over her, waiting in an awesome silence for the shotgun to be passed.

I drew my eyes away from the window and let them come to rest on the small, brown box that had arrived at my hotel that day. I went to the bed, picked it up, and began to open it slowly, ritualistically, as if I were uncovering a treasure of vast renown, some relic from an ancient faith.

It was no such awesome thing, of course. It was nothing more than Rebecca's book.

I stared at it, disappointed, exhausted, barely engaged enough to keep my eyes upon it. Still, it had its own dark allure. The jacket was rather melodramatically illustrated with the face of a sinister-looking paternal figure, but the title seemed as cool and academic as its author: *THESE MEN: Studies in Family Murder*, by Rebecca Soltero.

For the rest of the night, I sat at the window of my room and read Rebecca's study of 'these men'. One by one, she explored and exposed them, moving through those elements of character and background which united them, closing in on that single element which joined them together in a dark, exclusive brotherhood, the fact that they were, above all, deeply romantic men. So much so, that each of them had found a kind of talisman, an emblem for his extreme and irreducible yearning. 'Creatures of a visceral male romanticism,' Rebecca wrote, 'each of these men had found a symbol for what was missing in his life.'

True to her method, she then ticked these emblems off. Crude and childish, they would normally have seemed no more than the physical representations of men who had become locked in boyish fantasies. But under Rebecca's transforming eye, they took on an occult and totemic symbolism: Fuller's baseball bat, Parks's simple curl, Townsend's foreign stamps, Stringer's safari hat, and last, as Rebecca described them, 'the sleek racing bikes of William Patrick Farris'.

'By clinging to these symbols,' Rebecca wrote, 'these men made one last effort to control a level of violent romantic despair which women almost never reach.'

With the exception of my father, each of them had even gone so far as to take these totemic objects with them in their efforts to escape. Fuller had thrown the bloody bat into the back seat of his car; Stringer had worn his safari hat onto the plane he'd hoped to take to Africa; Townsend had stuffed his briefcase full of foreign stamps beneath the seat he'd purchased on an eastbound train; and Herbert Parks, though trying to disguise himself in other ways, had stubbornly maintained his enigmatic curl.

The tenacious hold of these symbols upon the imaginations of the men she'd studied led Rebecca unerringly to the final conclusion of her book:

> In the minds of these men, the most immediate need became the elimination of whatever it was that blocked their way to a mythically romantic life. That is to say, their families. Essentially, they could not bear the normal limits of a life lived communally, domestically, and grounded in the sanctity of enduring human relations. Instead, they yearned for a life based, as it were, on male orgasmic principles, one which rose toward thrilling, yet infinitely renewable, heights of romantic trial and achievement. In time, they came to hold any other form of life in what can only be described as a murderous contempt.

But even as I read this final passage, I wondered if it could actually be applied to my father. For where, in all the descriptions of vast romantic torment which dotted Rebecca's book, was the man who'd puttered with a bicycle in the basement and played Chinese checkers with a little girl, and who'd said of these simple, normal, intensely humble things, 'This is all I want.'

Once more, I read the section of Rebecca's book which dealt with my father. She'd written elegantly and well of my family's life, and even given my father an exalted place among her other subjects by suggesting that his particular totem, the Rodger and Windsor bikes, provided the most fitting symbol for the destructive male romanticism she had studied and at last condemned, 'a thing of high mobility and speed, self-propelled and guided, capable of supporting only one lone rider at a time'.

Only one?

Then to whom had he passed the shotgun that rainy afternoon?

Once more I imagined the 'someone else' with whom he might have joined in such murderous conspiracy, but even here, I found that there was still something missing, something that didn't fit.

And so, at last, I returned to the small stack of crime-scene photographs Rebecca had sent to me. Slowly, one by one, as the early morning light built outside my hotel window, I peered at each picture, my mother's body behind the floral curtains, her blood-encrusted house shoes on the floor beside her bed; Jamie, faceless, beneath the wide window, his biology book opened to the picture of a gutted frog; Laura, her body wrapped in a white terry-cloth robe, her bare feet stretched toward the camera as if trying to block its view.

By the time I'd returned the last of the pictures to the envelope that had contained them, I still was no closer to knowing if Rebecca had been right about my father. At least for me, she had not yet solved the mystery of his murderousness, but she had doubtless offered the only clue as to where and how it might be solved.

# FIFTEEN

R odger and Windsor.
 Rebecca had made an immensely persuasive case that the men
she'd studied had been unable to live without their private romantic
totems. In my desperate need to find him, it struck me at last that my
father might have been no less obsessed than the rest of them, that the
sleek red racing bikes he'd imported from England had perhaps made the
same romantic claim upon his mind as foreign stamps and safari hats had
made upon the other men in Rebecca's book.

It was a wet, fall day when I reached Rodger and Windsor's offices in
New York City. The cold drizzle I'd walked through had given me an
even more desolate appearance than usual, and because of that, the neat
young man who came out to the front desk to greet me seemed hesitant
to come too close.

'May I help you?' he said.

'I'm looking for my father,' I told him.

'Your father?' he asked me, puzzled. 'Does he work here?'

'No,' I answered.

Then, in all its appalling detail, I told him the story of my father's
crime. One by one I showed him the crime-scene photographs of my
mother, Laura, and Jamie. At each picture, he flinched a little.

'Your father did all that?' he asked finally.

I nodded, then took out Rebecca's book and read him the relevant passage. He listened with a rapt intensity.

'My father was obsessed with these bikes,' I told him, 'he wouldn't be
able to live without getting one.' I waited, then added, 'And I'm sure it
would be red.'

From the look on his face, I could tell that the young man in the
starched white shirt and plain gray tie had decided to do everything he
could to help me. Something exciting had unexpectedly come into his
life, and as I looked at the eagerness I could see building in his eyes, I
wondered if I had been like him on that day Rebecca had first arrived at

the offices of Simpson and Lowe. Had I been nothing more than a clerk with a clerk's long day looming before him? Was that the secret of my fall? Was it no more than the flight from boredom that had killed my wife and son?

I thought of my father, too, the way he'd trudged up the narrow aisles of his hardware store day after day. I saw the listlessness in his eyes, the weary rhythm of his gait, and it struck me more powerfully than ever before just how dangerous a man may become when he suddenly feels no compelling reason any longer to live as he has always lived.

The clerk nodded. 'And you want me to help you find him?'

'Yes,' I said, then added, 'I have reason to believe that my father crossed the border into Mexico.'

The clerk smiled. 'Then let's start in Mexico,' he said.

And so we began there, going back through the stacks of sales invoices that stretched toward the present from the distant year of 1959. With a continually deepening level of engagement, we stalked the passing years. It was the clerk who found the first hint of my father's new abode. He pulled a single sheet of paper from the file. 'Could it be this?' he asked.

I took the paper and looked at it. The order was dated March 17, 1962, and it was for a single red Rodger and Windsor bike. It had been received from a bicycle shop located in a small town on the western coast of Mexico. The man who'd signed the order had used the name Antonio Dias. There had been other orders from other places, of course, but this was the only bicycle shop that had ordered only one Rodger and Windsor, and that had specifically stipulated that its color must be red.

During the next twenty years, as the clerk discovered, this same Antonio Dias had ordered thirty-two red Rodger and Windsor bikes. The shipping invoices showed that during that same time he'd moved to nine different towns, each time farther south until he'd finally reached the border of Honduras.

In 1982, the orders had abruptly stopped. For the next three years there were no orders from Antonio Dias. Then, in November of 1985, one appeared again. This time, however, it had not come from Mexico, but from far more distant Spain, from a town about the size of Somerset, but located on the Mediterranean, and which bore the exotic and romantic name of Alicante. At the rate of nearly two a year, the orders had continued to arrive over the next seven years. The last one had been received only two months before.

The clerk looked at me significantly. 'If this Antonio Dias is your father,' he said, 'then my guess is, he's still in Alicante.'

And so I made my plans to go. I renewed my passport, then waited in my hotel room for it to arrive. During that time I watched no television nor read a book. I wrote no letters nor read any that I received. I didn't want to be distracted. As the days passed, I sank deeper into my own closed world. I no longer nodded to people on the street. I didn't answer when they spoke to me. The days passed, and my world grew smaller. At last, I shrank into a small, dark seed.

The passport arrived, and I bought a ticket to Madrid. From there, I took a bus to Alicante.

It was nearly midnight when I arrived. A foreigner, with no knowledge of the language, I took the first hotel room I could find and stretched out on the small, narrow bed to await the morning. Through the night, I thought of my father, of how near I sensed he was. I tried to imagine his face webbed in dark wrinkles, the sound of his voice as it spoke in a foreign language. But he remained as elusive as always, still as remote and towering as he had been the day he'd stood on the veranda and silenced all of us with nothing more commanding than his gaze.

I awoke very early, just after first light. Across from my bed, I could see a small sink, a wrinkled towel that hung limply from its bare metal rack, and a battered armoire. They didn't look the same as in my escapist dream, however. Nothing was the same. Outside my window, where light blue, rather than white, curtains lifted languidly in the warm morning breeze, there were no tiled roofs or dark spires. There was only a sprawling modern town gathered around a much older one.

It was still early when I left the hotel. Across the street was a large market, decked with bright-colored vegetables and row upon row of sleek, silvery fish. Pointing first to one thing, then another, I bought a piece of bread and a cup of coffee, eating as I continued on my way.

I'd written the address to which the last Rodger and Windsor had been sent on a piece of paper, and for nearly an hour after leaving the market, I moved from person to person, showing each the address, then following an array of hand signals, since I could not understand what was said to me. Block by block, turn by turn, I closed in on my father, moving deeper and deeper into the old Moorish quarter of the city. Perched on a high hill, a huge fortress loomed above me, its massive yellow walls glowing in the sun.

At last I found the street I'd been looking for. Madre de Dios it was called, Mother of God. It curled near the center of a warren of other narrow, nearly identical streets, and at its far end, half hidden in the shadows, I saw a sign. It was carelessly painted, and hung at an angle, the way I knew he would have painted and hung it. It read BICICLETAS.

I approached the store slowly, with a sensation of shrinking, of returning to the size of a little boy. I felt as I had felt that night I'd gone down the basement stairs, hesitant, unsure, eerily afraid of the man who stood behind the large black wheel.

And so, once I reached the shop, I found that I couldn't go in. Through a single, dusty window, I could see a figure moving in its dim interior, moving as he had moved, haphazardly from place to place, but I could not approach it. Each time my hand moved toward the door, it was seized by a terrible trembling, as if I expected the shotgun still to be cradled in his arms.

After a moment, I turned abruptly and walked across the street, standing rigidly, unable to move, while a stream of men and women, some with children at their sides, casually went in and out, ringing the little bell he'd hung above the door.

There was a small, dusty plaza just up from the store, a place of scrubby trees and cement benches. I went there and continued to watch the entrance of the shop. As the hours passed, I remained in place, my back pressed up against the spindly gray trunk of an olive tree. To the right, a gathering of women, their faces hung in black scarves, talked idly while young children scrambled playfully at their feet. At the far end of the square, old men in black berets tossed wooden balls across a dusty court, their faces shaded beneath a canopy of palms.

Time crawled by, minute by minute. The sun rose, then began to lower.

While I waited, I imagined it again.

I imagined following him as he made his way out of the little bicycle shop. Using the landscape that now surrounded me, I saw him trudge along the deserted street, winding uphill toward the ancient fortress, its gigantic walls glowing yellow above him, striking and unreal. I imagined stalking him steadily, as he crossed the little plaza, his feet shuffling cautiously over the rubble of its broken walkway. I saw myself close in upon him as he turned into a narrow, nearly unlighted alleyway, passed under a low, crumbling balcony, and disappeared behind its veil of hanging flowers. It was there I saw myself sweep in behind him, rushing beneath the balcony, the two of us suddenly gathered together behind the dense curtain. I heard myself say, 'Father,' then watch as he turned toward me. I knew that I would give him time to turn, time for him to see me, time for his body to stiffen as the word continued to echo in his mind, as he wondered hopelessly, and with a wrenching sense of terror, if it could be true.

Then and only then, I would strike, raising the blade above his trembling, horror-stricken face. 'This is for Laura,' I would tell him as I delivered the first blow. 'And this is for Peter and Marie.'

For the next hour or so, I continued to luxuriate in my father's murder, reliving it again and again, rejoicing in his agony, while the sun sank farther toward the sea, and still, he did not come out. By then the other shops had closed, their owners marching off to the nearest tavern to while away the remainder of the afternoon, while my father remained inside his shop. I'd seen the door of my father's shop close, as well, then a hand draw down a curtain, but nothing more. At first, I imagined him still inside, perhaps piddling with his latest Rodger and Windsor. But as the hours passed, a graver thought occurred to me. Perhaps he had escaped again. In my mind, I saw him crawling out a dusty window, then trotting down a narrow alley to where a small boat waited for him, bobbing lightly in a peaceful sea.

For a moment, I felt a great terror sweep over me, the fear not only that he'd escaped again, but that he'd escaped from me, as if, from the beginning, from that first flight into the rain, that had been his one true aim.

I stood up and peered out toward the shop, my eyes squinting against the still-bright sun, and almost at that instant the hand appeared again, and the curtain rose.

With the afternoon siesta over, customers began to come and go again. There were not many of them, as I noticed, but then my father had never been one to attract a steady clientele.

The light began to change with the final waning of the afternoon, darkening steadily until the first blue haze of evening descended upon the street. At last, the first lights began to shine from the shop windows that lined the narrow, winding route of Madre de Dios.

It was already full night when those lights began to blink off again. The one that shined beneath the tilted sign for BICICLETAS finally blinked off, too.

Seconds later, I saw him back out of the shop, pulling the door closed behind him, then turn slowly to face the plaza. A streetlight cast a silver veil over him, and in its light I could see that he was dressed like the other old men of the region, in a dark suit, with a faded white shirt that looked slightly frayed at the collar, and no tie.

He turned up the street, and then I saw his yellow cane as it hung limply from his hand. He placed it firmly on the ground and began to walk slowly up the hill, the cane tapping lightly in the nearly deserted street.

As he moved toward me, I could see that he was still tall, though bent now, his shoulders slightly rounded. His hair was white, and his face was brown and leathery, drier than I remembered it, parched by his long years in the sun. The only thing that remained the same was his piercingly blue eyes.

They didn't glance in my direction as he headed across the street, then into the little plaza, finally going by me at a distance of no more than ten or fifteen feet. A woman nodded toward him as she passed and an old man waved from the other end of the square, but my father didn't stop to talk to either of them.

He continued on, his feet plowing unsteadily across the dusty plaza. When he was near the middle of it, I stood up and watched him closely, as if expecting him to vanish magically into the air. In the distance, I could see him moving past the old men tossing balls in the courtyard, the women with their children, his feet raising a little cloud of dust behind him.

He was almost at the end of the plaza before I fell in behind him, trailing him at a distance, the eyes of the people in the square following me almost as intently as I followed my father.

Slowly, with an old man's gait, he made his way up a narrow street, then, to my surprise, turned abruptly to the right and entered a small tavern.

He'd already taken a seat behind a round, wooden table when I entered the same tavern seconds later. There were other men around him, men at other tables, old men who looked as weathered as he, their eyes deep-set and encircled by spidery webs of dark lines, their skin deeply furrowed. But they were shorter and rounder than my father, who still retained something of the tall, lean figure I remembered from my youth. It was clear that they knew him, perhaps even associated him with the American cowboys they'd seen in movies and on television, the silent, solitary, lethal men whose brave adventures made their dull, familial lives seem small and cowardly and of little worth.

I took a seat across the room and watched as my father ordered his first drink. When it came, I saw that it was sherry, a drink that struck me as quite bland for a man who on a rainy November day had, with the help of 'someone else', taken a shotgun to his family.

*Sherry*, I thought, *my father drinks sherry*, and suddenly I saw him as a man of tastes and appetites, an old man who walked slowly through the dusty streets, his shadow moving jaggedly along the flat stone walls. The specter of my youth, the gray figure in the basement, the slaughterer of my family, there he was before me, drinking sherry and wiping his wet lips with a soiled handkerchief.

There he was, but still I found that I couldn't approach him. And so I watched from a distant corner, my fingers tapping rhythmically against my knees, my eyes moving toward him, then away, as if fleeing a flash of brutal light.

The night deepened hour by hour, but my father didn't leave his chair.

One sherry, sipped slowly, was followed by another. He ordered a plate of sliced ham and a piece of bread smeared with tomato, eating his dinner at a leisurely pace, his blue eyes closing from time to time as he leaned back tiredly against the tiled wall.

From time to time, other men would sit down with him and chat awhile, but my father seemed to greet them distantly, talk to them absently, pay them little mind. As each one left, he merely nodded slowly and said, 'Adios,' in a tone that seemed faintly sorrowful, so that even in the grip of my hatred I sensed that there had been a loneliness to his exile, things he had endured, losses he had silently absorbed. For a moment, I was able to imagine the long night of his escape, the flight to a distant land, the constant shifting from town to town, the years of fear and dread. *What at 417 McDonald Drive*, I wondered, *could have been worth such a deep and endless sacrifice?*

At around ten, as he continued to sit alone and unmolested, an African trader in black trousers and a billowy purple shirt approached his table. A lavender turban was wound loosely around his head. He smiled at my father and drew several carved figures from a cloth bag, elephants of various sizes, a giraffe. He arranged them on my father's table. My father glanced at them, then shook his head.

The trader remained in place, persistent, trying to make a sale. My father shook his head again, then turned away, his eyes settling on one of the tile paintings that adorned the opposite wall, the head of a woman wreathed in luscious purple grapes. His eyes lingered on it, the eyelids slightly drooped, the skin wrinkled, but the eyes themselves still luminously blue, the way they'd looked that night as I'd stood, facing him from the third step.

The trader drew a wooden mask from the dark sack. It was crudely carved and sloppily lacquered, a work done without interest and for little pay. He placed it on my father's table, edging one of the elephants away.

My father didn't look at the mask, but only waved his hand languidly, refusing once again.

The trader returned the carvings to his bag, then glanced about the tavern, his eyes large and bulging, his black skin nearly blue in the dimly lighted room. He saw no other likely customers and headed for the door.

My father watched him as he walked away, the lavender turban weaving gently through a cloud of thick white smoke. A woman at the adjoining table gave my father a knowing glance, but my father only shrugged and lifted his glass in a faint, half-hearted toast.

As I sat only a few yards from him, I wondered to what it was he might still offer even so weak a toast. Was it to life? To death? Could he toast others, or were they only doll-sized figures on a featureless landscape, things like a wife and children, things he could do without?

It was nearly midnight when he rose suddenly, startling me far more than I had thought possible. I saw him rise and come toward me from the choking, smoke-filled depths of the tavern. He was upon me almost instantly, his shadow moving in a dark gray wave across my table. As he passed, I felt him brush my shoulder. I looked up and saw him glance down at me, nodding quickly, as if in apology, before he suddenly stopped dead and peered at me frozenly. For an instant, I thought he might have recognized me, and I quickly turned away. By the time I looked around again, he'd disappeared.

But he didn't go far, only a little way down the same narrow street, and into another tavern. It was emptier than the first, and he took a table at the back. I took a table not far away, and watched him more closely, as if afraid that he might vanish once again.

Under the light which hung above him, I could see the dust that had settled upon the shoulders of his jacket. There was dust on his sleeves, as well, and dust on his shoes. As I sat, watching him, I imagined dust in great brown lumps pressing in upon his guts, his lungs, his brain. I imagined his veins thick with dust, a brown mud clogging the valves of his heart. I could even envision a thick, dusty blood pouring from him as I jerked the blade upward, gutting him in one swift thrust.

He leaned back against the wall of the tavern and closed his eyes. I wondered if, at such a moment, he'd ever allowed his mind to return to McDonald Drive. Or did he go there only in a nightmare in which he watched helplessly as a little boy came down the basement stairs, stopped on the third step, and grimly leveled a shotgun at his panicked and unblinking eyes?

His eyes opened suddenly, and I saw that they were aimed at me. He glanced away and didn't look at me again. His hand lifted to his mouth, brushed against his lips, then drifted back down to his lap.

I could see a torpor in his movements, a languidness which seemed to pull even at the sharp, sudden darting of his eyes. Moments later, when a dark-haired beauty strolled past his table, he didn't follow her appreciatively, but simply let his eyes drop toward the glass he cradled gently in his right hand. At that moment he seemed quite shy, captured in shyness, almost shrunken, made of straw, himself a weightless miniature.

And yet I was still afraid of him, afraid of the scenes within his mind, the long walk up the stairs, the look on Jamie's still-living face, the backward plunge my sister's ruptured body must have made as the volley struck her, the plaintive, begging eyes of my mother as she'd crouched behind the cardboard box. I knew that there was a hideous gallery of such pictures in his brain, though the fact that he'd lived with them for so long seemed unimaginable to me.

Time passed, but my fear did not.

I could feel my hand tremble each time I thought of approaching him, and it struck me as unseemly to be so afraid of such a spiritless old man. What could he possibly do to me at this point in our lives? His physical force entirely diminished, his moral force long ago destroyed, he was nothing but an empty shell, a shadow.

And yet, I was afraid.

I was afraid because, for all his weakness and frailty, he was still my father, and the line that connected us was still a line that he somehow controlled. In his presence, I felt myself become the little boy who'd moved down the stairs, felt his gaze stop me dead.

I was afraid, and I knew why. I watched his eyes and knew exactly what I feared.

After all these months of hating him, I was afraid that when we met at last, and after I'd confronted him with everything he'd done, rubbed his face in the blood of those he'd murdered, that after all that excruciating pain had been unearthed again, and he sat, stunned, stricken, his blue eyes resting upon mine, that at that moment I would see again, know again, only this time with perfect clarity, that he had never loved me.

It was that which made me hate him again with a fierce, blinding passion. I hated him because he had not loved me enough to take me with him in his flight.

I felt my body rise suddenly, as if called to duty by an overwhelming need. I felt it move forward smoothly, righteously, with an angelic, missionary grace.

His eyes lifted toward me as I approached his table. Once I reached it, I started to speak, but to my amazement, he spoke first.

'Stevie,' he said.

Stunned at the sound of his voice, thrown entirely off track by the fact that he had spoken first, I didn't answer him.

'Stevie,' he repeated softly, 'sit down.'

Still, I couldn't speak. And so I snatched the envelope from my pocket instead, took out the three photographs, and arranged them quickly on the table before him. There, beneath the weaving candle, he could see them in a dreadful line, my mother in her bed, Jamie on his back, Laura sprawled across the floor of her room.

Then, at last, a voice leaped out at him. 'Why did you do this?'

He watched me, utterly calm. He seemed beyond fear or regret, beyond anything but the long travail of his seclusion. His eyes regarded me

378

coolly. His hands didn't tremble. The ancient power of his fatherhood surrounded him like a fortress wall.

'We had happy times,' he said at last. 'You remember them, don't you, Stevie?' He leaned back, the broad shoulders pressed firmly against the tile wall. His eyes dropped toward the photographs, then leaped back up at me. 'Happy times,' he said again.

The face that watched me seemed hardly recognizable, the 'happy times' little more than sparkling shards thrown up by a blasted family. I remembered other things, instead, the icy immobility of his face as he'd stared out at 'poor Dottie' from the smoky interior of the old brown van.

'You didn't love my mother, did you?' I asked.

He looked surprised by the question, but unwilling to lie.

'No,' he said.

'She was dying.'

Again the surprise, followed by the admission. 'Yes, she was, Stevie.'

'But you killed her anyway.'

He started to speak, but I rushed ahead. 'Why did you clean her up after that? Why did you put her in the bed that way?'

He shook his head slowly. 'Respect, maybe, I don't know.' He shrugged. 'Pity.'

I could feel my mouth curl down in a cruel rebuke. 'Respect? Pity? That's why you laid her out like that?'

'Yes, it is,' he answered firmly, as if it were a source of pride. 'She was a very modest woman. I didn't want her to be seen like that.'

'What about Jamie?' I shot back. 'You didn't care how he was seen, did you?'

'What do you mean?'

'Leaving him in his room the way you did,' I told him brutally, 'lying on his back like that, with his face blown off.'

He turned away, flinching slightly. It was the first emotion he had shown, and I felt a cruel delight in its suggestion that I had at least some small power to wound him.

'And what about Laura?' I asked tauntingly. 'What about her?'

He didn't answer.

I tapped the photograph that showed her on her back, her chest blown open, her bare, soiled feet pressing toward the lens.

'You left her like Jamie,' I said, 'lying in her blood.'

He nodded, almost curtly. 'Yes, I did.'

My legs dissolved beneath me as if I were being pressed down by the sudden weight of his complete admission. I sank down into the chair opposite him and released a long, exhausted breath.

'Why did you kill Laura?' I asked.

The light blue eyes squeezed together. 'Because I had to,' he said sharply, 'because I had no choice.'

It was a flat, factual response, with no hint of apology within it.

I scoffed at the notion of his being forced to carry out such a crime. 'You had to kill Laura?'

'Yes.'

'Why?'

The old rigidity returned to his face. He stared at me stonily. 'Once it started, I had to finish it.'

'Once it started?'

He shifted slightly and drew his hands back slowly until they finally dropped over the edge of the table. 'The killing.' His eyes darted away, then returned. 'It wasn't what I wanted, Stevie.'

Suddenly Swenson's words rushed toward me. *Someone else. Someone else was in that house.* I stared at him evenly. 'Who made you do it then?' I demanded. 'Who did you do it for?'

For the first time he seemed reluctant to answer.

I looked at him determinedly. 'Who wanted us all dead?'

His face tensed. I could see that he was going back now, that I was forcing him back.

I glared at him lethally. 'Tell me what happened that day.'

He looked at me as if I knew nothing, as if I'd just been born, something marvelous in its innocence, but which had to be despoiled.

'That's not when it began, that day,' he said. 'It didn't just happen, you know.'

'Of course not,' I told him. 'You'd planned it for a long time.'

'What do you mean?'

'Those two tickets, remember?' I said. Then, so that he could have no doubt as to just how much I already knew, I added, 'Those two tickets to Mexico City, the ones you bought in June.'

His face tightened. 'You knew about that?'

'Yes.'

'How did you know?'

'The police found out,' I said.

He looked strangely relieved. 'Oh,' he said, 'the police.'

'They found out everything,' I told him.

He leaned forward slowly, his hands clasped together on the table. 'No, they didn't,' he said.

'Everything except who helped you kill them,' I said.

'Helped me?'

'Yes.'

'No one helped me, Stevie,' he said. 'What I did, I did alone.'

I stared at him doubtfully. 'Two tickets,' I repeated, 'one for you, and one for someone else.' I paused a moment. 'Who was she?' I demanded, my voice almost a hiss, visions of Yolanda Dawes circling in my mind.

His face softened, his eyes resting almost gently upon me. 'Do you remember that morning when we were all having breakfast and Laura was talking about a report she'd done in school, and Jamie kept attacking her, belittling her?'

'Yes.'

He shook his head. 'Jamie was always at Laura,' he said, 'always trying to humiliate her, to take away her dreams.'

He was right, of course, and it was easy for me to see everything that had happened that morning, the terrible hatred my brother had shown for my sister, the delight he'd taken in chipping away at her vibrant, striving character. That morning he'd been even worse than usual, his small eyes focused upon her with a deadly earnest: *You're not going anywhere.*

My father turned away for a moment, drew in a deep breath, then looked back toward me. 'I couldn't take it that morning,' he said quietly. 'I couldn't stand to see what he was doing to your sister.' He smiled. 'I knew how much she wanted out of life, you see,' he went on, 'how much she wanted her life to be different.'

'Different from what?' I asked.

'Different from my life, Stevie,' he said. 'Different from your mother's life, and what Jamie's life would probably have been.' He stopped, as if remembering her again in the full glory of her extravagant desire. 'She talked to me about it, you know,' he added after a moment. 'About all she wanted to do in her life, all the places she wanted to go.' He smiled softly. 'She would come down in the basement where I was, and she would talk to me about it.' His eyes drifted away slightly. 'Always barefoot, remember?' he said, almost wistfully. 'I used to tell her to put on her shoes, but she never would. She was like that, untamed. She'd always go back up with her feet covered with that grit from the basement floor.' He grew silent for a moment, then shrugged. 'Anyway,' he said, 'that morning after Jamie had acted the way he did, I went out and sat down in that little room we had, the one with the vines.' He stopped, his voice a little harder when he spoke again. 'That's when I decided that it couldn't go on like it was, Stevie,' he said. 'That something had to be done about it.'

'You mean, something had to be done about Jamie?'

'About what he was doing to your sister,' my father answered. 'Something had to be done about that.'

I remembered the look on his face as he'd sat alone in the solarium that morning. It was a grim, determined face, all doubt removed. It was then that he'd decided that 'something had to be done', I supposed, not while he'd sat gazing at my mother as she stooped over the flower garden, but that spring morning when Jamie had launched his attack upon the daughter that my father loved.

My father's hands drew back, each of them finally drifting over the edge of the table. 'I told Laura about it a week later,' he said. 'She came down to the solarium one night. It must have been toward the middle of that last summer.' He drew in a deep breath. 'I told her what I wanted to do.'

I looked at him, astonished. 'Kill us,' I muttered.

His eyes widened, staring at me unbelievingly. 'What?'

'That you were going to kill us,' I said, 'you told Laura that?'

He shook his head. 'No, Stevie,' he said, 'not that.' He paused a moment, watching me brokenly. 'Never that.'

'What then?'

'I told her that I'd decided to take her away,' my father said, 'that I'd looked through a lot of travel brochures, and that I'd already decided on the place.' He looked at me solemnly. 'I told her that I'd already bought two tickets to Mexico, and that I was going to take her there.'

'And leave the rest of us?' I asked.

'Jamie wouldn't have cared,' my father said. 'And your mother, she'd always wanted to move back to Maine, where she'd grown up.' His face took on the look of a mournful revelation. 'There was someone there, Stevie. Waiting for her, you might say. Someone from way back. Someone she'd never forgotten.'

It was the phantom lover, of course, Jamie's real father, a man in a mountain cabin, as I imagined him at that moment, writing letters to my mother on soft blue paper.

'Jamie and your mother would both have been better off in another place,' my father said.

'And me?'

'You're what made it hard, Stevie,' my father said. 'I hadn't really decided about you.'

I stared at him bitterly. 'At the time you killed them, you mean?' I asked brutally.

My father did not so much as flinch. 'I chose to save my daughter,' he said with a grave resignation.

A strange pride gathered in his voice, and suddenly I recognized that at that moment when he'd told Laura of his plan to take her away, at that precise moment in his life, and perhaps for the only time, his love had taken on a fabled sweep, had become a thing of knights on horseback and maidens in dire distress, a romantic mission of preservation and defense, one far different from the type undertaken by those other men with whom Rebecca had already forever linked his name.

'I never saw Laura more happy when I told her about Mexico,' my father said.

In my mind, I saw them together in the little solarium with its windows draped in vines, my father in the white wicker chair, Laura below him, her face resting peacefully, as if she were still a little girl.

'Why didn't you go then?' I asked. 'Why didn't you just take her and go away?'

'Because toward the end of the summer I found out your mother was dying,' my father said. 'I couldn't leave her in a situation like that. So I canceled the tickets.' He shook his head helplessly. 'I didn't tell Laura right away, and when I did, she looked as if her whole world had collapsed.' He seemed to bring her back into his mind, fully, in all her furious need. 'Laura wasn't like me,' he said again, 'there was something great in her.' He stopped, then added, 'But there was something wrong, too, something out of control.'

'When did you tell Laura that you'd canceled the tickets?'

'Around the middle of October.'

'Did you tell her why?'

'I'd already told her that your mother was very sick,' he answered, 'but I'm not sure she realized that it had made me change our plans until I actually told her that I'd canceled the tickets, that we wouldn't be going to Mexico together.'

I stared at him evenly, remembering the sudden, wrenching illness that had gripped my mother the night of the fireworks. I remembered how Laura had prepared her a glass of milk after we'd returned.

'Laura tried to kill her, didn't she?' I asked coolly.

He nodded. 'Yes, she did,' he said. 'I thought it was over, after that. She'd done something terrible, but I thought that would be the end of it.' He looked at me pointedly. 'Until that day.'

That day.

'It was raining,' I said softly, 'that's almost all I remember.'

He drew in a quick breath. 'Yes, it was raining,' he said. He waited a moment, as if deciding whether or not to go on. 'I was at the store downtown like always,' he began finally. 'I was alone. There was so much rain. No one was on the streets.' The old mournfulness swept into his eyes. 'Then the phone rang,' he said. 'It was Laura. She said that your mother had gotten sick, and she told me to come home.'

'When was this?'

'Around a quarter after three, I guess,' my father said. 'I went home right away.'

I could feel a silence gather around us as we sat facing each other in the small tavern, vast and empty, as if ours were the only voices that had survived a holocaust.

'Laura met me in the kitchen,' my father said. 'She'd made me a ham sandwich, and for a minute, I thought that the long time she'd been so angry with me, that it was finally over.'

'Where was my mother?'

'Laura said that she was upstairs,' my father answered, 'that she was a little better, that she was taking a nap.'

And so, suspecting nothing, my father had sat down at the kitchen table, and taken a few bites of the ham sandwich Laura had made for him. She had disappeared upstairs almost immediately, and after a time my father had wandered out to the solarium and slumped down in one of its white wicker chairs.

'I wasn't there very long,' he said, 'when I heard someone coming down the stairs. It was your mother.'

Perhaps more fully than I had ever thought possible, I now saw my mother in all her lost and loveless beauty. I saw her move softly down the carpeted stairs in her fluffy house shoes, her hand clutching the throat of her blouse, a woman perhaps less foolish than any of us had thought, her mind already wondering which of her children would try to kill her next.

'From where I was sitting, I just saw her go by,' my father said. 'Then I heard the basement door open, and I knew she was going down there.'

He heard her feet move down the wooden stairs, then went back to the little book he'd found in the solarium, reading it slowly, as he always did, his eyes moving lethargically across the slender columns.

'Jamie came in after that,' he said.

Encased in a vast solitude, rudderless and without direction, my brother came through the kitchen door, trails of rainwater dripping from his hair. He glanced coldly toward my father, but didn't speak. Instead he simply bounded up the stairs.

'I heard him close the door to his room,' my father said. 'He made a point of slamming it.'

After that, but for only a few, precious moments, a silence had descended upon 417 McDonald Drive. For a time, as he read in the solarium, my father had heard nothing but the rain.

Then a blast of incredible magnitude rocked the house.

'I thought it was a gas explosion,' my father said, 'something like that. I couldn't imagine what else it might be.'

He jumped to his feet, the book sliding to the floor of the solarium. He stared around a moment, not knowing where to go. In a blur of speed, he saw Laura fly past the open space that divided the living room from the downstairs corridor.

'The way she was running, I thought something must have happened upstairs,' my father said, 'so I ran up there, thinking that Jamie might be hurt, that things might be on fire.'

And so he rushed up the stairs, taking them in broad leaps, plummeting down the corridor where he could see a blue smoke coming through the open door of Jamie's room.

'I ran into his room, thinking that he must be hurt, that I had to pull him out,' my father said.

What he saw was a boy without a face.

'And I still didn't know what had happened,' my father said, breathless, already exhausted, as if he had only now made that dreadful run. 'I still didn't realize at that point that Jamie had been shot,' he said wonderingly, as if, through all the years, this was the strangest thing of all.

He ran to him, picked him up slightly, his shoes already soaking up Jamie's rich, red blood. Still stunned, dazed, unable to think, he heard a roar from down below.

'Then I knew, I think,' he said, 'but even then ... even then ...'

Even then, he didn't know for sure that his family was being slaughtered.

'And so I just stood there, in the middle of Jamie's room,' my father said.

Just stood there, his eyes darting about wildly until he finally bolted toward the basement.

'From out of nowhere, I thought that it must be someone else,' he said, 'that some killer had broken into the house somehow.' He looked at me, the astonishment still visible in his face. 'I thought that it was this killer who must have chased Laura down the stairs, that she'd been running from someone else when I'd seen her fly past me that time before.'

And so he began to run again, into the bedroom across the hall, then down the stairs, taking long, desperate strides as he searched for 'someone else' in the living room, the dining room, the kitchen, his bloody tracks leading everywhere until, at last, they led down the basement stairs.

He stopped on the third step, stricken by what he saw.

'Your mother was behind a big cardboard box,' my father said. 'Laura was standing just a few feet away. My old shotgun was in her hands. The barrel was still smoking.' He looked at me unbelievingly. 'She was barefoot, like always.'

Barefoot, yes. Like she was in the photograph that should have told me everything, her bare feet stretched toward the camera, their upturned soles covered with the dark grit she'd picked up from the basement floor as she'd stood and aimed the shotgun at my mother.

Swenson's words came rushing back to me: 'Someone else. Someone in the house. Someone helping.'

Laura.

My father shook his head slowly. 'She just looked at me, and she said, 'Now we *have* to go!" He stared at me pointedly. 'She meant Mexico,' he said, 'that now, after what she'd done, that I had no choice but to take her there.'

After that, they'd gone back up to the kitchen together, my father shaken, lost, unable to register the events that had just swept over him.

'I knew she'd done something to your mother a month before,' he said, 'but I'd never dreamed that she would do the same to Jamie or to ...' He stopped and looked at me emptily.

'To me?' I said.

He leaned forward, his eyes very gentle. 'She wanted me to do it, Stevie,' he said. 'She said she couldn't.'

Then she had gone upstairs to her room, walking briskly up the stairs, like someone who'd just been released from prison.

'I stayed in the kitchen,' my father told me. 'I thought about it all for a while.'

For a while, but not for long. Only for that short interval which Mrs. Hamilton had noticed between the second shot and the final one.

'I knew Laura had to die,' my father said, 'and I knew that if I killed her, they would blame all of it on me, that you would never know what she'd done to them.'

Or had planned to do to me.

'So I wiped her fingerprints off the gun,' my father said. 'Then I walked upstairs and ...' He stopped, his eyes glancing away for a moment, then returning to me. 'It was instant,' he whispered.

I saw my sister turn, saw her eyes widen in disbelief, her hand lift futilely as he pulled the trigger.

'That left you,' my father said.

That left me, yes.

To live on, though alone, remembering the love of my sister.

My father watched me a moment, leaning back, as if to get a better view. He seemed infinitely relieved, though carrying the same, ancient burden he'd carried through it all.

'I hadn't really had time to think about anything,' my father said. 'But after Laura, I went downstairs and thought about what I should do. Later I went back upstairs to change my clothes.'

And so the bloody shoes had never gone below the third step, though by then I knew that my father had.

'But I decided to clean things up a little,' my father said. 'I knew you'd be coming home any minute, and I didn't want you to see . . .' He shrugged, the sentence trailing off into a brief silence before he began again. 'After I'd finished with your mother,' he said, 'I decided that maybe I should take you with me.' The blue eyes softened. 'So I waited for you, Stevie. I didn't do anything about Laura or Jamie. I just left them where they were and waited for you to come home.' He looked at me plaintively, as if in apology. 'But you never came,' he said. 'The phone kept ringing. I thought it might be you, but I was afraid to pick it up.'

And so, at last, he'd walked out into the rain.

'I went to the store and got what money I could,' he told me. 'Then I drove to Oscar's and bought a few things.' He looked at me tenderly. 'The last thing I did was call the house. I thought you might be there. Just come in, maybe. Not seen anything. I didn't think it was possible, but I wanted to give it one last chance.'

One last chance, to take me with him.

'But you still weren't there,' he said.

I looked away from him, stared at the wall. I felt my hand rise and press down upon my lips. I didn't speak.

'I did see you one more time, though,' he said. 'After I left the house that day, I drove up to a place near my parents' farm. I knew there was a cabin in the woods. You may remember it yourself. We all went up there one time.'

'I remember it,' I answered softly.

'I stayed there for over a month,' my father told me, 'then I decided to head south.' He paused a moment, his eyes settling gently on my face. 'On the way down, I drove by Somerset and took some flowers to the graves. I'd just finished putting some on Jamie's grave when I saw you and Edna coming up the hill.' His voice seemed about to break as he continued. 'I ran off into the woods. I could see you at the graves.' He fell silent for a time, then added, 'I've lived alone since then. I never married. Never had more children.' He watched me, as if not sure he had the right to inquire into my life.

'How about you, Stevie?' he asked finally, tentatively.

'Yes, I got married,' I told him quietly.

He seemed pleased, though he didn't smile. 'Any kids?' he asked.

'A son.'

'Where's your family now?'

I shrugged, but not indifferently.

'Gone,' I told him.

I saw a terrible bleakness come into his face, a father's grief for the losses of his son. 'Sorry,' was all he said.

Once again, we sat silently for a time, then walked out of the tavern together. It was very dark, and so my father guided me through the twisting, ebony streets, past the olives and the palms, through what was left of the labyrinth, until we reached the unlighted beach.

'Stevie?' my father began, then stopped, as if brought to a halt by the look he'd glimpsed upon my face.

I didn't answer.

Far in the distance, through the immense stillness, I could see a ship in the darkness, sailing blindly, it seemed to me, toward its nightbound home.

# THE CHATHAM SCHOOL AFFAIR

For Kate Miciak

*Sine qua non*

*He sees enough who doth his darkness see.*

LORD HERBERT OF CHERBURY

# PART I

# ONE

My father had a favorite line. He'd taken it from Milton, and he loved to quote it to the boys of Chatham School. Standing before them on opening day, his hands thrust deep into his trouser pockets, he'd pause a moment, facing them sternly. 'Be careful what you do,' he'd say, 'for evil on itself doth back recoil.' In later years he could not have imagined how wrong he was, nor how profoundly I knew him to be so.

Sometimes, particularly on one of those bleak winter days so common to New England, wind tearing at the trees and shrubbery, rain battering the roofs and windows, I feel myself drift back to my father's world, my own youth, the village he loved and in which I still live. I glance outside my office window and see the main street of Chatham as it once was – a scattering of small shops, a ghostly parade of antique cars with their lights mounted on sloping fenders. In my mind, the dead return to life, assume their earthly shapes. I see Mrs. Albertson delivering a basket of quahogs to Kessler's Market; Mr. Lawrence lurching forward in his homemade snowmobile, skis on the front, a set of World War I tank tracks on the back, all hooked to the battered chassis of an old roadster pickup. He waves as he goes by, a gloved hand in the timeless air.

Standing once again at the threshold of my past, I feel fifteen again, with a full head of hair and not a single liver spot, heaven far away, no thought of hell. I even sense a certain goodness at the core of life.

Then, from out of nowhere, I think of her again. Not as the young woman I'd known so long ago, but as a little girl, peering out over a glittering blue sea, her father standing beside her in a white linen suit, telling her what fathers have always told their children: that the future is open to them, a field of grass, harboring no dark wood. In my mind I see her as she stood in her cottage that day, hear her voice again, her words like distant bells, sounding the faith she briefly held in life. *Take as much as you want, Henry. There is plenty.*

\*

Church stood at the eastern entrance
ave for its tall, dark spire. There was a
f the church, marked by a stubby white
uses picked up and deposited passengers
d no liking for the train.

in 1926, I'd been sitting on the church steps,
itary history, my addiction at the time, when
yards away. From that distance I'd watched its
hinges creaking in the warm late-summer air. A
la_              o children emerged first, followed by an elderly man
who s_           _ and wore a navy blue captain's cap, the sort of 'old
salt' often s_      _ Cape Cod in those days. Then there'd been a moment
of suspension, when no one emerged from the shadowy interior of the
bus, so that I'd expected it to pull away, swing left and head toward the
neighboring town of Orleans, a trail of dust following behind it like an
old feather boa.

But the bus had stayed in place, its engine rumbling softly as it idled
by the road. I could not imagine why it remained so until I saw another
figure rise from a seat near the back. It was a woman, and she moved
forward slowly, smoothly, a dark silhouette. Near the door she paused,
her arm raised slightly, her hand suspended in midair even as it reached
for the metal rail that would have guided her down the stairs.

At the time I couldn't have guessed the cause for her sudden hesitation.
But in the years since then, I've come to believe that it was precisely at
that moment she must have realized just how fully separate our world was
from the one she'd lived in with her father during the many years they'd
traveled together, the things she'd seen with him, Florence in its summer
splendor, the canals of Venice, Paris from the steps of Sacre-Coeur. How
could anything in Chatham ever have compared with that?

Something at last urged her forward. Perhaps necessity, the fact that
with her father's recent death she had no other option. Perhaps a hope
that she could, in the end, make her life with us. I will never know.
Whatever the reason, she drew in a deep breath, grasped the iron rail, and
made her way down the stairs and into the afternoon stillness of a tiny
seacoast village where no great artist had ever lived, no great event ever
happened, save for those meted out by sudden storms or the torturous
movement of geologic time.

It was my father who greeted her when she stepped from the bus that
afternoon. He was headmaster of Chatham School, a man of medium
height, but whose manner, so expansive and full of authority, made him
seem larger than he was. In one of the many pictures I have of him from
that time, this one printed in the Chatham School Annual for 1926, he

is seated in his office, behind a massive oak desk, his hands resting on its polished surface, his eyes staring directly into the camera. It was the usual pose of a respectable and accomplished man in those days, one that made him appear quite stern, perhaps even a bit hard, though he was nothing of the kind. Indeed, when I remember him as he was in those days, it is usually as a cheerful, ebullient man with an energetic and kindly manner, slow to anger, quick to forgive, his feelings always visible in his eyes. 'The heart is what matters, Henry,' he said to me not long before his death, a principle he'd often voiced through the years, but never for one moment truly lived by. For surely, of all the men I've ever known, he was the least enslaved by passion. Now an old man too, it is hard for me to imagine how in my youth I could have despised him so.

But I did despise him. Silently. Sullenly. Giving him no hint of my low regard, so that I must have seemed a perfectly obedient son, given to moodiness, perhaps, but otherwise quite normal, rocked by nothing darker than the usual winds of adolescence. Remembering him, as I often do, I marvel at how much he knew of Cicero and Thucydides, and how little of the boy who lived in the room upstairs.

Earlier that morning he'd found me lounging in the swing on the front porch, given me a disapproving look, and said, 'What, nothing to do, Henry?'

I shrugged.

'Well, come with me, then,' he said, then bounded down the front steps and out to our car, a bulky old Ford whose headlights stuck out like stubby horns.

I rose, followed my father down the stairs, got into the car, and sat silently as he pulled out of the driveway, my face showing a faint sourness, the only form of rebellion I was allowed.

On the road my father drove at a leisurely pace through the village, careful to slow even further at the approach of pedestrians or horses. He nodded to Mrs. Cavenaugh as she came out of Warren's Sundries, and gave a short cautionary beep on the horn when he saw Davey Bryant chasing Hattie Shaw a little too aggressively across the lighthouse grounds.

In those days, Chatham was little more than a single street of shops. There was Mayflower's, a sort of general store, and Thompson's Haberdashery, along with a pharmacy run by Mr. Benchley, in which the gentlemen of the town could go to a back room and enjoy a glass of illegal spirits, though never to the point of drunkenness. Mrs. Jessup had a boardinghouse at the far end of Main Street, and Miss Hilliard a little school for 'dance, drama, and piano,' which practically no one ever attended, so that her main source of income came from selling cakes and pies, along with keeping house for several of the rich families that summered in spacious, sun-drenched homes on the bay. From a great height Chatham had to have looked idyllic, and yet to me it was a prison, its buildings like high, looming walls, its yards and gardens strewn around me like fields of concertina wire.

My father felt nothing of the kind, of course. No man was ever more suited to small-town life than he was. Sometimes, for no reason whatever, he would set out from our house and walk down to the center of the village, chatting with whoever crossed his path, usually about the weather or his garden, anything to keep the flow of words going, as if these inconsequential conversations were the very lubricant of life, the *numen*, as the Romans called it, that divine substance which unites and sustains us.

That August afternoon my father seemed almost jaunty as he drove through the village, then up the road that led to the white facade of the Congregationalist Church. Because of that, I knew that something was up. For he always appeared most happy when he was in the midst of doing some good deed.

'Do you remember that teacher I mentioned?' he asked as we swept past Warren's Sundries. 'The one who's coming from Africa.'

I nodded dully, faintly recalling the brief mention of such a person at dinner one night.

'Well, she's arriving this afternoon. Coming in on the Boston bus. I want you to give her a nice welcome.'

We got to the bus stop a few minutes later. My father took up his place by the white pillar while I wandered over to the steps of the church, slumped down on its bottom stair, and pulled the book I'd been reading from the back pocket of my trousers.

I was reading it a half hour later, by then lost in the swirling dusts of Thermopylae, when the bus at last arrived. I remained in place, grudgingly aware that my father would have preferred that I rush down to greet the new teacher. Of course, I was determined to do nothing of the kind.

And so I don't know how he reacted when he first saw Miss Channing emerge from the bus that afternoon, for I couldn't see his face. I do know how beautiful she was, however, how immaculately white her throat looked against the wine-red collar of her dress. I have always believed that as she stepped from the gray interior of the bus, her face suddenly captured in a bright summer light, her eyes settling upon my father with the mysterious richness I was to see in them as well, that at that moment, in that silence, he surely caught his breath.

# TWO

Inevitably, when I recall that first meeting, the way Miss Channing looked as she arrived in Chatham, so young and full of hope, I want to put up my hand and do what all our reading and experience tells us we can never do. I want to say 'Stop, please. Stop, Time.'

It's not that I want to freeze her there for all eternity, of course, a young woman arriving in a quaint New England town, but that I merely wish to break the pace long enough to point out the simple truth life unquestionably teaches anyone who lives into old age: since our passions do not last forever, our true task is to survive them. And one thing more, perhaps: I want to remind her how thin it is, and weaving, the tight-rope we walk through life, how the smallest misstep can become a fatal plunge.

Then I think, *No, things must be as they became.* And with that thought, time rolls onward again, and I see her take my father's hand, shake it briefly, then let it go, her face turning slightly to the left so that she must have seen me as I finally roused myself from the church steps and headed toward her from across its carefully tended lawn.

'This is my son, Henry,' my father said when I reached them.

'Hi,' I said, offering my hand.

Miss Channing took it. 'Hello, Henry,' she said.

I can clearly recall how she looked at that first meeting, her hair gathered primly beneath her hat, her skin a perfect white, her features beautiful in the way certain female portraits are beautiful, not so much sensuous as very finely wrought. But more than anything, I remember her eyes, pale blue and slightly oval, with a striking sense of alertness.

'Henry's going to be a sophomore this year,' my father added. 'He'll be one of your students.'

Before Miss Channing could respond to that, the bus driver came bustling around the back of the bus with two leather valises. He dropped them to the ground, then scurried back into the bus.

My father nodded for me to pick up Miss Channing's luggage. Which

I did, then stood, a third wheel, as he immediately returned the full force of his attention to Miss Channing.

'You'll have an early dinner with us,' he told her. 'After that we'll take you to your new home.' With that, he stepped back slightly, turned, and headed for the car, Miss Channing walking along beside him, I trudging behind, the two leather valises hanging heavily from my hands.

We lived on Myrtle Street in those days, just down from Chatham School, in a white house with a small porch, like almost all the others in the village. As we drove toward it, passing through the center of town on the way, my father pointed out various stores and shops where Miss Channing would be able to buy her supplies. She seemed quite attentive to whatever my father told her, her attention drawn to this building or that one with an unmistakable appreciativeness, like someone touring a gallery or a museum, her eyes intently focused on the smallest things, the striped awning of Mayflower's, the hexagonal bandstand on the grounds of the town hall, the knot of young men who lounged in front of the bowling alley, smoking cigarettes, and in whose desultory habits and loose morals my father claimed to glimpse the grim approach of the coming age.

A hill rose steadily from the center of town, curving to the right as it ascended toward the coastal bluff. The old lighthouse stood at the far end of it, its grounds decorated with two huge whitewashed anchors.

'We once had three lighthouses here in Chatham,' my father said. 'One was moved to Eastham. The second was lost in the storm of 'twenty-three.'

Miss Channing gazed at our remaining lighthouse as we drifted by it. 'It's more striking to have only one,' she said. She turned toward the backseat, her eyes falling upon me. 'Don't you think so, Henry?'

I had no answer for her, surprised as I was that she'd bothered to ask, but my father appeared quite taken by her observation.

'Yes, I think that's true,' he said. 'A second makes the first less impressive.'

Miss Channing's eyes lingered on me a moment, a quiet smile offered silently before she turned away.

Our house was situated at the end of Myrtle Street, and on the way to it we passed Chatham School. It was a large brick building with cement stairs and double front doors. The first floor was made up of classrooms, the second taken up by the dormitory, dining hall, and common room.

'That's where you'll be teaching,' my father told her, slowing down a bit as we drove by. 'We've made a special room for you. In the courtyard.'

Miss Channing glanced over to the school, and from her reflection in the glass, I could see that her eyes were very still, like someone staring into a crystal ball, searching for her future there.

We pulled up in front of our house a few seconds later. My father opened the door for Miss Channing and escorted her up the front stairs to the porch, where my mother waited to be introduced.

'Welcome to Chatham,' my mother said, offering her hand.

She was only a few years younger than my father, but considerably less agile, and certainly less spirited, her face rather plain and round, but with small, nervous eyes. To the people of Chatham, she'd been known simply as the 'music teacher' and more or less given up for a spinster. Then my father had arrived, thirty-one years old but still a bachelor, eager to establish a household in which he could entertain the teachers he'd already hired for his new school, as well as potential benefactors. My mother had met whatever his criteria had been for a wife, and after a courtship of only six weeks, he'd asked her to marry him. My mother had accepted without hesitation, my father's proposal catching her so completely by surprise, as she loved to tell the women in her sewing circle, that at first she had taken it for a joke.

But on that afternoon nearly twenty years later, my mother no longer appeared capable of taking anything lightly. She'd grown wide in the hips by then, her figure large and matronly, her pace so slow and ponderous that I often grew impatient with it and bolted ahead of her to wherever we were going. Later in life she sometimes lost her breath at the top of the porch stairs, coming to a full stop in order to regain it, one hand grasping a wooden supporting post, the other fluttering at her chest, her head arched back as she sucked in a long, difficult breath. In old age her hair grew white and her eyes dimmed, and she often sat alone in the front room, or lay curled on her bed, no longer able to read and barely able to attend to the radio. Even so, something fiery remained in her to the very end, fueled by a rage engendered by the Chatham School Affair, one that smoldered forever after that.

She died many years after the affair had run its frightful course, and by then much had changed in all our lives: the large house on Myrtle Street no more than a memory, my father living on a modest pension, Chatham School long closed, its doors locked, its windows boarded, the playing fields gone to weed, all its former reputation by then reduced to a dark and woeful legacy.

My mother had prepared a chowder for us that afternoon, buttery and thick with clams and potatoes, the sort typical of Cape Cod. We ate at the dining table, Sarah Doyle, the teenage servant girl my father had brought from Boston only two years before, ladling the fragrant chowder into large china bowls.

Sitting at the table, Miss Channing asked few questions as my father went through his usual remarks about Chatham School, what its philosophy was, how it had come to be, a lecture my mother had heard countless times, but which clearly engaged Miss Channing's interest.

'Why only boys?' she asked at one point.

'Because girls would change the atmosphere of the school,' my father answered.

'In what way?'

'The boys would feel their presence,' my father told her. 'It would cause them to show off, to act foolishly.'

Miss Channing thought a moment. 'But is that the fault of the girls or the boys, Mr. Griswald?'

'It's the fault of the mixture, Miss Channing,' my father told her, obviously surprised by the boldness he detected in her question. 'It makes the atmosphere more ... volatile.'

My father fully expected to have brought the subject to a close with that. An expectation I shared so completely that when Miss Channing suddenly spoke again, offering what amounted to a challenge, I felt something like a call to arms.

'And without the girls, what's the atmosphere?' she asked.

'Studious and serious,' my father answered. 'Disciplined.'

'And that's the atmosphere you want at Chatham School?'

'Yes,' my father replied firmly. 'It is.'

Miss Channing said nothing more on the subject, but sitting across from her, I sensed that there was more she might have said, thoughts that were in her head, bristling there, or firing continually, like small explosions.

At the end of the meal my father led Miss Channing and my mother into the little parlor at the front of the house for a cup of tea. I lingered at the table, watching Sarah clear away the dishes after she'd served them. Though my father had closed the French doors that separated the parlor from the dining room, it was still possible for me to see Miss Channing as she sat listening quietly to my father.

'So, what do you think of the new teacher?' I asked Sarah as she leaned over my shoulder and plucked a bowl from the table.

Sarah didn't answer, so I glanced up at her. She was not looking at me, but toward the parlor, where Miss Channing sat by the window, her hands held primly in her lap, the Joan Crawford hat sitting firmly on her head.

'Such a fine lady,' Sarah said in an almost reverential tone. 'The kind folks read about in books.'

I looked back toward Miss Channing. She was taking a sip from her cup as my father went on, her blue eyes peering just over the rim, sharp and evaluating, as if her mind ceaselessly sifted the material that passed through it, allowing this, dismissing that, her sense of judgment oddly final, a court, as it would prove to be, from which there could be no appeal.

I was in my room an hour later, perusing the latest issue of *Grady's Illustrated Magazine for Boys*, when my father summoned me downstairs.

'It's time to take Miss Channing home,' he told me.

I followed him out the door, then down the front stairs to where Miss Channing was already waiting in the car.

'It's only a short drive,' my father said to her as he pulled himself in behind the wheel. 'Perhaps I can get you there ahead of the rain.'

But he could not, for as we drove toward the cottage, the overhanging clouds suddenly disgorged their burden, thunderously and without warning, as if abruptly being called to account.

Once outside the village center, my father turned right, onto the coastal road, past the great summer houses that rose along the shore, then on toward the marsh, with its shanties and fishermen's houses, their unkempt yards scattered with stacks of lobster traps and tangled piles of gray netting.

Given the torrent, the drive was slow, the old Ford sputtering along, battered from all directions by sudden whipping gusts, the windshield wipers squeaking rhythmically as they swept ineffectually across the glass.

My father kept his eyes on the road, of course, but I noticed that Miss Channing's attention had turned toward the landscape of Cape Cod, its short, rounded hills sparsely clothed in tangles of brush and scrub oak, wind ripping through the sea grass that sprouted from the dunes.

'The Cape's pretty, don't you think, Miss Channing?' my father said cheerfully.

Her reply must have startled him.

'It looks tormented,' she said, staring out the window on the passenger side, her voice suddenly quite somber, as if it came from some darker part of her mind.

My father glanced toward her. 'Tormented? What do you mean?'

'It reminds me of the islands of the Florida Keys,' she answered, her eyes still concentrated on the landscape. 'The name the Spanish gave them.'

'What name was that?'

'Los Martires,' Miss Channing answered. 'Because they looked so tormented by the wind and the sea.'

'Forgive my ignorance,' my father said. 'But what does "Los Martires" mean?'

Miss Channing continued to gaze out the window. 'It means "the martyrs",' she said, her eyes narrowing somewhat, as if she were no longer looking at the dunes and the sea grass beyond her window, but at the racked and bleeding body of some ancient tortured saint.

My father drew his attention back to the road. 'Well, I've never thought of the Cape as looking like that,' he said. Then, to my surprise, I saw his eyes lift toward the rearview mirror, fix on mine. 'Have you ever thought of the Cape like that, Henry?'

I glanced out the window at my right, toward a landscape that no longer seemed featureless and inert, but beaten and bedeviled, lashed by gusts of wind and surging waters. 'Not until just now,' I said.

At about a mile beyond town we swung onto a stretch of road bordered on all sides by dense forest and covered with what had once been a layer of oyster shells, but which past generations of hooves and feet and wagon wheels had since ground into little more than a fine powder.

The woods had encroached so far into the road that I could hear the surrounding vegetation slap and scrape against the side of the car as we bumped along the road.

'It gets pretty deserted out this way,' my father said. He added nothing else as we continued in silence until the road forked, my father taking the one to the right, moving down it for perhaps a quarter mile, until it widened suddenly, then came to an abrupt dead end before a small white cottage.

'There it is,' my father said. 'Milford Cottage.'

It was tiny compared to our house on Myrtle Street, so dwarfed by the surrounding forest that it appeared to crouch fearfully within a fist of green, a dark stretch of water sweeping out behind it, still and lightless, its opaque depths unplumbed, like a great hole in the heart of things.

'That's Black Pond,' my father said.

Miss Channing leaned forward slightly, peering at the cottage very intently through the downpour, like a painter considering a composition, calculating the light, deciding where to put the easel. It was an expression I would see many times during the coming year, intense and curious, a face that seemed to draw everything into it by its own strange gravity.

'It's a simple place,' my father told her. 'But quite nice. I hope you'll at least find it cozy.'

'I'm sure I will,' she said. 'Who lived here?'

'It was never actually lived in,' my father answered. 'It was built as a honeymoon cottage by Mr. Milford for his bride.'

'But they never lived there?'

My father appeared reluctant to answer her but obligated to do so. 'They were both killed on the way to it,' he said. 'An automobile accident as they were coming back from Boston.'

Miss Channing's face suddenly grew strangely animated, as if she were imagining an alternative story in her mind, the arrival of a young couple who never arrived, the joys of a night they never spent together, a morning after that was never theirs.

'It's not luxurious, of course,' my father added quickly, determined, as he always was, to avoid disagreeable things, 'but it's certainly adequate.' His eyes rested upon Miss Channing for a moment before he drew them away abruptly, and almost guiltily, so that for a brief instant he looked rather like a man who'd been caught reading a forbidden book. 'Well, let's go inside,' he said.

With that, my father opened the door and stepped out into the rain. 'Quickly now, Henry.' He motioned for me to get Miss Channing's valises and follow him into the cottage.

He was already at the front door, struggling with the key, his hair wet and stringy by the time I reached them. Miss Channing stood just behind him, waiting for him to open the door. As he worked the key, twisting it right and left, he appeared somewhat embarrassed that it wouldn't turn, as if some element of his authority had been called into question. 'Everything rusts in this sea air,' I heard him murmur. He jerked at the key again. It gave, and the cottage door swung open.

'There's no electricity out this way,' my father explained as he stepped into the darkened cottage. 'But the fireplace has been readied for winter, and there are quite a few kerosene lamps, so you'll have plenty of light.' He walked to the window, parted the curtains, and looked out into the darkening air. 'Just as I explained in my letter.' He released the curtain and turned back to her. 'I take it that you're accustomed to things being a little ... primitive.'

'Yes, I am,' Miss Channing replied.

'Well, before we go, you should have a look around. I hope we didn't forget anything.'

He walked over to one of the lamps and lit it. A yellow glow spread through the room, illuminating the newly scrubbed walls, the recently hung lace curtains, the plain wooden floor that had been so carefully swept, a stone fireplace cleared of ash.

'The kitchen's been stocked already,' he told her. 'So you've got plenty of lard, flour, sugar. All of the essentials.' He nodded toward the bedroom. 'And the linens are in the wardrobe there.'

Miss Channing glanced toward the bedroom, her eyes settling upon the iron bedstead, the sheets stretched neatly over the narrow mattress, two quilts folded at the foot of the bed, a single pillow at its head.

'I know that things take getting used to, Miss Channing,' my father said, 'but I'm sure that in time you'll be happy here.'

I knew well what my father meant by the word 'happy', the contentment it signified for him, a life of predictable events and limited range, pinched and uninspired, a pale offering to those deeper and more insistent longings that I know must have called to him from time to time.

But as to what Miss Channing considered happiness, that I could not have said. I knew only that a strange energy surrounded her, a vibrancy and engagement that was almost physical, and that whatever happiness she might later find in life would have to answer to it.

'I hope you'll like Chatham as well,' my father said after a moment. 'It's quite a lovely little town.'

'I'm sure I will,' Miss Channing told him, though even as she said it, she might well have been comparing it to Rome or Vienna, the great cities she'd visited, the boulevards and spacious squares she'd strolled along, a wider world she'd long known but that I had only dreamed of.

'Well, we should be going now,' my father said. He nodded toward the two leather valises in my hands. 'Put those down, Henry.'

I did as I was told, and joined my father at the door.

'Well, good night, then, Miss Channing,' he said as he opened it.

'Good night, Mr. Griswald,' she said. 'And thank you for everything.'

Seconds later we were in the car again, backing onto Plymouth Road. Through the cords of rain that ran down the windshield as we pulled away, I could see Miss Channing standing at the threshold of the cottage, her face so quiet and luminous as she waved good-bye that I have often chosen to recall her as she was that first night rather than as she appeared at our last meeting, her hair clipped and matted, her skin lusterless, the air around her thick with a dank and deathly smell.

# THREE

My father's portrait hangs on the large wood-paneled wall opposite my desk and over the now-unused marble hearth, shelves of law books arrayed on either side. He is dressed in a black three-piece suit, the vest neatly buttoned, a formal style of dress common to portraiture at that time. But there is something unusual about the composition nonetheless. For although my father is dressed appropriately enough, he is not posed behind his desk or standing before a wall of books, but at a large window with dark red curtains held in place by gold sashes. Outside the window, it is clearly summer, but nothing in the landscape beyond the glass in the least resembles either Chatham or Cape Cod.

Instead, my father gazes out into a strange, limitless plain, covered in elephant grass and dotted with fire trees, a vast expanse that sweeps out in all directions until it finally dissolves into the watery reaches of a distant blue lake, his attention focused on something in the exotic distance, perhaps the farther shore of that same lake, an effect that gives his face a look of melancholy longing.

It is the tragic fate of goodness to lack the vast attraction of romance. Because of that, I have never been able to see my father as a man capable of the slightest allure. And yet, for all that, he was a man in love, I think. Though with a school, rather than a woman. Chatham School was his great passion, and the years during which he served as its founder and headmaster, a guiding spirit to its boys, a counselor to its teachers, he'd felt more deeply than he ever would again that his life was truly whole.

I have looked at this portrait countless times, studying it as a way of studying my father, concentrating upon what lies mysteriously within it. Inevitably, I turn from it in a mood of vague frustration and uneasiness, my eyes drawn to the artist's signature, her name written out in tiny broken letters: *Elizabeth Rockbridge Channing*.

The portrait was painted during the last days of that school year, my father standing at the window of his office, peering out, while Miss Channing remained stationed at her easel a few yards away, her body draped in a gray, paint-dabbled smock, her hair falling to her shoulders in a great unruly mass. By that April, she no longer looked as she had upon her arrival the previous August. The blush of youth was gone, a haggardness in its place, and glimpsing her alone in her classroom during those last days, or as she made her solitary way down the coastal road, I could see nothing left of the young woman who'd stood in the doorway of Milford Cottage only a few months before, waving good-bye as my father backed our car onto Plymouth Road.

I never knew precisely what Miss Channing did after my father and I drove away that evening, leaving her alone in the cottage. I have always imagined her opening the two valises and unpacking her things, putting her new hat on the narrow shelf at the top of the wardrobe, hanging her dresses on the wooden bar that ran nearly its entire length, tucking her undergarments in the drawers that rested at its base.

From the look of the cottage when I saw it again the next day, I know that she had found a nail already in place and hung a portrait of her father, one taken years before in the courtyard of the Uffizi, the Florentine sun pouring over him, dressed stylishly in white trousers, a navy blue jacket, and a straw bowler, his fingers around the silver head of a polished wooden cane.

I also know that the randomly placed kerosene lamps must have cast heavy shadows throughout her new home, because I could tell from the positions I later saw them in that at some point during her first night in the cottage she arranged them in different places throughout the rooms, moving them here and there until, at last, a steady, even glow pervaded its shadowy interior, its darkened corners now brushed with light.

But more than anything, and with a certainty I cannot claim for other things, I know that toward midnight, when the rain finally stopped, she strolled out to the very edge of the pond, glanced over the water, and noticed a faint movement on its otherwise unmoving surface. It was then that a bank of clouds parted, a shaft of moonlight falling upon the water so that she could see the white prow of a rowboat as it skirted briefly along the far rim of light, then disappeared into the covering darkness. There was a figure in the boat, almost completely draped in a black poncho, as she later described it, so that she could make out only one small square of flesh, a hand, large and masculine, gripping a single moving oar.

I know all this absolutely, because she said as much on a sweltering summer day nearly a year later, the crowd shifting frantically to get a better view of her, craning their necks and lifting their heads, muttering grimly as they did so, talking of death and suicide and murder, their eyes following with a macabre fascination as she moved across the room and took her seat upon the witness stand.

\*

In later life, after I'd returned to Chatham and begun my legal practice, I had only to glance out my office window to see the name of the man who'd cross-examined Miss Channing on that August afternoon in 1927. For in those days, Mr. Parsons' office had been located just across the street from where I now have mine, and which his son, Albert Parsons, Jr., still occupies, a lawyer who specializes in personal injury litigation and contract disputes, rather than the prosecution of criminal cases for which his father was renowned throughout the state.

The younger Parsons' shingle swings above the same little rectangle of grass where his father's once swung, and which I must have seen quite clearly on the very day my father picked up Miss Channing at the bus stop, our old Ford sweeping past it as we drove to our house on Myrtle Street, my father at the wheel, Miss Channing in the passenger seat, I crowded in the backseat with her luggage, so young and inexperienced, so lost to the iron laws of life that even had they been presented to me, I would have denied their right to hold me down. Certainly, I could not have known how often I would glance at Mr. Parsons' shingle in the coming years, hear his voice thunder out of the past: *It was you, Miss Channing, you and you alone who brought about this death.*

In those days Albert Parsons held the office of commonwealth attorney. A short, stocky man with wire-rimmed glasses, I often saw him making his way along the wooden sidewalk to his office, puffing his briar pipe and doffing his gray homburg to passersby. He'd appeared perfectly self-assured back then, confident in his own abilities, a man who expected to live out his life in a world whose rules were clear to him, a paradise, as he must have considered Chatham, poised on the rim of heaven.

I remember seeing Mr. Parsons in old age, when he would sit on the wooden bench in front of the town hall, tossing broken pieces of soda cracker to the pigeons gathered at his feet, his eyes watching them with a curious lack of focus. But before that, in the first years of his retirement, he'd built a workroom in his backyard, furnished it with metal book-shelves, a wooden desk, a brass reading lamp, and an old black typewriter. It was there that he'd written his account of the Chatham School Affair, utterly convinced that he had unearthed the darkest of its secrets.

Down through the years I've often thought of him, the pride he took in having discovered the cause of so much death, then the way he later strode the streets of Chatham, boldly, proudly, as if he were now the exclusive guardian of its health, Miss Channing no more than a dark malignancy he'd successfully cut out.

\*

It was a Saturday, clear and sunny, the last one before school was scheduled to begin, when I next saw Miss Channing.

My father had already left for Osterville, as my mother told me that morning, but he'd left instructions for me to look in on Milford Cottage, see if Miss Channing needed anything, then run whatever errands she required.

Milford Cottage was almost two miles from the center of Chatham, so it took me quite some time to walk there. I arrived at around ten, knocked lightly at the door, and waited for Miss Channing to open it. When there was no answer, I knocked again, this time more loudly. There was still no answer, so I rapped against the door a third time.

That's when I saw her. Not as I'd expected, a figure inside the cottage, or poised beside its open door, but strolling toward me from the edge of the woods, no longer dressed formally as she'd been before, but in a pale blue summer dress, billowy and loose-fitting, her black hair falling in a wild tangle to her shoulders.

She didn't see me at first, and so continued to walk in the woods, edging around trees and shrubs, her eyes trained on the ground, as if following the trail of something or someone who'd approached the cottage from the surrounding forest, lingered a moment, then retreated back into its concealing depths. At the very edge of the forest she stopped, plucked a leaf from a shrub, lifted it to the sun, and turned it slowly in a narrow shaft of light, staring at it with a kind of childlike awe.

When she finally glanced away from the leaf and saw me, I could tell she was surprised to find me at her door.

'Good morning, Miss Channing,' I called.

She smiled and began to walk toward me, the hem of her skirt trailing lightly over the still-moist ground.

'I didn't mean to scare you,' I said.

She appeared amused by such a notion. 'Scare me? You didn't scare me, Henry. Why would you think that?'

I shrugged, finding her gaze so penetrating that I began to sputter. 'Anyway, my father sent me to make sure that everything is all right. Particularly with the cottage. He wanted to know if anything else needed fixing. The roof, I mean. How it held up. Against the rain, that is. Leaks.'

'No, everything's fine,' Miss Channing said, watching me intently, as if memorizing my features, carefully noting their smallest dips and curves, the set of my jaw, the shape of my eyes.

It gave me an uncomfortable feeling of being exposed, my skin peeled away layer by layer, revealing what lay beneath, the bony tower, the circuitry of arteries and veins, the resentment I so carefully suppressed. I felt my hand toy with the button at my throat.

'Well, is there anything else you need?' I asked, still mindful of my father's instructions, but eager now to get away. 'I mean, between now and Monday, when school starts?'

'No, I don't think so.'

'All right, then,' I said. 'I guess I'll see you at school on Monday.'

With that, I nodded good-bye and started back toward the road, ambling slowly, not wanting to give an impression of flight.

I was halfway down the path that led from her door to the road when I heard her call to me.

'Are you walking back to the village, Henry?'

I stopped and turned toward her. 'Yes,' I said.

'Would you mind if I came along with you? I haven't really seen it yet.'

I didn't relish the idea of being seen with a teacher outside a classroom setting. 'It's a long way into town, Miss Channing,' I said, hoping to dissuade her.

She was undeterred. 'I'm used to long walks.'

Clearly, there was no way out. 'All right,' I said with an unenthusiastic shrug.

She came forward, quickening her pace slightly until she reached my side.

Sometime later, after I'd read her father's book and realized all the exotic places he'd taken her during the years they'd traveled together, it would strike me as very strange that she'd wanted to go into the village at all that morning. Certainly, given the breadth of her experience, Chatham could only have seemed quaint. And yet her curiosity seemed real, her need to explore our small streets and shops not in the least diminished by the fact that she'd strolled the narrow alleyways of Naples and the plazas of Madrid, her father at her side relating gruesome stories of Torquemada's Inquisition and the visions of Juana the Mad in that same tone of ominousness and impending death that later fathers would use as they led their children along the banks of Black Pond, grimly spinning out a tale whose dreadful course they thought had ended there.

# FOUR

I have always wondered if, during that first walk down Plymouth Road with Miss Channing, I should have noticed some hint of that interior darkness Mr. Parsons later claimed to have unearthed in her. Often, I've tried to see what he saw in his first interrogation of her, the 'eeriness' he described in his memoir, the sense that she had 'delved in black arts'.

She carefully kept pace with me that morning, a breeze playing lightly in her hair, her conversation generally related to the plant life we saw around us. She asked the names of the trees and flowers that bordered the road, often very common ones like beach plum or Queen Anne's lace.

'I guess you had different plants in Africa,' I said.

'Yes, very different,' she said. 'Of course, it wasn't at all the sort of place people think of when they think of Africa. It wasn't a jungle, or anything like that. It was a plain, mostly grasslands. With a river running through it, and animals everywhere.' She smiled. 'It was like living in the middle of an enormous zoo.'

'Did you like living there?'

'I suppose,' she answered. 'But I really didn't live there long. Only a few months after my father died. With my uncle and his family.' She stopped and peered out into the surrounding forest. 'It must have looked like this when the first explorers came.'

I could hardly have cared less about anything so distant. 'Why did you leave Africa?' I asked.

She drew her attention back to me. 'I needed a job. My uncle went to school with your father. He wrote to him, hoping he might know of a position. Your father offered me one at Chatham School.'

'What do you teach?'

'Art.'

'We've never had an art teacher,' I told her. 'You'll be the first one.'

She started to speak, then glanced toward the ground at the white dust that had begun to settle on her feet and shoes.

'It comes from the oyster shells,' I told her, merely as a point of information. 'That white dust, I mean.'

She turned toward me sharply. 'Oyster shells?'

'Yes. That's what they used to put on the roads around here.'

She nodded silently, then walked on, suddenly preoccupied, my first hint of the strange life she'd lived before coming to Chatham, how deeply it had formed her. 'That's what they killed Hypatia with,' she said.

She saw the question in my eyes, and immediately answered it. 'She was the last of the pagan astronomers. A Christian mob murdered her.' Her eyes drifted toward the road. 'They scraped her to death with oyster shells.'

I could tell by the look on her face that she was seeing the slaughter of Hypatia at the instant she described it, the mocking crowd in its frenzy, Hypatia sinking to the ground, bits of her flesh scooped from her body and tossed into the air.

'There was nothing left of her when it was over,' she said. 'No face. No body. Torn to bits.'

It was then I should have glimpsed it, I suppose, the fact that she had lived in many worlds, that they now lived in her, strange and kaleidoscopic, her mind a play of scenes. Some quite beautiful – Mont Saint Michel like a great ship run aground in dense fog. Others hung in death and betrayal – the harbor in which the last weary remnants of the Children's Crusade had trudged onto waiting ships, then disappeared into the desert wastes of Arab slavery.

But at the time I could only react to what Miss Channing had just told me. And so I grimaced, pretending a delicacy I didn't actually feel, knowing all the while that some part of her story had intrigued me.

'How do you know about Hypatia?' I asked.

'My father told me about her,' Miss Channing answered.

She said nothing more about her father, but merely began to move forward again, so that we walked on in silence for a time, the sound of our feet padding softly over the powdered shells as the wind rustled through the forest that bore in upon us from both sides.

When we reached the outskirts of Chatham, Miss Channing stopped for a moment and peered down the gently curving road that led from the center of the village to the lighthouse on the bluff. 'It looks very ... American,' she said.

I'd never heard anyone say anything quite so odd, and I suppose that it was at that moment I knew that something truly different had entered my life.

Of course, I kept that early intimation to myself, and so merely

413

watched silently as she stood at the threshold of our village. From there she would have been able to see all the way down Main Street, from the Congregationalist Church, where the bus had let her off the day of her arrival, to the courthouse, where she would later come to trial, hear the shouts of the crowd outside: *Murderess. Murderess.* If she'd looked closely enough, concentrating on the small details, she might even have seen the wooden bench where, years later, Mr. Parsons would sit alone in the afternoon, thinking of his memoir, convinced that he had plumbed the black depths of her heart.

I left Miss Channing on the outskirts of town, then walked up the hill that ran along the edge of the coastal bluff. At the top, I turned onto Myrtle Street, passing Chatham School as I made my way home.

By then some of the boys had begun to arrive. I could see them lugging their trunks and traveling cases down the long concrete walkway that led to the front of the building. From there I knew they would drag them up the stairs to the dormitory, then empty their contents into the old footlockers that rested at the end of each bed.

Many of the boys have blurred with time, but I can remember Ben Calder, who would later run a large manufacturing enterprise, and Ted Spencer, destined for the New York Stock Exchange, and Larry Bishop, who would go on to West Point and the leading his men toward the shores of Okinawa.

In general, they were from good families, and most of them were good boys who'd merely exhibited a bit of rude behavior their parents sought to correct by placing them at Chatham School. They were reasonably bright, at least adequately studious, and for the most part they later followed the route that had been prepared for them all along, taking up acceptable professions or running either their own businesses or those first established by their fathers or grandfathers. They did not seek a grandly romantic life, nor anticipate one. They had no particular talents, except, perhaps, for that peculiar one that enables us to persevere – often for a lifetime – in things that do not particularly interest us and for which we feel little genuine passion. In later life, after leaving Chatham School, they would do what had always been expected of them, marry, support themselves, have children of their own. I thought them dull and uninspired, while my father saw them as inestimably dutiful and fine.

I was sitting in the swing on our front porch when my father returned from Osterville at around five that afternoon. Coming up the stairs, he spotted me slouched languidly before him, my legs flung over the wooden arm of the swing, a posture he clearly didn't care for.

'So there wasn't much to do at Milford Cottage, I take it?' he asked doubtfully.

'No, there wasn't,' I told him.

'The roof didn't leak?'

'No.'

'You asked Miss Channing that directly?'

'Yes, sir. I told her you were concerned about it. She said it was fine.'

He nodded, still looking at me in that questioning way of his. 'Well, did you do anything at all for Miss Channing?'

'I walked her into town. That's all she wanted me to do.'

He thought a moment, then said, 'Well, get in the car, Henry. I want to make sure she's got everything she needs.'

Had I not gone with my father to Milford Cottage that afternoon, I might never have seen what Miss Channing later captured in her portrait of him, the look on his face as he peered through the red curtains, his eyes fixed on the exotic blue lake that so clearly beckoned to him with an unmistakable sensuousness, but toward which he would not go.

The cottage looked deserted when my father brought the car to a halt in front of it. The front door was securely closed, no lamp yet lighted, despite the fact that it was late afternoon by then, the sun already setting.

'Maybe she's still in the village,' I said as my father and I lingered in the car.

'Could be,' my father said. He stared at the cottage a moment longer, perhaps trying to decide whether to knock at the door or simply return to Chatham, content that he had at least done his duty in dropping by.

Then the door of the cottage opened, and Miss Channing walked out onto the cool grass of the front lawn. She was barefoot, and as she came toward us, I noticed that my father's eyes dropped toward her feet, his lips parting. Then, just as suddenly, he returned to himself, opened the door of the car, and stepped out.

'I have only a moment,' he said a little stiffly and hurriedly, like a man who had more important things to do.

Miss Channing continued to move toward him, her feet padding softly across the grass.

'But I wanted to make sure that everything was in order,' my father added in the same vaguely harried tone. I remained inside the car, but despite its dusty windshield, I could see that she had washed her hair so that it now hung wet and glistening in the darkening air, giving her that appearance of female dishabille that has forever after seemed so beautiful to me.

'I didn't mean to disturb you,' my father continued.

She came to a halt perhaps no more than three feet from where he stood. 'Thank you for sending Henry to me this morning,' she said. 'There was really nothing more for him to do.'

'Yes, he told me that.' My father paused for a moment, lifting his eyes upward slightly as he reached into the pocket of his jacket. 'I wanted to bring you this,' he said, drawing out a large envelope. 'It's the schedule for the school. It tells you when your classes are held, when you take lunch, that sort of thing. You should bring it with you Monday morning. I would have mailed it to you, of course,' my father added quickly as she took the envelope from him, 'as I generally do with the other teachers. But then, you were in Africa, and so … well …'

A silence fell over him and I expected him to break it with a quick good-bye, then get back into the car. Instead, he uttered a question that seemed very odd to me. 'Do you ever plan to have a family of your own, Miss Channing?'

I could tell that she'd never been asked such a question, so ordinary and domestic, nor once considered the way of life it suggested. 'I don't know,' she answered quietly.

'It has its compensations,' my father said, though more to himself, it seemed, than to her. 'Family life.'

She stared at him, puzzled, as I was, by his remark.

He looked suddenly embarrassed by what he'd said, like a man who'd inadvertently revealed some small, sad aspect of himself. Then he spoke hurriedly again, resuming his schoolmaster pose. 'Well, Henry and I had best be getting home. Good night, Miss Channing.'

'Good night,' she answered, the same quizzical look in her eyes as she watched my father stride back to his car, get in, and pull away.

We arrived back home a few minutes later. My mother had prepared one of her pot roasts and throughout the meal my father appeared no different than usual, eating with the same careful attention to manners, dabbing the white cloth napkin at the corners of his mouth after almost every bite.

But when it was over, rather than retiring to the parlor as was his custom, he walked down Myrtle Street to the school, saying only that he had 'a few last minute details' he wanted to look over before classes started the following Monday morning.

My mother didn't question him. Nor did I. But toward sunset, while I was sitting on the front steps of our house, I glanced up and saw my father standing in the school's bell tower, alone, facing out over the village. It was only minutes before nightfall, and a great stillness had settled over everything. I knew that from his place in the bell tower my father could stare out over all the roofs of Chatham and watch the low, unhurried beam of the lighthouse as it swept smoothly across the darkening sea, then over the village and finally beyond it, to the ebony waters of Black Pond.

I have always believed that at that moment he was thinking of Miss Channing, of her oval eyes and wet, glistening hair, seeing her again as he had earlier that afternoon, her bare feet nestled in a cool bed of dark green grass, his eyes closing for a moment as he reveled in that vision, then opening again, focused now upon the village, the school he'd labored all his life to build, the house on Myrtle Street, its small lights, his mind accepting without bitterness or rancor the path that he had taken, along with all the obligations it required, yet recognizing, too, as I believe he must have, that there was a certain shuddering ecstasy he would never know.

# FIVE

I've kept only a single photograph to remind me of what I was, what I did, all that followed after that. It is a grainy photograph, artlessly taken from the roof of one of the buildings across from the courthouse, its vista crosshatched with wooden poles and power lines, but clear enough to show the swarm of men and women who'd gathered around the building that day, their numbers pouring down its wide cement steps. And yet, it wasn't the crowd of people that had caught my attention when I'd first seen it, but a single, crudely written sign thrust up from among them, its message scrawled in huge black letters: *Hang her.*

It is a phrase that has returned to me often over the years, and which can still prompt my deepest speculations. Especially given the fact that on her arrival at Chatham School, no one would have been able to suggest that Miss Channing might ever stir up such violent emotions, or even that her time among us would be any different from that of the many other teachers who'd come and gone over the years.

On that first day, as I stood with the other boys, all of us gathered in front of the school to hear my father's customary opening remarks, I saw her turn onto Myrtle Street, her arms at her sides, no books or papers in them, no overstuffed briefcase dangling from her bare hand.

In all other ways, however, she'd done her best to blend in, wearing a plain white dress with a pleated skirt, and a pair of square-heeled black shoes with large silver buttons. She'd changed her hair as well, so that it was now wound in a tight bun at the back of her neck and secured with an ornate silver clasp. I could almost imagine her standing before the mirror in her bedroom a moment before leaving the cottage, looking herself over, her mind pronouncing an identity that – given the exalted vision of life her father had presented to her – she may well have found rather uninspired: *School marm –*

'Good morning, Miss Channing,' I said as she passed by.

She glanced toward me, smiled, then continued on across the lawn, over to where the other teachers were assembled. I saw a few of them turn and greet her, Mr. Corbett, the math teacher, even going so far as to remove his old felt hat. Later, some of them would tell their fellow villagers that she'd never really fit in, that from the very beginning she'd set herself apart, telling the boys grim and savage tales from her travels with her father, creating dark and bloody landscapes in their young minds. Some went even further, claiming powers of clairvoyance, as if they'd known all along that Miss Channing was destined to be the prime mover in what Professor Peyton would later call with typical hyperbole 'a grim Shakespearean orgy of violence and death'. 'I saw trouble the minute I laid eyes on her,' I heard my history teacher Mrs. Cooper say one afternoon in Warren's Sundries, though I'm sure she'd seen nothing of the kind.

Of course, the one thing that did unquestionably separate Miss Channing from the other teachers at Chatham School was her youth and beauty, and from the way my fellow students watched her as she approached that morning, it was clear that their interest in her went far deeper than the usual curiosity inspired by a new teacher.

'Who's that?' I heard Jamie Phelps ask Winston Bates, poking him with his elbow.

I took the opportunity to demonstrate the insider's knowledge I possessed as the headmaster's son. 'That's the new teacher,' I told them authoritatively. 'She came all the way from Africa.'

'That's where she got that bracelet, I guess,' Jamie said, pointing to the string of brightly colored wooden beads that circled Miss Channing's wrist, the very one Mr. Parsons would later find at the edge of Black Pond, broken by then, the beads scattered across the muddy ground.

As usual on the first day of classes, my father stood at the entrance of the school, the teachers and administrative staff to his left, the boys to his right, all of them dressed in what amounted to the uniform of Chatham School, white shirts, black trousers, gray ties, and black suspenders. Dark gray jackets would be added later in the fall.

'All right, let me have your attention, please,' my father began. 'I want to welcome all of you back to Chatham School. Most of us are very familiar with the routine, as well as each other, but we have a new teacher this year, and I want to introduce her to you.'

He motioned for Miss Channing to join him on the stairs, which she did, moving gracefully beside him, glancing first at her fellow teachers, then at the boys.

'This is Miss Channing,' my father said. 'She has come all the way from Africa to join us here at Chatham School, and she'll be teaching art.'

There was polite applause, then Miss Channing stepped back into the cluster of teachers and listened quietly while my father continued his introductory remarks, going over the necessary administrative details, reminding the boys of various school rules, that there was to be no cheating, no plagiarism, no profanity, no smoking, nor any drinking of alcoholic beverages, as he put it, 'anywhere, anytime, for any reason, ever'.

I have often wondered what came into Miss Channing's mind as she listened to my father recite the rules by which we were all to conduct ourselves at Chatham School, rules that stressed humility, simple honesty, and mutual faith, and which stood four-square against every form of recklessness and betrayal and self-indulgence. How different they must have seemed to the visionary teachings her father had laid down, how deeply rooted in the very kind of humble, uninspired, and profoundly predictable village life he had taught her to revile.

Once my father had finished, the boys already shifting restlessly and muttering impatiently to each other, he clapped his hands together once, then uttered a final remark whose tragic irony he could not have guessed. 'Welcome to another splendid year in the history of Chatham School,' he said.

I entered Miss Channing's class about an hour later.

It was a small room, formerly used to store school furniture and various supplies, but now converted to other purposes. It was not physically connected to the school, but stood apart from it in a little courtyard to the rear. Still, it seemed adequate enough, with three long tables lined up one behind the other in front of the much smaller one that served as Miss Channing's desk. On the far wall, half a dozen gray aprons hung from wooden pegs beside a metal cabinet upon which someone had painted the words ART SUPPLIES in large white letters. In the far corner a few wooden sculpting pedestals had been stacked base to base, the legs of the upper pedestals stretching almost to the room's tin ceiling.

As for art, there were portraits of George Washington and Abraham Lincoln, along with a framed photograph of the current president, Calvin Coolidge.

There were only five of us in the class, but we scattered ourselves widely throughout the room. Ralph Sherman and Miles Clayton took possession of the rear table, Biff Conners and Jack Slaughter the middle one, leaving the front table to me.

Miss Channing didn't smile at us or say a word of welcome as we entered the room. She'd already placed one of the sculpting pedestals in front of her, and as we filed in, she began to knead the clay gently, hardly glancing up from it as we took our seats. Then, once we'd taken our places, she drew her hands from the clay and looked at us, her eyes moving from one boy to another. She did not acknowledge me in any way.

'I've never taught art,' she said. 'Or been taught it by anyone else.'

Her fingers moved over the clay's wet surface, shaping it with slow, graceful strokes as she searched for her next remark.

'When my father died, I went to live with my uncle and his family in Africa,' she said finally. 'He had a mission near a village where the natives lived in wooden huts. It was just a clearing in the plain. The people who lived in the village did all their cooking in their huts, and there was no way for the smoke to get out except through a small hole in the roof. When they came out of their huts in the morning, a sheet of smoke trailed behind them.' Her eyes lifted toward us, and I saw them take on a certain wonder and delight. It was as if in telling stories, she could find a voice to teach in, a way of reaching us. 'Like wings that dissolved in the light,' she said.

'That's where I learned to paint.' She was kneading the clay more quickly now, in short, quick thrusts. 'In Africa.' She stopped suddenly and settled her eyes upon us. I could tell that a thought had just occurred to her, that in the very course of talking to us she'd discovered something. 'That's where I learned that to be a painter or a sculptor, you have to change your senses,' she said. 'Switch them around, so that you *see* with your fingertips and *feel* with your eyes.'

I didn't see Miss Channing again until much later that same day. The last class had been dismissed for nearly an hour, and I was busily doing my assigned tasks around the school.

Under my father's leadership, it was the policy of Chatham School to combine academics with physical labor, and so from the time of his arrival, each boy was assigned various chores. Some of the boys swept the classrooms and the dormitory, some washed the sheets and blankets, some worked on the grounds, pruning shrubbery or mowing grass or maintaining the playing fields. In the winter everyone shoveled snow or took turns unloading coal.

On that particular afternoon it was my job to return any books that lay on the library tables to their proper shelves, carefully keeping them in order according to the Dewey decimal system Mrs. Cartwright, the school librarian, had established. After that I was to dust the bookshelves with the old feather duster my mother had donated to the school after buying a new one at Mayflower's a month before.

It was nearly four by the time I'd finished. Mrs. Cartwright surveyed the now-empty tables and ran a finger over the top of one of the bookshelves. 'Very good, Henry,' she said when she found it clear of dust.

With that statement of satisfaction I was released for the remainder of the afternoon.

I remember the feeling of relief that swept over me each time I ran down the stairs, bolted through the broad double doors of Chatham School, and raced out into the open air. I don't know why I felt the weight of Chatham School so heavily, or so yearned to be rid of it, for it was by no means a prison, my father by no means a tyrant. And yet, in my raw youth, the days seemed to drag along behind me like a ball and chain. Every stricture burned like a lash, and sometimes, at night, I would feel as if my whole life lay smothered beneath a thick blanket of petty obligations and worn-out rules.

Miss Channing's class had offered a certain relief from that musty atmosphere, so that even on that first afternoon I found that I looked forward to the next one in a way that I'd never looked forward to Mr. Crawford's Latin lectures or the interminable recitations of Mrs. Dillard's history class. There'd been a freshness to her approach, a sense of something less hindered by the ancient forms of instruction, something young, as I was young, already free in a way I one day hoped to be.

As I came out of the school, already vaguely considering a quick stroll into the village, perhaps even a secret cigarette behind the bowling alley, I saw Miss Channing sitting on one of the wooden benches that rested near the edge of the coastal bluff. Normally it would not have occurred to me to approach a teacher outside of class, but she already seemed less a teacher to me than a comrade of some sort, both of us momentarily stranded at Chatham School, but equally destined to go beyond it someday.

She didn't appear surprised when I drifted past her, took hold of the rail that stretched along the edge of the bluff, and stared out to sea, my back to her, pretending that I hadn't noticed her sitting directly behind me.

'Hello, Henry,' she said.

I turned toward her. 'Oh, Miss Channing,' I said. 'I didn't see—'

'It's a marvelous view, isn't it?'

'Yes, it is.'

I glanced back over the bluff. Below, the sea was empty, but a few people strolled along the beach or lounged beneath striped umbrellas. I tried to see the view through her eyes. From behind me, I heard her say, 'It reminds me of the Lido.'

'The Lido?'

'A beach near Venice,' she said. 'It was always filled with striped umbrellas. The changing rooms were painted with the same stripes. Yellow. Bright yellow.' She shook her head. 'Actually, it doesn't remind me of the Lido at all,' she said, her voice a shade lower, as if now talking to me in confidence. 'It's just that I was thinking of it when you came up.'

'Why?' I asked, no other question occurring to me.

'Because my father died on the Lido,' Miss Channing said. 'That's what I was really thinking of just now.'

In later life we forget what it was like, the sweetness and exhilaration of being spoken to for the first time as something other than a child. And yet that was what I felt at that moment, sweetness and exhilaration, a sense that some part of my boyhood had been peeled away and cast aside, the man beneath allowed to take his first uneasy breaths.

'I'm sorry,' I said, immediately using a phrase I'd heard so many times on similar occasions.

Her expression did not change. 'There's nothing to be sorry for, really. He lived a good life.'

I could see the love she'd had for him and wondered what it was like to have had a father you admired.

'What did he do?' I asked.

'He was a writer. A travel writer.'

'And you traveled with him?'

'From the time I was four years old. That was when my mother died. After that we traveled all the time.'

As if my father had suddenly assumed my shape, I asked a question that seemed more his than mine. 'What about school?'

'My father was my school,' Miss Channing answered. 'He taught me everything.' She rose and joined me at the rail, the two of us now looking out over the beach below. 'He believed in going his own way.' She paused a moment, a line coming to her, one I later read in her father's book, and which she now repeated to me.

'An artist should follow only his passions,' she said. 'All else is a noose around his neck.'

Now, when I recall that line, the calm with which she said it, I feel its dreadful premonition, and in my mind see an old car hurling down a weedy, overgrown embankment, a figure turning at the water's edge, eyes wide, aghast, uncomprehending. And after that, forever after that, the long, unfading echo of her scream.

# SIX

In the years following Miss Channing's trial, my father assembled a small collection of materials concerning the Chatham School Affair, one he bequeathed to me at his death, and which I've been unable to discard. I've given other things away – my mother's knitting needles, my father's quill pen, stacks of books to the village library. But my father's collection has remained intact, tucked into the bottom corner of the bookshelf in my office, all but hidden by the floor lamp that stands in front of it. It is a slender archive, especially given the events it summons up. Madness and suicide and murder, the forlorn world left in their wake. And yet there are times when my attention lingers on it with a curious nostalgia. For I know that it holds the defining moment of my youth.

It consists of nothing more than a folder containing a single copy of the Chatham School Annual for 1927, a few newspaper clippings and photographs. There is even one of Sarah Doyle, though it was unintended. In the picture she is rushing down the little walkway beside the school. Her back is to the camera, and snow is falling all around her, gathering on her long, dark cape, while the boys in the yard – the real focus of the picture – playfully heave packed snowballs at each other, my father on the front steps of the school, arms folded over his chest, looking on with mock disapproval.

To these few things my father added three books, two of them directly related to what happened on Black Pond, one considerably less so.

The first is Mr. Parsons' memoir, the work he quickly put together and had privately published just after the trial. As a book, it leaves a great deal to be desired. In fact, it is little more than an assortment of quotations from the trial transcript awkwardly strung together by Mr. Parsons' own rather tedious narrative.

The second volume is more detailed. Titled *A Mortal Flaw*, it was written by one Wilfred M. Peyton, a professor of moral philosophy at Oberlin College. Scarcely a hundred pages long, it is essentially an extended essay published in 1929 by a small religious press, and hampered not only by

Professor Peyton's harsh, sermonizing tone, but by the way he singled out Miss Channing as the true villain in what he insists on calling – over and over again, like words from a warlock's chant – 'The Black Pond Murders'. Such was his rage against Miss Channing that whenever he spoke of her, it was with an Old Testament prophet's infuriated rebuke. 'To her father, she was "Libby",' he wrote in a typical passage, 'for by such endearment did he call her in her youth. But to the ages she should be more rightly known as Elizabeth, a cold and formal name that must be included among those of other women like herself: Delilah, Salome, and Jezebel.'

Of the three volumes of my father's archive, Professor Peyton's was the only one he clearly hated. So much so that he scribbled angry notes throughout its text, sometimes disputing a small, inconsequential fact (noting, for example, that the school library had three thousand books, not the mere two thousand attributed by Peyton), sometimes quarreling with an interpretation, but always seeking to undermine the book's authority to those who might later read it.

The reason my father so detested Professor Peyton's book is obvious. For it was not only an attack upon Miss Channing, but upon Chatham School itself, as an 'indulgent, coddling retreat for wealthy, dissolute boys.' Indeed, at the end of the book Professor Peyton flatly concluded that 'the unspeakable outrage which occurred on the otherwise tranquil surface of Black Pond on 29 May 1927 was emblematic of the moral relativism and contempt for established authority that has emerged in educational theory during the last two decades, and of which Chatham School is only the most odious example.' It never surprised me, of course, that this was a passage my father had underlined in black ink, then appended his own heartrending cry of 'NO! NO! NO!'

But for all its bluster and moral posturing, for all the pain it caused my father, *A Mortal Flaw* was, at last, a completely dismissible book, one which, after I read it, I never found the slightest need to pick up again.

I can't say the same for the final volume in my father's collection, however. For it was a book I have returned to many times, as if looking for some answer to what happened on Black Pond that day, perhaps even for what might have prevented it, some way to sedate our hearts, make them satisfied with less.

The third book is entitled *A View from the Window*, and on the back of the book's cover there is a photograph of its author, Jonathan Channing, a tall, somber man in his late forties, staring at the camera from the courtyard of the Louvre.

'You can take it if you want,' Miss Channing said the day she lent it to me.

It was late on a Friday afternoon, the first week of class now ended. My father had sent me to Miss Channing's classroom with a box of art books he'd picked up at a Boston bookstore the day before. Always somewhat impulsive, he'd been eager to get Miss Channing's opinion of them before turning them over to Mrs. Cartwright in the library on Monday morning.

She'd been standing at the cabinet, putting away her supplies, when I came through the door.

'My father wanted you to take a look at these.' I lifted the box slightly. 'Art books.'

She closed the door of the cabinet and walked to her desk. 'Let's see them,' she said.

I brought them to her, then watched while she looked through each book in turn, slowly turning the pages, pausing to gaze at the paintings she found reproduced there, sometimes mentioning the name of the gallery in which a painting now hung. 'This is in Florence,' she'd say, or 'I saw this at the Prado.' She turned the book toward me. 'This one always frightened me. What do you think, Henry?'

I looked at the painting. It showed a little girl with stringy blond hair, crouched before an enormous tree, its jagged limbs stretching to both sides of the canvas, the gnarled limbs hung with surreal images of floating heads and body parts, the colors livid, greens the color of bile, reds the color of fresh blood. Staring at the tree, the child appeared frozen by the terror and immensity of what she faced.

'Have you ever felt like her?' Miss Channing asked me quietly, her gaze fixed on the illustration, rife with its malicious and chaotic gore.

I shook my head. 'I don't think so, Miss Channing.' Which was true then, though it is no longer so.

She turned the book back around, leafing through it once again, until she came upon a photograph of the courtyard at the Louvre. 'There's a picture of my father standing here,' she told me. 'They used it for his book.'

'His book?'

'Yes,' Miss Channing said. 'He was a travel writer. He wrote a great many articles, but only one book.'

Out of mere politeness I said, 'I'd like to read it sometime.'

She took this as a genuine expression of interest, opened the drawer of her desk, and drew out a single volume. 'This is it,' she said as she handed it to me. 'The picture I mentioned is on the back.'

I turned the book over and looked at the photograph. It showed a tall, slender man, handsome in a roguish sort of way, dressed in dark trousers and a white dinner jacket, his hair slicked back in the fashion of the time, but with a wilder touch added in the form of a single black curl that fell just over the corner of his right eye.

'I was ten years old when that picture was taken,' Miss Channing said. 'We'd just gotten back from a visit to Rouen. My father was interested in the cathedral there.'

'Was he religious?'

'Not at all,' she said with a smile I found intriguing.

I lifted the book toward her, but she made no move to reclaim it.

'You can take it if you want,' she said.

I had not really wanted to read her father's book, but I took it with me anyway, reluctantly, unable to find an acceptable way to refuse it.

As it turned out, I read it that same afternoon, sitting alone on the coastal bluff, the other boys of Chatham School either engaged in a game of football on the playing field or gathered outside Quilty's Ice Cream Parlor in the village.

In earlier years I'd tried to be one of them. I'd joined them in their games, even participated in the general mischief, playing pranks on teachers or making up nicknames for them. But in the end it hadn't worked. For I was still the headmaster's son, a position that made it impossible for them to accept me as just another boy at Chatham School, one with whom they could be as vulgar and irreverent as they pleased, calling my father 'Old Grizzlewald', as I knew they often did.

Though never exactly ostracized, I'd finally turned bookish and aloof, a boy who could often be found reading in the porch swing or at the edge of the playing field, a 'scholarly lad' as my father sometimes called me, though in a tone that never struck me as entirely complimentary.

Recalling the boy I was in those days, so solitary and isolated, I've sometimes thought myself one of the victims of the Chatham School Affair, my life no less deeply wounded by the crime that rocked Black Pond. Then, as if to bring me back to what really happened there, my mind returns me to a little girl on a windy beach. She is running against the wind, an old kite whipping left and right behind her. Finally it lifts and she watches it joylessly, her eyes wreathed in that forsakenness that would never leave them after that. Remembering how she looked at that moment in her life, I instantly recognize who Black Pond's victims truly were, and in that captured moment perceive the terror I escaped, the full depth of a loss that was never mine.

I learned a great deal about Miss Channing the afternoon I read her father's book. I learned about her father too: the fact that he'd been born into a privileged Massachusetts family, educated at Harvard College, and worked as a journalist in Boston during the years following his graduation.

At twenty-three he'd married the former Julia Mason Rockbridge, also from a distinguished New England family. The two had taken up residence on Marlborough Street, near Boston Common, and in 1904 had a daughter, Elizabeth Rockbridge Channing. After that Mr. Channing continued to work for the *Boston Globe*, while his wife performed the usual functions of an upper-class woman of that time. Then, in the fall of 1908, Julia Channing fell ill. She lingered for some weeks, but finally died in January 1909, leaving four-year-old Elizabeth entirely to her father's care.

More than anything, *A View from the Window* is a day-to-day record of the years Miss Channing lived and traveled with her father, a period during which they'd never actually had a fixed abode of any kind, nor any permanent attachments, save for each other. The purpose of such a rootless life, Mr. Channing's purpose in insisting upon it, is revealed in the opening paragraphs of his narrative:

> *After my wife's death, to stay in Boston seemed doom to me. I walked about our house on Marlborough Street, gazing at the many luxuries she had acquired over the years, the velvet curtains, the Tiffany lamp, and a host of other appendages that, like Julia, were elegant in their way, but for which I could no longer feel any enduring affection. And so I decided to move on, to live in the world at large, to acquaint my daughter Libby with its most spacious and inaccessible climes.*
>
> *As to my reasoning in this matter, I have never hidden it, nor wished to hide it. I chose to educate my daughter as I saw fit. And with what purpose in mind? For none other than that she should live a life freed from the constrictive influence of any particular village or nation, nor ever be bound by the false constraints of custom, ideology, or blood.*

And yet, despite its grandly stated purpose, *A View from the Window* remained essentially a travelogue, though one that detailed not only sights and sounds and historical backgrounds, but the life Miss Channing and her father had lived as together they'd roamed the world.

It had been a vagabond life, the book made clear, a life lived continually in transit, with nothing to give it direction save for Mr. Channing's furious determination to teach his daughter his own unique philosophy of life, relentlessly driving it home by escorting young Libby, as he called her, to bizarre and tragic sites, locations he'd selected for the lessons he planned to teach.

Reading that philosophy on the bluff that afternoon, I felt myself utterly swept away by a view of life so different from my father's, from the governing assumptions of Chatham and of Chatham School, from any way of seeing things I'd ever encountered before, that I felt as if I'd suddenly entered a new galaxy, where, according to Mr. Channing, there should be 'no rules for the rule of life', nor any hindrance whatsoever to a man's unbridled passions.

It was a world directly opposite to the one I'd been taught to revere, everything reversed or turned topsy-turvy. Self-control became a form of slavery, vows and contracts mere contrivances to subdue the spirit, the moral law no more absolute than a passing fad. More than anything, it was a world in which even the darkest evils were given a strange and somber dignity:

*We took a boat from Sorrento, and disembarked a short time later at Marina Grande, on the eastern coast of Capri. The town was festive and welcoming, and Libby took great delight in its scents and in the winding labyrinth of its streets, skipping playfully ahead of me from time to time. She seemed captivated by the nearly tropical lushness of the place, particularly with the luxuriousness of its vegetation, forever plucking leaves and petals from the shrubs and flowers we encountered on the way.*

*But I had brought her to Capri for more than an afternoon's lark. Nor was it the quaint village byways and varied plant life I had brought her here to see. Mine was another purpose, as well as another destination, one I could but indistinctly glimpse from the town's narrow pathways.*

*And so we journeyed upward and upward for over an hour, baked in a nearly blinding summer heat, through the spectacular flowered hedges that lined both sides of the earthen walkway. The smell of flowers was everywhere, as were the sounds of small lizards, dozens of them, scurrying through the brush or darting like thin green ribbons across our path.*

*The walk was arduous, but the great ruin of the Villa di Giovi made infamous by Suetonius, loomed enticingly above, beckoning me with the same sinister and mysterious call the sirens had issued to Odysseus from the Bay of Naples far below. For like the ancient world of those mythic seamen, the place I journeyed to that morning had been bloody and perverse.*

*And yet there was something glorious here as well, something incontestably free in the wild pleasure gardens the emperor had designed, the human bodies he'd formed into living sculptures, even in the heedless and unrestrained delight he'd taken in their libidinous show. For it was in this place that Tiberius had exalted physical sensuality over spiritual aridness, breaking every known taboo, pairing boys with boys, girls with girls, covering his own wrinkled frame with the smooth bodies of the very young. And though hideous and unnatural as it might seem, still it remained the pagan world's most dramatic gesture toward the truly illimitable.*

*And so I brought Libby here, to walk with her within the bowers of this ruined yet still magnificent grove, and once there, I sat with her in full view of the infamous Salto di Tiberio and spoke to her of what life should be, the heights it should reach, the passions it should embrace, all this said and done in the hope that she might come to live it as a bird on the wing. For life is best lived at the edge of folly.*

An evening shade had fallen over the bluff, the deserted beach beneath it, the whole small realm of Chatham, when I finished *A View from the Window.* I tucked the book under my arm and wandered back down Myrtle Street toward home. On the way I saw Danny Sheen loping across the playing field, and Charlie Patterson lugging a battered trunk along the front walkway of Chatham School. Upstairs the lights were on, and I knew the boys were either studying in the library or talking quietly in the common room, that soon the bell would call them to their dinner, my father dining with them as he always did on Friday evenings, rising at the end of the meal, ringing his little bell, then dismissing them with some quotation he hoped might serve them in the years to come.

Thinking of all that, Myrtle Street like a flat, turgid stream flowing sluggishly ahead of me, I realized that I'd never known any way of life other than the one defined by Chatham School, nor felt that any other might be open to me. Certainly I'd never conceived of my destiny as anything but decided. I would graduate from Chatham School, go to college, make my living, have a family. I would do what my father had done, and his father before him. A different date marked my birth, and a different date would mark my death. Other than that, I would live as they had lived, die as they had died, find whatever joy or glory there might be in life along the same beaten path they'd trod before me through the misty ages.

But as I made my way home that evening, none of that seemed any longer as settled as it once had. The restlessness that seized me from time to time, the sullenness into which I fell, the way I cringed as my father offered his trusty platitudes to the assembled boys, the whole inchoate nature of my discontent began to take a certain shape and definition so that for the first time, I dimly began to perceive what I really wanted out of life.

It was simple. I wanted to be free. I wanted to answer only to myself, to strike out toward something. I didn't know at that moment how to gain my freedom, or what to do with it. I knew only that I had discovered what I wanted, and that with that discovery a great pall had lifted, a door opened. I didn't know where I was going, only that I had to go in a different direction than my father had gone, or that any of the other boys of Chatham School would likely go.

I ran down Myrtle Street, breathless, my mind glittering in a world of fresh ideas. Though night had nearly fallen by the time I reached home, it felt like dawn to me. I remember bounding up the stairs, stretching out on my bed, and reading Mr. Channing's book again, cover to cover. One sentence held for all time: Life is best lived at the edge of folly.

I remember that a fierce exhilaration seized me as I read and reread that line in my bedroom beneath the eaves, that it seemed to illuminate everything I had ever felt. Even now it strikes me that no darkness ever issued from a brighter flame.

# PART II

# SEVEN

In old age and semiretirement I'd finally come to a time in life when I never expected to think of her again. By then years had gone by with little to remind me of her, save the quick glimpse of an old woman moving heavily across a wide wooden porch or rocking slowly in her chair as I drove by. And so Miss Channing had at last grown distant. When I thought of her at all, it was as a faded thing, like a flower crushed within the pages of an ancient, crumbling book. Then, suddenly, my own life now drawing to a close, she came back to me by a route I'd never have expected.

I'd come to my office early that morning, the village street still empty, a fog sweeping in from the sea, curling around the corner of Dalmatian's Cafe and nestling under the benches outside the town hall. I was sitting at my desk, handling the few cases that still came my way, when I suddenly looked up and saw an old man standing at my door.

'Morning, Henry,' he said.

It was Clement Boggs, dressed as he always was, in a flannel shirt and baggy pants, an old hat pulled down nearly to his ears. I'd known Clement all my life, though never very well. He'd been one of the local rowdies who'd smoked in front of the bowling alley, the type my father had always warned me against, a rough, lower-class boy who'd later managed to pull himself together, make a good life, even put away a considerable fortune. I'd handled quite a few of his legal affairs, mostly closings in recent years, as he'd begun to divest himself of the property he'd accumulated throughout his life.

He sat down in one of the chairs in front of my desk, groaning slightly as he did so. 'I've got an offer on some land I bought a long time back,' he told me. 'Out on Plymouth Road.' He hesitated, as if the words themselves held all the terror, rather than the events that had happened there. ''Round Black Pond. The old Milford cottage.'

As if I'd suddenly been swept back to that terrible summer day, I heard Mr. Parsons say, *You often went to Milford Cottage, didn't you, Henry?* My answer simple, forthright, as all of them had been: *Yes, sir, I did.*

435

Clement watched me closely. 'You all right, Henry?'

I nodded. 'Yes,' I said. 'I'm fine.'

He didn't seem convinced, but continued anyway. 'Well, like I said, I've got an offer on that land 'round Black Pond.' He leaned back slowly, watching me intently, no doubt wondering at the scenes playing in my mind, the swirling water, a face floating toward me from the green depths. 'He wants to know if he can get a zoning variance. I thought you might look into it, see if the town might give him one.'

Clement sat only a few feet from me, but he seemed far way; Mr. Parsons bore in upon me so closely I could almost feel his breath upon my face. *When were you last on Black Pond?* Matter-of-factly, with no hint of passion, and certainly none of concealment, my answer came: *On May 29, 1927. That would be a Sunday? Yes.*

'You'll have to go out there, of course,' Clement said, his gaze leveled upon me steadily, his head cocked to the right, so that for an instant I wondered if he might also be reliving my day in the witness box, listening once again to Mr. Parsons' questions as they'd resounded through the crowded courtroom. *What happened on Black Pond that day?*

Clement's eyes narrowed, as if against a blinding light, and I knew that he could sense the upheaval in my mind no matter how hard I labored to contain it. 'I don't guess you've been out that way in quite some time,' he said.

'Not in years.'

'Looks the same.'

'The same as what?'

My question appeared to throw him into doubt as to what his answer should be. 'Same as it did in the old days,' he replied.

I said nothing, but I could feel myself helplessly returning to the days he meant. I saw an old car moving through the darkness, two beams of yellow light engulfing me as it came to a halt, a figure staring at me from behind the wheel, motioning now, whispering, *Get in.*

'Well, let me know what you find out,' Clement said, rising from his chair. 'About the variance, I mean.'

'I'll look into it right away.'

Once at the door, he turned back to face me. 'You don't have to stay out there for long, of course,' he told me, his way of lightening the load. 'Just get an idea of what the town might think of somebody developing it.'

I nodded.

He seemed unsure of what he should say next, or if it should be me to whom he said it. Finally, he spoke again. 'There's one more thing, Henry. The money. From the land, I mean. I want it to go to somebody in particular.' He paused a moment, then said her name. 'Alice Craddock.'

She swam into my mind, an old woman, immensely fat, her hair gray and bedraggled, her mind unhinged, the butt of a cruel school-yard poem I'd heard repeated through the years:

> Alice Craddock,
> Locked in the paddock
> Where's your mama gone?

'It just seems right that she should get whatever the land out there brings,' Clement said. 'I'm an old man. I don't need it. And they say Alice has come on bad times.'

I saw Alice as a middle-aged woman, slack-jawed, growing fat on potato chips and candy bars, her eyes dull and lightless, a gang of boys chasing after her, pointing, laughing, until Mr. Wallace chased them away, his words trailing after them as they fled down the street: *Leave her alone. She's suffered enough.*

'Not much left of what was given her,' Clement said.

'Not much, no.'

He shrugged. 'Well, maybe this can help a little,' he said, then turned and walked through the door.

Once he'd gone, I went to the window and looked out. I could see him trudging toward the dusty old truck he'd parked across the street. But I could see him, too, as he'd looked years before, during the days of the trial, the way he'd stood with his cronies on the courthouse steps as Miss Channing had been rushed down them, jeering at her as she swept past, the dreadful word I'd heard drop from his mouth as he glared at her: *Whore.*

It was not something I'd ever expected to do, see Milford Cottage again, feel the allure I'd known there, the passions it had stirred. But once Clement's old truck had pulled away, I felt myself drawn back to it, not in a mood of youthful reminiscence, but as someone forced to look at what he'd done, view the bodies in their mangled ruin, a criminal returning to the scene of his crime.

And so I drove out to Milford Cottage only an hour later. It was still early, the streets deserted, with only a few people having breakfast at Dalmatian's Cafe. Driving along Main Street, it seemed to me that the village had changed very little since the days of Miss Channing's trial, when the crowds had swirled around the courthouse or milled about in front of Quilty's and Mayflower's, muttering of murder and betrayal.

Once outside the village, I followed the road that led along the seashore.

There were bogs and marshes on either side, just as there'd always been, and from time to time I spotted a gull circling overhead, a crow skirting just over a distant line of trees.

A mile out of the village I turned onto Plymouth Road, taking the same route my father had taken the afternoon we'd first driven down it together, Miss Channing in the front seat, I in the back with her two valises. The forest thickness pressed in upon me no less thickly than it had that day, the green vines slapping once again against both sides of the car.

As I rounded the last curve, Milford Cottage swept into view.

It looked much smaller than it had the last time I'd seen it. But that wasn't the only change time had wrought. For the cottage had gone completely to ruin during the intervening years, the tar roof now ripped and curled, the screen door torn from its rusty hinges, the yard a field of weed and bramble, the whole structure so weathered and dilapidated that it seemed hardly able to hold its own against the changeless waters of Black Pond.

I stared at it, reviewing the story of its abandonment. I knew that no one would ever live there again, no young woman would ever rearrange the lanterns inside it or hang her father's picture on its walls. From the trial transcripts so generously quoted in Mr. Parsons' book, I knew what had been said in its small rooms, what had been felt as well. But I also knew that there'd been other voices, too, other feelings, things Mr. Parsons, for all his effort, had been unable to unearth. As if her lips were at my ear, I heard Miss Channing say, *I can't go on.* Then my reply, *What can I do to help?*

For a time I peered at the front door that had barred my father's way that first afternoon, remembering how Miss Channing had stood behind him, waiting silently in the rain as he'd struggled to unlock it. Then I walked up to it, gave a gentle push, and watched as it drifted back, revealing the emptiness inside.

I stepped into the cottage, my eyes moving along the leaf-strewn floor, settling for a moment on the old fireplace with its heap of gray ash. I heard Miss Channing say, *Get rid of this,* and closed my eyes abruptly, as if against a vision I expected to appear before them at any moment, Miss Channing standing at the hearth, staring into it with a steely glare, feeding letters into its leaping flames.

When I opened them again, the cottage was as empty as before, with nothing to give it sound or movement but the drama playing in my mind.

I glanced into the vacant bedroom, to where a little wooden bookshelf had once rested beside her bed. I could remember the books I'd seen collected there, the words of her father's heroes bound in dark vellum: Byron, Shelley, Keats.

A gust of wind slammed against the cottage, rattling what remained of its few dusty windowpanes. I saw a bare limb rake across the glass, a bony finger motioning me outside. And so I nodded silently, like someone agreeing to be led into another chamber, then walked to the back of the cottage, out the rear door, and across the yard to the water's edge.

The great willow still rose above the pond, the one Miss Channing had so often painted, its long, brown tendrils drooping toward the surface of the water. I wondered how many times during her first weeks in Chatham she'd stood beneath it, remembering the poems her father had so often read to her, sometimes in the very places where they'd been written, odes to nightingales and Grecian urns, pleasure domes and crystal seas, women who walk in beauty like the night. But there'd been other things as well, other titles on the shelf beside her bed, the speculations of Mesmer, the visions of Madame Blavatsky, the gruesome ravings of de Sade.

*All of that*, I thought, standing now where she had stood, my eyes fixed upon the motionless surface of Black Pond, *All of that was in her mind*. Then I looked out across the pond, and heard a voice, cold, lean, mouthing its grim question: *Do you want them dead?*

I was there when she saw him for the first time. Or, at least, I think I was. Of course, she'd already glimpsed him with the other teachers or disappearing into a classroom down the hall. But I don't think she'd actually *seen* him before, that is, picked him out from among the others, noticed something that distinguished him and drew her attention toward him more intently.

It was toward the middle of October, near the end of Miss Channing's first month at Chatham School. She was standing behind a sculptor's pedestal, as she often did, though this time there was no mound of clay. We were only to imagine it there, she said, shape it only in our minds.

'When you imagine the muscles, you have to feel their power,' she told us. 'You have to feel what is *beneath* the figure you're working with. What is *inside* it.' She picked up a large book she'd previously placed on her desk and turned it toward us, already open to the page she'd selected to illustrate her point.

'This is a picture of Rodin's *Balzac*.' She began to walk along the side of the room, the book still open, pressing the picture toward us. 'You can't see Balzac's body,' she added. 'He's completely covered in a long, flowing cape.'

She continued to move along the edge of the room, the boys now shifting in their seats to keep her in view. 'But if you opened the cape,' Miss

Channing went on, 'you'd see this.' With a purposely swift gesture, she turned the page, and there before us, in full view, was a monstrously fat and bulging Balzac, immense and naked, his belly drooping hugely toward his feet.

'This figure is actually under the cape,' she said. 'Rodin added the cape only *after* he'd sculpted the body beneath it. The actual body of Balzac.'

She closed the book and for a moment stared at us silently. Then she lifted her hands and wriggled her fingers. 'You must imagine what's *beneath* the skin of the figure you're working on. Feel the muscles stretch and contract.' She swept her hands back until they came to a halt at the sides of her face. 'Even the smallest muscles are important, like the tiny ones that open and close your eyes.'

We stared at her in shocked silence, stunned by the naked figure she'd just displayed to us, but awed by it as well.

'Remember all that when you start to work on your figures in class tomorrow,' Miss Channing said just as the bell sounded our dismissal.

It was her last class of the day, and I remember thinking that her first month of teaching at Chatham School had gone quite well. Even my father had commented upon it, mentioning to my mother over dinner one evening that Miss Channing had 'gotten a grip on things right away', that teaching seemed to 'fit her nature'.

I was already at the door that afternoon, the other boys rushing by, when I turned back and saw her alone, standing behind her sculpting pedestal. It seemed the perfect time to approach her.

'Miss Channing,' I said, coming toward her slowly.

She looked up. 'Yes, Henry?'

I took her father's book from my bag and held it out to her. 'I thought it was great,' I said. 'I've read it quite a few times. Even copied things out of it. I thought he was right about everything. About "living on the run."'

She did not take the book, and I felt certain that she could sense the life I craved, how much I needed to bound over the walls of Chatham School, race into the open spaces, live on the edge of folly. For a moment she seemed to be evaluating me, asking herself if I had the will to see it through, possessed the naked ruthlessness such freedom might require.

'It isn't easy to live the way my father did,' she said, her blue eyes focused powerfully. 'Most people can't do it.'

'But everything else ... the way people *do* live ...' I stammered. 'I don't want to live like my father does. I don't want to be like him ... a fool.'

She didn't seem in the least shocked by my ruthless evaluation of my father. 'How do you want to be, Henry?'

'Open to things. To new things.'

She watched me a moment longer, and I could see that she was think-ing of me in a way that no one else ever had, not merely as the boy I was, but as the man I might someday be. 'I've been noticing your drawing,' she said. 'It's really quite good, you know.'

I knew no such thing. 'It is?'

'There's a lot of feeling in it.'

I knew how strangely twisted my drawings were, how wreathed in a vampire blackness, but it had never occurred to me that such character-istics added up to 'feeling', that they might spring from something deep within me.

I shrugged. 'There's not much to draw around here. Just the sea. The lighthouse. Stuff like that.'

'But you put something into them, Henry,' Miss Channing said. 'Something extra. You should get a sketchbook and take it around with you. That's what I did in Africa. I found that just having it along with me made me look at things differently.' She waited for a response, then continued when I failed to offer one. 'Anyway, when you've done a few more drawings, bring them in and let me look at them.'

I'd never been complimented by a teacher before. Certainly none had ever suggested that I had a talent for anything but moodiness and soli-tude. To the other teachers I had always been a disappointment, someone tolerated because I was the headmaster's son, a boy of limited prospects and little ambition, a 'decent lad', as I'd once heard my father describe me in a tone that had struck me as deeply condescending, a way of saying that I was nothing, and never would be.

'All right, Miss Channing,' I said, immensely lifted by her having seen something in me the other teachers had not seen.

'Good,' she said, then returned to her work as I headed down the aisle and out the door.

I walked into the courtyard and drew in a deep, invigorating breath. It was autumn now, and the air was quite brisk. But my mood had been so heated up by Miss Channing's high regard that I could not feel its hint of winter chill.

A few hours later I took my seat for the final class of the day. I glanced out the window, then at the pictures that hung on the wall. Shakespeare. Wordsworth. Keats. My attention was still drifting aimlessly from one face to another when I heard the steady *thump ... thump ... thump* of the approaching teacher's wooden cane, soft and rhythmic, like the distant muffled beating of a drum.

Was he handsome, the man who came into the room seconds later, dressed, as always, in a chalk-smeared jacket and corduroy pants?

441

Yes, I suppose he was. In his own particular way, of course.

And yet it never surprised me that the people of the village later marveled that such fierce emotions could have stormed about in a so visibly broken frame.

He was tall and slender, but there was something in his physical arrangement that always struck me as subtly off kilter, the sense of a leaning tower, of something shattered at its base. For although he always stood erect, his back pressed firmly against the wall of his classroom while he spoke to us, his body often appeared to be of another mind, his left shoulder a few degrees lower than the right, his head cocked slightly to the left, like a bust whose features were classically formed yet eerily marred, perhaps distorted, the product of an unsteady hand.

Still, it was his face that people found most striking, the ragged black beard, lined here and there with gray, and the dark, deep-set eyes. But more particularly the cream-colored scar that ran crookedly from just beneath his left eye, widening and deepening until it finally disappeared into the thick bramble of his beard.

His name was Leland Reed.

I often recall my first glimpse of him. It was a summer afternoon several years before. I'd been slouched on the front porch of our house when I looked up to see a man coming down the street. He walked slowly, his shoulders dipping left and right like a little boat in a gently swelling sea. At last he came to a halt at the short metal gate that separated our house from the street. 'Good afternoon,' he said. 'I'm looking for Mr. Arthur Griswald.'

'That's my father,' I told him.

He did not open the gate, but merely peered at me like someone who could see both my past and my future in a single glimpse, how I had been reared, what I would become as a result.

'He's inside the house,' I said, stung by his inspection.

'Thank you,' Mr. Reed answered.

Seconds later I heard my father say, 'Ah, Mr. Reed,' as he opened the door and let him in. Not long after that I found my father and Mr. Reed in the parlor, my father so engrossed in interviewing Mr. Reed that he never noticed me standing at the door, listening with a little boy's curiosity for the world of men.

Mr. Reed had come from Boston, as it turned out, where he'd taught at the Boston Latin School for the past three years. He'd grown tired of the city, he said, then went on to provide other details in a self-confident, manly voice, but with something distant in it, too, a voice that later struck me as somewhat similar to his face, strong and forthright in its own way, but irreparably scarred.

'I'm surprised a man like yourself doesn't want to live in Boston,' my father said. 'I've always found it very stimulating.'

Mr. Reed gave no answer.

'Would you mind if I asked your age?'

'Twenty-eight.'

I could tell that my father had thought him older, perhaps because of the wisps of gray visible in his beard, or, more likely, because his manner was so deliberative, his eyes so still.

'Twenty-eight,' my father repeated. 'And ... single?'

'Yes.'

They talked for well over an hour that afternoon, and although I drifted past the parlor's open door on several occasions, idly listening as their conversation continued, there was only one small fragment of it that later struck me as revealing of the kind of man Mr. Reed actually was. It had come toward the end of the interview, my father's pipe now lying cold and smokeless in the ashtray beside his chair, Mr. Reed still seated opposite him, both feet pressed firmly on the floor.

'And what about travel,' my father asked. 'Have you done much of that?'

Mr. Reed shook his head. 'Only a little.'

'Where to, if I may ask?'

'France.'

My father seemed pleased. 'France. Now, that's a beautiful country. What part did you visit?'

'Only the countryside,' Mr. Reed answered quietly, adding nothing more, so that my father had to finally coax him forward with another question.

'You were there on business?'

Mr. Reed shook his head, and I saw one of his large hands move down to a right knee that had begun to tremble slightly.

'Just there on vacation, then?' my father asked lightly.

'No,' Mr. Reed answered, a single coal-black eyebrow arching suddenly, then lowering again. 'The war.'

I remember that his voice had become strained as he'd answered, and that his eyes had darted toward the window briefly. At that, both my father and I suddenly realized that the casualness of my father's question had plumbed an unexpectedly raw aspect of Mr. Reed's experience, miraculously revealing to us what Mr. Reed himself must have seen some years before, an exploded shell lifting mounds of muddy earth, men hurling upward, then plummeting down, his own body spinning in a cloud of smoke, bits of himself flying away in surreal tongues of flame.

'Oh,' my father said softly, glancing toward the cane. 'I didn't know.'

Mr. Reed drew his eyes back to my father but didn't speak.

'In your letter you didn't mention that you were a veteran. Most men do when they're applying for a job.'

Mr. Reed shrugged. 'I find it difficult to do that,' he said.

My father reached for his pipe, though I noticed that he didn't light it. 'Well, tell me why you think you'd like to teach at Chatham School.'

I don't remember Mr. Reed's answer, but only that my father had appeared satisfied with it, and that Mr. Reed left the house a few minutes later, presumably walking back to the bus stop in Chatham center, then boarding a bus for Boston. I didn't see him again until almost two months later, and even then only briefly, a man moving down the corridor of Chatham School, one hand clutching a book, the other a cane, whose steady, rhythmic thump announced him like a theme.

As it still did when I heard it tapping down the hallway that autumn afternoon seven years later, followed by the inevitable cautionary whispers of, 'Shhh. Mr. Reed is coming.'

However, on that particular day he didn't come into the room as he usually did, but stopped at the door instead, leaning one shoulder into it, so that he stood at a slant. 'There probably won't be many more days as pleasant as this one,' he said, nodding toward the window, the clear, warm air beyond it. 'So I thought we'd have class out in the courtyard this afternoon.'

With that, he turned and led us down the corridor to the rear of the school, then out into the little courtyard behind it. Once there, he positioned himself beside the large oak that stood near the center of the courtyard and motioned for us to sit down on the ground in a semicircle around him. Then, he leaned against the tree and glanced down at the book he'd brought with him. 'Today we're going to begin our study of Lord Byron,' he said, his voice a curious combination of something soft and rough, and which at times seemed almost physical, like the touch of a fine, unsanded wood. 'You should pay close attention, for Byron lived the poetry he wrote.'

As always, Mr. Reed began by giving us the details of the poet's life, concentrating on his travels and adventures, a wild vagabond existence that Mr. Reed clearly admired. 'Byron didn't settle for what the rest of us settle for,' he told us. 'He would find the lives we lead intolerably dull.'

During the next hour we learned that Byron had been raised in a place called Aberdeen, that as a child he'd been stricken with infantile paralysis, his right leg and foot so terribly contracted that he'd walked with a pronounced limp for the rest of his life. 'Like me,' Mr. Reed said with a quiet smile, nodding toward his cane, 'except that he refused to let it hinder him, or change his life in any way.'

Byron had had what Mr. Reed called 'an adventurous nature', throwing wild parties at his own castle, drinking burgundy from a human skull. 'He lived his ideas,' Mr. Reed declared. 'Nothing ever stood in his way.'

Class was nearly over by the time Mr. Reed finished telling us about Byron's life. But before releasing us completely, he opened the book he'd brought with him. 'I want you to listen now,' he said as he began flipping the pages briskly until he found the lines he'd been searching for. Then he looked toward us and smiled in that strange way I'd already noticed, a smile that seemed to require an undisclosed amount of effort. 'Words need to be heard sometimes,' he said. 'After all, in the beginning all poetry was spoken.'

With that he read the lines he'd selected for us, his voice low, almost a whisper, so that the words themselves sounded inordinately private, an intimate message sent by one whose peculiar sadness seemed at one with Mr. Reed's.

> Every feeling hath been shaken;
>   Pride, which not a world could bow,
> Bows to thee – by thee forsaken
>   Even my soul forsakes me now;
>
> But 'tis done – all words are idle –
>   Words from me are vainer still;
> But the thoughts we cannot bridle
>   Force their way without the will.

His voice trailed off at the end of the recitation, though his eyes remained on the lines a moment longer, his head bowed wearily, as if beneath the weight of thoughts he himself could not bridle.

'I think it's sometimes a good idea to end class with a poem,' he said at last. Then he paused, watching us silently, perhaps hoping for a response. When none came, he closed the book. 'All right, you may go,' he said.

We scrambled to our feet quickly, gathering our books into our arms, and began to disperse, some heading back into the building, others toward the rear entrance of the courtyard and the playing fields beyond. Only Mr. Reed stayed in place, his back pressed against the tree, the volume of Byron's poetry dangling from his hand. He looked as if he might crumple to the ground. But then I saw him draw in a long, reviving breath, straighten his shoulders, step away from the tree, and begin to make his way toward the building. 'Good night, Henry,' he said as he went by me.

'Good night, Mr. Reed,' I answered.

I picked up my books and turned to the right. Miss Channing's classroom was directly in front of me, and when I glanced toward it, I saw that she stood at one of the three large windows that overlooked the courtyard. Her eyes were fixed upon Mr. Reed with a clearly appreciative gaze, taking in the slight limp, the narrow cane, perhaps even the jagged cream-colored scar. I'd never seen a woman look at a man in exactly the same way, almost as if he were not a man at all, but a painting she admired for the boldness of its execution, the way the standard symmetries had been discarded in favor of jaggedness and instability, her earlier sense of beauty now adjusting to take it in, finding a place for mangled shapes.

# EIGHT

From my place beneath the willow, staring out across the water, I could barely make out the house in which Mr. Reed had lived so many years before, and so I stepped away from the tree and took a narrow footpath that hunters and swimmers and the occasional forest solitaire had maintained over the years, and which I knew to be the one Miss Channing had taken on that Saturday evening two weeks later, when she'd set out for Mr. Reed's house on the other side of Black Pond. As I began to move down that same path, I heard Mr. Parsons say, *So, from the beginning you were aware of their meetings?* My answer, *Yes, I was. And what were your impressions, Henry? I didn't see anything wrong with it. Do you now? Yes.*

A tangle of forest had surrounded Miss Channing that evening, and she might well have seen a lone white gull as it plummeted toward the surface of the pond. No doubt she heard the soft crunch of the leaves beneath her feet, but she may have heard an assortment of bird cries, too, or the scurrying of a field mouse, or the plop of a frog as it leaped into the water. For those were the things I saw and heard as I retraced her steps that morning, moving slowly, at an old man's pace.

Her dinner at Mr. Reed's house had been arranged several days before. By then my father had told Miss Channing that it was getting a bit too cold for her to continue walking back and forth from her cottage to Chatham School. He'd gone on to inform her that there was another teacher who lived on Black Pond. It would be a simple matter for him to drop by for her each morning and return her to Milford Cottage in the afternoon.

And so at some point before the end of October, I saw Mr. Reed escort Miss Channing to his car, a battered sedan, its wheels mud-spattered, its running board hardly more than a drooping sheet of rust, its windows streaked and scratched as if they'd been sandblasted with sea salt.

As to what they'd said to each other on that first drive, no one would ever have known had not Mr. Parsons later been so insistent on learning every word ever spoken between them, requiring revelations so detailed that I could still hear their voices whispering in the air around me as I struggled to make my way along the edges of Black Pond.

*I live just on the other side of the pond. You can probably see my house from your cottage.*

*Yes, I've seen it.*

*You may have seen me on the pond too. I go rowing on it occasionally.*

*Do you row at night?*

*Sometimes.*

*Then I think I saw you once. It was my first night in the cottage. I went out to stand by the pond. It was overcast, but I think I saw you for just a moment. Not you, exactly. Just part of the boat, and your hand. Why do you go out at night?*

*For the solitude, I suppose.*

*You don't live alone?*

*No. I have a wife and daughter. What about you? Do you live alone?*

*Yes.*

*You're not afraid? Living out here?*

*No.*

*Some people would be.*

*Then they should live elsewhere, I suppose.*

Listening to their voices as I continued my journey around Black Pond that morning, I realized that such a statement had to have struck Mr. Reed as amazingly self-possessed. How different she must have seemed from any other woman he had ever known.

*I've seen you teaching. The boys seem very interested in your class.*

*I hope they are.*

*They look very attentive.*

*I've seen you with your class too. You were reading to them in the courtyard.*

*Oh, yes, a couple weeks ago. I wanted to take advantage of what I thought might be the last day we could go outside before winter sets in.*

*It was from Byron.*

*You recognized it.*

*Yes, I did. My father read a great deal of Byron. Shelley too. And Keats.*

At that moment Miss Channing told him of her visit to the cluttered Roman apartment in which Keats had died. His books were still there, she said, along with pages written in Keats's own hand.

The interest Mr. Reed by then had come to feel for Miss Channing can be gauged by what he did next.

*I know this is rather sudden, Miss Channing. But I wonder if you'd like to have dinner with my family and me tomorrow evening?*

*I would like that very much, Mr. Reed.*

*Around six, then?*
*Yes.*
*Shall I pick you up?*
*No. I like to walk. Besides, your house is just on the other side of the pond.*

Only a ruin remained of Mr. Reed's house, and even that was so overgrown, I nearly missed it as I made my way along the water's edge that morning. Hung with vines, its roof covered with forest debris, a scattering of shattered lobster traps strewn across its grounds, it gave off a forlorn sense of having been abruptly abandoned, then left to rot forever.

The stairs creaked loudly as I climbed them, grabbing a shaky railing as I went, then stood silently on the porch for a moment, looking into the house, thinking of the terrible words that had been said within its cramped few rooms, wondering if some element of all that might linger still, like a poison mold growing on the walls. A tiny voice pierced the air. *Mama. Mama.*

It was then that I glanced back out into the yard, where for a single visionary instant I saw a small girl in a white boat closely tethered to the shore, playfully pulling at the oars, her blond hair held in place by a thin red ribbon.

From behind me, a second, disembodied voice called her name. *Mary, Mary.*

I turned and saw Mrs. Reed standing at the door of a house that was no longer overgrown with vines, its paint no longer peeling from wood gone black and sodden in the years since its abandonment. She seemed to stare directly through me, as if I were the ghostly one, she brought back to life. Then her eyes narrowed, and she brushed back a loose strand of red hair as she called to her daughter once again, her words echoing in the air, bounding and rebounding across the unresponsive surface of Black Pond. *Mary, come inside.*

I felt a cold wave rush through me, then saw Mary dart past her mother and into the house, laughing happily as she dissolved into its darkened space, her laughter growing faint in the distance, as if she were still running, though now down the passageway of a vast, unending tunnel.

Like a blast of arctic air, I felt all the terror of the past sweep over me in a breathless shiver, as if it were Mrs. Reed and her daughter who had drawn me back into their world rather than I who had returned them unwillingly to mine.

I peered into the interior of the house, its front door long ago pulled down. The walls were now stripped and bare, the fireplace crumbling, the floor little more than a loose assemblage of sagging wooden slats. The kitchen was at the rear of the house, silent, empty, a dusky shaft of light pouring in from the rear window, and with nothing but four rust-colored indentations in the floor to indicate the heavy iron stove Mrs. Reed had used to prepare dinner for her family.

From court testimony I knew that Mrs. Reed had made a special meal for Miss Channing that night, that it had consisted of cabbage and boiled ham, deviled eggs, and a rhubarb pie. I knew that after dinner Mary Reed had busied herself in the front room while the Reeds and Miss Channing lingered over a pot of coffee whose phantom aroma I could almost smell, as if, down all the passing years, it had continued to waft out of the deserted kitchen, filter through the long-abandoned rooms, drift out onto the creaky, leaf-strewn porch where I stood.

Throughout dinner Mr. Reed had kept the conversation centered on Miss Channing, forever returning her to one place or another from her travels, so that during the course of the dinner she'd described everything from the look of Vesuvius as it loomed menacingly over the ruins of Pompeii to the tiny Danish village beloved by Christian Andersen. 'How interesting,' had been Mr. Reed's repeated responses. 'How the boys at school must enjoy listening to you.'

As for Abigail Reed, she'd listened quietly, watching her husband as he watched Miss Channing, smiling politely from time to time, nodding occasionally, perhaps already beginning to sense that something unexpected had entered her life, a woman in a pretty dress, talking of the books she'd read, the things she'd seen, a world Mrs. Reed had never known, nor thought it important to know. Mr. Parsons' voice echoed in the air around me. *How well did you know Abigail Reed?* Her face appeared before me, floating wide-eyed in the green depths. *Not very well.*

The dinner had come to an end at around ten o'clock. By then Mary had drifted out of the front room and disappeared into the darkness surrounding the house. On the porch Miss Channing had politely thanked Mr. Reed and Abigail for the dinner, then turned and headed down the stairs and out toward the narrow path that followed along the water's edge. From a distance she heard Mr. Reed calling for his daughter, then Mrs. Reed's assurance that there was nothing for him to be worried about, that she was only playing near the shed.

It had never occurred to me that it might still be there, but as I eased myself down the stairs of what was left of Mr. Reed's house, I looked to the left and saw it. In contrast to the house, it was remarkably well-preserved, an unpainted wooden shed, tall and narrow, with a roof of corrugated tin. It stood in a grove of Norway spruce, perhaps a hundred yards on the other side of the Reed house. The trail that had once led to it was overgrown, and the tin roof was covered with pine needles, but the terrible weathering and neglect that had left the Reed house and Milford Cottage in such disrepair seemed hardly to have affected it.

I approached it reluctantly, as anyone might who knew the terror that had shivered there, the sound of small fingers clawing at its door, the whimpering cries that had filtered through the thick wooden slats, *Daddy, Daddy*.

It was windowless, its walls covered with tar paper, the heavy door trimmed in black rubber, creating a tight seal. Though very dark inside, it nonetheless gave off a sense of spaciousness because of the high roof, the great boards that ran its length nearly ten feet above, the large, rusty hooks that pierced the base of the boards and hung toward the floor like crooked red fingers. During Miss Channing's trial, Mr. Parsons had repeatedly referred to it as a 'slaughterhouse', but it had never been any such thing. Rather, it was one of those outbuildings, common at the time, in which large slabs of meat were hung for smoking or salting or simply to be carved into pieces fit for cooking. The floor had been slightly raised, with half-inch spaces between the boards, so that blood could trickle through it, be soaked up by the ground beneath. Mr. Reed had rarely used it, although it rested on his land, but Mary had often been seen playing both inside it and nearby.

It was this latter fact that had finally brought Captain Lawrence P. Hamilton of the Massachusetts State Police to its large gray door that afternoon. The captain had already searched Mr. Reed's house by then, the little earthen basement beneath it, the cramped, unlighted attic overhead. That's where he'd found a battered cardboard box, a knife, and length of rope inside, along with an old primer curiously inscribed. But Captain Hamilton had not been looking for such things when he'd first come to the Reed house that day. His concerns had been far more immediate than that. For although Mrs. Reed had already been found by then, Mary was still missing.

# NINE

It was nearly ten in the morning when I returned to my car, pulled myself behind the wheel, and headed back toward Chatham. By then, the atmosphere of the places I'd just revisited – Milford Cottage, Mr. Reed's house, the little shed Captain Hamilton had warily approached on that sweltering May afternoon – had sunk into my memory like a dark, ineradicable stain. I thought of all that had followed the events of that terrible day, some immediately, some lingering through all the intervening years. I remembered my father at his desk, desperately trying to reclaim some part of a dream already lost, my mother staring at him bitterly, locked in her own sullen disillusionment. I saw a young world grow old, the boys of Chatham School expanding into adulthood, then shrinking into old age just as I had, though with less than they had to show for my time on earth, wifeless, childless, a man known primarily for a single boyhood act.

Then, in the midst of all that dead or aged company, I glimpsed the youthful face of Sarah Doyle.

I remember that it was a Saturday afternoon in early November, only a week following Miss Channing's dinner with Mr. Reed and his family. I was sitting on a bench at the edge of the coastal bluff. On the beach below I could see several people strolling about or lounging under large striped umbrellas. There was no one in the water, of course, the season for swimming having passed by then. But far out to sea, I could make out the white sail of a fifteen-footer as it skirted along the shore-line. Watching it drift by, I yearned to be on it, to be cutting across an illimitable blue vastness.

Sarah was wearing a long blue skirt and red blouse when she came up to me that morning, and she'd wrapped a flowered scarf over her shoulders, the knot tied loosely at her throat. Her hair was long and extraordinarily dark, and had a continually frazzled and unruly look to it, as if she'd just been taken by the heels, turned upside down, and shaken violently, her hair left in tangled disarray.

Still, for all that, she was quite a lovely girl, the same age I was, and I often found my attention drawn to her as she swept past my room or bounded up the stairs, but most particularly when I found her lounging on the porch swing, her arms at her sides, her eyes half-closed and languid, as if lost in a dream of surrender.

In those days, of course, the classes were more rigidly divided than they have since become, and so I knew that whatever my feelings for Sarah might be, they would always have to be carefully guarded. For unlike the other deadly sins, lust is sometimes joined to love, and such a prospect would no doubt have met with stern disapproval from my mother. And so, up until that day, I'd allowed myself only those hidden thoughts and secret glances that were within my sphere, thinking of Sarah at night, but by day returning her to the status of a servant girl.

'And hello to you, sir,' she said as she approached me, the Irish lilt now striking me as somewhat thrilling and exotic.

I nodded. 'Hi, Sarah.'

She smiled brightly, but seemed unsure of what to do next. 'Well, should I sit with you, then?' she asked.

'Sure,' I said casually, as if the nearness of her body meant no more to me than that of the lamppost a block away.

She sat down and looked out over the water. I did the same, careful to conceal the fact that all I could think of was her skin, the color of milk, her hair black as coal, the mysteries of her body infinitely enticing.

As to her history, I knew only the broad details. But from the bits and pieces of conversation I'd overheard as I roamed the house on Myrtle Street, I'd learned of her mother's early death in Limerick and had some picture of the bleak coastal village she'd grown up in after that. She'd had three brothers, two killed in the Great War, one an aimless drifter who'd disappeared into the dreary slums of East London. As to her father, he'd died of tuberculosis five years before, leaving her with only enough money to book passage to America. I'd heard my father speak grimly of that passage, the horrors of the steerage, the way the men had leered at her in the dank quarters of the ship's belly, the stale bread and dried beef that alone had sustained her until she'd finally disembarked at the Port of Boston.

After that Sarah had fallen upon the mercy of the Irish Immigrant Aid Society, who'd fed, clothed, and given her shelter until she'd landed a job as a serving girl in a great Boston house. It was there she'd met my father three years later, told him how much she longed for village life again, particularly if the village happened to be located near the sea. By all accounts she had spoken to my father with great earnestness, and my father, never one to remain deaf to such heartfelt solicitations, had first cleared it with her employer, then offered her a place in our house at Chatham, one she'd taken without a moment's further thought and performed dutifully ever since.

But as I looked at her that morning nearly two years later, she seemed not altogether pleased with her earlier decision. There was a melancholy wistfulness in her eyes, a deep dissatisfaction.

'Something's bothering you,' I said bluntly, my own intense restlessness now spilling over into a general sense of radical impatience.

Her eyes shot over to me, as if I'd accused her of stealing the silverware. 'Now, why do you say that?' she asked in a sharp, defensive tone.

I gave her a knowing look.

She turned her head away, touched her cheek. 'I've nothing to complain about. I'll not be thought of as a whiner.'

I was too consumed with my own complaint to feel much tenderness toward Sarah's, so I said nothing more.

This seemed to jar her. 'Well I want you to know that I don't at all regret coming to Chatham. Not at all, that's for sure. I wouldn't ever want your father to think I wasn't grateful for what he's done for me. It's just that I didn't come to America to be a serving girl. I'm after more than that. I want to better myself, to break away from the cleaning and cooking. To *be* something, don't you know. Not just a serving girl ... like I am now.' She shook her head violently. 'It's no good, feeling like I do. Like I'm all tied up in ropes.'

I could see it in her face, a vast, billowing need to leap beyond the mundane and unglamorous life she otherwise seemed destined for, and which, since reading Mr. Channing's book, I had also begun to feel far more powerfully than I ever had before. Watching her agitation, the restlessness that swept over her, I suddenly felt absolutely in league with her, the two of us castaways on a narrow strip of land whose strictures and limitations both appalled and threatened to destroy us. I saw my father as grimly standing in our way, reading his ancient books, mouthing their stony maxims. In my mind I heard his steady drone: *Do this, do that. Be this, be that.* I had never felt such a deep contempt for everything he stood for.

'Maybe you should just take off, Sarah,' I told her. 'Just take the train to Boston and disappear.'

Even as I said it, I saw myself doing it. It would be a moment of wild flight, the real world dissolving behind me, all its gray walls crumbling, the sky a vast expanse before me, my life almost as limitless as the unbounded universe.

'You should do whatever you have to, Sarah,' I continued boldly. Then, as if to demonstrate my zeal, I said, 'If I can help you in any way, let me know.'

Her response came as a question that utterly surprised me. For it had nothing to do with flight, with night trains to Boston, or disappearing into the multitude. Instead, she studied me intently, then said, 'Do you remember Miss Channing? The lady that came to the house at the end of summer, the one that's teaching art?'

'I'm in her class.'

'Such a fine lady, the way she talks and all. So smart, don't you think?'

'Yes, she is.'

Sarah hesitated, now suddenly reluctant to ask what she had perhaps come to ask me all along. Then the wall fell, and she spoke. 'Do you think that such a fine lady as Miss Channing is – talking so fine the way she does – that she might be of a mind to teach me how to read?'

We headed down Myrtle Street together the following Sunday morning, Sarah walking beside me, a basket of freshly baked cookies hanging from one arm, her offering to Miss Channing.

At the bluff we swung to the left, passed beneath the immense shadow of the lighthouse, then down the curving road that led into the village.

'What if Miss Channing says no,' Sarah asked. 'What if she won't teach me?'

'I don't think she'll say no, Sarah,' I said, though I know that part of me hoped that she would, wanted Sarah to be refused so that she would have to consider the other choice I'd already suggested, far bolder, as it seemed to me, edged in that frenzied sense of escape whose attractions had begun to overwhelm me.

'But what if she doesn't want to?'

I answered with a determination that was new to me, an icy ruthless-ness already in my voice. 'Then we'll find another way.'

This appeared to satisfy her. She smiled brightly and took my arm with her free hand.

Still, by the time we'd turned onto Plymouth Road, her fear had taken root again. She walked more slowly, her feet treading very softly over the bed of oyster shells, as if it were an expensive carpet and she did not want to mar it with her prints.

'I hope I look all right, then,' she said as we neared Miss Channing's cottage.

She'd dressed as formally as she knew how, in what looked like her own schoolgirl version of the Chatham School uniform. Her skirt was long and dark, her blouse an immaculate white. She'd tied a black bow at her throat and pinned a small cameo to her chest, one that had belonged to her mother, her sole inheritance, she told me.

It was not a look I admired, and even as I gazed at her, I imagined her quite differently, dressed like Ramona in *The Gypsy Band*, bare-shouldered, with large hoop earrings, a lethal glint in her eye, a knife clutched between her teeth as she danced around the raging campfire. It was as adolescent a fantasy as any I had ever had, and yet it was also tinged with a darkness that was very old, a sense of woman as most lusty and desirable when poised at the edge of murder.

At Milford Cottage Sarah glanced down at her skirt and frowned. 'There's dust all over the hem.' She bent forward and brushed at the bottom of her skirt. 'Sticks like glue,' she said, finally giving up. Then she lifted her head determinedly and I felt her hand tighten around my arm. 'All right,' she said. 'I'm ready.'

We walked down the little walkway that led to the door of the cottage. Without a pause Sarah knocked gently, glanced at me with a bright, nervous smile, and waited.

When no one answered, she looked at me quizzically.

'Try again,' I said. 'It's early. She must be here.'

Sarah did as I told her, but still there was no answer.

I remembered the occasion several weeks before, when I'd come to the cottage at nearly the same time, found it empty, as it now appeared to be, Miss Channing strolling along the edge of the forest.

'Sometimes she takes a walk in the morning,' I told Sarah confidently, although I could not be sure of any such thing. 'Let's look around.'

We stepped away from the door, walked to the far side of the cottage, then around it to the rear yard, toward the pond. A heavy morning mist still hung over the water, its lingering cloud rolling out over the edges of the land, covering it in fog.

For a moment Sarah and I stood, facing the pond, the impenetrable mist that drifted out from it covering the small area behind the cottage.

Nothing moved, or seemed to move, neither the air, nor the mist that cloaked the water, nor anything around us, until suddenly I saw a figure drift slowly toward us, the thick gray fog thinning steadily as she came nearer so that she appeared to rise toward us smoothly, like a corpse floating up from a pool of clouded water.

'Miss Channing,' Sarah said.

Miss Channing smiled slightly. 'I was out by the pond,' she said. 'I thought I heard someone at the door.' Dimly I could see the easel she'd set up at the water's edge, a large pad of drawing paper already in place upon it, all of it still shrouded in curling wisps of gray cloud.

'This is Sarah Doyle,' I told her. 'You may remember her from when you had dinner at our house the night you first came to Chatham.'

Sarah lifted the basket toward her. 'I brought you some cookies, Miss Channing,' she said nervously. 'I baked them special for you. As payment, ma'am.'

'Payment?' Miss Channing asked. 'For what?'

For an instant, Sarah hesitated, and I could see that she believed her entire future to be at stake at that moment in her life, all her limitless prospects to be placed in someone else's hands.

'For teaching me to read,' she said boldly, eyes on Miss Channing's face. 'If you'd be willing to do it, ma'am.'

Miss Channing did not pause a beat in her response. 'Of course I will,' she said, and stepped forward to take the basket from Sarah's trembling hand.

An hour later they were still at it. From my place at the edge of the water I could see Miss Channing sitting at a small table she'd brought from the cottage and placed beneath the willow tree. Sarah sat opposite her, a writing pad before her, along with a sheet of paper upon which Miss Channing had written the alphabet in large block letters.

I heard Miss Channing say, 'All right. Begin.'

Sarah kept her eyes fixed upon Miss Channing's, careful not to let them stray toward the page as she began. 'A, B, C . . .'

She continued through the alphabet, stumbling here and there, pausing until Miss Channing finally provided the missing letter, then rushing on gleefully until she reached the end.

'Good,' Miss Channing said quietly. 'Now. Once more.'

Again Sarah made her way through the alphabet, this time stopping only once, at U, then plunging ahead rapidly, completing it in a flourish of pride and breathlessness.

When she'd gotten to the end of it, Miss Channing offered her an encouraging smile. 'Very good,' she said. 'You're a very bright girl, Sarah.'

'Thank you,' Sarah said, a broad smile lighting her face.

They continued their work until almost noon, when I heard Miss Channing say, 'Well, I think we had a very good lesson, Sarah.'

Sarah rose, then did a small curtsy, a servant girl once again, taking leave of her superior. 'Thank you, Miss Channing.' Her earlier nervousness had now completely returned. 'Do you think we could have another lesson sometime, then?' she asked hesitantly.

'Yes, of course we could,' Miss Channing told her. 'Actually, we should have a lesson once a week. Would Sunday mornings be all right?'

'Oh, yes, ma'am,' Sarah burst out, a great relief and happiness sweeping over her. 'You can depend on it, Miss Channing. I'll be here every Sunday morning from this day on.'

'Good,' Miss Channing said. 'I'll be waiting for you.' She turned to me. I could see that something was on her mind. 'You didn't bring a sketchbook with you, Henry,' she said.

I shrugged. 'I guess I didn't ...'

'You should have it with you all the time,' Miss Channing told me. She smiled, then said a line I later repeated to Mr. Parsons. 'Art is like love. It's all or nothing.'

With that she quickly walked into the cottage, then returned, this time with a sketchbook in her hand.

'Take one of mine,' she said as she handed it to me. 'I have a few left from my time in Africa.'

I looked at the book, the soft burgundy cover, the clean, thick paper that rested beneath it. Nothing had ever looked more beautiful to me. I felt as if she'd passed me a golden locket or a strand of her hair.

'Now, don't let me see you without a sketchbook ever again, Henry,' she said with a mocking sternness.

I tucked the book beneath my arm. 'I won't,' I told her.

She gazed at me a moment, then nodded toward the table and chairs. 'Would you mind taking all this back into the cottage?' she asked.

'Not at all.'

I grasped one chair in each hand and headed for the cottage. On the way I heard Sarah say, 'So you were painting this morning, were you?' And Miss Channing's reply, 'Yes. I often do in the morning.'

Inside the cottage I placed the chairs at the wooden table in the kitchen. Through the rear window I could see Miss Channing and Sarah as they strolled toward the easel that still stood at the water's edge, the pages of the drawing book fluttering slightly in a breeze from off the pond. Miss Channing had opened the drawing book and was showing one of her sketches to Sarah. Sarah had folded her hands before her in the way Miss Channing often did, and was listening attentively to her every word.

After a while I turned and walked back into the small living room at the front of the cottage. The picture of Miss Channing's father still hung in the same place. But since that time, several sketches had been added to the wall, carefully wrought line drawings that she had brought out of Africa and which portrayed vast, uncluttered vistas, borderless and uncharted, devoid of both animals and people, the land and sky stretching out into a nearly featureless infinity. This, I knew, was her father's world, unlimited and unrestrained.

I stared at her drawings a few seconds longer, then walked outside again, retrieved the table, placed it just inside the cottage door, and made my way over to where Miss Channing and Sarah still stood at the edge of the pond.

'I like that one,' Sarah said brightly, her eyes on one of the drawings Miss Channing had just displayed.

'It's not finished yet,' Miss Channing told her. 'I was working on it this morning.'

I peered at the drawing. It showed a body of water that only faintly resembled Black Pond. For it was much larger, as well as being surrounded by a world of empty hills and valleys that appeared to roll on forever. So much so, that the mood of the drawing, its immensity and sense of vast, unbounded space struck me as very similar to the ones I'd just seen inside the cottage. But there was something different about it too. For near the center of the drawing, hovering near the middle of a huge, unmoving water, Miss Channing had drawn a man at the oars of a small boat. His face was caught in a shaft of light, his eyes locked on the farther shore.

Sarah leaned forward, looking closely at the figure in the boat. 'That man there, isn't that—'

'Leland Reed,' Miss Channing said, the first time I'd ever heard her say his name.

Sarah smiled. 'Yes, Mr. Reed. From Chatham School.'

Miss Channing let her eyes settle upon the painting. She drew in a deep breath and let it out slowly, a gesture which, months later, after I'd described it to Mr. Parsons, he forever called 'a lover's sigh'.

# TEN

I was still thinking of Miss Channing's drawing a few minutes later when I brought my car to a halt in front of Dalmatian's Cafe. It had long been my favorite place in Chatham, not only because it had been the place where the boys of Chatham School had sometimes gathered after a game or on the weekends, but because it had pretty much remained unchanged from that now-distant time. The grill and counter were still in the same place; so were the booths by the window. Even the old rusty plow blade that Mrs. Winthrop, the cafe's first owner, claimed her great-grandfather had used to break ground on their family farm in 1754 still hung on the back wall, though now hemmed in by bright neon signs hawking beer and soft drinks.

I took my usual seat in the booth farthest from the door, the one that nestled in a corner by the window, and from which I could look out and watch the village's activities. And without warning I saw Dr. Craddock pull up in front of our Myrtle Street house just as he had on that night so long ago, driving the sleek black sedan in which he paid house calls in the twenties, saw him as he walked through the rain to where my father stood gloomily on the porch. The doctor had been dressed in a black suit, and had taken off his hat as he came up the stairs, his question delivered almost like a plea. *I'm sorry to trouble you, Arthur, but could we talk about the little girl?*

And as I sat there hearing the doctor's voice, time reversed itself, old buildings replacing more recent ones, the blue pavement of Main Street suddenly buried beneath a stretch of earth marked by both wooden wagon wheels and the narrow rubber tread of clanging Model A's.

Far in the distance I saw an old iron bell materialize out of the motionless air of the long-empty bell tower of what had once been Chatham School, then begin to move, as if it had been pushed by an invisible hand, its implacable toll reverberating over the buildings and playing fields of Chatham School summoning us to our classes in the morning, and releasing us from them in the afternoon, ringing matins and vespers with an authority and sense of purpose that had little diminished from the time of monks and kings.

And then, as if from some high aerie where I sat perched above them, I saw the boys pour out of the great wooden doors at the front of the school, sweep down its wide cement stairs, and fan out into the surrounding streets, myself among them, the gray school jacket now draped over my shoulders, its little shield embroidered on the front pocket, along with the single phrase, *Veritas et Virtus*, truth and virtue, the words my father had long ago selected as the motto of Chatham School.

It was a Friday afternoon in late November, around three weeks after I'd taken Sarah to Miss Channing's cottage for her first reading lesson. By then Sarah and I had become somewhat closer, she no longer simply a servant girl, I no longer simply the son of her master. Her yearning to make something of herself fired my own emerging vision of living an artist's life, a life lived 'on the run', as Jonathan Channing had called it, and whose vast ambitions Sarah's own great hope seemed to mirror in some way.

We were on our way to the lighthouse that afternoon, Sarah in a cheerful mood, strolling almost gaily over a carpet of red and yellow leaves, Sarah with a new purse she'd bought at a village shop, I with my sketchbook tucked firmly beneath my arm.

'I just want you to look at them before I show them to Miss Channing,' I told her as we strode across the street, then onto the broad yard that swept out from the whitewashed base of the lighthouse. 'And if they're bad, Sarah, I want you to tell me so. I don't want Miss Channing to see them if they're bad.'

Sarah flashed me a smile. 'Give them to me, Henry, and stop going on so about it,' she said, playfully snatching the sketchbook from my hand.

'It's just pictures of places around here mostly,' I added as she opened it. 'Just beaches and stuff.'

But to me they were anything but local scenes. For what they portrayed was not Chatham, but my view of it. As such, they were moody drawings of shrouded seascapes and gloomy woods, each done with an unmistakable intensity, everything oddly torn and twisted, as if I'd begun with an ordinary scene in mind, some commonplace beach or village lane, then dipped it in black ink and put it through a grinder.

And yet, for all their adolescent excess, they'd had a certain sense of balance and proportion, the intricate bark of a distant tree, the grittiness of beach sand, drawings that suggested not only the look of things, but their physical textures. There was a vision of the world in them as well, a feeling for the claustrophobia of life, so that even the vistas, wide though they seemed, appeared pinched and walled in at the same time, the earth, for all its spinning vastness, no more than a single locked room from which nothing seemed able to escape.

Sarah remained silent while she flipped through my sketchbook. Then, with a quick flick of her hand, she closed it, a wry smile on her lips.

'I like them, Henry,' she said happily. 'I like them a lot.'

She no doubt expected a smile to burst onto my face, but nothing of the sort happened. Instead, I stared at her with a decidedly troubled look. 'But do you think Miss Channing will like them?' I demanded.

She looked at me as if the question were absurd. 'Of course she will,' she said. She gave me a slight nudge. 'Besides, even if Miss Channing didn't like your drawings, all she'd want to do is teach you how to make them better.'

'All right,' I said, drawing the sketchbook from her hand as I got to my feet.

I walked a short distance away from her across the lighthouse grounds, then stopped and glanced back to where she remained seated on the little cement bench. 'Thank you, Sarah,' I said.

She watched me closely, clearly sensing my insecurity, her teasing, carefree mood now entirely vanished. 'Do you want me to come with you, Henry?'

I knew she'd read my mind. 'Yes, I think I do.'

'All right,' Sarah said, coming to her feet with a sweep of her skirt. 'But only as far as the courtyard, not into Miss Channing's room. When you show her your drawings, you should do it on your own.'

I'd expected to find her alone, doing what she normally did at the end of the school day, washing the tables and putting away her supplies. It was only after I'd reached the door of her classroom and peered inside that I realized she was not. Even so, I don't know why it surprised me so, finding Mr. Reed in her room, leaning casually against the front table while she stood a few feet away, her back to him, washing the blackboard with a wet cloth. After all, I'd often seen them arriving at school in the morning and leaving together in the afternoon, Mr. Reed behind the wheel of his sedan, Miss Channing seated quite properly on the passenger side. I'd seen them together at other times as well, strolling side by side down the school corridor, or sitting on the steps, having lunch, usually with a gathering of other teachers, yet slightly off to the side, a mood surrounding them like an invisible field, so that even in the midst of others, they seemed intimately alone.

'Hello,' Miss Channing said when she turned away from the blackboard and saw me standing at the door. 'Please, come in, Henry.'

I came into her room with a reluctance and sense of intrusion that

I still can't entirely explain, unless, from time to time, we are touched by the opposite of aftermath, feel not the swirling eddies of a retreating wave, but the dark pull of an approaching one.

'Hello, Henry,' Mr. Reed said.

I nodded silently as I came down the aisle, sliding the sketchbook back slightly, trying to conceal it.

'I thought you'd be at the game,' Mr. Reed said, referring to the lacrosse match that had been scheduled for that same afternoon. 'It's against New Bedford Prep, you know.' He glanced toward Miss Channing. 'Traditionally, New Bedford Prep has been our most dreaded opponent.'

I said nothing, tormented now with second thoughts about showing my drawings to Miss Channing since Mr. Reed would be there to see them too. I'm not sure I would have shown them at all had not Miss Channing's eyes drifted down to the sketchbook beneath my arm.

'Did you bring that for me?' she asked.

She could see my reluctance to hand it over. To counteract it, she smiled and said, 'You know, my father used to stand me in front of a bare wall. He'd say, "Look closely, Libby. On that wall there is a great painting by someone who was afraid to show it." If no one ever sees your work, Henry, then what's the point of doing it at all? Let's see what you've done.'

I drew the sketchbook from beneath my arm and handed it to her.

She placed it on the table and began to turn the pages, studying one drawing at a time, commenting from time to time, mentioning this detail or that one, how the trees appeared to bulge slightly, something in them trying to get out, or the way the sea tossed and heaved.

'They have a certain – I don't know – a certain *controlled uncontrol* about them, don't you think?' she asked Mr. Reed.

He nodded, his eyes on her. 'Yes, I do.'

She drew in a long breath. 'If we could only live that way,' she said, her eyes still on one of my drawings.

She'd said it softly, without undue emphasis, but I saw Mr. Reed's face suddenly alter. 'Yes,' he said, his voice little more than a whisper, yet oddly charged as well, as if he were responding not to an idle remark made in an open room, but to a note slipped surreptitiously beneath his chamber door.

I left Miss Channing's room a few minutes later, reasonably satisfied with her response, but in other ways somewhat troubled and ill at ease, as if something had been denied me, a moment alone with her.

'I knew she'd like them,' Sarah said firmly when I told her what had happened.

She'd waited for me at the back of the school, the two of us now moving down its central corridor, other boys brushing past us, a few turning to get a better look at Sarah after she'd gone by.

Once outside, we returned to our little cement bench beside the lighthouse. From it we could see Chatham School just across the street.

'I wish I could leave here,' I said abruptly, almost spitefully, my mind turning from my drawings to the escape route they represented for me. Not art, as I know now, but an artist's life as I then imagined it.

Sarah looked surprised by the depth of my contempt. 'But you have everything, Henry. A family. Everything.'

I shook my head. 'I don't care. I hate this place.'

'Where do you want to go?'

'I don't know. Somewhere else, that's all.'

She looked at me knowingly. 'There are lots of places worse than Chatham,' she said.

It was then that Miss Channing and Mr. Reed came out the front door of the school and began strolling slowly toward the parking lot. Despite the formal distance they maintained, the fact that they at no point touched, there was something in the way they walked along together that drew my attention to them, called forth those first small suspicions that would later grow to monstrous size.

'I'll bet they'd like to go someplace else too,' I said.

Sarah said nothing, but only turned toward the school and watched as Mr. Reed and Miss Channing continued toward Mr. Reed's car. When they reached it, he opened the door for Miss Channing, waited until she'd gotten in, then closed it once again.

The car rumbled past us a few seconds later, Mr. Reed at the wheel as always, and Miss Channing seated beside the passenger door. A late afternoon chill had settled over the village by that time, and I noticed that she'd rolled her window up to shut it out. Her face, mirrored in the glass, seemed eerily translucent as the car swept by.

More than anything, I remember that she appeared to sit in a great stillness as the car drifted by. Just as she would some months later, after the verdict had been rendered, and she'd been hustled down the courthouse stairs and rushed into the backseat of a black patrol car. She'd sat next to the window on that occasion too, staring straight ahead as the car inched through the noisy, milling crowd, slowly picking up speed as it continued forward, bearing her away.

# ELEVEN

I found that I couldn't go directly to my office after leaving Dalmatian's Cafe that morning. For there was yet another place that called to me even more darkly than Milford Cottage or Mr. Reed's house or the silent reaches of Black Pond. For although the final act had occurred there, its tragic origins lay somewhere else, a different conspiracy entirely from the one Mr. Parsons felt so certain he'd unmasked in the courtroom the day I took the stand.

And so, after a second cup of coffee at Dalmatian's Cafe, I walked back to my car, pulled out of the parking space, and headed up the steadily ascending coastal road that curved along the outerbank to Myrtle Street.

At the top of the bluff I wheeled to the right. The lighthouse gleamed in the bright morning air as I drove past it, a vast blue sky above, with only wisps of skirting clouds to suggest the tearing wind and rain that had rocked us during most of the preceding week.

Dolphin Hall rose just down the street from the lighthouse, and even at that early hour there were a couple of cars parked in its lot. One of them, a sleek BMW, bright red with thin lines of shimmering chrome, was parked beneath the same ancient oak that had once shaded the battered chassis of Mr. Reed's old Model T.

I pulled in next to it and stopped. Through my windshield I could see the gallery a few yards away, its red brick portico little changed since the days when the building had housed the boys of Chatham School.

Other things had been altered, of course. The tall, rattling windows had been replaced by sturdy double-paned glass, and a wide metal ramp now glided up the far right side of the cement stairs, granting access to the handicapped.

But more than any of these obvious changes, I noticed that a tall plaster replica of the lighthouse had been placed on the front lawn in almost exactly the spot where Miss Channing's column of faces had briefly stood, my own face near the center of the column, my father's near the bottom, where a circular bed of tulips had been planted.

465

On the day the school's governing board ordered it battered down, my father had stood with his arms folded over his chest, listening to the ring of the hammer as it shattered the plaster faces one by one. Standing rigidly with his back to the small group of people who'd come to observe its destruction, clothed in his neatly pressed black suit, he'd watched it all silently and with complete dignity. It was only after it had been done, the faces gathered in a dusty pile, that he'd glanced back toward me, his head cocked at an angle that allowed the morning sun to touch his face, its brief glimmer caught in the tears of his eyes.

The cement walkway to the gallery had been replaced by a more attractive cobblestone, but the path itself was still as straight and narrow as before.

At the door, a small cardboard sign read simply WELCOME, so I opened the door and walked inside, entering what had once been Chatham School for the first time in all the many years that had passed since its closing.

From the foyer I could see the wide central corridor that had led from the front of the school all the way to the rear courtyard, the stairs that rose toward the second floor dormitory, and even the door of what had once been my father's office, its brass knob reflecting the newly installed halogen lights.

Beside the front window there was a little table filled with information about the various exhibitors represented in the gallery. I reached for the one nearest me and moved down the corridor, more or less pretending to read it, acting quite unnecessarily like some secret agent who'd been sent from the past to bring back news from the present, inform the ghostly legions as to how it had turned out.

I'd gotten only a little way down the corridor before I was intercepted.

'Well, Mr. Griswald. Hello.'

I recognized the man who greeted me as Bill Kipling, the gallery's owner, and whose grandfather, Joe Kipling, had once played lacrosse for Chatham School. Joe had been a lanky, energetic boy, later a town selectman and real estate baron, more recently an old man who'd swallowed handfuls of vitamins and food supplements before he'd finally died of liver cancer in a private hospital room in Hyannis.

'Well, what made you decide to drop by after all this time?' the younger Kipling asked cheerily.

'Just thinking about old times, I guess. When Chatham School was here.'

'My grandfather went to Chatham School, you know.'

'Yes, I remember him.'

And saying that, I saw Joe Kipling not as a boy rushing forward with a

466

lacrosse stick raised in the air, but as he'd stood beside the gray column, a sledgehammer in his hand, swinging it fiercely at the plaster faces Miss Channing had fashioned, a layer of dust gathering upon the shoulders of his school jacket.

'My father loved Chatham School,' his grandson told me now.

'We all did.'

Some few minutes of small talk followed, then he left me to browse through the gallery undisturbed, knowing that I had not really come to see the pictures he'd hung from its walls, but to hear the shouts and laughter of the boys as they'd tumbled chaotically down the wide stair-case at seven-thirty sharp, some fully dressed, others still looping their suspenders over their shoulders or pulling on their jackets, but always under the watchful eye of my father. For each morning he'd taken up his position at the bottom of the stairs, his arms folded over his chest like a Roman centurion, greeting each boy by name, then adding a quick 'Work well, play well.' I could still remember how embarrassed I'd felt at such a scene each morning, the boys rushing by, trying so hard to please, to be what my father wanted them to be, sturdy, upright 'good citizens'. At those times he'd appeared almost comical to me, a caricature of the Victorian schoolmaster, an artifact from that dead time, bloodless as a bone dug out of an ancient pit. Of all the mired and passionless things I did not wish to be, my father was chief among them. As for the 'good life' about which he sometimes spoke, standing before the boys in his Ciceronian pose, it struck me as little more than a life lived without vitality or imagination, a life hardly worth living, and from which death could come only as a sweet release.

His office had faced the staircase, and its great mahogany door was still in place. Stepping up to it, I could almost hear him uttering the ominous words I'd overheard as I'd swept down the stairs that faced his office on that drizzly afternoon in May of 1927. The door had still been fully open when I'd begun to make my way from the upper landing, but he'd begun to close it, his attention so focused on the people already inside his office that he hadn't seen me descending the stairs. 'This is Mr. Parsons, the commonwealth attorney,' I'd heard him say as he stepped farther into his office, slowly drawing the door behind him.

I'd been able to glance inside the office and see a man in a dark suit, a homburg held in his hand. He stood in front of my father's desk, a large cardboard box in the chair beside him. 'Please sit down, Miss Channing,' I heard him say.

Through the narrowing space that remained open as I reached the bot-tom of the stairs, I could see Miss Channing standing stiffly before Mr. Parsons, her hands folded together at her waist, her hair in a tight bun.

As the door closed, I heard her reply to him, her words spoken softly, but in a tone that struck me as deathly cold. 'I prefer to stand,' she said.

The door to what had formerly been my father's office now had a little sign tacked to it, one that read 'Private', so I could not go in. I stood, facing it, remembering that a completely different sign had once been there, one that had read 'Arthur H. Griswald, Headmaster'.

My father had removed that sign himself, placed it in a shoe box, and kept it in the cellar of the little house we rented after leaving Chatham School. But it was not very difficult for me to imagine that it was still in place, and that beyond the door his desk was still there too, along with the crystal inkwell my mother had given him on their tenth anniversary, the ceremonial quill pen he'd used to sign important documents, even the brass lamp with the dark green shade that had given the room an indisputable authority.

I knew that a whole world had once held its ground in that small room, made what amounted to its last stand. How fully all of that had been visible in my father's face the day he'd marched onto the front lawn of the school, then instructed Joe Kipling to take his place before Miss Channing's carved column of faces. He'd paused a moment, his gaze lingering on the column, then turned to Joe and given the order with a single word: *Begin.*

I felt my eyes close against the awesome spectacle of that moment, the sound of the hammer as it slammed into the column, the severe and unsmiling faces of the people who watched as Joe Kipling pounded it into dust.

I turned away from the door. On either side, large rooms were filled with paintings of more or less modern design, the paint splattered upon the canvas or lathered over it in chaotic swirls, fragments of color pressed jag-gedly one against another. I could only imagine how their disharmony would have offended my father, how much he would have preferred the idyllic scenes and passive landscapes he'd scrupulously selected for these same corridors during his tenure as headmaster, works governed by order and design, harmony and the laws of reason, a vision of life he'd striven to maintain at Chatham School ... and failed.

Toward the rear of the corridor I stepped into the room that had once been Mr. Reed's. Able to accommodate no more than ten or twelve student desks, its large windows looked out into the courtyard. Through them he had been able to see the little converted storeroom where Miss Channing taught. How often he must have glanced out those windows and caught her in his eyes, a slender young woman with raven black hair and light blue eyes, standing behind a sculpting pedestal or before an easel, spinning stories of fabled lands and tragic people while she worked with paint and clay. Although I never saw it happen, I'm sure that from time to time Miss Channing must have glanced toward her own window and caught Mr. Reed watching her from across the courtyard, at first through veils of autumn rain, then through swirls of windblown snow, and finally through the shimmering air of that final spring, their eyes now locked in a dreadful stare, a look as desperate and harrowing as the words I'd heard them speak: *How do you want to do it? Without looking back.*

I didn't remain in Mr. Reed's classroom for very long. For I could feel a heat and sharpness in the air, as if it had begun to sizzle.

And so I turned and fled to the courtyard where the outbuilding that had once been Miss Channing's classroom still stood, though it had long been converted into the gallery's framing shop.

The door was open, and standing at its threshold I could see the wide counter that ran along the rear of the building, stacks of empty frames leaning against the wall behind it. Frame samples of various colors and materials – brass, wood, aluminum – hung from a large square of pressed board. To the right, where I'd once sat at the front of the room, a work space had been created, complete with a large table and circular saw. A layer of sawdust and wood chips coated the floor beneath the table, and a bright red metal toolbox rested alongside.

Clearly, of the several places I visited that day, it was Miss Channing's room that had been most transformed. No trace remained of the tables and chairs where the boys had sat watching her sculpt and paint, nor of the sculpting pedestals and easels and canvases we'd used to fashion our own crude works of art; nor the cabinet where she'd returned the room's modest supplies before joining Mr. Reed for their drive home each afternoon; nor even the portraits of Washington and Lincoln that had watched us from the room's opposite walls, their faces stern but kindly, like two old-fashioned fathers.

And yet, for all that, I sensed Miss Channing's presence more within that transformed and cluttered space than in any of the other places I'd revisited. And I could feel Mr. Reed as well, the two of them together as I had found them on that long-ago afternoon, she behind the front table, he at the far door, moving toward her irrevocably, his words spoken so softly that I'd barely been able to hear them: *Because I love you, I can do it.*

It was more than I could bear. And so I wheeled around and walked back through the courtyard and down the central corridor of the building, then swiftly out of it, like someone in flight from a surging fire.

At last I came to a halt at the little cement bench where Sarah and I had sat together years before, the lighthouse behind us, the school in front. In my mind I saw Miss Channing and Mr. Reed walk once again to the car beneath the oak, Mr. Reed open the door, Miss Channing slip inside, the car begin to move, turning out of the parking lot and onto Myrtle Street, finally drifting by me as it had that day so many years before, Miss Channing staring straight ahead, so silent and so still, with nothing but a dark strand of loosened hair to leave its mark upon her face.

I returned to my office, sat down at my desk, my eyes involuntarily drifting over to the archive my father had long ago assembled, perhaps as something to remind him of his fall, though without in the least knowing that it had been mine as well.

I rose and walked to the file cabinet beneath my father's portrait. Glancing up at it, I heard his voice in old age, hung with the bleakness of his final years, perhaps even the deepest of its disappointments: *So there'll never be a wife, Henry? Never a child?* My answer as stark as it had always been: *No.*

I turned away from the portrait, opened the cabinet, and pulled out the forms I would need to begin my work for Clement Boggs, already considering what the last phase of that work would inevitably require, the cruel lyrics of a dreadful song playing in my mind as I made my way back to my desk:

> Alice Craddock
> Locked in a paddock
> Where's your daddy gone?

# PART III

# TWELVE

During the final years of his life, with my mother gone, and few means of passing the idle hours, my father took to walking through the countryside. I was a middle-aged bachelor by then, with little to engage me but my legal practice. And so I often accompanied him on his rambles, the two of us first driving to a particular spot, then setting off into the woods. Usually we went to Nickerson State Park, where the trails were easiest. But from time to time we would wander into some more remote area, park the car along the road, then follow a less well-defined path around a nearby hill or up a gently angled slope.

Most of these walks were routine affairs, my father talking quietly about whatever he'd read most recently, a book or magazine article that had briefly held his attention. The past, particularly his years at Chatham School, seemed nearly to have disappeared from his consciousness altogether.

Then, one afternoon only a year before his death, we found ourselves on a hilltop outside Chatham, the spires and roofs of the village in the distance, and down below, like a dark, sightless eye, the unruffled waters of Black Pond.

He remained silent for a time, but I could see that he was struggling to say something, release some pronouncement he'd long kept inside. It was a struggle that surprised me. For except for those times when my mother had insisted upon bringing up the subject, my father had seemed more than satisfied to let all thought of the Chatham School Affair sink unmourned into oblivion.

'So much death, Henry,' he said finally. 'Down there on Black Pond. So much destruction.'

I saw bodies swirling in green water, small hands clawing at a strip of black rubber, a boat lolling in an empty sea, a middle-aged woman rocking on her front porch, her eyes vacant and emotionless, staring into nowhere, her hair a sickly yellow streaked with gray.

My father continued to peer down at the pond, his hands behind his back, two wrinkled claws. 'I sometimes forget that I ever really knew them. Miss Channing and Mr. Reed, I mean.' He shook his head. 'How about you, Henry? Do you ever think of them?'

I glanced about, recalling the slow trudge we'd all made up the hill that morning, Mr. Reed in the lead, Miss Channing just behind him. I could still feel the cold November air that had surrounded us, how we'd had to brush snowflakes from our eyes.

'I came up here with them,' I said. 'To the top of this same hill. Sarah came with us too.' My eyes settled on the very place where we'd stood together and looked out over the pond. 'It all seemed harmless at the time.'

I remembered Miss Channing and Mr. Reed strolling through Chatham, pausing to gaze in shop windows, or standing beside the fence at London Livery, Miss Channing stroking the muzzle of one of the horses. Once I'd come upon them in Warren's Sundries, Mr. Reed with a model boat in his hand, turning it at various angles, pointing out its separate parts, the mast, the spinnaker, the fluttering sail, his words spoken quietly, bearing, at the time, no grave import. *It wouldn't be hard to do it.*

My father's eyes searched the near rim of the pond. The thick summer foliage blocked the spot I knew he was looking for.

'Why did you go to Milford Cottage so often?' he asked, still peering down the hillside.

'Because of Sarah. I went to her reading lessons.'

'But why?'

'I don't know.'

My father kept his tone matter-of-fact, but I knew how charged his feelings were, how many questions still plagued him. At last he asked one he'd kept inside for a long time. 'Were you in love with her, Henry?'

I remembered the night I'd gone to her room, how gently she'd received me, her eyes shy and downcast, her body beneath a white nightgown, a satin ribbon dangling just above her chest. 'She was a lovely girl,' I said. 'And living in our house the way she did, I might have—'

'I wasn't talking about Sarah,' my father said, interrupting me. 'I was talking about Miss Channing.'

I heard rain batting against the windowpanes of Milford Cottage as it had that night, wind slamming at the screen door, saw candles burning in her bedroom, a yellow light pouring over her, the stillness in her eyes when she spoke. *Will you do it, Henry?* Then my reply, obedient as ever, *Yes.*

'I always thought that was the reason you took it so hard,' my father added. 'Because you had a certain ... feeling for Miss Channing.'

Her face dissolved in a haze of yellow light, and I saw her as she'd appeared the day we'd stood there on the hill, snow clinging to her hair and gathered along the shoulders of her long blue coat. 'I wanted her to be free,' I said.

'To do what?'

'Live however she wanted to.'

He shook his head. 'It didn't turn out that way.'

'No, it didn't.'

I felt my father's arm settle on my shoulders, embrace me like a child. 'Never forget, Henry,' he said, offering his final comment on the Chatham School Affair, 'never forget that some part of it was good.'

I'm not sure I ever fully believed that, though I couldn't deny that there'd been good moments, especially at the beginning. One of those moments had been the very day we'd all gone up the hill and stood together in the first snow of the season.

Sarah and I had walked to Milford Cottage that November morning, Sarah eager to get on with her lessons, confident that she would soon master the skills she needed to 'better' herself, childlike in her enthusiasm, adult in her determination.

Not long after we'd left Chatham it had begun to snow, so that by the time we'd finally reached Milford Cottage we were cold and wet.

As we neared the cottage, I saw Miss Channing part the plain white curtains of one of its small windows and peer out. She was wearing a white blouse, the sleeves rolled up to the elbow, and her hair fell loosely over her shoulders. From the look on her face, I could tell that she was somewhat surprised to see us.

'You didn't have to come, you know,' she called to us as she opened the door. 'I would have understood that the weather—'

Sarah shook her head vigorously. 'Oh, no, Miss Channing,' she said, 'I wouldn't think of missing a lesson.'

Miss Channing eased back into the cottage and motioned us inside. 'Well, come in quickly, then,' she said. 'You must be frozen stiff.'

We walked into the cottage, and I realized that it looked considerably different from when I'd last been inside. Some of Miss Channing's older sketches had been replaced by more recent ones, quiet village scenes, along with intricate line drawings, beautifully detailed, of various leaves and vegetation she'd found in the surrounding woods, some of which now rested in a large glass vase on her mantel.

'You've made it very cozy inside the house here,' Sarah said. She glanced about the room, taking in other changes, the hooked rug in front of the fireplace, the bookshelf in the far corner, the small red pillows that rested against the wooden backs of the room's two chairs. 'You've made it look like a regular house,' she added, drawing her scarf from her head.

'It's quite grand, Miss Channing.' She lifted the basket she'd brought with her from Myrtle Street. 'I brought a fruitcake for you. There's a bit of spirits in it though.' Her mischievous smile flickered. 'So we shouldn't be having too much of it, or we won't stay clearheaded, you know.'

Miss Channing took the cake and deposited it on the small table by the window. 'We'll have some after the lesson,' she said.

They got down to their lessons right away, Miss Channing opening the notebook Sarah had brought along, peering at the writing inside, evaluating it closely before commenting. 'Good,' she said warmly. 'Very good, Sarah.'

After that they went to work in the usual way, Miss Channing writing short, simple sentences which Sarah then read back to her. From my place in a chair not far away, I could see how well they got along, how much Sarah admired Miss Channing, perhaps even dreamed of being like her, 'a fine lady,' as she'd always said.

I suppose it was something in that 'fineness' that made me take out my sketchbook that morning and begin to draw Miss Channing, concentrating on the way she leaned forward, her head cocked slightly, her hair falling in a dark wave across her shoulders. I found that I could capture her general appearance, but that there was something else I couldn't get, the way her eyes sometimes darkened, as if a small light had gone off behind them, and which Mr. Parsons later described as 'sinister', the very word he used at her trial.

She was still working with Sarah when I heard a car coming down Plymouth Road, its engine rattling chaotically as it slid to a halt in the driveway of the cottage.

Miss Channing rose, walked to the window, and looked out.

'We have a guest,' she said. There was a hint of excitement in her voice, something Sarah must have heard too, for her eyes swept over to me with a quizzical expression in them.

By then Miss Channing had walked to the door and opened it, a gust of wind sweeping her black hair across her face.

'Well, good morning,' she called, waving her arm. She turned toward Sarah and me. 'It's Mr. Reed,' she said.

I walked to the window. At the edge of the yard I could see Mr. Reed as he got out of his car. He was wearing a heavy wool coat, brown boots, and a gray hat he'd pulled somewhat raffishly to the left. He waved to Miss Channing, then came tramping down the walkway, the snow nearly an inch deep by then.

'You're just in time for fruitcake,' Miss Channing told him as he neared the door.

'Fruitcake,' Mr. Reed said. 'Well, it's certainly the right weather for

476

it.' For a moment he stood on the threshold of the cottage, facing Miss Channing from the bottom of the stairs, his eyes lifted toward her, gazing at her. 'I wanted to—' he began, then stopped when he saw Sarah and me inside the cottage. 'Oh, I see you have company,' he said, his manner now stiffening slightly.

'Yes, I do,' Miss Channing said. 'Sarah's here for her reading lesson. She made the fruitcake I mentioned.'

Mr. Reed appeared at a loss as to what he should do next, whether he should come into the cottage or leave immediately. 'Well, I wouldn't want to disturb Sarah's lesson,' he said.

'No, no. We've just finished it,' Miss Channing told him. She stepped back into the room. 'Please, come in.'

Mr. Reed hesitated a moment, but then came into the cottage and took a seat by the window as Sarah and Miss Channing disappeared into the kitchen to serve the cake.

For a time Mr. Reed said nothing. I could tell that my presence disturbed him. Perhaps at that time he thought me an informer, certain that I'd rush back to Chatham, tell my father about his visit to Miss Channing's cottage. Then he glanced at me with a certain apprehensiveness I'd never seen in him before. 'Well, Henry, are you enjoying your classes this year?'

'I guess so,' I answered.

He smiled thinly and returned his attention to the window.

He was still staring out of it a few seconds later, when Miss Channing and Sarah came back into the room. Miss Channing placed the cake on the table in front of him and began to cut. The first piece went to Sarah, the second to Mr. Reed. Then, turning to me, she said, 'Would you like a large piece?'

I shook my head, trying to be polite.

She smiled, no doubt sensing my hunger, then spoke a line that life forever proves to be a lie. 'Take as much as you want, Henry. There is plenty.'

A few minutes later the four of us walked out of Miss Channing's cottage, swung to the left, and followed Mr. Reed as he led us down Plymouth Road, then up a gentle slope to a clearing at the top of a nearby hill.

Once there, we sat down on a fallen tree, the four of us in a single line, facing back down the hill toward Black Pond. The snow had thickened by then; a layer of white gathered on the leafless trees and settled onto the brim of Mr. Reed's hat.

'A snow like this,' Miss Channing said. 'The flakes so small, but so many of them. Like confetti.'

Mr. Reed smiled at her. 'Is that how you'd paint it, Elizabeth? As confetti?'

She smiled, but didn't answer him. Instead, she walked a few paces farther on, while Mr. Reed remained in place, watching her as she reached the crest of the hill, then stood, peering out over the pond. For a moment she remained very still, as if lost in thought. Then she lifted her arms and drew them around her shoulders. It was a gesture made against the cold, quite unselfconsciously, I think, but one Mr. Reed must have experienced as a vision so beautiful and so brief that it remained with him forever after that, set the mark against which everything else would ultimately be measured.

We stood in a ragged line at the crest of the hill, facing east, across Black Pond, to where a curl of chimney smoke could be seen rising from the trees along its most distant bank.

'That smoke must be coming from your house, Mr. Reed,' Sarah said, pointing to it.

Mr. Reed nodded, his manner now strangely somber. 'I should be getting back home,' he said, glancing toward Miss Channing. 'Abigail is waiting.'

'It looks just like a Christmas card, if you ask me,' Sarah said happily. 'The house by the pond. The snow. Just like a Christmas card, don't you think so?'

Mr. Reed smiled, but with a curious wistfulness, as if it were something he remembered fondly from a distant past. 'Yes,' he said, his eyes now fixed on the far bank of the pond. 'Yes, it looks just like a Christmas card.' Then he turned away and I saw his eyes light upon Miss Channing, linger upon her profile for a moment.

'And are you going away for the Christmas holiday then?' Sarah asked him. The cold air had caused the color to rise in her cheeks and her eyes sparkled with excitement.

He seemed reluctant to answer, but did so anyway. 'Yes,' he said. 'I'm going to Maine for a couple of weeks. We always do that, go to Maine.'

With that, he turned quickly and led us back down the hill to Miss Channing's cottage.

Mr. Reed stopped when he reached his car. 'I'll be getting home now,' he said, his eyes on Miss Channing.

'I'm glad you dropped by,' she told him, her voice quite soft, almost inaudible.

'Perhaps I'll come again,' Mr. Reed said in a tone that struck me as subtly imploring, as if he were asking for some sign from her that he should return.

If she gave him one, I didn't see it. Instead, she shivered slightly. 'It's really quite cold.'

'Yes, it is,' Mr. Reed answered, his voice now entirely matter-of-fact. 'Would you like a ride into the village?' he asked Sarah and me.

We accepted his offer and climbed into the car. Mr. Reed remained outside it, facing Miss Channing, the snow falling between and around them. He spoke to her again, words I couldn't hear, then stepped forward and offered his hand. She took it, held it for just an instant, then let it go, smiling quietly as he stepped away. It was then I saw it in all its naked force, the full measure of the love that had begun to overwhelm Mr. Reed, perhaps even some hint of the exquisite agony that was inseparable from it, not yet fierce, and certainly not explosive, but the fuse already lit.

Instead of going directly to Chatham, Mr. Reed swung to the right and drove to his own house on the other side of the pond. 'I should tell my wife that I'm going to the marina,' he told us.

'The marina?' Sarah asked.

Mr. Reed nodded. 'Yes,' he said. 'I rented a boathouse there a few years ago. I'm building a boat in it. A fifteen-footer.'

Sarah stared at him admiringly, the thought of such a grand endeavor playing in her eyes. 'When will it be finished?' she asked.

'With a little help, I could probably finish it by summer,' Mr. Reed answered.

Impulsively, without giving it the slightest thought, I suddenly made an offer that has pursued me through the years, following me through time, like a dog through the night, its black muzzle forever sniffing at my heels. 'I could help you finish it,' I said. 'I'd like to learn about boats.'

Mr. Reed nodded, his eyes fixed on the road ahead. 'Really, Henry? I didn't know you were interested in that sort of thing.'

'Yes, I am,' I told him, though even now I don't know why I felt such an interest. I do know that it had not come from the seafaring adventure novels I often read, though that was the reason I offered Mr. Parsons the day we walked through the boathouse together. More likely, it had sprung from a voyeur's dark urge, the allure of the forbidden already working like a drug in my mind.

We reached his house a few minutes later. Sarah and I remained in the car while Mr. Reed went inside.

'He's such a nice man,' Sarah said. 'Not an old fogy like some of them at Chatham School.'

I nodded. 'Yes, he is.'

He came back out of the house almost immediately, a long roll of white paper beneath his arm, bound with twine, like a scroll. I watched as he made his way across the yard, his daughter Mary rushing down the stairs behind him while Mrs. Reed stood at the edge of the porch, wiping her hands on her apron as she watched him trudge back toward us through the falling snow. She was still in that position when he pulled himself into the car, but Mary had bounded toward us, then stopped, smiling mischievously as she attempted to roll a snowball in her hands.

Once inside the car, Mr. Reed started the engine and began to pull away. We'd drifted back only a few feet, when Mary suddenly rushed forward and hurled the snowball toward us. It landed on the hood and exploded just at the base of the windshield, sending a flurry of white onto the glass. Mr. Reed turned on the wipers, and as they swept across the windshield, I saw Mrs. Reed still standing on the porch, watching motionlessly as Mr. Reed continued backward, away from her, leaving two dark cuts in the snow.

I told my father about that scene as we stood together on the hill over-looking Black Pond.

'Do you think she'd already sensed it?' my father asked me when I'd finished the story. 'I mean, before Christmas. Before they all went to Maine together? Do you think Mrs. Reed already suspected something?'

I shrugged. 'I don't know.'

His eyes shifted to the left, and I could tell he was gazing in the general direction of where Mr. Reed had once lived with his wife and daughter. 'If she did know, or if she already suspected something by that time, then she had to have dealt with it for a long time before ...'

'Yes, she had,' I said. And with those words I saw her again, Abigail Reed standing beside me as she had in the boathouse that day, her eyes staring down into a cardboard box, fixed on the things that lay inside it – the rope, the knife, a nautical map with a route already drawn in red ink.

'So what finally broke her, I wonder. Sent her over the edge, I mean.'

I said nothing.

He looked at me, his puzzlement returning once again. 'We'll never get to the bottom of it, will we, Henry? We'll never know what she was thinking in the end.'

I did not answer him, but in my mind I saw her in that final moment, a face pressing toward me out of the murky depths, her red hair waving behind her like a shredded banner.

# THIRTEEN

But despite those times when I was forced to consider the end of it, as I had that day on the hill with my father, I found that I more often hearkened back to its beginning, particularly to a story Miss Channing told in class only a few days after we'd all had fruitcake and gone for a walk in the snowy woods.

At Chatham School, the lunch break was one hour, from twelve to one, and after having lunch in the upstairs dining hall I'd walked into the village, made my way to Peterson's Hardware Supply, idly fiddled with a fancy new fishing pole, then headed back up the snow-covered hill toward the school.

As I neared Myrtle Street, I saw Miss Channing sitting on a wooden bench near the edge of the cliff, Mr. Reed standing behind her, leaning on his cane, the wind blowing back his jacket and riffling through his hair, so that he seemed momentarily captured in that passionate wildness Mr. Parsons would later describe as the origins of murder. I saw his hand touch her shoulder, then leap back, as if from a red-hot stove. Then he said something, and she glanced back at him and smiled.

That's when she caught me with her eye, peered at me an instant, then rose and began to stride toward me.

She was wearing a long, dark coat, and as she moved toward me from the crest of the bluff, the high collar raised up against the back of her neck, I remember thinking that she looked like someone from an earlier century, one of those women we'd read about in Mr. Reed's literature class the previous year, Eustacia Vye, perhaps, or Madame Bovary, wild and passionately driven, capable of that lethal wantonness Mr. Parsons later described to the jury, and in whose presence, he said, Mr. Reed was 'little more than a piece of kindling before a raging flame.'

And yet, on that particular morning Miss Channing hardly looked wanton. She had dressed herself conservatively, as she usually did, her hair tied with a dark blue ribbon, a cameo at her throat.

It was Mr. Reed who appeared somewhat emboldened, standing very erect beside her, his face full of purpose as he spoke.

'Have you seen Sarah?' he asked.

I shook my head. 'Not since this morning.'

Miss Channing drew a book from beneath her arm. It was old, with a peeling cover and frayed yellow pages, its spine long ago broken, so that some of the pages were barely held in place. 'I wanted to give her this,' she told me.

'It's my primer,' Mr. Reed explained. 'From grade school. I've kept it all these years, and now Miss Channing thinks she can use it in her lessons with Sarah.'

I looked at Miss Channing. 'If you want, I could give it to her when I go home after school.'

'Thank you, Henry,' Miss Channing said. She handed me the book. 'Just tell Sarah to bring it when she comes for her lesson next Sunday.'

I nodded.

'Thank you again, Henry,' Miss Channing said. Then she turned, and the two of them walked back to the bench beside the cliff, Mr. Reed now sitting beside her, though still at a discreet distance, his cane resting between them like a strictly imposed divide.

I didn't see Miss Channing again until that same afternoon, this time as she stood behind the table at the front of her classroom.

'Today we're going to start something new,' she said. 'Landscapes.' She turned and made a broad arc over nearly the entire length of the blackboard, then flattened its upper reaches with a few quick strokes. 'This is the general shape,' she said, 'of a volcano.'

With that, her face took on the curious intimacy I'd become accustomed to by then, the odd intertwining of her teaching and her life. 'Nothing on earth, not even the sea, will ever make you feel as small as a volcano makes you feel,' she said.

Then she told us the story of the day her father had taken her to Mount Etna. Its immensity could hardly be grasped by anyone who had not seen it firsthand, she said. It soared from its base to a height of nearly two miles, and the railway that circled it was over ninety miles long, roughly the same distance from Chatham School to Boston. 'My father was in awe of the violence of Etna,' she said. 'Of how powerful it was, and how indifferent to everything but itself. He wanted me to see how the lava from one of its eruptions had once flowed all the way to the sea, destroying everything in sight.'

She seemed to envision that vast smoldering flow as it had rolled down the slopes, then flowed across the valley, devouring everything in flames, consuming whole villages as it swept toward the sea.

Then, rather suddenly her face brightened. 'But what I remember best about Mount Etna,' she said, 'is that there were flowers everywhere. On the slope and in the valley. So many of them that even near the rim, where I could see smoke and steam rising from the crater itself, even at that point, where everything else was so desolate, I could still smell the flowers down below.' She appeared genuinely amazed at the process she described. 'Flowers grown from ash.'

During all the years since then, I've thought of the Chatham School Affair in exactly opposite terms, the whole process utterly reversed, something that flowered briefly, gave off an exquisite sweetness, then, in a harrowing instant, turned everything to ash.

And so, just as my father later said, some part of it was good. Especially for Mr. Reed, since, as I later learned, he'd never before experienced that form of passion that turns our eyes to the far horizon, erases the past like chalk dust from a board, raises us from the dead as surely as it consigns all others to the grave.

I showed up at his rented boathouse just after Miss Channing's class that day, images of smoldering volcanos still playing in my mind, my sketchbook already filled with my own attempts at rendering an explosive and primeval violence I was certain I would never experience.

Mr. Reed was sitting at the little wooden desk he'd placed in the corner, a pile of papers spread out across it. He turned to face me as I came through the door.

'Hello, Henry,' he said.

'I wondered if you still needed help on the boat.'

He smiled. 'So, you're still interested?' he asked, already reaching for his cane.

'Yes.'

'Well, there she is,' he said, indicating the boat. 'What do you think?'

The boat rested on a wooden frame that stretched nearly the entire length of the room. The inner shell had only been partially fitted, so I could see into its still-unfinished interior. Hoisted upon the frame, without a mast, and with slats missing from its outer wrapping, it looked more like the skeleton of some ancient beast than a boat.

'As you can see,' Mr. Reed said, 'there's still a lot to do. But not as much as you might think. Toward the end, it all comes together rather suddenly.' He paused, gauging my response. Then he said, 'We can start now, if you're still interested.'

We set to work right away, Mr. Reed giving me my first basic lesson in boat-building, the patience it required, the precision of measurement. 'You have to go slowly,' he said at one point. 'Just let things fall

483

into place.' He offered a wry smile. 'It's like a woman who can't be rushed.'

As we continued to work that afternoon, it struck me that something had fallen away from Mr. Reed, some part of the impenetrable weariness I'd seen during all the years I'd known him, and which had served to cloak him in a melancholy that seemed inseparable from his character. A new and vital energy had begun to take its place. It was as if a fire were slowly burning off the detritus of his former life, making him more alert and animated than I'd ever seen him, a sense of buoyancy replacing the ponderousness that had so deeply marked him until then, and which I have since come to recognize not as the product of a dream already fulfilled, but only of a hope precariously revived.

We worked together all that afternoon, Mr. Reed more talkative than he'd ever been outside the classroom. He spoke of writers he admired, quoted lines from their works, though not so much in the manner of a teacher as simply of a man whose mind and heart had been informed and uplifted by his reading. He talked about his boat as well, its speed and durability, what its capacities were. 'A boat this size, built this way,' he said at one point, 'you could sail it around the world.' He thought a moment, as if considering such a possibility. 'You'd have to sail along the coastline and skip from island to island,' he added. 'But it could be done.'

Only once did the old melancholy appear to settle over him again. 'Just one life, Henry,' he said, staring out the window of the boathouse, his eyes fixed on the bay, and, beyond it, the open sea. 'Just one life, and no more chances after that.' He turned back to me. 'That's the whole tragedy, right there.'

It seemed the perfect moment to add my own comment. 'That's what Miss Channing's father says,' I told him. 'In his book. He says that if you look back on your life and ask What did I do?, then it means that you didn't do anything.'

Mr. Reed nodded thoughtfully, and I could tell he was turning the line over in his mind. 'Yes, that's true. Do you think Miss Channing believes that?'

With no evidence whatsoever, I answered, 'Yes, I do.'

He seemed pleased by my answer. 'Well, it *is* true, Henry. Absolutely true. Whether most people want to believe it or not.'

I suppose that from then on I felt in league with Mr. Reed, willing to work on his boat every afternoon and weekend if that's what it took to finish it, willing to listen to him in all the weeks that followed, his tone bright and buoyant at first, then darkening steadily until, toward the end, he seemed mired in endless night.

It was nearly evening when I finally headed back toward home. And I remember that as I walked up the coastal road, the autumn drizzle felt more like a spring rain, the bare limbs not destined for a deeper chill, but on the very brink of budding.

The table had already been set for dinner by the time I reached home, my mother and father in their usual places at opposite ends of it, Sarah moving smoothly from one to the other, humming softly under her breath so my mother could not hear her.

My father glanced at his pocket watch as I took my seat. 'Are you aware of the time, Henry?'

I wasn't, but said I was, then gave him a reason that I knew would justify my tardiness. 'I was down at the marina, helping Mr. Reed.'

'Helping Mr. Reed?' my mother asked doubtfully. 'To do what?'

'He's building a boat,' I answered. I glanced toward Sarah, saw her give me a quick conspiratorial smile. 'He's been working on it for a long time,' I added. 'He wants to finish it by summer.'

My mother could not conceal her disapproval. 'It's his house over on the pond that could use a little work, if you ask me,' she sniffed. 'More than some fool boat down at the marina.'

'Now, Mildred,' my father cautioned, always careful that teachers at Chatham School not be criticized in front of me. 'What Mr. Reed does in his spare time is his own business. But being on time for dinner is your responsibility, Henry, and be sure you look to it from now on.'

'Yes, sir,' I said, glancing once again toward Sarah, her smile even broader now, her eyes gleaming with a quick, mischievous fire.

Her room was in the attic.

The tap at the door must have surprised her. 'Who's there?' she asked, a hint of apprehension in her voice.

'It's me, Henry,' I said, standing in the utter darkness of the narrow stairway. 'Miss Channing wanted me to give you a book.'

She opened the door slightly, her face in candlelight. 'You shouldn't be up here, Henry,' she whispered. 'What if your ...'

'They're asleep,' I told her. I smiled mockingly. 'I know they are. I can hear my mother snoring.'

She laughed sharply, and swiftly covered her mouth. 'Be quick about it, then,' she urged as she opened the door.

The room was tiny, with a slanting ceiling, her bed pressed up against the far wall, a small desk and a chair at the other end, along with a short bureau with a porcelain wash basin and china pitcher on top. Now, when I recall that room, it seems smaller still, particularly compared to the aspirations of the girl who lived there, the life she yearned for.

'Miss Channing asked me to give you this,' I said, handing her Mr. Reed's primer.

She stepped over to her bed and sat down upon it. I stood a few feet away, watching as she opened the book and began to leaf through the pages.

'It's Mr. Reed's primer,' I said. 'The one he had in grade school. Miss Channing wants you to bring it with you on Sunday.'

She continued to glance through the book until she reached the end. Then she turned back to its beginning. 'Look, Henry,' she said, her eyes on the book's front page.

I walked over to the bed and sat down beside her.

'Look at what Mr. Reed wrote to Miss Channing,' she said.

The words were in dark blue ink, Mr. Reed's small, tortured hand immediately recognizable, though the words seemed far more tender than Mr. Reed himself ever had.

My dear Elizabeth,
I hope that you can make some use of this book, even though, like the owner of it, it is an old and worn-out thing.

With love,
Leland

Sarah's eyes lingered on the inscription for a time before she lifted them to me, her hand suddenly brushing mine very gently, almost silkily, with no more weight than a ribbon. 'Have you ever been in love, Henry?' she asked, the words coming with an odd hesitancy, her eyes upon me with a softness and sense of entreaty that have never left me since then, and which I often recall on those nights when the wind blows and drifts of snow climb toward the window, and I am alone with my memories of her.

My answer was quick and sure. 'No.'

I saw her shoulders fall slightly, felt her hand draw away. She closed the book and placed it on the bed beside her. 'You'd better go now,' she said, her eyes now averted.

I walked to the door, opened it, and stepped out onto the narrow landing. 'Well, good night, Sarah,' I said as I turned to close the door again.

She did not look up, but kept her head bowed slightly so that a dark curtain of black hair fell over the right side of her face. 'Good night, Henry,' was all she said.

I closed the door and returned to my room. I don't recall thinking of Sarah again that night. But I have thought of her often since then, wondered if things might have turned out differently on Black Pond had I lingered a moment longer in her room. Perhaps I might finally have grasped the ribbon that dangled from her gown, given it a slow, trembling pull, and thus come to know both the power of that first encounter, and then the later pleasures of enduring love. I don't know if Sarah would have given herself to me that night, but if she had, I might have gone to her from then on rather than to the boathouse or Milford Cottage. I might have experienced love up close and through all its changing seasons, and by doing that, come to feel spring as something other than a cruel deception, winter the dreadful truth of things.

# FOURTEEN

But in the end, I chose to think of life rather than to live it.

I said as much in my office one afternoon. I'd been talking to Mr. Parsons' son, Albert Parsons, Jr., the two of us in our middle fifties by then, with the elder Mr. Parsons now impossibly old and senile, a figure rooted on a bench outside the town hall, muttering to himself and flinging crumbs to the pigeons.

'So many books, Henry,' he said in a tone that seemed vaguely accusatory. 'Have you read them all?'

I offered him a mirthless smile. 'They're what I have instead of a wife and children.'

Albert laughed. 'You're a pistol, Henry. A real barnyard philosopher.' He sat back and let his eyes roam the bookshelves in my office, squinting at the titles. 'Greeks and Romans. Why them in particular?'

'They were my father's favorites.'

'Why's that?'

I shrugged. 'Maybe because he thought they saw it more clearly.'

'Saw what?'

'Life.'

He laughed again. 'You're a pistol, Henry,' he repeated.

We'd just come to a settlement that each of us felt our clients would accept, his being the aggrieved party in a construction contract dispute, mine, a local contractor named Tom Cannon.

'You know, Henry, I was a little surprised that Tom ever got named in a lawsuit like this,' Albert said. 'He's done plenty of work for me, and I've never had any trouble with him.' He took a sip of the celebratory brandy I'd just poured him. 'He even built that little office my father used when he was working on his memoirs.'

Some part of the old time abruptly reasserted itself in my mind, and I saw Mr. Parsons as he'd stood before the jury on the last day of Miss Channing's trial, a man in his early forties then, still young and vigorous, no doubt certain that he'd found the truth about her, revealed for all to see the murderous conspiracy she'd hatched with Leland Reed.

'How is Mr. Parsons these days?' I asked.

'Oh, he's as good as can be expected, I guess,' Albert answered. 'Of course, the way he is now, there's not a whole lot he can do but sit around.' He took a greedy sip from the brandy. 'He likes to hang around the courthouse for the most part. Or on that bench in front of the town hall.' He shrugged. 'He mutters to himself sometimes. Old age, you know.'

I saw Mr. Parsons on his lonely bench, his hand rhythmically digging into a paper bag filled with bread crumbs or popcorn, casting it over the lawn, a circle of pigeons sweeping out from around him like a pool of restless gray water.

Albert took a puff on his cigar, then flicked the ash into the amber-colored ashtray on my desk. 'He talks about my mother, of course, along with my sister and me,' he went on absently. 'Some of his big cases too. They come to mind once in a while.'

Before I could stop myself, I blurted, 'The Chatham School Affair.'

Albert looked at me, perhaps surprised that it had leaped into my mind so quickly. 'Yes, that one in particular,' he said. 'He got quite a shock from that woman ... what was her name?'

'Channing,' I said. 'Elizabeth Channing.'

Albert shook his head. 'Nobody could have imagined that that woman would cause so much trouble,' he added with a short laugh. 'Not even your father.'

Inevitably I recalled how the people of Chatham had finally laid a large portion of the blame for what happened on Black Pond at my father's feet. It was the price he'd paid for hiring Miss Channing in the first place, then turning what everyone considered a blind eye to her behavior, a delinquency that his neighbors had never been able to forget, nor his wife forgive.

'You think he ever suspected anything, Henry?'

I remembered the look on my father's face as he'd closed the door of his office that day, with Mr. Parsons in his dark suit, reaching into the box he'd placed on the chair beside him, drawing out a book with one hand, a length of gray rope with the other, Miss Channing standing before him in a white dress. 'Not of what they thought she did. No, I don't think he ever suspected her of that.'

'Why, I wonder,' Albert said casually, as if he were discussing no more than a local curiosity, 'I mean, she was pretty strange, wasn't she?'

For a moment I thought I saw her sitting silently on the other side of the room, staring at me as she had that last time, her hair oily, matted, unwashed, her skin a deathly pale, but still glowing incandescently from out of the surrounding shadows. In a low, unearthly whisper I heard her repeat her last words to me: *Go now, Henry. Please.*

'No, she wasn't strange,' I said. 'But what happened to her was.'

Albert shrugged. 'Well, I was just a little boy at the time, so really, about all I remember is that she was very pretty.'

I recalled my father's eyes the day she'd approached him across the summer lawn of Milford Cottage, her bare feet in the moist green grass, then the look on Mr. Reed's face as he'd gazed at her on the hill that snowy November morning. 'She was beautiful,' I told Albert Parsons, my eyes now drifting toward the window, then beyond it, to the lighthouse she'd fled from that terrible afternoon. 'But she couldn't help that, could she?'

'Well, one thing's for sure,' Albert said. 'It was the man who was the real shocker in the whole thing. The other teacher, I mean.'

'Leland Reed.'

'That's right.' Albert released a quick, mocking laugh. 'I mean, God almighty, Henry, who'd have thought that a man like him would interest a young woman as pretty as that Channing woman was?' He shook his head at the curiousness of human beings, their woeful randomness and unpredictability, the impenetrable wilderness they make of life. 'Why, hell, that Reed fellow looked like a damn freak, as I remember it, always limping around, his face all scarred up. Just a rag of a man, that's what my father said. His very words. Just a rag of a man.'

I drew my eyes away from the lighthouse and settled them on the old oak that stood across the way, its bare limbs rising upward, twisting and chaotic, a web without design. Beyond it, down a distant street that led to the marina, I could make out the gray roof of the old boat-house where Mr. Reed and I had labored to build his boat. In my memory of those days I could see him working frantically through the night, painting, varnishing, making the final preparations for its maiden voyage. Like someone whispering invisibly in my ear, I heard him say, *Disappear, disappear*, the grim incantation of his final days.

'Of course that Channing woman certainly saw something in him,' Albert said. He smiled. 'What can you say, Henry? The mysteries of love.'

But the nature of what Miss Channing might have seen in Leland Reed seemed hardly to matter to Albert, Jr. He crushed his cigar into the ashtray. 'They didn't get away with it though,' he said. 'That's the main thing. I once heard my father say that he'd never have gotten to the bottom of it – that he'd have just thought it was all some kind of terrible accident – if it hadn't been for you.'

I felt something give in the thick wall I'd built around my memory of that time. In my mind I saw Mr. Parsons standing in front of me, the two of us on the playing field behind Chatham School, facing each other in a blue twilight, Mr. Parsons suddenly twisting his head in the general direction of Black Pond before returning his gaze to me, his hand coming to a soft paternal rest upon my shoulder. *Thank you, Henry. I know how hard it is to tell the truth.*

The newspaper headline stated the fact baldly: STUDENT TESTIFIES IN CHATHAM SCHOOL AFFAIR.

There'd been a photograph beneath the headline, a young man in dark trousers and a gray jacket, his black hair now slicked back and neatly combed, a figure that had not in the least resembled the wild-eyed boy who'd stood at the top of the lighthouse some weeks before, madly drawing one frenzied portrait after another, rendering Chatham as a reeling nightmare world.

Others in the village have no doubt forgotten what I said upon the stand, but I never have, nor ever will. So that on that day over forty years later, when I'd sat in my office with Albert Parsons, Jr., watching him light his second cigar, I'd seen it all unfold once again, myself in the witness box, dressed in the black trousers and gray jacket of Chatham School, my hair neatly combed, all my wild ideas of flight and freedom now brought to heel by Mr. Parsons' first question: *When did you first meet Elizabeth Channing?*

After that he'd continued gently, pacing back and forth while I sat rigidly in the witness box, a bright morning sun pouring in from the high windows, flashing rhythmically in the lenses of his glasses as he moved through blinding shafts of light.

*Mr. Parsons: Now, you are a student at Chatham School, are you not, Henry?*

*Witness: Yes, sir.*

*Mr. Parsons: And you took English with Mr. Leland Reed, I believe, and art with the defendant, Miss Elizabeth Channing?*

*Witness: Yes.*

*Mr. Parsons: And would you say that Mr. Reed took a special interest in you?*

*Witness: Yes, he did.*

*Mr. Parsons: And Miss Channing too?*

*Witness: Yes.*

*Mr. Parsons: How would you describe the interest Miss Channing took in you, Henry?*

*Witness: Well, mostly she was interested in my drawing. She told me that she thought I had talent, and that I should get a sketchbook and draw in my spare time.*

491

Sitting in the witness box, listening to my own voice, I remembered all the times I'd tucked that same sketch-book beneath my arm and set out from my house on Myrtle Street, a lone figure marching solemnly into the village or strolling down the beach, fired by the idea of an artistic life, of roaming the world as Miss Channing's father had, a creature with no fixed abode.

*Mr. Parsons: And did you do a great deal of drawing at this time?*
*Witness: Yes, I did.*
*Mr. Parsons: But that was not your only activity at this time, was it, Henry?*
*Witness: Activity?*
*Mr. Parsons: Well, you also became involved in another project during that year at Chatham School, didn't you? With Mr. Reed, I mean.*
*Witness: Yes, I did.*
*Mr. Parsons: And what activity was that?*
*Witness: I helped him build his boat.*

Even as I'd said it, I recalled how often I'd gone down to the boathouse Mr. Reed had rented near the harbor, the two of us drifting down the coastal road in his old car, Mr. Reed talking quietly, I listening silently, my fingers drumming incessantly on the sketchbook in my lap, increasingly extravagant visions playing in my mind, the vagabond life I so desperately wanted, trains hurling through mountain tunnels, night boats to Tangier.

But it hadn't been my boyish fantasies, nor even my relationship with Mr. Reed, that Mr. Parsons had been intent upon exploring the day he'd questioned me in court, and I remember how my body had tensed as he began to close in upon what I knew to be his sole intended prey:

*Mr. Parsons: So during this last year you spent at Chatham School, you came to know Miss Channing well?*
*Witness: Yes, I did.*
*Mr. Parsons: And sometimes you visited her at her cottage on Black Pond, isn't that so?*
*Witness: On Black Pond, yes, sir.*
*Mr. Parsons: In the company of Sarah Doyle, is that right?*
*Witness: Yes.*

I saw all those many occasions pass through my mind as the questions continued, my answers following, Mr. Parsons now beginning to lead the silent courtroom spectators into a steadily more sinister tale, my own mind working to avoid that part of it Mr. Parsons had not yet discovered, trying not to see again what I'd seen that fateful day, a woman seated on a porch, snapping beans from the large blue bowl that rested on her lap, dropping their severed ends into a bucket at her feet, then rising slowly as I came toward her from the distance, peering at me intently, a single freckled hand lifting to shield her eyes from the bright summer sun.

Concealing all of that, my answers had continued to take the form of Mr. Parsons' questions, adding nothing, going along with him, responding to questions that sounded innocent enough but which I knew to be lethally aimed at the only villain in the room.

*Mr. Parsons: Did you have occasion to meet with Miss Channing in her classroom at Chatham School on Friday afternoon, December 21, 1926?*
*Witness: Yes.*
*Mr. Parsons: Could you tell the court the substance of that meeting?*

It had happened during the last week of school before the Christmas break, I told the court, nearly a month after the time I'd come up the coastal road and noticed Miss Channing and Mr. Reed talking together at the edge of the bluff. I had left her class later that same afternoon, feeling rather low because she'd not seemed terribly enthusiastic about some of the drawings I'd shown her, wide seas and dense forests, suggesting that I try my hand at what she called 'a smaller canvas', a vase of flowers or a bowl of fruit.

During most of the next day I'd brooded over her suggestion. Then an idea had occurred to me, a way of regaining some measure of the esteem I so craved at that time. With that goal in mind, I'd returned to Miss Channing's classroom at the end of the following day.

*Mr. Parsons: Miss Channing was alone when you came to her classroom?*
*Witness: Yes, she was.*

Up until that moment in my testimony I'd answered Mr. Parsons' questions directly and with little elaboration. Then, rather suddenly, I began to supply unnecessary details. I'd gone to Miss Channing's room with a particular purpose in mind, I told him, my eyes fixed directly on Mr. Parsons, my voice low, almost a whisper, as if I'd convinced myself that whatever I said from then on would be kept strictly secret between Mr. Parsons and me, that there was no jury present, no benches filled with spectators, no reporters to record the things I said and send them out into the larger world.

Miss Channing had been preparing for the next day's classes, I told the court. I'd come through the door silently, so that she'd been slightly startled when she saw me.

*Mr. Parsons: Startled? Why was she startled?*
*Witness: Probably because she'd been expecting someone else.*
*Mr. Parsons: Who?*
*Witness: Mr. Reed, I suppose.*
*Mr. Parsons: What happened after that?*
*Witness: She spoke to me.*
*Mr. Parsons: What did she say?*

'Henry?' she said.
I stood at the door, facing her. From the way she looked at me, I could tell that she hadn't expected to see me there.
'What is it, Henry?' she asked.
I wanted to answer her directly, tell her frankly why I'd come to see her at that hour, but the look in her face silenced me.

*Mr. Parsons: What look was that, Henry?*
*Witness: Well, Miss Channing had a way of looking at you that made you ... made you ...*
*Mr. Parsons: Made you what?*
*Witness: I don't know. She was different, that's all. Different from the other teachers.*
*Mr. Parsons: In what way was she different?*
*Witness: Well, she taught her classes in a different way than the other teachers did. I mean, she told us stories about the places she'd been to, about things that had happened in these places.*
*Mr. Parsons: These 'things that had happened', were they pleasant things?*
*Witness: Not always.*
*Mr. Parsons: In fact, many of them were often very cruel things, weren't they? Stories about violence? About death?*
*Witness: Sometimes.*
*Mr. Parsons: She told the class about a certain Saint Lucia, isn't that right? A woman who'd gouged out her own eyes?*
*Witness: Yes. She told us about the church in Venice, where her body is.*
*Mr. Parsons: Another one of her stories involved the murder of children, didn't it?*
*Witness: Yes. The little princes. That's what she called them.*

Mr. Parsons had continued with similar questions, unearthing other of Miss Channing's stories, tales of children who'd been buried alive, women who'd been drowned, before returning at last to the afternoon I'd gone to her room.

*Mr. Parsons: All right. Now, tell me, Henry, did you finally tell Miss Channing why you'd come to her classroom?*
*Witness: Yes, I did.*
*Mr. Parsons: What did you tell her?*

'I want to draw you,' I told her.
'Draw me?' she asked. 'Why?'
'I tried to do it once before,' I said, concealing my true purpose in wanting a portrait of her. 'But it didn't come out very well.' I lifted the sketch pad I'd tucked beneath my arm. 'I thought I'd try again if you wouldn't mind.'
'You want me to pose for you, Henry?'
I nodded. 'Just until you ... go to Mr. Reed.'
I could see that the expression I'd used, the way I'd said 'go to Mr. Reed', had sounded suggestive to her, but I added nothing else.

*Mr. Parsons: And so you could tell, even at that early time, that Miss Channing was already aware that you were suspicious of her relationship with Mr. Reed?*
*Witness: I think so, yes.*
*Mr. Parsons: And how did she react to the fact that she might be coming under suspicion?*
*Witness: Like she didn't care.*
*Mr. Parsons: What gave you that impression?*
*Witness: What she said, and the way she said it.*

She lifted her head in a gesture that made her look very nearly prideful, and said, 'As a matter of fact, Mr. Reed will be here in just a few minutes.'
'I could draw you until he comes,' I told her. 'Even if it's only for a few minutes.' I took a short, uneasy step toward her, the afternoon light flooding over me from the courtyard window. 'Just for practice.'
'Where do you want me?' she asked.
I nodded toward the wooden table that served as her desk. 'Just sitting at your desk would be fine,' I said.

*Mr. Parsons: And so Miss Channing posed for you that afternoon?*
*Witness: It wasn't exactly a pose. She just sat at her desk, working, while I drew.*

*Mr. Parsons: How long did she do that?*

*Witness: For about an hour, I guess. Until Mr. Reed came for her. By then it was getting dark.*

*Mr. Parsons: As a matter of fact, it was already dark enough for you to turn on the light in the room, isn't that right, Henry?*

*Witness: Well, I could see her, but I needed more light, yes.*

*Mr. Parsons: What I'm trying to make clear is that it was very late in the afternoon by the time Mr. Reed came to Miss Channing's room.*

*Witness: Yes, it was.*

*Mr. Parsons: Could it reasonably be said that all the other teachers had left Chatham School by then?*

*Witness: Yes.*

*Mr. Parsons: And where were the other students?*

*Witness: In the dormitory, most of them. On the second floor. It was almost time for dinner.*

*Mr. Parsons: And so, when Mr. Reed arrived at Miss Channing's room, he probably expected to find her alone, is that right?*

*Witness: Yes.*

*Mr. Parsons: And when Miss Channing saw Mr. Reed come into her room, did you notice any reaction from her?*

*Witness: Yes, I did.*

*Mr. Parsons: What was that reaction?*

Miss Channing's eyes suddenly brightened, I told the court, and she smiled. 'I thought you'd forgotten me,' she said, her eyes gazing toward the front of the room.

I glanced over my shoulder and saw Mr. Reed standing at the door, leaning on his cane.

'Am I interrupting something, Elizabeth?' he asked as he stepped farther into the room, his eyes drifting over to me, then back to Miss Channing.

'No,' she answered. 'Henry just wanted to practice his drawing.' She rose and began to gather up her things. 'We'll have to continue this some other time,' she said to me.

I nodded and started to close the sketchbook, but by that time Mr. Reed had come down the aisle, his eyes on my drawing.

'Not bad,' he said, 'but the eyes need something.'

He looked at Miss Channing. 'It would be hard to capture your eyes.'

She smiled at him softly. 'I'm ready,' she said as she walked toward the front of the room. Mr. Reed stepped back and opened the door for her, then watched as she passed through it. 'Coming, Henry?' he asked, glancing back into the room. I closed my sketchbook and walked out into the courtyard, where Miss Channing stood beside the tree, a few books hugged to her chest.

'Well, good night, Henry,' she said as Mr. Reed joined her, the two of them now moving through the courtyard and into the school, I trailing behind at a short distance.

*Mr. Parsons: So you were more or less following Miss Channing and Mr. Reed, is that right?*

*Witness: Yes. But I stopped at the front door of the school. They went on to the parking lot. Toward Mr. Reed's car. Then they drove away.*

*Mr. Parsons: Do you know where they went?*

*Witness: I later found out where they went.*

*Mr. Parsons: How did you find that out, Henry?*

*Witness: Mr. Reed told me. The next day. On the way to Boston.*

*Mr. Parsons: So by this time you and Mr. Reed had developed the sort of relationship that allowed him to confide such things in you?*

*Witness: Yes, we had.*

*Mr. Parsons: Could you describe the nature of that relationship?*

It was in answer to that question that I told my only lie upon the witness stand, one whose enduring cruelty I had not considered until I told it. 'Mr. Reed was like a father to me,' I told Mr. Parsons, then glanced over to see my own father staring at me, a mournful question in his eyes. *Then what was I to you, my son?*

# FIFTEEN

Despite the answer I gave to Mr. Parsons that day, Mr. Reed was never really like a father to me. Nor like a brother nor even a friend. Instead, we seemed to move forward on parallel conspiracies, the two of us lost in separate but related fantasies, his focused on Miss Channing, mine upon a liberated life, both of us oblivious of what might happen should our romantic dreams converge.

It had developed rapidly, my relationship with Mr. Reed, so that only a few weeks after we'd begun to work on the boat together, it had already assumed the ironclad form that would mark it from then on, Mr. Reed still vaguely in the role of teacher, I in the role of student, but with an unexpected collusion that went beyond all that, as if we were privy to things others did not know, depositories of truths the world was too cowardly to admit.

To the other teachers and students of Chatham School during those last few months, we must have seemed a curious pair, Mr. Reed walking slowly with his cane, I trailing along beside him with a sketchbook beneath my arm, the two of us sometimes making our way up the lighthouse stairs, to stand at its circular iron railing, Mr. Reed pointing the tip of his cane out to sea, as if indicating some far, perhaps impossible place he yearned to sail for. 'Past Monomoy Point, it's open sea,' he told me once. 'There'd be nothing to stop you after that.'

We drove to Boston together the day before he was set to leave for Maine with Mrs. Reed and his daughter. He'd wanted to buy a breastplate for the boat, along with some rigging. 'The really elegant things are in Boston,' he explained. 'Things that are made not just to be used, but to be ... admired.'

We took the old route that curved along the coast, through Harwichport and Dennis, past Hyannis, and farther, until we reached the canal. It was no more than a muddy ditch in those days, Sagamore Bridge not yet built, so that we rumbled across the wooden trellis that had been flung over the water years before, a rattling construct of steel and timber, functional but inelegant, as Mr. Reed described it, the way much of life appeared to be.

Once over the bridge, the Cape receding behind me, I looked back. 'You know what Miss Channing said when she saw the Cape for the first time?' I asked.

Mr. Reed shook his head.

'That it looked tormented,' I told him. 'Like a martyr.'

'Yes, she would say something like that,' he said with a quiet, oddly appreciative smile. He grew silent for a moment, his eyes fixed on the wider road that led to Boston. 'I guess you noticed Miss Channing and me leaving school together yesterday afternoon.'

I pretended to make nothing of it. 'You always leave together.'

He nodded. 'I usually take her straight home,' he said. 'But yesterday we went to the old cemetery on Brewster Road.' He waited for a question. When none came, he continued. 'We wanted to talk awhile. To be alone.' He stared at the road, the strand of dark hair that had fallen across his brow now trembling slightly with the movement of the car. 'So we went to the cemetery. Just to get away from ... other people.' He smiled. 'I promised Miss Channing that I'd have her home before dark.'

The landscape swept by on either side. I had not been off the Cape in well over a year, and I felt an unmistakable exhilaration in the forward thrust of the car, the unfolding of the landscape, the vast, uncharted world that seemed to lie just beyond my grasp.

'I don't know why I picked that cemetery,' Mr. Reed went on as if he were circling around something he was not sure he wanted to reveal. 'Something about it, I suppose. Probably the quiet, the solitude.'

'Did Miss Channing like it?' I asked.

'Yes, she did. There's a little grove near the center of it. Some evergreen trees, with a little cement pool.' He forced a small laugh. 'I did most of the talking. You know, about my life.'

After that Mr. Reed told me a great deal of what he'd said to Miss Channing in the cemetery the previous afternoon, how he'd been born in a working class section of Boston, a noisy, pinched world of clattering factories and grimy tenements where people lived beneath clouds of industrial vapor and coal dust.

'My father left when I was just a boy. My mother was a ... well ... not like your mother, Henry.' He smiled. 'She looked a little like Sarah, though. With long black hair, I mean, and a light complexion. Black Irish, we call it. My mother wanted me to be a clerk of some sort. In a bank, something like that. To wear a white shirt and tie, that's what she wanted me to do, look respectable.' He peered down at the brown jacket, its worn sleeves, the chalk dust. 'But it didn't turn out that way.'

'How did you happen to become a teacher?' I asked.

'Just by reading books, I guess. There was a school in Braintree. That's where I went. The war interrupted things, but when I got back, I got a job at Boston Latin School.' I saw his fingers draw more tightly around the steering wheel. 'It's funny how you have to make so many decisions before you're prepared to make them. All the important ones, I guess. About your life. Your work. The person you marry.' Suddenly he looked at me with a striking earnestness. 'I hope you make all the right decisions, Henry. If you don't, life can be so ... treacherous. ... You can end up wondering why you should even bother to live it through.'

No one had ever talked to me so intimately, nor with such urgent regard for my own future happiness. It seemed to me that my father had spoken only of the rules of life, never of its possibilities, his world a straight, unbending road, Mr. Reed's a narrow lane of pits and snares and hairpin curves, a place I should be warned about before it was too late and I had become not what I wanted to be, but what my father already was.

'The main thing is not to settle too quickly,' Mr. Reed added after a moment. 'In life ... or in love.'

An immense longing swept into his face, as if he'd recognized for the first time just how lonely and bereft he was. I wanted to offer him something, a token of the high regard I had for him. 'Chatham School would be very different without you, Mr. Reed,' I said.

He appeared wholly unmoved by what I'd said. 'Yes, of course,' he replied dryly. 'What would the boys do without me?'

I said nothing else, but only watched as Mr. Reed continued to stare toward the road ahead, his face fixed in that intense yearning I'd wanted to ease somehow, and which I remembered in all the years to come, so that it finally seemed to me that we were not created in God's image at all, but in the image of Tantalus instead, the thing we most desire forever dancing before our eyes, and yet forever beyond our grasp.

Once in the city, Mr. Reed led me through a series of shops, picking up the items he'd come to buy, brass knobs and hinges that he often touched softly before buying, moving his fingers lightly over the smooth surface of the metal, or holding it up to the light, staring at it wonderingly sometimes with an admiring smile, like a pirate of the old time, his eyes feasting on a gold doubloon.

It was noon by the time we'd finished buying what Mr. Reed had come for. Bundled up in our winter coats, we had lunch on a bench in the Common, near the botanical gardens, facing the great facade of the

Ritz Hotel, the two of us munching sandwiches Mrs. Reed had prepared for us, and which Mr. Reed took from a metal lunch pail, along with a thermos of lemonade.

'I was tired of Boston before I moved to Chatham,' Mr. Reed told me. 'But now—'

'Now what?' I asked.

'Now I think I'm tired of Chatham.'

'Where do you want to go?'

He shrugged. 'Anywhere,' he said.

'Is Mrs. Reed tired of Chatham too?'

'No, she's quite content to live in Chatham,' he said, his eyes taking on a strange agitation. 'She always has been ... content.' He thought a moment, then added, 'She's afraid of things, Henry.' His eyes drifted toward me. 'Even afraid of me sometimes, I think.'

With that, he turned away, placed the thermos in the lunch pail, and snapped it shut. 'We'd better be on our way,' he said as he got to his feet, determined, or so it seemed, to end any further conversation about Mrs. Reed.

It was then I realized that Mr. Reed had already removed his wife to some remote and inaccessible place in his life, locked her in an imaginary attic or down in a dark cellar, where she sat in the shadows, isolated and alone, listening with whatever combination of anticipation or fear to his footsteps on the stairs.

On the way back to the car, Mr. Reed suddenly stopped at the window of a jewelry store on a side street not far from where we'd parked. 'Look how beautiful that is, Henry,' he said, pointing to a necklace made of colored glass. He stared at it as if it were a talisman, something that could magically transform an all too lusterless world.

'It's pretty expensive,' I said, my eyes on the small white price tag.

He looked at me as if I'd offered him a challenge. 'Maybe once in a while you have to do something foolish,' he said. 'Just to prove that you're still alive.' With that, he smiled and walked into the shop.

I followed him inside, then stood at the counter while the shopkeeper retrieved the necklace from the window and handed it to Mr. Reed. He turned it slowly, so that the colored glass in his hands glinted in the light. 'I'll take it,' he said.

The shopkeeper wrapped it in a piece of tissue and placed it in a small red box. Mr. Reed thanked him and put the box in his jacket pocket.

We were on the road a few minutes later, Mr. Reed's spirits suddenly quite high, as if he'd proved himself in some way by buying the necklace, his hand from time to time crawling into the pocket of his jacket, moving

501

slowly inside it, turning the box over delicately, fondling it with his fingertips, a curious excitement in his eyes.

It was nearly nightfall by the time we got back to Chatham. Mr. Reed drove me directly to my house on Myrtle Street, the old car shaking violently as it came to a halt in my driveway.

'Thanks for coming along, Henry,' Mr. Reed said.

I nodded, then glanced toward the house. I could see my mother peering down at me from behind the parlor curtains. 'I'd better get inside,' I said. 'My mother's suspicious.'

'Of what?' Mr. Reed asked.

I gave him a knowing smile. 'Everything.'

He laughed. 'Most people are, Henry,' he said.

I got out of the car and headed toward the stairs. I'd almost reached them when I heard Mr. Reed call to me. 'Henry? Are you going to Milford Cottage with Sarah tomorrow?'

'I guess.'

'Tell Miss Channing I'll drop by when I get back from Maine.'

'All right,' I answered, then turned and moved on up the stairs.

The rest of that evening went along routinely. I had dinner with my mother and father, then went for a short walk with Sarah, the two of us sitting on the bench by the bluff for a few minutes before the cold drove us back inside.

'I don't like winter on the Cape,' she said with a shiver.

'I don't either,' I told her. 'Or the fall or spring or summer.'

She laughed and gave me a playful nudge with her shoulder. 'You should have more patience, Henry,' she said. 'You'll be off to college soon enough. You don't ever have to come back here after that.'

I looked at her squarely. Only half jokingly, I said, 'If I do come back here, kill me.'

Her face darkened. 'Don't say things like that, Henry. Not even as a joke.' Then she said a line that has never left me since that time. 'I wish we could be happy just to be alive.'

A few minutes later, now alone in my room, I went back over the day I'd spent with Mr. Reed, my affection for him growing, along with my admiration, particularly for the boldness I could see rising in him, making it possible that he might actually break free from whatever it was that bound him so. I thought of the necklace he'd impulsively bought, then of the fact that Christmas was coming on. It struck me that I wanted to give Mr. Reed a present. I thought of something for the boat, a brass name-plate, perhaps, or a lantern for the small cabin we'd nearly completed by then. Then I noticed my sketchbook lying on top of my desk, and knew what the perfect gift would be.

But several months later, near the conclusion of my first hour of testimony, it was clear that Mr. Parsons was not interested in what I'd later decided to give Mr. Reed for Christmas. He was interested in another gift entirely. The necklace brought back from Boston.

*Mr. Parsons: What happened after Mr. Reed bought the necklace?*
*Witness: He put it in his pocket and we walked back to his car and came back to Chatham.*
*Mr. Parsons: Did Mr. Reed ever tell you who the necklace was for?*
*Witness: No, he didn't.*
*Mr. Parsons: Well, did you ever see it again?*
*Witness: Yes, I saw it again.*
*Mr. Parsons: Where did you see it?*
*Witness: At Milford Cottage. In Miss Channing's bedroom. It was lying on the bookshelf beside her bed.*
*Mr. Parsons: How did you happen to see it?*
*Witness: It was the Friday night before ... the deaths. Miss Channing went into her bedroom. That's where I saw it. She took it off the bookshelf, and gave it to me.*
*Mr. Parsons: What did she say when she gave it to you, Henry?*
*Witness: She said, 'Get rid of this.'*
*Mr. Parsons: And did you do that for her?*
*Witness: Yes.*
*Mr. Parsons: What did you do with the necklace?*
*Witness: I threw it into Black Pond.*

I will always remember the low murmur that rose from the people in the courtroom when I said that, then the rap of Judge Crenshaw's gavel, calling them to order. It was late in the afternoon by then, and so he adjourned the court for the day.

At dinner later that night, my father and mother and I sat silently at the table for a long time, a newly hired servant girl flitting in and out of the dining room, her hair a dazzling red. Then, her eyes aflame, my mother suddenly glanced at me. 'They thought they were above everything,' she said with that bitterness that would mark her life from then on, 'that woman and Mr. Reed. They thought they could do anything, and no one would ever know.'

My father's head jerked up from his plate, his eyes nearly bulging. 'Mildred, please.'

'Above all the rest of us, that's what they thought,' my mother went on relentlessly, her glare now leveled directly upon my father. 'They didn't care who they hurt.'

'Mildred, please,' my father repeated, though with little force. 'This is not the time or place to—'

'But they started in death and they ended in death,' my mother declared, referring now to the meeting in the cemetery I'd described in the courtroom only hours before. I could hear again the things I'd said, the answers I'd given, always careful to tell nothing but the truth, yet all the while listening as one truth followed another, the body of evidence accumulating one answer at a time, until, truth by truth, it assumed the shape of a monstrous lie.

My mother lifted her head proudly. 'I'm proud of you, Henry,' she said. 'For remembering the ones they murdered.'

I heard my father gasp. 'Mildred, you know perfectly well that—'

She raised her hand and silenced him. Her eyes fell upon me with a lethal force. 'Don't ever forget the ones that died, Henry.'

I never did. But in remembering them, I also remembered Miss Channing and Mr. Reed in a way my mother would have abhorred. For despite everything, and for a long, long time, I persisted in thinking of them as romantic figures, modern-day versions of Catherine and Heathcliff, standing together on a snowy hilltop or strolling beside a wintry sea rather than rushing toward each other across a windswept moor.

And yet, for all that, there were other times when I'd glimpse a row of marble headstones in the same cemetery where they'd gone to be alone that long-ago afternoon, and see Mr. Reed and Miss Channing as they'd appeared that final spring, Mr. Reed staring toward the courtyard, his eyes trained on Miss Channing as she worked on her column of faces.

But that had been toward the end of it, the curtain poised to close, all the characters already beginning to assume their positions for the final scene: Abigail Reed, scratching at her hands as she peered out across Black Pond; little Mary at the bottom of the stairs, her eyes trained on the distant, darkened shed; I trudging grimly down Plymouth Road through the sweltering summer woods, a single phrase circling in my mind, taken from William Blake and quoted by Mr. Reed, facing the courtyard when he said it, Miss Channing at work on her column only a few short yards away. *Sooner murder an infant in its bed than nurse unacted desire.*

# PART IV

# SIXTEEN

Mr. Reed and his family returned to Chatham from Maine on the third of January in the new year of 1927. I'd just come out of Warren's Sundries, a cup of hot apple cider steaming in my hand, when his car swept past me. Mrs. Reed was seated in the front seat, Mary in the back, an old trunk lashed to the top of the car, olive green, and with one of its corners slightly battered in.

Mr. Reed didn't see me as he drove by, nor did Mrs. Reed, for both were staring straight ahead, Mr. Reed's face cast in shadow beneath the brim of a floppy gray hat, Mrs. Reed's locked in stony silence, Mary's eyes drifting toward me as the car went by, a frail smile on her lips, her small hand lifted in a faint gesture of recognition. *Hi, Henry.*

It had been nearly two weeks since Mr. Reed's departure, and the sight of him returning to Chatham filled me with anticipation, as if, after a long intermission, the curtain had risen again on the adventure in which I'd joined him.

When I rushed home and told Sarah that I'd just seen Mr. Reed drive past Warren's Sundries, she'd seemed to share my excitement about his return. 'You can get on with the boat now,' she said, smiling. 'Maybe finish it by summer.'

During the Christmas break Sarah and I had often found ourselves alone in the house, my mother working at the church, helping other local women prepare for the Nativity play, my father busy in his office at Chatham School. The school vacation had given us a chance to talk more intimately and for longer periods than we ever had before. Sarah spoke eagerly of one day going to college, her glowing ambition no longer satisfied with attaining the most basic skills, but now set resolutely upon mastering the highest ones. In later years I sometimes thought that it was she who should have been my father's child, a proud and grateful graduate of Chatham School, I an illiterate boy shipped in from far away, the future author of its ruin.

For by then my own character and ambitions had moved very far from

507

my father's teaching. It was Mr. Reed to whom I was drawn, particularly to the passionate discontent I could sense in him, his need to do more, be more, break free of Chatham, discover some new world, as if life were a horn of plenty, vast and infinite, rather than a small basket, inadequately stocked, and from which, in choosing one fruit, we must forever lose another.

I found him in the boathouse the day after his return to Chatham. Coming through the door, the Christmas gift I'd brought for him held firmly beneath my arm, I'd expected to find him as I usually did, planing spruce for the rigging, caulking seams, or simply at work with sandpaper, paint, varnish.

But instead, he was sitting idly at the stern of the boat, his hands in his lap, the cane propped up against the bare, unpainted rail to his left.

He looked up sharply at my entrance, like someone pulled abruptly from a long period of deep concentration, his face still cast in that mood of troubled thoughtfulness I'd seen in it the day before.

'I thought you might be here,' I said. 'I saw you drive through town yesterday.'

He smiled faintly. 'Go warm yourself,' he said, pointing to the stove. 'Then we can start to work.'

I walked over to the stove, then stood with my back to it, watching silently as Mr. Reed began to apply a coat of sealant to the inner frame of the boat. He seemed preoccupied, very nearly distracted, his eyes narrowing from time to time, his lower lip moving very slightly, as if he were reciting lines beneath his breath.

'Did you enjoy your trip to Maine?' I asked, though I could tell he hadn't.

He shook his head, his eyes following the brush. 'Not much.'

I offered a possible reason, though one I doubted. 'It's probably even colder there than it is here in Chatham.'

Mr. Reed didn't look up from his work to answer me. 'I don't care for Maine. I'd rather have stayed here.' He added nothing else for a while. Then he said, 'Did you go over to Milford Cottage during the break?'

'Once,' I told him. 'With Sarah.'

The brush stopped. 'And Miss Channing ... how is she?'

'Fine, I guess.'

And yet, even as I answered him, I recalled that there'd been something in Miss Channing's manner that had seemed somewhat different from the other times I'd accompanied Sarah to Milford Cottage, more subdued than she'd been before, locked in what appeared the same concentration that I now noticed in Mr. Reed. Throughout the lesson she'd occasionally glanced out her front window, peering through the parted curtains to the empty lawn, her eyes filled with a subtle but detectible agitation, the way I imagined the wives of sailors to have gazed out from their widow's walks, apprehensively scanning the horizon for their husbands' ships. I now had no doubt that it was Mr. Reed she'd been thinking of at those moments.

Mr. Reed returned to his work, the brush moving rhythmically right and left.

I watched him for a few moments, knowing that he was thinking about Miss Channing. I could feel the present I'd made for him still cradled under my arm. It seemed the perfect time to give it to him.

'I have something for you,' I said, rising from the chair. 'A Christmas present. I finished it while you were in Maine. I hope you like it. Merry Christmas, Mr. Reed.'

I'd wrapped it in bright green paper and bound it together with a red ribbon. 'Thank you,' he said, lifting it slightly, smiling. By its shape he must have known that it was a drawing, although when he opened it, I could tell that what I'd done both surprised and pleased him.

'Miss Channing,' he murmured.

I'd drawn her with pen and ink, though in a pose far different than Mr. Reed would have expected, her hair falling over her bare shoulders in a tangled mass, her eyes intense and searching, lips full and slightly parted, her head tilted forward, but her gaze directed straight ahead, a figure both real and unreal, ethereal, yet beckoning, rendered in an unmistakable attitude of seduction.

'It's beautiful, Henry,' Mr. Reed said, his eyes fixed on the portrait. He gazed at it a moment longer, then walked over to the small table in the corner. 'I'll hang it here,' he said. He took a nail from his jacket pocket and drove it into the wall above the desk. But before he hung the portrait, he paused, as if another thought had come to him. 'You know, Henry, we should show it to Miss Channing.'

'Do you think she'd like it?'

'Of course she would.'

I was not so sure, but Mr. Reed seemed certain, so a few minutes later we were backing out of the driveway of the boathouse, headed for Milford Cottage, Mr. Reed's spirits considerably higher now, the framed portrait of Miss Channing pressed against his side.

And so, as it turned out, I didn't do any work on the boat that day. But during the next few weeks I often returned to the boathouse to do what remained of the caulking and sealing, construct the mast and the boom, assemble the rigging. Enough work so that, four months later, after the Coast Guard had found the boat adrift in Cape Cod Bay, towed it back to Chatham, and moored it in the harbor, I could still walk down to the water's edge, look out beyond the other boats to the far side of the marina, and see the white prow of the *Elizabeth* lolling emptily in the distance, my eyes forever focused upon that part of it, the naked mast, the rolled-up sail, that I had helped to make.

Miss Channing was standing at the edge of Black Pond when we pulled into the driveway, a place where Sarah and I would sometimes find her when we arrived at Milford Cottage on a Sunday morning, and where, in my mind, I still see her, dressed in white, her back to me, framed by a swath of dark water.

She'd turned as Mr. Reed's car came to a halt, rushed toward it briefly, then glimpsed me in the passenger seat, and instantly reined herself in, so that she was walking slowly by the time she reached us.

'Hello, Elizabeth,' Mr. Reed said softly as he got out of the car.

'Hello, Leland,' Miss Channing answered. It was the first time I'd ever heard her call Mr. Reed by his given name.

He drew the picture from beneath his arm. 'I want to show you something. It's a Christmas present. Henry gave it to me.'

She stared at the portrait much longer than I'd expected her to. Now I realize that she could not possibly have cared for the way I'd drawn her, that it was only a nakedly romantic vision of herself, fervidly adolescent, and as she'd continued to study it that afternoon, she might well have been thinking those very words she would later say to Mr. Parsons, her eyes downcast, staring at her hands. *It was never me.*

'Very nice,' she said softly at last. She looked at me, smiled thinly, then handed the portrait back to Mr. Reed. 'Would you like some tea?'

Mr. Reed didn't hesitate in his reply. 'Yes. Thank you.'

We went directly into the cottage.

'When did you get back?' Miss Channing asked Mr. Reed after she'd prepared the tea and served us.

'Just yesterday,' Mr. Reed answered.

'And how was Maine?'

'Like always,' Mr. Reed muttered. He took a quick sip, then said, 'And you? What did you do while I was away?'

'I stayed here,' she replied. 'Reading mostly.'

Mr. Reed drew in a slow breath. 'Tell me, Elizabeth ... do you sometimes think that you're living only in your head?'

She shrugged. 'Is that such a bad place?'

Mr. Reed smiled gravely. 'It depends on the head, I suppose.'

'Yes, of course,' Miss Channing said.

There was an interval of silence before Mr. Reed said, 'The boat will be finished by summer.'

Miss Channing said nothing, but only raised the cup to her lips, her eyes on Mr. Reed.

'After that it would be possible to' – he stopped, as if cautioning himself against speaking too rashly, then went on – 'possible to go anywhere, I suppose.'

Miss Channing lowered the cup to her lap. 'Where would you like to go, Leland?'

Mr. Reed stared at her intently. 'Places you've already been, I suppose.'

For an instant, they stared at each other silently, but with an unmistakable intensity and yearning that made the shortest distance between them seem more than they could bear. It was then I first recognized the full depth of what they'd come to feel for each other. It had emerged slowly, incrementally, building every day, word by word, glance by glance, until, at last, it had broken the surface of their long decorum, something irresistibly powerful now blazing up between them, turning all show of mere friendship into a lover's ruse.

We walked out of the cottage a few minutes later, Mr. Reed and Miss Channing just ahead of me as we strolled out toward the pond, then turned to the right and walked to the end of the old wooden pier that stretched out over the water.

'In the spring we'll go rowing,' Mr. Reed said. 'On the Bass River. All of us together.'

I could see his house in the distance, the small white boat pulled up on dry land. I remembered that only a few weeks before, as we'd stood in the snow on the hill, the sight of his own house had appeared to disturb Mr. Reed, work in his mind like an unpleasant memory. Now it seemed very nearly invisible to him.

It did not seem so to Miss Channing, however, and as she looked across the water toward it, I saw something in her eyes darken, a little light go out. 'You should be getting home, Leland,' she told him.

'Yes, I should,' he said, though he made no effort to do so. 'That was the first boat I ever built, that little rowboat you can see on the bank there,' he said, his words now turned deeply inward, as if it had been in the process of building it that he'd discovered some abandoned part of himself, a part that had grown steadily since then, and was now poised to consume him. 'I guess I wanted something that would let me drift by things,' he added. 'Not sail toward them. But just drift by. Hardly make a mark.' He drew in a slow, troubled breath. 'Your father would have despised me, Elizabeth,' he said.

Her eyes flashed toward him. 'Don't ever think that, Leland,' she told him. 'It isn't true.' She glanced at me, then away, clearly trying to determine exactly what she could do or say in my presence. Then, as if suddenly alarmed by the fact that I was there at all, she said sharply, 'You'd better go, Leland.'

Mr. Reed nodded silently, turned, and headed off the pier, Miss Channing at his side, the two of them moving slowly across the yard toward where his car rested in the driveway, I off to the right at a little distance, trying to give them all the privacy I could, knowing that it was far less than they desired.

'Well, I'll come for you on Monday morning,' Mr. Reed said to Miss Channing when we reached the car. 'We'll drive into school together, just like always.'

Miss Channing smiled very faintly, then, in a gesture that seemed to come from deep within her, she suddenly stepped forward and pressed her hand against the side of his face. 'Yes,' she whispered. 'Monday morning.'

It was the only act of physical intimacy I ever saw between them. And yet it was enough so that when Mr. Parsons asked his question several months later – *Was it your impression, Henry, that Miss Channing was in love with Mr. Reed at this time?* – I could answer, as always, with the truth:

*Witness: Yes.*

# SEVENTEEN

A nd so it never surprised me that in the photograph taken nearly two months later, they were still together, standing side by side, Mr. Reed holding to his cane, Miss Channing with her arms at her sides, the trees that tower over them still locked in the grip of that long winter, their limbs stripped and frigid, as bare and fruitless as a bachelor's life can sometimes be.

Mr. Reed and Miss Channing are not alone in the picture, however. To Mr. Parsons' dismay, no photograph of them alone was ever located. Instead, they stand amid a throng of teachers and students from Chatham School, along with its office and janitorial staff, everyone assembled on the school's front lawn, with my father standing proudly in front of them, the lordly captain of their tidy ship, dressed, as always, in his black suit and starched white shirt. The boys fan out to the left and right behind him, all of them dressed in their winter uniforms, shoes shined brightly, wool scarves around their necks, dark blue with gold fringes, the colors of Chatham School. I stand near the end of one flank, my sketch-book pressed manfully against my chest, a warrior behind his sturdy shield.

In every way, then, it was a picture typical of the time, a group photograph artlessly taken and presumed to have little value save to the people pictured in it. Nor would I ever have specifically recalled it had my father not cut it out of the school annual some months after its publication, then added it to his little archive, his reason for doing so made obvious by what he wrote on the back: *Chatham School, 7 March 1927, Last known photograph of Leland Reed.*

But for Mr. Parsons, the principal importance of the photograph was that it showed Mr. Reed and Miss Channing standing beside each other as late as the first week of March 1927, their 'illicit affair', as he called it, still clearly going on. For their arms are touching lightly, as he noted for the jury, a fact that indisputably suggested, as he said in his closing argument, 'that Elizabeth Channing and Leland Reed remained united

513

in a relationship whose adulterous and malevolent nature witness after witness has already made clear.'

The testimony of those witnesses was dutifully recorded in Mr. Parsons' book, but even had I never read it, I would have remembered what they said, a catalogue of random sightings that stretched through the winter and nosed into the following spring, a scattering of words snatched from longer conversations, often innocent in themselves, but within the context of what later happened on Black Pond, as profoundly sinister and unnerving as a trail of bloody footprints around a scene of slaughter.

*Trial Transcript, Commonwealth of Massachusetts vs. Elizabeth Rockbridge Channing, August 16, 1927.*

*Witness: Well, I was sitting on one of the dunes there on First Encounter Beach. That's when I saw two people coming up the beach, a man and a woman.*

*Mr. Parsons: Is it unusual for people to be on the beach in late January, Mr. Fletcher?*

*Witness: Yes, sir. The cold pretty much keeps people in. But I probably wouldn't have made much of it, except that the man had a cane, and you don't usually see a cripple like that out on the beach no matter when it is.*

*Mr. Parsons: What did these two people do on the beach that morning?*

*Witness: They walked on a little ways, then they sat down at the bottom of one of the dunes.*

*Mr. Parsons: And what did you observe at that point?*

*Witness: Well, they talked awhile, but I couldn't hear what they said, of course. They were sort of snuggled up together, with the man's arm around the woman's waist, pulling her up against him. They sat that way awhile, then I saw the man take a piece of paper out of his coat pocket. It was all rolled up, but he unrolled it, and they both looked at it. The man was talking and pointing out things on the paper.*

*Mr. Parsons: Do you remember the color of that paper?*

*Witness: It was greenish looking. Sort of light green.*

*Mr. Parsons: Did you recognize either the man or the woman you saw that morning?*

*Witness: No, I didn't recognize them until later. That is, when I saw their pictures in the paper.*

*Trial Transcript, Commonwealth of Massachusetts vs. Elizabeth Rockbridge Channing, August 17, 1927.*

*Mr. Parsons: Now, as the harbor master of Chatham harbor, Mr. Porter, you're in charge of maintaining various buildings and storage areas that are rented to people who use the harbor, are you not?*

*Witness: Yes.*

*Mr. Parsons: Do you remember renting such a building to Mr. Leland Reed in November of 1923?*

*Witness: Yes, I do. He planned to build a boat.*

*Mr. Parsons: Did he subsequently build that boat?*

*Witness: Yes, he did. He finished it toward the end of this last May.*

*Mr. Parsons: During the last weeks of the boat's construction, did you sometimes have occasion to step inside the building Mr. Reed rented?*

*Witness: I went in sometimes. To see how things were going.*

*Mr. Parsons: Did you ever happen to see a piece of paper unfolded on the desk inside that building?*

*Witness: Yes, sir. It was a nautical map is what it was. Of the East Coast, and down through the Caribbean.*

*Mr. Parsons: Did you notice anything about the map that struck you as unusual?*

*Witness: Well, I noticed that somebody had drawn a route on it. In red ink.*

*Mr. Parsons: Now, this route, this nautical route, it went from where to where?*

*Witness: From Chatham to Havana, Cuba.*

*Mr. Parsons: Do you remember the color of the paper?*

*Witness: It was the usual color for nautical maps. It was pale green.*

*Mr. Parsons: Now, Mr. Porter, did you ever see the defendant, Elizabeth Channing, with Mr. Reed in the building where he was building his boat?*

*Witness: Not in the building, no, sir. But I saw them out walking through the marina one time.*

*Mr. Parsons: And when was this?*

*Witness: Around the same time I saw the map, I guess. Early February, I'd say. Mr. Reed was pointing out into the bay there, sort of wheeling his cane around, like he was telling Miss Channing directions.*

*Mr. Parsons: And if a boat followed that route out of Chatham harbor, where would it go, Mr. Porter?*

*Witness: Into the open sea.*

*Mr. Parsons: On that occasion, did you notice anything else about Miss Channing and Mr. Reed?*

*Witness: Only that when they turned back toward the boathouse, Miss Channing sort of threw her head back and laughed.*

*Trial Transcript, Commonwealth of Massachusetts vs. Elizabeth Rockbridge Channing, August 19, 1927.*

*Mr. Parsons: What is your occupation, Mrs. Benton?*

*Witness: I teach Latin at Chatham School.*

*Mr. Parsons: Are you familiar with the defendant?*

*Witness: Yes, sir. Her place ... her room at the school, I mean ... it's just across the courtyard from mine.*

*Mr. Parsons: So you have a good vantage point to see what goes on in that classroom, is that correct?*

*Witness: Yes, sir.*

*Mr. Parsons: Did you ever see Mr. Leland Reed in that room?*

*Witness: Yes, sir.*

*Mr. Parsons: Often?*

*Witness: Just about every day. He would come there and have lunch with Miss Channing. Then he'd come again in the afternoon.*

*Mr. Parsons: Tell me, Mrs. Benton, situated as you were, so close to Miss Channing's room, did you ever hear any conversation pass between the defendant and Mr. Reed?*

*Witness: Yes, I did.*

*Mr. Parsons: How did that come about?*

*Witness: Well, I was coming along the side of Miss Channing's room, and I heard voices.*

*Mr. Parsons: Do you recall the approximate date when you heard the voices?*

*Witness: It was March fourth. I know because I had bought a birthday present for my son, and I was taking it home that afternoon.*

*Mr. Parsons: And the voices you heard that day, they were coming from Miss Channing's classroom?*

*Witness: Yes, they were, and so I looked in, just as I was passing, and I saw Miss Channing sort of turned away, facing the wall over there by the cabinets, and Mr. Reed was standing behind her.*

*Mr. Parsons: Did you hear any conversation at that time?*

*Witness: A little. 'We'll find another way.' That's what Mr. Reed said.*

*Mr. Parsons: And that was all?*

*Witness: Yes.*

*Mr. Parsons: Did Miss Channing reply to that?*

*Witness: Well, she kept her back to him, but I heard her say, 'There is no other way.'*

*Trial Transcript, Commonwealth of Massachusetts vs. Elizabeth Rockbridge Channing, August 20, 1927.*

*Mr. Parsons: Now, Mrs. Krantz, you're a clerk in Peterson's Hardware, is that right?*

*Witness: Yes, sir.*

*Mr. Parsons: I want to show you a receipt for a purchase made at Peterson's Hardware on March 15, 1927. Do you recognize this receipt?*

*Witness: Yes, sir.*

*Mr. Parsons: What items were purchased, according to the receipt?*

*Witness: Well, the first one is a bottle of arsenic.*

*Mr. Parsons: Do you recall the person who purchased that arsenic on March fifteenth?*

*Witness: Yes, I do.*

*Mr. Parsons: Who was it, Mrs. Krantz?*

*Witness: Mr. Leland Reed.*

*Mr. Parsons: Could you read the other items that Mr. Reed purchased that day?*

*Witness: It says here, a knife and twenty feet of rope.*

*Trial Transcript, Commonwealth of Massachusetts vs. Elizabeth Rockbridge Channing, August 20, 1927.*

*Mr. Parsons: What is your job, Mrs. Abercrombie?*

*Witness: I'm Mr. Griswald's secretary.*

*Mr. Parsons: by 'Mr. Griswald', you mean Arthur Griswald, the headmaster of Chatham School?*

*Witness: Yes, sir.*

*Mr. Parsons: Mrs. Abercrombie, did you ever see or hear anything transpire between the defendant and Mr. Leland Reed that indicated to you that the nature of their relationship was somewhat beyond what might be expected of two professional colleagues, or even two friends?*

*Witness: Yes, I did.*

*Mr. Parsons: Could you tell the court, please.*

*Witness: One afternoon – this was during the last week of March, I think – anyway, I was walking through the parking area. It was late. I mean, it was night already. Everybody had gone home. But Mr. Griswald had been preparing next year's budget, so I'd stayed late to help him. Anyway, I saw that Mr. Reed's car was still parked in the parking area, there beside the tree, where he usually put it, and as I went on by, I saw that he was sitting behind the wheel, and that Miss Channing was in the car with him.*

*Mr. Parsons: Miss Channing was sitting in the front seat, was she?*

*Witness: Yes, she was. And she had her hands sort of at her throat, and I saw Mr. Reed lean over and take her hands and pull them away.*

*Mr. Parsons: Now, Mrs. Abercrombie, in your capacity as assistant to Mr. Griswald, did you ever have a conversation with the headmaster about the behavior of Miss Channing and Mr. Reed, the very scene that you witnessed that evening in the parking lot of Chatham School?*

*Witness: Yes, I did. I felt like it was something he needed to know about. So I told him about what I'd seen that night in Mr. Reed's car, and I also told him that there was a lot of talk about Miss Channing and Mr. Reed among the other teachers.*

*Mr. Parsons: How did Mr. Griswald respond to what you told him?*

*Witness: He said he wasn't much for gossip.*

*Mr. Parsons: And that was the headmaster's only response to what you reported to him?*

*Witness: The only one I know of, yes.*

But it had not been the only response my father made, as I had known long before Mrs. Abercrombie took the stand. For one day during the very next week, he dropped in on Mr. Reed's afternoon class.

I remember how I'd entered Mr. Reed's room to find my father already stationed in one of the desks at the back. He nodded to each of us as we came into the room, then silently watched as Mr. Reed began his lesson, leaning back, trying to appear casual, but with a clearly visible sense of vigilance in his eyes.

My father remained in that position during the entire class, his gaze only occasionally drawn toward the courtyard, Miss Channing's room at the far end of it. Instead, he kept his attention intently focused upon Mr. Reed, no doubt listening not only to what he said, but how he said it, observing not just a teacher going through the motions, but the man behind the teacher, looking for that broken part of Mr. Reed that he so deeply feared and distrusted, not the part that had been shattered in the war, but long before, as he conceived it, in Adam's dreadful fall.

When the class was over, my father rose quietly and walked to the front of the room. He said something to Mr. Reed, nodded politely, then walked down the corridor to his office. I watched as he made his way down the hallway, his dark, ponderous frame like an ancient ship cutting through a stream of youthful, darting boys, silent, meditative, a melancholy figure in a black coat, head bowed, shoulders slumped, as if beneath the burden of our lost and implacable hearts.

# EIGHTEEN

Spring came at last, and toward the middle of April, we went rowing, just as Mr. Reed had promised we would on that cold January day when the three of us stood at the end of the pier together and looked out over Black Pond.

It was a Saturday, warm and sunny, with what my father called 'the glow of Easter' everywhere around us. During the preceding months I'd worked on the boat with Mr. Reed and attended classes with Miss Channing, but I'd actually seen them together only during their accustomed arrivals and departures from Chatham School. All their other 'secret rendezvous', as Mr. Parsons later called them, had been discreetly held outside my view.

I'd gotten to the boathouse early that morning, already at work when Mr. Reed arrived, fully expecting that we'd labor through the day, as we always did, finish up toward the end of the afternoon, then take a long walk on the beach near the marina.

Mr. Reed had arrived at the boathouse with a very different plan in mind, however, one he announced as soon as he opened the door and peered inside.

'It's too pretty to be cooped up in here,' he said, one foot inside the boathouse, the other still on the walkway outside it. He stepped out of the door and into the warm spring air. 'Come on, Henry,' he said, motioning me to follow after him.

I followed him out the door, then down the wooden walkway toward the road. In the distance I could see his car, half-concealed behind one of the marina's old outbuildings, but enough of it visible so that I could make out the small white rowboat roped to its top.

Mr. Reed was already pulling himself behind the wheel by the time I rounded the corner of the building. 'Come on, Henry,' he said, motioning me forward, hurrying me along. 'We want to get an early start.'

It was then I saw Miss Channing sitting on the passenger side, a large basket in her lap, her pale blue eyes like distant misty lights behind the dusty windshield.

'Hello, Miss Channing,' I said as I climbed into the backseat of the car.

She nodded but didn't answer, and I suppose that it was precisely at that moment I first noticed the peculiar tension and uneasiness that would never leave her after that, a sense of being trapped or constricted, the world's former breadth and expansiveness now drawing around her like a noose.

Mr. Reed leaned forward and hit the ignition. 'We're off to the Bass River,' he said in a cheerful tone that struck me as somewhat forced, as if he were trying to lift Miss Channing's spirits. He looked at her for a moment, offering a slender smile. 'We'll have the whole day, Elizabeth,' he told her. 'Just like I said we would.'

It took nearly an hour to reach the Bass River, a spot Mr. Reed had already selected, one he'd 'chosen for its remoteness and seclusion', as Mr. Parsons later described it, surrounded by high grass and at the bottom of a sloping embankment, so that neither the car nor the boat was visible from the main road a short hundred yards or so away.

'At this point in the river, it's nearly a mile from bend to bend,' Mr. Reed told us as he began to untie the ropes that bound the boat to the top of the car. 'We can row downstream, then come back with the tide.'

Miss Channing walked to the bank of the river, and stood, watching, as the current swept past her, bearing bits of wood and marsh debris, its slowly moving surface reflecting a cloudless sky.

Once the boat had been untied, Mr. Reed grasped the bow, pulled it toward him, then down, so that it slid off the roof of the car at a deep angle, its bow nosing into the soft ground. 'All right, Henry,' he said, 'take hold of the back there.'

I did as he told me, the two of us lugging the boat toward the water, then setting it down in the moist earth that bordered the river.

Miss Channing remained in place, still facing the water, her eyes fixed on a yellow film of pollen gathered in a pool on the farther shore.

'Are you ready, Elizabeth?' Mr. Reed asked gently, almost delicately, as if her mood were a fragile thing, a rare vase he feared breaking.

She nodded without turning around, and Mr. Reed offered her his hand. She took it and stepped inside the boat. 'Thank you,' she said as she released it.

'You're next, Henry,' Mr. Reed said.

I climbed into the boat, then looked back just as Mr. Reed pushed it forward again, drawing himself up and over the rail as he did so, a movement that struck me as very smooth and agile, his cane left on the bank behind us, the river lapping softly at its curved end.

I will always remember the few hours that followed, the slow drift of the boat down the narrow channel of the river, a wall of grass on either side, Mr. Reed at the oars, Miss Channing facing him from the opposite end of the boat, her right hand lowered toward the water, a single finger slicing it silently, leaving a glistening trail across its otherwise smooth surface.

At that moment she seemed as beautiful as any woman had ever been or would ever be. I picked up my sketchbook and began to draw, hoping to please her this time, to draw her as she really was. She was staring just off to the left as I began, her face in profile as she watched a gull prance along the far embankment. Turning back, she saw the sketchbook open in my lap, the drawing pencil in my hand, my eyes intent upon her. Her face suddenly grew taut, as if she thought I'd been sent to record her presence in the boat, use it later as evidence against her. 'No, Henry,' she said.

'But I was just ...'

She shook her head determinedly, her eyes locked in that steeliness Mr. Parsons would later associate with the coldness of her heart. 'No,' she repeated firmly. 'Put it down.'

I glanced at Mr. Reed, saw him turn away from me, fix his attention on the stream ahead, clearly unwilling to go against her.

'Yes, Miss Channing,' I said, then closed the book and placed it on the seat beside me.

There was an interminable silence after that, Miss Channing motionless on her seat as we drifted onward, the boat now moving through a labyrinth of narrow channels, Mr. Reed suddenly tugging more fiercely at the oars, as if already in flight from some grim, pursuing hand.

After a time we came to a bend in the river, but rather than rounding it, Mr. Reed rowed us to shore.

Once on the riverbank, we spread a checkered cloth a few feet from the water, the wind billowing it up briefly as we lowered it to the ground. Mr. Reed sat at one corner, Miss Channing at another, removing fruit and sandwiches from the basket.

We ate slowly, in what I later recognized as the kind of silence that falls when the last resort has been reached, all debate now closed, nothing to be taken back or reconsidered, the final decision irrevocably made, though perhaps still unstated.

In an effort to lighten that very atmosphere, Mr. Reed suddenly looked at Miss Channing and said, 'Tell us a story, Elizabeth.'

She shook her head.

Mr. Reed leaned forward slightly. 'Something from your travels,' he said softly, almost gingerly as if her feelings were a red-hot coal he feared to touch.

She shook her head again.

'Just one, Elizabeth.' Mr. Reed's tone was now so imploring it seemed almost beggarly.

Without a word she got to her feet and strode away from us, down along the water's edge, to where a tangle of driftwood lay on the bank, its limbs rising like fleshless bones from the moist ground.

Mr. Reed watched her leave us, then, moving slowly and unsteadily without his cane, walked down to where she stood.

I tried to turn away, but I found myself continually drawn back to them, their bodies so fully surrounded by walls of grass and coils of water, they looked utterly ensnared, like two animals captured in an invisible net, thrashing about, desperate to break free, and yet with every thrust and movement growing more fatally entangled. I thought of the delight in Mr. Reed's eyes as he'd bought the glass necklace in Boston, then of the look on Miss Channing's face as she'd pressed her hand against his cheek, traced its jagged scar, and finally of the hopelessness and futility that appeared to have overwhelmed them since that time. That the passion I was certain I'd seen between them should now be in the process of disintegration seemed inconceivable to me, and watching them, as they continued to talk intently only a few yards away, I felt a scalding surge of anger against the whole design of life, its web of duties and obligations, Chatham like a dark pit in which Miss Channing and Mr. Reed were now imprisoned, Mrs. Reed standing on its rim, grim and unrelenting, dressed in black, her implacable arms folded over her chest, the female version of my father.

'Well, Henry, I suppose we'd better be on our way now,' Mr. Reed told me solemnly when he and Miss Channing rejoined me. I helped them gather up the cloth and the basket.

At the boat Mr. Reed offered Miss Channing his hand. She grasped it lightly, stepped inside, and took her seat again at the stern.

'It'll be quick going back,' Mr. Reed told her as he pushed us off. 'The tide's coming in now.' He pulled himself over the rail and took hold of the oars, his gaze upon Miss Channing as he said, 'Parting is such sweet sorrow, and all that.'

It was a line from *Romeo and Juliet*, of course, and it must have lingered in Miss Channing's mind, for when the bend in the river had disappeared behind us, she broke her silence. 'I went to Juliet's house in Verona when

I was sixteen,' she said. 'There were lots of people there. It was like a shrine.' She gathered her arms more tightly around the basket that rested in her lap. 'My father pointed to the balcony and told me to stand where Juliet had, looking down at Romeo.' Her eyes took on an unmistakable intensity, as if she were reliving the moment again, she on the stone balcony, her father in the courtyard below, their eyes fixed upon each other. 'That's what he was searching for, I think,' she said. 'An ideal love.'

Mr. Reed drew back the oars slowly. 'If he'd ever found a love like that,' he said, 'I'm sure he'd have found a way to keep it too.'

Miss Channing said nothing, but only stared rigidly ahead as the boat moved swiftly inland, the nightbound tide now exerting its vast pull. No one ever looked more tortured by a grave resolve.

It was nearly night when we reached Milford Cottage. An evening mist drifted over the pond. I sat in the car while Mr. Reed walked Miss Channing to her door. They lingered on the threshold, Mr. Reed on the step beneath Miss Channing, she looking down at him. Finally, he took her hand, held it very briefly, then released it and headed back toward where I sat.

She'd lit a candle by the time Mr. Reed got into the car, a soft yellow glow now coming from the windows of the front room.

'It's so hard, Henry,' Mr. Reed said, his eyes on the cottage as he began to back away. 'It's the hardest thing in the world.'

I never mentioned his words to Mr. Parsons, since they'd seemed directed toward something larger than the Chatham School Affair, not the crime of forbidden love, which was Mr. Parsons' sole interest, but some deeper one, plotted at the core of life, and which inflexibly decrees that one love in flower must leave another in decay.

When we arrived at Mr. Reed's house on the other side of the pond, Mary was playing in the front yard, building a house of sticks and leaves as she sat near the water, nearly obscured in a blue twilight. She ran toward the car as we got out, then stood watching while we unlashed the boat and carried it toward its usual mooring by the tree at the water's edge.

'Did you catch a fish?' she asked Mr. Reed brightly as she skipped along beside him.

'We didn't go fishing,' he told her. 'Just rowing.' He glanced back toward me. 'Just Henry and me,' he added.

We set the boat down, and Mary climbed into it as Mr. Reed tethered it to the tree, taking a seat at the bow, bouncing slightly, her small hands clapping rhythmically to some beat in her mind.

'Where's your mother?' Mr. Reed asked her once he'd secured the boat.

Mary pointed to the porch. 'She's been sitting there all day.'

I turned toward the house. In the evening shade I had not seen her, but now I could make her out quite clearly. She sat in the far corner of the porch, rocking quietly, her green eyes peering dully out of the shadows like two small, unpolished stones.

# NINETEEN

After the Chatham School Affair, my father always believed that the deepest tragedies inevitably unfolded slowly, reached their climaxes in seizures of violence and grief, then lingered on forever in the minds of those who were near enough to feel their lethal force and yet survive.

Some, of course, do not survive at all.

Those who perished return to me most often in a newspaper photograph published during the trial, which I saw lying on my father's desk at Chatham School one evening, my father at his office window, his hands clutched behind his back, staring out into the courtyard, where the remnants of Miss Channing's sculpture had been gathered into a pile of gray rubble, an almost surreal mound of shattered faces.

In the photograph Mrs. Reed is seated in her husband's small white boat. Mary is on her wide lap. Both smile happily in a picture taken, according to the newspaper, by Mr. Reed during what it called 'happier times'.

I can still remember how wrenching I found that photograph the evening I first saw it. Because of that, it never surprised me that I sometimes took it from the little archive I inherited at my father's death, staring at it by the fire, letting it remind me of Mrs. Reed and her daughter, what they'd been, no longer were, and thus warn me away from the temptation I occasionally felt to find a wife, have children of my own.

Of course, there'd been plenty of testimony to remind me of them at the time, particularly of Mrs. Reed, neighbors and relatives who'd come at Mr. Parsons' bidding, and who, by answering the questions he put to them, had labored to bring her back to life, consistently portraying her as a dutiful and, for the most part, cheerful woman, faithful and hardworking, a good mother and a good wife, incontestably entitled to her husband's unswerving devotion.

I remembered Mrs. Hale, the coroner's wife, talking quietly of how well Mrs. Reed had taken care of her parents in their illness and old age. Then Mrs. Lancaster after her, speaking no less quietly about Mrs.

Reed's kindness toward her feebleminded sister, the way she'd never failed to bring her a cake and a jar of apple cider on her birthday.

But of all the people who testified about Abigail Reed, the witness I most remember was my mother.

As it turned out, she'd known Mrs. Reed almost all her life, remembered her as Abbey Parrish, the only daughter of William and Dorothy Parrish, he a fisherman who moored his boat in Chatham harbor, she a fisherwife of the old school, who hauled tubs of lobster and baskets of quahogs and slabs of smoked bluefish to the local market every day. As a child, Abigail had often accompanied her mother there, standing at her side, helping her sell the day's catch from behind a wooden table that had been placed beneath a tattered canvas roof, her hands made rough by the work, scarred by scales and fins.

On the stand, my mother had spoken in a somewhat more agitated manner than either Mrs. Hale or Mrs. Lancaster. Her voice took on an unmistakable edginess as she answered Mr. Parsons' questions, her eyes sometimes involuntarily flitting over to Miss Channing, little sparks of anger glinting in them, especially as she related the afternoon Mrs. Reed had turned up at our house on Myrtle Street, her manner quite desperate by then, as my mother described it, a chilling terror in her red-rimmed eyes.

Still, for all the impact of her testimony, my mother didn't do or say anything on the stand that stunned me as much as what happened only a few minutes after she left it.

'Walk your mother home, Henry,' my father told me as she stepped from the witness box and began to make her way down the aisle toward the back of the courtroom.

She was already passing through its large double doors by the time I caught up with her, moving at that brisk, determined pace she often assumed, as if something were chasing after her, she trying to outrun it.

'Are you thirsty, Mother?' I asked her as we made our way through the dense, crowd that had gathered on the courthouse steps. 'Do you want to stop and have something to drink?'

She stared straight ahead as she answered, roughly elbowing her way through the mob, her eyes glaring hotly toward the street. 'No, I want to go home,' she said.

At the bottom of the stairs, she wheeled to the right and strode up Main Street at the same nearly frantic pace, taking short, quick steps, her heavy black shoes thumping loudly along the walkway.

For nearly a block she kept silent, then, suddenly, under her breath, in a kind of bitter hiss, I heard her say, 'That woman should be hung.'

My eyes widened in dreadful horror at what she'd said. 'Miss

Channing?' I gasped, my complicity in her fate sweeping over me in a bitter wave. 'But she didn't ...'

My mother waved her hand, silencing me, as she continued forward at the same merciless pace, her eyes now glowing furiously.

I could tell by the hard look in them that she had no intention of saying more. So I simply rushed along beside her, glancing at the bustling crowds, the knots of people that had gathered on every street corner and in front of every shop. It looked as if the whole world had suddenly descended upon our village, all drawn by the dark specter of the Chatham School Affair.

'I don't understand why everybody is so caught up in this,' I said to my mother as she surged forward along the crowded street, an observation I only half believed but felt safe in making, so utterly neutral, as it seemed to me, edging neither toward my mother's testimony nor my own, neither to the error of her suspicions, nor the unbearable actuality of my crime.

Still she said nothing, oblivious, or so it appeared, not only of my last remark, but of the steady stream of traffic in the streets, the cars and people moving past us, the scores of men and women who spread out over the broad lawn of the town hall.

In that ceaselessly agitated surrounding, it seemed equally safe to offer another observation, one I'd desperately clung to during the previous weeks, as if, by clinging to it, I could stay afloat above the tragedy that had by then engulfed so many others. 'It's the love story that attracts them, I guess. Just that it's basically a love story.'

At that, my mother came to a halt so abrupt and violent, she appeared to have run into an invisible wall.

'A love story?' she asked, her eyes igniting with a fire I had never seen in them before and of which I had not believed her capable.

'Well, that's what Miss Channing and Mr.—'

'You think it's a love story, Henry?' My mother's words burst from her mouth like puffs of steam.

I could feel the air heat up around us, my mother's body begin to smolder.

'Well, in a way it is,' I said. 'I mean, Miss Channing just—'

'Miss Channing?' my mother cried. 'What about Mrs. Reed? What about her love for her husband? Isn't *that* a love story too?'

It seemed the sort of question Mr. Parsons might have posed to the twelve jurors who'd been asked to judge Miss Channing, and ultimately to condemn her, and I realized that I had no answer for my mother, that I had never known the kind of love she had just spoken of, one based on ancient vows and meant to last forever, the 'love story' of a marriage.

'All you do is think about that woman,' my mother said. 'That Miss

Channing. How romantic it all is. Her and Mr. Reed. Walking on the beach. Sailing in the boat. Where do you think Mrs. Reed was while all that was going on?'

In my mind I suddenly saw Mrs. Reed as she'd appeared on the porch the day we'd returned from the Bass River, heard her daughter's words again, the vast suffering and loneliness they now so powerfully conveyed. *She's been sitting there all day.*

'I'm ashamed of you, Henry,' my mother snapped angrily, her words hitting me like small iron pellets. 'Ashamed of the way you think.'

Staring at her mutely, I realized that I'd never understood how from the moment the trial began, my mother had done nothing but consider not the tale spun by my willful romantic imagination, but the dreadful anguish of Abigail Reed, the unbearable fear and rage and sense of betrayal that must have overwhelmed her as she'd watched her husband slip away.

'I'm sorry, Mother,' I whispered.

What she said next stunned me with its uncompromising force. 'You're all alike, Henry, all you men.'

She stared at me for one long, ghastly moment, then turned and walked away, leaving me in a world that had begun to move again, though differently than it had before, filled with greater complications, a weave of consequences and relations that seemed larger than romance, deeper and more enduring, though still distant from my understanding, a world I'd only just briefly glimpsed, as it were, through my mother's eyes.

My mother never again spoke to me directly about the Chatham School Affair. And I remember that a few hours later, after a nearly silent dinner, I went upstairs to my room, lay down upon my bed, and tried to think about Mrs. Reed, not in the panic and despair of her last seconds, as I'd continually thought of her throughout Miss Channing's trial, but before that, when she'd been a wife and mother.

Toward dawn I awoke, and there she was before me. Abigail Reed, as if she were alive again, with red hair and green eyes, watching me silently from the ruins of her shattered faith. And for the first time, as I lay in the shadowy early morning light, I found that I was able to imagine what it must have been like for her during those weeks when Mr. Reed had begun to drift from her, spending long hours with me in the boathouse, the two of us working deep into the night to complete his boat, while she remained at home, tending to their daughter, bathing her, clothing her in thick flannel sleeping gowns, putting her to bed.

I saw all those many nights when the hour had grown late, and still Mr. Reed had not returned. How she must have wondered about the changes that had come over her husband, how preoccupied and distracted he had become, as if he could not keep his mind from wandering away from her, and toward some distant attachment whose nature she could not let herself consider.

And yet she had to have considered it, had to have noticed that he no longer touched her with the same affection, nor with any great desire, and that although he still frolicked with Mary, he more often preferred to be alone with his daughter, taking her on long walks or even rowing her out into the center of Black Pond, where, bundled up against the cold of that long winter, they fished in the icy water.

Perhaps, in order to escape the unbearable implications of the changes she noticed in him, Mrs. Reed had sometimes recalled the moment when she'd first seen him, a tall, slender man, leaning on a cane as he bought his weekly supplies at the village store, the way they'd walked out together, he holding the door for her, nodding quickly as she passed, then falling in behind her for a little distance before she'd stopped, turned toward him and asked him bluntly if he was not Leland Reed, the new teacher at Chatham School.

But where had he gone, this man who'd lived with her for more than five years, who was the father of her daughter, and who'd provided for her and loved her as no man ever had or ever would again, but who now seemed to have receded, perhaps even beyond the promised gravity of home.

How Mrs. Reed must have suffered during all those long nights, I thought as the air lightened outside my bedroom window that morning. How she must have yearned to regain Mr. Reed once again, not just for a night, but forever.

But as I well knew, Mr. Reed had never returned to her. So that as the days passed one after the other, and the nights deepened and grew colder, I knew that she must have walked to the window at regular intervals, parted the curtains, and peered out into the darkness, her eyes now fixed on the empty road, searching for some sign of his approaching car. At such a moment, locked in dread, Mrs. Reed's face could not have looked at all like the women of romantic myth, Iseult beneath her billowing white sail, or Guenevere waiting heroically to be burned alive. And yet, for all that, she now seemed heroic to me somehow, as my mother had certainly thought of her when she fled the court that day, convinced, as she had every right to be, that no man, her son included, could ever conceive or even remotely comprehend the depth of her long pain.

# TWENTY

Nor do I think that my father ever really understood it. At least not at that time. For although he must have felt the deepest sympathy for Mrs. Reed, I believe that he remained captured in a different orbit, one that spun around Miss Channing, had *her* life, *her* loss, as its central star.

And so it never surprised me that he labored to defend her on that August afternoon when it came his turn to take the stand.

*Mr. Parsons: Now, you hired Miss Elizabeth Rockbridge Channing as a teacher at Chatham School, did you not, Mr. Griswald?*

*Witness: Yes, I did.*

*Mr. Parsons: And early on, did you have any reason to doubt the wisdom of choosing Miss Channing for her post at Chatham School?*

*Witness: No, I did not.*

*Mr. Parsons: Well, at a later time, did you begin to have reservations about Miss Channing's character?*

*Witness: Not exactly.*

*Mr. Parsons: But as you have already heard, Mr. Griswald, an earlier witness has testified that she told you about certain rumors having to do with Miss Channing's relationship with Leland Reed.*

*Witness: Yes, I was informed that certain people felt that way.*

*Mr. Parsons: But you chose to ignore their warnings?*

*Witness: I had no proof of anything, Mr. Parsons.*

*Mr. Parsons: But you had observed some rather odd behavior, had you not? In regard to both Mr. Reed and Miss Channing. Certain alarming behavior?*

*Witness: I wouldn't call it alarming.*

*Mr. Parsons: Well, isn't it true that both Mr. Reed and Miss Channing appeared extremely strained during the final weeks of the school year?*

*Witness: Yes, they did.*

*Mr. Parsons: And didn't this strain become obvious at one point in your own house, Mr. Griswald? At a party on, I believe, April twenty-third.*

*Witness: Yes, it did.*

*Mr. Parsons: Did Miss Channing and Mr. Reed come to that party to-gether?*

*Witness: No. Miss Channing came into my office the afternoon before the party and asked if I might pick her up.*

*Mr. Parsons: You, Mr. Griswald? She didn't wish to be picked up by Mr. Reed?*

*Witness: Evidently not.*

*Mr. Parsons: And did you agree to do that, to bring Miss Channing to your house that evening?*

*Witness: Yes, I did.*

And so, as he had so many times in the past, my father demanded that I come with him to Milford Cottage that evening, the two of us driving through a soft blue twilight to retrieve her. On the way, I remember that he had a certain agitated look in his eyes, like someone pressed into a service he'd rather have avoided but felt it his duty to perform. By then, of course, he must have known that something very grave had begun to darken the atmosphere of Chatham School, something he found it difficult to confront, or simply knew no way of confronting. I have often wondered what I might have said had he turned to me that evening and asked me bluntly what I knew about Miss Channing and Mr. Reed. Perhaps I would have lied to him, as I later did, claiming an innocence I did not deserve.

But he talked of the party instead, the long tables that had been placed on the back lawn, the Chinese lanterns he'd hung over them, how festive everything looked.

It was not until we neared Milford Cottage that he grew silent.

Miss Channing came out immediately, dressed in a long black skirt and a dark red blouse, her hair bound tightly in a bun. Her eyes seemed feverish and her skin was very pale.

I got out of the car, and held the door open for her. 'Thank you, Henry,' she said as she got into the front seat beside my father.

'Good evening, Miss Channing,' my father said.

She nodded softly. 'Good evening, Mr. Griswald.'

They hardly spoke for the first few minutes of the drive back toward Chatham. Then, out of nowhere, my father suddenly blurted out, 'I was thinking of offering you a commission, Miss Channing. A private commission, that is. A portrait of myself.' He glanced toward her, then back to the road. 'Do you do portraits?'

'Yes,' she said. 'I've done a few. My uncle. His wife. When I was in Africa.'

'So, do you think you'd like to take a crack at it?'

She smiled slightly. 'Yes, I would.'

My father seemed pleased. 'Splendid.'

They went on to arrange various times when my father would be available to sit for her, and during the next few weeks I saw them often in his office together, the door always open, of course, Miss Channing in her gray smock, standing behind her easel, my father posed beside the window, looking out onto the courtyard, his body caught in a shaft of light.

During the rest of the drive, my father talked rather absently about the spring term, how brief it always seemed compared to fall and winter, warning Miss Channing that the boys would become 'increasingly rambunctious' as the end of the school year approached. 'So keep a firm hand on them,' he told her, 'because they'll certainly need it.' It was not until we'd turned onto the main road back to Chatham that he suddenly said, 'By the way, Mr. Reed may not be able to join us this evening.'

My attention sprang to Miss Channing, and I saw her body grow tense at the mention of Mr. Reed's name.

'It seems that Mrs. Reed has taken ill,' my father went on. 'Something to do with her stomach.'

Miss Channing turned away from my father and toward the window at her side, a quick reflexive gesture made, or so it seemed to me at the time, in order to shield her face from his view. Watching her, I recalled the way she'd sat so stiffly in the boat as we'd made our way down the Bass River only a week or so before, her manner now even more enclosed than it had appeared that day, so that she seemed oddly frightened of the very movement her life had taken, as if it were a blade swinging above her head.

It was warm enough for my father to have rolled the window down on the driver's side, and as we made our way along the coastal road he peered out over the fields of sea grass that rose from the marshes and the bogs. 'I love the spring on Cape Cod. Summer, too, of course. Do you plan to stay here on the Cape for the summer, Miss Channing?'

'I haven't really thought about the summer,' she murmured as if such a possibility had not occurred to her.

'Well, there's still plenty of time to think about it,' my father told her, then let the subject drop.

We pulled into the driveway of our house seconds later. I got out and opened the door for Miss Channing. 'Thank you, Henry,' she said as she stepped out of the car.

Some of the other teachers had already arrived, the rest coming only a few minutes later, everyone serving themselves from the plentiful buffet my mother and Sarah had arranged on a long table in the backyard, then sitting in small groups on chairs my father and I had placed throughout the grounds earlier that afternoon.

It was my job to help Sarah serve the guests at the buffet table, and from that position I could see Miss Channing as she sat with a group not far away, my mother facing her directly, Mr. Corbett to her right, Mrs. Benton, the Latin teacher, to her left, and finally Mrs. Abercrombie, my father's assistant, just a bit outside the circle, her long, thin legs requiring somewhat more room.

My mother was doing her best to be sociable that evening, talking in that slightly rapid way of hers about whatever matter she thought might interest the people gathered around her.

At one point I heard her say, 'Well, Chatham is small, but I think there must be quite a few eligible young men.' Then she turned to Miss Channing, the only unmarried woman in the group, and asked, 'Don't you think so, Elizabeth?'

I remember that Miss Channing seemed unable to answer my mother's question, perhaps suspecting that she had some ulterior motive in asking it.

In that brief silence, I saw my mother's eyes narrow slightly as she added, 'I mean to say, I was wondering what your experience had been.'

Still, Miss Channing did not answer, and in that interval of silence I noticed Mrs. Benton glance knowingly at Mrs. Abercrombie.

Finally, Miss Channing said, 'I wouldn't know about that.'

I expected my mother to let the answer go, but she didn't. 'You wouldn't?' she said, clearly surprised. 'So you've not become acquainted with any of the young men in Chatham since you arrived?'

Miss Channing shook her head. 'No, I haven't.'

My mother gave her a slow, evaluating look. 'Well, I'm sure someone will come along,' she said with a stiff smile.

They went on to other topics after that. Each time I glanced Miss Channing's way, she appeared fixed in the same position, her hands in her lap, her back erect, a plate of uneaten food nestled in the grass beside her chair.

By nine most everyone had departed. It was April, a chill still present in the evening air, and so my father invited the few guests who remained to join him in the parlor.

My mother took her usual chair by the fireplace, my father the wooden rocker a few feet away. Mrs. Abercrombie and Mrs. Benton shared the small settee, while Miss Channing chose a chair somewhat off to the side. I pulled out the piano stool and sat by the window.

I don't remember what they talked about for the next few minutes, only that Miss Channing said very little, her face more or less expression-less as she listened to the others, her hands still in her lap, as they had been all evening.

It was an attitude she might have remained in for the rest of the night had she not caught the sound of a car rumbling down Myrtle Street. She clearly recognized its distinctive clatter, turned toward the window, parted the curtains, and peered outside, her face suddenly bathed in light as the car wheeled into our driveway and came to a halt. I saw her eyes widen, her lips part silently as she watched a figure move down the drive-way and up the stairs to our front door. One of her hands crawled into the other as she turned away from the window, listening first to the knock at the door, then Sarah's cheery greeting when she opened it. 'Well, good evening, Mr. Reed.'

He came directly into the parlor, his hat in his hand, the old brown jacket draped over his shoulders, like a cape.

'Hello,' he said. 'I hope I'm not intruding.'

'No, not at all. Please, come in,' my father told him, though not with his usual enthusiasm. There was something rather stiff in the way he rose from his chair to shake Mr. Reed's hand. 'I hope Mrs. Reed is feeling better.'

Mr. Reed nodded. 'Yes, she is,' he said.

'Please, sit down,' my father told him.

Mr. Reed took a seat near the door, glancing about until his eyes fell upon Miss Channing. And though his lips lifted in a thin smile, his eyes seemed utterly mirthless and unsmiling. 'Hello, Miss Channing,' he said.

She nodded coolly. 'Mr. Reed.'

My father glanced back and forth between them. 'Well, now,' he said loudly, clearly trying to draw Mr. Reed's attention back to the group, 'we were all discussing the possibility of adding a course in Shakespeare to next year's curriculum.'

Mr. Reed turned toward him but offered no reply.

'We were wondering who might best be able to teach such a course,' my father went on.

Mr. Reed stared my father dead in the eye. 'I really don't know,' he said with what must have struck my father as a shocking sense of indif-ference, as if Chatham School had ceased to play any significant part in his life, but only continued to hang from it, numb, limp, useless, like an atrophied appendage waiting to be cut away.

It was a tone that clearly disturbed my father, and which he could not confront, so he merely drew in a quick, troubled breath and returned his attention to the others. 'Well, how about a round of port?' he asked them.

All heads nodded, and with that my father summoned Sarah to serve the port.

'We're so lucky to have Sarah,' my mother said after she'd finished serving and left the room. 'We had a wonderful Negro girl before her. Amelia was her name, and she was quite able.' She glanced at Miss Channing. 'As a matter of fact, Amelia would have been very interested in talking to you, Elizabeth.'

Miss Channing's fingers tightened around her glass. 'Why is that?' she asked evenly.

'Because she'd have wanted to hear all about your life in Africa,' my mother answered. She'd picked her knitting from a basket beside her chair and the long silver needles flashed in the lamplight as she flicked them right and left.

'Amelia was a follower of Marcus Garvey, you see,' my father said. 'She was quite taken with this idea of going back to Africa, living free, and all that.' He shrugged. 'It was all terribly unrealistic, of course, the whole business.' Drawing a pipe from the rack that rested on the table beside his chair, he began to fill its dark briar bowl with tobacco. 'But what can you do about such a romantic notion?'

It was a question he'd asked rhetorically, not expecting an answer, least of all a brutal one.

'You can crush it,' Mr. Reed blurted out harshly, his eyes darting over to Miss Channing, then back to my father.

My father looked at him quizzically, his hand now suspended motionlessly above the bowl of his pipe, his eyes widening to take him in. 'Crush it, Mr. Reed?' he asked.

'That's right,' Mr. Reed said. 'You can tell her how foolish such an idea of freedom is. How foolish and preposterous it is to believe that you can ever escape anything or change anything, or live in a way that—'

He stopped, his eyes now turning toward Miss Channing, who only glared at him, her face taut and unmoving.

Then my father said, 'Well, that would be rather cruel, wouldn't it, Mr. Reed?' His voice was surprisingly gentle and restrained as he continued, his eyes leveled upon Mr. Reed's. 'Perhaps you could simply remind her – Amelia, I mean – that there is much in life beyond such extreme desires.'

Mr. Reed shook his head, drawing his gaze from Miss Channing, and waved his hand. 'It doesn't matter anyway,' he said wearily.

There was an exchange of glances among the guests, then, as if to lower the heat within the room, Mrs. Benton chirped, 'It's a lovely room you have here, Mrs. Griswald. The curtains are ... lovely.'

With that, the conversation took a different and decidedly less volatile turn, although I can't remember what was said, only that neither Mr. Reed nor Miss Channing said anything at all. Mrs. Abercrombie left within a few minutes, then Mrs. Benton, each of them nodding cordially as they bade my father and mother good night.

Mr. Reed rose directly after that. He seemed weary beyond measure, as if his earlier outburst had weakened him profoundly. At the entrance to the parlor he turned back. 'Do you need a ride home, Miss Channing?' he asked, though with an unmistakable hopelessness, her answer already made clear to him by the ravaged look in her eyes.

'No,' she said, adding nothing else as he turned from her and moved silently out the door.

And so it was my father and I who drove Miss Channing home that night, gliding through the now-deserted village, then out along Plymouth Road to where we finally came to a halt at the very end of it, the headlights of my father's car briefly illuminating the front of Milford Cottage before dissolving into the impenetrable depths of Black Pond.

'Well, good night, Miss Channing,' he said to her quietly.

I expected Miss Channing to get out of the car, but she remained in place. 'Mr. Griswald,' she said. 'I wonder if I might ask you something?'

My heart stopped, for I felt sure that she was about to tell him everything, reveal the whole course and nature of her relationship with Mr. Reed, ask my father for that wise guidance I know he would have given if she had done so.

But she did nothing of the kind. Instead, she said, 'I was thinking of making something for the school. A piece of sculpture. Plaster masks of all the boys and the teachers, everyone at the school. I could arrange them on a column. It would be a record of everyone at Chatham School this year.'

'That would be a lot of work for you, wouldn't it, Miss Channing?' my father asked.

'Yes, it would. But for the next few weeks—' She stopped, as if trying to decide what to say. 'For the next few weeks,' she began again, 'I'd just like to keep myself busy.'

My father leaned forward slightly, peering at her closely, and I knew that whatever he had refused to see before that moment he now saw in all its fatal depth, Miss Channing's misery and distress so obvious that when Mr. Parsons finally asked his question, *You knew, didn't you, Mr. Griswald, that by the night of your party Miss Channing had reached a desperate point?*, he could not help but answer, *Yes.*

But that night at Milford Cottage he only said, 'Yes, very well, Miss Channing. I'm sure your sculpture will be something the school can be proud of.'

Miss Channing nodded, then got out of the car and swiftly made her way down the narrow walkway to her cottage.

My father watched her go with an unspoken sympathy for a plight he seemed to comprehend more deeply than I would have expected, and which later caused me to wonder if perhaps somewhere down a remote road or along the outer bank, some woman had once waited for him, one he wished to go to but never did, and in return for that refusal received this small unutterably painful addition to his understanding.

If such a woman ever lived, her call unanswered, he never spoke of it.

And as to Miss Channing, as he watched her make her way toward the cottage that night, 'God help her' was all he said.

# TWENTY-ONE

I think it was the somberness of my father's words that awakened me early the next morning, sent me downstairs, hoping that I wasn't too late to catch up with Sarah as she set off for her weekly reading lesson.

She was already at the end of Myrtle Street when I called to her. She waited, smiling, as I came up to her.

'I thought I'd go with you this morning,' I told her.

This seemed to please her. 'That would be grand,' she said, then turned briskly and continued on down the street, the basket swinging between us as we made our way toward Milford Cottage.

We reached it a short time later, the morning air bright and warm, with more of summer in it now than spring. Miss Channing was sitting outside, on the steps of the cottage, her body so still she looked as if she'd been in the same position for a long time.

'Good morning,' she said as we came down the walkway, her tone less open and welcoming than I had ever heard it, her eyes squeezed together slightly, like someone wincing with an inward pain.

It was only a few minutes later, after she'd begun Sarah's lesson, that Miss Channing grew less distracted in her voice and manner. She began to smile occasionally, though less vibrantly than in the past, so that her overall mood remained strangely subdued.

The lesson ended at eleven, just as it usually did.

'Good, Sarah,' Miss Channing said as she rose from the table and began to gather up the books and writing pads. 'You're coming along splendidly. I'll see you again next Sunday.'

Sarah looked at me quizzically, then turned back to Miss Channing, clearly worried by the distress she saw in her, perhaps even afraid to leave her in such a troubled state. 'Would you like to take a stroll, Miss Channing?' she asked softly. 'There's a little parade or something in the village today.' She looked at me for assistance. 'What is it, Henry, that parade?'

'It's to celebrate the beginning of the Revolution,' I said. 'The shot heard 'round the world.'

Sarah kept her eyes on Miss Channing. 'We could all walk into town together,' she said. 'It's such a pretty day.'

For a moment Miss Channing seemed thrown into a quandary by Sarah's invitation. Finally, she said, though still with some reluctance, 'Well, yes, I suppose I could do that.'

We set off right away, the three of us walking at a leisurely pace down Plymouth Road. It was deep enough into spring for the first greenery to have appeared, budding trees and ferns and a few forest wildflowers, a rich pungency in the air around us. 'There was once a French king who was very fond of sweet smells,' Miss Channing said after a moment, 'and when he gave parties in the ballroom, he would have his servants pour different perfumes over live pigeons, then release them into the air.' She stopped and drew in a long breath. 'It must have been like this,' she told us, 'a tapestry of smells.'

She began to walk again, adding nothing more, but I would always remember that this was the final story I would hear from her, the slender smile she offered at the end of it, the last that I would see upon her face.

At noon the streets of Chatham were already filled with people who'd come into the village for the day's festivities. We found a vacant spot on the hill in front of the town hall and stood, along with everyone else, waiting for the parade. Below us, on the crowded sidewalks, we could see the people moving back and forth, trying to find a clear view of the street. Miss Channing remained silent most of the time, nearly motionless as well, save that her eyes had a tendency to follow knots of children as they darted along the sidewalk or across the lawn.

We were still standing on the lawn of the town hall when the local fife and bugle corps marched by, followed by a ragged gang of villagers dressed in Revolutionary costumes, my father among them, doffing a tricornered hat. The town's new fire engine came next, festooned with flags and bunting, and after it, a small contingent of the Massachusetts State Police, riding horseback, a tall, slender man in the lead, with gray hair and a formal manner, his silver badge winking in the afternoon light, and whom I later recognized as Captain Lawrence Hamilton.

The crowd began to disperse soon afterward, children rushing here and there as their parents summoned them to their sides, groups of young people heading off toward Quilty's for ice cream and soda, couples strolling idly toward the outskirts of town, no doubt headed for the beach, where a clambake had been scheduled for later in the day.

'Well, I guess that's it for the parade,' I said absently, looking to the right, toward Miss Channing.

She didn't answer me, or even turn her eyes in my direction. Instead, she continued to peer across the street. I glanced toward where she was staring, and saw Mrs. Reed standing on the opposite corner, with Mary in her arms.

For a moment Mrs. Reed held her attention on the parade. Then, at a pace that seemed surreally slow, she turned to face us, her gaze suddenly leveled upon Miss Channing, cold, steady, hateful, yet strangely haunted too, features that seemed locked forever in a ghostly rage.

It must have been a look that Miss Channing could not bear, for she whirled around immediately, like someone wrenching herself from a murderous, invisible grip, and began to push forward through the crowd, leaving Sarah and me in her wake, watching, astonished, as she plunged away from us, darting left and right through the milling crowd until she finally disappeared into the throng.

'What's the matter with Miss Channing?' Sarah asked, both of us still staring off in the direction where she'd gone.

'I don't know,' I answered. But I did.

For a long time I believed that it was what Miss Channing saw that afternoon, Mrs. Reed in all her wounded anguish, little Mary helpless in her arms, that determined the nature of the conversation I overheard the very next day.

It happened late in the afternoon, a blue haze already settling over the school courtyard, hovering in the trees and over the pebbled walkway. Miss Channing had just completed a portrait session with my father, for I remember seeing her in his office only moments before, my father at the window where she'd placed him, she a few feet away, peering toward him from around the side of her easel.

He'd offered to drive her home, as he later told me, but she had declined, telling him that she wanted to begin work on the other project she had proposed, the column of faces that was to be her gift to Chatham School. After that she'd returned to her classroom, brought out a lump of clay, and begun to fashion a model of the sculpture she was soon to make.

She was still at it sometime later when I walked through the courtyard, glanced to the right, and saw her standing at her sculpting pedestal, her hands sunk deep in the pockets of her smock. She was looking toward the front of the room, but until I moved farther west, heading toward the rear door of the school, I couldn't make out what she was looking at, for the large tree that stood near the center of the courtyard blocked my view. And so it was not until I'd passed beyond it that I saw Mr. Reed standing at the entrance to her room.

It was a scene that startled me, the two of them facing each other so silently and at such a physical distance that they looked like duelists in an evening shade. And so I stopped and drew back behind the tree, listening like a common eavesdropper as their voices came toward me from the open windows of Miss Channing's room.

'What do you want, Leland?'

'Something impossible.'

'You know what has to be done.'

'How do you want me to do it?'

'Without looking back.'

There was a pause, then I heard Mr. Reed speak again.

'Because I love you, I can do it.'

'Then do.'

'Let me take you home now. We can—'

'No.'

'Why?'

'You know why, Leland.'

Another pause. Then he said it.

'Do you want her dead?'

I heard no answer, but only the sound of Miss Channing's footsteps as she headed toward the door, and after I that her voice again, anguished, pleading.

'Leland, please. Let me go.'

'But don't you see that—'

'Don't touch me.'

'Elizabeth, you can't—'

I heard the door of the room fly open, then saw Miss Channing rush quickly past where I stood beside the tree, and into the school, her black hair flying like a dark pennant in her wake. Watching her go, then glancing back into her room to see Mr. Reed now slumped in a chair, his head in his hands, I felt the same soaring anger I'd glimpsed in Mrs. Reed's face as she'd glared at Miss Channing the day before, but with Mrs. Reed now the object at *my* rage, Miss Channing and Mr. Reed the birds I wished to free from her bony, strangling grasp.

I was still seething nearly an hour later, Mr. Reed's words echoing in my mind – *Do you want her dead?* – when Sarah found me on the front steps of the house on Myrtle Street.

'Your father sent me to get you,' she told me as she lowered herself onto the step just beneath me. 'He's at the school. He has something he wants you to do.'

'Tell him you couldn't find me,' I replied sullenly.

I felt her hand touch mine.

'What's the matter, Henry?'

I shook my head, unable to answer her.

For a moment she watched me silently, then she said, 'Why are you so unhappy, Henry?'

I gave her the only answer I had at the time. 'Because no one's free, Sarah. None of us.'

Her question sprang from an ancient source. 'What would happen if we were? Free, I mean.'

My answer signaled the dawning of a self-indulgent age. 'We'd be happy,' I said angrily. 'If we were free to do what we want, don't you think we'd be happy?'

She had no answer for me, of course. Nor should I have expected one, since she was young, as I was, the hard fact that our lives cannot accommodate the very passions they inspire still a lesson waiting to be learned.

Sarah got to her feet again. 'You'd better go to your father, Henry. He's expecting you.'

I didn't move. 'In a minute,' I told her.

'I'll go tell him that you're on your way,' Sarah said.

With that, she walked away, leaving me to sit alone, watching as she reached Myrtle Street, then swung left and headed for the school, my mind by then already returning to its lethal imaginings, thoughts so malicious and ruthless that several weeks later, as Mr. Parsons and I made our way around that playing field, he could ask his question in a tone of stark certainty, *So it was murder, wasn't it, Henry?* and to my silence he could add nothing more than *How long have you known?*

# TWENTY-TWO

I never answered Mr. Parsons' question, but even as he asked it I recalled the very moment when I first thought of murder.

It was late on a Saturday afternoon, the first week of May. I was alone in the boathouse, Mr. Reed having gone to Mayflower's for a bag of nails. The boat was nearing completion by then, its sleek sides gleaming with a new coat of varnish, the mast now fitted with ropes, its broad sail wrapped tightly and tied in place.

The lights were on inside the boathouse, but Mr. Reed had covered its windows with burlap sacks, the whole room shrouded, so that it resembled something gloomy and in hiding rather than the bright departure point of the great adventure it had once seemed to me.

I was standing near the stove, gathering the last few nails from the bottom of a toolbox, when the door suddenly opened. I turned toward it, expecting to see Mr. Reed, then felt my breath catch in my throat.

'You're Henry,' she said.

She stood in the doorway, a bright noon light behind her, facing me, one hand on the door, the other at her side, the sun behind her turning the red tint of her hair into a fiery aurora.

'Mildred Griswald's son,' she added.

Leveled upon me as they were, her green eyes shone out of the spectral light, wide and unblinking, like fish eyes from a murky tank.

I nodded. 'Yes, ma'am.'

She stepped through the door, her gaze upon me with a piercing keenness, alert and wolfish. 'You're helping him,' she said. 'Helping him build the boat.'

'Yes, I am.'

Her eyes drifted from me over to the gleaming side of the boat. Then, in a quick, nearly savage movement, they shot back to me.

'Where is he?' she asked.

'Gone to buy nails.'

She came toward me, and I felt my body tense. For there was something in her manner, a sense of having been slowly devoured over many weeks, fed upon by thousands of tiny, gnawing doubts, that gave her a strangely cadaverous appearance, as if the bones were already beginning to appear beneath the pale, nearly translucent film that had become her skin.

'Your mother and I were friends when we were girls,' she said with a faint, oddly painful smile.

She continued to come forward, and seconds later, when she spoke to me again, I could feel her breath on my face. 'The boat's nearly finished.'

'Yes, it is,' I said hollowly.

She glanced about the room, her eyes moving randomly until, with a terrible suddenness, they fixed on the drawing I'd made of Miss Channing, which now hung over the desk in the far corner. Her face became instantly expressionless and void, as if an invisible acid were being poured over her features, melting her identity away.

'Does she come here?' she asked, her gaze still concentrated upon the drawing.

I shrugged. 'I don't know.'

She lifted her head and twisted it sharply to the left, her attention now focused on the cardboard box that rested on the desk, just below the portrait. Like someone lifted on a cushion of smoky air, she drifted toward it effortlessly, soundlessly, the world held in a motionless suspension until she reached it, dropped her head forward, and peered inside.

I knew what she was looking at. A map. A knife. A coil of gray rope. And in the corner, a small brown bottle, the letters printed boldly in black ink: ARSENIC.

She stared into the box for what seemed a long time, like someone recording everything she saw. Then she raised her head in what I will always remember as a slow, steady movement, as if drawing it from the dark, airless water in which it had been submerged, and turned to face me once again. 'Is it just me?' she asked.

'Just you?'

'Is it just me? Or is it Mary too?'

'I don't know what you mean, Mrs. Reed.'

During all the years that have passed since that moment, I have seen my share of fear and uncertainty and sorrow, but I don't think I ever saw it in the same combination again, terror so delicately blended with pain, pain so inseparably mingled with confusion, that the final effect was of a shivering, anguished bafflement.

That was what I saw in Mrs. Reed's face. It is what I still see when I remember her. It was clear and vivid, all her misery in her eyes. Anyone might have seen it. It could hardly have been more obvious. The only mystery is why her plight, so dark and terrible, did not move me in the least.

It was my mother that it moved.

It was late in the afternoon when I returned home that same day. Sarah was in the dining room, setting places for the evening meal, but she stopped when she saw me enter the house, and rushed into the foyer. I could tell that she was alarmed. 'Henry, I have to talk to you,' she said urgently. 'Mrs. Reed came here today. To talk to your mother.'

As Mrs. Reed had turned up at our door only a short time after she'd appeared in the boathouse, I had little doubt as to the purpose of her visit. Still, I kept that earlier encounter to myself, allowing Sarah to go on with her story as if I had no hint of where it might be headed.

'She looked odd, Henry,' Sarah said. 'Mrs. Reed did. An odd look in her eye.' She shivered slightly. 'It gave me a ... a creepy feeling, the way she looked.'

'What did she want?'

'She asked to speak with your mother.'

'Did they speak?'

'Oh, yes, they spoke, all right. Your mother called for tea, and I brought it to them. Right in the parlor. With the door closed, of course.'

I could see my mother and Mrs. Reed sitting beside the empty hearth of the parlor, our best china teacups in their hands, Mrs. Reed tormented beyond measure, telling of her husband's betrayal, my mother growing more and more angry and alarmed as she listened to her story.

'I couldn't hear what they said,' Sarah added. 'But it looked serious.'

'Where are they now?'

'They went for a walk, the two of them.' Sarah gave me a piercing look. 'What's this all about, Henry?' she demanded.

'I don't know,' I lied, then turned away and mounted the stairs to my room.

I was still there an hour later when my father returned from his office at Chatham School. He called me downstairs and asked me directly where my mother was. I glanced toward where Sarah stood silently at the entrance of the dining room, waiting for my answer.

'She went out for a walk,' I said.

'A walk?' my father asked. 'At this hour? With whom?'

'With Mrs. Reed,' I told him.

He could not conceal his troubled surprise at such a visit. 'Mrs. Reed? Mrs. Reed came here?'

'Yes. She came by this afternoon.'

'What did she want?'

'Just to see Mother, I guess.'

He nodded casually, determined to put the best possible light on such a meeting. 'Well, they were neighbors, you know,' he said. 'Your mother and Mrs. Reed. They're probably talking about old times, that sort of thing.'

'I didn't know they were neighbors,' I said.

'Yes, they were,' my father said, obviously reluctant to provide any further details. 'Well, go on about your business, then, son,' he added, then turned and walked into the parlor.

I stood at the parlor door. 'When were they neighbors?' I asked.

He sat down, picked up the newspaper from the table beside his chair, and began turning the pages, still trying to avoid any further discussion of the matter. 'When they were young. Your mother lived next to the people Mrs. Reed worked for after she was—' He stopped and looked at me suddenly. 'Mrs. Reed was abandoned, Henry. When she was a young woman.'

'Abandoned?'

'Left at the altar, as they say.' My father's eyes now retreated behind the paper once again. 'And so your mother has a certain ... well, a certain sympathy, I suppose you'd call it. For Mrs. Reed, I mean.' He drew in a long breath. 'For what she's gone through in her life.'

He said nothing more about Mrs. Reed, so that I left the parlor shortly after, returned to my room upstairs, and stayed there until I heard the creak of the front gate, glanced out the window, and saw my mother striding up the walkway to the front stairs.

I had one of those premonitions children often have, moments when they sense that things are about to fly apart. Perhaps it was the firm, heavy-footed way my mother took the stairs, or the hard slap of the screen door as it closed behind her.

In any event, I went downstairs to find her in the parlor with my father. He'd lowered the paper and gotten to his feet, facing her from what looked like a defensive position beside the mantel.

'A woman knows, Arthur,' I heard my mother say.

'That's preposterous, Mildred, and you know it.'

'You won't face it, that's the problem.'

'There has to be some sort of—'

'A woman knows,' my mother cried. 'A woman doesn't need proof.'

'Yes, but I do, Mildred,' my father told her. 'I can't just bring two respected teachers into my office and—'

'Respected?' My mother spat out the word. 'Why should they be respected?'

'That's enough,' my father said.

My mother sank briefly into a fuming silence. Then, in a calm, deadly voice she said, 'If you won't do something about this, Arthur, then I'll have no respect for you either.'

My father's voice filled with dismay. 'How can you say such a thing to me?'

'Because I mean it,' my mother said. 'I married you because I respected you, Arthur. You seemed like a good man to me. Honest. Steady. But if you don't do something about this situation between Mr. Reed and that woman – well, then, the way I see it, you're not the man I married.'

What I have always remembered most from that dreadful moment is that as my mother listed those things that had drawn her to my father, she never once mentioned love.

For a few smoldering seconds they faced each other without speaking. Then my father walked to his chair and slumped down into it. 'It doesn't matter anyway, Mildred,' he said softly, his eyes now drifting toward the window. 'Miss Channing is leaving Chatham School. She will not return next year.' He picked up the newspaper from the floor beside his chair but did not open it. 'She resigned this afternoon. Whatever it is that Mrs. Reed thinks must be going on between Miss Channing and ... well ... you can tell her that it has come to an end.'

My mother stood rigidly in place. 'You men always feel the same way. That when it's over, a woman can just forget that it ever happened.'

Wearily, my father shook his head. 'I didn't say that, Mildred, and you know it.'

What my mother said next amazed me. 'Have you ever betrayed me, Arthur?'

My father looked at her with an astonishment exactly like my own. 'What?' he blurted out. 'My God, Mildred, what's gotten into you? How could you ask me such a question?'

'Answer it, Arthur.'

He stared at her, curiously silent, before he finally took a breath and gave his answer. 'No, Mildred,' he said evenly. 'I have never betrayed you.'

I looked at my mother, her eyes upon my father with a lethal gaze, and it struck me that she did not believe him, or at least that she would never be sure that he'd told her the truth.

For a moment they simply faced each other silently. Then my mother walked past him, edging her way through the parlor door as she headed for the kitchen. 'Dinner in an hour' was all she said.

The dinner we sat through an hour later was extremely tense. My father and mother spoke only of trivial things – my father's plan to include a couple of new courses in the curriculum, my mother's to have a larger summer garden at the back of the house. When it was over, my mother walked into the parlor, where she stayed, knitting by the unlighted hearth, until she went up to her bed. My father went back to the school, where he worked in his office until nearly nine, returning home only after my mother had already gone upstairs.

I was sitting in my customary spot in the swing on the front porch when I saw him coming down the street, his gait very slow, his head lowered slightly, the posture he always assumed when he was deep in thought.

He nodded to me as he came up the stairs.

'Nice evening, isn't it, Henry?'

I expected him to go directly into the house, as he usually did. But instead, he came over to the swing and sat down beside me. At first I didn't know what to do in regard to the exchange I'd heard between him and my mother a few hours before, but after a time my curiosity got the better of me, so I decided to bring it up.

Still, I didn't want to approach things too directly, so I said, 'When I was coming downstairs this afternoon, I thought I heard you say that Miss Channing was leaving Chatham School.'

He did not appear surprised that I'd overheard him, nor particularly alarmed by it, so that I felt the faint hope that, perhaps for the first time, he'd begun to see me not as a little boy from whom life must be concealed behind a wall of secrecy and silence, but as someone on the brink of adulthood to whom, however painfully, its truths must be revealed.

'Yes, she's leaving, Henry.'

'Where's she going?'

'I don't know.' He glanced toward me, then away again. 'But I wouldn't worry about Miss Channing. She'll do quite well, I'm sure. She's a very able teacher. Very able. I'm sure she'll find another post somewhere else.'

The subject seemed closed. Then, abruptly, my father turned to me. 'Henry, you must keep quiet about whatever you've heard at home,' he said. 'About Miss Channing and Mr. Reed, I mean.'

I could tell that he was trying to find the words for some other, deeper thought. 'Life is inadequate, Henry,' he said finally, his eyes upon me very solemnly. 'Sometimes the most we can give, or get, is trust.' With that he leaned forward, patted my leg, rose, and went inside. Nor did he ever make any further attempt to explain what he'd said to me. But over the years, as he grew older and I grew older, I came to understand what he'd meant that night, that hunger is our destiny, faith what we use to soothe its dreadful pang.

I know now that my father had tried to reach out to me that night, show the path ahead, but I remember that as I watched him trudge wearily through the door, he seemed smaller to me than he ever had. I felt a malevolent wave of contempt for everything he stood for. It was swift and boiling, and in its wake I felt an absolute determination never to be like my father, never so pathetic, nor so beaten down.

Now, when I think of that moment in my life, of what I felt, and later did, the inevitable strikes me as nothing more than that which has just happened unexpectedly.

# PART V

# TWENTY-THREE

Some years ago I happened upon a line in Tacitus. It came near the end of the section of *Germania* that described the utter subjugation of the barbaric German tribes at the hands of the more tightly regimented Roman legions, a campaign that had stripped the Germans of the last vestiges of their savagery, all their primitive rites and rituals taken from them, their dances, songs, and stories. 'They have made a wilderness,' Tacitus wrote, 'and call it peace.'

In the brief period that remained before it closed for the summer, a similarly bare and withered peace appeared to descend upon Chatham School, turning it into a passionless world, as it seemed to me at the time, very nearly a void, all its former vibrancy, the tingling sense of intrigue and desire, now buried beneath a layer of stark propriety.

During this time Miss Channing no longer arrived and departed with Mr. Reed, but walked back and forth from Milford Cottage alone. In the morning I would often see her moving up our street, her pace slow, meditative, so that she appeared to be in continual conversation with herself. At school she remained in her room, eating her lunch there, or sitting by the cabinet, reading, between clases. There were no more strolls into the village with Mr. Reed, no more meetings with him by the coastal bluff. And when the day was over, she would head back toward Black Pond, moving through the evening shade with the same thoughtful air with which she'd arrived at school that same morning.

Her classes took on a similar mood of withdrawal. She became more formal than she had before, her demeanor more controlled, as if she now felt it necessary to conceal every aspect of her life, both past and present, from the many prying eyes she'd sensed around her for so long.

During these final three weeks it was the column of faces that occupied most of her time. She covered a table with a dark green tarpaulin, and one by one the teachers and students of Chatham School came to her room and lay down upon it to have plaster masks made of their faces. Once I saw Mrs. Benton lying there, her eyes closed, her body tense and rigid,

Miss Channing poised above her, staring down, a single finger daubed with moist clay drawing a line across her throat.

My turn came during the middle of May.

'Hello, Miss Channing,' I said as I stepped into her classroom.

It was after six in the evening, the air outside growing dark, a soft breeze rustling gently through the late spring leaves of the old oak that stood in the courtyard.

She was wearing a long blue dress, but she'd thrown on one of the gray smocks she used to protect her clothing. Her hair was pulled back and tied with what appeared to be a piece of ordinary twine.

'Hello, Henry,' she said in that aloof and oddly brittle tone she'd fallen into by that time. 'What do you want?'

'I've come to get a cast made of my face,' I told her. 'For the column.'

She nodded toward the table. 'Lie down,' she said.

I walked to the table, pulled myself onto it, and lay on my back, my eyes turned toward the ceiling.

'I'm sorry I've come so late,' I said.

She stepped up to the table, dipped her fingers in the wet clay, then began to apply it smoothly, first across my forehead, then along the sides of my face. 'Close your eyes,' she said.

I did as she told me, breathing softly as she coated my eyelids, her touch very tender, almost airy.

'This is the way they make a death mask, isn't it?' I asked.

'Yes,' she said. 'It is.' She continued to work, covering my face with a cold, thin layer of clay.

Once she'd finished applying the clay, I lay on the table while it dried, listening as she moved about the room. I could hear the soft tread of her feet as she walked from the tables to the cabinet, putting things away, and I recalled how she'd drifted across the summer grass toward my father on that now-distant afternoon, the look in his eyes as he'd caught sight of her bare feet.

After a time she returned to me, removed the cast, then wiped away the residue from my face with a moist towel.

'It's done,' she said as she dropped the towel into a basket by the table. 'You can go.'

I pulled myself to a sitting position, then got to my feet. By then Miss Channing was several feet away, where many other masks lay faceup on a wide table, eyes closed, lips pressed tightly together, cadaverously gray.

'Well, good night, Miss Channing,' I said when I reached the door.

'Good night, Henry,' she answered, her eyes now fixed on the mask she'd just made of my face as she wrapped it in a length of white cloth.

I remained at the door, wanting to reach her somehow, remove her from the pall she seemed imprisoned in, tell her what she should do, how she must follow her father's lead, live the life he'd prepared her for. I could almost see her rushing through the dark marina, a red cape flowing behind her, Mr. Reed waiting in the boat, lifting her into it, the hunger of their embrace, that thirsty kiss.

'Is there something else, Henry?' she asked, now staring at me intently, her fingers still wet and glistening, bits of moist clay in her hair. She appeared strikingly similar to the way I'd later see her, rising from the water, her hair soaked and stringy, hung with debris from the depths of Black Pond, her question asked in the same bloodless tone, *Is she dead?* My answer delivered as passionlessly as my life would be lived from then on, *Yes*.

Miss Channing finished the column only a few days later, and it was erected on the eighteenth of May in a ceremony my father arranged for the occasion. The ceremony took place on the front lawn of the school, and in the photograph taken that morning, and later included in my father's archive of the Chatham School Affair, Miss Channing stands to the right of the sculpture, her arms clasped to her sides, my father to its left, one hand tucked beneath his coat, Napoleonic fashion. All the teachers and students of the Chatham School are gathered around them, along with Sarah, who stands just off to the side, dressed up for the occasion, smiling brightly, her long black hair tucked inside a straw hat with a wide ribbon trailing off the back.

Miss Channing didn't speak to the assembly that morning, but my father did. He thanked her for her work, not only on the sculpture, but as a teacher who, he said, had done a 'remarkable job all round'. At the end of the speech he announced that Miss Channing would not be returning to Chatham School the following year, and that she would be 'deeply, deeply missed'.

Mr. Reed was the only teacher who did not attend the ceremony that morning. Nor did I expect him to. For during the preceding two weeks he'd grown increasingly remote, arriving alone at school just before his first class and leaving alone directly after the last one. During the school day he no longer lingered in the hallway with students, nor took them into the courtyard for a recitation, despite the unseasonable warmth of those first days of summer. Instead, he conducted his classes in the usual manner, lecturing and reading, but with much of the spirit he'd once brought to it now drained away. From time to time, as he stood at the front of the room, he would let his gaze wander toward the window, where, across the courtyard, he could see Miss Channing with her own students before her. At those moments he appeared frozen in a grim and futile yearning, and seemed unable to draw his eyes away from her, until, at last, they would dart back to us, his head jerking slightly as they did so, like someone who'd been slapped.

Still, despite the furious melancholy that so clearly hovered around him, Mr. Reed continued to work on his boat. It was finished by the third week in May, and the following Saturday he asked me to join him for the maiden voyage.

The boat had already been taken from the boathouse when I arrived at the marina that morning, the wooden rack that had once held it now empty, the tools and supplies that had been used in its construction put away. The top of the desk had been cleared as well, the cardboard box in which Mrs. Reed had found such an assortment of disturbing things already taken to the house on Black Pond and placed in the attic where Captain Hamilton would later find it, the small brown bottle of arsenic still huddled in the corner, its cap tightly fitted, but the contents nearly gone.

Only my drawing of Miss Channing still remained in its former place, though it now hung slightly askew, its surface coated with a thin layer of dust. It would still be there two weeks later, when I showed it to Mr. Parsons, his comment destined to linger in my mind forever after that. *She's what did it to him, Henry, she's what drove him mad.*

But on that foggy Saturday morning, so strange an eventuality seemed inconceivable, and the boathouse appeared merely like a structure that had weathered a violent but departed storm rather than one about to be blown apart by an approaching one.

'All right, let's try her out,' Mr. Reed said as he led me out of the boathouse and down the wooden pier to where I could see the *Elizabeth* lolling softly in the undulating water, its tall mast weaving rhythmically left and right, a white baton in the surrounding fog.

Once we'd climbed into the boat, Mr. Reed untied the rope that held it to its mooring, adjusted the sail so that we briefly drifted backward, then took the rudder and guided it out of the marina.

We followed what appeared to be a predetermined course, exactly like the one I'd seen drawn on Mr. Reed's nautical map, along the western coast of Monomoy Island, past Hammond's Bend and Powder Hole, and finally around the tip of the island at Monomoy Point and into the open sea. Mr. Reed kept his eyes forward for the most part, but from time to time he would peer about, like someone scouting dangers all around, so that for a single, exhilarating instant I felt once again a party to some desperate and wildly romantic conspiracy, this early morning voyage, begun before the harbor master had arrived at work, with the marina deserted and the coastline shrouded in mist, serving as our practice run.

'A man could vanish into a fog like this,' he said at one point. 'Disappear. Disappear.'

It was nearly ten o'clock when we sailed back into Chatham harbor. The early morning fog had now burned off entirely; the air around us was crystal clear. Mr. Reed guided the boat into its place in the marina, then looped the rope to the wooden pylon, mooring it in the same dock where we'd found it earlier that same morning.

But rather than being uplifted by the maiden voyage of a boat he'd been working on for three years, Mr. Reed remained solemn and downcast. I moved along beside him, down the long wooden pier and into the boathouse, wondering what I might do to lift his spirits, draw him out of the dreadful despair that had fallen over him, renew the vitality and soaring discontent I'd so admired before, perhaps even point the way to some victory that might still be his.

Mr. Reed drew himself up on the desk in the corner of the boathouse, resting his cane against it, his hands folded one over the other. For a few minutes he talked about the Galápagos Islands, the ones off the coast of South America that Darwin had written of in *The Voyage of the Beagle*. 'Everything must have looked new to him,' he told me. 'Everything in life brand new.' He shook his head with a strange mirthlessness. 'Imagine that,' he said. 'A whole new world.'

Watching him from my place a few feet away, I felt coldly stricken, like a boy at a deathwatch, helplessly observing the slow disintegration of someone he'd admired.

As for Mr. Reed, he seemed hardly aware that I was in the room at all. At times his mind appeared to drift directionlessly from one subject to the next, his eyes sometimes fixed in a motionless frieze, sometimes roaming from place to place about the room, as if in flight from the one object he would not let them light upon, the portrait of Miss Channing that still hung on the far wall, her face forever captured in what must have come to strike him as a cruelly beckoning gaze.

During all that afternoon he spoke only once about the boat, the long labor of the last few years, his eyes locked on the empty rack that had once held its lofty frame. 'Well, she was seaworthy, at least,' he said. Then he grasped his cane, edged himself off the desk, and walked to one of the windows that looked out into the harbor. It was still covered with a strip of burlap, and for a moment Mr. Reed simply stared at the rough, impenetrable cloth. Then, with a sudden, violent jerk he yanked it down, a sheet of dust and a shaft of hard incandescent light pouring over him, and into which, for a single, surreal instant, he seemed to disappear.

# TWENTY-FOUR

I often felt as if I had disappeared as well, vanished into the same dusky light that had briefly engulfed Mr. Reed.

For with the boat now finished, I saw him only occasionally, either in his classroom or at a distance, a figure who seemed perpetually in flight, walking rapidly down a far corridor or turning the corner of Myrtle Street, silent, harried, like someone running beneath the lash of invisible whips.

As for Miss Channing, I rarely saw her anywhere but in her room, so I felt once again like one student among many, with nothing to distinguish me or set me apart from the rest, watching silently, just as they did, while she gave her final lessons with a formality that struck me as very nearly rigid, all the ease and spontaneity that had marked her former relationship with us completely cast aside, leaving her distant and preoccupied, her focus turned inward with a deadly gravity.

Left more or less to myself, I became increasingly agitated as the end of the school year approached. I fidgeted nervously through Miss Channing's classes, my attention drifting toward the window, not with the lack of interest that sometimes afflicted the other boys, but in an attitude of barely controlled hostility and contempt, as if she were a lover who had led me on and then betrayed me, and whom I now despised.

I felt bereft and abandoned, deserted by my closest allies. And so I poured all my energy into my drawing, watching helplessly as those darker elements that had earlier marked it now took on a demonic blackness, the village forever hung in gothic shadows, the sea disappearing into a grim invading horde of thunderclouds. The angles and perspectives changed as well, tilting Chatham on a cruel axis, its crooked streets plunging in jagged lines toward a central maelstrom, houses careening left or right, a world of colliding shapes. Stranger still, I drew my distortions as if they were not really distortions at all, but our village seen rightly, caught in the actual warp and wrench of the world, a grotesque deformity its true face.

During this time I had only Sarah to remind me of everything that had once seemed so exciting, the piercing intensity I'd felt the day we'd all stood on the snowy hilltop together and gazed down at Black Pond, how open life had seemed at that moment, how thrillingly romantic. All of that now appeared smothered and inert. So much so that I even began to avoid Sarah, closing my bedroom door at the sound of her approach, as if she were nothing more than a bitter reminder of some lost ideal, a charred locket that had once hung from a lover's neck.

Sarah no doubt sensed the way I felt, but she refused to withdraw from me despite it. Instead, she often came to where I lay in my room, knocked at the door, and demanded that I join her for a walk along the beach or accompany her on a shopping trip to the village.

On the final Thursday of that school year, she found me sitting at the edge of the playing field. It was late in the afternoon. The teachers had already gone home to prepare the final examinations of the coming week, and some of the boys had decided to play a game of touch football before going to their rooms for a night of study.

'What are you doing here, Henry?' she asked as she strode up and lowered herself onto the ground beside me.

I shrugged silently, pretending that my attention was on the boys as they continued at the game, their movements dictated by its unbending rules, no hitting, scratching, kicking, rules that must have, in the end, given them comfort, the limits laid out so clearly, but which I saw as yet another example of their strapped and adventureless lives.

'You hate it, don't you, Henry?' Sarah demanded. 'You hate Chatham School.'

The game dissolved. I looked at her evenly, the truth bursting from me. 'Yes, I do.'

Sarah nodded, and to my surprise read my thoughts with perfect accuracy. 'Don't run away, Henry. You'll be leaving for college soon. After that, you won't have to ...'

I turned away from her and nodded toward the boys. 'What if I end up like them?'

She settled her gaze on the playing field, watching and listening as the boys darted about and called to one another. From the look in her eyes I could tell that she did not think them so bad, the boys of Chatham School, nor even the lives they would later make. For she was already mature enough to sense that the wilder life I so yearned for might finally come to little, the road less traveled end in nothing more than the dull familiarity of having traveled it.

But I lacked that same maturity, and so Sarah's rebel spirit now seemed as dead as Mr. Reed's and Miss Channing's, the whole world mired in a vile dispiritedness and cowardice. 'When you get right down to it, you're just like them, Sarah,' I told her sneeringly, nodding toward the boys, my words meant to strike deep, leave her soul bleeding on the ground. 'You're a girl. That's the only difference.'

I might have said more, struck at her with an even greater arrogance and cruelty, but a loud crash suddenly stopped me. It was hard and metallic, and it had come from the lighthouse. Glancing toward it, I saw Miss Channing rush out its open door, a red scarf whipping behind her as she made her way across the lawn.

Sarah's eyes widened. 'Miss Channing,' she whispered.

Miss Channing reached the street, wheeled to the right, and headed down it, her stride long and rapid until she came to the coastal road. For a moment she stopped, briefly dropped her head into her hands, then lifted it again and whirled around, glaring toward the lighthouse for an instant before she turned away and rushed down the road toward town.

It was then that we looked back toward the lighthouse. Mr. Reed stood in its still-open door, his head drooping forward as he leaned, exhausted, upon his cane.

'Why don't they just run away together?' I blurted out with a vehemence so deep the words seemed directed less to them than to me. 'Why are people such cowards?'

Sarah watched me softly, gently, the harsh words I'd just said to her already put aside. 'They're not cowards, Henry,' she told me firmly.

'Then why don't they just go ahead and do what they want to do and forget everything else?'

She did not answer me. And when I recall that moment now, I realize that she could not possibly have answered. For we have never discovered why, given the brevity of life and the depth of our need and the force of our passions, we do not pursue our own individual happiness with an annihilating zeal, throwing all else to the wind. We know only that we don't, and that all our goodness, our only claim to glory, resides in this inexplicable devotion to things other than ourselves.

I turned back toward the lighthouse. Its open door was now empty, for Mr. Reed had mounted the stairs to its top by then. I could see him standing there, staring out over the village, his hands gripped to the iron rail, posed exactly as I would no doubt have painted him, a crippled silhouette against a bloodred sky.

'She's killing him,' I said, my mind now so fierce and darkly raging that I all but trembled as I said it. 'They're killing each other. Why don't they just get in his boat and sail away from all this?'

Sarah looked at me intently. I could tell that she hardly had the courage for her next question, but felt that she had to ask it anyway. 'Is that what you were doing, Henry?' she asked. 'Building a boat for them to run away in?'

I thought of all I'd seen and heard over the last few weeks, the hours of labor I'd devoted to helping Mr. Reed build his boat, the unspoken purpose I'd come to feel in the building of it. I looked at her boldly, proud of what I'd done, regretful only that so much work had come to nothing. 'Yes,' I told her. 'That's what I was building it for. So that they could run away.'

Sarah's eyes widened in dismay. 'But, Henry, what about—' She stopped, and for a moment we faced each other silently. Then, with no further word, she rose and walked away, taking her place, as it seemed to me, among that numb and passionless legion forever commanded by my father.

For the next few hours, lying sullenly in my bed upstairs, I felt nothing but my own inner seething. The most ordinary sounds came to me as an unbearable clamor, the heaviness of my mother's footsteps like the thud of horses' hooves, my father's voice a mindless croaking. The house itself seemed arrayed against me, my own room closing in upon me like a vise, the air inside it so thick and acrid that I felt myself locked in a furiously smoldering chamber.

It was nearly nine when I finally rushed down the stairs and out into the night. My mother had gone to a neighbor's house, so she didn't see me leave. As for my father, I could see the lights of his office at Chatham School as I slunk down Myrtle Street, and knew that he was at work there, curled like a huge black bear over the large desk beside the window, his quill pen jerking left and right as he signed 'important documents'.

I didn't know where I was going as I continued toward the bluff, only that it vaguely felt like I was running away, doing exactly what Sarah had warned me not to do, fleeing Chatham School on a wave of impulse, casting everything aside, throwing my future to the wind.

I knew that I was not really doing that, of course, but I kept moving anyway, down through the streets of the village I so despised, past its darkened shops, and further still, out along the road that ran between the marshes and the sea, to where Plymouth Road suddenly appeared, a powdery lane of oyster shells, eerily pale as a bank of clouds parted and a shaft of moonlight fell upon it, abruptly rendering it as gothic and over-wrought as I would no doubt have drawn it, its route stretching toward me like a ghostly hand.

In my mind I saw Miss Channing as she'd rushed from the lighthouse hours before, the red scarf trailing after her, Mr. Reed left behind, his head bowed, his hand clutching his cane. They had never appeared more tragically romantic to me than at that moment, more deserving to be together, to find the sort of happiness that only people like themselves, so fierce and passionately driven, can find, or even deserve to find.

I turned onto Plymouth Road with little specific intention in mind, recalling the many times I'd strolled down it with Sarah to find Miss Channing sitting on the steps of Milford Cottage or standing beside the pond. I remembered the snowy day in November when we'd all walked to the top of a nearby hill, how happy everyone had been that day, how open all our lives had briefly appeared, how utterly and permanently closed they now did.

I reached Milford Cottage with no prior determination to go there. Had I found the lights off, I would have turned away. Had a car been parked in the drive, I would have retreated back into the darkness and returned to Myrtle Street. But the lights were on, and no car blocked my path. Perhaps even more important, it began to rain. Not softly, but with a deafening burst of thunder, so that I knew it would be over quickly, that I would need the shelter of Milford Cottage only just long enough for the storm to pass, and then be on my way.

When she opened the door, I saw a face unlike any I had ever seen, her eyes so pale they seemed nearly colorless, two black dots on a field of white, dark crescents beneath them, her hair thrown back and tangled as if she had been shaken violently, then hurled against a wall. Never had anyone looked more cursed by love than Miss Channing did at that dreadful instant.

'Henry,' she said, squinting slightly, trying to bring me into focus, her voice a broken whisper. 'What are you doing here?'

'I was just out walking,' I explained, speaking rapidly, already stepping back into the night, aware that I had come upon her in a grave moment. 'Then it started to rain and so ...'

She drew back into the cottage, opening the door more widely as she did so. 'Come in,' she told me.

Candles were burning everywhere inside the cottage, but there was also a fire in the hearth, a stack of letters on the mantel, some of them, as I could see, already burning in the flames. The air inside was thick and overheated, a steam already gathering in the corners of the windows.

'I was just getting rid of a few things,' Miss Channing told me, her voice tense, almost breathless, beads of sweat gathered on her forehead and along the edge of her upper lip, her long fingers toying distractedly at the collar of her blouse. 'Before I leave,' she added. Her eyes shot toward the window, the rain that could be seen battering against it. 'Things I don't want,' she said as she glanced back to me.

I didn't know what to say, so I said only, 'What can I do to help?'

Her gaze was directed toward me with a terrible anguish, all her feeling spilling out. 'I can't go on,' she said, her eyes now glistening in the candlelight.

I stepped toward her. 'Anything, Miss Channing,' I said. 'I just want to help.'

She shook her head. 'There's nothing you can do, Henry,' she told me.

I looked at her imploringly. 'There must be something,' I insisted.

I saw a strange steeliness come into her face, a sense of flesh turning into stone, as if, in that single instant, she had determined that she would survive whatever it was that love had done to her. With a quick backward step she drew away from me and walked into the adjoining bedroom. For a moment she stood beside the bookshelf near her bed, staring down at it with a cold, inflexible glare. Then she plucked a necklace from its top shelf, her fingers clutching it like pale talons as she returned to me.

'Get rid of this,' she said.

'But, Miss Channing . . .'

She grabbed my hand, placed the necklace in its open palm, and closed my fingers around it. 'That's all I want you to do, Henry,' she said.

The rain had stopped when I left Milford Cottage a few minutes later, Miss Channing standing in the door, framed by the interior light. She was still there when I rounded the near bend and, with that turn, swept out of her view.

I walked on in darkness, moving slowly over the wet ground, thinking of what I'd glimpsed in Miss Channing's face, shaken by what I'd seen, the awful ruin of the passions she'd once shared with Mr. Reed, unable to imagine anything that might return her to its earlier joy save for the one that had always presented itself, the two of them in Mr. Reed's boat, a high wind sweeping through its white sails, propelling them around Monomoy Point and into the surging, boundless sea.

For a time I was locked in pure fantasy, as if I were with them, sweeping southward, a Caribbean wind whipping the tropical waters off the coast of Cuba, Miss Channing's face radiantly tanned, her black hair flying free in warm sea breezes, Mr. Reed at the helm, miraculously cured of his limp, the scar erased forever from his face, the winters of New England, with all their frozen vows, unable to reach them now or call them back to anything.

It was the headlights of an approaching car that brought my attention back to Plymouth Road. They came forward slowly, almost stalkingly, like two yellow eyes, covering me in so bright a shaft of blinding light that it was only after the car had come to a halt beside me that I saw Mr. Reed behind the wheel, his eyes hidden beneath the shadows of his hat.

'Get in,' he said.

I got in and he pulled away, continuing down Plymouth Road, but turning to the left at the fork, moving toward his house on the other side of the pond rather than Milford Cottage.

'What are you doing out here, Henry?'

'Just walking.'

He kept his eyes trained on the road, his fingers wrapped tightly around the wheel. 'Were you with Miss Channing?'

'Yes,' I told him.

'Why?'

'I was out walking and it started to rain. I went there to get out of the rain.'

The car continued forward, two shafts of yellow light dimly illuminating the glistening road ahead.

'What did she tell you?' Mr. Reed asked.

'Tell me?'

His eyes swept over to me. 'About this afternoon. At the lighthouse.'

I shook my head. 'Nothing,' I answered.

For a moment he seemed not to believe me. We sped on for a few seconds, his attention held on the road ahead. Then I saw his shoulders fall slightly, as if a great weight had suddenly been pressed down upon them. He lifted his foot from the accelerator and pressed down on the brake, bringing the car to a skidding halt. In the distance I could see the lights of his house glowing softly out of the darkness. 'Sometimes I wish that she were dead,' he whispered. Then he turned to me, his face nearly as gray and lifeless as the masks of Miss Channing's column. 'You'd better get home now, Henry' was all he said.

I did as he told me, then watched as he pulled away, the taillights of his car glaring back toward me like small mad eyes.

Mr. Reed did not come to school the next day, but Miss Channing did, her mood very somber, the agitation of the night before now held within the iron grip of her relentless self-control.

It was the Friday before final examinations, and we all knew that since she was leaving Chatham School, it would be the last class we would ever have with her. Other departing teachers, those who had retired or found better posts, even the few whose abilities my father had found unacceptable and sent packing, had always taken a moment to say good-bye to us, usually with a few casual words about how much they had enjoyed being with us and hoped we'd stay in touch. I suppose that as the class neared its final minutes that day, we expected Miss Channing to do something similar, perhaps give a vague indication of what she intended to do after leaving Chatham School.

But Miss Channing didn't do any of that. Instead, she raced through a review of the major things she'd taught us, her manner brittle, giving only the most clipped answers to our questions, ending it all with a single, lifeless comment. 'It's time to go,' she said only a few seconds before the final bell. Then she strode down the aisle and stationed herself at the entrance to her classroom.

The bell sounded, and as we all rose and filed out of the room, Miss Channing nodded to each of us as we went past, her final word only a quick, barely audible, 'Good-bye.'

'We don't have to say good-bye now,' I told her when I reached the door. 'I'll be coming over with Sarah on Sunday.'

She nodded briskly. 'All right,' she said, then swiftly turned her attention to the boy behind me. 'Good-bye, William,' she said as he stepped forward and took her hand.

For the rest of the day Miss Channing spent her time cleaning out the small converted shed that had served as her room and studio for the preceding nine months. She put away her materials, stacked the sculpting pedestals, folded up the dropcloth she'd placed over the tables on which she'd fashioned the masks for the column on the front lawn.

By four in the afternoon she'd nearly finished most of the work and was now concentrating upon the final details of the cleanup. Mrs. Benton saw her washing the windows with the frantic wiping motions she later described to Mr. Parsons and Captain Hamilton. Toward evening, the air in the courtyard now a pale blue, Mrs. Abercrombie saw the lights go out in her classroom, then Miss Channing step out of it, closing the door behind her. For a moment she peered back inside it, Mrs. Abercrombie said, then she turned and walked away. A few seconds later Mr. Taylor, a local banker who lived in the one great house on Myrtle Street, saw her standing beside the column on the front lawn of Chatham School, her fingers lightly touching one of its faces. And finally, just before nightfall, with a line of storm clouds advancing along the far horizon, my father came out of the front door of the school, glanced idly to the left, and saw her standing on the bluff, the tall white lighthouse to her back, her long black hair tossing wildly in the wind as she stared out over the darkening sea.

During the next day, Saturday, May 28, 1927, no one saw Miss Channing at all. The local postman said the cottage was deserted when he delivered her mail at eleven o'clock, and a hunter by the name of Marcus Lowe, caught in the same sort of sudden thunderstorm that had swept over the Cape two nights before, later said that he'd stood for nearly half an hour on the small porch of Milford Cottage and heard no stirring inside it. Nor had any of its lamps been lighted, he added, despite the gloom that had by then settled along the outer reaches of Black Pond.

# TWENTY-FIVE

It's quite possible that from the time Miss Channing left Chatham School on that last Friday before final exams, no one at all saw her until the following Sunday morning, when Sarah arrived for her final reading lesson.

The storm of the previous evening had passed, leaving the air glistening and almost sultry as we walked down Plymouth Road that morning. Sarah appeared hardly to have remembered the sharp words I'd said to her as we'd sat at the edge of the playing field two days before. Once she even took my arm, holding it lightly as we continued down the road, her whole manner cheerful and confident, the timid girl of a year before completely left behind.

'I'll miss Miss Channing,' she told me. 'But I'm not going to stop studying.'

She had mastered the basics of reading and writing by then, and from time to time during the past few weeks I'd seen her sitting in the kitchen, an open book in her lap, her beautiful eyes fiercely concentrated on the page, getting some of the words, clearly stumped by others, but in general making exactly the sort of progress I would have expected in one so dedicated and ambitious and eager to escape the life she might otherwise have been trapped in.

She released my arm and looked at me determinedly. 'I'm not going to ever give up, Henry,' she said.

She'd dressed herself quite formally that morning, no doubt in a gesture of respect toward Miss Channing. She wore a white blouse and a dark red skirt, and her hair fell loosely over her shoulders and down her back in a long, dark wave. She'd made something special as well, not merely cookies or a pie, but a shawl, dark blue with a gold fringe, the colors of Chatham School.

'Do you think Miss Channing will like it?' she asked eagerly as she drew it from the basket.

I shrugged. 'I don't know,' I answered, recalling how distant and unhappy Miss Channing had seemed in her final class on Friday, the way she'd only nodded to us as we'd left her room. But even that distance seemed better than the torment I'd seen two nights before, the look in her eyes as she'd placed the necklace in my hand, the cold finality of the words she'd said, *Get rid of this*.

But I hadn't gotten rid of it, so that by the time Sarah and I reached the fork in Plymouth Road, I could feel it like a small snake wriggling in my trouser pocket, demanding to be set free.

I stopped suddenly, knowing what I would do.

'What's the matter, Henry?' Sarah asked.

I felt my hand slide into my pocket, the glass necklace curl around my fingers. 'I have to go over to Mr. Reed's for a minute,' I told her.

'Mr. Reed's? Why?'

'I have to give him something. I'll come to Miss Channing's after that.'

Sarah nodded, then turned and headed on down the road, taking the fork that led to Milford Cottage while I took the one that led to Mr. Reed's.

I arrived at his house a few minutes later. His car was sitting in the driveway, but the yard was deserted, and I heard no sounds coming from the house.

Then I saw her, Mrs. Reed walking toward me from the old gray shed that stood in the distance, her body lumbering heavily across the weedy ground, so deep in thought she did not look up until she'd nearly reached the front steps of the house.

'Good morning, Mrs. Reed,' I said.

She stopped abruptly, startled, her hand rising to shield her eyes from the bright morning sun, gazing at me with a strange wariness, as if I were a shadow she'd suddenly glimpsed in the forest or something she'd caught lurking behind a door.

'I'm Henry Griswald,' I reminded her. 'The boy you—'

'I know who you are,' she said, her chin lifting with a sudden jerk, as if in anticipation of a blow. 'You helped him with the boat.'

I could hear the accusation in her voice, but decided to ignore it. 'Is Mr. Reed home?'

The question appeared to throw her into distress. 'No,' she answered in a voice now suddenly more agitated. 'He's out somewhere, walking.' Her eyes shot toward the pond, the little white cottage that rested on its far bank. 'I don't know where he is.'

'Do you know when he'll be back?'

'No, I don't,' she answered, her manner increasingly tense, brittle, a single reddish eyebrow arching abruptly, then lowering slowly, like a dying breath. 'Why are you here?' she asked, peering at me with a grave distress, as if I were diving toward her from a great height, a black bird in fatal descent. 'What did you come here for?'

'I just wanted to see Mr. Reed.'

Another thought appeared to strike her, her mind now twisting in a new direction.

'Is he running away?' she demanded, her eyes upon me with a savage spite, her voice very thin, a cutting wire drawn taut. 'Leaving me and Mary?' She tilted her head to the left, toward the pond. 'Running away with *her*?'

I shrugged. 'I ... don't ...'

Something seemed to ignite in her mind. 'He wouldn't be the first, you know. The first one to leave me.'

I said nothing.

She was watching me apprehensively, as if I were not a boy at all, but someone sent to do her harm, my fingers wrapped not around a frail glass necklace, but a length of gray rope, the steel grip of a knife.

'I just wanted to see Mr. Reed,' I told her. 'I'll come back some other time.'

She stared at me angrily. 'You tell him I'll not have it again,' she said loudly, distractedly, as if she were speaking to someone in the distance. 'He said he would be home.'

'I'm sure he'll be back in a few minutes,' I said.

She remained silent, locked in what now seemed an impenetrable distraction, her eyes drifting, unhinged, so that they seemed unable to focus on anything more definite than the old apron her fingers now began to squeeze and jerk.

Looking at her at that moment, I could not imagine that she would ever embrace Mr. Reed again, draw him into her bed, or even go walking with him through the woods on a snowy afternoon. How could he possibly live the rest of his life with her, eating a milky chowder while she stared at him from the other side of the table, babbling about the price of lard, but thinking only of betrayal?

Suddenly, the alternative to such a fate presented itself more forcefully than it ever had, and I saw Miss Channing rushing from the lighthouse, Mr. Reed at her side, the two of them making their way down the coastal road, through the village streets, until they reached the *Elizabeth*, its broad sails magnificently unfurled, the trade winds waiting like white stallions to carry them away.

It was then, in a moment of supreme revelation, that the answer came to me. Someone else had to do it. Someone else had to set them free. Miss Channing and Mr. Reed were helplessly imprisoned in the dungeon of Chatham School, my father its grim warden, Mrs. Reed the guardian of the gate. It was up to me to be the real hero of their romance, turn the iron key, pull back the heavy door.

And so I leveled my eyes upon Mrs. Reed and said, 'Let them go, Mrs. Reed. They want to be free.'

Her eyes froze, everything in her face tightening, her features now a twisted rope. 'What did you say?'

'They want to be free,' I repeated, now both astonished and emboldened by my own daring.

She stared at me stonily. 'Free?'

I glanced toward the pond. In the distance I could see the willow behind Milford Cottage, the pier that stretched out over the water. I thought of the moment when Miss Channing had pressed a trembling hand against Mr. Reed's cheek, the look in his eyes as he'd felt her touch.

It was a vision that urged me onward with a ruthless zeal. 'Yes,' I said coldly. 'To be free. That's what they want. Miss Channing and Mr. Reed.'

For a moment she stared at me silently, her eyes now strangely dull, her features flat and blunted, as if they'd been beaten down by a heavy rod. Then her body stiffened, like someone jerked up by a noose, and she whirled around and bolted away from me, calling out as she did so, *Mary, come inside*, her voice pealing through the surrounding woods as she swept up the stairs and disappeared into the house, a little girl darting around its far corner only seconds later, climbing up the wooden stairs, laughing brightly as she vanished into its unlighted depths.

Miss Channing and Sarah were inside Milford Cottage when I arrived there a few minutes later, standing very erectly in their midst, still in awe of the great thing I felt sure I had just accomplished.

Sarah had obviously waited for my arrival before giving Miss Channing her present. 'This is for you,' she said, smiling delightedly, as she brought the shawl from her basket.

'Thank you,' Miss Channing said, taking it from her gently, as if it were an infant. 'It's beautiful, Sarah.'

We were all standing in the front room of the cottage. Many of Miss Channing's belongings were now packed into the same leather traveling cases I'd brought there nearly a year before, along with a few boxes in which she'd placed a small number of things she'd acquired since then. In my mind I saw myself loading them onto Mr. Reed's boat, then standing at the edge of the pier, waving farewell as they drifted out of the moonlit marina, never to be seen again at Chatham School.

'I have something for you too,' Miss Channing said to Sarah. She walked into her bedroom, then came out with the African bracelet in her hand, its brightly colored beads glinting in the light. 'For all your work,' she said as she handed it to Sarah.

Sarah's eyes widened. 'Oh, thank you, Miss Channing,' she said as she put it on.

Miss Channing nodded crisply. 'Well, we should start our lesson now,' she said.

They took their seats at the table by the window, Sarah arranging her books while Miss Channing read over the writing she'd assigned the Sunday before.

I left them to their work, strolled to the edge of the pond. In the distance I could see Mr. Reed's house half concealed within a grove of trees, his car sitting motionless in the driveway.

I was still at the water's edge an hour later, when I saw Sarah and Miss Channing come walking toward me, Sarah chatting away, as she often did at the end of a lesson.

'Where is it you will be going now?' she asked Miss Channing as they strolled up to me.

Miss Channing's answer came more quickly than I'd expected, since I hadn't heard anyone in my household mention her intentions.

'Boston, perhaps,' she said. 'At least for a while.'

Sarah smiled excitedly. 'Now, that's a fine city,' she said. 'And what do you plan to be doing once you're settled in?'

Miss Channing shrugged. 'I don't know.' It was a subject that appeared to trouble her. To avoid it, she said to me, 'Henry, I have some books from the school library. Would you mind taking them back for me?'

'Of course, Miss Channing.'

She turned and headed toward the cottage, walking so briskly that I had to quicken my pace in order to keep up with her. Once inside, she retrieved a box of books from her bedroom. 'Henry, I'd like to apologize for the state I was in when you came to the cottage the other night,' she said as she handed it to me.

'There's nothing to apologize for, Miss Channing,' I told her, smiling inwardly at how much she might soon have to thank me for, the fact that I'd taken the fatal step, done what neither she nor Mr. Reed had been able to do, struck at the heavy chain that bound them to Chatham.

After that we walked out of the cottage to stand together near the willow. It was nearly noon by then, quiet, windless, the long tentacles of the tree falling motionlessly toward the moist ground. To the right I could see Sarah moving toward the old wooden pier. At the end of it she hesitated for a time, as if unsure of its stability, then strolled to its edge, a slender, erect figure in her finest dress.

'I hope you'll look after Sarah,' Miss Channing said, watching her from our place beside the willow. 'Encourage her to keep at her studies.'

'I don't think she'll need much encouragement,' I said, glancing out across the pond toward Mr. Reed's house, where I suddenly saw Mrs. Reed as she rushed down the front steps, dragging Mary roughly behind her. At the bottom of the stairs she paused a moment, her head rotating left and right, like someone looking for answers in the air. Then she wheeled to the left and headed toward the shed, moving swiftly now, Mary trotting along beside her.

For a time they disappeared behind a wall of foliage. Then Mrs. Reed emerged again, marching stiffly toward the car. She'd begun to pull away when I glanced at Miss Channing and saw that she was staring across the pond, observing the same scene.

'She's crazy,' I said. 'Mrs. Reed.'

Miss Channing's eyes shot over to me. She started to speak, then stopped herself. I could see something gathering in her mind. I suppose I expected her to add some comment about Mrs. Reed, but she said nothing of the kind. 'Be like your father, Henry,' she said. 'Be a good man, like your father.'

I stared at her, shocked by the high regard she'd just expressed for my father, and searching desperately for some way to lower her regard for him. But I found that I could discover nothing that, in saying it, would not lower Miss Channing's regard for me as well. Because of that, we were still standing silently at the water's edge when we suddenly heard a car approaching from Plymouth Road, its engine grinding fiercely, the sound rising steadily as it neared us, becoming at last a shuddering roar.

I turned to the right and saw it thunder past us in a thick cloud of white dust, a wall of black hurling down the weedy embankment, its ancient chassis slamming left and right as it plunged at what seemed inhuman speed toward the rickety wooden pier.

For a single, appalling instant, I felt utterly frozen in place, watching like a death mask fixed to a lifeless column until Miss Channing's scream set the world in motion again, and I saw Sarah wheel around, the car then jerk to the right, as if to avoid her, but too late, so that it struck her with full force, her body tumbling over the left side of the hood and into the water, the car plowing past her, then lifting off the end of the pier like a great black bird, heavy and wingless as it plummeted into the depths of Black Pond, then sank with a terrible swiftness, its rear tires still spinning madly, throwing silver arcs of water into the summer air.

We rushed forward at the same time, Miss Channing crashing into the water, where she sank down and gathered Sarah's broken body into her arms. I ran to the edge of the pier and dove into the still wildly surging water.

When I surfaced again only a minute or so later, drenched and shaken, my mind caught in a dreadful horror of what I had just seen, I found Miss Channing slumped at the edge of the pond, Sarah cradled in her arms.

'It's Mrs. Reed,' I told her as I trudged out of the water.

She looked at me in shock and grief. 'Is she dead?'

My answer came already frozen in that passionlessness that would mark me from then on. 'Yes.'

# TWENTY-SIX

I've never been able to remember exactly what happened after I came out of the water. I know that I ran over to where Miss Channing now sat, drenched and shivering, on the bank, with Sarah's head resting in her lap. I remember that Sarah's eyes were open as I approached her, blank and staring, but that I saw them close slowly, then open again, so that I felt a tremendous wave of hope that she might be all right.

At some point after that I took off down Plymouth Road, soaking wet, with my hair in my eyes, and flagged down the first passing car. There was an old man behind the wheel, a local cranberry farmer as I later found out, and he watched in disbelief as I sputtered about there having been an accident on Black Pond, that he had to get a doctor, the police, that he had to please, please hurry. I remember how he sprang into action suddenly, his movements quick and agile, as if made young by a desperate purpose. 'Be right back, son,' he promised as he sped away, the old gray car thundering toward Chatham.

After that I rushed back to Milford Cottage. Miss Channing was still where she'd been when I left her, Sarah cradled in her arms, alive, though unconscious, her eyes closed, her breath rattling softly, a single arrowhead of white bone protruding from the broken skin of her left elbow, but otherwise unmarked.

We sat in an almost unbroken silence with nothing but the lapping of the pond and an occasional rustle of wind through the trees to remind us that it was real, that it had actually happened, that Sarah had been struck down, and that beneath the surface of Black Pond, Mrs. Reed lay curled over the steering wheel of the car.

Dr. Craddock was the first to arrive. His sleek new sedan barreled down Plymouth Road, then noisily skidded to a halt in front of Milford Cottage. He leaped from the car, then bolted toward us, a black leather bag dangling from his hand.

'What happened?' he asked as he knelt down, grabbed Sarah's arm, and began to feel for her pulse.

'A car,' I blurted out. 'She was hit by a car.'

He released Sarah's arm, swiftly opened his bag, and pulled out a stethoscope. 'What car?' he asked.

I saw Miss Channing's eyes drift toward the pond as she waited for my answer.

'It's in the water,' I said. 'The car's in the water. It went off the pier.'

Dr. Craddock gave me a quick glance as he pressed the tympanum against Sarah's chest. 'And this young woman was driving it?'

'No,' I told him. 'There's someone in the car.'

I saw the first glimmer of that astonished horror that was soon to overtake our village settle like a gray mist upon his face.

'It's a woman,' I added, unable to say her name, already trying to erase her from my memory. 'She's dead.'

'Are you sure?'

'Yes.'

He returned the stethoscope to the bag, then brought out a hypodermic needle and a vial of clear liquid. 'How about you, are you all right?' he asked me.

'Yes.'

He looked at Miss Channing. 'And you?' he asked as he pierced the vial with the needle, then pressed its silver point into Sarah's arm.

'I'm all right,' Miss Channing said, her features now hung in that deep, strangely impenetrable grief that would forever rest upon her face.

'The woman in the car,' Dr. Craddock said. 'Who is she?'

'Abigail Reed,' Miss Channing answered. Then she looked down at Sarah and drew back a strand of glossy wet hair. 'And this is Sarah Doyle,' she said.

Sarah had already been taken away when Captain Lawrence P. Hamilton of the Massachusetts State Police arrived at Milford Cottage. He was a tall man, with gray hair and a lean figure, his physical manner curiously graceful, but with an obvious severity clinging to him, born, perhaps, of the dark things he had seen.

Miss Channing and I were standing beside the cottage when he arrived, the once-deserted lawn now dotted with other people, the village constable, the coroner, two of Chatham's four selectmen, the tiny engine of local officialdom already beginning to crank up.

Captain Hamilton was not a part of that local establishment, as every aspect of his bearing demonstrated. There was something about him that suggested a breadth both of authority and of experience that lay well beyond the confines of Chatham village, or even of Cape Cod. It was in the assuredness of his stride as he walked toward us, the command within his voice when he spoke, the way he seemed to know the answers even before he posed the questions.

'You're Henry Griswald?' he asked me.

'Yes.'

He looked at Miss Channing. 'You live here at the cottage, Miss Channing?'

She nodded mutely and gathered her arms around herself as if against a sudden chill.

'I have most of the details,' Captain Hamilton said. 'About the accident, I mean.' His eyes shifted toward the pond. A tractor had been backed to its edge, and I could see a man walking out into the water, dressed in a bathing suit, a heavy chain in his right hand.

'We're going to pull the car out now,' Captain Hamilton told us.

The man in the water curled over and disappeared beneath the surface of the pond, his feet throwing up small explosions of white foam.

'There's a husband, I understand,' Captain Hamilton said. 'Leland Reed?'

Odd though it seems to me now, I had not thought of Mr. Reed at all before that moment, nor of the other person Captain Hamilton mentioned almost in the same breath.

'And there's a little girl, I'm told. A daughter. Have you seen her?'

'No.'

'Could she have been in the car?'

I shook my head. 'No.'

'Well, nobody seems to be at home over there,' Captain Hamilton said, nodding out across the pond. 'Do you have any idea where Mr. Reed and the little girl might be?'

I remembered the last thing I'd seen at Mr. Reed's house, Mrs. Reed bolting across the lawn, Mary trotting at her side, both of them headed for the old gray shed.

'I think I know where she is,' I said.

Captain Hamilton appeared surprised to hear it. 'You do?'

'In the shed,' I answered.

'What shed?'

'There's a shed about a hundred and fifty yards or so from the house.'

Captain Hamilton watched me closely. 'Would you mind showing it to me, Henry?'

I nodded. 'All right,' I said, though the very thought of returning to Mr. Reed's house sent a dreadful chill through me.

Captain Hamilton glanced at Miss Channing, then touched the brim of his hat. 'We'll be talking again,' he said as he took my arm and led me away.

Moments later, as he would testify the following August, Captain Hamilton and I made our way along the edges of Black Pond. The old shed stood in a grove of trees, its door tightly closed, locked from the outside with a large, rusty eyebolt.

Only a few feet away we heard a sound coming from inside. It was low and indistinct, a soft whimper, like a kitten or a puppy.

'Step back, son,' Captain Hamilton said when we reached the door.

I did as he told me, waiting a short distance away from the shed as he opened the door and peered in. 'Don't be afraid,' I heard him say as he disappeared inside it. Seconds later he stepped back out into the light, now with Mary in his arms, her clothes drenched with her own sweat, her long blond hair hanging in a tangle over her shoulders, her blue eyes staring fearfully at Captain Hamilton, asking her single question in a soft, uncomprehending voice – *Where's my mama gone?* – and which she would hear answered forever after in a cruel school-yard song:

Into Black Pond
Is where she's gone
Drowned by a demon lover

Mr. Reed's car had already been dragged from the pond when Captain Hamilton and I got back to Milford Cottage. Mrs. Reed's body had been taken from it by then, transported to Henson's Funeral Parlor, as I later learned, where it was placed on a metal table and covered with a single sheet.

Miss Channing and I were standing near the cottage when my father arrived. He looked very nearly dazed as he moved toward us.

'Dear God, is it true, Henry?' he asked, staring at me.

I nodded.

He looked at Miss Channing, and in that instant I saw a terrible dread sweep into his face, a sense that there were yet darker things to be learned from Black Pond. Without a word he stepped forward, took her arm, and escorted her inside the cottage, where they remained for some minutes, talking privately, my father standing by the fireplace, Miss Channing in a chair, looking up at him.

They had come back outside again by the time Captain Hamilton strode up to the cottage. He nodded to my father in a way that made it obvious that they already knew each other.

'Your son's a brave boy, Mr. Griswald,' Captain Hamilton said. 'He tried his best to save her.'

I felt my eyes close slowly, saw Mrs. Reed staring at me through a film of green water.

577

'The car looks fine,' Captain Hamilton added, now talking to all of us. 'No problem with the brakes or the steering column. No reason for an ... accident. Henry, when the car went by, could you see Mrs. Reed behind the wheel?'

I shook my head. 'I didn't notice anything but the car.'

Captain Hamilton started to ask another question, but my father intervened.

'Why would that matter, Captain?' he asked. 'Whether Henry saw Mrs. Reed or not?'

'Because if there was nothing wrong with the car, then we begin to wonder if there was something wrong with the person driving it.' He shrugged. 'I mean something like a seizure or a heart attack, some reason for Mrs. Reed to lose control the way she did.'

For a moment, no one spoke. Then Captain Hamilton turned his attention to Miss Channing. 'This young woman, Sarah Doyle. Did Mrs. Reed know her?'

Miss Channing shook her head. 'I don't think so.'

Captain Hamilton appeared to turn this over in his mind, come to some conclusion about it before going on to his next thought. 'And what about you, Miss Channing? Did Mrs. Reed know you?'

'Only slightly.'

'Had she ever visited you here at the cottage?'

'No.'

The captain's eyes drifted toward the road, remained there briefly, then returned to Miss Channing. 'Well, if Mrs. Reed didn't know you, why would she have been coming this way?' he asked her. 'It's a dead end, you see. So if she didn't have any business with you, Miss Channing, then why would she have been headed this way at all?'

Miss Channing replied with the only answer available to her. 'I don't know, Captain Hamilton,' she said.

With that, my father suddenly stepped away, tugging me along with him. 'I have to get my son home now,' he explained. 'He needs a change of clothes.'

Captain Hamilton made no attempt to stop us, and within a few seconds we were in my father's car. It was the middle of the afternoon by then, the air impossibly bright and clear. As we backed away, I saw Captain Hamilton tip his hat to Miss Channing, then step away from her and head out toward the pier, where, at the very end of it, I could see Mr. Parsons facing out over the water, clothed in his dark suit, his homburg set firmly on his head.

# TWENTY-SEVEN

Once we got back home, my father told me to change quickly and come downstairs. Sarah had been taken to Dr. Craddock's clinic, he said, and all of us were to come to her bedside as soon as possible. I did as I was told, pulling off clothes that had once been soaked through but were now only damp, then rushed back downstairs to find my father waiting edgily on the front porch, my mother already in the car.

'I knew something bad was coming,' she said as I climbed into the backseat of the car. 'A woman knows.'

Dr. Craddock's clinic was situated in a large house on the eastern end of Chatham. It had once been the home of a prosperous sea captain, but now functioned as what amounted to a small hospital, complete with private rooms on the second floor.

He met us at the door, dressed in a long white coat, a stethoscope dangling from his neck.

'How is she?' my father asked immediately.

'She's still unconscious,' Dr. Craddock replied. 'I think you should prepare for the worst.'

'Do you mean she may die?'

Dr. Craddock nodded. 'She's in shock. That's always very dangerous.' He motioned us into the building, then up the stairs to where we found Sarah in her bed, her eyes still closed, but now motionless behind the lids, her breathing short and erratic.

'Oh, Lord,' my mother whispered as she stepped over to the bed. 'Poor Sarah.'

Looking at her, it was hard to imagine that she was in such peril. Her face was unmarked and lovely, like a sleeping beauty, her long black hair neatly combed, as I found out later, by Dr. Craddock himself. A gesture that has always struck me as infinitely kind.

My father moved to touch her cheek, then drew back his hand and turned toward Dr. Craddock. 'When will you know if she's ... if she's going to be all right?'

'I don't know,' Craddock answered. 'If there's no brain injury, then it's possible she could—' He stopped, clearly unwilling to offer unfounded hope. 'I'll know more in the next few hours.'

'Please let me know if there are any changes, or if there's anything I can do,' my father said.

Dr. Craddock nodded. 'How long has she been with you?'

'Nearly two years,' my father answered. He looked down at her tenderly. 'Such a lovely child. Bright. Ambitious. She was learning to read.'

Watching her from where I stood directly beside the bed, it was hard to imagine that only a few hours before she'd been so fully alive, so proud of the progress she'd made in her lessons with Miss Channing, drawing the African bracelet onto her wrist as if it were an emblem of her newfound mastery. Nothing had ever made life I seem so tentative to me, so purely physical, and therefore utterly powerless to secure itself against the terrible assaults of accident or illness or even the invisible deadliness of time. It was just a little point of light, this life we harbored, just a tiny beam of consciousness, frail beyond measure, brief and unsustainable, the greatest lives like the smallest ones, delicately held together by the merest thread of breath.

We returned home that afternoon in an icy silence, my mother in the front seat of the car, fuming darkly, my father with his eyes leveled on the road, no doubt trying to fix this latest catastrophe within his scheme of things, give it the meaning it deserved, perhaps even some imagined grace.

As for me, I found that I could not bear to think of what had happened on Black Pond, either to Sarah or to Mrs. Reed, could not bear to hold such devastation in my mind, envision Sarah's shattered bones or the last hellish gasps of Mrs. Reed.

And so I concentrated only on Miss Channing, imagining her alone in her cottage or out wandering in the nearby woods. It seemed entirely unfitting that she should be left to herself under such circumstances. And so, as we neared Myrtle Street, I said, 'What about Miss Channing? Do you think we should ...'

'Miss Channing?' my mother blurted out, twisting around to face me. 'Yes.'

'What about her?'

'Well, she may be all alone. I was thinking that we might bring her ...'

'Here?' my mother demanded sharply. 'Bring her here? To our home?'

I glanced at my father, clearly hoping for some assistance, but he continued to keep his eyes on the road, his mouth closed, unwilling to confront the roaring flame of my mother's rage.

'That woman will never set foot in our house again,' my mother declared. 'Is that clear, Henry?'

I nodded weakly and said nothing else.

The atmosphere in the house on Myrtle Street had grown so sullen by nightfall that I was happy to leave it. My father dropped me off in front of Dr. Craddock's clinic, saying only that someone would relieve me at midnight.

The doctor met me at the door. He said that Sarah's condition hadn't changed, that she appeared reasonably comfortable. 'There's a nurse at the end of the corridor,' he added. 'Call her if you notice Sarah experiencing any distress.'

'I will,' I told him, then watched as he moved down the stairs, got into his car and drove away.

Sarah lay in the same position as before, on her back, a sheet drawn up to her waist, her shattered arm in a plaster cast. In the light from the lamp beside her bed, her face took on a bloodless sheen, all its ruby glow now drained into a ghostly pallor.

I watched her a moment longer, touched her temple with my fingertips, then settled into the chair beside the window to wait with her through the night. I'd brought a book with me, some thick seafaring tale culled from the limited collection available from the school library. I would concentrate on it exclusively, I'd told myself as I'd quickly pulled it from the shelf, let it fill my mind to the brim, allow no other thoughts inside it.

But I'd gotten through only twenty pages or so when I saw someone emerge out of the dimly lighted hallway, tall and slender, her dark hair hung like a wreath around her face.

'Hello, Henry,' Miss Channing said.

I got to my feet, unable to speak, her presence like a splash of icy water thrown into my face, waking me up to what I'd done.

'How is she?'

I let the book drop onto my chair. 'She hasn't changed much since the ... since ...'

She came forward slowly and stood by the bed, peering down. She was wearing a plain white dress, the shawl Sarah had knitted for her draped over her shoulders. She watched Sarah silently for a time, then let her eyes drift over to where I continued to stand beside my empty chair. 'Tell your father that I'd like to sit with Sarah tomorrow,' she said.

'Yes, Miss Channing.'

'For as long as she needs me.'

'I'll tell him.'

She pressed her hand against the side of Sarah's face, then turned and walked past me, disappearing from the room as quickly as she'd entered it.

I know that for the rest of that long night she remained alone in her cottage, no doubt staring at the old wooden pier as she sat in her chair by the window, the unlighted hearth only a few feet away, the ashes of Mr. Reed's letters still resting in a gray heap where, three days later, Mr. Parsons would find them when he came to question her about what he called 'certain things' he'd heard at Chatham School.

As for me, I remained at Sarah's bedside, trying to lose myself in the book, but unable to shut out the sound of her breathing, the fact that as the hours passed, it grew steadily more faint. From time to time a soft murmur came from her, but I never saw any sign of the 'distress' Dr. Craddock had warned me about. If anything, she appeared utterly at peace, so that I often found myself looking up from my book, imagining her unconsciousness, wondering if, locked so deeply within the chamber of herself, she could feel things unfelt by the rest of us, the slosh of her blood through the valves of her heart, the infinitesimal firings of her brain, perhaps even the movement of those tiny muscles Miss Channing had once spoken of, and which any true artist must come to understand.

And so I didn't know until nearly midnight when Dr. Craddock came into the room, walked over to her bed, took hold of her wrist, held it briefly, then released it, shaking his head as he did so, that whatever small sensations Sarah might have felt from the depths of that final privacy, she now could feel no more.

My father had already been told that Sarah had died when he came for me. As he trudged toward me from down the hallway he looked as if he were slogging through a thick, nearly impenetrable air. He drew in a long breath as he gathered me into his arms. 'So sad, Henry,' he whispered, 'so sad.'

We went directly home, drifting slowly through the center of the village, its shops closed, the streets deserted, no one stirring at all save for the few fishermen I saw as we swept past the marina. Glancing out over its dark waters, I could see Mr. Reed's boat lolling peacefully. The *Elizabeth's* high white mast weaved left and right, and for a moment, I remembered it all again, he and Miss Channing sitting together on the steps of Chatham School or on the bench beside the bluff, the cane like a line drawn between them. By spring, as I recalled, they'd begun to stroll through the village together, companionably, shoulder to shoulder, their love growing steadily by then. No, not growing, as I thought suddenly, but tightening around them like a noose, around Mrs. Reed and Sarah, too, and even little Mary, so that love no longer seemed a high, romantic thing to me at all, no longer a fit subject for our poems and for songs, nor even to be something we should seek.

And so I never sought it after that.

'We'll have to make an announcement in school tomorrow morning,' my father told my mother as he came into the parlor. 'The boys have to be told. And Captain Hamilton wants to question a few people tomorrow afternoon.'

My mother, working fiercely at her knitting, so much death burning in her mind, did not seem in the least surprised by such a development. 'No doubt there'll be plenty of questions,' she said without looking up.

'Who do they want to question?' I asked my father.

'Me, of course,' he answered, now trying to pretend that it was merely some kind of police routine, a formality. 'Some of the teachers.'

'They'll want to talk to me as well,' my mother said, her eyes glowing hotly, clearly looking forward to the prospect.

'Why would they want to talk to you, Mildred?' my father asked.

'Because of what Mrs. Reed told me,' she answered, her eyes fixed on her knitting. 'About that woman and Mr. Reed.'

For the first time, I saw my father bristle. 'You're not to be spreading tales, Mildred,' he told her.

My mother's head shot up, her eyes narrowing fiercely. 'Tales?' she said. 'I'm not talking about tales, Arthur. I'm talking about what Mrs. Reed told me right here in this room, things she asked me to keep quiet about, and so I did ... until now.'

'And what are these "things", may I ask?'

'She thought that there were bad things afoot,' my mother replied. 'In the boathouse. Down at the marina. She thought there was a plot against her.'

Aghast, my father looked at her. 'You can't be serious.'

My mother stood her ground. 'She thought he might murder her. Mr. Reed, I mean. She was terrified of that.'

'But Mrs. Reed wasn't murdered, Mildred,' my father replied. 'It was an accident.'

The needles stopped. My mother leaned forward, glaring at him. 'She saw a knife, Arthur. A rope too. And they'd already mapped out where they were running to.' Her eyes narrowed menacingly. 'And poison too.'

I felt my breath abruptly stop. 'Poison?'

My mother nodded. 'A bottle of arsenic. That's what she saw. Right there with the knife and the rope.'

I could hardly believe my ears. 'That was for the rats,' I told her. 'In the boathouse. I helped Mr. Reed spread it myself.'

She appeared not to have heard me, or to have ignored what she heard. She eased herself back, the needles whipping frantically again. 'Oh, there're going to be questions all right,' she said. 'Lots of questions, that's for sure.'

I suppose it was at that moment that the further consequences of what had happened on Black Pond that afternoon first occurred to me. It would not end with Mrs. Reed dead behind the wheel or Sarah dead in her bed at Dr. Craddock's clinic. Their deaths were but the beginning of more destruction still.

# TWENTY-EIGHT

Throughout that long night I floated in green water, saw Mrs. Reed's head plunge toward me from out of the murky depths, her features pressed frantically against the glass, eyes wide and staring.

By morning I was exhausted, and I felt as if I could barely stand with the other boys when they assembled on the front lawn of Chatham School and listened as my father told them all he thought they needed to know about the previous day's events, the fact that 'a tragic accident' had occurred on Black Pond, that Mrs. Reed's car had 'gone out of control', and that both she and Sarah Doyle were now dead.

As to the state of Mr. Reed and Miss Channing, my father told them nothing whatsoever, save that they remained in their respective homes, Mr. Reed tending to his daughter, Miss Channing continuing to prepare for her departure from Chatham. He did not know if either of them would return to Chatham School before it closed for the summer, and asked the boys to 'keep them in their thoughts'.

For most of the rest of that long day I stayed in my room, almost in an attitude of concealment, not wanting to meet my mother's gaze as she stormed about the house, nor talk to any of the boys of Chatham School, since it was only natural that they'd ply me with questions about what had happened on Black Pond. Most of all, however, I wanted to avoid any chance meeting with Captain Hamilton, the way I felt when he looked at me, as if I were a small animal scurrying across a strip of desert waste, he the great bird diving toward me at tremendous speed and from an impossible height, looking only for the truth.

And so I was in my room when I heard a knock at the front door, cautiously peered downstairs and saw Mr. Parsons, his hat in his hand, facing my mother in the foyer. 'Is Mr. Griswald here?' he asked.

'No. He's at the funeral parlor,' my mother told him. 'Making arrangements for Sarah.'

Mr. Parsons nodded. 'Well, would you tell him to call me when he returns?'

My mother said she would, but added nothing else.

Mr. Parsons smiled politely and turned to leave. I thought my mother was going to let him go, that she had decided to hold her tongue. But abruptly, the door still open, Mr. Parsons halfway through it, she said, 'Such a terrible thing, what happened to Sarah ... and, of course ... Mrs. Reed.'

Mr. Parsons nodded. 'Yes, terrible,' he said, though with little emphasis, heading out the door, other matters clearly on his mind.

'She came to see me, you know,' my mother added. 'Mrs. Reed did.'

Mr. Parsons stopped and turned to face her. 'When was that, Mrs. Griswald?' he asked.

'Only a short time ago,' my mother answered. She paused a moment, then added with a grim significance, 'She seemed quite troubled.'

'About what?'

'Family matters. Troubles in the family.'

Mr. Parsons eased himself back into the foyer. 'Would you be willing to talk about that conversation, Mrs. Griswald?' he asked.

I saw my mother nod, then lead him into the parlor and close the door.

My father returned home an hour or so later. Mr. Parsons had left by then, but my mother made no attempt to conceal his visit, nor what she had told him during it. From the top of the stairs, crouched there like a court spy, I listened to her tell my father exactly what had transpired.

'I wasn't making accusations,' my mother said. 'Just speaking the plain truth, that's all.'

'What truth is that, Mildred?'

'Just what Mrs. Reed said.'

'About Mr. Reed?'

'Him and that woman.'

'You mentioned Miss Channing? You mentioned her to Mr. Parsons?'

'Yes.'

'Why?'

'Because Mrs. Reed said she saw her picture in the boathouse. She knew it was her that Mr. Reed was involved with.'

'What did you tell him?'

'That she suspected something. Between the two of them. That it frightened her.'

'Frightened her?'

'That she was afraid of them, the two of them. What they might do. Run off together. Or worse.'

'Or worse?'

'What she found in the boathouse. The knife she saw, and the ...'

'You told Mr. Parsons that?'

'I told him what Mrs. Reed said. That's all.'

I waited for something more, but there was only silence. From my place at the top of the stairs I saw my father walk out the door, my mother behind him, then both of them in the car, pulling out of the driveway, no doubt headed for the funeral parlor where Sarah now lay in a room decked with flowers sent by the teachers of Chatham School.

When they returned home sometime later, the air grown dark by then, the same silence enveloped them. They sat silently in the parlor, and silently through dinner. Nor did they ever speak to each other with any real tenderness again.

I spent the rest of the next day in my room, lying on my bed. Downstairs, I could hear my mother doing the chores that had once been Sarah's. I suppose from time to time I drifted into sleep, but if so, I don't remember it.

By noon the summer heat had begun to make the room unbearable, and so I walked out onto the porch and sat down in the swing, drifting slowly back and forth, recalling Sarah in random pieces of memory, words and glances flying through my mind like bits of torn paper in a whirling wind. At some point my mother brought me a sandwich and a glass of water, but the sandwich was never eaten, nor the water drunk.

Later I decided to take a short walk, perhaps to the beach, where I hoped to get some relief from the terrible scenes playing in my mind. I made my way down Myrtle Street, the bluff widening before me. To my left I could see the now-deserted grounds of Chatham School, Miss Channing's column of faces still standing in the bright summer light, and to my right, the lighthouse, a dazzling white tower, motionless and eternal, as if in mute contradiction to the human chaos sprawled around it.

I made it to the bluff but did not go down. So a few minutes later I was still sitting on the same bench that had once accommodated Miss Channing and Mr. Reed, when I saw Mr. Parsons' car mount the hill, then glide to the left and come to a stop directly before me.

'Hello, Henry,' Mr. Parsons said as he got out.

I nodded.

He walked to the bench and sat down beside me. 'I wonder if we might have a talk,' he said.

I said nothing, but rather than press the issue, Mr. Parsons sat quietly for a moment, then said, 'Let's go for a little walk, Henry.'

We both rose and headed down Myrtle Street, past Chatham School, and, still strolling at a leisurely pace, made our way out toward the playing field and then around it.

'I've talked to quite a few people at Chatham School,' Mr. Parsons said.

I stared straight ahead, gave him no response.

'Your name has been mentioned quite a few times, Henry. Everybody seems to think that you were pretty close to both of them. Miss Channing and Mr. Reed, I mean.'

I nodded, but offered nothing more.

'They say that you spent a lot of time with Mr. Reed. In a boathouse he's got down at the harbor. That you helped him build a boat, that's what they say.' He stopped and turned toward me. 'The thing is, Henry, we've begun to wonder how all this happened. I mean, we've begun to wonder what Mrs. Reed was intending when she drove over to Milford Cottage last Sunday.'

I said nothing.

Mr. Parsons began to walk again, gently tugging me along with him. 'Now, you're a brave young man,' he said. 'Nobody can question that. You did your best to save Mrs. Reed. But now you've got another duty. We know that Mrs. Reed was pretty sure that her husband was involved with another woman. And we know that that other woman was Elizabeth Channing.'

I felt my eyes close slowly as we walked along, as if by such a motion I could erase everything that had happened on Black Pond.

'We think she was after Miss Channing that day,' Mr. Parsons said. 'That it wasn't an accident, what happened on Black Pond.'

I kept silent.

'We think Mrs. Reed mistook Sarah Doyle for Elizabeth Channing, and so killed her instead.'

We walked a few seconds more, then Mr. Parsons once again stopped, his eyes bearing into me. 'So it was murder, wasn't it, Henry? It was murder Mrs. Reed intended when she aimed that car at Sarah Doyle.'

He saw the answer in my eyes.

'How long have you known?'

I shrugged.

'Look, Henry, everybody's proud of you, of how you went into the water and all. But like I said before, you have another duty now. To tell the truth, the whole truth ... I'll bet you know the rest of it.'

'And nothing but the truth,' I said, my voice barely above a whisper.

'That's right,' Mr. Parsons said. He placed his hand on my shoulder. 'Let's go down to the boathouse, son, and talk a little more.'

I gave him a private tour of the boathouse, watching as his eyes continually returned to my drawing of Miss Channing. 'She's what did it to him,' he said with a certainty that astonished me. 'She's what drove him mad.' Then he walked to the back window. In the distance we could see the *Elizabeth* bobbing gently in the quiet water. 'Somebody has to pay for all this, Henry,' he said without looking back toward me. 'There're just too many deaths to let it go.'

We left the boathouse together shortly after that, walked to his car, and drove back up the coastal road to the house on Myrtle Street. Before pulling away, he made a final remark. 'What we can't figure out is what finally set her off,' he said almost absently, a mere point of curiosity. 'Mrs. Reed, that is. I mean, she'd known about her husband and Miss Channing for quite some time. We just wonder what happened on that particular day that sent her over the edge like that, made her go after Miss Channing the way she did, kill that poor girl instead.'

He never posed it as a question, and so I never answered him, but only stepped away from the car and watched as it pulled away, my silence drawing around me like a cloak of stone.

# TWENTY-NINE

It was not until many years later that I learned exactly what had happened the next day. I knew only that Mr. Parsons and Captain Hamilton arrived at our house early that morning, that my father ushered them quickly into the parlor, then departed with them a few minutes later, sitting grimly in the backseat of Captain Hamilton's patrol car as it backed out of our driveway. He returned in the same car a few minutes later, this time with a little girl in a light blue dress in his arms, her long blond hair tumbled about her face, and whom I immediately recognized as Mary Reed.

'They want us to keep Mary for a while,' he explained to me. Then he sent me off on a picnic with her, my mother having packed a basket for the occasion, the same one Sarah had used to bring cakes and cookies to Miss Channing. 'Take her to the beach and try to keep her mind off things, Henry,' he told me. 'She's going to be pretty scared for a while.'

And so, before leaving that morning, I ran up to my room and got an old kite I hadn't flown in years. At the beach I taught Mary Reed how to string it, then to run against the wind so that it would be taken up. For a long time we watched it soar beneath the blue, and I will always remember the small, thin smiles that sometimes rose precariously to her lips, then vanished without a trace, her face darkening suddenly, so that I knew the darkness came from deep within.

'It was because they suspected that Mr. Reed might have been plotting to kill his wife, that's why they took Mary,' my father told me many years later when I was a grown man, and he an old one, the two of us sitting in the tiny, cluttered room he used as his private chamber. 'To make sure she was safe, that's what Mr. Parsons told me when he drove me over to Mr. Reed's house that morning.'

What my father witnessed on Black Pond a few minutes later stayed with him forever, the anguish in Mr. Reed's face so pure, so unalloyed by any other feeling, that it seemed, he told me, 'like something elemental'.

At first Mr. Reed had appeared puzzled to find so many men at his door, my father told me. Not only himself, Mr. Parsons, and Captain Hamilton, but two uniformed officers of the Massachusetts State Police as well.

It was Mr. Parsons who spoke first. 'We'd like to talk to you for a moment, Mr. Reed.'

Mr. Reed nodded, then walked outside, closing the door behind him.

'We've been looking into a few things,' Mr. Parsons said. He glanced inside the house and saw Mary's face pressed against the screen of an otherwise open window. 'Let's go into the yard,' he said, taking Mr. Reed by the elbow and guiding him down the stairs and out into the yard, where he stood by the pond, encircled by the other men.

'Mr. Reed,' Mr. Parsons began. 'We've become concerned about the welfare of your daughter.'

It was then, my father said, that Mr. Reed appeared to understand that something serious was upon him, though he may well not have grasped exactly what it was. 'Concerned about Mary?' he asked. 'Why are you concerned about Mary?'

'We've heard some suggestions,' Mr. Parsons told him. 'Having to do with your relationship with Mrs. Reed.'

'What suggestions?'

'There's no need to go into them at this time,' Mr. Parsons said. 'But they have caused the commonwealth to feel some concern about your daughter.'

'What kind of concern?'

'For her safety.'

'She's perfectly safe,' Mr. Reed said firmly.

Mr. Parsons shook his head, then drew a piece of paper from his jacket pocket and handed it to Mr. Reed. 'There's been enough death. We can't take the chance on there being any more.'

Mr. Reed stared at Mr. Parsons, still vaguely puzzled. 'What are you talking about?' he asked. He glanced at the paper. 'What is this?'

'We're going to take custody of your daughter,' Mr. Parsons told him. 'Mr. Griswald has agreed to look after her until certain things can be cleared up.'

Mr. Reed thrust the paper toward Mr. Parsons. 'You're not going to take Mary,' he said. 'You're not going to do that.'

Mr. Parsons' voice hardened. 'I'm afraid we are, Mr. Reed.'

Mr. Reed began to back away, the men gathering around him as he did so. 'No,' he said, 'you can't do that.'

Captain Hamilton stepped forward. 'Mr. Reed, your daughter doesn't need to see us use force, does she?'

Mr. Reed glanced toward the porch, where Mary now stood, a little girl in a pale blue dress, staring down at him. 'Please, don't do this,' he said in a desperate whisper, his attention now riveted on Mr. Parsons. 'Not now. Not with her mother just—' He gazed imploringly at my father. 'Please, Mr. Griswald, can't you—'

'It's only until we can clear things up,' Mr. Parsons said, interrupting him. 'But for now we have to be sure that your daughter is safe.'

Suddenly, Mr. Reed shook his head and began to push his way out of the circle. The men closed in upon him, and as he thrashed about, he lost his grip on his cane, crumpled to the ground and lay sprawled before them, laboring to get up, but unable to do so. It was then, my father said, that a cry broke from him, one that seemed to offer up the last frail measure of his will.

'He looked like a different man when he got to his feet,' my father told me. 'Like everything had been drained out of him. He didn't say anything. He just looked over to the porch, where Mary was, and waved for her to come to him. At first she wouldn't. She was so scared, of course. All those men she didn't know. The way they'd surrounded her father.' He shook his head. 'You can imagine how she felt, Henry.'

But at last the child came. Mr. Reed met her, lifted her into his arms, kissed her softly, then handed her to my father, his words oddly final as he did so: *She'll be better off this way.* He reached out and touched her hair; he never said good-bye.

Only an hour or so after those harrowing events, Mary walked to the beach with me, the two of us flying my old red striped kite until the first line of thunderclouds appeared on the horizon, its jagged bolts of lightning still far away, so that we'd gotten home well in advance of the rain.

By nightfall the rain had subsided, but a few hours later it began again. It was still falling when Dr. Craddock's car came to a halt in front of our house. The doctor was wearing a long raincoat and a gray hat which he drew from his head as he mounted the stairs to where my father sat in a wicker chair a few feet away, I in the swing nearby.

'I've come about the little girl,' he said. 'Mary Reed.'

My father got to his feet, puzzled. 'Mary Reed? What about her?'

Dr. Craddock hesitated a moment, and I could tell that something of vast importance lay in the balance for him. 'I'm sure you know that my wife and I ... that we've ... that we have no children.'

My father nodded.

'Well, I wanted to let you know that we would be very interested in taking Mary in,' Dr. Craddock said. 'My wife would be a good mother for her, I'm sure. And I believe that I would be a good father.'

'Mary has a father,' my father answered with an unexpected sternness, as if he were talking to one who wished to steal a child.

Dr. Craddock stared at him, surprised. 'You've not heard?' he asked.

'Heard what?'

I remember rising slowly and drifting across the porch toward my father as Dr. Craddock told him that Mr. Reed's boat had been found adrift in the bay, with nothing but his old wooden cane inside it, save for a note written on a piece of sail and tacked to the mast. *Please see to it that Mary is treated well, and tell her that I do this out of love.*

I think that over the years Mary Reed was well-treated, that, overall, despite the many problems that later arose, the howling phantoms that consumed her, the bleak silences into which she sometimes fell, that despite all that, Dr. Craddock and his wife continued to love her and strive to help her. At first it looked as though they had succeeded, that Mary had come to think of them as her parents, put her own dreadful legacy behind her. By the time she entered the local school, she'd come to be called by her middle name, which was Alice, as well as that of her adoptive parents, which was Craddock.

It was a deliverance my father had hoped for, and perhaps even believed to be possible. 'In time, she'll heal,' I heard him say as Dr. Craddock took her small white hand and led her down the stairs and out into the rain.

But she never did.

Mr. Reed's death left only Miss Channing upon whom the law could now seek retribution, and so, after a few more days of investigation, and at Mr. Parsons' direction, the grand jury charged her in a two-count indictment, the first count being the most serious, conspiracy to murder Abigail Reed, but the second also quite grave at that time, adultery.

It was my father who delivered the news of the indictment to Miss Channing, allowed to do so by Captain Hamilton, whose duty it otherwise would have been.

'Get in the car, Henry,' my father said the morning we made our final drive to Milford Cottage. 'If she becomes ... well ... difficult ... I might need your help.'

But Miss Channing did not become difficult that morning. Instead, she stood quite still, listening as my father told her that the two indictments had been handed down, that she would have to stand trial, then went on to recommend a local attorney who was willing to defend her.

'I don't want a lawyer, Mr. Griswald,' Miss Channing said.

'But these are serious charges, Miss Channing,' my father said somberly. 'There are witnesses against you. People who should be questioned as to whatever it is they're claiming to have seen or heard.' I could feel the pain his next words caused him. 'My wife will be one of those witnesses,' he told her. 'Henry too.'

I'd expected her eyes to shoot toward me at that moment, freeze me in a hideous glare, but she did not shift her attention from my father's face. 'Even so' was all she said.

We left a few minutes later, and I didn't say a single word to Miss Channing that morning, but only gazed at her stonily, my demeanor already forming into the hard shell it would assume on the day I testified against her, answering every question with the truth, the whole truth, and nothing but the truth, knowing all the while that there was one question Mr. Parsons would never ask me, nor even remotely suspect that I had the answer to: *What really happened on Black Pond that day?*

# THIRTY

Miss Channing came to trial that August. During that interval I never saw her, nor knew of anyone who did. My father was now more or less banned from any further contact with her by my mother's abject fury.

As to the charges against her, the evidence was never very great. But bit by bit it was presented to the jury, tales of odd sightings and snatches of conversation, a portrait hung in a boathouse, an old primer curiously inscribed, a nautical map with what Mr. Parsons called an 'escape route' already drawn, a boat named *Elizabeth*, a pile of letters hastily burned in an otherwise empty hearth, a knife, a piece of rope, a bottle of arsenic.

Against all that, as well as Chatham's ferocious need to 'make someone pay', Miss Channing stood alone. She listened as the witnesses were called, people who had seen and heard things distantly, as well as the more compelling testimony that I gave, shortly followed by my mother.

Through it all she sat at the defense table in so deep a stillness, I half expected her not to rise when the time finally came and the bailiff called her to the stand.

But she did rise, resolutely, her gaze trained on the witness box until she reached it and sat, waiting as Mr. Parsons approached her from across the room, the eyes of the jurors drifting from her face to her white, unmoving fingers, peering at them intently, as if looking for bloodstains on her hands.

I will always remember that my father watched Miss Channing's testimony with a tenderness so genuine that I later came to believe that understanding and forgiveness were the deepest passions that he knew.

My mother's expression was more severe, of course, less merciful thoughts no doubt playing in her mind – memories of people she had known, a husband's career now in the balance, a school teetering on the brink of ruin. Her eyes were leveled with an unmistakable contempt upon the woman she held responsible for all that.

As for me, I found that I glanced away from Miss Channing as she rose

595

and walked toward the witness box, unable to bear the way she looked, so set upon and isolated that she resembled a figure out of ancient drama, Antigone or Medea, a woman headed for a sacrificial doom, and in relation to whom I felt like a shadow crouched behind a tapestry, the secret agent of her fall.

She wore a long black dress that day, ruffled at the throat and at the ends of the sleeves. But more than her dress, more than the way she'd pulled back her hair and bound it tightly with a slender black ribbon, I noticed how little she resembled the young woman I'd seen get off a Boston bus nearly a year before, how darkly seasoned, as if she'd spent the last few weeks reviewing the very events about which she'd now, at her own insistence, been called to speak.

I know now that even at that moment, and in the wake of such awesome devastation, some part of me still lingered in the throes of the high romantic purpose that had seized me on Black Pond, driven me to the reckless and destructive act I was still laboring to conceal. And yet, despite all the pain and death that had ensued, I still wanted Miss Channing to speak boldly of love and the right to love, use the same brave and uncompromising words her father had used in his book. I wanted her to rise and take the people of Chatham on like Hypatia had taken on the mobs of Alexandria, standing in her chariot, lashing at them with a long black whip. I wanted her to be as ruthless and determined with Mr. Parsons and all he represented as I had been toward Mrs. Reed, to justify, at least for a brief but towering moment, the dreadful thing that I'd done to her, and through her, to Sarah Doyle. For it seemed the only thing that might yet be salvaged from the wreckage of Black Pond, a fierce, shimmering moment when a woman stood her ground, defied the crowd, sounded the truth with a blazing trumpet. All else, it seemed to me, was death and ruin.

But Miss Channing did not do what I wanted her to do on the stand that day. Instead, she meekly followed along as Mr. Parsons began to question her about the early stages of her 'relationship' with Mr. Reed, convinced, as he was, that everything that had later transpired on Black Pond had begun in the quiet drives she and Mr. Reed had taken back and forth from Milford Cottage to their classes at Chatham School, their leisurely strolls into the village, the idle hours they'd spent together, seated on a bench on the coastal bluff, all of which had flowed like an evil stream toward what he insisted on calling the 'murders' on Black Pond.

Through it all, Miss Channing sat rigidly in place, her hands in her lap, as prim and proper as any maiden, her voice clear and steady, while she did the opposite of what I'd hoped, lied and lied and lied, shocking me with the depths of her lies, claiming that her relationship with Mr. Reed had never gone beyond 'the limits of acceptable contact'.

At those words, I saw myself again at Milford Cottage on a cold January day, her fingers trembling as she pressed them against Mr. Reed's cheek, then, weeks later, in the cottage, the rain battering against the window, the anguish in her face when she'd said, 'I can't go on.' That she could now deny the depths of her own passion appalled me and filled me with a cold contempt, made everything I'd done, the unspeakably cruel step I'd taken on her behalf, seem like little more than a foolish adolescent act that had gone fatally awry.

Watching her as she sat like a schoolmarm, politely responding to Mr. Parsons' increasingly heated questions, I felt the full force of her betrayal. For I knew now how Mrs. Reed must have felt, that I had given love and devotion, and in return received nothing but lies and deception.

And so I felt a kind of hatred rise in me, a sense that I'd been left to swing from the gallows of my own conscience, while Miss Channing now attempted to dismiss as mere fantasy that wild romantic love I'd so clearly seen and which it seemed her duty to defend, if not for me, then for Mr. Reed, perhaps even her own father.

In such a mood, I began to root for Mr. Parsons as he worked to expose Miss Channing, ripping at her story even as she labored to tell it, continually interrupting her with harsh, accusatory questions. *When you went driving with Mr. Reed, you knew he was married, didn't you, Miss Channing? You knew he had a child?*

As she'd gone on to give her answers, I recalled the many times I'd seen her in Mr. Reed's car, growing more animated as the days passed, happy when he dropped by her cottage on that snowy November day when we'd all eaten Sarah's fruitcake together, happy to sit with him on the bluff, stroll with him along the village streets, chat with him in her classroom at the end of day. If, during all that, the 'limits of acceptable contact' had never been breached, then I'd played my fatal card for nothing, worshipped at the altar of a love that had never truly existed, save in my own perfervid imagination.

And yet, as Miss Channing continued, so self-contained and oddly persuasive, I began to wonder if indeed I *had* made it all up, seen things that weren't there, eyes full of yearning, trembling fingers, a romantic agony that was only in my head.

Because of that, I felt an immense relief sweep over me when Mr. Parsons suddenly asked, 'Are you saying, Miss Channing, that you were *never* in love with Leland Reed?'

Her answer came without the slightest hesitation:

*Witness: No. I am not saying that. I would never say that. I loved Leland Reed. I have never loved anyone else as I loved him.*

In a voice that seemed to have been hurled from Sinai, Mr. Parsons asked, 'But you knew that he was married, didn't you, Miss Channing? You knew he had a child?'

*Witness: Yes, of course I knew he was married and had a child.*
*Mr. Parsons: And each time Mr. Reed left you – whether it was at your cottage or in some grove in the middle of a cemetery, or after you'd strolled along some secluded beach – he returned to the home across the pond that he shared with his wife and daughter, did he not?*
*Witness: Yes, he did.*
*Mr. Parsons: And what did the existence of a wife and child mean to you, Miss Channing?*

Her answer lifted me like a wild wind.

*Witness: It didn't mean anything to me, Mr. Parsons. When you love someone the way I loved Leland Reed, nothing matters but that love.*

Heroic as her statement seemed to me, it was the opening Mr. Parsons had no doubt dreamed of, and he seized it.

*Mr. Parsons: But they did exist, didn't they? Mrs. Reed and little Mary?*
*Witness: Yes, they did.*
*Mr. Parsons: And had Mr. Reed told you that he and Mrs. Reed had had terrible arguments during the past two weeks, and that his daughter had witnessed these arguments?*
*Witness: No, he had not.*
*Mr. Parsons: Had he told you that Mrs. Reed had become suspicious of his relationship with you?*
*Witness: No.*
*Mr. Parsons: That she had even come to suspect that he was plotting her murder?*
*Witness: No, he didn't.*
*Mr. Parsons: Well, isn't it true that Mr. Reed wanted to be rid of his wife?*

Sitting in the courtroom at that moment, I recalled the last time I'd heard Mr. Reed speak of Mrs. Reed, the two of us in his car together, a yellow shaft of light disappearing down the road ahead, his own house in the distance, his eyes upon its small square windows, the coldness of his words: *Sometimes I wish that she were dead.*

Because of that, Miss Channing's answer, coming on the heels of the proud figure she'd only recently begun to assume, utterly astonished me.

*Witness: No, he did not want to be rid of his wife, Mr. Parsons.*
*Mr. Parsons: He never spoke ill of Mrs. Reed?*
*Witness: No, he never did.*
*Mr. Parsons: Nor conspired to murder her?*
*Witness: Of course not.*
*Mr. Parsons: Well, many people have testified that Mr. Reed was very upset during the last days of the school year. Do you deny that?*
*Witness: No, I don't.*
*Mr. Parsons: And in that state he did peculiar things. He named his boat after you, Miss Channing, rather than his wife or daughter.*
*Witness: Yes.*
*Mr. Parsons: He made some rather ominous purchases as well. He bought a rope and a knife. He bought poison. It would seem that at least during his last few weeks at Chatham School, Mr. Reed surely wanted to rid himself of somebody, don't you think, Miss Channing?*

It was a question Mr. Parsons had asked rhetorically, for its effect upon the jury, knowing that he had no evidence whatever that any of these things had been purchased for the purpose of murdering Abigail Reed. Because of that, I'd expected Miss Channing to give him no more than a quick, dismissive denial. But that was not what she did.

*Witness: Yes, he wanted to be rid of someone, Mr. Parsons. But it was not Mrs. Reed.*
*Mr. Parsons: Well, if it wasn't Mrs. Reed, then who did he want to be rid of, Miss Channing?*
*Witness: He wanted to be rid of me.*
*Mr. Parsons: You? You're saying he wanted to be rid of you?*
*Witness: Yes, he did. He wanted me to leave him alone. To go away. He told me that in the strongest possible terms.*
*Mr. Parsons: When did he tell you these things?*
*Witness: The last time I saw him. When we met in the lighthouse. That's when he told me he wanted to be rid of me. He said that he wished that I were dead.*

When I left the courthouse that afternoon, the final seconds of Miss Channing's testimony were still playing in my mind:

*Mr. Parsons: Leland Reed said that to you, Miss Channing? He said that he wished that you were dead?*

*Witness: Yes.*

*Mr. Parsons: And is it also your testimony, Miss Channing, that Mr. Reed never actually loved you?*

*Witness: He may have loved me, Mr. Parsons, but not enough.*

*Mr. Parsons: Enough for what?*

*Witness: Enough to abandon other loves. The love he had for his wife and his daughter.*

*Mr. Parsons: You are saying that Mr. Reed had already rejected you and wished to be rid of you and return to his wife and daughter, that he had already come to that decision when Mrs. Reed died?*

*Witness: He never really left them. There was never any decision to be made. They were the ones he truly cared about and wished to be with, Mr. Parsons. It was never me.*

In my mind I saw Mrs. Reed rushing up the stairs as she had on that final day, calling to Mary, then back down them again sometime later, dragging her roughly toward the shed. After that it was a swirl of death, a car's thunderous assault, Sarah's body twisting in the air, Mrs. Reed staring at me from infinite green depths, Mr. Reed lowering his cane to the bottom of the boat, slipping silently into the engulfing waves. Had all of that come about over a single misunderstood remark? *Sometimes I wish that she were dead.* Had it really been Miss Channing whom Mr. Reed, rocked by such vastly conflicting loves, had sometimes wanted dead? Had I gotten it all wrong, and in doing that, recklessly done an even greater wrong? I thought of the line I'd so admired in Mr. Channing's book – *Life is best lived at the edge of folly* – and suddenly it seemed to me that of all the reckless, ill-considered lies I'd ever heard, this was the deepest, the gravest, the most designed to lead us to destruction.

# THIRTY-ONE

At the end of Miss Channing's testimony, the prosecution rested its case. The jury began its deliberations. During the next two days, a hush fell over Chatham. The crowds no longer gathered on the front steps of the courthouse. Nor huddled in groups on street corners or on the lawn of the town hall.

In the house on Myrtle Street we waited in our own glum silence, my mother puttering absently in her garden, my father working unnecessarily extended hours at the school, I reading in my room, or going for long walks along the beach.

On the following Monday morning, at nine A.M., the jury returned to its place in the courtroom. The foreman handed the verdict to the bailiff, who in turn gave it to Judge Crenshaw. In a voice that was resolutely measured, he delivered the news that Elizabeth Rockbridge Channing had been found not guilty on the first count of the indictment, conspiracy to murder. I remember glancing at my father to see a look of profound relief sweep into his face, then a stillness gather on it as the verdict on the second count was read.

*Court: On the charge of adultery, how do you find the defendant, Elizabeth Rockbridge Channing?*

A smile of grim satisfaction fluttered onto my mother's lips as the foreman gave his answer: *Guilty.*

I glanced at the defense table where Miss Channing stood, facing the judge, her face emotionless, save that her eyes closed briefly and she released a soft, weary breath. Minutes later, as she was led down the stairs to the waiting car, the crowd pressing in around her, I saw her glance toward my father, nod silently. In return, he took off his hat with a kind of reverence, which, given the nature of her testimony, the portrait of herself as little more than a wanton temptress, struck me as the oddest thing he had ever done.

I don't think Miss Channing saw me at all, since I'd stationed myself farther from her, the crowd wrapped around me like a thick wool cloak. But I could see her plainly nonetheless, her face once again held in that profound sense of self-containment I'd first glimpsed months before, her eyes staring straight ahead, lips tightly closed, as if determined – perhaps like proud Hypatia – to hold back her cry.

She was sentenced to three years' imprisonment, the maximum allowed by Massachusetts law, and I remember that my father greeted the severity of her punishment with absolute amazement, my mother as if it had been handed down from heaven. 'It's finally over,' she said with obvious relief. She didn't mention the trial again during the rest of that week, but she did insist upon visiting Sarah's grave, as well as Mrs. Reed's, carrying vases of fresh flowers for each of them. Mr. Reed had been buried only a short distance from them, but I never saw my mother give his grave so much as a sideward glance.

It was not over, of course, despite my mother's declaration. At least not for my father. For there was still the matter of Chatham School to deal with.

During the next few weeks its fate hung in the balance. My father labored to restore its reputation, along with that part of his own good name that had been tarnished by the tragedy on Black Pond. A governing board was established to look into the school's affairs and consider its future prospects. One by one, over the few weeks that remained of that summer, benefactors dropped away and letters came from distant fathers to say that their sons would not be returning to Chatham School next fall.

At last, all hope for the school's survival was abandoned, and on a meeting in late September, it was officially closed, my father given two weeks' severance pay and left to find his way.

He found it in a teaching job at a public school in neighboring Harwichport, and during that long, rain-swept autumn, he rose early, pulled on his old gray duster, and trudged to the car from our new, much smaller house to the east of Chatham.

Others at Chatham School made similar accommodations to their abrupt unemployment. Mrs. Benton took a job as a clerk at Warren's Sundries, Mrs. Abercrombie as a secretary for Mr. Lloyd, a prominent local banker. Other teachers did other things, of course, although most of them, in the end, drifted away from Chatham to take jobs in Boston or Fall River or other towns along the Cape.

The first snows did not arrive until the last of the village Christmas decorations had been pulled down and returned to their boxes in the basement of the town hall. By February, when the snows were deepest and the sky hung in a perpetual gloom of low-slung clouds, the building that had once housed Chatham School had been converted into a small dressmaking factory, its second floor stacked with bolts of cloth and boxes of thread and buttons, the sound of sewing machines humming continually from its lower rooms.

But in other ways, things went back to normal, and there seemed to be little thought of Miss Channing, with only quick glimpses of Mary Reed sitting between Dr. and Mrs. Craddock at Quilty's or building a snowman on her front lawn to remind me of her fate.

And so the years passed as they always do, faster than we can grasp where we have been or may be going to. New buildings replaced older ones. Streets were paved, new lights hung. And high above the sea, the great bluff crumbled in that slow, nearly undetectable way that our bodies crumble before time, and our dreams before reality, and the life we sought before the one we found.

Then, in December of the final year of Miss Channing's imprisonment, when I was home for the Christmas break of my freshman year in Princeton, a letter came, addressed to my father, in an envelope sent from Hardwick Women's Prison, and which he later slipped into the little brown folder that became his archive of the Chatham School Affair.

The letter read:

Dear Mr. Griswald:

I write concerning one of my prisoners, Elizabeth Rockbridge Channing, and in order to inform you that she has fallen ill. Her file lists neither relatives nor friends who, under such circumstances, should be contacted. However, in conversations with Miss Channing, I have often heard mention of your name, of her time in, I take it, your employ, and I wonder if you could provide me with the names and addresses of any relatives or other close associates who should be informed of her condition.

Best regards,
Mortimer Bly
Warden, Hardwick Women's Prison

My father replied immediately, sending the name and address of Miss Channing's uncle in British East Africa. But he did more than that as well, did it with an open heart and against the firmly stated wishes of my mother, who seemed both shocked and appalled by the words he said to her that same night over dinner: *I've decided to look in on Miss Channing, and take Henry with me.*

Four days later, on a cold, rainy Saturday, my father and I arrived at the prison in which Miss Channing had been kept for the last three years. We were greeted by Warden Bly, a small, owlish man, but whose courtly manner seemed almost aristocratic. He assured us that Miss Channing was slated to be taken to the prison hospital as soon as a bed was available, and thanked us for coming. 'I'm sure it will brighten her spirits,' he said.

After that, my father and I were directed into the heart of the prison, walking down a long corridor, the bars rising on either side, our ears attuned to the low murmur of the women who lived behind them, dressed in gray frocks, smelly and unkempt, their bare feet padding softly across the concrete floor as they shuffled forward to stare at us, their faces pressed against the bars, their eyes following us with what seemed an absolute and irreparable brokenness.

'She's at the back, all by herself,' the guard said, the keys on the metal ring jangling as he pulled it from his belt. 'She ain't one for mixing.'

We continued to walk alongside him, our senses helplessly drawn toward the cells that flowed past us on either side, the dank odor that emanated from them, the faces that peered at us from behind the steel bars, women in their wreckage.

Finally, we reached the end of the corridor. There the guard turned to the left and stopped, his body briefly blocking our view into the cell. While we waited, he inserted the key, gave it a quick turn, and swung open the door. 'In here, gentlemen,' he said, waving broadly. 'Step lively.'

With that, he drew away, and my father and I saw her for the first time since the trial, so much smaller than I remembered her, a figure sitting on the narrow mattress of an iron bed, her long hair now cut short, but still blacker than the shadows that surrounded her, her pale eyes staring out from those same shadows like two small blue lights.

'Miss Channing,' I heard my father murmur.

Standing together, silent and aghast, we saw her rise and come toward us, her body shifting beneath the gray prison dress, her hand reaching out first to my father, then to me, cold when he took it, no warmer when I let it go.

'How good of you to come, Mr. Griswald,' she said, her voice low and unexpectedly tender, her eyes still piercingly direct, yet oddly sunken now, as if pressed inward by the dungeon's leaden air. 'And you, Henry,' she said as she settled them upon me.

'I'm so sorry I never came before,' my father told her, expressing what I recognized as a true regret.

For an instant she glanced away, a gray light sweeping over her face, revealing the purple swell of her lips, the weedy lines that had begun to gather at her eyes. 'I had no wish to trouble you,' she said as she turned back to us.

My father smiled delicately. 'You were never a trouble to me, Miss Channing,' he said.

She nodded softly, then said, 'And how are things at Chatham School?'

My father shot me a pointed look. 'Just fine,' he said quickly. 'Quite back to normal, as you can imagine. We think we may beat New Bedford come next spring. Several of the new boys are very good at the game.'

I watched her silently as my father went on, noting the ragged cut of her hair, oily and unwashed, a nest of damp black straw, remembering how she'd looked at Chatham School and laboring to make myself believe that there was some part of her fate that she deserved.

For the next few minutes they continued to talk together, and at no time did my father let slip the true state of our affairs, or of what had happened to Chatham School. Instead, he spoke of things that had long passed, a school that had once existed, a marriage for a time not frozen in a block of ice, villagers who never whispered of his poor judgment from places safe behind his back.

Finally, we heard a watchman call out to us, and rose to leave her.

'It was good seeing you, Miss Channing,' I said as lightly as I could.

'You too, Henry,' she replied.

My father draped his arm over my shoulder. 'Henry won a scholarship to Princeton, you know. All he does is study now.'

She looked at me as if nothing had changed since our first meeting. 'Be a good man, Henry,' she told me.

'I will try, Miss Channing,' I said. Though I knew that it was already too late for so high a word as goodness ever to distinguish me.

She nodded, then turned to my father. 'I so regret, Mr. Griswald, that you and the school were ever brought into my—'

My father lifted his hand to silence her. 'You did nothing wrong, Miss Channing. I have never doubted that.'

'Still, I regret that—'

In an act whose unexpected courage has never left my mind, my father suddenly stepped forward and gathered her gently into his arms. 'My dear, dear child,' he said.

Standing beside them, I saw Miss Channing draw him closer and closer, holding him very tightly, and for what seemed a long time, until, at last, she let him go.

'Thank you, Mr. Griswald,' she said as she released him and stepped away.

'We will come again,' my father told her. 'I promise you that.'

'Thank you,' Miss Channing said.

We stepped out of her cell, my father quickly moving away from it and back down the corridor, while I remained, my eyes fixed upon her as she retreated to the rear of her cell, to the place where we had found her. For a time she stared at her hands, then her eyes lifted and she saw me lingering in the corridor. 'Go, Henry,' she said. 'Please.'

I wanted to do exactly that, even felt the impulse to rush down the corridor as my father had, unable to bear a moment longer the tragedy before me. But I found that for the briefest instant I couldn't draw my eyes away from her, and as she turned away, I saw her once again as she'd first appeared, so beautiful as she'd stared out at the landscape of Cape Cod, pronounced it a world of stricken martyrs. It was then I felt something break in me, a little wall that had held through all my nightmarish dreams of Sarah and Mrs. Reed, of women floating in dark water. I thought of the rash and terrible thing I'd done and knew that I would never be able to trust myself again. And so the only answer seemed never to get close to anyone, to hold books as my sole companions, accept a bloodless, unimpassioned life, revere the law's steadfast clarity against the lethal chaos of the heart.

I was silent for a long time after that, silent as I turned from her cell, silent as I walked down the corridor to where my father waited, hollow-eyed, before the iron door, silent as we drove back to Chatham, a clear night sky above us.

'What is it, Henry?' my father asked finally as we crossed the bridge from the mainland, the old car rumbling over the wooden trellis.

I shook my head. 'You can never take anything back,' I said, feeling for the first time the full call of confession, wanting to let it go, to tell him what had really happened on Black Pond.

He looked at me worriedly, his eyes filled with a father's care. 'What do you mean, Henry?'

I shrugged, closing myself off again, retreating, as Miss Channing had, into the shadowy darkness of my own cell.

'Nothing,' I told him.

And I never told him more.

I'm sure that my father fully intended to visit Miss Channing again, despite the objections my mother had already voiced. But he still had the remainder of the school year to contend with, and so it was not until summer that he began to mention making such a visit.

I had returned home from college by then, taken a summer job as a clerk in a law office in Chatham, its cordial atmosphere a pleasant respite from the mood at home, the way my mother and father forever bickered over small matters, while leaving the great one that had long ago divided them buried deep inside.

And so I was once again in Chatham when another letter arrived suddenly from Hardwick Prison, addressed to my father, just as the first one had been, but this time bearing graver news.

My father read it in the small room he'd turned into a cluttered study, sitting in one of the great chairs that had once been in the parlor of our house on Myrtle Street and which seemed to fill up the entire room.

'Here, Henry,' he said, lifting it toward me after he'd read it.

I took the letter from him and read it while standing beside his chair. It had been written by Warden Bly, and it informed us in language that was decidedly matter-of-fact that following a short recovery, Miss Channing had fallen ill again, that she had finally been transferred to the prison clinic, then to a local hospital, where, two days after her admittance, she had died. Her body was currently being housed in the local morgue, Warden Bly said, and he wished instructions as to what should be done with it.

I will always remember how curiously exhausted my father looked after reading this letter, how his hands sank down into his lap, his shoulders slumped. 'Poor child,' he murmured, then rose and went to his room, where he remained alone throughout that long afternoon.

The next day he telegraphed Miss Channing's uncle, informing him of his niece's death and requesting instructions as to the disposition of her body. Two days later, Edward Channing replied with a telegram requesting my father to make whatever arrangements he deemed necessary, and to forward him 'a bill for all expenses incurred in the burial of my unfortunate niece'.

Miss Channing was buried in the little cemetery on Brewster Road four days later. Her plain wooden coffin was drawn by four uniformed guards from a prison hearse and carried on their shoulders to her grave.

'Would you be wanting us to hang about?' one asked my father, no doubt noticing that no one else had come to, as he put it, 'see her off'.

'No,' my father answered. 'You didn't know her. But thank you for asking.'

With that, the guards left, the prison wagon sputtering along the far edge of the cemetery, past the grove with its cement pond, then disappearing down Brewster Road.

My father opened the old black Bible he'd brought with him, and while

I stood silently at his side, read a few verses from the Song of Songs, *Lo, the winter is past, the rain is over and gone.*

'We'll need to send her things back to her uncle,' he said when he'd finished and we'd begun to make our way out of the cemetery.

My father had gotten permission to store Miss Channing's things at Milford Cottage, fully expecting that she would one day return to Chatham to reclaim them. When we walked into its front room, we found most everything still in place, the table by the window, the red cushions on the chairs.

Everything else had been packed away. We found three boxes stacked neatly in Miss Channing's bedroom, along with the two leather valises she'd brought with her from Africa. Only the black dress she'd worn on the day she'd taken the stand hung inside the large wooden armoire. My father took it out, opened one of the boxes, and placed it inside. Then he turned and looked at me, his face suddenly very grave. 'Someone should know the truth, Henry,' he said. 'If I died suddenly, no one would.'

I said nothing, but only stood before him, a grim apprehensiveness settling upon me.

'The truth about Miss Channing,' he added. 'About what really happened.'

I felt my heart stop. 'On Black Pond?' I asked, trying to keep the dread out of my voice.

He shook his head. 'No. Before that. In the lighthouse.' He lowered himself onto the bed, paused a moment, then looked up. 'You remember when I came here the day of the ... accident?'

I nodded.

'And Miss Channing and I went into the cottage alone to have a private talk?'

'Yes,' I said, remembering how he'd stood by the mantel, Miss Channing in a chair, her eyes lifted toward him.

'That's when she told me, Henry,' my father said. 'The truth.'

Then he told me what she'd said.

She had not wanted to go to the lighthouse that afternoon, Miss Channing told my father, had not wanted to meet Mr. Reed, be alone with him again. For it seemed to her that each time they were together, something unraveled inside of him. Still, he'd asked her to meet him one last time, asked her in letter after letter during that last month, until she'd finally agreed to do it.

He was standing against the far wall of the lighthouse when she entered it, his back pressed into its softly rounded curve, the old brown jacket draped over his shoulders, his black hair tossed and unruly.

'Elizabeth,' he whispered. 'I've missed you.'

She closed the metal door behind her but did not move toward him. 'I've missed you too, Leland,' she said, though careful to keep a distance in her voice.

He smiled delicately, in that way she'd noticed the first time she'd seen him, a frail, uneasy smile. 'It feels strange to be alone with you again.'

She remembered the few times they'd been alone in the way he meant, with his arms around her, his breath on her neck, the warmth of his skin next to hers.

'You haven't forgotten, have you?' he asked.

She shook her head. 'No,' she admitted.

He drew himself from the wall, staring at her silently. The chamber's single light glowed faintly from behind a cage of wire mesh, throwing a gray crosshatch of shadows over his face. 'How has it been for you, Elizabeth? Being away from me?'

She looked at him sadly, mournfully, knowing that she would never allow herself to be taken into his arms again. 'We have to go on, Leland,' she said.

'Go on to what?' he asked. 'To nothing?' He seemed on the verge of sweeping toward her.

'I can't stay long,' she told him quickly, then glanced out the small square window of the door, the playing field beyond it, the boys of Chatham School scurrying about in a game of touch football.

'Is it so hard to be with me now?' he asked, an edginess in his voice.

She shook her head wearily, now regretting that she'd come at all. 'Leland, there's no point in this. The only answer is for me to leave.'

'And what will I do then, Elizabeth?'

'What you did before.'

His eyes darkened, as if she had insulted him. 'No. Never. I can never go back to the life I used to live.' He began to pace back and forth, his cane tapping sharply on the cement floor. 'I can never do that, Elizabeth.' He stopped, his eyes now glaring at her. 'Do you want to just throw me away? Is that what you want?'

She felt a sudden surge of anger toward herself, the fact that she had ever let him love her as he did, or loved him in return, ever pretended that they lived in a world where no one else lived, where no other hearts could be broken.

'We can go away, Elizabeth,' he said. 'We can do what I always planned for us to do.'

The very suggestion returned her to her own childhood, to a father with grand notions of freedom he never followed out of love for her, how bereft she would have felt, how worthless and unloved, had he been taken from her by any force less irresistible than death. 'You know I won't do that,' she said. 'Or let you do it.'

He stepped toward her, opening his arms. 'Elizabeth, please.'

She lifted her hand, warning him away. 'I have to go, Leland.'

'No, don't. Not yet.'

She looked at him imploringly. 'Leland, please. Let me leave, still loving you.'

He stepped forward again, closing the space between them, staring at her needfully, but now with a terrible cruelty in his eyes. 'Sometimes I wish I'd never met you,' he told her. 'Sometimes I wish that you were dead.'

She shook her head. 'Stop it.'

He closed in upon her, his hands reaching for her shoulders.

She turned and grabbed the handle of the door, but he suddenly swept up behind her and jerked her around to face him, his hands grasping at her waist.

'Stop it,' she repeated. 'Let me go.'

His grip tightened around her, drawing her into a violent embrace.

'Stop it. Leland ... Leland ...'

He thrust up and pushed her hard against the door, then spun her roughly to the right, away from the door, and pressed her against the wall, so that she could feel it, hard and gritty, at her back.

'I can't let you go,' he said, his eyes now shining wildly in the gray light.

She pressed her hands flat against his shoulders. 'Stop it!' she cried, now thrusting, right and left, desperately trying to get free.

But each time she moved, he pressed in upon her more violently, until she stopped suddenly, drew in a deep breath, leveled her eyes upon him, her body now completely still, her voice an icy sliver when she spoke. 'Are you going to rape me, Leland? Is that what you've become?'

He rocked backward, stricken by her words.

'I'm sorry,' he whispered, releasing her, stepping away, his eyes now fixed upon her with a shattered, unbelieving gaze. 'Elizabeth, I only—'
He stopped and looked at her brokenly, saying nothing more as she turned and fled toward the door, her red scarf flowing behind her like a blood-soaked cloth.

My father watched me silently for a moment, then rose and walked to the window, his hands behind his back as he stared out into the yard.

I kept my place by the door, my eyes fixed on the two leather valises beside the bed as I tried to keep the rhythm of my breath quiet and steady, so that it would not reveal the upheaval in my mind. 'So it was all a lie,' I said at last. 'What Miss Channing said in court. About never going beyond the 'acceptable limits'. They *were* lovers.'

'Yes, they were, Henry,' my father said. 'But at the trial Miss Channing didn't want Mary to ever know that.'

I saw the *Elizabeth* sailing in an open sea, a ghost ship now, drifting eerily through a dense, engulfing fog.

My father walked over to me and placed his hand on my shoulder. 'Miss Channing had a good heart, Henry,' he said, then added pointedly, as if it were the central truth of life, 'Never forget, that it's the heart that matters.'

We left Milford Cottage a few minutes later, took Miss Channing's belongings to the post office, then returned home. My mother was preparing dinner, and so my father and I retired to his office. He sat down in his chair, took out his pipe. I sat opposite him, still thinking about what Miss Channing had told him, how much she must have trusted him to have done so, my eyes studying the portrait she'd painted of him, not as the staid schoolmaster I'd so despised at the time, but as a man who had something restless and unquenchable in him, something that stared out toward the thin blue lake that shimmered seductively in the distance. It was then I realized that Miss Channing had painted my father not as himself alone, but in some sense as herself as well, perhaps as all of us, stranded as we are, equally tormented by conflicting loves, trying, as best we can, to find a place between passion and boredom, ecstasy and despair, the life we can but dream of and the one we cannot bear.

'I'm glad I told you what I did this afternoon,' he said. 'You deserved to know the truth. Especially since you were there on Black Pond that day.' He shook his head. 'The sad thing is that it was all over between Miss Channing and Mr. Reed. She was going away. And in the end, he would have taken up his life again.' He seemed captured by the mystery of things, how dark and unforgiving the web can sometimes be. 'Nothing would have happened if Mrs. Reed hadn't died in Black Pond that day.'

'No,' I said. 'Nothing.'

He leaned back in his chair. 'So that's the whole story, Henry,' he said, bringing the pipe toward his lips. 'There's nothing more to know about the Chatham School Affair.'

I didn't answer him. But I knew that he was wrong.

# THIRTY-TWO

Many years have passed since then, and all the others have departed now, taking with them, one by one, small pieces of the Chatham School Affair, my mother and father, Mr. Parsons and Captain Hamilton, the last of the teachers who taught at Chatham School that year, even the boys who went there, all dead now, or living far away, probably in decrepitude, near death, with their final year at Chatham School no more than a faint remembrance of a curious and unhappy time.

Through all these many years, only Alice Craddock has remained to remind me of what happened on Black Pond, first as a little girl with melancholy eyes, then as a teenager, sullen and withdrawn, later as a woman of late middle age, grown monstrously fat and slovenly by then, friendless, alone, the village madwoman, chased by little boys, and finally as an old woman, rocking on her porch, with nothing but Dr. Craddock's steadily dwindling fortune to sustain her.

I know that sometimes I would simply shake my head as she went by, dressed so strangely, as she often was, her toenails painted green, her mind so often lost in a sea of weird imaginings. Once, standing beside Mrs. Benton on the village square, I saw her attention drawn to Alice as she drifted vacantly down the opposite street, wrapped in a ragged shawl, feet in rubber thongs. 'Now, there's a batty one,' Mrs. Benton said, then added in a tone so casual it shocked me with its flippancy. 'Probably end up like her mother.'

But as the years had proven, Alice had not 'ended up' like Mrs. Reed, so that after I'd done my work for Clement Boggs, gotten the zoning variance he needed to sell the land around Black Pond, it finally became my duty to deliver the money he'd received for it to the old house where Alice still lived, wandering aimlessly through its many dusty rooms, a candle sometimes in her hand, so people said, despite the fact that all the lights were on.

At first I'd declined to do it, not wanting to face Alice up close, see what time had wrought, along with suicide and murder. But Clement,

612

determined that his gift remain anonymous, had refused the task himself, and so it had fallen to me to do it for him. 'It's only right that it should be you who tells her about the money, Henry,' he said. 'After all, you knew her father, and it was you at the pond when her mother died.'

It was an argument I had no defense against. And so, late on a clear December night, I drove to the house on the bay, the very one that had once housed Dr. Craddock's clinic, and in which Sarah Doyle had died so many years before.

It was quite cold, but she was sitting on the large side porch when I arrived, wrapped in a thick blanket, her huge frame rocking softly in a high-backed chair.

She turned when she heard my footsteps on the stairs, squinting into the darkness, yet with a strange, expectant air, as if she had been waiting for some important guest.

'Hello, Alice,' I said as I came up the stairs, moving slowly, closing the space between us. 'You remember me, don't you?'

She watched me silently, her eyes moving up and down.

'I'm Henry,' I told her. 'Henry Griswald.'

She stared at me, uncomprehending.

'I knew you when you were Mary Reed,' I said. 'Back when you lived on Black Pond.'

Her face brightened instantly. 'With Mama,' she said.

'Yes.'

She smiled suddenly, a little girl's smile, then stood, lumbered heavily to a wide bench that rested, facing the sea, at the far end of the porch. She sat down and patted the space beside her, offering another slender smile. 'You can sit here,' she said.

I did as she told me, lowering myself unsteadily onto the bench, my eyes averted from her briefly before I forced myself to look at her again.

'I have something for you,' I told her, drawing the envelope from the pocket of my overcoat. 'It's a gift. From a friend. A check. I'm going to deposit it in your account tomorrow. Mr. Jamison, at the bank, he'll handle it for you.'

She glanced at the envelope but did not take it from my hand. 'Okay,' she said, then returned her gaze to the sea. 'Boats go by,' she said. 'Sailboats.'

I nodded. 'Yes, they do.'

I saw her as a little girl again, heard her laughter as she'd darted up the stairs, answering her mother's call, *Mary, come inside*, then later, on the beach, her eyes so still as she'd watched the red striped kite dip and weave in the empty sky.

'We flew a kite once,' I told her. 'Do you remember that?'

She did not look at me, nor give an answer.

I looked away, out toward the nightbound sea, and suddenly it shattered, all of it around me, the great shell I had lived in all my life. I felt the air warm up around me, a green water spread out before me, my body plunging into it from off the wooden pier, the world instantly transformed into a dense, suffocating green as I surged forward, first toward the rear end of the car, then along its side, my eyes open, searching, everything held in a deathly stillness as I peered inside, staring frantically into what seemed an impenetrable wall of green. Then I saw her face swim out of the murky darkness, her red hair waving behind her, her eyes open, staring at me helplessly, her mouth agape, a wave of blood pouring from it as she gasped for breath. I grabbed the handle of the door, started to jerk it open, free her from a watery grave, then heard a voice pierce the depths, cold and cruel, as if the dark mouth of Black Pond were whispering in my ear: *Sometimes I wish that she were dead.* I felt my fingers wrap more tightly around the metal handle, Mrs. Reed now staring at me desperately, her face pressed against the glass, her green eyes blinking through the swirl of blood that had gathered around her head, her mouth moving wordlessly, unable to cry or scream, her eyes growing large, bulging, gaping at me with a strange incomprehension as I faced her through the glass, my hand on the handle, poised to pull open the door, but pressing against it instead, holding it in place. For a moment she saw it in my face, knew exactly what was happening. Her lips parted with her last words, *Please, no.* Then a wave of bloody water came from her mouth, and I saw her hands lift with an immense heaviness, her fingers claw almost gently at the glass as the seconds fell upon her like heavy weights, and her eyes dimmed, and the last bubbles rose, and her body began to drift backward, rising slowly as the weight of life deserted her, so that the last thing I saw was her body as it made a slow roll, then began to descend again, curling finally over the jutting wheel, her eyes lifted upward in the final moment, searching for the surface of the pond, its distant glimmer of bright summer air.

I closed my eyes and felt winter gather around me once again, the faintly sweet odor of Alice Craddock's blanket wafting over me. I could feel my fingers trembling as I returned the envelope to my jacket pocket, listening first to my father's voice as it rang over the boys of Chatham School, *Evil on itself doth back recoil,* then to the last stanza of a song I'd heard repeated all my life and whose every word had served to prove him wrong:

> For the fear and slaughter
> In the dark green water
> Miss Channing pays alone.

I started to rise, now wanting only to rush away, back to my house, my books, retreat once again behind the shield of my isolation, but I felt Alice's soft, fleshy hand grab my coat, draw me back down onto the place beside her.

'You can stay with me awhile,' she said in a voice that sounded like a child's command.

I eased myself back down upon the bench. 'All right,' I said. 'I'll stay awhile.'

She smiled softly, unwrapped her blanket, and draped it over both of us.

We sat very still for a long time, then I felt her fingers reach for my hand and close around it. 'Pretty night,' she said.

I nodded, waited a moment, then, because I couldn't stop them, let the words fall from my lips. 'I'm sorry, Mary,' I told her.

Her fingers tightened around mine. 'Oh, that's all right,' she said almost lightly, a child's forgiveness for some small slight, but her gaze lifting toward the sky, a curious gravity gathering in them, so that for a moment she seemed to take on the greater burden, a whole world of broken bodies, mangled hearts, her eyes searching through the vastness for some reason that would explain their ruin, past stars and worlds of stars, the boundless depths, the last dim light, where still there was no answer to her *Why?*

I put my arm around her shoulders, and drew her close against my side. It seemed so little, all I had. 'You're right,' I told her. 'It is a pretty night.'